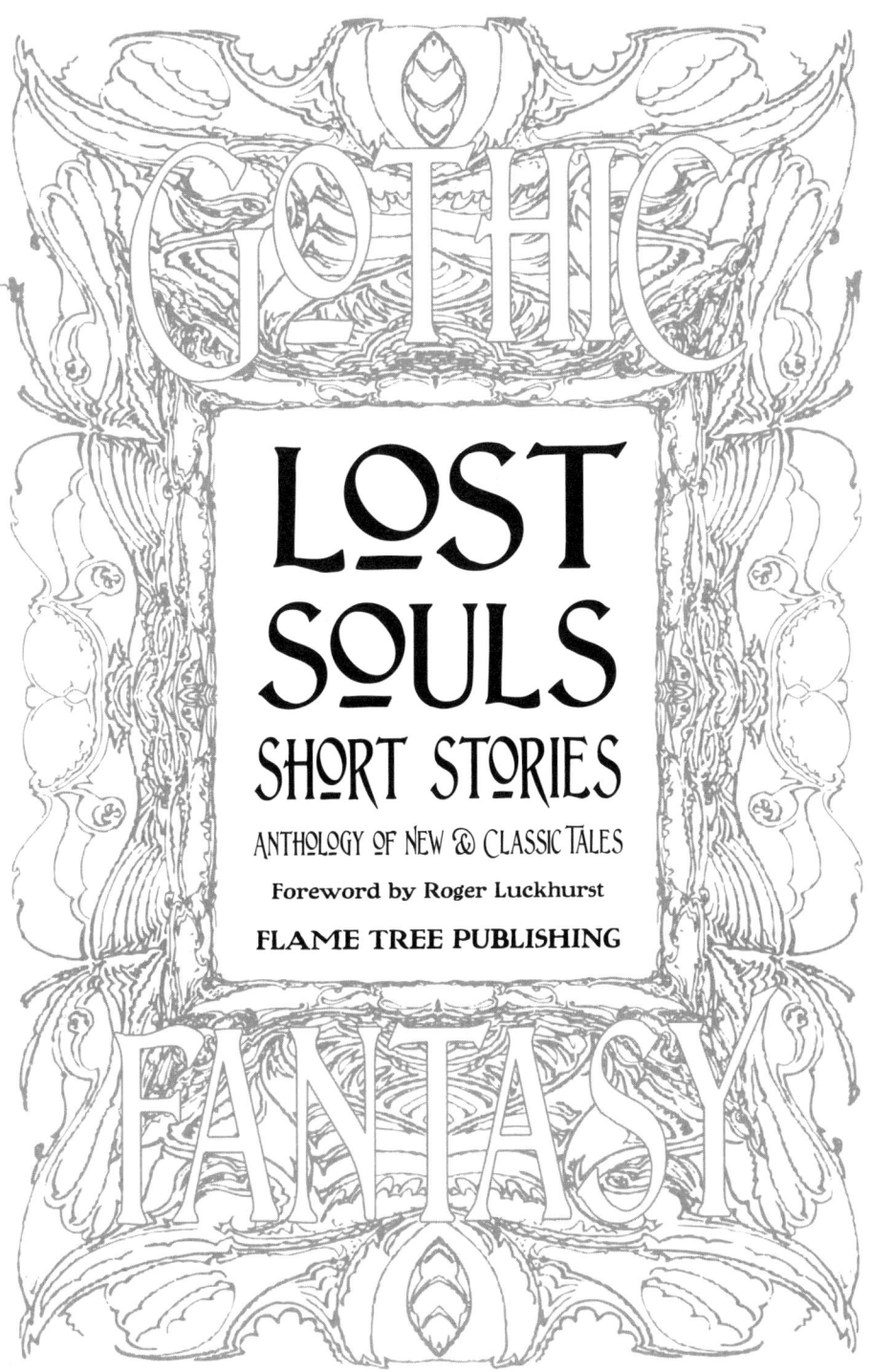

GOTHIC

LOST SOULS

SHORT STORIES

ANTHOLOGY OF NEW & CLASSIC TALES

Foreword by Roger Luckhurst

FLAME TREE PUBLISHING

FANTASY

This is a FLAME TREE Book

Publisher & Creative Director: Nick Wells
Project Editor: Laura Bulbeck
Editorial Board: Gillian Whitaker, Josie Mitchell, Catherine Taylor

Publisher's Note: Due to the historical nature of the classic text, we're aware that there may be some language used which has the potential to cause offence to the modern reader. However, wishing overall to preserve the integrity of the text, rather than imposing contemporary sensibilities, we have left it unaltered.

FLAME TREE PUBLISHING
6 Melbray Mews, Fulham,
London SW6 3NS, United Kingdom
www.flametreepublishing.com

First published 2018

Copyright © 2018 Flame Tree Publishing Ltd

Stories by modern authors are subject to international copyright law, and are licensed for publication in this volume.

18 20 22 21 19
1 3 5 7 9 10 8 6 4 2

ISBN: 978-1-78664-805-1

All rights reserved. No part of this publication may be reproduced, stored in a retrieval system, or transmitted in any form or by any means, electronic, mechanical, photocopying, recording or otherwise, without the prior written permission of the publisher.

The cover image is created by Flame Tree Studio
based on artwork by Slava Gerj and Gabor Ruszkai.

A copy of the CIP data for this book is available from the British Library.

Printed and bound in China

See our new fiction imprint
FLAME TREE PRESS | FICTION WITHOUT FRONTIERS
New and original writing in Horror, Crime, SF and Fantasy
flametreepress.com

Contents

Foreword by Roger Luckhurst..8

Publisher's Note..9

They Lived in the House on Cherry Street..................12
Sara Dobie Bauer

The Outcast...19
E.F. Benson

An Inhabitant of Carcosa..30
Ambrose Bierce

The Moonlit Road...33
Ambrose Bierce

The Cold Embrace...39
Mary Elizabeth Braddon

Joined..45
Sarah L. Byrne

The Doll's Ghost..51
F. Marion Crawford

Some Souls Stay..59
Rachael Cudlitz

Purgatorio (First Terrace – Pride)....................................61
Dante

The Trial for Murder..70
Charles Dickens

Was It an Illusion?..77
Amelia B. Edwards

Shut-In..89
C.R. Evans

The Child That Went with the Fairies 94
    Sheridan le Fanu

The Pontianak's Doll 100
    Geneve Flynn

The Lost Ghost 108
    Mary E. Wilkins Freeman

Soul Cakes 119
    Adele Gardner

Perfect Mother 125
    Anne Gresham

Thalassa's Pool 133
    Sara M. Harvey

The Beast with Five Fingers 137
    W.F. Harvey

The Searcher of the End House 154
    William Hope Hodgson

The Elementary Spirit 169
    E.T.A. Hoffmann

Mary Burnet 192
    James Hogg

Only Bella 205
    Kurt Hunt

The Adventure of the German Student 208
    Washington Irving

The Jolly Corner 212
    Henry James

The Haunted Dolls' House 232
    M.R. James

The Man of Science 239
    Jerome K. Jerome

Thurnley Abbey **243**
                Perceval Landon

The Death-Bride **252**
                Friedrich Laun

The Strange High House in the Mist **272**
                H.P. Lovecraft

The Inmost Light **278**
                Arthur Machen

The Bowmen **295**
                Arthur Machen

Until There Is Only Hunger **297**
                Michael Matheson

Melmoth the Wanderer (abridged version) **305**
                Charles Maturin

Every Time She Kills Him **328**
                J.A.W. McCarthy

The Price of Forever **338**
                John M. McIlveen

Man-Size in Marble **343**
                E. Nesbit

The Obstinate One **351**
                Jessica Nickelsen

The Open Door **355**
                Margaret Oliphant

Orpheus and Eurydice **375**
                A Retelling of the Myth from Ovid's Metamorphoses

The Phone Call **377**
                Michael Penncavage

Morella **382**
                Edgar Allan Poe

Last Long Night...386
                      Lina Rather

A Good Thing and a Right Thing.................................388
                      Alexandra Renwick

Scare Tactics...395
                      Aeryn Rudel

The Tapestried Chamber...402
                      Walter Scott

This House Is My Cage...411
                      Lizz-Ayn Shaarawi

Lullaby for the Dead..415
                      Erin Skolney

Abandonment Option...420
                      Lucy A. Snyder

Casualty of Peace...427
                      David Tallerman

The Storm..435
                      Sarah Elizabeth Utterson

Sing Me Your Scars..440
                      Damien Angelica Walters

The Triumph of Night..450
                      Edith Wharton

Biographies & Sources...466

Foreword: Lost Souls Short Stories

IN THE NINETEENTH CENTURY, science declared war on old-time superstitions. Charles Darwin offered a purely biological explanation of the origins of man: there was no divine spark, no soul, only the process of evolution through natural selection. Geologists read in the stones that the Earth was far older than Biblical history suggested. Folklorists collected old stories and myths because they believed the accelerating progress of the modern world would shortly kill off all memory of them. Anthropologists suggested that superstitions about ghosts and wandering spirits, or hexes needed to ward off evil, were evidence of 'survivals' from the mind of savages – a scientific education would end the more primitive beliefs.

Yet even as Enlightenment philosophers became more confident in expressing these modern positions, superstition and magical thinking persisted: suicides were still buried outside church grounds and sometimes staked to the earth to stop their spirits from floating around; murderers were buried at crossroads, to confuse their souls damned to eternal wandering. A whole new religious movement called Spiritualism emerged in the 1840s, which promised to put the bereaved in touch with their dead relatives and friends, and hundreds of thousands of eminently respectable Victorians explored the world of the séance. Earnest Cambridge dons invented 'psychical research' in the 1880s to use scientific methods to 'prove' the existence of survival of bodily death.

And there was also an explosion of supernatural fiction. The first wave of the Gothic (running from the 1760s to the 1820s) was often written in a religious framework. It was full of tyrannical Catholic priests, torturers from the Inquisition, and scary nuns doing unspeakable things in mouldering convents. This was the kind of stuff that scared readers in the relatively young democracies of Protestant England and America.

This has never quite gone away. 'Melmoth the Wanderer' in this collection was written by the Irish Protestant minister Charles Maturin, who wrote rabid anti-Catholic tracts. But in the main the Gothic was transformed by the rapid arrival of the modern world. Instead of being set in the deep past and in ruins and castles in Italy or Spain, ghost stories began to appear in modern houses and in the present day. Writers like Charles Dickens and Mary Braddon began to shift the locations into a recognizable contemporary world, the more to spook a wider readership. Modern horror was about the fears of the physical body, of decay, of the very absence of religious consolation – a significant change that is represented in the work of writers like Edgar Allan Poe or Ambrose Bierce. The famous doyen of 'weird fiction', H.P. Lovecraft, was an implacable atheist: for him, horror came from the utter indifference of the universe to the puny man, not from the terrors of eternal damnation.

Haunting became the problem less of ancient family curses and more of rental properties long off the market (as in E.F. Benson's 'The Outcast') or anonymous houses in horrible suburban developments (as in Arthur Machen's 'The Inmost Light'). Ghosts did less lecturing on moral wrongs – like Hamlet's father – and became more fugitive, wispy and uncertain. They started to be emanations of psychological states, and sometimes we're not even sure if they exist at all. In Henry James's 'The Jolly Corner' it might even be that the main character who inherits this New York house is somehow haunting *himself*.

After 1880, it is often said that we enter the 'golden age' of the ghost story. A new magazine market wanted short sensational tales, and the lost souls in stories about haunting became perfectly poised between offering a shudder of old superstitions revived and a new way of talking about dreamy psychological states. As Sigmund Freud reflected, we might be living in the modern world, but the creak of a floorboard or the glimpse of a figure on the landing might instantly plunge us back into primitive psychological states of dread or terror.

This is part of the pleasure of reading fiction about lost souls, of course. May I wish you plentiful shivers as you read through this selection of stories.

Roger Luckhurst

Publisher's Note

LOST SOULS HAVE long intrigued us – whether it be ghostly apparitions, wanderings in the afterlife or Faustian deals – this fantastic new collection evokes haunting tales from the darkest corners of literature and legend. Musings on the afterlife and visitations from the dead are infused in mythologies all over the world, and we've included one such example from the Greeks here. That fascination has stayed with us, culminating in nineteenth and early twentieth century ghost stories, which turned out to be a particularly golden age for female writers like Edith Wharton, E. Nesbit and Mary E. Wilkins Freeman, to name but a few. We also could not consider an anthology on lost souls without looking at Dante's seminal work *The Divine Comedy*, and his vivid imaginings of Purgatory in particular. The dark scenes within mingle seamlessly with the later tales of William Hope Hodgson or Arthur Machen.

We received an incredible number of new submissions for this anthology, and have loved plunging into the icy chills of wraiths, spirits and shadows. It is always fascinating to see the different takes on a theme – do those that return seek revenge, justice, or simply recognition? Just where do souls go when they leave this earthly plane? Making the final selection is always an incredibly hard decision, but ultimately we chose a collection of stories we hope sit alongside each other and with the classic fiction, to provide a fantastic *Lost Souls* book for all to enjoy.

They Lived in the House on Cherry Street

Sara Dobie Bauer

AFTER THE FUNERAL, I explained to my husband I wanted time alone in the homestead – the place I grew up. He understood, of course, and took our teenage daughters home.

I don't know why the old house held such wonder for me still. My mother had been in assisted living for months. With the help of my husband, we'd removed every trace of her and my father from the place where I grew up – the brick monument on Cherry Street Daddy designed and built for us.

I expected nothing but silence and the stale smell of age when I walked through the breezeway and turned the familiar key in the familiar side door lock. Imagine my surprise when I smelled cigarettes and heard the rickety echo of Glenn Miller's orchestra on a turntable.

The side door led into the kitchen, which I could see was filled with blue smoke, illuminated by early evening light through windows that led to the backyard.

Then, I heard her voice: Mom.

"Home at last," she said.

The kitchen was as it once was: filled with blooming cacti and framed cross-stitch phrases in Italian. Beneath the cigarette smoke, I smelled tomato sauce. My mother stood at the counter, salting pasta, dousing it in olive oil, and stirring, stirring with a wooden spoon.

She must have been thirty years old: carefully curled black hair, red lipstick, a tiny waist, and a simple stained apron that belonged to my father but that she claimed was her favorite.

Mom turned to face me and smiled. She wiped her hands on her apron and opened her arms. "Give me a hug, Sandi. And why are you so late from school?"

We'd burned her decrepit, sick body three days before. She was ashes in the ground at St. Rose Cemetery, where all the Catholics ended up.

One of my knees gave out, so I reached for the edge of the stove for balance. I shouted and pulled my hand back from the heat, which made my mother run to me and yell, "Albert!"

I felt her hands on me – not the paper-thin flesh of a dying old woman but the strong, supple hands of a lifetime cook who kept our Cherry Street house clean and made my bed every morning. Her hands wrapped around my thin wrists and led me to the kitchen table that wasn't supposed to be there. No, we'd sold the family table at the estate sale.

She pushed me into a wrought iron chair with a cream-colored pillow and rushed to the sink to wet a washcloth. She pressed the cloth to my hand, and I smelled her perfume: Chanel No. 5.

"What's all the ruckus, Ella?"

Dad stood in the doorway that led from kitchen to living room – the place where we'd spent over forty Christmas morns. His head was already bald, but his hair was still brown around the sides of his head. He looked strong, the Naval officer he once was, not the wasted sack of bones he became the night he died in their bedroom ten years before.

I ignored the cold cloth on my scalded hand and ran to him. He almost dropped his newspaper at my exuberance. He smelled like smoke and Old Spice. He felt warm and soft, full around the middle from all the new-fangled light beer. He stuck his face in my hair and whispered, "Sandi, baby, are you all right?"

I cried, and Mom tutted. "She just burned her hand, silly thing." She grabbed at me and again shoved the cloth against my palm. "Now, sit down, you two. Time to eat."

With shaking hands and knees, I sat at the kitchen table. Dad sat at the head and folded his paper, leaving it to soak up extra tomato sauce near the edge of his plate. Mom sat across from me and smiled, not a wrinkle in her young, tanned skin. She reached for me. We all joined hands and said grace. Daddy crossed himself and said, "Amen."

I watched them eat in fascination.

"How was your day at school, Sandi?" Dad asked.

"What?"

"Your day at school," Mom repeated. "And why were you late? You weren't spending time with James, were you?"

I took a bite of steaming spaghetti. My tongue tingled at the memory of the sweet sauce Mom made before she got old and started burning things. We had to get live-in help then, and the food was never the same. By the time I thought to ask for a recipe, she was too far gone.

"You look beautiful, Mom," I said.

She tilted her chin down and gave me the smile she saved only for me, her only child.

After dinner, Mom made a pot of decaf coffee. We sat around the dinner table and played Scrabble. Daddy won. I watched in wonder as his hands didn't shake, not like the last time we played together, a month before he died.

The new pastel green fridge hummed in the corner: a special gift for Mom's thirty-fifth birthday. There were only two photos so far: one of Mom and Dad on a beach in Hawaii and one of me – my senior picture, all glasses and big teeth.

Mom said, "Off to bed, baby. School in the morning."

"Yes," I said.

She ushered me up the steep staircase that led to my bedroom and the spare room for guests. It was all there: my posters of the Beatles, of far-off beaches. A flower wreath decorated the small lamp by my bed. Mom pulled down the covers and picked up my aged red teddy bear I'd slept with since birth. She tucked me in tight but not before I gave her a hug.

"I love you, Mom," I said.

"Love you, Sandi." She kissed my nose and glanced back at me from the door. I didn't remember her like this, beautiful and young, smelling of smoke, tomatoes, and perfume. I only remembered her as the woman in the sick bed: tired and tortured, unable to speak. In the sick bed, she used to pretend to sleep when I was there. The nurses said she was embarrassed.

* * *

I woke on the carpeted living room floor. My cell phone rang and rang. I sat up, and my parents' house was empty. The horrible smell was there again: the smell of age. The house was silent except for the ringing. I answered, "Hello?"

"Sandi. Where are you?" my husband said.

I looked at the bare walls. "I fell asleep. I'm sorry."

"It's okay. Just come home."

I stood in my wrinkled black funeral suit and dragged my feet across the carpet into the kitchen – empty, empty. I drove home, only a couple blocks, but it seemed much further. As soon as I walked into our two-story dream house, my twins wandered in from the TV room and gave me quiet, muttering hugs.

I kissed their foreheads. "My babies." I hid my shaking hands by running my fingers through their soft, long hair.

James stood behind them. His lips wore a smile but his eyes worried. I walked past my daughters and hugged him. I heard footsteps as the girls returned to the TV, happy to have a day away from the pressures of their senior year.

"Are you all right?" he whispered.

I buried my nose against his neck and smelled the familiar scent of bar soap and coffee. "Yeah. I mean…."

He rubbed his hands up and down my back. "I know. Your family's coming over at noon."

"Shit."

He brushed the hair away from my face. "You look like a wreck. Go take a shower. I'll make another pot of coffee."

I nodded and drifted upstairs. It was only when I turned on the water in the shower that I realized my hand was burnt.

* * *

The afternoon was spent discussing financial details and the sale of the house on Cherry Street. Since I had no siblings, I was in charge of everything – the executor of the will. Every decision deferred to me, but thank God I had James to calm aunts and uncles if things got heated. I kept looking at my hand, wrapped in a bandage. I told James I didn't know how it happened, and he got that look: the one he used to get back when we first married, when I was drinking too much and cutting my skin to deal with stress. Long before the twins.

Everyone left around three, most of them to the local bar where people in town were known to celebrate births, deaths, and weddings. I went to Cherry Street. James offered to come, and I told him no.

From the outside, the house looked empty. I told myself it was empty. I walked through the breezeway and unlocked the front door. I pushed inside and heard laughter. Must have been Wednesday.

Mom and Dad danced through a haze of smoke to the tune of Frank Sinatra. Empty martini glasses were on the kitchen counter, and when Dad saw me, he dipped Mom halfway to the floor. Her hair was longer; Dad's was gray. He twirled her, and she shouted, "Sandi!" in that singsong way she did when she'd had half a martini.

"Sandi, baby!" Dad echoed.

Mom spun toward me and took both my hands in hers. She had slight wrinkles on the outside of her eyes, and the red lipstick of her thirties had changed to a deep orange. "Where's James?"

I glanced at the green fridge and saw our wedding picture front and center: me in a bodice of lace and James with his moustache and shaggy haircut. God, five years had passed in an afternoon.

"He couldn't make it," I said.

"You want a martini? Light on the vermouth." Dad did a cha-cha toward the family shaker, decorated with men on horseback in red and black polo attire. He was in his gold chain phase. He'd picked up the habit in Key West, where all the older guys wore gold chains to decorate copious chest hair.

"No thanks, Daddy." I hadn't touched a drink in years.

Mom took my elbows in her hands. Her skin felt less supple. She moved my arms back and forth until I danced with her. "You're just in time for a fast dinner!" She laughed, revealing rows of white teeth, stained on the edges from all the cigarettes.

"Fast dinner" was what she called dinner consisting of eggs and bacon. My whole life I hated Mom's eggs. No one made a less thrilling pile of yellow fluff. In that moment, I couldn't wait. All I wanted was my mom's eggs to the tune of 'The Way You Look Tonight'.

I knew I couldn't spend another night sleeping there, which of course, my parents understood. I was a married woman, after all, Mom said, with a handsome husband waiting. Mom gave me one of her sloppy lipstick kisses that stained my cheek. Daddy leaned in and gave me a gentle peck on the forehead.

Before I left, I turned and watched them from the side door. They danced like I wasn't there. I left like they weren't.

Back in my car, I looked in the rearview mirror. I wiped the lipstick off before I got home.

* * *

Due to family tragedy, I didn't have to go back to work at the newspaper – not yet. I had a full week before going back to the office, so the next morning, once the girls returned to school and James went into the city to pour over legal briefs, I went to the house on Cherry Street.

I was surprised to find our real estate agent, Leslie, in the front yard. She grinned when she saw me. "Sandi! You're looking well." She leaned in for an awkward hug. She wore some flowery perfume that reminded me of funerals.

"Leslie. What are you doing here?"

"Well, James said it's time to put up the sign." She gestured to the base of the ancient pine tree in my parents' front yard. Underneath was a placard that announced, loudly, FOR SALE.

"Oh. He didn't mention it to me."

"I don't think he wanted you to have to think about it. Losing your mother is so hard." She ran her hand up and down my arm. Her skin felt cold through my t-shirt.

I nodded.

"Let's hope we get some bites. It's such a beautiful neighborhood and a very historic house. It's so romantic that your family lived here all these years. Some young couple will probably fall in love with the story more than the house." She smiled. Her gums showed when she smiled. "Anyway, you'll be hearing from me for showings. I told James you might want to light candles inside. People like the smell of candles."

She meant that people don't like the smell of old people.

I nodded again.

"You doing okay, Sandi?"

"I'm fine. Thank you."

She waddled off toward her swanky blue car and gave me a wave. One of the diamonds on her hand shimmered in the sun.

I walked through the breezeway and unlocked the front door. The kitchen was empty but clean. Dishes dried in the sink rack. A glass mobile hung in the window and cast rainbows on a bouquet of pink tulips on the counter.

"Sandi?" I heard Daddy's voice from the TV room.

There were more pictures of James and me on the fridge: one from when he got his law degree.

So seven years gone.

In the back room, they sat in their respective recliners watching tennis. Pictures of family were everywhere and even a painting I did in college of a decrepit house I'd seen down by the river. The family ficus tree stood in the corner, mauled by Mom's sheering. It was the only thing I'd ever seen my parents fight about: the way she chopped that poor tree within an inch of its life.

Andre Agassi was on the television with his long, Samson hair.

I looked at my parents, looked at them close. Daddy's hair was bright white. He wore glasses. He was losing weight already. Mom had dyed her hair from gray to a deep orange that matched her lipstick. She carried weight around her middle. Her tiny toes were painted the color of a shell's insides.

Daddy moved to stand. "Sandi, baby!" He held his arms open, and I crushed him in my embrace. He still smelled like Old Spice, mixed with some menthol gel he used on his lower back. The house didn't smell like smoke; they'd given up the habit by then.

I sat on the couch between their chairs. I reached out and took my mother's hand, already on its way to fragility.

I couldn't leave the house on Cherry Street. I couldn't lose them again.

* * *

I was helping Mom do dishes in the kitchen when someone knocked on the side door. We'd just finished rolling ravioli. Mom insisted we make it from scratch. We'd used her homemade stuffing: spinach, ground beef, garlic, and ricotta. I dried my hands on a towel and said, "I'll get it."

When I answered the door, my husband was there. His light brown eyes were wide. He hadn't shaved in perhaps two days, and his light hair stood up around the edges. He never could get it to behave in the summer heat. He'd come right from work, still in a suit and tie, although the tie was crooked. He smelled like sweat.

"Where the hell have you been?" He walked past me.

When I turned to follow, my mom was gone. So were the dishes. So was the smell of garlic.

"You haven't been answering your phone. I thought…." He reached for my hand and looked at my wrist. He pulled me to him, crushed me against his chest. "Sandi, it's been two days."

"What?" I backed away. "No, I was just…."

"I wanted to give you space," he said. "I know how hard this is. I remember what it was like when we lost your dad, but you need to come home. There's nothing here."

What could I say?

"There have been calls about the house. Leslie is ready to show it, but she needs your approval, and since you haven't been answering your phone…." He shook his head and put his hands on his hips.

"I'm sorry. I'm sorry." I touched his face and pressed my lips to his. He responded, holding me in his arms.

"I can't lose you," he said.

"No." I hugged him back.

"Please come home."

I nodded. I went to see my daughters.

* * *

Four different couples walked through the house on Cherry Street. Leslie said there was a lot of discussion about updates. The stove would need replacing. The basement smelled like mold. The windows didn't insulate well in winter. We might have to drop the price.

I busied myself being a mother and wife. I made love to James. I gave the twins cash for their school lunches and talked about college. We watched *Jeopardy!* as a family at night. I laughed when the girls made up answers. I pretended to sleep.

Two days later, I made it back to my parents' house alone.

I walked through the breezeway, unlocked the door. The house was silent. I thought maybe I'd imagined the whole thing until I smelled cigarette smoke. My mom started smoking again after…

She was at the kitchen table. Her hair was gray. Her skin had begun to sag, and her orange lipstick was crooked. On the fridge were pictures of my girls back when they were short, smiling, and in soccer uniforms.

"Mom?" I said.

"He's dead," she said. "Your father is dead."

Salt burned my eyes. "No."

Her voice caught before she asked, "Where have you been?" She stared up at me, nothing but malice in her gaze. "Where have you been, Sandra?"

"I'm sorry, Mom."

"You should have been here," she said.

"Mom, I –"

"You should have been here!" She hit the table with her fist.

The night my father died, I went home to get some sleep. He'd been sick for weeks. Their marriage bed was his prison. He stopped eating. He barely recognized any of us. I couldn't take it. I had to get away. I went home and I slept and he died.

She lit another cigarette. "How did I get so old, Sandi? How did this happen to us?"

I stepped closer, afraid to touch her.

"Remember how we used to dance?"

I nodded.

"Your father was the best dancer. He loved dancing with his little girl." She looked up at me.

I shuddered out a sob. "Mom, please don't go."

"Then, stay with me, Sandi."

I heaved a breath. I knew how it went from here. I knew what happened after Daddy died, how Mom started drinking again – how she would get so drunk she wouldn't remember he was dead. I would have to remind her, again and again. Then, she would slowly give in. She would eat to fill the space he'd left, her husband of fifty-five years. She would grow obese until she became bedridden. Then, she would turn ugly and angry. She would yell at me, at the hospice nurses. On Christmas, she would have a stroke and stop talking. She would live for nine months in an unfamiliar hospital that smelled of piss and vomit. Then, one night, she would open her eyes wide, stare into the corner of her hospice room, and die.

"Don't make me watch," I begged. "I don't want to do this again, Mom. Don't make me remember you like this."

The ghost of my mother looked at me knowingly. She knew what awaited her, awaited me. She lit another cigarette. "We were happy here, weren't we, baby?"

"So happy."

"You should go home," she said. "Go home to James and your girls. Don't waste a day."

"I love you."

She hid behind a veil of smoke.

I faced the green fridge and looked at the old, curled photos from Hawaii, the new ones they'd stacked one on top of another as their little girl grew up, married, had little girls of her own. There was one I'd scanned and tried to retouch: one photo of Mom and Daddy on a beach with an inner tube wrapped around their waists, before I was even born.

I walked away from her and knew she was dead.

* * *

The couple that bought the house on Cherry Street have a daughter. I heard from the neighbors they gutted the kitchen and replaced the old windows. They cut down the pine tree out front. I wouldn't know. I don't drive past the homestead anymore, because it's not mine.

I spend a lot of time looking at James and wonder what would have happened if I'd stayed in the house with my parents. I could have stayed for years before anyone got sick – gotten to know them again the way they were before diapers and drool and death.

I wonder if I would have grown younger, too. Or died with them.

The Outcast

E.F. Benson

WHEN MRS. ACRES bought the Gate-house at Tarleton, which had stood so long without a tenant, and appeared in that very agreeable and lively little town as a resident, sufficient was already known about her past history to entitle her to friendliness and sympathy. Hers had been a tragic story, and the account of the inquest held on her husband's body, when, within a month of their marriage, he had shot himself before her eyes, was recent enough, and of as full a report in the papers as to enable our little community of Tarleton to remember and run over the salient grimness of the case without the need of inventing any further details – which, otherwise, it would have been quite capable of doing.

Briefly, then, the facts had been as follows. Horace Acres appeared to have been a heartless fortune-hunter – a handsome, plausible wretch, ten years younger than his wife. He had made no secret to his friends of not being in love with her but of having a considerable regard for her more than considerable fortune. But hardly had he married her than his indifference developed into violent dislike, accompanied by some mysterious, inexplicable dread of her. He hated and feared her, and on the morning of the very day when he had put an end to himself he had begged her to divorce him; the case he promised would be undefended, and he would make it indefensible. She, poor soul, had refused to grant this; for, as corroborated by the evidence of friends and servants, she was utterly devoted to him, and stated with that quiet dignity which distinguished her throughout this ordeal, that she hoped that he was the victim of some miserable but temporary derangement, and would come to his right mind again. He had dined that night at his club, leaving his month-old bride to pass the evening alone, and had returned between eleven and twelve that night in a state of vile intoxication. He had gone up to her bedroom, pistol in hand, had locked the door, and his voice was heard screaming and yelling at her. Then followed the sound of one shot. On the table in his dressing-room was found a half-sheet of paper, dated that day, and this was read out in court. "The horror of my position," he had written, "is beyond description and endurance. I can bear it no longer: my soul sickens...." The jury, without leaving the court, returned the verdict that he had committed suicide while temporarily insane, and the coroner, at their request, expressed their sympathy and his own with the poor lady, who, as testified on all hands, had treated her husband with the utmost tenderness and affection.

For six months Bertha Acres had travelled abroad, and then in the autumn she had bought Gate-house at Tarleton, and settled down to the absorbing trifles which make life in a small country town so busy and strenuous.

* * *

Our modest little dwelling is within a stone's throw of the Gate-house; and when, on the return of my wife and myself from two months in Scotland, we found that Mrs. Acres was installed as a neighbour, Madge lost no time in going to call on her. She returned with a series of pleasant impressions. Mrs. Acres, still on the sunny slope that leads up to the tableland of life which begins at forty years, was extremely handsome, cordial, and charming in manner, witty and agreeable, and wonderfully well dressed. Before the conclusion of her call Madge, in country fashion, had begged her to dispose with formalities, and, instead of a frigid return of the call, to dine with us quietly next day. Did she play bridge? That being so, we would just be a party of four; for her brother, Charles Alington, had proposed himself for a visit....

I listened to this with sufficient attention to grasp what Madge was saying, but what I was really thinking about was a chess-problem which I was attempting to solve. But at this point I became acutely aware that her stream of pleasant impressions dried up suddenly, and she became stonily silent. She shut speech off as by the turn of a tap, and glowered at the fire, rubbing the back of one hand with the fingers of another, as is her habit in perplexity.

"Go on," I said.

She got up, suddenly restless.

"All I have been telling you is literally and soberly true," she said. "I thought Mrs. Acres charming and witty and good-looking and friendly. What more could you ask from a new acquaintance? And then, after I had asked her to dinner, I suddenly found for no earthly reason that I very much disliked her; I couldn't bear her."

"You said she was wonderfully well dressed," I permitted myself to remark.... If the Queen took the Knight –

"Don't be silly!" said Madge. "I am wonderfully well dressed too. But behind all her agreeableness and charm and good looks I suddenly felt there was something else which I detested and dreaded. It's no use asking me what it was, because I haven't the slightest idea. If I knew what it was, the thing would explain itself. But I felt a horror – nothing vivid, nothing close, you understand, but somewhere in the background. Can the mind have a 'turn', do you think, just as the body can, when for a second or two you suddenly feel giddy? I think it must have been that – oh! I'm sure it was that. But I'm glad I asked her to dine. I mean to like her. I shan't have a 'turn' again, shall I?"

"No, certainly not," I said.... If the Queen refrained from taking the tempting Knight –

"Oh, do stop your silly chess-problem!" said Madge. "Bite him, Fungus!"

Fungus, so-called because he is the son of Humour and Gustavus Adolphus, rose from his place on the hearth-rug, and with a horse laugh nuzzled against my leg, which is his way of biting those he loves. Then the most amiable of bull-dogs, who has a passion for the human race, lay down on my foot and sighed heavily. But Madge evidently wanted to talk, and I pushed the chessboard away.

"Tell me more about the horror," I said.

"It was just horror," she said – "a sort of sickness of the soul...."

I found my brain puzzling over some vague reminiscence, surely connected with Mrs. Acres, which those words mistily evoked. But next moment that train of thought was cut short, for the old and sinister legend about the Gate-house came into my mind as accounting for the horror of which Madge spoke. In the days of Elizabethan religious persecutions it had, then newly built, been inhabited by two brothers, of whom the elder, to whom it belonged, had Mass said there every Sunday. Betrayed by the younger, he was arrested and racked to death. Subsequently the younger, in a fit of remorse, hanged himself in the panelled parlour. Certainly there was a story that the house was haunted by his strangled apparition dangling from the beams, and the late tenants of the house (which now had stood vacant for over three years) had quitted it after a month's occupation, in consequence, so it was commonly said, of unaccountable and horrible sights. What was more likely, then, than that Madge, who from childhood has been intensely sensitive to occult and psychic phenomena, should have caught, on that strange wireless receiver which is characteristic of 'sensitives', some whispered message?

"But you know the story of the house," I said. "Isn't it quite possible that something of that may have reached you? Where did you sit, for instance? In the panelled parlour?"

She brightened at that.

"Ah, you wise man!" she said. "I never thought of that. That may account for it all. I hope it does. You shall be left in peace with your chess for being so brilliant."

* * *

I had occasion half an hour later to go to the post-office, a hundred yards up the High Street, on the matter of a registered letter which I wanted to despatch that evening. Dusk was gathering, but the red glow of sunset still smouldered in the west, sufficient to enable me to recognise familiar forms and features of passers-by. Just as I came opposite the post-office there approached from the other direction a tall, finely built woman, whom, I felt sure, I had never seen before. Her destination was the same as mine, and I hung on my step a moment to let her pass in first. Simultaneously I felt that I knew, in some vague, faint manner, what Madge had meant when she talked about a 'sickness of the soul'. It was no nearer realisation to me than is the running of a tune in the head to the audible external hearing of it, and I attributed my sudden recognition of her feeling to the fact that in all probability my mind had subconsciously been dwelling on what she had said, and not for a moment did I connect it with any external cause. And then it occurred to me who, possibly, this woman was....

She finished the transaction of her errand a few seconds before me, and when I got out into the street again she was a dozen yards down the pavement, walking in the direction of my house and of the Gate-house. Opposite my own door I deliberately lingered, and saw her pass down the steps that led from the road to the entrance of the Gate-house. Even as I turned into my own door the unbidden reminiscence which had eluded me before came out into the open, and I cast my net over it. It was her husband, who, in the inexplicable communication he had left on his dressing-room table, just before he shot himself, had written 'my soul sickens'. It was odd, though scarcely more than that, for Madge to have used those identical words.

* * *

Charles Alington, my wife's brother, who arrived next afternoon, is quite the happiest man whom I have ever come across. The material world, that perennial spring of thwarted ambition, physical desire, and perpetual disappointment, is practically unknown to him. Envy, malice, and all uncharitableness are equally alien, because he does not want to obtain what anybody else has got, and has no sense of possession, which is queer, since he is enormously rich. He fears nothing, he hopes for nothing, he has no abhorrences or affections, for all physical and nervous functions are in him in the service of an intense inquisitiveness. He never passed a moral judgment in his life, he only wants to explore and to know. Knowledge, in fact, is his entire preoccupation, and since chemists and medical scientists probe and mine in the world of tinctures and microbes far more efficiently than he could do, as he has so little care for anything that can be weighed or propagated, he devotes himself, absorbedly and ecstatically, to that world that lies about the confines of conscious existence. Anything not yet certainly determined appeals to him with the call of a trumpet: he ceases to take an interest in a subject as soon as it shows signs of assuming a practical and definite status. He was intensely concerned, for instance, in wireless transmission, until Signor Marconi proved that it came within the scope of practical science, and then Charles abandoned it as dull. I had seen him last two months before, when he was in a great perturbation, since he was speaking at a meeting of Anglo-Israelites in the morning, to show that the Scone Stone, which is now in the Coronation Chair at Westminster, was for certain the pillow on which Jacob's head had rested when he saw the vision at Bethel; was addressing the Psychical Research Society in the afternoon on the subject of messages received from the dead through automatic script, and in the evening was, by way of a holiday, only listening to a lecture on reincarnation. None of these things could, as yet, be definitely proved, and that was why he loved them. During the intervals when the occult and the fantastic do not occupy him, he is, in spite of his fifty years and wizened mien, exactly like a schoolboy of eighteen back on his holidays and brimming with superfluous energy.

I found Charles already arrived when I got home next afternoon, after a round of golf. He was betwixt and between the serious and the holiday mood, for he had evidently been reading to Madge from a journal concerning reincarnation, and was rather severe to me....

"Golf!" he said, with insulting scorn. "What is there to know about golf? You hit a ball into the air –"

I was a little sore over the events of the afternoon.

"That's just what I don't do," I said. "I hit it along the ground!"

"Well, it doesn't matter where you hit it," said he. "It's all subject to known laws. But the guess, the conjecture: there's the thrill and the excitement of life. The charlatan with his new cure for cancer, the automatic writer with his messages from the dead, the reincarnationist with his positive assertions that he was Napoleon or a Christian slave – they are the people who advance knowledge. You have to guess before you know. Even Darwin saw that when he said you could not investigate without a hypothesis!"

"So what's your hypothesis this minute?" I asked.

"Why, that we've all lived before, and that we're going to live again here on this same old earth. Any other conception of a future life is impossible. Are all the people who have been born and have died since the world emerged from chaos going to become inhabitants of some future world? What a squash, you know, my dear Madge! Now, I know what you're going to ask me. If we've all lived before, why can't we remember it? But that's so simple! If you remembered being Cleopatra, you would go on behaving like Cleopatra; and what would Tarleton say? Judas Iscariot, too! Fancy knowing you had been Judas Iscariot! You couldn't get over it! You would commit suicide, or cause everybody who was connected with you to commit suicide from their horror of you. Or imagine being a grocer's boy who knew he had been Julius Caesar.... Of course, sex doesn't matter: souls, as far as I understand, are sexless – just sparks of life, which are put into physical envelopes, some male, some female. You might have been King David, Madge and poor Tony here one of his wives."

"That would be wonderfully neat," said I.

Charles broke out into a shout of laughter.

"It would indeed," he said. "But I won't talk sense any more to you scoffers. I'm absolutely tired out, I will confess, with thinking. I want to have a pretty lady to come to dinner, and talk to her as if she was just herself and I myself, and nobody else. I want to win two-and-sixpence at bridge with the expenditure of enormous thought. I want to have a large breakfast tomorrow and read *The Times* afterwards, and go to Tony's club and talk about crops and golf and Irish affairs and Peace Conferences, and all the things that don't matter one straw!"

"You're going to begin your programme tonight, dear," said Madge. "A very pretty lady is coming to dinner, and we're going to play bridge afterwards."

Madge and I were ready for Mrs. Acres when she arrived, but Charles was not yet down. Fungus, who has a wild adoration for Charles, quite unaccountable, since Charles has no feelings for dogs, was helping him to dress, and Madge, Mrs. Acres, and I waited for his appearance. It was certainly Mrs. Acres whom I had met last night at the door of the post-office, but the dim light of sunset had not enabled me to see how wonderfully handsome she was. There was something slightly Jewish about her profile: the high forehead, the very full-lipped mouth, the bridged nose, the prominent chin, all suggested rather than exemplified an Eastern origin. And when she spoke she had that rich softness of utterance, not quite hoarseness, but not quite of the clear-cut distinctness of tone which characterises northern nations. Something southern, something Eastern....

"I am bound to ask one thing," she said, when, after the usual greetings, we stood round the fireplace, waiting for Charles – "but have you got a dog?"

Madge moved towards the bell.

"Yes, but he shan't come down if you dislike dogs," she said. "He's wonderfully kind, but I know –"

"Ah, it's not that," said Mrs. Acres. "I adore dogs. But I only wished to spare your dog's feelings. Though I adore them, they hate me, and they're terribly frightened of me. There's something anti-canine about me."

It was too late to say more. Charles's steps clattered in the little hall outside, and Fungus was hoarse and amused. Next moment the door opened, and the two came in.

Fungus came in first. He lolloped in a festive manner into the middle of the room, sniffed and snorted in greeting, and then turned tail. He slipped and skidded on the parquet outside, and we heard him bundling down the kitchen stairs.

"Rude dog," said Madge. "Charles, let me introduce you to Mrs. Acres. My brother, Mrs. Acres: Sir Charles Alington."

* * *

Our little dinner-table of four would not permit of separate conversations, and general topics, springing up like mushrooms, wilted and died at their very inception. What mood possessed the others I did not at that time know, but for myself I was only conscious of some fundamental distaste of the handsome, clever woman who sat on my right, and seemed quite unaffected by the withering atmosphere. She was charming to the eye, she was witty to the ear, she had grace and gracefulness, and all the time she was something terrible. But by degrees, as I found my own distaste increasing, I saw that my brother-in-law's interest was growing correspondingly keen. The 'pretty lady' whose presence at dinner he had desired and obtained was enchaining him – not, so I began to guess, for her charm and her prettiness; but for some purpose of study, and I wondered whether it was her beautiful Jewish profile that was confirming to his mind some Anglo-Israelitish theory, whether he saw in her fine brown eyes the glance of the seer and the clairvoyante, or whether he divined in her some reincarnation of one of the famous or the infamous dead. Certainly she had for him some fascination beyond that of the legitimate charm of a very handsome woman; he was studying her with intense curiosity.

"And you are comfortable in the Gate-house?" he suddenly rapped out at her, as if asking some question of which the answer was crucial.

"Ah! But so comfortable," she said – "such a delightful atmosphere. I have never known a house that 'felt' so peaceful and homelike. Or is it merely fanciful to imagine that some houses have a sense of tranquillity about them and others are uneasy and even terrible?"

Charles stared at her a moment in silence before he recollected his manners.

"No, there may easily be something in it, I should say," he answered. "One can imagine long centuries of tranquillity actually investing a home with some sort of psychical aura perceptible to those who are sensitive."

She turned to Madge.

"And yet I have heard a ridiculous story that the house is supposed to be haunted," she said. "If it is, it is surely haunted by delightful, contented spirits."

Dinner was over. Madge rose.

"Come in very soon, Tony," she said to me, "and let's get to our bridge."

But her eyes said, "Don't leave me long alone with her."

Charles turned briskly round when the door had shut.

"An extremely interesting woman," he said.

"Very handsome," said I.

"Is she? I didn't notice. Her mind, her spirit – that's what intrigued me. What is she? What's behind? Why did Fungus turn tail like that? Queer, too, about her finding the atmosphere of the Gate-house so tranquil. The late tenants, I remember, didn't find that soothing touch about it!"

"How do you account for that?" I asked.

"There might be several explanations. You might say that the late tenants were fanciful, imaginative people, and that the present tenant is a sensible, matter-of-fact woman. Certainly she seemed to be."

"Or –" I suggested.

He laughed.

"Well, you might say – mind, I don't say so – but you might say that the – the spiritual tenants of the house find Mrs. Acres a congenial companion, and want to retain her. So they keep quiet, and don't upset the cook's nerves!"

Somehow this answer exasperated and jarred on me.

"What do you mean?" I said. "The spiritual tenant of the house, I suppose, is the man who betrayed his brother and hanged himself. Why should he find a charming woman like Mrs. Acres a congenial companion?"

Charles got up briskly. Usually he is more than ready to discuss such topics, but tonight it seemed that he had no such inclination.

"Didn't Madge tell us not to be long?" he asked. "You know how I run on if I once get on that subject, Tony, so don't give me the opportunity."

"But why did you say that?" I persisted.

"Because I was talking nonsense. You know me well enough to be aware that I am an habitual criminal in that respect."

* * *

It was indeed strange to find how completely both the first impression that Madge had formed of Mrs. Acres and the feeling that followed so quickly on its heels were endorsed by those who, during the next week or two, did a neighbour's duty to the newcomer. All were loud in praise of her charm, her pleasant, kindly wit, her good looks, her beautiful clothes, but even while this *Lob-gesang* was in full chorus it would suddenly die away, and an uneasy silence descended, which somehow was more eloquent than all the appreciative speech. Odd, unaccountable little incidents had occurred, which were whispered from mouth to mouth till they became common property. The same fear that Fungus had shown of her was exhibited by another dog. A parallel case occurred when she returned the call of our parson's wife. Mrs. Dowlett had a cage of canaries in the window of her drawing-room. These birds had manifested symptoms of extreme terror when Mrs. Acres entered the room, beating themselves against the wires of their cage, and uttering the alarm-note.... She inspired some sort of inexplicable fear, over which we, as trained and civilised human beings, had control, so that we behaved ourselves. But animals, without that check, gave way altogether to it, even as Fungus had done.

Mrs. Acres entertained; she gave charming little dinner-parties of eight, with a couple of tables at bridge to follow, but over these evenings there hung a blight and a blackness. No doubt the sinister story of the panelled parlour contributed to this.

This curious secret dread of her, of which as on that first evening at my house, she appeared to be completely unconscious differed very widely in degree. Most people, like myself, were conscious of it, but only very remotely so, and we found ourselves at the Gate-house behaving quite as usual, though with this unease in the background. But with a few, and most of all with Madge, it grew into a sort of obsession. She made every effort to combat it; her will was entirely set against it, but her struggle seemed only to establish its power over her. The pathetic and pitiful part was that Mrs. Acres from the first had taken a tremendous liking to her, and used to drop in continually, calling first to Madge at the window, in that pleasant, serene voice of hers, to tell Fungus that the hated one was imminent.

Then came a day when Madge and I were bidden to a party at the Gate-house on Christmas evening. This was to be the last of Mrs. Acres's hospitalities for the present, since she was leaving immediately afterwards for a couple of months in Egypt. So, with this remission ahead, Madge almost gleefully accepted the bidding. But when the evening came she was seized with so violent an attack of sickness and shivering that she was utterly unable to fulfil her engagement. Her doctor could find no physical trouble to account for this: it seemed that the anticipation of her evening alone caused it, and here was the culmination of her shrinking from our kindly and pleasant neighbour. She could only tell me that her sensations, as she began to dress for the party, were like those of that moment in sleep when somewhere in the drowsy brain nightmare is ripening. Something independent of her will revolted at what lay before her....

* * *

Spring had begun to stretch herself in the lap of winter when next the curtain rose on this veiled drama of forces but dimly comprehended and shudderingly conjectured; but then, indeed, nightmare ripened swiftly in broad noon. And this was the way of it.

Charles Alington had again come to stay with us five days before Easter, and expressed himself as humorously disappointed to find that the subject of his curiosity was still absent from the Gate-house. On the Saturday morning before Easter he appeared very late for breakfast, and Madge had already gone her ways. I rang for a fresh teapot, and while this was on its way he took up *The Times*.

"I only read the outside page of it," he said. "The rest is too full of mere materialistic dullnesses – politics, sports, money-market –"

He stopped, and passed the paper over to me.

"There, where I'm pointing," he said – "among the deaths. The first one."

What I read was this:

> Acres, Bertha. Died at sea, Thursday night, 30th March, and by her own request buried at sea. (Received by wireless from P. & O. steamer Peshawar.)

He held out his hand for the paper again, and turned over the leaves.

"Lloyd's," he said. "The *Peshawar* arrived at Tilbury yesterday afternoon. The burial must have taken place somewhere in the English Channel."

* * *

On the afternoon of Easter Sunday Madge and I motored out to the golf links three miles away. She proposed to walk along the beach just outside the dunes while I had my round, and return to the club-house for tea in two hours' time. The day was one of most lucid spring: a warm south-west wind bowled white clouds along the sky, and their shadows jovially scudded over the sandhills. We had told her of Mrs. Acres's death, and from that moment something dark and vague which had been lying over her mind since the autumn seemed to join this fleet of the shadows of clouds and leave her in sunlight. We parted at the door of the club-house, and she set out on her walk.

Half an hour later, as my opponent and I were waiting on the fifth tee, where the road crosses the links, for the couple in front of us to move on, a servant from the club-house, scudding along the road, caught sight of us, and, jumping from his bicycle, came to where we stood.

"You're wanted at the club-house, sir," he said to me. "Mrs. Carford was walking along the shore, and she found something left by the tide. A body, sir. 'Twas in a sack, but the sack was torn, and she saw – it's upset her very much, sir. We thought it best to come for you."

I took the boy's bicycle and went back to the club-house as fast as I could turn the wheel. I felt sure I knew what Madge had found, and, knowing that, realised the shock.... Five minutes later she was telling me her story in gasps and whispers.

"The tide was going down," she said, "and I walked along the high-water mark.... There were pretty shells; I was picking them up.... And then I saw it in front of me – just shapeless, just a sack...and then, as I came nearer, it took shape; there were knees and elbows. It moved, it rolled over, and where the head was the sack was torn, and I saw her face. Her eyes were open, Tony, and I fled.... All the time I felt it was rolling along after me. Oh, Tony! She's dead, isn't she? She won't come back to the Gate-house? Do you promise me...? There's something awful! I wonder if I guess. The sea gives her up. The sea won't suffer her to rest in it...."

The news of the finding had already been telephoned to Tarleton, and soon a party of four men with a stretcher arrived. There was no doubt as to the identity of the body, for though it had been in the water for three days no corruption had come to it. The weights with which at burial it had been laden must by some strange chance have been detached from it, and by a chance stranger yet it had drifted to the shore closest to her home. That night it lay in the mortuary, and the inquest was held on it next day, though that was a bank-holiday. From there it was taken to the Gate-house and coffined, and it lay in the panelled parlour for the funeral on the morrow.

Madge, after that one hysterical outburst, had completely recovered herself, and on the Monday evening she made a little wreath of the spring-flowers which the early warmth had called into blossom in the garden, and I went across with it to the Gate-house. Though the news of Mrs. Acres's death and the subsequent finding of the body had been widely advertised, there had been no response from relations or friends, and as I laid the solitary wreath on the coffin a sense of the utter loneliness of what lay within seized and encompassed me. And then a portent, no less, took place before my eyes. Hardly had the freshly gathered flowers been laid on the coffin than they drooped and wilted. The stalks of the daffodils bent, and their bright chalices closed; the odour of the wallflowers died, and they withered as I watched.... What did it mean, that even the petals of spring shrank and were moribund?

* * *

I told Madge nothing of this; and she, as if through some pang of remorse, was determined to be present next day at the funeral. No arrival of friends or relations had taken place, and from the Gate-house there came none of the servants. They stood in the porch as the coffin was brought out of the house, and even before it was put into the hearse had gone back again and closed the door. So, at the cemetery on the hill above Tarleton, Madge and her brother and I were the only mourners.

The afternoon was densely overcast, though we got no rainfall, and it was with thick clouds above and a sea-mist drifting between the grave-stones that we came, after the service in the cemetery-chapel, to the place of interment. And then – I can hardly write of it now – when it came for the coffin to be lowered into the grave, it was found that by some faulty measurement it could not descend, for the excavation was not long enough to hold it.

Madge was standing close to us, and at this moment I heard her sob.

"And the kindly earth will not receive her," she whispered.

There was awful delay: the diggers must be sent for again, and meantime the rain had begun to fall thick and tepid. For some reason – perhaps some outlying feeler of Madge's obsession had wound a tentacle round me – I felt that I must know that earth had gone to earth, but I could not suffer Madge to wait. So, in this miserable pause, I got Charles to take her home, and then returned.

Pick and shovel were busy, and soon the resting-place was ready. The interrupted service continued, the handful of wet earth splashed on the coffin-lid, and when all was over I left the cemetery, still feeling, I knew not why, that all was *not* over. Some restlessness and want of certainty possessed me, and instead of going home I fared forth into the rolling wooded country inland, with the intention of walking off these bat-like terrors that flapped around me. The rain had ceased, and a blurred sunlight penetrated the sea-mist which still blanketed the fields and woods, and for half an hour, moving briskly, I endeavoured to fight down some fantastic conviction that had gripped my mind in its claws. I refused to look straight at that conviction, telling myself how fantastic, how unreasonable it was; but as often as I put out a hand to throttle it there came the echo of Madge's words: "The sea will not suffer her; the kindly earth will not receive her." And if I could shut my eyes to that there came some remembrance of the day she died, and of half-forgotten fragments of Charles's superstitious belief in reincarnation. The whole thing, incredible though its component parts were, hung together with a terrible tenacity.

* * *

Before long the rain began again, and I turned, meaning to go by the main-road into Tarleton, which passes in a wide-flung curve some half-mile outside the cemetery. But as I approached the path through the fields, which, leaving the less direct route, passes close to the cemetery and brings you by a steeper and shorter descent into the town, I felt myself irresistibly impelled to take it. I told myself, of course, that I wished to make my wet walk as short as possible; but at the back of my mind was the half-conscious, but none the less imperative need to know by ocular evidence that the grave by which I had stood that afternoon had been filled in, and that the body of Mrs. Acres now lay tranquil beneath the soil. My path would be even shorter if I passed through the graveyard, and so presently I was fumbling in the gloom for the latch of the gate, and closed it again behind me. Rain was falling now thick and sullenly, and in the bleared twilight I picked my way among the mounds and slipped on the dripping grass, and there in front of me was the newly turned earth. All was finished: the grave-diggers had done their work and departed, and earth had gone back again into the keeping of the earth.

It brought me some great lightening of the spirit to know that, and I was on the point of turning away when a sound of stir from the heaped soil caught my ear, and I saw a little stream of pebbles mixed with clay trickle down the side of the mound above the grave: the heavy rain, no doubt, had loosened the earth. And then came another and yet another, and with terror gripping at my heart I perceived that this was no loosening from without, but from within, for to right and left the piled soil was falling away with the press of something from below. Faster and faster it poured off the grave, and ever higher at the head of it rose a mound of earth pushed upwards from beneath. Somewhere out of sight there came the sound as of creaking and breaking wood, and then through that mound of earth there protruded the end of the coffin. The lid was shattered: loose pieces of the boards fell off it, and from within the cavity there faced me white features and wide eyes. All this I saw, while sheer terror held me motionless; then, I suppose, came the breaking-point, and with such panic as surely man never felt before I was stumbling away among the graves and racing towards the kindly human lights of the town below.

I went to the parson who had conducted the service that afternoon with my incredible tale, and an hour later he, Charles Alington, and two or three men from the undertaker's were on the spot. They found the coffin, completely disinterred, lying on the ground by the grave, which was now three-quarters full of the earth which had fallen back into it. After what had happened it was decided to make no further attempt to bury it; and next day the body was cremated.

* * *

Now, it is open to anyone who may read this tale to reject the incident of this emergence of the coffin altogether, and account for the other strange happenings by the comfortable theory of coincidence. He can certainly satisfy himself that one Bertha Acres did die at sea on this particular Thursday before Easter, and was buried at sea: there is nothing extraordinary about that. Nor is it the least impossible that the weights should have slipped from the canvas shroud, and that the body should have been washed ashore on the coast by Tarleton (why not Tarleton, as well as any other little town near the coast?); nor is there anything inherently significant in the fact that the grave, as originally dug, was not of sufficient dimensions to receive the coffin. That all these incidents should have happened to the body of a single individual is odd, but then the nature of coincidence is to be odd. They form a startling series, but unless coincidences are startling they escape observation altogether. So, if you reject the last incident here recorded, or account for it by some local disturbance, an earthquake, or the breaking of a spring just below the grave, you can comfortably recline on the cushion of coincidence....

* * *

For myself, I give no explanation of these events, though my brother-in-law brought forward one with which he himself is perfectly satisfied. Only the other day he sent me, with considerable jubilation, a copy of some extracts from a mediaeval treatise on the subject of reincarnation which sufficiently indicates his theory. The original work was in Latin, which, mistrusting my scholarship, he kindly translated for me. I transcribe his quotations exactly as he sent them to me.

"We have these certain instances of his reincarnation. In one his spirit was incarnated in the body of a man; in the other, in that of a woman, fair of outward aspect, and of a pleasant conversation, but held in dread and in horror by those who came into more than casual intercourse with her.... She, it is said, died on the anniversary of the day on which he hanged himself, after the betrayal, but of this I have no certain information. What is sure is that, when the time came for her burial, the kindly earth would receive her not, but though the grave was dug deep and well it spewed her forth again.... Of the man in whom his cursed spirit was reincarnated it is said that, being on a voyage when he died, he was cast overboard with weights to sink him; but the sea would not suffer him to rest in her bosom, but slipped the weights from him, and cast him forth again on to the coast.... Howbeit, when the full time of his expiation shall have come and his deadly sin forgiven, the corporal body which is the cursed receptacle of his spirit shall at length be purged with fire, and so he shall, in the infinite mercy of the Almighty, have rest, and shall wander no more."

An Inhabitant of Carcosa

Ambrose Bierce

FOR THERE BE divers sorts of death – some wherein the body remaineth; and in some it vanisheth quite away with the spirit. This commonly occurreth only in solitude (such is God's will) and, none seeing the end, we say the man is lost, or gone on a long journey – which indeed he hath; but sometimes it hath happened in sight of many, as abundant testimony showeth. In one kind of death the spirit also dieth, and this it hath been known to do while yet the body was in vigor for many years. Sometimes, as is veritably attested, it dieth with the body, but after a season is raised up again in that place where the body did decay.

Pondering these words of Hali (whom God rest) and questioning their full meaning, as one who, having an intimation, yet doubts if there be not something behind, other than that which he has discerned, I noted not whither I had strayed until a sudden chill wind striking my face revived in me a sense of my surroundings. I observed with astonishment that everything seemed unfamiliar. On every side of me stretched a bleak and desolate expanse of plain, covered with a tall overgrowth of sere grass, which rustled and whistled in the autumn wind with heaven knows what mysterious and disquieting suggestion. Protruded at long intervals above it stood strangely shaped and somber-colored rocks, which seemed to have an understanding with one another and to exchange looks of uncomfortable significance, as if they had reared their heads to watch the issue of some foreseen event. A few blasted trees here and there appeared as leaders in this malevolent conspiracy of silent expectation.

The day, I thought, must be far advanced, though the sun was invisible; and although sensible that the air was raw and chill my consciousness of that fact was rather mental than physical – I had no feeling of discomfort. Over all the dismal landscape a canopy of low, lead-colored clouds hung like a visible curse. In all this there were a menace and a portent – a hint of evil, an intimation of doom. Bird, beast, or insect there was none. The wind sighed in the bare branches of the dead trees and the gray grass bent to whisper its dread secret to the earth; but no other sound nor motion broke the awful repose of that dismal place.

I observed in the herbage a number of weather-worn stones, evidently shaped with tools. They were broken, covered with moss and half sunken in the earth. Some lay prostrate, some leaned at various angles, none was vertical. They were obviously headstones of graves, though the graves themselves no longer existed as either mounds or depressions; the years had leveled all. Scattered here and there, more massive blocks showed where some pompous tomb or ambitious monument had once flung its feeble defiance at oblivion. So old seemed these relics, these vestiges of vanity and memorials of affection and piety, so battered and worn and stained – so neglected, deserted, forgotten the place, that I could not help thinking myself the discoverer of the burial-ground of a prehistoric race of men whose very name was long extinct.

Filled with these reflections, I was for some time heedless of the sequence of my own experiences, but soon I thought, "How came I hither?" A moment's reflection seemed to make this all clear and explain at the same time, though in a disquieting way, the singular character with which my fancy had invested all that I saw or heard. I was ill. I remembered now that I had been prostrated by a sudden fever, and that my family had told me that in my periods of delirium I had constantly cried out for liberty and air, and had been held in bed to prevent my escape out-of-doors. Now I had eluded the vigilance of my attendants and had wandered hither to – to where? I could not conjecture. Clearly I was at a considerable distance from the city where I dwelt – the ancient and famous city of Carcosa.

No signs of human life were anywhere visible nor audible; no rising smoke, no watch-dog's bark, no lowing of cattle, no shouts of children at play – nothing but that dismal burial-place, with its air of mystery and dread, due to my own disordered brain. Was I not becoming again delirious, there beyond human aid? Was it not indeed *all* an illusion of my madness? I called aloud the names of my wives and sons, reached out my hands in search of theirs, even as I walked among the crumbling stones and in the withered grass.

A noise behind me caused me to turn about. A wild animal – a lynx – was approaching. The thought came to me: If I break down here in the desert – if the fever return and I fail, this beast will be at my throat. I sprang toward it, shouting. It trotted tranquilly by within a hand's breadth of me and disappeared behind a rock.

A moment later a man's head appeared to rise out of the ground a short distance away. He was ascending the farther slope of a low hill whose crest was hardly to be distinguished from the general level. His whole figure soon came into view against the background of gray cloud. He was half naked, half clad in skins. His hair was unkempt, his beard long and ragged. In one hand he carried a bow and arrow; the other held a blazing torch with a long trail of black smoke. He walked slowly and with caution, as if he feared falling into some open grave concealed by the tall grass. This strange apparition surprised but did not alarm, and taking such a course as to intercept him I met him almost face to face, accosting him with the familiar salutation, "God keep you."

He gave no heed, nor did he arrest his pace.

"Good stranger," I continued, "I am ill and lost. Direct me, I beseech you, to Carcosa."

The man broke into a barbarous chant in an unknown tongue, passing on and away.

An owl on the branch of a decayed tree hooted dismally and was answered by another in the distance. Looking upward, I saw through a sudden rift in the clouds Aldebaran and the Hyades! In all this there was a hint of night – the lynx, the man with the torch, the owl. Yet I saw – I saw even the stars in absence of the darkness. I saw, but was apparently not seen nor heard. Under what awful spell did I exist?

I seated myself at the root of a great tree, seriously to consider what it were best to do. That I was mad I could no longer doubt, yet recognized a ground of doubt in the conviction. Of fever I had no trace. I had, withal, a sense of exhilaration and vigor altogether unknown to me – a feeling of mental and physical exaltation. My senses seemed all alert; I could feel the air as a ponderous substance; I could hear the silence.

A great root of the giant tree against whose trunk I leaned as I sat held inclosed in its grasp a slab of stone, a part of which protruded into a recess formed by another root. The stone was thus partly protected from the weather, though greatly decomposed. Its edges were worn round, its corners eaten away, its surface deeply furrowed and scaled. Glittering particles of mica were visible in the earth about it – vestiges of its decomposition. This stone had apparently marked the grave out of which the tree had sprung ages ago. The tree's exacting roots had robbed the grave and made the stone a prisoner.

A sudden wind pushed some dry leaves and twigs from the uppermost face of the stone; I saw the low-relief letters of an inscription and bent to read it. God in Heaven! *My* name in full! – the date of *my* birth! – the date of *my* death!

A level shaft of light illuminated the whole side of the tree as I sprang to my feet in terror. The sun was rising in the rosy east. I stood between the tree and his broad red disk – no shadow darkened the trunk!

A chorus of howling wolves saluted the dawn. I saw them sitting on their haunches, singly and in groups, on the summits of irregular mounds and tumuli filling a half of my desert prospect and extending to the horizon. And then I knew that these were ruins of the ancient and famous city of Carcosa.

Such are the facts imparted to the medium Bayrolles by the spirit Hoseib Alar Robardin.

The Moonlit Road

Ambrose Bierce

I
Statement of Joel Hetman, Jr.

I AM THE most unfortunate of men. Rich, respected, fairly well educated and of sound health – with many other advantages usually valued by those having them and coveted by those who have them not – I sometimes think that I should be less unhappy if they had been denied me, for then the contrast between my outer and my inner life would not be continually demanding a painful attention. In the stress of privation and the need of effort I might sometimes forget the somber secret ever baffling the conjecture that it compels.

I am the only child of Joel and Julia Hetman. The one was a well-to-do country gentleman, the other a beautiful and accomplished woman to whom he was passionately attached with what I now know to have been a jealous and exacting devotion. The family home was a few miles from Nashville, Tennessee, a large, irregularly built dwelling of no particular order of architecture, a little way off the road, in a park of trees and shrubbery.

At the time of which I write I was nineteen years old, a student at Yale. One day I received a telegram from my father of such urgency that in compliance with its unexplained demand I left at once for home. At the railway station in Nashville a distant relative awaited me to apprise me of the reason for my recall: my mother had been barbarously murdered – why and by whom none could conjecture, but the circumstances were these: my father had gone to Nashville, intending to return the next afternoon. Something prevented his accomplishing the business in hand, so he returned on the same night, arriving just before the dawn. In his testimony before the coroner he explained that having no latchkey and not caring to disturb the sleeping servants, he had, with no clearly defined intention, gone round to the rear of the house. As he turned an angle of the building, he heard a sound as of a door gently closed, and saw in the darkness, indistinctly, the figure of a man, which instantly disappeared among the trees of the lawn. A hasty pursuit and brief search of the grounds in the belief that the trespasser was someone secretly visiting a servant proving fruitless, he entered at the unlocked door and mounted the stairs to my mother's chamber. Its door was open, and stepping into black darkness he fell headlong over some heavy object on the floor. I may spare myself the details; it was my poor mother, dead of strangulation by human hands!

Nothing had been taken from the house, the servants had heard no sound, and excepting those terrible finger-marks upon the dead woman's throat – dear God! That I might forget them! – no trace of the assassin was ever found.

I gave up my studies and remained with my father, who, naturally, was greatly changed. Always of a sedate, taciturn disposition, he now fell into so deep a dejection that nothing could hold his attention, yet anything – a footfall, the sudden closing of a door – aroused in him a fitful interest; one might have called it an apprehension. At any small surprise of the senses he would start visibly and sometimes turn pale, then relapse into a melancholy apathy deeper than before. I suppose he was what is called a 'nervous wreck'. As to me, I was younger then than now – there is much in that. Youth is Gilead, in which is balm for every wound. Ah, that I might again dwell in that enchanted land! Unacquainted with grief, I knew not how to appraise my bereavement; I could not rightly estimate the strength of the stroke.

One night, a few months after the dreadful event, my father and I walked home from the city. The full moon was about three hours above the eastern horizon; the entire countryside had the solemn stillness of a summer night; our footfalls and the ceaseless song of the katydids were the only sound aloof. Black shadows of bordering trees lay athwart the road, which, in the short reaches between, gleamed a ghostly white. As we approached the gate to our dwelling, whose front was in shadow, and in which no light shone, my father suddenly stopped and clutched my arm, saying, hardly above his breath:

"God! God! What is that?"

"I hear nothing," I replied.

"But see – see!" he said, pointing along the road, directly ahead.

I said: "Nothing is there. Come, father, let us go in – you are ill."

He had released my arm and was standing rigid and motionless in the center of the illuminated roadway, staring like one bereft of sense. His face in the moonlight showed a pallor and fixity inexpressibly distressing. I pulled gently at his sleeve, but he had forgotten my existence. Presently he began to retire backward, step by step, never for an instant removing his eyes from what he saw, or thought he saw. I turned half round to follow, but stood irresolute. I do not recall any feeling of fear, unless a sudden chill was its physical manifestation. It seemed as if an icy wind had touched my face and enfolded my body from head to foot; I could feel the stir of it in my hair.

At that moment my attention was drawn to a light that suddenly streamed from an upper window of the house: one of the servants, awakened by what mysterious premonition of evil who can say, and in obedience to an impulse that she was never able to name, had lit a lamp. When I turned to look for my father he was gone, and in all the years that have passed no whisper of his fate has come across the borderland of conjecture from the realm of the unknown.

II
Statement of Caspar Grattan

TODAY I AM SAID to live; tomorrow, here in this room, will lie a senseless shape of clay that all too long was I. If anyone lift the cloth from the face of that unpleasant thing it will be in gratification of a mere morbid curiosity. Some, doubtless, will go further and inquire, "Who was he?" In this writing I supply the only answer that I am able to make – Caspar Grattan. Surely, that should be enough. The name has served my small need for more than twenty years of a life of unknown length. True, I gave it to myself, but lacking another I had the right. In this world one must have a name; it prevents confusion, even when it does not establish identity. Some, though, are known by numbers, which also seem inadequate distinctions.

One day, for illustration, I was passing along a street of a city, far from here, when I met two men in uniform, one of whom, half pausing and looking curiously into my face, said to his companion, "That man looks like 767." Something in the number seemed familiar and horrible. Moved by an uncontrollable impulse, I sprang into a side street and ran until I fell exhausted in a country lane.

I have never forgotten that number, and always it comes to memory attended by gibbering obscenity, peals of joyless laughter, the clang of iron doors. So I say a name, even if self-bestowed, is better than a number. In the register of the potter's field I shall soon have both. What wealth!

Of him who shall find this paper I must beg a little consideration. It is not the history of my life; the knowledge to write that is denied me. This is only a record of broken and apparently unrelated memories, some of them as distinct and sequent as brilliant beads upon a thread, others remote and strange, having the character of crimson dreams with interspaces blank and black – witch-fires glowing still and red in a great desolation.

Standing upon the shore of eternity, I turn for a last look landward over the course by which I came. There are twenty years of footprints fairly distinct, the impressions of bleeding feet. They lead through poverty and pain, devious and unsure, as of one staggering beneath a burden –

Remote, unfriended, melancholy, slow.

Ah, the poet's prophecy of Me – how admirable, how dreadfully admirable!

Backward beyond the beginning of this *via dolorosa* – this epic of suffering with episodes of sin – I see nothing clearly; it comes out of a cloud. I know that it spans only twenty years, yet I am an old man.

One does not remember one's birth – one has to be told. But with me it was different; life came to me full-handed and dowered me with all my faculties and powers. Of a previous existence I know no more than others, for all have stammering intimations that may be memories and may be dreams. I know only that my first consciousness was of maturity in body and mind – a consciousness accepted without surprise or conjecture. I merely found myself walking in a forest, half-clad, footsore, unutterably weary and hungry. Seeing a farmhouse, I approached and asked for food, which was given me by one who inquired my name. I did not know, yet knew that all had names. Greatly embarrassed, I retreated, and night coming on, lay down in the forest and slept.

The next day I entered a large town which I shall not name. Nor shall I recount further incidents of the life that is now to end – a life of wandering, always and everywhere haunted by an overmastering sense of crime in punishment of wrong and of terror in punishment of crime. Let me see if I can reduce it to narrative.

I seem once to have lived near a great city, a prosperous planter, married to a woman whom I loved and distrusted. We had, it sometimes seems, one child, a youth of brilliant parts and promise. He is at all times a vague figure, never clearly drawn, frequently altogether out of the picture.

One luckless evening it occurred to me to test my wife's fidelity in a vulgar, commonplace way familiar to everyone who has acquaintance with the literature of fact and fiction. I went to the city, telling my wife that I should be absent until the following afternoon. But I returned before daybreak and went to the rear of the house, purposing to enter by a door with which I had secretly so tampered that it would seem to lock, yet not actually fasten. As I approached it, I heard it gently open and close, and saw a man steal away into the darkness. With murder in my heart, I sprang after him, but he had vanished without even the bad luck of identification. Sometimes now I cannot even persuade myself that it was a human being.

Crazed with jealousy and rage, blind and bestial with all the elemental passions of insulted manhood, I entered the house and sprang up the stairs to the door of my wife's chamber. It was closed, but having tampered with its lock also, I easily entered and despite the black darkness soon stood by the side of her bed. My groping hands told me that although disarranged it was unoccupied.

"She is below," I thought, "and terrified by my entrance has evaded me in the darkness of the hall."

With the purpose of seeking her I turned to leave the room, but took a wrong direction – the right one! My foot struck her, cowering in a corner of the room. Instantly my hands were at her throat, stifling a shriek, my knees were upon her struggling body; and there in the darkness, without a word of accusation or reproach, I strangled her till she died!

There ends the dream. I have related it in the past tense, but the present would be the fitter form, for again and again the somber tragedy reenacts itself in my consciousness – over and over I lay the plan, I suffer the confirmation, I redress the wrong. Then all is blank; and afterward the rains beat against the grimy window-panes, or the snows fall upon my scant attire, the wheels rattle in the squalid streets where my life lies in poverty and mean employment. If there is ever sunshine I do not recall it; if there are birds they do not sing.

There is another dream, another vision of the night. I stand among the shadows in a moonlit road. I am aware of another presence, but whose I cannot rightly determine. In the shadow of a great dwelling I catch the gleam of white garments; then the figure of a woman confronts me in the road – my murdered wife! There is death in the face; there are marks upon the throat. The eyes are fixed on mine with an infinite gravity which is not reproach, nor hate, nor menace, nor anything less terrible than recognition. Before this awful apparition I retreat in terror – a terror that is upon me as I write. I can no longer rightly shape the words. See! They –

Now I am calm, but truly there is no more to tell: the incident ends where it began – in darkness and in doubt.

Yes, I am again in control of myself: 'the captain of my soul'. But that is not respite; it is another stage and phase of expiation. My penance, constant in degree, is mutable in kind: one of its variants is tranquillity. After all, it is only a life-sentence. 'To Hell for life' – that is a foolish penalty: the culprit chooses the duration of his punishment. Today my term expires.

To each and all, the peace that was not mine.

III
Statement of the Late Julia Hetman, Through the Medium Bayrolles

I HAD RETIRED EARLY and fallen almost immediately into a peaceful sleep, from which I awoke with that indefinable sense of peril which is, I think, a common experience in that other, earlier life. Of its unmeaning character, too, I was entirely persuaded, yet that did not banish it. My husband, Joel Hetman, was away from home; the servants slept in another part of the house. But these were familiar conditions; they had never before distressed me. Nevertheless, the strange terror grew so insupportable that conquering my reluctance to move I sat up and lit the lamp at my bedside. Contrary to my expectation this gave me no relief; the light seemed rather an added danger, for I reflected that it would shine out under the door, disclosing my presence to whatever evil thing might lurk outside. You that are still in the flesh, subject to horrors of the imagination, think what a monstrous fear that must be which seeks in darkness security from malevolent existences of the night. That is to spring to close quarters with an unseen enemy – the strategy of despair!

Extinguishing the lamp I pulled the bed-clothing about my head and lay trembling and silent, unable to shriek, forgetful to pray. In this pitiable state I must have lain for what you call hours – with us there are no hours, there is no time.

At last it came – a soft, irregular sound of footfalls on the stairs! They were slow, hesitant, uncertain, as of something that did not see its way; to my disordered reason all the more terrifying for that, as the approach of some blind and mindless malevolence to which is no appeal. I even thought that I must have left the hall lamp burning and the groping of this creature proved it a monster of the night. This was foolish and inconsistent with my previous dread of the light, but what would you have? Fear has no brains; it is an idiot. The dismal witness that it bears and the cowardly counsel that it whispers are unrelated. We know this well, we who have passed into the Realm of Terror, who skulk in eternal dusk among the scenes of our former lives, invisible even to ourselves and one another, yet hiding forlorn in lonely places; yearning for speech with our loved ones, yet dumb, and as fearful of them as they of us. Sometimes the disability is removed, the law suspended: by the deathless power of love or hate we break the spell – we are seen by those whom we would warn, console, or punish. What form we seem to them to bear we know not; we know only that we terrify even those whom we most wish to comfort, and from whom we most crave tenderness and sympathy.

Forgive, I pray you, this inconsequent digression by what was once a woman. You who consult us in this imperfect way – you do not understand. You ask foolish questions about things unknown and things forbidden. Much that we know and could impart in our speech is meaningless in yours. We must communicate with you through a stammering intelligence in that small fraction of our language that you yourselves can speak. You think that we are of another world. No, we have knowledge of no world but yours, though for us it holds no sunlight, no warmth, no music, no laughter, no song of birds, nor any companionship. O God! What a thing it is to be a ghost, cowering and shivering in an altered world, a prey to apprehension and despair!

No, I did not die of fright: the Thing turned and went away. I heard it go down the stairs, hurriedly, I thought, as if itself in sudden fear. Then I rose to call for help. Hardly had my shaking hand found the doorknob when – merciful heaven! – I heard it returning. Its footfalls as it remounted the stairs were rapid, heavy and loud; they shook the house. I fled to an angle of the wall and crouched upon the floor. I tried to pray. I tried to call the name of my dear husband. Then I heard the door thrown open. There was an interval of unconsciousness, and when I revived I felt a strangling clutch upon my throat – felt my arms feebly beating against something that bore me backward – felt my tongue thrusting itself from between my teeth! And then I passed into this life.

No, I have no knowledge of what it was. The sum of what we knew at death is the measure of what we know afterward of all that went before. Of this existence we know many things, but no new light falls upon any page of that; in memory is written all of it that we can read. Here are no heights of truth overlooking the confused landscape of that dubitable domain. We still dwell in the Valley of the Shadow, lurk in its desolate places, peering from brambles and thickets at its mad, malign inhabitants. How should we have new knowledge of that fading past?

What I am about to relate happened on a night. We know when it is night, for then you retire to your houses and we can venture from our places of concealment to move unafraid about our old homes, to look in at the windows, even to enter and gaze upon your faces as you sleep. I had lingered long near the dwelling where I had been so cruelly changed to what I am, as we do while any that we love or hate remain. Vainly I had sought some method of manifestation, some way to make my continued existence and my great love and poignant pity understood by my husband and son. Always if they slept they would wake, or if in my desperation I dared approach them when they were awake, would turn toward me the terrible eyes of the living, frightening me by the glances that I sought from the purpose that I held.

On this night I had searched for them without success, fearing to find them; they were nowhere in the house, nor about the moonlit lawn. For, although the sun is lost to us forever, the moon, full-orbed or slender, remains to us. Sometimes it shines by night, sometimes by day, but always it rises and sets, as in that other life.

I left the lawn and moved in the white light and silence along the road, aimless and sorrowing. Suddenly I heard the voice of my poor husband in exclamations of astonishment, with that of my son in reassurance and dissuasion; and there by the shadow of a group of trees they stood – near, so near! Their faces were toward me, the eyes of the elder man fixed upon mine. He saw me – at last, at last, he saw me! In the consciousness of that, my terror fled as a cruel dream. The death-spell was broken: Love had conquered Law! Mad with exultation I shouted – I *must* have shouted, "He sees, he sees: he will understand!" Then, controlling myself, I moved forward, smiling and consciously beautiful, to offer myself to his arms, to comfort him with endearments, and, with my son's hand in mine, to speak words that should restore the broken bonds between the living and the dead.

Alas! Alas! His face went white with fear, his eyes were as those of a hunted animal. He backed away from me, as I advanced, and at last turned and fled into the wood – whither, it is not given to me to know.

To my poor boy, left doubly desolate, I have never been able to impart a sense of my presence. Soon he, too, must pass to this Life Invisible and be lost to me forever.

The Cold Embrace

Mary Elizabeth Braddon

HE WAS AN ARTIST – such things as happened to him happen sometimes to artists.

He was a German – such things as happened to him happen sometimes to Germans.

He was young, handsome, studious, enthusiastic, metaphysical, reckless, unbelieving, heartless. And being young, handsome and eloquent, he was beloved.

He was an orphan, under the guardianship of his dead father's brother, his uncle Wilhelm, in whose house he had brought up from a little child; and she who loved him was his cousin – his cousin Gertrude, whom he swore he loved in return.

Did he love her? Yes, when he first swore it. It soon wore out, this passionate love; how threadbare and wretched a sentiment it became at last in the selfish heart of the student! But in its first golden dawn, when he was only nineteen, and had just returned from his apprenticeship to a great painter at Antwerp, and they wandered together in the most romantic outskirts of the city at rosy sunset, by holy moonlight, or bright and joyous morning, how beautiful a dream!

They keep it a secret from Wilhelm, as he has the father's ambition of a wealthy suitor for his only child – a cold and dreary vision beside the lover's dream.

So they are betrothed; and standing side by side when the dying sun and the pale rising moon divide the heavens, he puts the betrothal ring upon her finger, the white and taper finger whose slender shape he knows so well. This ring is a peculiar one, a massive golden serpent, its tail in its mouth, the symbol of eternity; it had been his mother's, and he would know it amongst a thousand. If he were to become blind tomorrow, he could select it from amongst a thousand by the touch alone.

He places it on her finger, and they swear to be true to each other for ever and ever – through trouble and danger – sorrow and change – in wealth or poverty. Her father must needs be won to consent to their union by-and-by, for they were now betrothed, and death alone could part them.

But the young student, the scoffer at revelation, yet the enthusiastic adorer of the mystical asks:

"Can death part us? I would return to you from the grave, Gertrude. My soul would come back to be near my love. And you – you, if you died before me – the cold earth would not hold you from me; if you loved me, you would return, and again these fair arms would be clasped round my neck as they are now."

But she told him, with a holier light in her deep-blue eyes than had ever shone in his – she told him that the dead who die at peace with God are happy in heaven, and cannot return to the troubled earth; and that it is only the suicide – the lost wretch on whom sorrowful angels shut the door of Paradise – whose unholy spirit haunts the footsteps of the living.

The first year of their betrothal is passed, and she is alone, for he has gone to Italy, on a commission for some rich man, to copy Raphaels, Titians, Guidos, in a gallery at Florence. He has gone to win fame, perhaps; but it is not the less bitter – he is gone!

Of course her father misses his young nephew, who has been as a son to him; and he thinks his daughter's sadness no more than a cousin should feel for a cousin's absence.

In the meantime, the weeks and months pass. The lover writes – often at first, then seldom – at last, not at all.

How many excuses she invents for him! How many times she goes to the distant little post-office, to which he is to address his letters! How many times she hopes, only to be disappointed!

How many times she despairs, only to hope again!

But real despair comes at last, and will not be put off anymore. The rich suitor appears on the scene, and her father is determined. She is to marry at once. The wedding-day is fixed – the fifteenth of June.

The date seems burnt into her brain.

The date, written in fire, dances for ever before her eyes.

The date, shrieked by the Furies, sounds continually in her ears.

But there is time yet – it is the middle of May – there is time for a letter to reach him at Florence; there is time for him to come to Brunswick, to take her away and marry her, in spite of her father – in spite of the whole world.

But the days and weeks fly by, and he does not write – he does not come. This is indeed despair which usurps her heart, and will not be put away.

It is the fourteenth of June. For the last time she goes to the little post-office; for the last time she asks the old question, and they give her for the last time the dreary answer, "No; no letter."

For the last time – for tomorrow is the day appointed for her bridal. Her father will hear no entreaties; her rich suitor will not listen to her prayers. They will not be put off a day – an hour; tonight alone is hers – this night, which she may employ as she will.

She takes another path than that which leads home; she hurries through some by-streets of the city, out on to a lonely bridge, where he and she had stood so often in the sunset, watching the rose-coloured light glow, fade, and die upon the river.

He returns from Florence. He had received her letter. That letter, blotted with tears, entreating, despairing – he had received it, but he loved her no longer. A young Florentine, who has sat to him for a model, had bewitched his fancy – that fancy which with him stood in place of a heart – and Gertrude had been half-forgotten. If she had a rich suitor, good; let her marry him; better for her, better far for himself. He had no wish to fetter himself with a wife. Had he not his art always? – His eternal bride, his unchanging mistress.

Thus he thought it wiser to delay his journey to Brunswick, so that he should arrive when the wedding was over – arrive in time to salute the bride.

And the vows – the mystical fancies – the belief in his return, even after death, to the embrace of his beloved? O, gone out of his life; melted away for ever, those foolish dreams of his boyhood.

So on the fifteenth of June he enters Brunswick, by that very bridge on which she stood, the stars looking down on her, the night before. He strolls across the bridge and down by the water's edge, a great rough dog at his heels, and the smoke from his short meerschaum-pipe curling in blue wreaths fantastically in the pure morning air. He has his sketch-book under his arm, and attracted now and then by some object that catches his artist's eye, stops to draw: a few weeds and pebbles on the river's brink – a crag on the opposite shore – a group of pollard willows in the distance. When he has done, he admires his drawing, shuts his sketch-book, empties the ashes from his pipe, refills from his tobacco-pouch, sings the refrain of a gay drinking-song, calls to his dog, smokes again, and walks on. Suddenly he opens his sketch-book again; this time that which attracts him is a group of figures: but what is it? It is not a funeral, for there are no mourners.

It is not a funeral, but a corpse lying on a rough bier, covered with an old sail, carried between two bearers.

It is not a funeral, for the bearers are fishermen – fishermen in their everyday garb.

About a hundred yards from him they rest their burden on a bank – one stands at the head of the bier, the other throws himself down at the foot of it.

And thus they form a perfect group; he walks back two or three paces, selects his point of sight, and begins to sketch a hurried outline. He has finished it before they move; he hears their voices, though he cannot hear their words, and wonders what they can be talking of. Presently he walks on and joins them.

"You have a corpse there, my friends?" he says.

"Yes; a corpse washed ashore an hour ago."

"Drowned?"

"Yes, drowned. A young girl, very handsome."

"Suicides are always handsome," says the painter; and then he stands for a little while idly smoking and meditating, looking at the sharp outline of the corpse and the stiff folds of the rough canvas covering.

Life is such a golden holiday for him – young, ambitious, clever – that it seems as though sorrow and death could have no part in his destiny.

At last he says that, as this poor suicide is so handsome, he should like to make a sketch of her.

He gives the fishermen some money, and they offer to remove the sailcloth that covers her features.

No; he will do it himself. He lifts the rough, coarse, wet canvas from her face. What face?

The face that shone on the dreams of his foolish boyhood; the face which once was the light of his uncle's home. His cousin Gertrude – his betrothed!

He sees, as in one glance, while he draws one breath, the rigid features – the marble arms – the hands crossed on the cold bosom; and, on the third finger of the left hand, the ring which had been his mother's – the golden serpent; the ring which, if he were to become blind, he could select from a thousand others by the touch alone.

But he is a genius and a metaphysician – grief, true grief, is not for such as he. His first thought is flight – flight anywhere out of that accursed city – anywhere far from the brink of that hideous river – anywhere away from remorse – anywhere to forget.

He is miles on the road that leads away from Brunswick before he knows that he has walked a step.

It is only when his dog lies down panting at his feet than he feels how exhausted he is himself, and sits down upon a bank to rest. How the landscape spins round and round before his dazzled eyes, while his morning's sketch of the two fishermen and the canvas-covered bier glares redly at him out of the twilight!

At last, after sitting a long time by the roadside, idly playing with his dog, idly smoking, idly lounging, looking as any idle, light-hearted travelling student might look, yet all the while acting over that morning's scene in his burning brain a hundred times a minute; at last he grows a little more composed, and tries presently to think of himself as he is, apart from his cousin's suicide.

Apart from that, he was no worse off than he was yesterday. His genius was not gone; the money he had earned at Florence still lined his pocket-book; he was his own master, free to go whither he would.

And while he sits on the roadside, trying to separate himself from the scene of that morning – trying to put away the image of the corpse covered with the damp canvas sail – trying to think of what he should do next, where he should go, to be farthest away from Brunswick and remorse, the old diligence comes rumbling and jingling along. He remembers it; it goes from Brunswick to Aix-la-Chapelle.

He whistles to his dog, shouts to the postillion to stop, and springs into the coupé.

During the whole evening, through the long night, though he does not once close his eyes, he never speaks a word; but when morning dawns, and the other passengers awake and begin to talk to each other, he joins in the conversation. He tells them that he is an artist, that he is going to Cologne and to Antwerp to copy Rubenses, and the great picture by Quentin Matsys, in the museum. He remembered afterwards that he talked and laughed boisterously, and that when he was talking and laughing loudest, a passenger, older and graver than the rest, opened the window near him, and told him to put his head out. He remembered the fresh air blowing in his face, the singing of the birds in his ears, and the flat fields and roadside reeling before his eyes. He remembered this, and then falling in a lifeless heap on the floor of the diligence.

It is a fever that keeps him for six long weeks on a bed at a hotel in Aix-la-Chapelle.

He gets well, and, accompanied by his dog, starts on foot for Cologne. By this time he is his former self once more. Again the blue smoke from his short meerschaum curls upwards in the morning air – again he sings some old university drinking-song – again stops here and there, meditating and sketching.

He is happy, and has forgotten his cousin – and so on to Cologne.

It is by the great cathedral he is standing, with his dog at his side. It is night, the bells have just chimed the hour, and the clocks are striking eleven; the moonlight shines full upon the magnificent pile, over which the artist's eye wanders, absorbed in the beauty of form.

He is not thinking of his drowned cousin, for he has forgotten her and is happy.

Suddenly someone, something from behind him, puts two cold arms round his neck, and clasps its hands on his breast.

And yet there is no one behind him, for on the flags bathed in the broad moonlight there are only two shadows, his own and his dog's. He turns quickly round – there is no one – nothing to be seen in the broad square but himself and his dog; and though he feels, he cannot see the cold arms clasped round his neck.

It is not ghostly, this embrace, for it is palpable to the touch – it cannot be real, for it is invisible.

He tries to throw off the cold caress. He clasps the hands in his own to tear them asunder, and to cast them off his neck. He can feel the long delicate fingers cold and wet beneath his touch, and on the third finger of the left hand he can feel the ring which was his mother's – the golden serpent – the ring which he has always said he would know among a thousand by the touch alone. He knows it now!

His dead cousin's cold arms are round his neck – his dead cousin's wet hands are clasped upon his breast. He asks himself if he is mad. 'Up, Leo!' he shouts. 'Up, up, boy!' and the Newfoundland leaps to his shoulders – the dog's paws are on the dead hands, and the animal utters a terrific howl, and springs away from his master.

The student stands in the moonlight, the dead arms around his neck, and the dog at a little distance moaning piteously.

Presently a watchman, alarmed by the howling of the dog, comes into the square to see what is wrong.

In a breath the cold arms are gone.

He takes the watchman home to the hotel with him and gives him money; in his gratitude he could have given that man half his little fortune.

Will it ever come to him again, this embrace of the dead?

He tries never to be alone; he makes a hundred acquaintances, and shares the chamber of another student. He starts up if he is left by himself in the public room at the inn where he is staying, and runs into the street. People notice his strange actions, and begin to think that he is mad.

But, in spite of all, he is alone once more; for one night the public room being empty for a moment, when on some idle pretence he strolls into the street, the street is empty too, and for the second time he feels the cold arms round his neck, and for the second time, when he calls his dog, the animal slinks away from him with a piteous howl.

After this he leaves Cologne, still travelling on foot – of necessity now, for his money is getting low. He joins travelling hawkers, he walks side by side with labourers, he talks to every foot-passenger he falls in with, and tries from morning till night to get company on the road.

At night he sleeps by the fire in the kitchen of the inn at which he stops; but do what he will, he is often alone, and it is now a common thing for him to feel the cold arms around his neck.

Many months have passed since his cousin's death – autumn, winter, early spring. His money is nearly gone, his health is utterly broken, he is the shadow of his former self, and he is getting near to Paris. He will reach that city at the time of the Carnival. To this he looks forward. In Paris, in Carnival time, he need never, surely, be alone, never feel that deadly caress; he may even recover his lost gaiety, his lost health, once more resume his profession, once more earn fame and money by his art.

How hard he tries to get over the distance that divides him from Paris, while day by day he grows weaker, and his step slower and more heavy!

But there is an end at last; the long dreary roads are passed. This is Paris, which he enters for the first time – Paris, of which he has dreamed so much – Paris, whose million voices are to exorcise his phantom.

To him tonight Paris seems one vast chaos of lights, music, and confusion – lights which dance before his eyes and will not be still – music that rings in his ears and deafens him – confusion which makes his head whirl round and round.

But, in spite of all, he finds the opera-house, where there is a masked ball. He has enough money left to buy a ticket of admission, and to hire a domino to throw over his shabby dress. It seems only a moment after his entering the gates of Paris that he is in the very midst of all the wild gaiety of the opera-house ball.

No more darkness, no more loneliness, but a mad crowd, shouting and dancing, and a lovely Débardeuse hanging on his arm.

The boisterous gaiety he feels surely is his old light-heartedness come back. He hears the people round him talking of the outrageous conduct of some drunken student, and it is to him they point when they say this to him, who has not moistened his lips since yesterday at noon, for even now he will not drink; though his lips are parched, and his throat burning, he cannot drink.

His voice is thick and hoarse, and his utterance indistinct; but still this must be his old light-heartedness come back that makes him so wildly gay.

The little Débardeuse is wearied out – her arm rests on his shoulder heavier than lead – the other dancers one by one drop off.

The lights in the chandeliers one by one die out.

The decorations look pale and shadowy in that dim light which is neither night nor day.

A faint glimmer from the dying lamps, a pale streak of cold grey light from the new-born day, creeping in through half-opened shutters.

And by this light the bright-eyed Débardeuse fades sadly. He looks her in the face. How the brightness of her eyes dies out! Again he looks her in the face. How white that face has grown!

Again – and now it is the shadow of a face alone that looks in his.

Again – and they are gone – the bright eyes, the face, the shadow of the face. He is alone; alone in that vast saloon.

Alone, and, in the terrible silence, he hears the echoes of his own footsteps in that dismal dance which has no music.

No music but the beating of his breast. For the cold arms are round his neck – they whirl him round, they will not be flung off, or cast away; he can no more escape from their icy grasp than he can escape from death. He looks behind him – there is nothing but himself in the great empty salle; but he can feel – cold, deathlike, but O, how palpable! – the long slender fingers, and the ring which was his mother's.

He tries to shout, but he has no power in his burning throat. The silence of the place is only broken by the echoes of his own footsteps in the dance from which he cannot extricate himself.

Who says he has no partner? The cold hands are clasped on his breast, and now he does not shun their caress. No! One more polka, if he drops down dead.

The lights are all out, and, half an hour after, the gendarmes come in with a lantern to see that the house is empty; they are followed by a great dog that they have found seated howling on the steps of the theatre. Near the principal entrance they stumble over – the body of a student, who has died from want of food, exhaustion, and the breaking of a blood-vessel.

Joined

Sarah L. Byrne

WHEN YOUR HEART BROKE, I felt it too. We were walking through the city park when it happened; together but apart, because that was the way we'd become by then, wasn't it? There was an arm's-length distance and a silence as wide as a desert between us, but we were still joined, which meant we were sharing the scent of the lilac blossoms, the cool of the spring air on our skin, sharing the guarded edges of each other's feelings. Then your heart just tore itself apart.

It wasn't exactly your heart, I know – that's poetic license I'd add in later, because you weren't around to do it – but it was close enough. A catastrophic aortic rupture. But because we were joined, I felt the tearing pain rip through your body, and for a moment my breath choked off as the blood drained from your aorta into your chest. But only for a moment. My blood pressure fell only enough that I sank slowly to my knees on the gravel, while yours dropped to nothing as you crumpled to the ground. My heart went on beating while yours gave a last desperate flutter then just stopped.

Voices, footsteps, people rushing to surround you as you lay there on your back in the middle of the path, your skin waxy pale, your eyes open and dilated black. You were already gone. They didn't know it, but I did. I felt it happen.

Now I feel nothing.

* * *

It was a strange experience for a while, this feeling nothing. At least, if *nothing* is what you can call it. Feeling only my own feelings, thinking my own thoughts; alone in my own head after so long. The nothing I'd wanted for so long.

Six years back when we got our license, getting joined had seemed like such a romantic idea: for your partner to be truly your other half, to share each other's everyday joys and sorrows, to literally feel each other's pain and pleasure, one brain to the other through a real-time upload and download. So we registered, one of the first couples to do it, along with the marriage license – I, Tracy, do take you, Alana – and received our neural implants, just a painless injection, harmless nanoparticles that targeted the nerve fibres and grew rapidly along them, twined around them like wisteria, no different from the kind they use for paralysis and prosthetics. Then in only a matter of weeks we were fully joined.

Sex was double the fun, of course. That's what everyone wanted to talk about at first. But for some of us it went further. Beyond sharing physical sensations and basic emotions, into thoughts and memories too. Even dreams, because wasn't it all the same thing really? All just neural connections, electrical impulses jumping synaptic gaps and neuropeptides docking with receptors. All of it picked up, encoded and transmitted by the implant.

It would be impossible to hurt each other, when you were joined, that's what people said. They were wrong: it wasn't just possible, it was easy. No, it was more than easy; it was inevitable. In those days we were wound so tight around each other it was hard to believe we were separate people. So you knew when things started changing between us, because I had no secrets from you – but you didn't want to know. You didn't want to know how cloying I'd begun to find your presence, pretending not to notice how my mind flinched away from yours when you reached out to me. And I pretending not to feel your hurt. It was grotesque, wasn't it? But we went on for more than a year like that, alone together, until that day your heart finally broke.

I lied when I said I felt nothing that day. What I felt was relief.

* * *

I'm trying to sleep in the attic room under the roof windows, like I usually do these nights. I like it up here under the sky, and since you've been gone, the thought of sleeping alone in the bed we used to share is unthinkable. Tonight, it's one of those clear summer nights when the temperature drops, the stars come out clear and the heat of the day fades into refreshing coolness. I'll get to sleep eventually, even with it playing over and over in my mind like it does most nights: you falling away from me, falling out of me; the life fading out of your eyes, the blood draining out of your heart.

We were told that a weakening of the arteries was a rare risk of the implants. Your blood pressure must have been too high. You knew you were supposed to quit smoking after we were joined, but you never could. You tried – for me, mostly, because I didn't like the taste – but somehow you never quite could give it up. I still felt the desperation of your cravings too as they clawed at you over the hours and the days: so I gave in. We called it a compromise.

Now, I block out the thought of the pack of cigarettes in the drawer downstairs. Sleep comes.

It's a feeling that wakes me. *Cold.* I turn over in bed, tugging the sheet up around my bare shoulder. Did I leave a window open? No. I did not. But there's a coldness creeping over my skin still. It's distant and alien, still entirely familiar.

"Alana?"

"I'm cold," you say. Or don't say, but you *think* it and my brain responds to your thought. Your feelings flood my senses, the old intensity of them, and for a moment it's like it always was.

But it's not.

"You're not real," I say into the empty darkness.

There's a hesitation, then your thought comes at me heavy with accusation, hits me hard. There'd be that little catch in your voice now if you still had one; there'd be hurt in your blue eyes if they weren't burned to ashes and scattered on the cold earth. And I'd look away.

"How can you say that?" you demand. "Don't you understand what's happening? I've come back to you. Tracy, don't you want us to be together again?"

I do, of course I do, that part of me that's lost its other half. The part of me that wants to believe death isn't a black oblivion waiting for all of us someday, maybe sooner than we think. The part that grieves for all those years back then when we were happy, for laughter and dancing, sex and snuggling under a blanket together, or staying up half the night sharing thoughts and feelings because it was like a well of cool water, yet however deep we drank we couldn't get enough of each other. There's an ache inside me, how badly I want that again.

But it wasn't like that towards the end. It was over. I know it and you know it too. Or you would if you were really here, if there was any *you* anymore.

You've gone quiet now. I don't feel anything from you. I curl up on my side and try to sleep again. But no matter what I do now, I just can't get warm.

* * *

Everything seems better in the morning, doesn't it always? I call the customer helpline to report the bug. My dead wife is in my head, I explain. She's talking to me. Something's gone wrong, some data cached in the system that should have been deleted; outdated settings somewhere in the cloud.

"Mmm-hmm," the bored-sounding assistant on the other end of the line says, like it's some everyday thing. "We'll look into it for you."

Maybe this happens a lot. Maybe he doesn't believe a word of it. Most likely he's just sticking to his script and doesn't care particularly either way. Why should he, after all?

You come again that night.

"I'm cold," you say. "I want to come back. I want us to be together again."

"That's not possible."

"Maybe it is. We've got to try, haven't we? We've been given a second chance, surely it's happening for a reason?"

"I was going to leave you," I say. "It wasn't working out. We were going to separate, you knew that. We both knew."

"No," you say. A flood of images and feelings surge through me before I can stop you – happy times, good times, rose-tinted smiles – and I shove them back at you.

"Yes." You never could face a truth you didn't like, could you? "Alana, listen, I didn't want it to happen like this. I wanted you to be happy. I hoped you'd meet someone else, forget about me –"

"That would never have happened." You cut me off with a pulse of thought so sharp it hurts. "I'm not like you. I can't just switch off my feelings."

And apparently I can't switch off your feelings either.

I turn over, bury my face in the pillow. If you were here, for real, I'd feel your touch now. Your fingers sliding down my shoulders, the warmth of your body against mine, the scent of your hair. I'd feel what you feel and know you felt it right back; I'd hate myself for it but I'd turn over and pull you down to me. But you're not here. I don't know why I'm even having this conversation.

It's a while before you speak again: "Just do one thing for me."

"What?"

"I need a smoke. Just one. I'm desperate."

I let my breath out slowly against the pillow. We both know you've got me.

"All right."

I get out of bed, make my way downstairs and outside. I light the cigarette in the garden, awkward and clumsy despite the familiar feel of it against my fingers and lips, but when I inhale the sudden burn of the hot smoke in my lungs makes me cough it out sharply.

"Slowly," you tell me, your mind taut with impatience, with need. I breathe the smoke in steadily, holding it inside me this time, and feel the familiar nicotine-adrenaline rush through my veins, the familiar relief that's yours, not mine.

"Don't you miss this too?" you ask.

"No," I lie, letting the smoke out slowly. I take another drag.

If you could still smile, you would. You can't, but when you do, I feel it all the same.

* * *

It was a mistake, letting you have that one smoke. But then it was always a mistake to let you have your way, giving in to one of your 'compromises'. You had a way of sensing weakness, and you'd push for more, always more, never satisfied with what I could give you.

You come to me in the daytime now, as well as at night. You're there when I wake up, craving your morning coffee; you know I hate coffee, but somehow the smell of it drifts through my kitchen every morning these days. When I'm dressing, you're there with suggestions of perfume, how you miss it. Silk camisoles like you used to wear under your shirts, the smoothness against your skin. Darling, why don't you try your hair like this?

And now here I am, huddled under a flimsy shelter outside the entrance to the hospital where I'm supposed to be at work. My coat collar turned up against the wind, hands cupped around the dwindling end of a cigarette to protect it from the driving rain.

"Hey, Tracy. I didn't know you smoked."

I look up, startled, one of my co-workers standing there. I don't recognise him for a moment.

"I don't," I manage to say eventually.

He quirks an eyebrow before walking on, and I drop what's left of the cigarette, without looking down to see it fizzle out on the wet tarmac. I turn and head into the building.

I know what you want, Alana. To use my body, for us to share it. We're half-way there already.

But I'm saying no to you this time. Brushing the drops of water out of my hair and pulling off my wet jacket, I walk to my lab with more purpose than I have had in the months since this all started, because now I know what I have to do.

I shrug into my lab coat, glance at the samples waiting on my bench. I've always done my job in a detached way. It's just samples to analyse; blood in a vial, cells on a plate. I've made a point of not really thinking about where they come from. But that doesn't change the facts. There are dead people in the basement.

You want a body, Alana? I'll find you one. One all of your own. I'll inject you into it, you can worm your way through its veins, animate its dead nerves.

Just stay out of mine.

* * *

It's cold down here. I feel the chill as soon as I step out of the elevator, into this underground place where the dead people are.

"Help you?" The uninterested desk clerk glances up. I don't know her, she doesn't know me, but a glimpse of my lab coat and badge is enough that she's not going to ask difficult questions.

"Some samples didn't make it upstairs this morning, I need to talk to Mark," I lie.

It isn't difficult. If I can lie to my telepathic dead wife in my head – if I can lie so well to myself – it was never going to be hard to lie a stranger.

"He's inside." she says.

"Thanks."

I slide past the closed door of Mark's examination room, where he's conducting an autopsy, murmuring reports into his recording device. Down to the end of the corridor and into the storage room at the back. I pull on nitrile gloves, tug open one of the drawers, stare at the dead man, the stranger lying there. The cold body that doesn't look like anything that was ever alive, or ever will be again.

This is not going to be any use, I realise. I don't know what I was thinking, how I thought this was going to work, what I'm doing here. It never even made any sense. I push the drawer closed, start to turn away. But then I'm pulling open another drawer, and then another.

It's not me doing it. You're in my head. Suddenly, down here in the chill of this windowless cavern, you're here, guiding me, moving my hands for me. Drawing me to you.

Because when I open the third drawer, I stop, heart thudding against my ribs so hard it stops my breath.

Alana.

It's you. Just like you looked lying on the gravel under the lilacs that day.

You can't be here. I said my goodbyes to you. I organised the memorial service, stood there tearless with your parents weeping and casting me haunted looks – the one who broke their daughter's heart, who sent tendrils creeping through her veins to tie her forever to me and beguiled her to her death – if only they knew how it really was. I received your ashes in a wooden urn, startlingly heavy, to scatter in the park where we walked that day under the lilacs. Joined corpses have to be cremated for fear of contamination, irrational dread of the nanothings creeping free and making their way through the earth to wreak some unknown havoc. It couldn't happen, of course, they die when we do. Except when they don't.

You touch me, your fingertip down the back of my neck.

I tear off my gloves, turn and run into the corridor, and straight into Mark. He grabs me to steady me.

"Hey, Tracy, you all right?"

I jerk away from his touch, because it feels so wrong, so alien, to have anyone touch me but you. I find my breath, my voice, and it comes out harsh and angry.

"What's Alana doing here? She's not supposed to be here."

"What?"

He's staring at me like I've gone crazy, and I can't blame him, the way I must look.

I shoulder past him and don't look back, just keep walking until I'm outside. I breathe in the air, the summer storm clearing now to leave a clean-washed blue sky and the sun breaking through the last rain drops.

I wonder if I might really be going crazy. Because the implant can do that to a person; as well as breaking your heart, it can send your mind spooling loose into free fall. There've been documented cases, and I feel myself falling now, endlessly falling, and I'd grab at anything in desperation. I wonder if that's how you feel, drifting formless in the void.

I can't blame you for grabbing onto me like you did. Can't blame you at all.

I want you, suddenly, Alana. Want to hold you close and not let go, because I'm falling. Nothing makes sense anymore and I'm just falling.

* * *

It was a mistake, it turns out. An administrative error, they say. Your body was mixed up with another woman's: someone else's daughter, someone else's wife. A body that was supposed to be donated to science, but instead ended up burnt to ashes, scattered under the lilacs and denied my tears. These things happen, they say.

And that left you still there, cold and waiting in that drawer. Your implant still functioning – perhaps – still reaching out from that dark place, still calling out to me. Although that shouldn't really be possible. Maybe it isn't. Maybe it was only ever *my* circuitry reaching out, trailing through the empty space inside me, twisting back on itself?

Either way, it all gets sorted out in time, as such things always do. Compensation paid and apologies made, paperwork redone. The body – your body – cremated for real this time.

Life goes on.

I don't have another memorial service. I don't scatter ashes, because I did that already. The time for that is past, drifted away with the spring blossoms, the fading, falling lilac petals. Instead, your urn sits on my bookshelf, silent.

You don't talk to me so much these days. But I like having you there. It's comforting, in a way. Funny that, I like you better dead than I did alive. Funny how things work out sometimes. I head outside, cigarette pack and lighter in hand. I never could quite kick the habit. Don't think I ever will. And honestly, I'm not sure I want to. I've gotten a taste for it lately. It might break my heart someday, but then I already know how that feels.

Out in the garden, the leaves swirl autumn brown around my feet, the year turning. I breathe in, inhaling the smoke deep along with the cool air.

Your smile touches the corners of my mouth, and I know you're here. You'll always be here.

And I'm fine with that. We're joined.

It would break my heart to lose you.

The Doll's Ghost

F. Marion Crawford

IT WAS A TERRIBLE ACCIDENT, and for one moment the splendid machinery of Cranston House got out of gear and stood still. The butler emerged from the retirement in which he spent his elegant leisure, two grooms of the chambers appeared simultaneously from opposite directions, there were actually housemaids on the grand staircase, and those who remember the facts most exactly assert that Mrs. Pringle herself positively stood upon the landing. Mrs. Pringle was the housekeeper. As for the head nurse, the under nurse, and the nursery maid, their feelings cannot be described. The head nurse laid one hand upon the polished marble balustrade and stared stupidly before her, the under nurse stood rigid and pale, leaning against the polished marble wall, and the nursery-maid collapsed and sat down upon the polished marble step, just beyond the limits of the velvet carpet, and frankly burst into tears.

The Lady Gwendolen Lancaster-Douglas-Scroop, youngest daughter of the ninth Duke of Cranston, and aged six years and three months, picked herself up quite alone, and sat down on the third step from the foot of the grand staircase in Cranston House.

"Oh!" ejaculated the butler, and he disappeared again.

"Ah!" responded the grooms of the chambers, as they also went away.

"It's only that doll," Mrs. Pringle was distinctly heard to say, in a tone of contempt.

The under nurse heard her say it. Then the three nurses gathered round Lady Gwendolen and patted her, and gave her unhealthy things out of their pockets, and hurried her out of Cranston House as fast as they could, lest it should be found out upstairs that they had allowed the Lady Gwendolen Lancaster-Douglas-Scroop to tumble down the grand staircase with her doll in her arms. And as the doll was badly broken, the nursery-maid carried it, with the pieces, wrapped up in Lady Gwendolen's little cloak. It was not far to Hyde Park, and when they had reached a quiet place they took means to find out that Lady Gwendolen had no bruises. For the carpet was very thick and soft, and there was thick stuff under it to make it softer.

Lady Gwendolen Douglas-Scroop sometimes yelled, but she never cried. It was because she had yelled that the nurse had allowed her to go downstairs alone with Nina, the doll, under one arm, while she steadied herself with her other hand on the balustrade, and trod upon the polished marble steps beyond the edge of the carpet. So she had fallen, and Nina had come to grief.

When the nurses were quite sure that she was not hurt, they unwrapped the doll and looked at her in her turn. She had been a very beautiful doll, very large, and fair, and healthy, with real yellow hair, and eyelids that would open and shut over very grown-up dark eyes. Moreover, when you moved her right arm up and down she said "Pa-pa", and when you moved the left she said "Ma-ma", very distinctly.

"I heard her say 'Pa' when she fell," said the under nurse, who heard everything. "But she ought to have said 'Pa-pa'."

"That's because her arm went up when she hit the step," said the head nurse. "She'll say the other 'Pa' when I put it down again."

"Pa," said Nina, as her right arm was pushed down, and speaking through her broken face. It was cracked right across, from the upper corner of the forehead, with a hideous gash, through the nose and down to the little frilled collar of the pale green silk Mother Hubbard frock, and two little three-cornered pieces of porcelain had fallen out.

"I'm sure it's a wonder she can speak at all, being all smashed," said the under nurse.

"You'll have to take her to Mr. Puckler," said her superior. "It's not far, and you'd better go at once."

Lady Gwendolen was occupied in digging a hole in the ground with a little spade, and paid no attention to the nurses.

"What are you doing?" enquired the nursery-maid, looking on.

"Nina's dead, and I'm diggin' her a grave," replied her ladyship thoughtfully.

"Oh, she'll come to life again all right," said the nursery-maid.

The under nurse wrapped Nina up again and departed. Fortunately a kind soldier, with very long legs and a very small cap, happened to be there; and as he had nothing to do, he offered to see the under nurse safely to Mr. Puckler's and back.

* * *

Mr. Bernard Puckler and his little daughter lived in a little house in a little alley, which led out off a quiet little street not very far from Belgrave Square. He was the great doll doctor, and his extensive practice lay in the most aristocratic quarter. He mended dolls of all sizes and ages, boy dolls and girl dolls, baby dolls in long clothes, and grown-up dolls in fashionable gowns, talking dolls and dumb dolls, those that shut their eyes when they lay down, and those whose eyes had to be shut for them by means of a mysterious wire. His daughter Else was only just over twelve years old, but she was already very clever at mending dolls' clothes, and at doing their hair, which is harder than you might think, though the dolls sit quite still while it is being done.

Mr. Puckler had originally been a German, but he had dissolved his nationality in the ocean of London many years ago, like a great many foreigners. He still had one or two German friends, however, who came on Saturday evenings, and smoked with him and played picquet or 'skat' with him for farthing points, and called him 'Herr Doctor', which seemed to please Mr. Puckler very much.

He looked older than he was, for his beard was rather long and ragged, his hair was grizzled and thin, and he wore horn-rimmed spectacles. As for Else, she was a thin, pale child, very quiet and neat, with dark eyes and brown hair that was plaited down her back and tied with a bit of black ribbon. She mended the dolls' clothes and took the dolls back to their homes when they were quite strong again.

The house was a little one, but too big for the two people who lived in it. There was a small sitting-room on the street, and the workshop was at the back, and there were three rooms upstairs. But the father and daughter lived most of their time in the workshop, because they were generally at work, even in the evenings.

Mr. Puckler laid Nina on the table and looked at her a long time, till the tears began to fill his eyes behind the horn-rimmed spectacles. He was a very susceptible man, and he often fell in love with the dolls he mended, and found it hard to part with them when they had smiled at him for a few days. They were real little people to him, with characters and thoughts and feelings of their own, and he was very tender with them all. But some attracted him especially from the first, and when they were brought to him maimed and injured, their state seemed so pitiful to him that the tears came easily. You must remember that he had lived among dolls during a great part of his life, and understood them.

"How do you know that they feel nothing?" he went on to say to Else. "You must be gentle with them. It costs nothing to be kind to the little beings, and perhaps it makes a difference to them."

And Else understood him, because she was a child, and she knew that she was more to him than all the dolls.

He fell in love with Nina at first sight, perhaps because her beautiful brown glass eyes were something like Else's own, and he loved Else first and best, with all his heart. And, besides, it was a very sorrowful case. Nina had evidently not been long in the world, for her complexion was perfect, her hair was smooth where it should be smooth, and curly where it should be curly, and her silk clothes were perfectly new. But across her face was that frightful gash, like a sabre-cut, deep and shadowy within, but clean and sharp at the edges. When he tenderly pressed her head to close the gaping wound, the edges made a fine grating sound, that was painful to hear, and the lids of the dark eyes quivered and trembled as though Nina were suffering dreadfully.

"Poor Nina!" he exclaimed sorrowfully. "But I shall not hurt you much, though you will take a long time to get strong."

He always asked the names of the broken dolls when they were brought to him, and sometimes the people knew what the children called them, and told him. He liked "Nina" for a name. Altogether and in every way she pleased him more than any doll he had seen for many years, and he felt drawn to her, and made up his mind to make her perfectly strong and sound, no matter how much labour it might cost him.

Mr. Puckler worked patiently a little at a time, and Else watched him. She could do nothing for poor Nina, whose clothes needed no mending. The longer the doll doctor worked, the more fond he became of the yellow hair and the beautiful brown glass eyes. He sometimes forgot all the other dolls that were waiting to be mended, lying side by side on a shelf, and sat for an hour gazing at Nina's face, while he racked his ingenuity for some new invention by which to hide even the smallest trace of the terrible accident.

She was wonderfully mended. Even he was obliged to admit that; but the scar was still visible to his keen eyes, a very fine line right across the face, downwards from right to left. Yet all the conditions had been most favourable for a cure, since the cement had set quite hard at the first attempt and the weather had been fine and dry, which makes a great difference in a dolls' hospital.

At last he knew that he could do no more, and the under nurse had already come twice to see whether the job was finished, as she coarsely expressed it.

"Nina is not quite strong yet," Mr. Puckler had answered each time, for he could not make up his mind to face the parting.

And now he sat before the square deal table at which he worked, and Nina lay before him for the last time with a big brown paper box beside her. It stood there like her coffin, waiting for her, he thought. He must put her into it, and lay tissue paper over her dear face, and then put on the lid, and at the thought of tying the string his sight was dim with tears again. He was never to look into the glassy depths of the beautiful brown eyes anymore, nor to hear the little wooden voice say 'Pa-pa' and 'Ma-ma'. It was a very painful moment.

In the vain hope of gaining time before the separation, he took up the little sticky bottles of cement and glue and gum and colour, looking at each one in turn, and then at Nina's face.

And all his small tools lay there, neatly arranged in a row, but he knew that he could not use them again for Nina. She was quite strong at last, and in a country where there should be no cruel children to hurt her she might live a hundred years, with only that almost imperceptible line across her face to tell of the fearful thing that had befallen her on the marble steps of Cranston House.

Suddenly Mr. Puckler's heart was quite full, and he rose abruptly from his seat and turned away.

"Else," he said unsteadily, "you must do it for me. I cannot bear to see her go into the box."

So he went and stood at the window with his back turned, while Else did what he had not the heart to do.

"Is it done?" he asked, not turning round. "Then take her away, my dear. Put on your hat, and take her to Cranston House quickly, and when you are gone I will turn round."

Else was used to her father's queer ways with the dolls, and though she had never seen him so much moved by a parting, she was not much surprised.

"Come back quickly," he said, when he heard her hand on the latch. "It is growing late, and I should not send you at this hour. But I cannot bear to look forward to it anymore."

When Else was gone, he left the window and sat down in his place before the table again, to wait for the child to come back. He touched the place where Nina had lain, very gently, and he recalled the softly tinted pink face, and the glass eyes, and the ringlets of yellow hair, till he could almost see them.

The evenings were long, for it was late in the spring. But it began to grow dark soon, and Mr. Puckler wondered why Else did not come back. She had been gone an hour and a half, and that was much longer than he had expected, for it was barely half a mile from Belgrave Square to Cranston House. He reflected that the child might have been kept waiting, but as the twilight deepened he grew anxious, and walked up and down in the dim workshop, no longer thinking of Nina, but of Else, his own living child, whom he loved.

An undefinable, disquieting sensation came upon him by fine degrees, a chilliness and a faint stirring of his thin hair, joined with a wish to be in any company rather than to be alone much longer. It was the beginning of fear.

He told himself in strong German-English that he was a foolish old man, and he began to feel about for the matches in the dusk. He knew just where they should be, for he always kept them in the same place, close to the little tin box that held bits of sealing-wax of various colours, for some kinds of mending. But somehow he could not find the matches in the gloom.

Something had happened to Else, he was sure, and as his fear increased, he felt as though it might be allayed if he could get a light and see what time it was. Then he called himself a foolish old man again, and the sound of his own voice startled him in the dark. He could not find the matches.

The window was grey still; he might see what time it was if he went close to it, and he could go and get matches out of the cupboard afterwards. He stood back from the table, to get out of the way of the chair, and began to cross the board floor.

Something was following him in the dark. There was a small pattering, as of tiny feet upon the boards. He stopped and listened, and the roots of his hair tingled. It was nothing, and he was a foolish old man. He made two steps more, and he was sure that he heard the little pattering again. He turned his back to the window, leaning against the sash so that the panes began to crack, and he faced the dark. Everything was quite still, and it smelt of paste and cement and wood-filings as usual.

"Is that you, Else?" he asked, and he was surprised by the fear in his voice.

There was no answer in the room, and he held up his watch and tried to make out what time it was by the grey dusk that was just not darkness. So far as he could see, it was within two or three minutes of ten o'clock. He had been a long time alone. He was shocked, and frightened for Else, out in London, so late, and he almost ran across the room to the door. As he fumbled for the latch, he distinctly heard the running of the little feet after him.

"Mice!" he exclaimed feebly, just as he got the door open.

He shut it quickly behind him, and felt as though some cold thing had settled on his back and were writhing upon him. The passage was quite dark, but he found his hat and was out in the alley in a moment, breathing more freely, and surprised to find how much light there still was in the open air. He could see the pavement clearly under his feet, and far off in the street to which the alley led he could hear the laughter and calls of children, playing some game out of doors. He wondered how he could have been so nervous, and for an instant he thought of going back into the house to wait quietly for Else. But instantly he felt that nervous fright of something stealing over him again. In any case it was better to walk up to Cranston House and ask the servants about the child. One of the women had perhaps taken a fancy to her, and was even now giving her tea and cake.

He walked quickly to Belgrave Square, and then up the broad streets, listening as he went, whenever there was no other sound, for the tiny footsteps. But he heard nothing, and was laughing at himself when he rang the servants' bell at the big house. Of course, the child must be there.

The person who opened the door was quite an inferior person, for it was a back door, but affected the manners of the front, and stared at Mr. Puckler superciliously under the strong light.

No little girl had been seen, and he knew "nothing about no dolls".

"She is my little girl," said Mr. Puckler tremulously, for all his anxiety was returning tenfold, "and I am afraid something has happened."

The inferior person said rudely that "nothing could have happened to her in that house, because she had not been there, which was a jolly good reason why"; and Mr. Puckler was obliged to admit that the man ought to know, as it was his business to keep the door and let people in. He wished to be allowed to speak to the under nurse, who knew him; but the man was ruder than ever, and finally shut the door in his face.

When the doll doctor was alone in the street, he steadied himself by the railing, for he felt as though he were breaking in two, just as some dolls break, in the middle of the backbone.

Presently he knew that he must be doing something to find Else, and that gave him strength. He began to walk as quickly as he could through the streets, following every highway and byway which his little girl might have taken on her errand. He also asked several policemen in vain if they had seen her, and most of them answered him kindly, for they saw that he was a sober man and in his right senses, and some of them had little girls of their own.

It was one o'clock in the morning when he went up to his own door again, worn out and hopeless and broken-hearted. As he turned the key in the lock, his heart stood still, for he knew that he was awake and not dreaming, and that he really heard those tiny footsteps pattering to meet him inside the house along the passage.

But he was too unhappy to be much frightened any more, and his heart went on again with a dull regular pain, that found its way all through him with every pulse. So he went in, and hung up his hat in the dark, and found the matches in the cupboard and the candlestick in its place in the corner.

Mr. Puckler was so much overcome and so completely worn out that he sat down in his chair before the work-table and almost fainted, as his face dropped forward upon his folded hands. Beside him the solitary candle burned steadily with a low flame in the still warm air.

"Else! Else!" he moaned against his yellow knuckles. And that was all he could say, and it was no relief to him. On the contrary, the very sound of the name was a new and sharp pain that pierced his ears and his head and his very soul. For every time he repeated the name it meant that little Else was dead, somewhere out in the streets of London in the dark.

He was so terribly hurt that he did not even feel something pulling gently at the skirt of his old coat, so gently that it was like the nibbling of a tiny mouse. He might have thought that it was really a mouse if he had noticed it.

"Else! Else!" he groaned right against his hands.

Then a cool breath stirred his thin hair, and the low flame of the one candle dropped down almost to a mere spark, not flickering as though a draught were going to blow it out, but just dropping down as if it were tired out. Mr. Puckler felt his hands stiffening with fright under his face; and there was a faint rustling sound, like some small silk thing blown in a gentle breeze. He sat up straight, stark and scared, and a small wooden voice spoke in the stillness.

"Pa-pa," it said, with a break between the syllables.

Mr. Puckler stood up in a single jump, and his chair fell over backwards with a smashing noise upon the wooden floor. The candle had almost gone out.

It was Nina's doll voice that had spoken, and he should have known it among the voices of a hundred other dolls. And yet there was something more in it, a little human ring, with a pitiful cry and a call for help, and the wail of a hurt child. Mr. Puckler stood up, stark and stiff, and tried to look round, but at first he could not, for he seemed to be frozen from head to foot.

Then he made a great effort, and he raised one hand to each of his temples, and pressed his own head round as he would have turned a doll's. The candle was burning so low that it might as well have been out altogether, for any light it gave, and the room seemed quite dark at first. Then he saw something. He would not have believed that he could be more frightened than he had been just before that. But he was, and his knees shook, for he saw the doll standing in the middle of the floor, shining with a faint and ghostly radiance, her beautiful glassy brown eyes fixed on his. And across her face the very thin line of the break he had mended shone as though it were drawn in light with a fine point of white flame.

Yet there was something more in the eyes, too; there was something human, like Else's own, but as if only the doll saw him through them, and not Else. And there was enough of Else to bring back all his pain and to make him forget his fear.

"Else! My little Else!" he cried aloud.

The small ghost moved, and its doll-arm slowly rose and fell with a stiff, mechanical motion.

"Pa-pa," it said.

It seemed this time that there was even more of Else's tone echoing somewhere between the wooden notes that reached his ears so distinctly, and yet so far away. Else was calling him, he was sure.

His face was perfectly white in the gloom, but his knees did not shake any more, and he felt that he was less frightened.

"Yes, child! But where? Where?" he asked. "Where are you, Else?"

"Pa-pa!"

The syllables died away in the quiet room. There was a low rustling of silk, the glassy brown eyes turned slowly away, and Mr. Puckler heard the pitter-patter of the small feet in the bronze kid slippers as the figure ran straight to the door. Then the candle burned high again, the room was full of light, and he was alone.

Mr. Puckler passed his hand over his eyes and looked about him. He could see everything quite clearly, and he felt that he must have been dreaming, though he was standing instead of sitting down, as he should have been if he had just waked up. The candle burned brightly now. There were the dolls to be mended, lying in a row with their toes up. The third one had lost her right shoe, and Else was making one. He knew that, and he was certainly not dreaming now. He had not been dreaming when he had come in from his fruitless search and had heard the doll's footsteps running to the door. He had not fallen asleep in his chair. How could he possibly have fallen asleep when his heart was breaking? He had been awake all the time.

He steadied himself, set the fallen chair upon its legs, and said to himself again very emphatically that he was a foolish old man. He ought to be out in the streets looking for his child, asking questions, and enquiring at the police stations, where all accidents were reported as soon as they were known, or at the hospitals.

"Pa-pa!"

The longing, wailing, pitiful little wooden cry rang from the passage, outside the door, and Mr. Puckler stood for an instant with white face, transfixed and rooted to the spot. A moment later his hand was on the latch. Then he was in the passage, with the light streaming from the open door behind him.

Quite at the other end he saw the little phantom shining clearly in the shadow, and the right hand seemed to beckon to him as the arm rose and fell once more. He knew all at once that it had not come to frighten him but to lead him, and when it disappeared, and he walked boldly towards the door, he knew that it was in the street outside, waiting for him. He forgot that he was tired and had eaten no supper, and had walked many miles, for a sudden hope ran through and through him, like a golden stream of life.

And sure enough, at the corner of the alley, and at the corner of the street, and out in Belgrave Square, he saw the small ghost flitting before him. Sometimes it was only a shadow, where there was other light, but then the glare of the lamps made a pale green sheen on its little Mother Hubbard frock of silk; and sometimes, where the streets were dark and silent, the whole figure shone out brightly, with its yellow curls and rosy neck. It seemed to trot along like a tiny child, and Mr. Puckler could almost hear the pattering of the bronze kid slippers on the pavement as it ran. But it went very fast, and he could only just keep up with it, tearing along with his hat on the back of his head and his thin hair blown by the night breeze, and his horn-rimmed spectacles firmly set upon his broad nose.

On and on he went, and he had no idea where he was. He did not even care, for he knew certainly that he was going the right way.

Then at last, in a wide, quiet street, he was standing before a big, sober-looking door that had two lamps on each side of it, and a polished brass bell-handle, which he pulled.

And just inside, when the door was opened, in the bright light, there was the little shadow, and the pale green sheen of the little silk dress, and once more the small cry came to his ears, less pitiful, more longing.

"Pa-pa!"

The shadow turned suddenly bright, and out of the brightness the beautiful brown glass eyes were turned up happily to his, while the rosy mouth smiled so divinely that the phantom doll looked almost like a little angel just then.

"A little girl was brought in soon after ten o'clock," said the quiet voice of the hospital doorkeeper. "I think they thought she was only stunned. She was holding a big brown-paper box against her, and they could not get it out of her arms. She had a long plait of brown hair that hung down as they carried her."

"She is my little girl," said Mr. Puckler, but he hardly heard his own voice.

He leaned over Else's face in the gentle light of the children's ward, and when he had stood there a minute the beautiful brown eyes opened and looked up to his.

"Pa-pa!" cried Else, softly, "I knew you would come!"

Then Mr. Puckler did not know what he did or said for a moment, and what he felt was worth all the fear and terror and despair that had almost killed him that night. But by and by Else was telling her story, and the nurse let her speak, for there were only two other children in the room, who were getting well and were sound asleep.

"They were big boys with bad faces," said Else, "and they tried to get Nina away from me, but I held on and fought as well as I could till one of them hit me with something, and I don't remember any more, for I tumbled down, and I suppose the boys ran away, and somebody found me there. But I'm afraid Nina is all smashed."

"Here is the box," said the nurse. "We could not take it out of her arms till she came to herself. Should you like to see if the doll is broken?"

And she undid the string cleverly, but Nina was all smashed to pieces. Only the gentle light of the children's ward made a pale green sheen in the folds of the little Mother Hubbard frock.

Some Souls Stay

Rachael Cudlitz

TO HEAR my grandmother tell it, these woods have been haunted from the time The Almighty raised his Holy hand and created Eden. The forest is filled with haints. The spirits of Chinook elders swirl between the bows of cedar and Douglas fir, stalking the lonely souls of trappers dipping their shadow hands into icy waters, grasping at beaver pelts long lost to time and rot. Behind dilapidated mountain cabins, pioneer women still hang out wash in freshly cleared meadows, while their husbands endlessly chop wood to feed fires. I was but a child, sitting at my grandmother's knee, rapt by the rhythm and glory of her voice while she told tales of ghostly Indian women standing on the river's shore mourning lost children, the echoes of their long dead cries skipping along the water's currents.

"If you sit real still," she'd say. "You'll hear them. And if you come to the river in the winter on the night of a waning moon, you'll see the children's spirits run through the forest to their mother's arms. The mothers will sing and cradle their babies at the feet of the ancient cedars, blessed in their reunion hidden by the shadows on the forest floor."

Of course, those stories are only true if you listen to the tales of a fanciful and somewhat addled old woman. She's dead and I am no longer a child. I've wandered these woods for a while now, remembering my grandmother's stories. I've spent many winter nights watching the moon and the river's edge. I've stared into the trees and dipped my hands into the cold waters. I can tell you there are no Chinook elders, no trappers. The dead Indian children and mourning mothers do not rejoice under the waning moon. My grandmother didn't know what the hell she was talking about.

The only spirit I've seen in this forest is a small girl stuck on the child-side of puberty – perhaps eleven, or twelve. Clearly she's been dead a long time, she's nothing like today's girls wrapped in Juicy Couture and spandex. Dressed in petticoats and aprons, her long auburn hair lays over her shoulders in two neat plaits, as fresh as the morning her mother braided it. And a faded yellow bonnet, tied around her throat, hangs limply against her back. The left side of her skull is fractured and covered in gore – a blow to the head from a rock, or maybe a club. Rivulets of dried blood arc across her face and stain the collar of her blouse. She says she doesn't remember how she died, and it doesn't hurt anymore, so the conversation, she says, is pointless.

Besides, she's told me countless times I look much worse.

I have to trust her. The river moves too quickly for me to see my reflection and all of the glass is broken in our cabin's windows. The girl's told me the story of my death many times. You see, she sat with me while it happened. Watched me as I begged him not to do it. Watched me fight and claw and kick and die. My screams echoing through the trees, disappearing into the wild thicket. She told me the first cut made me scream the most. By the time the saw's jagged teeth dragged across my throat, she said I had nothing left in me but a whimper.

This man's come back. I didn't remember him, but she pointed him out while we were watching trout shimmer in the river. He walks the hidden deer trails and along the river's rocky edge. Knows how to hide out here. Knows he's safe to linger without interruption. Thinks he has only the owl and the coyote as audience.

He doesn't know he has us, the girl and me. We watch him.

But we're not here for him. We're here for you. You see, we've been following him lately, watching him mark the trail you've left: the small indentations in the meadow grass, the well smothered fire in the copse beneath the Douglas fir. You've been careful to leave no trace, you're a good visitor in our beautiful home. But the forest knows you're here and the man does too.

In fact, he's watching you right now.

You've once again carefully put out your fire and are comfortably burrowed in a sleeping bag. You spent the last few moments before sleep scanning through the photographs you took today. The one of the large, mossy boulder with the twisted tree growing from the crag in its side is particularly good. You made a note in your book: *Cover?*

It's a shame you can't hear me. I want to tell you what will happen next. I want to tell you not to be afraid. I want to tell you you'll think you can save yourself, you'll pray someone or maybe even God will come and rescue you. They won't. I want to tell you that even though you'll feel you're alone and that no one will know how you died and that your existence will be severed completely by this man and his jagged saw – it's not true. The girl and I are with you now – watching you. We will be with you when you scream and kick and die. We want you to know you will still exist once this man has done his work and your body lays in pieces on the forest floor.

My grandmother didn't understand most souls – like the Chinook elders, the pioneers and folks like herself – most souls shoot to the heavens to dance among the stars. But some souls stay. Souls like the girl's and mine, and soon yours too. We get to walk the earth and live forever in its beauty and brutality. We stay, ready to bear witness and welcome our murdered kin home.

You still have some time left. He likes to wait till dawn – better light. Until then, just rest.

And remember, it won't hurt forever.

Purgatorio
First Terrace – Pride
Dante

Canto X

*When we had passed the threshold of the gate
(Which the soul's ill affection doth disuse,
Making the crooked seem the straighter path),
I heard its closing sound. Had mine eyes turn'd,
For that offence what plea might have avail'd?
We mounted up the riven rock, that wound
On either side alternate, as the wave
Flies and advances. "Here some little art
Behooves us," said my leader, "that our steps
Observe the varying flexure of the path."
Thus we so slowly sped, that with cleft orb
The moon once more o'erhangs her wat'ry couch,
Ere we that strait have threaded. But when free
We came and open, where the mount above
One solid mass retires, I spent, with toil,
And both, uncertain of the way, we stood,
Upon a plain more lonesome, than the roads
That traverse desert wilds. From whence the brink
Borders upon vacuity, to foot
Of the steep bank, that rises still, the space
Had measur'd thrice the stature of a man:
And, distant as mine eye could wing its flight,
To leftward now and now to right dispatch'd,
That cornice equal in extent appear'd.
Not yet our feet had on that summit mov'd,
When I discover'd that the bank around,
Whose proud uprising all ascent denied,
Was marble white, and so exactly wrought
With quaintest sculpture, that not there alone
Had Polycletus, but e'en nature's self
Been sham'd. The angel (who came down to earth
With tidings of the peace so many years
Wept for in vain, that op'd the heavenly gates
From their long interdict) before us seem'd,*

In a sweet act, so sculptur'd to the life,
He look'd no silent image. One had sworn
He had said, "Hail!" for she was imag'd there,
By whom the key did open to God's love,
And in her act as sensibly impress
That word, "Behold the handmaid of the Lord,"
As figure seal'd on wax. "Fix not thy mind
On one place only," said the guide belov'd,
Who had me near him on that part where lies
The heart of man. My sight forthwith I turn'd
And mark'd, behind the virgin mother's form,
Upon that side, where he, that mov'd me, stood,
Another story graven on the rock.
I passed athwart the bard, and drew me near,
That it might stand more aptly for my view.
There in the self-same marble were engrav'd
The cart and kine, drawing the sacred ark,
That from unbidden office awes mankind.
Before it came much people; and the whole
Parted in seven quires. One sense cried, "Nay,"
Another, "Yes, they sing." Like doubt arose
Betwixt the eye and smell, from the curl'd fume
Of incense breathing up the well-wrought toil.
Preceding the blest vessel, onward came
With light dance leaping, girt in humble guise,
Sweet Israel's harper: in that hap he seem'd
Less and yet more than kingly. Opposite,
At a great palace, from the lattice forth
Look'd Michol, like a lady full of scorn
And sorrow. To behold the tablet next,
Which at the back of Michol whitely shone,
I mov'd me. There was storied on the rock
The' exalted glory of the Roman prince,
Whose mighty worth mov'd Gregory to earn
His mighty conquest, Trajan th' Emperor.
A widow at his bridle stood, attir'd
In tears and mourning. Round about them troop'd
Full throng of knights, and overhead in gold
The eagles floated, struggling with the wind.
The wretch appear'd amid all these to say:
"Grant vengeance, sire! for, woe beshrew this heart
My son is murder'd." He replying seem'd;
"Wait now till I return." And she, as one
Made hasty by her grief; "O sire, if thou
Dost not return?" – "Where I am, who then is,
May right thee." – "What to thee is other's good,
If thou neglect thy own?" – "Now comfort thee,"

At length he answers. "It beseemeth well
My duty be perform'd, ere I move hence:
So justice wills; and pity bids me stay."
He, whose ken nothing new surveys, produc'd
That visible speaking, new to us and strange
The like not found on earth. Fondly I gaz'd
Upon those patterns of meek humbleness,
Shapes yet more precious for their artist's sake,
When "Lo," the poet whisper'd, "where this way
(But slack their pace), a multitude advance.
These to the lofty steps shall guide us on."
Mine eyes, though bent on view of novel sights
Their lov'd allurement, were not slow to turn.
Reader! I would not that amaz'd thou miss
Of thy good purpose, hearing how just God
Decrees our debts be cancel'd. Ponder not
The form of suff'ring. Think on what succeeds,
Think that at worst beyond the mighty doom
It cannot pass. "Instructor," I began,
"What I see hither tending, bears no trace
Of human semblance, nor of aught beside
That my foil'd sight can guess." He answering thus:
"So courb'd to earth, beneath their heavy teems
Of torment stoop they, that mine eye at first
Struggled as thine. But look intently thither,
An disentangle with thy lab'ring view,
What underneath those stones approacheth: now,
E'en now, mayst thou discern the pangs of each."
Christians and proud! O poor and wretched ones!
That feeble in the mind's eye, lean your trust
Upon unstaid perverseness! Know ye not
That we are worms, yet made at last to form
The winged insect, imp'd with angel plumes
That to heaven's justice unobstructed soars?
Why buoy ye up aloft your unfleg'd souls?
Abortive then and shapeless ye remain,
Like the untimely embryon of a worm!
As, to support incumbent floor or roof,
For corbel is a figure sometimes seen,
That crumples up its knees unto its breast,
With the feign'd posture stirring ruth unfeign'd
In the beholder's fancy; so I saw
These fashion'd, when I noted well their guise.
Each, as his back was laden, came indeed
Or more or less contract; but it appear'd
As he, who show'd most patience in his look,
Wailing exclaim'd: "I can endure no more."

Canto XI

O thou Almighty Father, who dost make
The heavens thy dwelling, not in bounds confin'd,
But that with love intenser there thou view'st
Thy primal effluence, hallow'd be thy name:
Join each created being to extol
Thy might, for worthy humblest thanks and praise
Is thy blest Spirit. May thy kingdom's peace
Come unto us; for we, unless it come,
With all our striving thither tend in vain.
As of their will the angels unto thee
Tender meet sacrifice, circling thy throne
With loud hosannas, so of theirs be done
By saintly men on earth. Grant us this day
Our daily manna, without which he roams
Through this rough desert retrograde, who most
Toils to advance his steps. As we to each
Pardon the evil done us, pardon thou
Benign, and of our merit take no count.
'Gainst the old adversary prove thou not
Our virtue easily subdu'd; but free
From his incitements and defeat his wiles.
This last petition, dearest Lord! is made
Not for ourselves, since that were needless now,
But for their sakes who after us remain."
Thus for themselves and us good speed imploring,
Those spirits went beneath a weight like that
We sometimes feel in dreams, all, sore beset,
But with unequal anguish, wearied all,
Round the first circuit, purging as they go,
The world's gross darkness off. In our behalf
If there vows still be offer'd, what can here
For them be vow'd and done by such, whose wills
Have root of goodness in them? Well beseems
That we should help them wash away the stains
They carried hence, that so made pure and light,
They may spring upward to the starry spheres.
"Ah! So may mercy-temper'd justice rid
Your burdens speedily, that ye have power
To stretch your wing, which e'en to your desire
Shall lift you, as ye show us on which hand
Toward the ladder leads the shortest way.
And if there be more passages than one,
Instruct us of that easiest to ascend;
For this man who comes with me, and bears yet
The charge of fleshly raiment Adam left him,

Despite his better will but slowly mounts."
From whom the answer came unto these words,
Which my guide spake, appear'd not; but 'twas said
"Along the bank to rightward come with us,
And ye shall find a pass that mocks not toil
Of living man to climb: and were it not
That I am hinder'd by the rock, wherewith
This arrogant neck is tam'd, whence needs I stoop
My visage to the ground, him, who yet lives,
Whose name thou speak'st not him I fain would view.
To mark if e'er I knew him? And to crave
His pity for the fardel that I bear.
I was of Latiun, of a Tuscan born
A mighty one: Aldobranlesco's name
My sire's, I know not if ye e'er have heard.
My old blood and forefathers' gallant deeds
Made me so haughty, that I clean forgot
The common mother, and to such excess,
Wax'd in my scorn of all men, that I fell,
Fell therefore; by what fate Sienna's sons,
Each child in Campagnatico, can tell.
I am Omberto; not me only pride
Hath injur'd, but my kindred all involv'd
In mischief with her. Here my lot ordains
Under this weight to groan, till I appease
God's angry justice, since I did it not
Amongst the living, here amongst the dead."
List'ning I bent my visage down: and one
(Not he who spake) twisted beneath the weight
That urg'd him, saw me, knew me straight, and call'd,
Holding his eyes with difficulty fix'd
Intent upon me, stooping as I went
Companion of their way. "O!" I exclaim'd,
"Art thou not Oderigi, art not thou
Agobbio's glory, glory of that art
Which they of Paris call the limmer's skill?"
"Brother!" said he, "with tints that gayer smile,
Bolognian Franco's pencil lines the leaves.
His all the honour now; mine borrow'd light.
In truth I had not been thus courteous to him,
The whilst I liv'd, through eagerness of zeal
For that pre-eminence my heart was bent on.
Here of such pride the forfeiture is paid.
Nor were I even here; if, able still
To sin, I had not turn'd me unto God.
O powers of man! how vain your glory, nipp'd
E'en in its height of verdure, if an age

Less bright succeed not! Cimabue thought
To lord it over painting's field; and now
The cry is Giotto's, and his name eclips'd.
Thus hath one Guido from the other snatch'd
The letter'd prize: and he perhaps is born,
Who shall drive either from their nest. The noise
Of worldly fame is but a blast of wind,
That blows from divers points, and shifts its name
Shifting the point it blows from. Shalt thou more
Live in the mouths of mankind, if thy flesh
Part shrivel'd from thee, than if thou hadst died,
Before the coral and the pap were left,
Or ere some thousand years have passed? And that
Is, to eternity compar'd, a space,
Briefer than is the twinkling of an eye
To the heaven's slowest orb. He there who treads
So leisurely before me, far and wide
Through Tuscany resounded once; and now
Is in Sienna scarce with whispers nam'd:
There was he sov'reign, when destruction caught
The madd'ning rage of Florence, in that day
Proud as she now is loathsome. Your renown
Is as the herb, whose hue doth come and go,
And his might withers it, by whom it sprang
Crude from the lap of earth." I thus to him:
"True are thy sayings: to my heart they breathe
The kindly spirit of meekness, and allay
What tumours rankle there. But who is he
Of whom thou spak'st but now?" – "This," he replied,
"Is Provenzano. He is here, because
He reach'd, with grasp presumptuous, at the sway
Of all Sienna. Thus he still hath gone,
Thus goeth never-resting, since he died.
Such is th' acquittance render'd back of him,
Who, beyond measure, dar'd on earth." I then:
"If soul that to the verge of life delays
Repentance, linger in that lower space,
Nor hither mount, unless good prayers befriend,
How chanc'd admittance was vouchsaf'd to him?"
"When at his glory's topmost height," said he,
"Respect of dignity all cast aside,
Freely He fix'd him on Sienna's plain,
A suitor to redeem his suff'ring friend,
Who languish'd in the prison-house of Charles,
Nor for his sake refus'd through every vein
To tremble. More I will not say; and dark,
I know, my words are, but thy neighbours soon

Shall help thee to a comment on the text.
This is the work, that from these limits freed him."

Canto XII

With equal pace as oxen in the yoke,
I with that laden spirit journey'd on
Long as the mild instructor suffer'd me;
But when he bade me quit him, and proceed
(For "here," said he, "behooves with sail and oars
Each man, as best he may, push on his bark"),
Upright, as one dispos'd for speed, I rais'd
My body, still in thought submissive bow'd.
I now my leader's track not loth pursued;
And each had shown how light we far'd along
When thus he warn'd me: "Bend thine eyesight down:
For thou to ease the way shall find it good
To ruminate the bed beneath thy feet."
As in memorial of the buried, drawn
Upon earth-level tombs, the sculptur'd form
Of what was once, appears (at sight whereof
Tears often stream forth by remembrance wak'd,
Whose sacred stings the piteous only feel),
So saw I there, but with more curious skill
Of portraiture o'erwrought, whate'er of space
From forth the mountain stretches. On one part
Him I beheld, above all creatures erst
Created noblest, light'ning fall from heaven:
On th' other side with bolt celestial pierc'd
Briareus: cumb'ring earth he lay through dint
Of mortal ice-stroke. The Thymbraean god
With Mars, I saw, and Pallas, round their sire,
Arm'd still, and gazing on the giant's limbs
Strewn o'er th' ethereal field. Nimrod I saw:
At foot of the stupendous work he stood,
As if bewilder'd, looking on the crowd
Leagued in his proud attempt on Sennaar's plain.
O Niobe! in what a trance of woe
Thee I beheld, upon that highway drawn,
Sev'n sons on either side thee slain! O Saul!
How ghastly didst thou look! On thine own sword
Expiring in Gilboa, from that hour
Ne'er visited with rain from heav'n or dew!
O fond Arachne! thee I also saw
Half spider now in anguish crawling up
Th' unfinish'd web thou weaved'st to thy bane!
O Rehoboam! Here thy shape doth seem

  Louring no more defiance! But fear-smote
With none to chase him in his chariot whirl'd.
  Was shown beside upon the solid floor
How dear Alcmaeon forc'd his mother rate
That ornament in evil hour receiv'd:
How in the temple on Sennacherib fell
His sons, and how a corpse they left him there.
Was shown the scath and cruel mangling made
By Tomyris on Cyrus, when she cried:
"Blood thou didst thirst for, take thy fill of blood!"
Was shown how routed in the battle fled
Th' Assyrians, Holofernes slain, and e'en
The relics of the carnage. Troy I mark'd
In ashes and in caverns. Oh! How fall'n,
How abject, Ilion, was thy semblance there!
What master of the pencil or the style
Had trac'd the shades and lines, that might have made
The subtlest workman wonder? Dead the dead,
The living seem'd alive; with clearer view
His eye beheld not who beheld the truth,
Than mine what I did tread on, while I went
Low bending. Now swell out; and with stiff necks
Pass on, ye sons of Eve! Veil not your looks,
Lest they descry the evil of your path!
  I noted not (so busied was my thought)
How much we now had circled of the mount,
And of his course yet more the sun had spent,
When he, who with still wakeful caution went,
Admonish'd: "Raise thou up thy head: for know
Time is not now for slow suspense. Behold
That way an angel hasting towards us! Lo
Where duly the sixth handmaid doth return
From service on the day. Wear thou in look
And gesture seemly grace of reverent awe,
That gladly he may forward us aloft.
Consider that this day ne'er dawns again."
  Time's loss he had so often warn'd me 'gainst,
I could not miss the scope at which he aim'd.
The goodly shape approach'd us, snowy white
In vesture, and with visage casting streams
Of tremulous lustre like the matin star.
His arms he open'd, then his wings; and spake:
"Onward: the steps, behold! are near; and now
Th' ascent is without difficulty gain'd."
  A scanty few are they, who when they hear
Such tidings, hasten. O ye race of men
Though born to soar, why suffer ye a wind

So slight to baffle ye? He led us on
Where the rock parted; here against my front
Did beat his wings, then promis'd I should fare
In safety on my way. As to ascend
That steep, upon whose brow the chapel stands
(O'er Rubaconte, looking lordly down
On the well-guided city,) up the right
Th' impetuous rise is broken by the steps
Carv'd in that old and simple age, when still
The registry and label rested safe;
Thus is th' acclivity reliev'd, which here
Precipitous from the other circuit falls:
But on each hand the tall cliff presses close.
As ent'ring there we turn'd, voices, in strain
Ineffable, sang: "Blessed are the poor
In spirit." Ah how far unlike to these
The straits of hell; here songs to usher us,
There shrieks of woe! We climb the holy stairs:
And lighter to myself by far I seem'd
Than on the plain before, whence thus I spake:
"Say, master, of what heavy thing have I
Been lighten'd, that scarce aught the sense of toil
Affects me journeying?" He in few replied:
"When sin's broad characters, that yet remain
Upon thy temples, though well nigh effac'd,
Shall be, as one is, all clean razed out,
Then shall thy feet by heartiness of will
Be so o'ercome, they not alone shall feel
No sense of labour, but delight much more
Shall wait them urg'd along their upward way."
Then like to one, upon whose head is plac'd
Somewhat he deems not of but from the becks
Of others as they pass him by; his hand
Lends therefore help to assure him, searches, finds,
And well performs such office as the eye
Wants power to execute: so stretching forth
The fingers of my right hand, did I find
Six only of the letters, which his sword
Who bare the keys had trac'd upon my brow.
The leader, as he mark'd mine action, smil'd.

The complete and unabridged text is available online, *from flametreepublishing.com/extras*

The Trial for Murder

Charles Dickens

I HAVE ALWAYS noticed a prevalent want of courage, even among persons of superior intelligence and culture, as to imparting their own psychological experiences when those have been of a strange sort. Almost all men are afraid that what they could relate in such wise would find no parallel or response in a listener's internal life, and might be suspected or laughed at. A truthful traveller, who should have seen some extraordinary creature in the likeness of a sea-serpent, would have no fear of mentioning it; but the same traveller, having had some singular presentiment, impulse, vagary of thought, vision (so-called), dream, or other remarkable mental impression, would hesitate considerably before he would own to it. To this reticence I attribute much of the obscurity in which such subjects are involved. We do not habitually communicate our experiences of these subjective things as we do our experiences of objective creation. The consequence is, that the general stock of experience in this regard appears exceptional, and really is so, in respect of being miserably imperfect.

In what I am going to relate, I have no intention of setting up, opposing, or supporting, any theory whatever. I know the history of the Bookseller of Berlin, I have studied the case of the wife of a late Astronomer Royal as related by Sir David Brewster, and I have followed the minutest details of a much more remarkable case of Spectral Illusion occurring within my private circle of friends. It may be necessary to state as to this last, that the sufferer (a lady) was in no degree, however distant, related to me. A mistaken assumption on that head might suggest an explanation of a part of my own case – but only a part – which would be wholly without foundation. It cannot be referred to my inheritance of any developed peculiarity, nor had I ever before any at all similar experience, nor have I ever had any at all similar experience since.

It does not signify how many years ago, or how few, a certain murder was committed in England, which attracted great attention. We hear more than enough of murderers as they rise in succession to their atrocious eminence, and I would bury the memory of this particular brute, if I could, as his body was buried, in Newgate Jail. I purposely abstain from giving any direct clue to the criminal's individuality.

When the murder was first discovered, no suspicion fell – or I ought rather to say, for I cannot be too precise in my facts, it was nowhere publicly hinted that any suspicion fell – on the man who was afterwards brought to trial. As no reference was at that time made to him in the newspapers, it is obviously impossible that any description of him can at that time have been given in the newspapers. It is essential that this fact be remembered.

Unfolding at breakfast my morning paper, containing the account of that first discovery, I found it to be deeply interesting, and I read it with close attention. I read it twice, if not three times. The discovery had been made in a bedroom, and, when I laid down the paper, I was aware of a flash – rush – flow – I do not know what to call it – no word I can find is satisfactorily descriptive – in which I seemed to see that bedroom passing through my room, like a picture impossibly painted on a running river. Though almost instantaneous in its passing, it was perfectly clear; so clear that I distinctly, and with a sense of relief, observed the absence of the dead body from the bed.

It was in no romantic place that I had this curious sensation, but in chambers in Piccadilly, very near to the corner of St. James's Street. It was entirely new to me. I was in my easy-chair at the moment, and the sensation was accompanied with a peculiar shiver which started the chair from its position. (But it is to be noted that the chair ran easily on castors.) I went to one of the windows (there are two in the room, and the room is on the second floor) to refresh my eyes with the moving objects down in Piccadilly. It was a bright autumn morning, and the street was sparkling and cheerful. The wind was high. As I looked out, it brought down from the Park a quantity of fallen leaves, which a gust took, and whirled into a spiral pillar. As the pillar fell and the leaves dispersed, I saw two men on the opposite side of the way, going from West to East. They were one behind the other. The foremost man often looked back over his shoulder. The second man followed him, at a distance of some thirty paces, with his right hand menacingly raised. First, the singularity and steadiness of this threatening gesture in so public a thoroughfare attracted my attention; and next, the more remarkable circumstance that nobody heeded it. Both men threaded their way among the other passengers with a smoothness hardly consistent even with the action of walking on a pavement; and no single creature, that I could see, gave them place, touched them, or looked after them. In passing before my windows, they both stared up at me. I saw their two faces very distinctly, and I knew that I could recognise them anywhere. Not that I had consciously noticed anything very remarkable in either face, except that the man who went first had an unusually lowering appearance, and that the face of the man who followed him was of the colour of impure wax.

I am a bachelor, and my valet and his wife constitute my whole establishment. My occupation is in a certain Branch Bank, and I wish that my duties as head of a Department were as light as they are popularly supposed to be. They kept me in town that autumn, when I stood in need of change. I was not ill, but I was not well. My reader is to make the most that can be reasonably made of my feeling jaded, having a depressing sense upon me of a monotonous life, and being 'slightly dyspeptic'. I am assured by my renowned doctor that my real state of health at that time justifies no stronger description, and I quote his own from his written answer to my request for it.

As the circumstances of the murder, gradually unravelling, took stronger and stronger possession of the public mind, I kept them away from mine by knowing as little about them as was possible in the midst of the universal excitement. But I knew that a verdict of Wilful Murder had been found against the suspected murderer, and that he had been committed to Newgate for trial. I also knew that his trial had been postponed over one Sessions of the Central Criminal Court, on the ground of general prejudice and want of time for the preparation of the defence. I may further have known, but I believe I did not, when, or about when, the Sessions to which his trial stood postponed would come on.

My sitting-room, bedroom, and dressing-room, are all on one floor. With the last there is no communication but through the bedroom. True, there is a door in it, once communicating with the staircase; but a part of the fitting of my bath has been – and had then been for some years – fixed across it. At the same period, and as a part of the same arrangement – the door had been nailed up and canvased over.

I was standing in my bedroom late one night, giving some directions to my servant before he went to bed. My face was towards the only available door of communication with the dressing-room, and it was closed. My servant's back was towards that door. While I was speaking to him, I saw it open, and a man look in, who very earnestly and mysteriously beckoned to me. That man was the man who had gone second of the two along Piccadilly, and whose face was of the colour of impure wax.

The figure, having beckoned, drew back, and closed the door. With no longer pause than was made by my crossing the bedroom, I opened the dressing-room door, and looked in. I had a lighted candle already in my hand. I felt no inward expectation of seeing the figure in the dressing-room, and I did not see it there.

Conscious that my servant stood amazed, I turned round to him, and said: "Derrick, could you believe that in my cool senses I fancied I saw a –" As I there laid my hand upon his breast, with a sudden start he trembled violently, and said, "O Lord, yes, sir! A dead man beckoning!"

Now I do not believe that this John Derrick, my trusty and attached servant for more than twenty years, had any impression whatever of having seen any such figure, until I touched him. The change in him was so startling, when I touched him, that I fully believe he derived his impression in some occult manner from me at that instant.

I bade John Derrick bring some brandy, and I gave him a dram, and was glad to take one myself. Of what had preceded that night's phenomenon, I told him not a single word. Reflecting on it, I was absolutely certain that I had never seen that face before, except on the one occasion in Piccadilly. Comparing its expression when beckoning at the door with its expression when it had stared up at me as I stood at my window, I came to the conclusion that on the first occasion it had sought to fasten itself upon my memory, and that on the second occasion it had made sure of being immediately remembered.

I was not very comfortable that night, though I felt a certainty, difficult to explain, that the figure would not return. At daylight I fell into a heavy sleep, from which I was awakened by John Derrick's coming to my bedside with a paper in his hand.

This paper, it appeared, had been the subject of an altercation at the door between its bearer and my servant. It was a summons to me to serve upon a Jury at the forthcoming Sessions of the Central Criminal Court at the Old Bailey. I had never before been summoned on such a Jury, as John Derrick well knew. He believed – I am not certain at this hour whether with reason or otherwise – that that class of Jurors were customarily chosen on a lower qualification than mine, and he had at first refused to accept the summons. The man who served it had taken the matter very coolly. He had said that my attendance or non-attendance was nothing to him; there the summons was; and I should deal with it at my own peril, and not at his.

For a day or two I was undecided whether to respond to this call, or take no notice of it. I was not conscious of the slightest mysterious bias, influence, or attraction, one way or other. Of that I am as strictly sure as of every other statement that I make here. Ultimately I decided, as a break in the monotony of my life, that I would go.

The appointed morning was a raw morning in the month of November. There was a dense brown fog in Piccadilly, and it became positively black and in the last degree oppressive East of Temple Bar. I found the passages and staircases of the Court-House flaringly lighted with gas, and the Court itself similarly illuminated. I *think* that, until I was conducted by officers into the Old Court and saw its crowded state, I did not know that the Murderer was to be tried that day. I *think* that, until I was so helped into the Old Court with considerable difficulty, I did not know into which of the two Courts sitting my summons would take me. But this must not be received as a positive assertion, for I am not completely satisfied in my mind on either point.

I took my seat in the place appropriated to Jurors in waiting, and I looked about the Court as well as I could through the cloud of fog and breath that was heavy in it. I noticed the black vapour hanging like a murky curtain outside the great windows, and I noticed the stifled sound of wheels on the straw or tan that was littered in the street; also, the hum of the people gathered there, which a shrill whistle, or a louder song or hail than the rest, occasionally pierced. Soon afterwards the Judges, two in number, entered, and took their seats. The buzz in the Court was awfully hushed. The direction was given to put the Murderer to the bar. He appeared there. And in that same instant I recognised in him the first of the two men who had gone down Piccadilly.

If my name had been called then, I doubt if I could have answered to it audibly. But it was called about sixth or eighth in the panel, and I was by that time able to say, "Here!" Now, observe. As I stepped into the box, the prisoner, who had been looking on attentively, but with no sign of concern, became violently agitated, and beckoned to his attorney. The prisoner's wish to challenge me was so manifest, that it occasioned a pause, during which the attorney, with his hand upon the dock, whispered with his client, and shook his head. I afterwards had it from that gentleman, that the prisoner's first affrighted words to him were, "*at all hazards, challenge that man!*" But that, as he would give no reason for it, and admitted that he had not even known my name until he heard it called and I appeared, it was not done.

Both on the ground already explained, that I wish to avoid reviving the unwholesome memory of that Murderer, and also because a detailed account of his long trial is by no means indispensable to my narrative, I shall confine myself closely to such incidents in the ten days and nights during which we, the Jury, were kept together, as directly bear on my own curious personal experience. It is in that, and not in the Murderer, that I seek to interest my reader. It is to that, and not to a page of the Newgate Calendar, that I beg attention.

I was chosen Foreman of the Jury. On the second morning of the trial, after evidence had been taken for two hours (I heard the church clocks strike), happening to cast my eyes over my brother jurymen, I found an inexplicable difficulty in counting them. I counted them several times, yet always with the same difficulty. In short, I made them one too many.

I touched the brother jurymen whose place was next me, and I whispered to him, "Oblige me by counting us." He looked surprised by the request, but turned his head and counted. "Why," says he, suddenly, "we are thirt–; but no, it's not possible. No. We are twelve."

According to my counting that day, we were always right in detail, but in the gross we were always one too many. There was no appearance – no figure – to account for it; but I had now an inward foreshadowing of the figure that was surely coming.

The Jury were housed at the London Tavern. We all slept in one large room on separate tables, and we were constantly in the charge and under the eye of the officer sworn to hold us in safe-keeping. I see no reason for suppressing the real name of that officer. He was intelligent, highly polite, and obliging, and (I was glad to hear) much respected in the City. He had an agreeable presence, good eyes, enviable black whiskers, and a fine sonorous voice. His name was Mr. Harker.

When we turned into our twelve beds at night, Mr. Harker's bed was drawn across the door. On the night of the second day, not being disposed to lie down, and seeing Mr. Harker sitting on his bed, I went and sat beside him, and offered him a pinch of snuff. As Mr. Harker's hand touched mine in taking it from my box, a peculiar shiver crossed him, and he said, "Who is this?"

Following Mr. Harker's eyes, and looking along the room, I saw again the figure I expected, – the second of the two men who had gone down Piccadilly. I rose, and advanced a few steps; then stopped, and looked round at Mr. Harker. He was quite unconcerned, laughed, and said in a pleasant way, "I thought for a moment we had a thirteenth juryman, without a bed. But I see it is the moonlight."

Making no revelation to Mr. Harker, but inviting him to take a walk with me to the end of the room, I watched what the figure did. It stood for a few moments by the bedside of each of my eleven brother jurymen, close to the pillow. It always went to the right-hand side of the bed, and always passed out crossing the foot of the next bed. It seemed, from the action of the head, merely to look down pensively at each recumbent figure. It took no notice of me, or of my bed, which was that nearest to Mr. Harker's. It seemed to go out where the moonlight came in, through a high window, as by an aerial flight of stairs.

Next morning at breakfast, it appeared that everybody present had dreamed of the murdered man last night, except myself and Mr. Harker.

I now felt as convinced that the second man who had gone down Piccadilly was the murdered man (so to speak), as if it had been borne into my comprehension by his immediate testimony. But even this took place, and in a manner for which I was not at all prepared.

On the fifth day of the trial, when the case for the prosecution was drawing to a close, a miniature of the murdered man, missing from his bedroom upon the discovery of the deed, and afterwards found in a hiding-place where the Murderer had been seen digging, was put in evidence. Having been identified by the witness under examination, it was handed up to the Bench, and thence handed down to be inspected by the Jury. As an officer in a black gown was making his way with it across to me, the figure of the second man who had gone down Piccadilly impetuously started from the crowd, caught the miniature from the officer, and gave it to me with his own hands, at the same time saying, in a low and hollow tone – before I saw the miniature, which was in a locket:

'I was younger then, and my face was not then drained of blood.'

It also came between me and the brother juryman to whom I would have given the miniature, and between him and the brother juryman to whom he would have given it, and so passed it on through the whole of our number, and back into my possession. Not one of them, however, detected this.

At table, and generally when we were shut up together in Mr. Harker's custody, we had from the first naturally discussed the day's proceedings a good deal. On that fifth day, the case for the prosecution being closed, and we having that side of the question in a completed shape before us, our discussion was more animated and serious. Among our number was a vestryman – the densest idiot I have ever seen at large, – who met the plainest evidence with the most preposterous objections, and who was sided with by two flabby parochial parasites; all the three impanelled from a district so delivered over to Fever that they ought to have been upon their own trial for five hundred Murders. When these mischievous blockheads were at their loudest, which was towards midnight, while some of us were already preparing for bed, I again saw the murdered man. He stood grimly behind them, beckoning to me. On my going towards them, and striking into the conversation, he immediately retired. This was the beginning of a separate series of appearances, confined to that long room in which we were confined. Whenever a knot of my brother jurymen laid their heads together, I saw the head of the murdered man among theirs. Whenever their comparison of notes was going against him, he would solemnly and irresistibly beckon to me.

It will be borne in mind that down to the production of the miniature, on the fifth day of the trial, I had never seen the Appearance in Court. Three changes occurred now that we entered on the case for the defence. Two of them I will mention together, first. The figure was now in Court continually, and it never there addressed itself to me, but always to the person who was speaking at the time. For instance: the throat of the murdered man had been cut straight across. In the opening speech for the defence, it was suggested that the deceased might have cut his own throat. At that very moment, the figure, with its throat in the dreadful condition referred to (this it had concealed before), stood at the speaker's elbow, motioning across and across its windpipe, now with the right hand, now with the left, vigorously suggesting to the speaker himself the impossibility of such a wound having been self-inflicted by either hand. For another instance: a witness to character, a woman, deposed to the prisoner's being the most amiable of mankind. The figure at that instant stood on the floor before her, looking her full in the face, and pointing out the prisoner's evil countenance with an extended arm and an outstretched finger.

The third change now to be added impressed me strongly as the most marked and striking of all. I do not theorise upon it; I accurately state it, and there leave it. Although the Appearance was not itself perceived by those whom it addressed, its coming close to such persons was invariably attended by some trepidation or disturbance on their part. It seemed to me as if it were prevented, by laws to which I was not amenable, from fully revealing itself to others, and yet as if it could invisibly, dumbly, and darkly overshadow their minds. When the leading counsel for the defence suggested that hypothesis of suicide, and the figure stood at the learned gentleman's elbow, frightfully sawing at its severed throat, it is undeniable that the counsel faltered in his speech, lost for a few seconds the thread of his ingenious discourse, wiped his forehead with his handkerchief, and turned extremely pale. When the witness to character was confronted by the Appearance, her eyes most certainly did follow the direction of its pointed finger, and rest in great hesitation and trouble upon the prisoner's face. Two additional illustrations will suffice. On the eighth day of the trial, after the pause which was every day made early in the afternoon for a few minutes' rest and refreshment, I came back into Court with the rest of the Jury some little time before the return of the Judges. Standing up in the box and looking about me, I thought the figure was not there, until, chancing to raise my eyes to the gallery, I saw it bending forward, and leaning over a very decent woman, as if to assure itself whether the Judges had resumed their seats or not. Immediately afterwards that woman screamed, fainted, and was carried out. So with the venerable, sagacious, and patient Judge who conducted the trial. When the case was over, and he settled himself and his papers to sum up, the murdered man, entering by the Judges' door, advanced to his Lordship's desk, and looked eagerly over his shoulder at the pages of his notes which he was turning. A change came over his Lordship's face; his hand stopped; the peculiar shiver, that I knew so well, passed over him; he faltered, "Excuse me, gentlemen, for a few moments. I am somewhat oppressed by the vitiated air"; and did not recover until he had drunk a glass of water.

Through all the monotony of six of those interminable ten days – the same Judges and others on the bench, the same Murderer in the dock, the same lawyers at the table, the same tones of question and answer rising to the roof of the court, the same scratching of the Judge's pen, the same ushers going in and out, the same lights kindled at the same hour when there had been any natural light of day, the same foggy curtain outside the great windows when it was foggy, the same rain pattering and dripping when it was rainy, the same footmarks of turnkeys and prisoner day after day on the same sawdust, the same keys locking and unlocking the same heavy doors – through all the wearisome monotony which made me feel as if I had been Foreman of the Jury for a vast cried of time, and Piccadilly had flourished coevally with Babylon, the murdered man never lost one trace of his distinctness in my eyes, nor was he at any moment less distinct than anybody else. I must not omit, as a matter of fact, that I never once saw the Appearance which I call by the name of the murdered man look at the Murderer. Again and again I wondered, "Why does he not?" But he never did.

Nor did he look at me, after the production of the miniature, until the last closing minutes of the trial arrived. We retired to consider, at seven minutes before ten at night. The idiotic vestryman and his two parochial parasites gave us so much trouble that we twice returned into Court to beg to have certain extracts from the Judge's notes re-read. Nine of us had not the smallest doubt about those passages, neither, I believe, had anyone in the Court; the dunder-headed triumvirate, having no idea but obstruction, disputed them for that very reason. At length we prevailed, and finally the Jury returned into Court at ten minutes past twelve.

The murdered man at that time stood directly opposite the Jury-box, on the other side of the Court. As I took my place, his eyes rested on me with great attention; he seemed satisfied, and slowly shook a great gray veil, which he carried on his arm for the first time, over his head and whole form. As I gave in our verdict, "Guilty", the veil collapsed, all was gone, and his place was empty.

The Murderer, being asked by the Judge, according to usage, whether he had anything to say before sentence of Death should be passed upon him, indistinctly muttered something which was described in the leading newspapers of the following day as 'a few rambling, incoherent, and half-audible words, in which he was understood to complain that he had not had a fair trial, because the Foreman of the Jury was prepossessed against him.' The remarkable declaration that he really made was this:

> "My Lord, I knew I was a doomed man, when the Foreman of my jury came into the box. My Lord, I knew he would never let me off, because, before I was taken, he somehow got to my bedside in the night, woke me, and put a rope round my neck."

Was It an Illusion?
A Parson's Story
Amelia B. Edwards

THE FACTS which I am about to relate happened to myself some sixteen or eighteen years ago, at which time I served Her Majesty as an Inspector of Schools. Now, the Provincial Inspector is perpetually on the move; and I was still young enough to enjoy a life of constant travelling.

There are, indeed, many less agreeable ways in which an unbeneficed parson may contrive to scorn delights and live laborious days. In remote places where strangers are scarce, his annual visit is an important event; and though at the close of a long day's work he would sometimes prefer the quiet of a country inn, he generally finds himself the destined guest of the rector or the squire. It rests with himself to turn these opportunities to account. If he makes himself pleasant, he forms agreeable friendships and sees English home – life under one of its most attractive aspects; and sometimes, even in these days of universal common – placeness, he may have the luck to meet with an adventure.

My first appointment was to a West of England district largely peopled with my personal friends and connections. It was, therefore, much to my annoyance that I found myself, after a couple of years of very pleasant work, transferred to what a policeman would call 'a new beat', up in the North. Unfortunately for me, my new beat – a rambling, thinly populated area of something under 1,800 square miles – was three times as large as the old one, and more than proportionately unmanageable. Intersected at right angles by two ranges of barren hills and cut off to a large extent from the main lines of railway, it united about every inconvenience that a district could possess. The villages lay wide apart, often separated by long tracts of moorland; and in place of the well-warmed railway compartment and the frequent manor-house, I now spent half my time in hired vehicles and lonely country inns.

I had been in possession of this district for some three months or so, and winter was near at hand, when I paid my first visit of inspection to Pit End, an outlying hamlet in the most northerly corner of my county, just twenty-two miles from the nearest station. Having slept overnight at a place called Drumley, and inspected Drumley schools in the morning, I started for Pit End, with fourteen miles of railway and twenty-two of hilly cross-roads between myself and my journey's end. I made, of course, all the enquiries I could think of before leaving; but neither the Drumley schoolmaster nor the landlord of the Drumley 'Feathers' knew much more of Pit End than its name. My predecessor, it seemed, had been in the habit of taking Pit End 'from the other side', the roads, though longer, being less hilly that way. That the place boasted some kind of inn was certain; but it was an inn unknown to fame, and to mine host of the 'Feathers'. Be it good or bad, however, I should have to put up at it.

Upon this scant information I started. My fourteen miles of railway journey soon ended at a place called Bramsford Road, whence an omnibus conveyed passengers to a dull little town called Bramsford Market. Here I found a horse and 'trap' to carry me on to my destination; the horse being a rawboned grey with a profile like a camel, and the trap a ricketty high gig which had probably done commercial travelling in the days of its youth. From Bramsford Market the way lay over a succession of long hills, rising to a barren, high-level plateau. It was a dull, raw afternoon of mid-November, growing duller and more raw as the day waned and the east wind blew keener... "How much further now, driver?" I asked, as we alighted at the foot of a longer and a stiffer hill than any we had yet passed over.

He turned a straw in his mouth, and grunted something about "fewer or foive mile by the rooad".

And then I learned that by turning off at a point which he described as 't'owld tollus', and taking a certain footpath across the fields, this distance might be considerably shortened. I decided, therefore, to walk the rest of the way; and, setting off at a good pace, I soon left driver and trap behind. At the top of the hill I lost sight of them, and coming presently to a little road-side ruin which I at once recognized as the old toll-house, I found the footpath without difficulty.

It led me across a barren slope divided by stone fences, with here and there a group of shattered sheds, a tall chimney, and a blackened cinder-mound, marking the site of a deserted mine. A light fog, meanwhile, was creeping up from the east, and the dusk was gathering fast.

Now, to lose one's way in such a place and at such an hour would be disagreeable enough, and the footpath – a trodden track already half obliterated – would be indistinguishable in the course of another ten minutes. Looking anxiously ahead, therefore, in the hope of seeing some sign of habitation, I hastened on, scaling one stone stile after another, till I all at once found myself skirting a line of park-palings. Following these, with bare boughs branching out overhead and dead leaves rustling underfoot, I came presently to a point where the path divided; here continuing to skirt the enclosure, and striking off yonder across a space of open meadow.

Which should I take?

By following the fence, I should be sure to arrive at a lodge where I could enquire my way to Pit End; but then the park might be of any extent, and I might have a long distance to go before I came to the nearest lodge. Again, the meadow-path, instead of leading to Pit End, might take me in a totally opposite direction. But there was no time to be lost in hesitation; so I chose the meadow, the further end of which was lost to sight in a fleecy bank of fog.

Up to this moment I had not met a living soul of whom to ask my way; it was, therefore, with no little sense of relief that I saw a man emerging from the fog and coming along the path. As we neared each other – I advancing rapidly; he slowly – I observed that he dragged the left foot, limping as he walked. It was, however, so dark and so misty, that not till we were within half a dozen yards of each other could I see that he wore a dark suit and an Anglican felt hat, and looked something like a dissenting minister. As soon as we were within speaking distance, I addressed him.

"Can you tell me", I said, "if I am right for Pit End, and how far I have to go?"

He came on, looking straight before him; taking no notice of my question; apparently not hearing it.

"I beg your pardon," I said, raising my voice; "but will this path take me to Pit End, and if so –" He had passed on without pausing; without looking at me; I could almost have believed, without seeing me!

I stopped, with the words on my lips; then turned to look after – perhaps, to follow – him.

But instead of following, I stood bewildered.

What had become of him? And what lad was that going up the path by which I had just come – that tall lad, half-running, half-walking, with a fishing-rod over his shoulder? I could have taken my oath that I had neither met nor passed him. Where then had he come from? And where was the man to whom I had spoken not three seconds ago, and who, at his limping pace, could not have made more than a couple of yards in the time? My stupefaction was such that I stood quite still, looking after the lad with the fishing-rod till he disappeared in the gloom under the park-palings.

Was I dreaming?

Darkness, meanwhile, had closed in apace, and, dreaming or not dreaming, I must push on, or find myself benighted. So I hurried forward, turning my back on the last gleam of daylight, and plunging deeper into the fog at every step. I was, however, close upon my journey's end. The path ended at a turnstile; the turnstile opened upon a steep lane; and at the bottom of the lane, down which I stumbled among stones and ruts, I came in sight of the welcome glare of a blacksmith's forge.

Here, then, was Pit End. I found my trap standing at the door of the village inn; the rawboned grey stabled for the night; the landlord watching for my arrival.

The 'Greyhound' was a hostelry of modest pretensions, and I shared its little parlour with a couple of small farmers and a young man who informed me that he 'travelled in' Thorley's Food for Cattle. Here I dined, wrote my letters, chatted awhile with the landlord, and picked up such scraps of local news as fell in my way.

There was, it seemed, no resident parson at Pit End; the incumbent being a pluralist with three small livings, the duties of which, by the help of a rotatory curate, he discharged in a somewhat easy fashion. Pit End, as the smallest and furthest off, came in for but one service each Sunday, and was almost wholly relegated to the curate. The squire was a more confirmed absentee than even the vicar. He lived chiefly in Paris, spending abroad the wealth of his Pit End coalfields.

He happened to be at home just now, the landlord said, after five years' absence; but he would be off again next week, and another five years might probably elapse before they should again see him at Blackwater Chase.

Blackwater Chase! The name was not new to me; yet I could not remember where I had heard it. When, however, mine host went on to say that, despite his absenteeism, Mr. Wolstenholme was "a pleasant gentleman and a good landlord", and that, after all, Blackwater Chase was "a lonesome sort of world-end place for a young man to bury himself in", then I at once remembered Phil Wolstenholme of Balliol, who, in his grand way, had once upon a time given me a general invitation to the shooting at Blackwater Chase. That was twelve years ago, when I was reading hard at Wadham, and Wolstenholme – the idol of a clique to which I did not belong – was boating, betting, writing poetry, and giving wine parties at Balliol.

Yes; I remembered all about him – his handsome face, his luxurious rooms, his boyish prodigality, his utter indolence, and the blind faith of his worshippers, who believed that he had only 'to pull himself together' in order to carry off every honour which the University had to bestow. He did take the Newdigate; but it was his first and last achievement, and he left college with the reputation of having narrowly escaped a plucking. How vividly it all came back upon my memory – the old college life, the college friendships, the pleasant time that could never come again! It was but twelve years ago; yet it seemed like half a century. And now, after these twelve years, here were Wolstenholme and I as near neighbours as in our Oxford days! I wondered if he was much changed, and whether, if changed, it were for the better or the worse.

Had his generous impulses developed into sterling virtues, or had his follies hardened into vices?

Should I let him know where I was, and so judge for myself? Nothing would be easier than to pencil a line upon a card tomorrow morning, and send it up to the big house. Yet, merely to satisfy a purposeless curiosity, was it worthwhile to reopen the acquaintanceship? Thus musing, I sat late over the fire, and by the time I went to bed, I had well nigh forgotten my adventure with the man who vanished so mysteriously and the boy who seemed to come from nowhere.

Next morning, finding I had abundant time at my disposal, I did pencil that line upon my card – a mere line, saving that I believed we had known each other at Oxford, and that I should be inspecting the National Schools from nine till about eleven. And then, having dispatched it by one of my landlord's sons, I went off to my work. The day was brilliantly fine. The wind had shifted round to the north, the sun shone clear and cold, and the smoke-grimed hamlet, and the gaunt buildings clustered at the mouths of the coalpits round about, looked as bright as they could look at any time of the year. The village was built up a long hill-side; the church and schools being at the top, and the 'Greyhound' at the bottom. Looking vainly for the lane by which I had come the night before, I climbed the one rambling street, followed a path that skirted the churchyard, and found myself at the schools. These, with the teachers' dwellings, formed three sides of a quadrangle; the fourth side consisting of an iron railing and a gate. An inscribed tablet over the main entrance – door recorded how 'These school-houses were rebuilt by Philip Wolstenholme, Esquire: AD 18—.'

Mr. Wolstenholme, sir, is the Lord of the Manor," said a soft, obsequious voice.

I turned, and found the speaker at my elbow, a square – built, sallow man, all in black, with a bundle of copy-books under his arm.

"You are the – the schoolmaster?" I said; unable to remember his name, and puzzled by a vague recollection of his face.

"Just so, sir. I conclude I have the honour of addressing Mr. Frazer?"

It was a singular face, very pallid and anxious-looking. The eyes, too, had a watchful, almost a startled, look in them, which struck me as peculiarly unpleasant.

"Yes," I replied, still wondering where and when I had seen him. "My name is Frazer. Yours, I believe, is – is –," and I put my hand into my pocket for my examination papers.

"Skelton – Ebenezer Skelton. Will you please to take the boys first, sir?"

The words were commonplace enough, but the man's manner was studiously, disagreeably deferential; his very name being given, as it were, under protest, as if too insignificant to be mentioned.

I said I would begin with the boys; and so moved on. Then, for we had stood still till now, I saw that the schoolmaster was lame. In that moment I remembered him. He was the man I met in the fog.

"I met you yesterday afternoon, Mr. Skelton," I said, as we went into the school-room.

"Yesterday afternoon, sir?" he repeated.

"You did not seem to observe me," I said, carelessly. "I spoke to you, in fact; but you did not reply to me."

"But – indeed, I beg your pardon, sir – it must have been someone else," said the schoolmaster, "I did not go out yesterday afternoon."

How could this be anything but a falsehood? I might have been mistaken as to the man's face; though it was such a singular face, and I had seen it quite plainly. But how could I be mistaken as to his lameness? Besides, that curious trailing of the right foot, as if the ankle was broken, was not an ordinary lameness.

I suppose I looked incredulous, for he added, hastily: "Even if I had not been preparing the boys for inspection, sir, I should not have gone out yesterday afternoon. It was too damp and foggy. I am obliged to be careful – I have a very delicate chest."

My dislike to the man increased with every word he uttered. I did not ask myself with what motive he went on heaping lie upon lie; it was enough that, to serve his own ends, whatever those ends might be, he did lie with unparalleled audacity.

"We will proceed to the examination, Mr. Skelton," I said, contemptuously.

He turned, if possible, a shade paler than before, bent his head silently, and called up the scholars in their order.

I soon found that, whatever his shortcomings as to veracity, Mr. Ebenezer Skelton was a capital schoolmaster. His boys were uncommonly well taught, and as regarded attendance, good conduct, and the like, left nothing to be desired. When, therefore, at the end of the examination, he said he hoped I would recommend the Pit End Boys' School for the Government grant, I at once assented. And now I thought I had done with Mr. Skelton for, at all events, the space of one year. Not so, however. When I came out from the Girls' School, I found him waiting at the door.

Profusely apologizing, he begged leave to occupy five minutes of my valuable time. He wished, under correction, to suggest a little improvement. The boys, he said, were allowed to play in the quadrangle, which was too small, and in various ways inconvenient; but round at the back there was a piece of wasteland, half an acre of which, if enclosed, would admirably answer the purpose. So saying, he led the way to the back of the building, and I followed him.

"To whom does this ground belong?" I asked.

"To Mr. Wolstenholme, sir."

"Then why not apply to Mr. Wolstenholme? He gave the schools, and I dare say he would be equally willing to give the ground."

"I beg your pardon, sir. Mr. Wolstenholme has not been over here since his return, and it is quite possible that he may leave Pit End without honouring us with a visit. I could not take the liberty of writing to him, sir."

"Neither could I in my report suggest that the Government should offer to purchase a portion of Mr. Wolstenholme's land for a playground to schools of Mr. Wolstenholme's own building." I replied. "Under other circumstances".

I stopped and looked round.

The schoolmaster repeated my last words.

"You were saying, sir – under other circumstances?"

I looked round again.

"It seemed to me that there was someone here," I said; "some third person, not a moment ago."

"I beg your pardon, sir – a third person?"

"I saw his shadow on the ground, between yours and mine."

The schools faced due north, and we were standing immediately behind the buildings, with our backs to the sun. The place was bare, and open, and high; and our shadows, sharply defined, lay stretched before our feet.

"A – a shadow?" he faltered. "Impossible."

There was not a bush or a tree within half a mile. There was not a cloud in the sky. There was nothing, absolutely nothing, that could have cast a shadow.

I admitted that it was impossible, and that I must have fancied it; and so went back to the matter of the playground... "Should you see Mr. Wolstenholme," I said, "you are at liberty to say that I thought it a desirable improvement."

"I am much obliged to you, sir. Thank you – thank you very much," he said, cringing at every word. "But – but I had hoped that you might perhaps use your influence –"

"Look there!" I interrupted. "Is that fancy?"

We were now close under the blank wall of the boys' schoolroom. On this wall, lying to the full sunlight, our shadows – mine and the schoolmaster's – were projected. And there, too – no longer between his and mine, but a little way apart, as if the intruder were standing back – there, as sharply defined as if cast by lime-light on a prepared background, I again distinctly saw, though but for a moment, that third shadow. As I spoke, as I looked round, it was gone!

"Did you not see it?" I asked.

He shook his head.

"I – I saw nothing," he said, faintly. "What was it?"

His lips were white. He seemed scarcely able to stand.

"But you must have seen it!" I exclaimed. "It fell just there – where that bit of ivy grows. There must be some boy hiding – it was a boy's shadow, I am confident."

"A boy's shadow!" he echoed, looking round in a wild, frightened way. "There is no place – for a boy – to hide."

"Place or no place," I said, angrily, "if I catch him, he shall feel the weight of my cane!"

I searched backwards and forwards in every direction, the schoolmaster, with his scared face, limping at my heels; but, rough and irregular as the ground was, there was not a hole in it big enough to shelter a rabbit.

"But what was it?" I said, impatiently.

"An – an illusion. Begging your pardon, sir – an illusion."

He looked so like a beaten hound, so frightened, so fawning, that I felt I could with lively satisfaction have transferred the threatened caning to his own shoulders.

"But you saw it?" I said again.

"No, sir. Upon my honour, no, sir. I saw nothing – nothing whatever."

His looks belied his words. I felt positive that he had not only seen the shadow, but that he knew more about it than he chose to tell. I was by this time really angry. To be made the object of a boyish trick, and to be hoodwinked by the connivance of the schoolmaster, was too much. It was an insult to myself and my office.

I scarcely knew what I said; something short and stern at all events. Then, having said it, I turned my back upon Mr. Skelton and the schools, and walked rapidly back to the village.

As I neared the bottom of the hill, a dog-cart drawn by a high-stepping chestnut dashed up to the door of the 'Greyhound', and the next moment I was shaking hands with Wolstenholme, of Balliol. Wolstenholme, of Balliol, as handsome as ever, dressed with the same careless dandyism, looking not a day older than when I last saw him at Oxford! He gripped me by both hands, vowed that I was his guest for the next three days, and insisted on carrying me off at once to Backwater Chase. In vain I urged that I had two schools to inspect tomorrow ten miles the other side of Drumley; that I had a horse and trap waiting; and that my room was ordered at the 'Feathers'. Wolstenholme laughed away my objections.

My dear fellow," he said, "you will simply send your horse and trap back with a message to the 'Feathers', and a couple of telegrams to be dispatched to the two schools from Drumley station. Unforeseen circumstances compel you to defer those inspections till next week!"

And with this, in his masterful way, he shouted to the landlord to send my portmanteau up to the manor-house, pushed me up before him into the dog-cart, gave the chestnut his head, and rattled me off to Backwater Chase.

It was a gloomy old barrack of a place, standing high in the midst of a sombre deer-park some six or seven miles in circumference. An avenue of oaks, now leafless, led up to the house; and a mournful heron-haunted tarn in the loneliest part of the park gave to the estate its name of Blackwater Chase. The place, in fact, was more like a border fastness than an English north-country mansion. Wolstenholme took me through the picture gallery and reception rooms after luncheon, and then for a canter round the park; and in the evening we dined at the upper end of a great oak hall hung with antlers, and armour, and antiquated weapons of warfare and sport.

"Now, tomorrow," said my host, as we sat over our claret in front of a blazing log-fire; "tomorrow, if we have decent weather, you shall have a day's shooting on the moors; and on Friday, if you will but be persuaded to stay a day longer, I will drive you over to Broomhead and give you a run with the Duke's hounds. Not hunt? My dear fellow, what nonsense! All our parsons hunt in this part of the world. By the way, have you ever been down a coal pit? No? Then a new experience awaits you. I'll take you down Carshalton shaft, and show you the home of the gnomes and trolls."

"Is Carshalton one of your own mines?" I asked.

"All these pits are mine," he replied. "I am king of Hades, and rule the underworld as well as the upper. There is coal everywhere underlying these moors. The whole place is honeycombed with shafts and galleries. One of our richest seams runs under this house, and there are upwards of forty men at work in it a quarter of a mile below our feet here every day. Another leads right away under the park, heaven only knows how far! My father began working it five and twenty years ago, and we have gone on working it ever since; yet it shows no sign of failing."

"You must be as rich as a prince with a fairy godmother!"

He shrugged his shoulders.

"Well," he said, lightly, "I am rich enough to commit what follies I please; and that is saying a good deal. But then, to be always squandering money – always rambling about the world – always gratifying the impulse of the moment – is that happiness? I have been trying the experiment for the last ten years; and with what result? Would you like to see?"

He snatched up a lamp and led the way through a long suite of unfurnished rooms, the floors of which were piled high with packing cases of all sizes and shapes, labelled with the names of various foreign ports and the addresses of foreign agents innumerable. What did they contain?

Precious marbles from Italy and Greece and Asia Minor; priceless paintings by old and modern masters; antiquities from the Nile, the Tigris, and the Euphrates; enamels from Persia, porcelain from China, bronzes from Japan, strange sculptures from Peru; arms, mosaics, ivories, wood-carvings, skins, tapestries, old Italian cabinets, painted bride-chests, Etruscan terracottas; treasures of all countries, of all ages, never even unpacked since they crossed that threshold which the master's foot had crossed but twice during the ten years it had taken to buy them!

Should he ever open them, ever arrange them, ever enjoy them? Perhaps – if he became weary of wandering – if he married – if he built a gallery to receive them. If not – well, he might found and endow a museum; or leave the things to the nation. What did it matter? Collecting was like fox-hunting; the pleasure was in the pursuit, and ended with it!

We sat up late that first night, I can hardly say conversing, for Wolstenholme did the talking, while I, willing to be amused, led him on to tell me something of his wanderings by land and sea.

So the time passed in stories of adventure, of perilous peaks ascended, of deserts traversed, of unknown ruins explored, of 'hairbreadth 'scapes' from icebergs and earthquakes and storms; and when at last he flung the end of his cigar into the fire and discovered that it was time to go to bed, the clock on the mantel-shelf pointed far on among the small hours of the morning.

Next day, according to the programme made out for my entertainment, we did some seven hours' partridge-shooting on the moors; and the day next following I was to go down Carshalton shaft before breakfast, and after breakfast ride over to a place some fifteen miles distant called Picts' Camp, there to see a stone circle and the ruins of a prehistoric fort.

Unused to field sports, I slept heavily after those seven hours with the guns, and was slow to wake when Wolstenholme's valet came next morning to my bedside with the waterproof suit in which I was to effect my descent into Hades.

"Mr. Wolstenholme says, sir, that you had better not take your bath till you come back," said this gentlemanly vassal, disposing the ungainly garments across the back of a chair as artistically as if he were laying out my best evening suit. "And you will be pleased to dress warmly underneath the waterproofs, for it is very chilly in the mine."

I surveyed the garments with reluctance. The morning was frosty, and the prospect of being lowered into the bowels of the earth, cold, fasting, and unwashed, was anything but attractive.

Should I send word that I would rather not go? I hesitated; but while I was hesitating, the gentlemanly valet vanished, and my opportunity was lost. Grumbling and shivering, I got up, donned the cold and shiny suit, and went downstairs.

A murmur of voices met my ear as I drew near the breakfast-room. Going in, I found some ten or a dozen stalwart colliers grouped near the door, and Wolstenholme, looking somewhat serious, standing with his back to the fire.

"Look here, Frazer," he said, with a short laugh, "here's a pleasant piece of news. A fissure has opened in the bed of Blackwater tarn; the lake has disappeared in the night; and the mine is flooded! No Carshalton shaft for you today!"

"Seven foot o' wayter in Jukes's seam, an' eight in th' owd north and south galleries," growled a huge red-headed fellow, who seemed to be the spokesman.

"An' it's the Lord's own marcy a' happened o' noight-time, or we'd be dead men all," added another.

"That's true, my man," said Wolstenholme, answering the last speaker. "It might have drowned you like rats in a trap; so we may thank our stars it's no worse. And now, to work with the pumps! Lucky for us that we know what to do, and how to do it."

So saying, he dismissed the men with a good-humoured nod, and an order for unlimited ale.

I listened in blank amazement. The tarn vanished! I could not believe it. Wolstenholme assured me, however, that it was by no means a solitary phenomenon. Rivers had been known to disappear before now, in mining districts; and sometimes, instead of merely cracking, the ground would cave in, burying not merely houses, but whole hamlets in one common ruin. The foundations of such houses were, however, generally known to be insecure long enough before the crash came; and these accidents were not therefore often followed by loss of life.

"And now," he said, lightly, "you may doff your fancy costume; for I shall have time this morning for nothing but business. It is not every day that one loses a lake, and has to pump it up again!"

Breakfast over, we went round to the mouth of the pit, and saw the men fixing the pumps.

Later on, when the work was fairly in train, we started off across the park to view the scene of the catastrophe. Our way lay far from the house across a wooded upland, beyond which we followed a broad glade leading to the tarn. Just as we entered this glade – Wolstenholme rattling on and turning the whole affair into jest – a tall, slender lad, with a fishing-rod across his shoulder, came out from one of the side paths to the right, crossed the open at a long slant, and disappeared among the tree-trunks on the opposite side. I recognized him instantly. It was the boy whom I saw the other day, just after meeting the schoolmaster in the meadow.

"If that boy thinks he is going to fish in your tarn," I said, "he will find out his mistake."

"What boy?" asked Wolstenholme, looking back.

"That boy who crossed over yonder, a minute ago."

"Yonder! In front of us?"

"Certainly. You must have seen him?"

"Not I."

"You did not see him? A tall, thin boy, in a grey suit, with a fishing-rod over his shoulder. He disappeared behind those Scotch firs."

Wolstenholme looked at me with surprise.

"You are dreaming!" he said. "No living thing – not even a rabbit – has crossed our path since we entered the park gates."

"I am not in the habit of dreaming with my eyes open," I replied, quickly.

He laughed, and put his arm through mine.

"Eyes or no eyes," he said, "you are under an illusion this time!"

An illusion – the very word made use of by the schoolmaster! What did it mean? Could I, in truth, no longer rely upon the testimony of my senses? A thousand half-formed apprehensions flashed across me in a moment. I remembered the illusions of Nicolini, the bookseller, and other similar cases of visual hallucination, and I asked myself if I had suddenly become afflicted in like manner.

"By Jove! This is a queer sight!" exclaimed Wolstenholme. And then I found that we had emerged from the glade, and were looking down upon the bed of what yesterday was Blackwater Tarn.

It was indeed a queer sight – an oblong, irregular basin of blackest slime, with here and there a sullen pool, and round the margin an irregular fringe of bulrushes. At some little distance along the bank – less than a quarter of a mile from where we were standing – a gaping crowd had gathered. All Pit End, except the men at the pumps, seemed to have turned out to stare at the bed of the vanished tarn.

Hats were pulled off and curtsies dropped at Wolstenholme's approach. He, meanwhile, came up smiling, with a pleasant word for everyone.

"Well," he said, "are you looking for the lake, my friends? You'll have to go down Carshalton shaft to find it! It's an ugly sight you've come to sue, anyhow!"

"Tes an ugly soight, squoire," replied a stalwart blacksmith in a leathern apron; "but thar's summat uglier, mebbe, than the mud, ow'r yonder."

"Something uglier than the mud?" Wolstenholme repeated.

"Wull yo be pleased to stan' this way, squoire, an' look strite across at yon little tump o' bulrashes – doan't yo see nothin'?"

"I see a log of rotten timber sticking half in and half out of the mud," said Wolstenholme; "and something – a long reed, apparently...by Jove! I believe it's a fishing rod!"

"It is a fishin' rod, squoire," said the blacksmith with rough carnesmess; "an' if yon rotten timber bayn't an unburied corpse, mun I never stroike hammer on anvil agin!"

There was a buzz of acquiescence from the bystanders. 'Twas an unburied corpse, sure enough. Nobody doubted it... Wolstenholme made a funnel with his hands, and looked through it long and steadfastly.

"It must come out, whatever it is," he said presently. "Five feet of mud, do you say? Then here's a sovereign apiece for the first two fellows who wade through it and bring that object to land!"

The blacksmith and another pulled off their shoes and stockings, turned up their trousers, and went in at once.

They were over their ankles at the first plunge, and, sounding their way with sticks, went deeper at every tread. As they sank, our excitement rose. Presently they were visible from only the waist upwards. We could see their chests heaving, and the muscular efforts by which each step was gained. They were yet full twenty yards from the goal when the mud mounted to their armpits... a few feet more, and only their heads would remain above the surface!

An uneasy movement ran through the crowd.

"Call 'em back, for God's sake!" cried a woman's voice.

But at this moment – having reached a point where the ground gradually sloped upwards – they began to rise above the mud as rapidly as they had sunk into it. And now, black with clotted slime, they emerge waist-high... now they are within three or four yards of the spot... and now...now they are there!

They part the reeds – they stoop low above the shapeless object on which all eyes are turned – they half-lift it from its bed of mud – they hesitate – lay it down again – decide, apparently, to leave it there; and turn their faces shorewards. Having come a few paces, the blacksmith remembers the fishing-rod; turns back; disengages the tangled line with some difficulty, and brings it over his shoulder.

They had not much to tell – standing, all mud from head to heel, on dry land again – but that little was conclusive. It was, in truth, an unburied corpse; part of the trunk only above the surface. They tried to lift it; but it had been so long under water, and was in so advanced a stage of decomposition, that to bring it to shore without a shutter was impossible. Being cross-questioned, they thought, from the slenderness of the form, that it must be the body of a boy.

"Thar's the poor chap's rod, anyhow," said the blacksmith, laying it gently down upon the turf.

I have thus far related events as I witnessed them. Here, however, my responsibility ceases. I give the rest of my story at second-hand, briefly, as I received it some weeks later, in the following letter from Philip Wolstenholme:

Blackwater Chase, Dec. 20th, 18—

Dear Frazer,

My promised letter has been a long time on the road, but I did not see the use of writing till I had something definite to tell you. I think, however, we have now found out all that we are ever likely to know about the tragedy in the tarn; and it seems that – but, no; I will begin at the beginning. That is to say, with the day you left the Chase, which was the day following the discovery of the body.

You were but just gone when a police inspector arrived from Drumley (you will remember that I had immediately sent a man over to the sitting magistrate); but neither the inspector nor anyone else could do anything till the remains were brought to shore, and it took us the best part of a week to accomplish this difficult operation. We had to sink no end of big stones in order to make a rough and ready causeway across the mud. This done, the body was brought over decently upon a shutter. It proved to be the corpse of a boy of perhaps fourteen or fifteen years of age.

There was a fracture three inches long at the back of the skull, evidently fatal. This might, of course, have been an accidental injury; but when the body came to be raised from where it lay, it was found to be pinned down by a pitchfork, the handle of which had been afterwards whittled off, so as not to show above the water, a discovery tantamount to evidence of murder. The features of the victim were decomposed beyond recognition; but enough of the hair remained to show that it had been short and sandy. As for the clothing, it was a mere mass of rotten shreds; but on being subjected to some chemical process, proved to have once been a suit of lightish grey cloth.

A crowd of witnesses came forward at this stage of the inquiry – for I am now giving you the main facts as they came out at the coroner's inquest – to prove that about a year or thirteen months ago, Skelton the schoolmaster had staying with him a lad whom he called his nephew, and to whom it was supposed that he was not particularly kind. This lad was described as tall, thin, and sandy-haired. He habitually wore a suit corresponding in colour and texture to the shreds of clothing discovered on the body in the tarn; and he was much addicted to angling about the pools and streams, wherever he might have the chance of a nibble.

And now one thing led quickly on to another. Our Pit End shoemaker identified the boy's boots as being a pair of his own making and selling. Other witnesses testified to angry scenes between the uncle and nephew. Finally, Skelton gave himself up to justice, confessed the deed, and was duly committed to Drumley gaol for wilful murder.

And the motive? Well, the motive is the strangest part of my story. The wretched lad was, after all, not Skelton's nephew, but Skelton's own illegitimate son. The mother was dead, and the boy lived with his maternal grandmother in a remote part of Cumberland. The old woman was poor, and the schoolmaster made her an annual allowance for his son's keep and clothing. He had not seen the boy for some years, when he sent for him to come over on a visit to Pit End. Perhaps he was weary of the tax upon his purse. Perhaps, as he himself puts it in his confession, he was disappointed to find the boy, if not actually half-witted, stupid, wilful, and ill brought-up. He at all events took a dislike to the poor brute, which dislike by and by developed into positive hatred.

Some amount of provocation there would seem to have been. The boy was as backward as a child of five years old. That Skelton put him into the Boys' School, and could do nothing with him; that he defied discipline, had a passion for fishing, and was continually wandering about the country with his rod and line, are facts borne out by the independent testimony of various witnesses. Having hidden his fishing-tackle, he was in the habit of slipping away at school-hours, and showed himself the more cunning and obstinate the more he was punished.

At last there came a day when Skelton tracked him to the place where his rod was concealed, and thence across the meadows into the park, and as far as the tarn. His (Skelton's) account of what followed is wandering and confused. He owns to having beaten the miserable lad about the head and arms with a heavy stick that he had brought with him for the purpose; but denies that he intended to murder him. When his son fell insensible and ceased to breathe, he for the first time realized the force of the blows he had dealt. He admits that his first impulse was one, not of remorse for the deed, but of fear for his own safety. He dragged the body in among the bulrushes by the water's edge, and there concealed it as well as he could. At night, when the neighbours were in bed and asleep, he stole out by starlight, taking with him a pitchfork, a coil of rope, a couple of old iron-bars, and a knife. Thus laden, he struck out across the moor, and entered the park by a stile and footpath on the Stoneleigh side; so making a circuit of between three and four miles. A rotten old punt used at that time to be kept on the tarn. He loosed this punt from its moorings, brought it round, hauled in the body, and paddled his ghastly burden out into the middle of the lake as far as a certain clump of reeds which he had noted as a likely spot for his purpose. Here he weighted and sunk the corpse, and pinned it down by the neck with his pitchfork. He then cut away the handle of the fork; hid the fishing-rod among the reeds; and believed, as murderers always believe, that discovery was impossible. As regarded the Pit End folk, he simply gave out that his nephew had gone back to Cumberland; and no one doubted it.

Now, however, he says that accident has only anticipated him; and that he was on the point of voluntarily confessing his crime. His dreadful secret had of late become intolerable. He was haunted by an invisible Presence. That Presence sat with him at table, followed him in his walks, stood behind him in the school-room, and watched by his bedside. He never saw it; but he felt that it was always there. Sometimes he raves of a shadow on the wall of his cell. The gaol authorities are of opinion that he is of unsound mind.

I have now told you all that there is at present to tell. The trial will not take place till the spring assizes. In the meanwhile I am off tomorrow to Paris, and thence, in about ten days, on to Nice, where letters will find me at the Hotel des Empereurs.

Always, dear Frazer.
Yours, etc.
P.W.

P.S. – Since writing the above, I have received a telegram from Drumley to say that Skelton has committed suicide. No particulars given. So ends this strange eventful history.

By the way, that was a curious illusion of yours the other day when we were crossing the park; and I have thought of it many times. Was it an illusion? That is the question.

Ay, indeed! That is the question; and it is a question which I have never yet been able to answer.

Certain things I undoubtedly saw – with my mind's eye, perhaps – and as I saw them, I have described them; withholding nothing, adding nothing, explaining nothing. Let those solve the mystery who can. For myself, I but echo Wolstenholme's question: was it an illusion?

Shut-In

C.R. Evans

I DON'T KNOW if it's been seconds or hours.

It's too dark to see anything, and I don't dare move in case anyone is hiding in here as well. The only measure of time I have is my heartbeat, which drowns out everything else. The crashing, the shooting. The screaming.

* * *

It has been months since I last saw the outside world in person. We are isolated in the middle of a wasteland, an unending landscape of featureless white. The screens showing the external cameras may as well have been painted the same as the grey walls of the base for all that they actually show.

Of the last two staff who went outside to collect the air-dropped supplies, one reported that the blizzard showed no sign of abating. The other did not return. You would think that the isolation and time would have made us 'thick as thieves', but it has actually made us as misanthropic and as standoffish as I would imagine any other group of criminals locked together. Then again, they don't send the most valuable or most sociable employees out here. Just the expendable ones, who valued the remuneration more than two years at home with their nearest and dearest. With the state of our group as it was, there was little mourning, and only a ceremonial mention of an attempt to recover the body for a proper burial. It was immediately decided that we would make searches for the dearly departed if the weather cleared and it was safe to venture outside. This was the same as the decision to not collect him at all, but tinged with kindness instead of practicality. Which is why I suggested it.

And so, life continued. Ours, anyway. Somewhere out in the distance were the remains of a poor soul, unmourned by us, whose death would remain unknown to those who cared until we were able to return to civilisation months from then. When the weather cleared and our two-year contracts were up, we would begin the journey to the coast to be collected. Then the next crew would find their way here, which would be surprisingly easy. Our base is a bright eyesore in the middle of a pallid hell. It sits, an orange and white fortress, upon an accordion base of black struts. To get in, one would need to jump three metres in the air, or have the ladder lowered to them, which only a member of staff would be able to do by waving the microchip embedded in their sleeve in front of the scanner below.

We were sat in the dining room, playing cards and chatting superficially, as we did almost every night. Without sunlight outside, daily rituals were all that separated the interminable days. It had been a week since Jamie had returned without Robert, and it was the first time he had elected to join us since then. He sat in silence, smiling and listening, but not adding much. He looked relieved to be amongst us, but not quite enough at ease to act like everything was normal. I supposed it might have been survivor's guilt – his telling of the 'incident' had been consistent, if somewhat vague. They had the supplies loaded on the sled, were walking back, and Robert fell.

He didn't get up.

Didn't move.

No pulse.

Goddamnit, I'm telling you he just dropped. Maybe an aneurysm or something. There wasn't enough room on the sled, and we needed the supplies.

I'd heard that story enough times that I had it down by rote. Jamie kept repeating it when he got back, shivering and alone. But, he had the supplies, and if cinema has taught me anything, it's not to start throwing around murder accusations in an isolated base in the middle of the Antarctic. I'm not well-liked or attractive enough to survive that scenario.

As it was, the evening was comfortable enough. The mood was lifted by the whiskey passed between eager hands, and there was enough chatter between the dozen-odd of us to feel almost homely.

That feeling was shattered the moment we heard a pounding at the door.

In an instant there was silence. Every eye was turned to the door. I don't think any of us breathed until we heard the crackling of the intercom. Marie gasped. I was stock-still, waiting to see what happened next. I didn't have to wait long.

There was a further crackle.

"*Hello*?!"

We did not reply.

"Open the door! *Please*!"

Marie rushed towards the intercom, then stopped short, looking back to us for some reason. Approval, I supposed. Jamie was on his feet, pale and shaking. Sweat had soaked through his shirt in an instant and he looked closer to death than I've ever seen another person.

He shook his head and begged in a whisper heard by all. "Don't. Please, please *don't*".

It was impossible to tell if he was speaking to Marie, or to the person outside.

The intercom crackled again.

"It's me, Rob! Jesus Christ, I'm freezing, I need to get in!" the desperate voice was certainly familiar.

Others began to speak up, in shocked voices about how we need to open the door.

Jamie spoke again, louder this time. "No! There's no way we let him in!"

A deep voice boomed over the others "We're not leaving someone out there, we're opening the door, *now*"

It was Valerie, our leader. She had a habit of yelling like a drill sergeant when she wanted to be heard, and this might be the first time in her life it had ever been necessary.

Jamie, eyes bulging, slammed his palms on the table so hard I heard the bone against the wood. "He's dead! He died a week ago and *that is not him*."

Marie interjected, "Clearly he must have been alive! You made a mistake, and he was just unconscious! He's okay and found his way back". She spoke with such hope, I really believed she thought it was true.

I finally found my voice. "Even if he wasn't dead, he couldn't have survived out in *that*" – I point towards one of the static screens on the wall – "not for a *week*". The camera meant to show our front door was completely covered in snow, and the others were similarly unclear.

Valerie spoke again, her voice even louder this time. "There is a person out there! We can find our answers later, but right now we get them in here. If you want to question him after, go right ahead, but I'm not letting someone die because the logic doesn't line up!"

"You're goddamn *right* it doesn't," Jamie was moving now, putting himself between us and the door. He was shaking, but the glint in his eyes did not lead me to believe he'd let any of us past him alive.

"Get out of the way!" Her voice reverberated. I'd never heard Valerie that loud before. She strode to the door quicker than I'd seen. Jamie stood in front of her, arms stretched. Jamie was hyperventilating. Even with the murmuring and shuffling around the room, his breathing was like hearing my heartbeat in my ears, overpowering and desperate.

There was a pause. Valerie tried to reach for the door, and Jamie pushed her, hard. She fell backwards, and five crew ran forwards before she could even react.

Jamie was now pressed against the door, looking around. His eyes turned to the ceiling, but his gaze went beyond it. He was praying, wordlessly.

As Valerie was helped up, he noticed he was surrounded. Taking a shuddering breath, he seemed to let go of something.

"Fine! I'll show you!"

He whirled around and slammed his hand on the intercom, turning on our side's microphone. "Hey, Rob, it's me! Jamie!" he spat out the words with such vitriol.

"Jamie! Let me in! I'm freezing! Goddamnit, don't let me die out here!"

Jamie pressed the button again, but had started laughing even before that. "I'm not letting you die out there, Rob. You died a week ago." This sentence ended with a sob and I saw his frame shake.

"I bloody didn't! I'm alive, for fucking now, unless you don't open this door! Look, I woke up in the snow, my nose and toes got frostbit off, but I'm definitely alive!"

"How's your head, then?" Jamie said, monotonously. I had edged my way to the back of the room by this point.

"It's cold, like everything else! Now use yours for once and *Let. Me. In.*"

"No" came Jamie's monotone reply. "No, because a week ago I finally caved in your head. I know you're not alive now, because a week ago I watched you die with your brains and blood pouring out of a crack that I made."

Absolute silence.

Then movement. Marie wailing. Valerie shouting orders, others gasping, sobbing, crying, swearing. A tousle. Jamie laughing, begging, pleading. He kept describing what had happened, why he did it, in the hope that a clearer picture would explain why Robert should not and could not be outside. Finally, the handle being turned, a screeching, metallic noise and the sound of air rushing in as it was finally opened.

The lights went out, and I ran. I had the door to the hall at my back, and my God, I slammed it behind me. As I ran, I heard screaming and panic. I heard the hallway door reopen and footsteps behind me, but I did not stop, I did not help, I did not look back, because something was wrong. I had seen it when I looked at the screen. The ladder had never been lowered.

* * *

From the dining hall I had tried to run towards my bedroom, with the childish notion of hiding under the bed until it was all over. I remember I paused, thinking I was overreacting to Jamie's theatrics. After all, it was more likely that the very-much alive Robert had come through that door, than an avenging spirit or frozen corpse. When I heard more screaming, I assumed it was Jamie still fighting, having a nervous breakdown. Certainly the blackout wouldn't help matters, and would explain why I heard other screams of terror. Plus, if there was an electrical failure, maybe the signal for the bridge being lowered was broken?

I tucked myself into the first door I saw, leaving it ajar. It was a cupboard. I waited for things to calm down so I could reappear. I could claim I was looking for the first aid supplies, I decided.

Then I heard footsteps sprinting past the room I was in. And then the gunshots from the direction they were running. After that I ran from room to room until I found this one. In the darkness I felt warm puddles on the floor. I heard shuffling behind doors, and panicked whispers. I heard a plea for help nearby, but I never stopped moving.

* * *

I am crouched, pressed against the door, with cold metal against my forehead. My hand is still clutching the handle, but it has gone numb while my legs cramp. It is absolute agony, but I don't move in case I make any noise and draw attention to this room, or from anyone else already in this room. It was pitch-black when I first hurled myself through the doorway, and I don't know if anyone might have found their way here first.

I fear making any noise at all, but I have finally reached the point where the need to move away from the door and get away from the screams outside is now outweighing the fear.

Very, very slowly I straighten legs which creak and burn. My hand is filled with pins and needles, and a surge of agony as blood reaches it again. I stumble slightly and turn to press my back against the door.

"OH GOD PLEASE OPEN, PL–"

A loud thump against the door. Too hard. Too solid.

Too silent now.

I try to take a step forward. My knee buckles and a hand thrown out finds the wall. I feel my way to the light switch.

* * *

The room is plain. There are two cots against one wall, and several monitors on desks against the other. The walls are plain concrete, and the floor is linoleum. It has a tiled pattern which is only broken where blood-splatter covers it.

Sprawled halfway onto the desk is a body. The hair is matted with blood, and it is face-down. I cannot recognise who it is, but the amount of blood on the desk tells me that they are dead without needing to get any closer.

This room is central to the base, and it is well secured. It's supposed to act as our fallout shelter in case of several scenarios I'm not allowed to know about, but was expected to run three drills a week in case of. It looks like I'm not the only person to consider this room, but I'm clearly the first person to lock the door properly behind me.

I can see the clock on the far wall. It's 21:00.

I take very, very slow steps forward. The body remains still, until I push it to the ground. He's facing me now. His throat has been torn out, and it's a small mercy that his eyes are closed, because the terror is written clearly on the rest of his face.

I sit in the now vacant chair and put my face into my hands. I'm safe. I'm secure, I repeat this over and over until I believe it.

It is now 21:25, and from behind me, there is a knock on the door.

There is a pause, then another knock.

"Hello, you there?"

The voice is muffled, but obviously nervous.

"Oh God.... Please open the door, *please*!"

I hurry to the door, but hesitate to grab the handle.

I press my ear to the door and can almost hear heavy breathing.

"Who's out there?" I call as loud as I dare.

"Oh thank God! I-It's Ryan! Ryan Sinclair! Look, just let me in, please, I've called for help and they're coming but we need to hide until they're here!"

"Is there anyone else out there?"

"No one's with me, but I don't know if there's anyone else alive. But that thing isn't here! Just let me in before it finds me!"

"I...I can't do that"

"Why?! God please you know what it'll do if it gets me, I..." he breaks off with a sob.

"How did you get away?"

"I fucking ran! I just ran and it got the others but I made it *and you're going to fucking let it get me too!*"

"No. It's not going to get you." I turn to look at the blood-soaked desk. "Look, I need to enter a code to let you in, it's going to take a minute to kick in, though"

"Ok! Ok...just... Open the door, please...."

He sounds relieved.

"While it's going, can you hear anything in the base? Anything moving?"

He pauses.

"Shit, yeah! I can hear the chopper! It must be the same one from the supply drop, come back! Oh God, ok. You need to get out here, we'll get to the roof and we'll signal them."

"It's going to take a minute longer" I reply.

I walk to the desk and press a key on the blood-covered keyboard.

The monitors light up. Most cameras for the facility are broken. I can't see if anyone is moving or if anything is arriving. The remaining cameras aren't much better. In fact, there's one camera left correctly functioning: the one sweeping the hall outside the door. It's about halfway up, but swivels to see the entire hallway when operated.

"Hey, are you opening the door? The storm's gone for now but they might leave if they don't see someone living!"

My finger hovers over the button, my eyes focussed on the monitor. The camera is facing the far end of the hall. Nothing is coming that way, yet.

I call back, much louder than would have been sensible, "No! I'm staying right here."

"Look, please just come out, we can make it!"

I chuckle slightly. "No, I'm not going. And neither are you."

"What? Look I can barely hear you, just come on!"

I turn to the monitor. The press of one button will swing the camera to face the other side of the door.

"Just let me in! We can figure a way out!"

I turn away from the monitor and pull a blanket off one of the cots.

"Please, I don't want to die!"

I cover Ryan's body as best I can and again consider adjusting the camera.

The Child That Went with the Fairies

Sheridan Le Fanu

EASTWARD OF the old city of Limerick, about ten Irish miles under the range of mountains known as the Slieveelim hills, famous as having afforded Sarsfield a shelter among their rocks and hollows, when he crossed them in his gallant descent upon the cannon and ammunition of King William, on its way to the beleaguering army, there runs a very old and narrow road. It connects the Limerick road to Tipperary with the old road from Limerick to Dublin, and runs by bog and pasture, hill and hollow, straw-thatched village, and roofless castle, not far from twenty miles.

Skirting the healthy mountains of which I have spoken, at one part it becomes singularly lonely. For more than three Irish miles it traverses a deserted country. A wide, black bog, level as a lake, skirted with copse, spreads at the left, as you journey northward, and the long and irregular line of mountain rises at the right, clothed in heath, broken with lines of grey rock that resemble the bold and irregular outlines of fortifications, and riven with many a gully, expanding here and there into rocky and wooded glens, which open as they approach the road.

A scanty pasturage, on which browsed a few scattered sheep or kine, skirts this solitary road for some miles, and under shelter of a hillock, and of two or three great ash-trees, stood, not many years ago, the little thatched cabin of a widow named Mary Ryan.

Poor was this widow in a land of poverty. The thatch had acquired the grey tint and sunken outlines, that show how the alternations of rain and sun have told upon that perishable shelter.

But whatever other dangers threatened, there was one well provided against by the care of other times. Round the cabin stood half a dozen mountain ashes, as the rowans, inimical to witches, are there called. On the worn planks of the door were nailed two horse-shoes, and over the lintel and spreading along the thatch, grew, luxuriant, patches of that ancient cure for many maladies, and prophylactic against the machinations of the evil one, the house-leek. Descending into the doorway, in the *chiaroscuro* of the interior, when your eye grew sufficiently accustomed to that dim light, you might discover, hanging at the head of the widow's wooden-roofed bed, her beads and a phial of holy water.

Here certainly were defences and bulwarks against the intrusion of that unearthly and evil power, of whose vicinity this solitary family were constantly reminded by the outline of Lisnavoura, that lonely hillhaunt of the 'Good people', as the fairies are called euphemistically, whose strangely dome-like summit rose not half a mile away, looking like an outwork of the long line of mountain that sweeps by it.

It was at the fall of the leaf, and an autumnal sunset threw the lengthening shadow of haunted Lisnavoura, close in front of the solitary little cabin, over the undulating slopes and sides of Slieveelim. The birds were singing among the branches in the thinning leaves of the melancholy ash-trees that grew at the roadside in front of the door. The widow's three younger children were playing on the road, and their voices mingled with the evening song of the birds. Their elder sister, Nell, was 'within in the house', as their phrase is, seeing after the boiling of the potatoes for supper.

Their mother had gone down to the bog, to carry up a hamper of turf on her back. It is, or was at least, a charitable custom – and if not disused, long may it continue – for the wealthier people when cutting their turf and stacking it in the bog, to make a smaller stack for the behoof of the poor, who were welcome to take from it so long as it lasted, and thus the potato pot was kept boiling, and hearth warm that would have been cold enough but for that good-natured bounty, through wintry months.

Moll Ryan trudged up the steep 'bohereen' whose banks were overgrown with thorn and brambles, and stooping under her burden, re-entered her door, where her dark-haired daughter Nell met her with a welcome, and relieved her of her hamper.

Moll Ryan looked round with a sigh of relief, and drying her forehead, uttered the Munster ejaculation:

"Eiah, wisha! It's tired I am with it, God bless it. And where's the craythurs, Nell?"

"Playin' out on the road, mother; didn't ye see them and you comin' up?"

"No; there was no one before me on the road," she said, uneasily; "not a soul, Nell; and why didn't ye keep an eye on them?"

"Well, they're in the haggard, playin' there, or round by the back o' the house. Will I call them in?"

"Do so, good girl, in the name o' God. The hens is comin' home, see, and the sun was just down over Knockdoulah, an' I comin' up."

So out ran tall, dark-haired Nell, and standing on the road, looked up and down it; but not a sign of her two little brothers, Con and Bill, or her little sister, Peg, could she see. She called them; but no answer came from the little haggard, fenced with straggling bushes. She listened, but the sound of their voices was missing. Over the stile, and behind the house she ran – but there all was silent and deserted.

She looked down toward the bog, as far as she could see; but they did not appear. Again she listened – but in vain. At first she had felt angry, but now a different feeling overcame her, and she grew pale. With an undefined boding she looked toward the heathy boss of Lisnavoura, now darkening into the deepest purple against the flaming sky of sunset.

Again she listened with a sinking heart, and heard nothing but the farewell twitter and whistle of the birds in the bushes around. How many stories had she listened to by the winter hearth, of children stolen by the fairies, at nightfall, in lonely places! With this fear she knew her mother was haunted.

No one in the country round gathered her little flock about her so early as this frightened widow, and no door 'in the seven parishes' was barred so early.

Sufficiently fearful, as all young people in that part of the world are of such dreaded and subtle agents, Nell was even more than usually afraid of them, for her terrors were infected and redoubled by her mother's. She was looking towards Lisnavoura in a trance of fear, and crossed herself again and again, and whispered prayer after prayer. She was interrupted by her mother's voice on the road calling her loudly. She answered, and ran round to the front of the cabin, where she found her standing.

"And where in the world's the craythurs – did ye see sight o' them anywhere?" cried Mrs. Ryan, as the girl came over the stile.

"Arrah! Mother, 'tis only what they're run down the road a bit. We'll see them this minute coming back. It's like goats they are, climbin' here and runnin' there; an' if I had them here, in my hand, maybe I wouldn't give them a hiding all round."

"May the Lord forgive you, Nell! The childhers gone. They're took, and not a soul near us, and Father Tom three miles away! And what'll I do, or who's to help us this night? Oh, wirristhru, wirristhru! The craythurs is gone!"

"Whisht, mother, be aisy: don't ye see them comin' up?"

And then she shouted in menacing accents, waving her arm, and beckoning the children, who were seen approaching on the road, which some little way off made a slight dip, which had concealed them. They were approaching from the westward, and from the direction of the dreaded hill of Lisnavoura.

But there were only two of the children, and one of them, the little girl, was crying. Their mother and sister hurried forward to meet them, more alarmed than ever.

"Where is Billy – where is he?" cried the mother, nearly breathless, so soon as she was within hearing.

"He's gone – they took him away; but they said he'll come back again," answered little Con, with the dark brown hair.

"He's gone away with the grand ladies," blubbered the little girl.

"What ladies – where? Oh, Leum, asthora! My darlin', are you gone away at last? Where is he? Who took him? What ladies are you talkin' about? What way did he go?" she cried in distraction.

"I couldn't see where he went, mother; 'twas like as if he was going to Lisnavoura."

With a wild exclamation the distracted woman ran on towards the hill alone, clapping her hands, and crying aloud the name of her lost child.

Scared and horrified, Nell, not daring to follow, gazed after her, and burst into tears; and the other children raised high their lamentations in shrill rivalry.

Twilight was deepening. It was long past the time when they were usually barred securely within their habitation. Nell led the younger children into the cabin, and made them sit down by the turf fire, while she stood in the open door, watching in great fear for the return of her mother.

After a long while they did see their mother return. She came in and sat down by the fire, and cried as if her heart would break.

"Will I bar the doore, mother?" asked Nell.

"Ay, do – didn't I lose enough, this night, without lavin' the doore open, for more o' yez to go; but first take an' sprinkle a dust o' the holy waters over ye, acuishla, and bring it here till I throw a taste iv it over myself and the craythurs; an' I wondher, Nell, you'd forget to do the like yourself, lettin' the craythurs out so near nightfall. Come here and sit on my knees, asthora, come to me, mavourneen, and hould me fast, in the name o' God, and I'll hould you fast that none can take yez from me, and tell me all about it, and what it was – the Lord between us and harm – an' how it happened, and who was in it."

And the door being barred, the two children, sometimes speaking together, often interrupting one another, often interrupted by their mother, managed to tell this strange story, which I had better relate connectedly and in my own language.

The Widow Ryan's three children were playing, as I have said, upon the narrow old road in front of her door. Little Bill or Leum, about five years old, with golden hair and large blue eyes, was a very pretty boy, with all the clear tints of healthy childhood, and that gaze of earnest simplicity which belongs not to town children of the same age. His little sister Peg, about a year older, and his brother Con, a little more than a year elder than she, made up the little group.

Under the great old ash-trees, whose last leaves were falling at their feet, in the light of an October sunset, they were playing with the hilarity and eagerness of rustic children, clamouring together, and their faces were turned toward the west and storied hill of Lisnavoura.

Suddenly a startling voice with a screech called to them from behind, ordering them to get out of the way, and turning, they saw a sight, such as they never beheld before. It was a carriage drawn by four horses that were pawing and snorting, in impatience, as it just pulled up. The children were almost under their feet, and scrambled to the side of the road next their own door.

This carriage and all its appointments were old-fashioned and gorgeous, and presented to the children, who had never seen anything finer than a turf car, and once, an old chaise that passed that way from Killaloe, a spectacle perfectly dazzling.

Here was antique splendour. The harness and trappings were scarlet, and blazing with gold. The horses were huge, and snow white, with great manes, that as they tossed and shook them in the air, seemed to stream and float sometimes longer and sometimes shorter, like so much smoke – their tails were long, and tied up in bows of broad scarlet and gold ribbon. The coach itself was glowing with colours, gilded and emblazoned. There were footmen in gay liveries, and three-cocked hats, like the coachman's; but he had a great wig, like a judge's, and their hair was frizzed out and powdered, and a long thick 'pigtail', with a bow to it, hung down the back of each.

All these servants were diminutive, and ludicrously out of proportion with the enormous horses of the equipage, and had sharp, sallow features, and small, restless fiery eyes, and faces of cunning and malice that chilled the children. The little coachman was scowling and showing his white fangs under his cocked hat, and his little blazing beads of eyes were quivering with fury in their sockets as he whirled his whip round and round over their heads, till the lash of it looked like a streak of fire in the evening sun, and sounded like the cry of a legion of 'fillapoueeks' in the air.

"Stop the princess on the highway!" cried the coachman, in a piercing treble.

"Stop the princess on the highway!" piped each footman in turn, scowling over his shoulder down on the children, and grinding his keen teeth.

The children were so frightened they could only gape and turn white in their panic. But a very sweet voice from the open window of the carriage reassured them, and arrested the attack of the lackeys.

A beautiful and 'very grand-looking' lady was smiling from it on them, and they all felt pleased in the strange light of that smile.

"The boy with the golden hair, I think," said the lady, bending her large and wonderfully clear eyes on little Leum.

The upper sides of the carriage were chiefly of glass, so that the children could see another woman inside, whom they did not like so well.

This was a black woman, with a wonderfully long neck, hung round with many strings of large variously-coloured beads, and on her head was a sort of turban of silk striped with all the colours of the rainbow, and fixed in it was a golden star.

This black woman had a face as thin almost as a death's-head, with high cheekbones, and great goggle eyes, the whites of which, as well as her wide range of teeth, showed in brilliant contrast with her skin, as she looked over the beautiful lady's shoulder, and whispered something in her ear.

"Yes; the boy with the golden hair, I think," repeated the lady.

And her voice sounded sweet as a silver bell in the children's ears, and her smile beguiled them like the light of an enchanted lamp, as she leaned from the window with a look of ineffable fondness on the golden-haired boy, with the large blue eyes; insomuch that little Billy, looking up, smiled in return with a wondering fondness, and when she stooped down, and stretched her jewelled arms towards him, he stretched his little hands up, and how they touched the other children did not know; but, saying, "Come and give me a kiss, my darling," she raised him, and he seemed to ascend in her small fingers as lightly as a feather, and she held him in her lap and covered him with kisses.

Nothing daunted, the other children would have been only too happy to change places with their favoured little brother. There was only one thing that was unpleasant, and a little frightened them, and that was the black woman, who stood and stretched forward, in the carriage as before. She gathered a rich silk and gold handkerchief that was in her fingers up to her lips, and seemed to thrust ever so much of it, fold after fold, into her capacious mouth, as they thought to smother her laughter, with which she seemed convulsed, for she was shaking and quivering, as it seemed, with suppressed merriment; but her eyes, which remained uncovered, looked angrier than they had ever seen eyes look before.

But the lady was so beautiful they looked on her instead, and she continued to caress and kiss the little boy on her knee; and smiling at the other children she held up a large russet apple in her fingers, and the carriage began to move slowly on, and with a nod inviting them to take the fruit, she dropped it on the road from the window; it rolled some way beside the wheels, they following, and then she dropped another, and then another, and so on. And the same thing happened to all; for just as either of the children who ran beside had caught the rolling apple, somehow it slipt into a hole or ran into a ditch, and looking up they saw the lady drop another from the window, and so the chase was taken up and continued till they got, hardly knowing how far they had gone, to the old cross-road that leads to Owney. It seemed that there the horses' hoofs and carriage wheels rolled up a wonderful dust, which being caught in one of those eddies that whirl the dust up into a column, on the calmest day, enveloped the children for a moment, and passed whirling on towards Lisnavoura, the carriage, as they fancied, driving in the centre of it; but suddenly it subsided, the straws and leaves floated to the ground, the dust dissipated itself, but the white horses and the lackeys, the gilded carriage, the lady and their little golden-haired brother were gone.

At the same moment suddenly the upper rim of the clear setting sun disappeared behind the hill of Knockdoula, and it was twilight. Each child felt the transition like a shock – and the sight of the rounded summit of Lisnavoura, now closely overhanging them, struck them with a new fear.

They screamed their brother's name after him, but their cries were lost in the vacant air. At the same time they thought they heard a hollow voice say, close to them, "Go home."

Looking round and seeing no one, they were scared, and hand in hand – the little girl crying wildly, and the boy white as ashes, from fear, they trotted homeward, at their best speed, to tell, as we have seen, their strange story.

Molly Ryan never more saw her darling. But something of the lost little boy was seen by his former playmates.

Sometimes when their mother was away earning a trifle at haymaking, and Nelly washing the potatoes for their dinner, or 'beatling' clothes in the little stream that flows in the hollow close by, they saw the pretty face of little Billy peeping in archly at the door, and smiling silently at them, and as they ran to embrace him, with cries of delight, he drew back, still smiling archly, and when they got out into the open day, he was gone, and they could see no trace of him anywhere.

This happened often, with slight variations in the circumstances of the visit. Sometimes he would peep for a longer time, sometimes for a shorter time, sometimes his little hand would come in, and, with bended finger, beckon them to follow; but always he was smiling with the same arch look and wary silence – and always he was gone when they reached the door. Gradually these visits grew less and less frequent, and in about eight months they ceased altogether, and little Billy, irretrievably lost, took rank in their memories with the dead.

One wintry morning, nearly a year and a half after his disappearance, their mother having set out for Limerick soon after cockcrow, to sell some fowls at the market, the little girl, lying by the side of her elder sister, who was fast asleep, just at the grey of the morning heard the latch lifted softly, and saw little Billy enter and close the door gently after him. There was light enough to see that he was barefoot and ragged, and looked pale and famished. He went straight to the fire, and cowered over the turf embers, and rubbed his hands slowly, and seemed to shiver as he gathered the smouldering turf together.

The little girl clutched her sister in terror and whispered, "Waken, Nelly, waken; here's Billy come back!"

Nelly slept soundly on, but the little boy, whose hands were extended close over the coals, turned and looked toward the bed, it seemed to her, in fear, and she saw the glare of the embers reflected on his thin cheek as he turned toward her. He rose and went, on tiptoe, quickly to the door, in silence, and let himself out as softly as he had come in.

After that, the little boy was never seen anymore by any one of his kindred.

'Fairy doctors', as the dealers in the preternatural, who in such cases were called in, are termed, did all that in them lay – but in vain. Father Tom came down, and tried what holier rites could do, but equally without result. So little Billy was dead to mother, brother, and sisters; but no grave received him. Others whom affection cherished, lay in holy ground, in the old churchyard of Abington, with headstone to mark the spot over which the survivor might kneel and say a kind prayer for the peace of the departed soul. But there was no landmark to show where little Billy was hidden from their loving eyes, unless it was in the old hill of Lisnavoura, that cast its long shadow at sunset before the cabin-door; or that, white and filmy in the moonlight, in later years, would occupy his brother's gaze as he returned from fair or market, and draw from him a sigh and a prayer for the little brother he had lost so long ago, and was never to see again.

The Pontianak's Doll
Geneve Flynn

LING HEI'S UNCLE was a mountain: a man so mighty that he was afraid of nothing.

He bred German shepherds as a side to his contracting business and the six great dogs in his stable would trail him like a pack of wolves – tails slung low, quick to bolt if Uncle's temper was poor.

When the mood took him, he would descend upon Ling Hei in a cloud of bitter Marlboro smoke and sweet Bryl hair cream, clamp his large, calloused hands around her head and lift her up, erupting with laughter. She would laugh with him even though it seemed that her body would tear away, leaving her head in his hands.

Ling Hei loved him with all her heart, but she was not mighty; she was very small. So, when he came to her with the doll, it was no surprise that she could not refuse.

* * *

The mosquitoes were singing outside her window and she was on the very edge of sleep. It was the monsoon season and the night was hot and heavy with an unbroken storm. Ling Hei kicked off her thin sheet and drowsed, wishing for a drink of water when Uncle came into her room. He sat, his weight bumping up her side of the bed. When he turned on the side table light, Ling Hei saw that he was streaked with mud and his eyes rolled and bulged in his face. Startled, she tried to sit up. Uncle stopped her with a finger pressed to his lips. He took a bundle from inside his coat and carefully undid its bindings. He brought out the doll and pressed it close to her side. She turned and stared at it, eye to eye.

It was an ugly thing, not at all like the ones in Orchard Road Plaza. Those dolls had shiny hair and eyes that clicked open and shut. They wore pretty clothes and came with a little hairbrush and a bottle of milk that never spilled. This doll was bald and its face was almost completely smooth. There was a suggestion of eyes, nose and mouth. Ling Hei shifted and saw that it had a split between its legs, like hers, so it must be a girl. It smelled faintly of frangipani and the earthen floor of the jungle.

"I have brought you a gift, Ling Hei," Uncle whispered. His words blew across her face, hot and sour. He leaned in close. "This is a very special present that I give to you, do you understand?"

Ling Hei nodded warily.

"You must take very special care of this doll."

The banana trees outside the window rustled and Uncle sat up sharply, a ragged gasp caught in his throat. He stared long and hard into the darkness outside.

"Uncle, what is it?" Ling Hei asked, inching away from the doll as much as she dared. Something warm and soft still tickled her cheek even though Uncle's breath no longer filled her nostrils.

Uncle let out his breath with a broken laugh. "Nothing. It is nothing." He leant in again, lifting Ling Hei's arms and placing the doll upon her chest. Its body was unpleasantly pliant and limp.

"My sweet Ling Hei," Uncle whispered. "I trust you with this very special duty. Will you do this for me?"

Ling Hei's heart swelled despite her revulsion. Uncle had come to her and entrusted her with something vital. He needed her help. "Yes, of course, Uncle."

Uncle smiled. "Good girl. You are a good girl." He reached for the doll but recoiled. Instead he laid his heavy hand upon Ling Hei's arm. "I ask that you keep this doll with you at all times. Wherever you go, so too must this doll. You are to treat her as your own child. If you eat, you must offer some to her. Just as we make offerings to our ancestors. If you play, she plays. But you must never, ever let her out of your sight."

Ling Hei opened her mouth.

His fingers tightened around her flesh. "Listen! This is the most important thing to remember: at night you must always, always wrap her until not an inch of her can be seen. She must be kept hidden until the sun rises. Do you understand?"

The pressure on her arm was unbearable and Ling Hei nodded hurriedly. Uncle sagged and let go. He took up the wrappings from his lap and carefully bound the doll, round and around until all that could be seen was a tattered bundle. He replaced the doll in Ling Hei's arms and sat back, scrubbing his face with his hands and smoothing his pompadour. "Good. That is settled then." He laid his big, hard hands against the sides of her head and stared into her eyes.

He sighed. "What I would give for a son."

After a long moment, he seemed to come to a decision and he released her. "Go to sleep. Tomorrow I have someone for you to meet."

* * *

The young woman was the most beautiful thing Ling Hei had ever seen. With the grace of a swan, the stranger glided around the breakfast table, laying out the condiments and utensils for the morning rice broth. Her skin glowed like the face of the moon and the braid down her back seemed to be made of the finest black silk. When the young woman looked up and saw Ling Hei at the door, she smiled, the bow of her mouth curving so sweetly that Ling Hei felt giddy. The old apron tied around the young woman's waist and the shabby confines of their kitchen only made her seem even more glorious.

Uncle stood up and came to the woman's side. Ling Hei started. She had not even noticed him in the room.

He drew the young woman close to him, a possessive hand at her hip. "Ling Hei, this is your new auntie."

Auntie nodded silently.

Ling Hei dipped her head in respect. "Good morning Auntie," she murmured.

Uncle grunted in approval and returned to his seat. Auntie began ladling out the steaming broth. Ling Hei pulled out a chair and placed her doll upon it, then took the next seat. Uncle glanced at Auntie before swiftly dropping his gaze to his breakfast. Auntie's porcelain brow furrowed for a moment but her beautiful eyes skipped over the chair with the doll and settled on Ling Hei. She smiled and offered Ling Hei a bowl, the faint perfume of a frangipani flower following her movements.

"Why doesn't Auntie speak?" Ling Hei asked.

Uncle's hand whipped out and slapped Ling Hei hard across the cheek. "It is enough that she is a good wife," he said with a scowl. "Eat your broth and ask no more questions."

Ling Hei blinked back her tears and bent her head to her bowl. The entire side of her head was a burning chime. She did not dare look up until the sounds of Uncle slurping and the clink of his spoon had stopped and he had scraped his chair back and departed for work.

When she raised her head, she saw Auntie still bustling around the small kitchen. The sting in the side of her face faded away as she watched the young woman working. Ling Hei became lulled by the graceful way Auntie went about her chores and was startled each time she caught a glimpse of Auntie's face. She truly was the most beautiful thing Ling Hei had ever seen.

* * *

Ling Hei opened her eyes to darkness. She lay lost in the fog of sleep, wondering distantly what had awoken her. Perhaps a night bird had screamed. Perhaps the dogs were fighting. Her cheek ached. The pain must have pulled her up from sleep. After several minutes, the night continued to slumber on, with only the call of the cicadas to break the silence. Ling Hei's eyes were drifting closed when she heard a shuffling step outside her door.

It stopped at the sound of her soft gasp. Ling Hei was certain that the thing outside was listening just as intently as she. She trapped her breath behind her two hands, eyes wide in the dark.

The hall light was on, and a pair of women's slippers cast twin shadows in the gap beneath Ling Hei's door. The door handle dipped and rose. The handle dipped lower again. Was Auntie lost? Had she gone to pass water in the middle of the night and forgotten the way back to Uncle's bed? Surely not. Apart from Ling Hei's room and Uncle's, there was only one other bedroom, the kitchen, dining room, toilet and bathroom. Still, it was the young woman's first night in a strange place. Ling Hei supposed Auntie must have forgotten which room she shared with Uncle and was trying to return without waking anyone. Ling Hei crawled off her bed and went to the door. When she pulled it open, the scent of frangipani washed over her and she saw a hunched figure in the hall, its back to her. Auntie's long braid gleamed in the faint light.

Ling Hei reached out. "Auntie? Are you alright?"

Auntie slowly twisted around. When they were face to face, a cold snake slithered down Ling Hei's spine. Auntie was just as beautiful as ever, but her eyes were as still and senseless as water at the bottom of a well. The young woman lifted her chin and sniffed deeply. Her gaze flicked around Ling Hei's room, alighting on the little stool, the wardrobe, the window, the bed. She seemed not to see Ling Hei at all.

"Are you dreaming, Auntie?" Ling Hei asked. That must be it. Why else wouldn't she answer? A good measure of relief filled Ling Hei. All she had to do was steer Auntie back towards Uncle's bed. She reached for Auntie's arm but the young woman pushed past into the room. Auntie shuffled from corner to corner, following the edge of the skirting board, her fingers hovering just above the surface of every object she encountered. Her lips moved in silent muttering. She froze at the head of Ling Hei's bed, a small frown on her face. Ling Hei went to her side and reached out with trembling fingers.

"Ling Hei!" Uncle rushed into the room. He took Auntie by the elbow, guiding her out. Ling Hei followed them to her door, and watched as he led Auntie back to his room. Uncle saw her. "Go back inside."

She turned and hurried back to her bed. She heard his door click shut and his heavy footsteps returning.

Uncle took Ling Hei's little chair and sat in it, his face pale and stern. "Come to me."
She stepped into the circle of his arms and he took her shoulders.
"Was the doll covered?" he asked.
Ling Hei turned and pointed to the small bundle by her pillow. "Yes, Uncle."
His brow creased and he stared in the direction of his room with troubled eyes.
"Auntie is not well," he said gravely. "She has trouble sleeping and sometimes she wanders. It is your duty and mine, to keep her from harm."
"I thought she was dreaming, or lost."
After some thought, Uncle nodded. "She was both."

* * *

The dry season had come and gone and they were once again trapped in the close heat of a coming storm. Ling Hei lay restless and wakeful under the light of the full moon that shone through her window. Uncle had gone into town for business. He had promised her a packet of salted plums on his return. Ling Hei had not eaten all of her rice in anticipation but Uncle had been delayed, and now her stomach rumbled emptily and she regretted her foolishness.

To distract herself, she listened hard for the sounds of Auntie's nightly travels. Auntie did not have trouble sleeping; Auntie *never* slept. At first it had been strange, knowing that someone was ceaselessly pacing the halls and rooms but after a time, Auntie's shuffling footsteps had become a comfort: something else that signalled that night had fallen. But tonight, it seemed that Auntie was finally still. Even the dogs were not roaming. There had been reports of poachers in the area and Uncle had locked them away in his absence.

Ling Hei sighed and turned onto her side. Her doll lay on the bed beside her, tightly bound in its wrappings. Ling Hei took up the edge of one of the cloths and rubbed it between her fingers. After many months of wrapping and unwrapping, the material had become worn and soft. She sat up, glanced around, her teeth worrying at her bottom lip. She unwound the cloth a little further.

What would happen?

She had done everything Uncle had asked of her with the doll. She had offered it grains of her rice, tipped her cup against its lips and shared her toys with it. She had kept it with her at all times. It even sat watch while Ling Hei squatted over the toilet. Most importantly of all, when the light began to fade from the sky and the cicadas began to call, she brought the doll inside with her, took out the bindings from beneath her pillow and bound the doll head to foot so that not an inch of it could be seen.

But tonight, Ling Hei was restless in spirit as well as body. She supposed she had been pondering this question for many nights and days now, and it was only tonight, when her stomach was grumbling along with the storm, that she thought to answer it. With a second furtive glance around her, Ling Hei slowly unwrapped the doll. In a fevered burst, her hands worked faster and faster, tugging and pulling at the cloths until the doll was bare.

Ling Hei sat back and waited, panting slightly. A monkey whooped a lonely call somewhere in the forest. The cicadas paused to listen, found nothing of interest, and took up their singing once again. A stray mosquito whined around her head. The doll lay naked and still on her pile of bindings, as ugly and featureless as ever. Ling Hei flushed red. So, the duty Uncle had asked of her was nothing more than a stupid game. Nothing would happen if she failed him. All those months feeding and playing with the doll and wrapping it each night, and Uncle and Auntie were probably laughing at her.

Look at Ling Hei! What a silly little girl she is!

She raised her hand to sweep the doll to the floor when she heard a shuffling step outside her door.

A soft sob. It seemed to be filled with every sorrow imaginable.

"Auntie?"

A listening silence answered her. Ling Hei's scalp prickled and the skin all over her body drew tight. In all the months since the young woman had come to live with them, she had not uttered a single sound. Even when Uncle lay with her, and Ling Hei could hear his grunting through the wall, Auntie remained voiceless.

Who, then, was crying outside her door?

Ling Hei drew her sheet over her doll. She swung her feet over the edge of her bed and stepped down to the floor. On trembling legs, she crept forwards. A soft knock came through the flimsy wood.

The sweet scent of frangipani filled Ling Hei's nose and she closed her eyes in relief. She crossed the room with sure steps and opened the door. Auntie stood outlined by the faint hall light. She bowed to Ling Hei and held out a comb. With a hopeful smile she patted her braid, which had begun to come undone. Strands of long, dark hair hung around her face and curled at her neck.

Auntie had never asked Ling Hei to help with anything before and although her heart still thrummed quickly, Ling Hei was pleased. Perhaps one day Auntie would find her voice and Ling Hei would be the first to hear it. She hoped that Auntie's voice would be just as beautiful as her face. She could not imagine it any other way.

The comb was made of dappled turtle shell and when Ling Hei took it, it felt wonderfully smooth and cool in her hand. She beckoned for Auntie to enter, hurried to her little stool and gestured to the seat. Auntie hesitated, her eyes lighting on the wardrobe, the side table, the bed, and Ling Hei's few toys in the corner. Her brow creased as if in frustration.

"Auntie, please sit," Ling Hei said.

A smile broke over Auntie's face and she bobbed her head, coming to sit with her back to Ling Hei on the stool. Ling Hei untied the band that held Auntie's braid in place, careful not to pull. She drew her fingers through the strands, marvelling at how soft and heavy the hair was. With slow and deliberate strokes, Ling Hei began combing. Auntie's shoulders rose and sagged in a noiseless sigh. Long strokes, top to bottom, creating a waterfall of shimmering black silk. On the fourth stroke, the comb snagged. Ling Hei frowned and drew the comb out. She gently parted the hair and saw the nail that had been driven deep into the nape of Auntie's neck.

A tiny shriek escaped her. Ling Hei dropped the precious comb. She stumbled backwards, remembering too late that the wall was only a step or two behind her. Auntie slowly swivelled on the stool, her hair a long black curtain about her face. Ling Hei's mouth opened and closed but no air went into her. She squeezed her eyes shut; she did not want to see.

A cool hand stroked Ling Hei's cheek. The reek of frangipani crawled down her throat, thick as syrup. She shrank back against the wall, praying and praying that Uncle would return soon.

The softest sob, filled with all the sorrows of the world, blew against her ear. Unable to help herself, Ling Hei opened her eyes.

Auntie sat with her head bowed, her pale hands clutched in her lap. Silver tears trickled down her cheeks to dot her apron with dark circles. Some of Ling Hei's fear melted away.

She inched forward and laid a shaking hand on Auntie's fingers. Auntie returned her kindness with a weak squeeze. Again, her shoulders rose and fell with a silent sigh.

"Auntie, what happened?"

Auntie raised her face and smiled sadly. She shook her head and said nothing.

"Why will you not speak?" Ling Hei asked. "Can you not tell me who has done this to you?"

Auntie raised a tentative hand to the back of her neck. Her fingers were hesitant and Ling Hei knew with certainty that it must hurt very much. Auntie touched her throat and then the nape of her neck, shaking her head.

Ling Hei's brow cleared. "Is it the nail that has stolen your voice?" she asked excitedly.

Auntie nodded vigorously.

"Can we not take you to the doctor to remove it?"

An equally vigorous shake of her head. Auntie took Ling Hei's hand and pressed it to the nail. It was unpleasantly warm and Ling Hei jerked away. Auntie captured Ling Hei's hand. Auntie's grasp was like iron and pull as she might, Ling Hei could not free herself.

The rattle of Uncle's truck sounded down the road. The dogs were up and baying, calling to be let out. Auntie sat up, rigid and ashen in the chair, her grip on Ling Hei forgotten. Ling Hei's eyes flew to the shape of the doll under her bed sheet. Hot and cold flashed through her, covering her in a sheen of sweat. She heard Uncle's voice deep in her head, "*at night you must always, always wrap her until not an inch of her can be seen. She must be kept hidden until the sun rises*".

Ling Hei pulled free and scuttled to her bed. She threw back the sheet and grabbed up the doll.

A sharp gasp from behind.

With a whirl and a clatter, Auntie shoved her aside, snatched the doll and leapt through the window, leaving only Ling Hei's overturned chair and the memory of her perfume.

Ling Hei stared at the torn screen in horror, the useless bindings hanging from her hands.

* * *

A sick knot throbbed in Ling Hei's stomach as she hurried through the moist dark of the jungle. Vines dangled and clung from every tree, brushing at her with thick, heavy leaves, and feathery ferns shivered as she pushed past. Every now and then moonlight broke through the canopy and lit her way. Damp leaf litter clung to her feet, and the smell of earth and rotting vegetation rose up around her. Her feet were torn and aching and she could not catch her breath, but she did not dare slow down. Auntie was no more than a pale shade flitting ahead, drawing Ling Hei further and further into the forest.

The dogs had been let out and she could hear their frantic barking and yelping.

"Ling Hei!" Uncle bellowed. Ling Hei jumped and glanced behind. He sounded so close. The beam of his torchlight danced a little way off. The knot in her middle tightened. If only she had ignored her own wayward nature. If only she had done as Uncle had asked, none of this would have happened. She swallowed the bitter taste on the back of her tongue and wiped her damp palms on her nightie. She spun and searched for the flit of Auntie's white dress among the trees.

All around her was darkness. She listened hard, but she could only hear the cries of the dogs. She spun a full circle, praying for a flash of white. With a whimper, Ling Hei faced what she thought was the last place she had seen Auntie. Before she could take a step, hard hands closed about her shoulders and she was lifted off the forest floor.

"Ling Hei," Uncle breathed into her ear, his voice shaking with fury, "where is your doll?"

Ling Hei could make no sound.

Uncle spun her around. "Where is Auntie?"

She shook her head. Uncle threw her to the ground. Her side struck a root but she did not dare cry out. She curled into herself and wept silent tears as the dogs rushed past, growling low in their throats, snuffling and scenting. Their tails vanished into the night. Uncle grabbed up his torch and swept the wall of trees and vines around them with a trembling beam.

"Call her."

Ling Hei looked up and blinked. "Uncle?"

Uncle swung his torchlight from side to side. "She will come if you call."

"Why –"

"Call her!" Uncle clamped his fingers around her arm and dragged her to her feet.

Her shoulder screamed in agony. Ling Hei cried out and clawed at his hand. Uncle thrust his face into hers. "Call her."

"Auntie! Auntie, please come!"

In the distance, a dog yelped then shrieked. The others howled and one by one were silenced. Finally, the last one screamed, an ululating cry that shook the darkness. Uncle's fingers grew slack and Ling Hei tumbled from his grip. In the quiet that followed, Ling Hei heard a baby crying. It was strident and close, floating around them like the mournful call of a night bird. Uncle trained his torchlight on the trees, chasing the cries with the shaking beam.

"Did you remove the nail?" Uncle asked, his voice a broken whisper.

"No. I did not touch it."

Uncle ran his hand over his face and nodded. "Good. That is good."

"Uncle, who put the nail into Auntie's neck? Who would do such a thing?"

His right hand smoothed his pompadour and scrubbed his face over and over. He did not seem to have heard her.

The crying faded. Uncle stared out into the darkness. After a long moment, he lowered his torch. He bowed his head, eyes closed tiredly.

Ling Hei saw a movement beyond Uncle's legs. Auntie floated out of the shadows. She cradled Ling Hei's doll in one arm, her other arm raised, finger to her lips. Ling Hei glanced up at Uncle, cold all over.

"Uncle," she croaked.

He spun and saw. "No!"

Auntie slowly stepped closer, her face a pale circle in the night. She seemed more radiant than ever, and when she looked down at the doll, the tenderness in her expression made her lovelier still. Ling Hei's breath caught in her throat. The doll was no longer featureless and bald. Instead, it had wrinkled, pink skin and eyes that were nearly swollen shut. Fine dark hair capped its head. Its tiny hands waved and its tiny legs kicked. A weak cry escaped its toothless mouth. Ling Hei saw that it had a protruding belly button, and a split between its legs, just as she did and so must be a girl. A baby. Auntie's baby.

Uncle grabbed Ling Hei and backed away from Auntie. Auntie smiled and took another floating step. He thrust Ling Hei forward. The beautiful young woman did not slow her approach. "Make her stop," Uncle hissed.

Ling Hei felt her heart break. Uncle was no longer mighty and he was very, very afraid. Auntie continued towards them, one slow step at a time, her eyes never leaving Uncle.

"Please, Ling Hei!" Uncle sobbed. "Call her off! She will listen to you!"

"How can I?" Ling Hei asked.

Uncle covered his face with his hands, shaking. "She is your mother. She is your mother."

Ling Hei stared at Auntie and knew that Uncle spoke the truth. Auntie knelt before Ling Hei and bowed her head. She took Ling Hei's hand and pressed her fingers to the nape of her neck.

"No!" Uncle lunged forward. Auntie snapped her head up, her eyes black and malevolent. Uncle cried out and shied away. Ling Hei shivered and pulled her fingers back. Auntie turned her gaze on Ling Hei. Her eyes cleared and instead were filled with a depthless sorrow. Ling Hei swallowed and took hold of the spike. It loosened with a wet tug. As it slid free, inch by inch, Auntie shuddered. The sweet scent of frangipani became the stench of rotting flesh and old bones. Auntie's porcelain skin shrivelled and her eyes sunk into her skull. A dark stain grew in the centre of Auntie's back, spreading until a ragged, bloody gash opened in the white of her night dress, revealing the gaping hole where her spine should have been.

Ling Hei was not afraid. She remembered now. She remembered the large, rough hands that clamped on either side of her head as she struggled to be born. She remembered being torn from her mother's womb through the hole in her back. She remembered the earthen smell of her mother's grave, mingled with the sharp bite of Marlboro cigarettes and sweet Bryl hair cream.

Ling Hei's mother smiled; the curve of her lips so sweet Ling Hei swayed on her feet. She laid the baby in Ling Hei's arms. Ling Hei drew her baby sister close to her face and breathed in her smell. The baby reached out and batted at Ling Hei's cheek. Ling Hei smiled. *I have cared well for you, Mei-Mei.* When her mother stood, hands drawn into claws, Ling Hei did not bar her way.

Uncle, Ling Hei's father, scrambled backwards. His pompadour had become a wild and greasy nest. His shirt had come untucked and his eyes bulged in the light of his fallen torch. "Ling Hei, please!"

Ling Hei's mother descended, her sharp nails driving deep into his hard belly.

The screams died down and once more the night was still. Ling Hei rocked her sister gently. Mosquitoes whined around her ears and she absently waved them away. The rotting musk of the undergrowth stirred by Uncle's struggles filled the air. It was not unpleasant.

Ling Hei's mother glowed in the moonlight. Some of her vitality had returned and she looked as beautiful as ever. She laid a hand on Ling Hei's cheek.

"Ling Hei – my sweet black spirit."

The ground around Uncle's torn body had collapsed, creating a hollow. Ling Hei's mother sank down face-to-face beside Uncle, leaving room enough for her two daughters. Ling Hei carefully stepped over her father's splayed legs and handed Mei-Mei – *little sister* – to her mother and snuggled down, her father's broad chest firm against her back. The baby nuzzled against her mother's breast and suckled contentedly. Ling Hei looked at her mother and smiled. The cold, slick earth caused her no discomfort as it tumbled and rolled over them all. The quiet rustle of the undergrowth as it reached out long tendrils and sinuous roots were of no concern. The only thing that mattered was that at long last, they were all where they belonged.

The Lost Ghost

Mary E. Wilkins Freeman

MRS. JOHN EMERSON, sitting with her needlework beside the window, looked out and saw Mrs. Rhoda Meserve coming down the street, and knew at once by the trend of her steps and the cant of her head that she meditated turning in at her gate. She also knew by a certain something about her general carriage – a thrusting forward of the neck, a bustling hitch of the shoulders – that she had important news. Rhoda Meserve always had the news as soon as the news was in being, and generally Mrs. John Emerson was the first to whom she imparted it. The two women had been friends ever since Mrs. Meserve had married Simon Meserve and come to the village to live.

Mrs. Meserve was a pretty woman, moving with graceful flirts of ruffling skirts; her clear-cut, nervous face, as delicately tinted as a shell, looked brightly from the plumy brim of a black hat at Mrs. Emerson in the window. Mrs. Emerson was glad to see her coming. She returned the greeting with enthusiasm, then rose hurriedly, ran into the cold parlour and brought out one of the best rocking-chairs. She was just in time, after drawing it up beside the opposite window, to greet her friend at the door.

"Good afternoon," said she. "I declare, I'm real glad to see you. I've been alone all day. John went to the city this morning. I thought of coming over to your house this afternoon, but I couldn't bring my sewing very well. I am putting the ruffles on my new black dress skirt."

"Well, I didn't have a thing on hand except my crochet work," responded Mrs. Meserve, "and I thought I'd just run over a few minutes."

"I'm real glad you did," repeated Mrs. Emerson. "Take your things right off. Here, I'll put them on my bed in the bedroom. Take the rocking-chair."

Mrs. Meserve settled herself in the parlour rocking-chair, while Mrs. Emerson carried her shawl and hat into the little adjoining bedroom. When she returned Mrs. Meserve was rocking peacefully and was already at work hooking blue wool in and out.

"That's real pretty," said Mrs. Emerson.

"Yes, I think it's pretty," replied Mrs. Meserve.

"I suppose it's for the church fair?"

"Yes. I don't suppose it'll bring enough to pay for the worsted, let alone the work, but I suppose I've got to make something."

"How much did that one you made for the fair last year bring?"

"Twenty-five cents."

"It's wicked, ain't it?"

"I rather guess it is. It takes me a week every minute I can get to make one. I wish those that bought such things for twenty-five cents had to make them. Guess they'd sing another song. Well, I suppose I oughtn't to complain as long as it is for the Lord, but sometimes it does seem as if the Lord didn't get much out of it."

"Well, it's pretty work," said Mrs. Emerson, sitting down at the opposite window and taking up her dress skirt.

"Yes, it is real pretty work. I just *love* to crochet."

The two women rocked and sewed and crocheted in silence for two or three minutes. They were both waiting. Mrs. Meserve waited for the other's curiosity to develop in order that her news might have, as it were, a befitting stage entrance. Mrs. Emerson waited for the news. Finally she could wait no longer.

"Well, what's the news?" said she.

"Well, I don't know as there's anything very particular," hedged the other woman, prolonging the situation.

"Yes, there is; you can't cheat me," replied Mrs. Emerson.

"Now, how do you know?"

"By the way you look."

Mrs. Meserve laughed consciously and rather vainly.

"Well, Simon says my face is so expressive I can't hide anything more than five minutes no matter how hard I try," said she. "Well, there is some news. Simon came home with it this noon. He heard it in South Dayton. He had some business over there this morning. The old Sargent place is let."

Mrs. Emerson dropped her sewing and stared.

"You don't say so!"

"Yes, it is."

"Who to?"

"Why, some folks from Boston that moved to South Dayton last year. They haven't been satisfied with the house they had there – it wasn't large enough. The man has got considerable property and can afford to live pretty well. He's got a wife and his unmarried sister in the family. The sister's got money, too. He does business in Boston and it's just as easy to get to Boston from here as from South Dayton, and so they're coming here. You know the old Sargent house is a splendid place."

"Yes, it's the handsomest house in town, but –"

"Oh, Simon said they told him about that and he just laughed. Said he wasn't afraid and neither was his wife and sister. Said he'd risk ghosts rather than little tucked-up sleeping-rooms without any sun, like they've had in the Dayton house. Said he'd rather risk *seeing* ghosts, than risk being ghosts themselves. Simon said they said he was a great hand to joke."

"Oh, well," said Mrs. Emerson, "it is a beautiful house, and maybe there isn't anything in those stories. It never seemed to me they came very straight anyway. I never took much stock in them. All I thought was – if his wife was nervous."

"Nothing in creation would hire me to go into a house that I'd ever heard a word against of that kind," declared Mrs. Meserve with emphasis. "I wouldn't go into that house if they would give me the rent. I've seen enough of haunted houses to last me as long as I live."

Mrs. Emerson's face acquired the expression of a hunting hound.

"Have you?" she asked in an intense whisper.

"Yes, I have. I don't want any more of it."

"Before you came here?"

"Yes; before I was married – when I was quite a girl."

Mrs. Meserve had not married young. Mrs. Emerson had mental calculations when she heard that.

"Did you really live in a house that was –" she whispered fearfully.

Mrs. Meserve nodded solemnly.

"Did you really ever – see – anything –"

Mrs. Meserve nodded.

"You didn't see anything that did you any harm?"

"No, I didn't see anything that did me harm looking at it in one way, but it don't do anybody in this world any good to see things that haven't any business to be seen in it. You never get over it."

There was a moment's silence. Mrs. Emerson's features seemed to sharpen.

"Well, of course I don't want to urge you," said she, "if you don't feel like talking about it; but maybe it might do you good to tell it out, if it's on your mind, worrying you."

"I try to put it out of my mind," said Mrs. Meserve.

"Well, it's just as you feel."

"I never told anybody but Simon," said Mrs. Meserve. "I never felt as if it was wise perhaps. I didn't know what folks might think. So many don't believe in anything they can't understand, that they might think my mind wasn't right. Simon advised me not to talk about it. He said he didn't believe it was anything supernatural, but he had to own up that he couldn't give any explanation for it to save his life. He had to own up that he didn't believe anybody could. Then he said he wouldn't talk about it. He said lots of folks would sooner tell folks my head wasn't right than to own up they couldn't see through it."

"I'm sure I wouldn't say so," returned Mrs. Emerson reproachfully. "You know better than that, I hope."

"Yes, I do," replied Mrs. Meserve. "I know you wouldn't say so."

"And I wouldn't tell it to a soul if you didn't want me to."

"Well, I'd rather you wouldn't."

"I won't speak of it even to Mr. Emerson."

"I'd rather you wouldn't even to him."

"I won't."

Mrs. Emerson took up her dress skirt again; Mrs. Meserve hooked up another loop of blue wool. Then she begun:

"Of course," said she, "I ain't going to say positively that I believe or disbelieve in ghosts, but all I tell you is what I saw. I can't explain it. I don't pretend I can, for I can't. If you can, well and good; I shall be glad, for it will stop tormenting me as it has done and always will otherwise. There hasn't been a day nor a night since it happened that I haven't thought of it, and always I have felt the shivers go down my back when I did."

"That's an awful feeling," Mrs. Emerson said.

"Ain't it? Well, it happened before I was married, when I was a girl and lived in East Wilmington. It was the first year I lived there. You know my family all died five years before that. I told you."

Mrs. Emerson nodded.

"Well, I went there to teach school, and I went to board with a Mrs. Amelia Dennison and her sister, Mrs. Bird. Abby, her name was – Abby Bird. She was a widow; she had never had any children. She had a little money – Mrs. Dennison didn't have any – and she had come to East Wilmington and bought the house they lived in. It was a real pretty house, though it was very old and run down. It had cost Mrs. Bird a good deal to put it in order. I guess that was the reason they took me to board. I guess they thought it would help along a little. I guess what I paid for my board about kept us all in victuals. Mrs. Bird had enough to live on if they were careful, but she had spent so much fixing up the old house that they must have been a little pinched for awhile.

"Anyhow, they took me to board, and I thought I was pretty lucky to get in there. I had a nice room, big and sunny and furnished pretty, the paper and paint all new, and everything as neat as wax. Mrs. Dennison was one of the best cooks I ever saw, and I had a little stove in my room, and there was always a nice fire there when I got home from school. I thought I hadn't been in such a nice place since I lost my own home, until I had been there about three weeks.

"I had been there about three weeks before I found it out, though I guess it had been going on ever since they had been in the house, and that was most four months. They hadn't said anything about it, and I didn't wonder, for there they had just bought the house and been to so much expense and trouble fixing it up.

"Well, I went there in September. I begun my school the first Monday. I remember it was a real cold fall, there was a frost the middle of September, and I had to put on my winter coat. I remember when I came home that night (let me see, I began school on a Monday, and that was two weeks from the next Thursday), I took off my coat downstairs and laid it on the table in the front entry. It was a real nice coat – heavy black broadcloth trimmed with fur; I had had it the winter before. Mrs. Bird called after me as I went upstairs that I ought not to leave it in the front entry for fear somebody might come in and take it, but I only laughed and called back to her that I wasn't afraid. I never was much afraid of burglars.

"Well, though it was hardly the middle of September, it was a real cold night. I remember my room faced west, and the sun was getting low, and the sky was a pale yellow and purple, just as you see it sometimes in the winter when there is going to be a cold snap. I rather think that was the night the frost came the first time. I know Mrs. Dennison covered up some flowers she had in the front yard, anyhow. I remember looking out and seeing an old green plaid shawl of hers over the verbena bed. There was a fire in my little wood-stove. Mrs. Bird made it, I know. She was a real motherly sort of woman; she always seemed to be the happiest when she was doing something to make other folks happy and comfortable. Mrs. Dennison told me she had always been so. She said she had coddled her husband within an inch of his life. 'It's lucky Abby never had any children,' she said, 'for she would have spoilt them.'

"Well, that night I sat down beside my nice little fire and ate an apple. There was a plate of nice apples on my table. Mrs. Bird put them there. I was always very fond of apples. Well, I sat down and ate an apple, and was having a beautiful time, and thinking how lucky I was to have got board in such a place with such nice folks, when I heard a queer little sound at my door. It was such a little hesitating sort of sound that it sounded more like a fumble than a knock, as if someone very timid, with very little hands, was feeling along the door, not quite daring to knock. For a minute I thought it was a mouse. But I waited and it came again, and then I made up my mind it was a knock, but a very little scared one, so I said, 'Come in.'

"But nobody came in, and then presently I heard the knock again. Then I got up and opened the door, thinking it was very queer, and I had a frightened feeling without knowing why.

"Well, I opened the door, and the first thing I noticed was a draught of cold air, as if the front door downstairs was open, but there was a strange close smell about the cold draught. It smelled more like a cellar that had been shut up for years, than out-of-doors. Then I saw something. I saw my coat first. The thing that held it was so small that I couldn't see much of anything else. Then I saw a little white face with eyes so scared and wishful that they seemed as if they might eat a hole in anybody's heart. It was a dreadful little face, with something about it which made it different from any other face on earth, but it was so pitiful that somehow it did away a good deal with the dreadfulness. And there were two little hands spotted purple with the cold, holding up my winter coat, and a strange little far-away voice said: 'I can't find my mother.'

"'For Heaven's sake,' I said, 'who are you?'

"Then the little voice said again: 'I can't find my mother.'

"All the time I could smell the cold and I saw that it was about the child; that cold was clinging to her as if she had come out of some deadly cold place. Well, I took my coat, I did not know what else to do, and the cold was clinging to that. It was as cold as if it had come off ice. When I had the coat I could see the child more plainly. She was dressed in one little white garment made very simply. It was a nightgown, only very long, quite covering her feet, and I could see dimly through it her little thin body mottled purple with the cold. Her face did not look so cold; that was a clear waxen white. Her hair was dark, but it looked as if it might be dark only because it was so damp, almost wet, and might really be light hair. It clung very close to her forehead, which was round and white. She would have been very beautiful if she had not been so dreadful.

"'Who are you?' says I again, looking at her.

"She looked at me with her terrible pleading eyes and did not say anything.

"'What are you?' says I. Then she went away. She did not seem to run or walk like other children. She flitted, like one of those little filmy white butterflies, that don't seem like real ones they are so light, and move as if they had no weight. But she looked back from the head of the stairs. 'I can't find my mother,' said she, and I never heard such a voice.

"'Who is your mother?' says I, but she was gone.

"Well, I thought for a moment I should faint away. The room got dark and I heard a singing in my ears. Then I flung my coat onto the bed. My hands were as cold as ice from holding it, and I stood in my door, and called first Mrs. Bird and then Mrs. Dennison. I didn't dare go down over the stairs where that had gone. It seemed to me I should go mad if I didn't see somebody or something like other folks on the face of the earth. I thought I should never make anybody hear, but I could hear them stepping about downstairs, and I could smell biscuits baking for supper. Somehow the smell of those biscuits seemed the only natural thing left to keep me in my right mind. I didn't dare go over those stairs. I just stood there and called, and finally I heard the entry door open and Mrs. Bird called back:

"'What is it? Did you call, Miss Arms?'

"'Come up here; come up here as quick as you can, both of you,' I screamed out; 'quick, quick, quick!'

"I heard Mrs. Bird tell Mrs. Dennison: 'Come quick, Amelia, something is the matter in Miss Arms' room.' It struck me even then that she expressed herself rather queerly, and it struck me as very queer, indeed, when they both got upstairs and I saw that they knew what had happened, or that they knew of what nature the happening was.

"'What is it, dear?' asked Mrs. Bird, and her pretty, loving voice had a strained sound. I saw her look at Mrs. Dennison and I saw Mrs. Dennison look back at her.

"'For God's sake,' says I, and I never spoke so before – 'for God's sake, what was it brought my coat upstairs?'

"'What was it like?' asked Mrs. Dennison in a sort of failing voice, and she looked at her sister again and her sister looked back at her.

"'It was a child I have never seen here before. It looked like a child,' says I, 'but I never saw a child so dreadful, and it had on a nightgown, and said she couldn't find her mother. Who was it? What was it?'

"I thought for a minute Mrs. Dennison was going to faint, but Mrs. Bird hung onto her and rubbed her hands, and whispered in her ear (she had the cooingest kind of voice), and I ran and got her a glass of cold water. I tell you it took considerable courage to go downstairs alone, but they had set a lamp on the entry table so I could see. I don't believe I could have spunked up enough to have gone downstairs in the dark, thinking every second that child might be close to me. The lamp and the smell of the biscuits baking seemed to sort of keep my courage up, but I tell you I didn't waste much time going down those stairs and out into the kitchen for a glass of water. I pumped as if the house was afire, and I grabbed the first thing I came across in the shape of a tumbler: it was a painted one that Mrs. Dennison's Sunday school class gave her, and it was meant for a flower vase.

"Well, I filled it and then ran upstairs. I felt every minute as if something would catch my feet, and I held the glass to Mrs. Dennison's lips, while Mrs. Bird held her head up, and she took a good long swallow, then she looked hard at the tumbler.

"'Yes,' says I, 'I know I got this one, but I took the first I came across, and it isn't hurt a mite.'

"'Don't get the painted flowers wet,' says Mrs. Dennison very feebly, 'they'll wash off if you do.'

"'I'll be real careful,' says I. I knew she set a sight by that painted tumbler.

"The water seemed to do Mrs. Dennison good, for presently she pushed Mrs. Bird away and sat up. She had been laying down on my bed.

"'I'm all over it now,' says she, but she was terribly white, and her eyes looked as if they saw something outside things. Mrs. Bird wasn't much better, but she always had a sort of settled sweet, good look that nothing could disturb to any great extent. I knew I looked dreadful, for I caught a glimpse of myself in the glass, and I would hardly have known who it was.

"Mrs. Dennison, she slid off the bed and walked sort of tottery to a chair. 'I was silly to give way so,' says she.

"'No, you wasn't silly, sister,' says Mrs. Bird. 'I don't know what this means any more than you do, but whatever it is, no one ought to be called silly for being overcome by anything so different from other things which we have known all our lives.'

"Mrs. Dennison looked at her sister, then she looked at me, then back at her sister again, and Mrs. Bird spoke as if she had been asked a question.

"'Yes,' says she, 'I do think Miss Arms ought to be told – that is, I think she ought to be told all we know ourselves.'

"'That isn't much,' said Mrs. Dennison with a dying-away sort of sigh. She looked as if she might faint away again any minute. She was a real delicate-looking woman, but it turned out she was a good deal stronger than poor Mrs. Bird.

"'No, there isn't much we do know,' says Mrs. Bird, 'but what little there is she ought to know. I felt as if she ought to when she first came here.'

"'Well, I didn't feel quite right about it,' said Mrs. Dennison, 'but I kept hoping it might stop, and anyway, that it might never trouble her, and you had put so much in the house, and we needed the money, and I didn't know but she might be nervous and think she couldn't come, and I didn't want to take a man boarder.'

"'And aside from the money, we were very anxious to have you come, my dear,' says Mrs. Bird.

"'Yes,' says Mrs. Dennison, 'we wanted the young company in the house; we were lonesome, and we both of us took a great liking to you the minute we set eyes on you.'

"And I guess they meant what they said, both of them. They were beautiful women, and nobody could be any kinder to me than they were, and I never blamed them for not telling me before, and, as they said, there wasn't really much to tell.

"They hadn't any sooner fairly bought the house, and moved into it, than they began to see and hear things. Mrs. Bird said they were sitting together in the sitting-room one evening when they heard it the first time. She said her sister was knitting lace (Mrs. Dennison made beautiful knitted lace) and she was reading the Missionary Herald (Mrs. Bird was very much interested in mission work), when all of a sudden they heard something. She heard it first and she laid down her Missionary Herald and listened, and then Mrs. Dennison she saw her listening and she drops her lace. 'What is it you are listening to, Abby?' says she. Then it came again and they both heard, and the cold shivers went down their backs to hear it, though they didn't know why. 'It's the cat, isn't it?' says Mrs. Bird.

"'It isn't any cat,' says Mrs. Dennison.

"'Oh, I guess it *must* be the cat; maybe she's got a mouse,' says Mrs. Bird, real cheerful, to calm down Mrs. Dennison, for she saw she was 'most scared to death, and she was always afraid of her fainting away. Then she opens the door and calls, 'Kitty, kitty, kitty!' They had brought their cat with them in a basket when they came to East Wilmington to live. It was a real handsome tiger cat, a tommy, and he knew a lot.

"Well, she called 'Kitty, kitty, kitty!' and sure enough the kitty came, and when he came in the door he gave a big yawl that didn't sound unlike what they had heard.

"'There, sister, here he is; you see it was the cat,' says Mrs. Bird. 'Poor kitty!'

"But Mrs. Dennison she eyed the cat, and she give a great screech.

"'What's that? What's that?' says she.

"'What's what?' says Mrs. Bird, pretending to herself that she didn't see what her sister meant.

"'Somethin's got hold of that cat's tail,' says Mrs. Dennison. 'Somethin's got hold of his tail. It's pulled straight out, an' he can't get away. Just hear him yawl!'

"'It isn't anything,' says Mrs. Bird, but even as she said that she could see a little hand holding fast to that cat's tail, and then the child seemed to sort of clear out of the dimness behind the hand, and the child was sort of laughing then, instead of looking sad, and she said that was a great deal worse. She said that laugh was the most awful and the saddest thing she ever heard.

"Well, she was so dumbfounded that she didn't know what to do, and she couldn't sense at first that it was anything supernatural. She thought it must be one of the neighbour's children who had run away and was making free of their house, and was teasing their cat, and that they must be just nervous to feel so upset by it. So she speaks up sort of sharp.

"'Don't you know that you mustn't pull the kitty's tail?' says she. 'Don't you know you hurt the poor kitty, and she'll scratch you if you don't take care. Poor kitty, you mustn't hurt her.'

"And with that she said the child stopped pulling that cat's tail and went to stroking her just as soft and pitiful, and the cat put his back up and rubbed and purred as if he liked it. The cat never seemed a mite afraid, and that seemed queer, for I had always heard that animals were dreadfully afraid of ghosts; but then, that was a pretty harmless little sort of ghost.

"Well, Mrs. Bird said the child stroked that cat, while she and Mrs. Dennison stood watching it, and holding onto each other, for, no matter how hard they tried to think it was all right, it didn't look right. Finally Mrs. Dennison she spoke.

"'What's your name, little girl?' says she.

"Then the child looks up and stops stroking the cat, and says she can't find her mother, just the way she said it to me. Then Mrs. Dennison she gave such a gasp that Mrs. Bird thought she was going to faint away, but she didn't. 'Well, who is your mother?' says she. But the child just says again 'I can't find my mother — I can't find my mother.'

"'Where do you live, dear?' says Mrs. Bird.

"'I can't find my mother,' says the child.

"Well, that was the way it was. Nothing happened. Those two women stood there hanging onto each other, and the child stood in front of them, and they asked her questions, and everything she would say was: 'I can't find my mother.'

"Then Mrs. Bird tried to catch hold of the child, for she thought in spite of what she saw that perhaps she was nervous and it was a real child, only perhaps not quite right in its head, that had run away in her little nightgown after she had been put to bed.

"She tried to catch the child. She had an idea of putting a shawl around it and going out – she was such a little thing she could have carried her easy enough – and trying to find out to which of the neighbours she belonged. But the minute she moved toward the child there wasn't any child there; there was only that little voice seeming to come from nothing, saying 'I can't find my mother,' and presently that died away.

"Well, that same thing kept happening, or something very much the same. Once in awhile Mrs. Bird would be washing dishes, and all at once the child would be standing beside her with the dish-towel, wiping them. Of course, that was terrible. Mrs. Bird would wash the dishes all over. Sometimes she didn't tell Mrs. Dennison, it made her so nervous. Sometimes when they were making cake they would find the raisins all picked over, and sometimes little sticks of kindling-wood would be found laying beside the kitchen stove. They never knew when they would come across that child, and always she kept saying over and over that she couldn't find her mother. They never tried talking to her, except once in awhile Mrs. Bird would get desperate and ask her something, but the child never seemed to hear it; she always kept right on saying that she couldn't find her mother.

"After they had told me all they had to tell about their experience with the child, they told me about the house and the people that had lived there before they did. It seemed something dreadful had happened in that house. And the land agent had never let on to them. I don't think they would have bought it if he had, no matter how cheap it was, for even if folks aren't really afraid of anything, they don't want to live in houses where such dreadful things have happened that you keep thinking about them. I know after they told me I should never have stayed there another night, if I hadn't thought so much of them, no matter how comfortable I was made; and I never was nervous, either. But I stayed. Of course, it didn't happen in my room. If it had I could not have stayed."

"What was it?" asked Mrs. Emerson in an awed voice.

"It was an awful thing. That child had lived in the house with her father and mother two years before. They had come – or the father had – from a real good family. He had a good situation: he was a drummer for a big leather house in the city, and they lived real pretty, with plenty to do with. But the mother was a real wicked woman. She was as handsome as a picture, and they said she came from good sort of people enough in Boston, but she was bad clean through, though she was real pretty spoken and most everybody liked her. She used to dress out and make a great show, and she never seemed to take much interest in the child, and folks began to say she wasn't treated right.

"The woman had a hard time keeping a girl. For some reason one wouldn't stay. They would leave and then talk about her awfully, telling all kinds of things. People didn't believe it at first; then they began to. They said that the woman made that little thing, though she wasn't much over five years old, and small and babyish for her age, do most of the work, what there was done; they said the house used to look like a pig-sty when she didn't have help. They said the little thing used to stand on a chair and wash dishes, and they'd seen her carrying in sticks of wood most as big as she was many a time, and they'd heard her mother scolding her. The woman was a fine singer, and had a voice like a screech-owl when she scolded.

"The father was away most of the time, and when that happened he had been away out West for some weeks. There had been a married man hanging about the mother for some time, and folks had talked some; but they weren't sure there was anything wrong, and he was a man very high up, with money, so they kept pretty still for fear he would hear of it and make trouble for them, and of course nobody was sure, though folks did say afterward that the father of the child had ought to have been told.

"But that was very easy to say; it wouldn't have been so easy to find anybody who would have been willing to tell him such a thing as that, especially when they weren't any too sure. He set his eyes by his wife, too. They said all he seemed to think of was to earn money to buy things to deck her out in. And he about worshiped the child, too. They said he was a real nice man. The men that are treated so bad mostly are real nice men. I've always noticed that.

"Well, one morning that man that there had been whispers about was missing. He had been gone quite a while, though, before they really knew that he was missing, because he had gone away and told his wife that he had to go to New York on business and might be gone a week, and not to worry if he didn't get home, and not to worry if he didn't write, because he should be thinking from day to day that he might take the next train home and there would be no use in writing. So the wife waited, and she tried not to worry until it was two days over the week, then she run into a neighbour's and fainted dead away on the floor; and then they made inquiries and found out that he had skipped – with some money that didn't belong to him, too.

"Then folks began to ask where was that woman, and they found out by comparing notes that nobody had seen her since the man went away; but three or four women remembered that she had told them that she thought of taking the child and going to Boston to visit her folks, so when they hadn't seen her around, and the house shut, they jumped to the conclusion that was where she was. They were the neighbours that lived right around her, but they didn't have much to do with her, and she'd gone out of her way to tell them about her Boston plan, and they didn't make much reply when she did.

"Well, there was this house shut up, and the man and woman missing and the child. Then all of a sudden one of the women that lived the nearest remembered something. She remembered that she had waked up three nights running, thinking she heard a child crying somewhere, and once she waked up her husband, but he said it must be the Bisbees' little girl, and she thought it must be. The child wasn't well and was always crying. It used to have colic spells, especially at night. So she didn't think any more about it until this came up, then all of a sudden she did think of it. She told what she had heard, and finally folks began to think they had better enter that house and see if there was anything wrong.

"Well, they did enter it, and they found that child dead, locked in one of the rooms. (Mrs. Dennison and Mrs. Bird never used that room; it was a back bedroom on the second floor.)

"Yes, they found that poor child there, starved to death, and frozen, though they weren't sure she had frozen to death, for she was in bed with clothes enough to keep her pretty warm when she was alive. But she had been there a week, and she was nothing but skin and bone. It looked as if the mother had locked her into the house when she went away, and told her not to make any noise for fear the neighbours would hear her and find out that she herself had gone.

"Mrs. Dennison said she couldn't really believe that the woman had meant to have her own child starved to death. Probably she thought the little thing would raise somebody, or folks would try to get in the house and find her. Well, whatever she thought, there the child was, dead.

"But that wasn't all. The father came home, right in the midst of it; the child was just buried, and he was beside himself. And – he went on the track of his wife, and he found her, and he shot her dead; it was in all the papers at the time; then he disappeared. Nothing had been seen of him since. Mrs. Dennison said that she thought he had either made way with himself or got out of the country, nobody knew, but they did know there was something wrong with the house.

"'I knew folks acted queer when they asked me how I liked it when we first came here,' says Mrs. Dennison, 'but I never dreamed why till we saw the child that night.'

"I never heard anything like it in my life," said Mrs. Emerson, staring at the other woman with awestruck eyes.

"I thought you'd say so," said Mrs. Meserve. "You don't wonder that I ain't disposed to speak light when I hear there is anything queer about a house, do you?"

"No, I don't, after that," Mrs. Emerson said.

"But that ain't all," said Mrs. Meserve.

"Did you see it again?" Mrs. Emerson asked.

"Yes, I saw it a number of times before the last time. It was lucky I wasn't nervous, or I never could have stayed there, much as I liked the place and much as I thought of those two women; they were beautiful women, and no mistake. I loved those women. I hope Mrs. Dennison will come and see me sometime.

"Well, I stayed, and I never knew when I'd see that child. I got so I was very careful to bring everything of mine upstairs, and not leave any little thing in my room that needed doing, for fear she would come lugging up my coat or hat or gloves or I'd find things done when there'd been no live being in the room to do them. I can't tell you how I dreaded seeing her; and worse than the seeing her was the hearing her say, 'I can't find my mother.' It was enough to make your blood run cold. I never heard a living child cry for its mother that was anything so pitiful as that dead one. It was enough to break your heart.

"She used to come and say that to Mrs. Bird oftener than to anyone else. Once I heard Mrs. Bird say she wondered if it was possible that the poor little thing couldn't really find her mother in the other world, she had been such a wicked woman.

"But Mrs. Dennison told her she didn't think she ought to speak so nor even think so, and Mrs. Bird said she shouldn't wonder if she was right. Mrs. Bird was always very easy to put in the wrong. She was a good woman, and one that couldn't do things enough for other folks. It seemed as if that was what she lived on. I don't think she was ever so scared by that poor little ghost, as much as she pitied it, and she was 'most heartbroken because she couldn't do anything for it, as she could have done for a live child.

"'It seems to me sometimes as if I should die if I can't get that awful little white robe off that child and get her in some clothes and feed her and stop her looking for her mother,' I heard her say once, and she was in earnest. She cried when she said it. That wasn't long before she died.

"Now I am coming to the strangest part of it all. Mrs. Bird died very sudden. One morning – it was Saturday, and there wasn't any school – I went downstairs to breakfast, and Mrs. Bird wasn't there; there was nobody but Mrs. Dennison. She was pouring out the coffee when I came in. 'Why, where's Mrs. Bird?' says I.

"'Abby ain't feeling very well this morning,' says she; 'there isn't much the matter, I guess, but she didn't sleep very well, and her head aches, and she's sort of chilly, and I told her I thought she'd better stay in bed till the house gets warm.' It was a very cold morning.

"'Maybe she's got cold,' says I.

"'Yes, I guess she has,' says Mrs. Dennison. 'I guess she's got cold. She'll be up before long. Abby ain't one to stay in bed a minute longer than she can help.'

"Well, we went on eating our breakfast, and all at once a shadow flickered across one wall of the room and over the ceiling the way a shadow will sometimes when somebody passes the window outside. Mrs. Dennison and I both looked up, then out of the window; then Mrs. Dennison she gives a scream.

"'Why, Abby's crazy!' says she. 'There she is out this bitter cold morning, and – and –' She didn't finish, but she meant the child. For we were both looking out, and we saw, as plain as we ever saw anything in our lives, Mrs. Abby Bird walking off over the white snow-path with that child holding fast to her hand, nestling close to her as if she had found her own mother.

"'She's dead,' says Mrs. Dennison, clutching hold of me hard. 'She's dead; my sister is dead!'

"She was. We hurried upstairs as fast as we could go, and she was dead in her bed, and smiling as if she was dreaming, and one arm and hand was stretched out as if something had hold of it; and it couldn't be straightened even at the last – it lay out over her casket at the funeral."

"Was the child ever seen again?" asked Mrs. Emerson in a shaking voice.

"No," replied Mrs. Meserve; "that child was never seen again after she went out of the yard with Mrs. Bird."

Soul Cakes

Adele Gardner

IN 1841, my brother Edmund died, the victim of the dark angel that haunted Mama's tower room. I was only eight. The day after the funeral, Papa left on a business trip to New York – he'd just perfected his new 'Incorruptible' automaton model, a clockwork bank clerk that could handle all routine teller operations. He didn't even wait till Mama's tears dried. With New York business, he said, he couldn't afford to wait a day.

When he rode off in his carriage with its clockwork driver, Mama took to her bed. She didn't even change clothes. She lay there in mourning on the white counterpane like a raven in the snow.

She wouldn't eat. She scarcely drank. She refused a doctor – and threatened to dismiss anyone who tried to help. She said she was just tired, exhausted with the loss of her boy. Her voice cracked and sank away, and her hair floated out over her pillow like Ophelia's, gone down in silence instead of singing.

I wanted to believe the lies she told – that she was fine; that she just needed time to gather heart. I sat at the foot of her bed, reading aloud. She only sighed as I repeated another endless favorite. Sometimes I stretched out beside her and held her hand while we watched the light slowly shift across the ceiling. But as scared as I was for her, something in Mama's stillness scared me more. I knew that if the dark angel came back, this time for her, she would not fight. So I fled each night, before the darkness grew too great. Before I left, I lit the gas lamps on her mantle and dresser. And that was the last sight I had of her each night – a dark fold in that bed of white, her eyes fixed on the ceiling.

Mama took fourteen days to die. My heart dwindled with her as she melted into her sharpest essence, the shape of her bones. I spoke fast, as if I could keep her alive. I lay with my arms wrapped around her, singing songs, telling her stories I made up – or that the spirits whispered in my ear. Edmund and I had been born in this house, and we'd heard them before we learned to speak.

At last Mama turned to look at me and stroked my hair with a touch so delicate I shivered. Her lips moved soundlessly. She tried again. "I love you, sweetheart. Never forget that. Take my ring. Yes, Great-Grandma's blessed ring. Keep it with you always, and the shadows won't dare to harm you."

All this in a whisper. I struggled not to cry. "I can't take it from you, Mama, don't ask me to take it –" I felt certain that if I took the wedding ring from her hand, she would soon be dead.

"Take it, Azure!" she said harshly. She worked to free her left arm from my embrace and wrenched at the ring. She folded my hand around it. "Hide it. It would grieve Papa if he saw it, and he might try to take it away. Promise me you will care for it…keep it safe…hide it from your father."

"Yes, Mama, I promise."

My brother Edmund's death had been a crushing weight. That sorrow weighed me down like the snow that bowed the peach tree, snapping branches and splitting the trunk. But the tree had sprouted again with spring: and though Edmund died, I had lived. That was the pain of it: I was still alive; and my brother, my best friend, was dead.

But this was an entirely different kind of pain. If Mama died, I'd have to give up breathing. Till now, I'd stood in the shallows – the water might rise to my neck, but it always receded with the tides. The threat of Mama's death was a great wave sweeping in, to carry me out at last.

"Remember me, and I will always be with you." Her hand slowed on my hair. Her eyes lingered on me, full of love and sorrow. And then she seemed to recede from them. She lay beside me, embracing me still; but she was gone.

I hugged her tighter. If I buried my head in her waves of hair, if I did not look in her eyes, I could imagine she was still alive.

She grew cold and stiff in my arms as darkness fell like an endless series of veils. Alone. I was entirely alone.

I heard horses whinny as Papa's carriage rolled into the drive.

I jumped up and ran, clutching the ring. In my room, I sewed it into the hem of my dress. I heard footsteps in the hall, but no noise from the tower where Mama lay.

Someone knocked. I had just enough time to hide the sewing things. Papa opened the door. He held out his arms. I ran to him. He hugged me tight without a word. She'd left us both.

That night, we ate supper alone together. Though he said little, his looks were thoughtful, his manners kind. For one night at least, gone was my angry, blustery father. In his place, the wind roared around the grand house, sending twigs to beat the windows. As I listened, I grew aware of a faint singing – a mournful tune without words. I tried to hum along until I felt Papa's fork clattered to his plate. He was so pale. That's when I first recognized Mama's voice.

After the funeral, Papa spent even less time at home; and when we saw each other, we were formal. Though I knew he could not have stopped their deaths, I blamed him for the long absence during which they'd died. Wrapped in a dark cloud, he gradually turned over more of the household management to me, though I never felt I'd earned more than his patience. Yet I was grateful that he never brought another woman to share our home. And as I proved my competence, he began to train me in his business of gears and levers, of cams and counterweights. I had a particular genius for solving problems and improving upon his ideas. At last my designs won his praise. He took a grudging pride in me, the only replacement for his lost son.

As the years passed, the memory of my living mother blurred and dimmed to an unearthly hue like the pale glow after sunset. But I had something stronger than memory to anchor me by then: Mama's ghost.

Mama's presence was not something I could discuss. Everyone knew that the world was populated by spirits; a large old house always had a sizeable congregation, and ours held unnamed generations of ghosts, some no more than a whisper now. But this one was special. My secret. I knew she would be angry if I revealed her to Papa; nothing was worth the risk of losing her.

She was the invisible presence who combed my hair between the strokes of my own brush, the song hummed into my ears with the warbling of doves in the morning. When I lay in bed under the moon, she would tell me tales about our family, things my grandparents had done, things we had all done together. She never mentioned Edmund directly, and we never spoke about her death.

As I grew older, I found I could actually see her if I squinted just right through dusk. She appeared to me in the half-light, by candlelight, or in the drifting motes of early morning.

Though gossamer and blurred, she looked as happy and carefree as I first remembered her – with an innocence that I myself had lost.

And yet, at the sound of Papa's tread, she always vanished. Sometimes she would not come back for days.

* * *

By seventeen, I'd grown bold through unrelenting loneliness, the confidence of one devoted ghost, and the power to whisper secrets with family spirits. I had become what Papa loathed most – a strong-willed girl. In his eyes, the blessings of my household management and my genius with our mechanical inventions were eclipsed by the curse of my stubbornness. When I refused to marry his business partner, Papa threatened, "If you're so strong, my girl, prove it by spending a night in the tower!" Through his glare, I saw fear in his eyes.

"Very well, Papa." I matched his stare with the stony look I used to manage human servants. I got my cursed stubbornness from him.

We climbed the final stair to the tower and stood before what had once been my favorite room. Here Edmund and I played for hours. Here Mama taught me to sew. Here she died. No one had set foot here for years. Papa had tried the room on guests, but they suffered. Some went mad. Others died. Now the maids did not enter even by day.

I was terrified. I thought I knew what occupied this room – the dark angel that had claimed Edmund and sapped Mama's spirit. All the dark souls. All the sorrow, the grief that clung like tar to the bottom of my heart.

Papa knew the danger as well as I. He didn't want to see me die – just bend me to his will. So he allowed my preparations. I filled a bag with garlands, blessed candles, and soul cakes I'd baked from Mama's recipe. I wore her wedding dress – and the wedding ring.

As we stood on the steps, Papa asked me one last time: "Will you marry Seymour?" There was an odd quaver in his voice. He looked at me so strangely – as if he wanted to beg me not to go.

But I shook my head hard, then turned the knob with a sharp crack.

Papa locked the door behind me.

I entered slowly, drinking it all in. In the midst of my fright, I felt a prickling excitement. The air hung heavy with dust and old perfume – the intangible essence of other lives. It was all as I remembered it: her dresser with its fringe-shaded lamps and swivel mirror; medieval brasses on the walls; closets with child-sized doors. Beyond the mullioned window, the setting sun sparkled like a star through the trees. I lit the gas lamps and arranged the blessed candles about the room. I strung my garlands and laid out the soul cakes.

When the last touch of evening died, I shivered. The hearth held leaves and nests. I dared not light a fire.

Here in her room, I missed Mama terribly. I stood before the dresser mirror, wearing her clothes, her ring. Around the band, medieval script inched in sharp-edged blocks: "Guard my heart well." As a child, I had turned the ring on Mama's finger to see the crosses between the words, the tiny heart that lay at midpoint in the phrase.

Her ring glowed in the mirror, silvery and pale. I stared at its reflection and let my eyes blur. I tried to imagine that I was she. We had the same high-swept brows and cheeks, the same deep-set brown eyes, the same raven curls.

"Mama, are you there?" If traces of her remained – even traces dark and sad – wouldn't they help guard me against evil?

Shadows stretched blue from the corners, whispering of cruelty. Darkness pressed against dirty windows. The shutters slapped the walls.

"Mama, dear, can you hear me?" The wind rattled down the chimney. Pinecones dropped on the roof with a heavy clatter. The shadows in the corners pressed closer. Sorrow oozed from the walls like mildew, with the stink of regret.

I wished Mama would show herself soon. My nerves were fraying, and my heart, like my hands, grew cold.

I picked up her hand-mirror. The back was encrusted with small silver figures – a tiny sea king, a cat, a heart-shaped lock. I lifted the matching brush. But it was not the same without her hands stroking my hair.

A decanter of cut crystal sparkled like a rainbow. Would there still be a trace of Mama's favorite perfume? I drew that smooth, cold stopper. Though it should have evaporated, the scent filled the room, a full-bodied fragrance, as if she stood before me. I reached to cap the bottle and glanced in the mirror.

And there she was.

I gasped. I dropped the stopper. It wobbled wildly. The bottle tipped, then steadied, as if by an unseen hand.

I reached for her. Her palms clapped mine, cold as ice. Her face bore all the marks of my terror: mouth open, dark eyes wide, hands like talons where our fingers touched.

"Mama!" I whispered. Behind her, the darkness gathered, rising in crazy tendrils over her shoulders. I turned: in the mirror over the mantle, Mama whirled to face them.

She swept her arm: I raised my fist. Silver shone on my shaking hand, cutting wild arcs in the darkness.

The room got darker blink by blink. The candles guttered, then snuffed out one by one. Darkness oozed from the cracks in the walls. Mama's lamps cast long, pointed shadows. There were only ragged crumbs where the soul cakes had been: not enough to appease these ghosts.

An icy touch clamped my shoulder – her hand. Her voice rose from the mirror – or my throat. "Leave her alone! I shall entertain you instead!"

The shadows folded back. Waiting.

I was shivering head to foot. But at least Mama stood around me, wherever a mirror lay. Each one told the same story: it was not Azure standing here.

Her eyes were bright and lively. Her skin, impossibly pale. Her hair curled black and lustrous, and her teeth shone white. How she spoke! So lively, with tales I longed to hear – stories that were strange to me; stories blurred by time; stories I'd thought lost forever.

She danced through the shadows, and they leapt to join her, hanging from her arms. My flesh crawled at their cold, gelatinous touch, but she laughed and twirled, her dark hair flying in the mirrors, as merry as could be.

Her stories grew dark. She wept as she told them, the wrenching sobs catching in my own breast. Then she cackled in derision. She mocked me: "So you miss your mother, precious lamb? Let me tell you something. She loved this house more than anything in the world. Her love for your brother failed before this house. She could have fled with Edmund to save his life. But she was afraid if she left, your Papa would never allow her to come back."

"That's not true! You tried to save Edmund, but you couldn't stop the dark angel –"

"It came for me. Not Edmund." She laughed bitterly. "Don't you remember his nightmares? He clung to me so tightly. He dreamed my death. That dark angel was the spirit of my family home. The ring prevented the angel from taking me, so he took Edmund instead."

The shadows in front of me had grown. Their grins reminded me of Mama's. They passed through my hands, leaving them as cold as ice – cold that hurt so much I felt my fingers had been stripped to the bone.

From all around, her voice echoed: "Why do you think I haunt this place? The one thing I wanted was never to leave!"

"I know you loved me. When you were my ghost, you were so kind –"

She laughed. "When I was your ghost, I couldn't help but be kind. I hadn't the strength for anything else."

In the mirror, glimpses of my fright struggled through her face. I lifted my arms and pressed my fingers to the glass. Ring to ring. They matched. They clinked where metal touched metal, touched glass: mirror opposites. Mirror twins.

"Yes," she said, sober for a moment. "I love you. But that doesn't change what I did. Why I'm here."

"To protect me, Mama. To watch over me."

She shook her head.

I said, "I don't care why you're here. I'm glad we're together!"

Her face seemed to be crumpling, aging in the mirror. Through the cracks, I caught glimpses of my face. In my agitation – in her grief – we paced the room, wringing our hands. Whenever I passed a mirror, she watched me with cold, accusing eyes.

"You feel I sacrificed myself to your father."

"No, Mama! I admire you!"

"You admire me? My life, or my death?" She strode in front of a mirror and ripped open her dress. "Is this what you admire?"

Her ribs protruded through thin skin, the bare bones sticking out like needles. I whirled away.

"You can't run from the truth," she said. "I embraced death beside you, knowing I'd die in your arms."

The dark shapes whirled about the room. I began to understand certain things. They bruised my heart as they passed through. The danger in this room had begun with the shadow of Mama's death. And since she'd appeared, all the shades deferred to her.

Whatever the dark angel had once been...I feared it was now my mother.

I thought about all the times I'd met her ghost. The sweet scratch of her whisper. A listless angel. Was that only one fragment of her? Here, she was a raging torrent. The dark spirits were drawn to her with the gravity of a deep well.

"You know some part of you still loves me. Otherwise, I'd be dead."

She snarled. The cramps in my sides told me I might not have much longer.

"Azure, pretty Azure...I want to walk in the world again. In your skin."

"Papa would know the difference. And my skin won't last long, without a soul."

She chuckled. As she turned past the windows, I saw the first faint touch of gold. "What makes you think he won't welcome my return?"

I concentrated on the ring, this charm she'd given me before she died. Tears had trickled from her eyes, soaking the pillows. If there was a damp place, a dead place in the room, it was here, where she'd lain, already dressed for her coffin.

"You may have killed yourself for spite, but you loved me in the end. You came back to me."

I wrenched her around to the dresser, took up the little mirror with the scalloped shells and silvered figurines. I had helped her decorate it. Her hands and mine, our raven heads bent together in the sunlight.

As I held up the mirror, her face softened slightly – just enough. "Mama," I murmured, "Mama, I love you. Mama, come be with me, as you promised. You don't have to take my life – you can share it."

I summoned all my courage and ignored the shades dancing in the mirror. I focused on Mama, whose mouth had softened. I opened my heart to her, the dark and the light. Mama, who could never be all dark to me, no matter what she'd become.

A great sigh filled the room. In the periphery of sight, at the edge of hearing, the shadows rustled with feathery beats. "Please, Mama," I begged. "I want you to live, even if it's my life." I spread my arms wide.

And then, to seal my words, I let myself go. Fell backward onto the bed, into that hole. My arms still outstretched, as if to float on water.

The whirling room, the freakish light and shadow – stopped. A great clap of thunder – from the walls, from the rooftops. Vertigo, and a torrent through my soul.

I opened my eyes on gold, diffused like the sun underwater. Mama held my hand.

She smiled at me, the smile passing through her like light, like the glow from the windows. Her hand was solid and warm in mine, as if she'd never left me. My skin prickled, limbs waking up, as though I'd just come to life.

We glided above the floor. I wanted to tell her how much I'd missed her, my heart so full it hurt.

She turned toward me, a finger on her lips. She placed her hands on the sides of my head. I felt a slight coolness, as though touched by a cloud, or water. I held very still as she looked at me. For a time, I could not have told my name. I slept, in that dress, atop yellowing lace, amid the stiff smell of dusty years.

Dawn broke into my eyes like revelation as I woke to the grating of the lock. They found me curled in her bed, the silver mirror in one hand. I laughed softly – giddiness spilling like foam. I was alive. With the rise of day, Mama had settled into me, snuggled down like a cat. I felt languid with peace.

As the women advanced with looks of fear and pity, I rose on one elbow, then gingerly climbed to my feet. All whole.

Papa strode in. The corners of his frown seemed to twitch with a smile of admiration.

"Good morning, Azure. I hope you passed a pleasant night."

"Indeed, Papa – thank you. If you don't mind, I'd like to keep this room. I don't think I've ever had such restful sleep."

He nodded, with his sharp smile. If he was the least unsettled, he didn't show it. I even thought he looked proud.

And so I moved my things up to Mama's bedroom. Peace and quiet. And the peace was greater for seeing Mama smile in the mirror – as any girl sees her mother.

A little in the nose. A lot in the hair.

And everywhere in the eyes.

Perfect Mother

Anne Gresham

IT WAS ONLY a little blood at first, though much more would follow.

The pink lipstick-like smear in Mallory's underwear was unexpected and out of place, like finding a Doritos wrapper in a baptismal font.

Spotting is common, she told herself, trying to talk over the clamoring murmur in the back of her brain that knew exactly what was happening. *It's probably nothing.*

Outside her stall, she could hear the mumbled shuffling of other conference goers comparing notes, planning routes to their next session, complaining that the coffee was too hot, the food options too limited, the venue to hard to navigate.

Mallory closed her eyes and tried to focus on the hot tingling ache blooming inside each of her breasts. It hadn't been unpleasant for her at all – if anything, the ache made her feel powerful, magical, an unexpectedly godlike creature capable of meting out life itself.

You aren't pregnant anymore, a darker corner of her gut whispered. *It's over.*

She heard her phone vibrating in her purse. Her lock screen was full of notifications from Jonathan.

> *how about benjamin?*
> *cassie for a girl?*
> *its gonna be a boy though*
> *wanna bet on it??*
> *I love you so much*

She stared at her phone, her stained underwear around her ankles. When she'd seen the positive test, she'd stopped breathing. She'd felt like she'd missed the final step of a staircase. Jonathan, on the other hand, burst into simultaneous laughter and tears and wrapped her up in his arms, shouting, "Oh my god oh my god oh my god!"

While he clung to her, she started to cry too. She didn't know how to tell him she was unsure, and she didn't know how to say that she already felt like a terrible mother for her ambivalence.

Blighted ovum, wasn't that what they called it? All smoke and no fire. An elaborate hormonal dress rehearsal played with enthusiasm for an empty house.

She'd call the birth center when she got back to the hotel, and then she'd text Jonathan. There wasn't much blood. This wasn't an emergency yet. Worrying wasn't going to help. She flushed the toilet and stood up. She had just enough time to make the next session, 'Eco Burial for Total Beginners'.

* * *

Her boss Laura had pursed her lips every time Mallory brought up green burial. "The bereaved," she'd said, looking even more camel-like than usual, "need time to say goodbye.

They need to see the person they loved one last time. And I don't care *what* you've been reading on the internet."

But even if Laura was overly hung up on the importance of an open casket, Mallory loved working with her. Laura had taught her why it was important to slip a pillow under a cadaver's head on the cold metal gurney, to hold his or her hand while you inserted a cannula into an artery to begin the embalming process, to hold space for friends and family that had no idea what to do in the face of the most predictable and most unimaginable human circumstance. "That's our job," Laura had told her. "We know what to do."

Still, Mallory grinned a bit disloyally when she slipped into the Magnolia Room. The hall was full of combat boots, tattoos, and friendly morticians her own age – people ready to talk about the value of letting family wash the body, to question embalming as standard practice, to consider new ways of doing things.

She took a seat in the back as her phone buzzed again.

> *we could name him after your dad, maybe*
> *but i really like benjamin*
> *benji for short!*

The real cramp started three slides into the internet-meme-laden PowerPoint. As the woman at the front of the room discussed the environmental damage caused by mercury in dental fillings, the pain grew more and more intense, tightening around her like a belt.

Some cramping is normal, she reminded herself. She repeated it over and over again, losing track of the presentation, until finally she couldn't pretend any more.

She left before the Q and A, clutching her stomach. She caught the conference shuttle back to the hotel, sitting on her complementary tote bag in an effort to preserve the bus's upholstery.

As soon as she got to her room, she called the birth center. She and Jonathan had called almost before the test strip had dried two weeks ago. Mallory had already known that she wanted a natural birth, and the center was warm, tastefully decorated, and enthusiastic. She had envisioned herself laboring powerfully while Jonathan held her hand and a midwife gently wiped her brow and whispered encouragement.

The midwife on duty told her what she already knew. With strong cramps and that much blood at six weeks, there wasn't much point in going to the hospital unless she started going through more than one pad in an hour. Something had been set in motion that couldn't be stopped.

"It's not your fault," the midwife told her. "These things happen. It's sad, but perfectly natural." Three days ago, the same woman had chirped that giving birth was what Mallory's body was designed to do. *Guess I'm perfectly naturally fucking broken, then.*

As soon as she hung up, her phone buzzed again, and again, and again – Jonathan sending a volley of links to cribs and car seats on Amazon. For the next hour he contentedly carried on a one-sided conversation about each model's virtues while Mallory sobbed alone on the hotel bed, curled protectively around the tight painful center of the end of her pregnancy.

* * *

Her breasts were still sore the next morning, but the ache was already fading with her plummeting hCG levels. She stared at the continental breakfast pastry and rubbed her stomach. It was only bloated, not rounded by a tiny, starfish-handed spark of a future nestled deep inside her, gently drifting on the warm tide of her pulse. This was nothing but gas and water retention that would resolve itself soon.

She flipped listlessly through the conference program. Only a few minutes before the next session. She had a sudden urge to be at work, where she could care for someone, massage moisturizer into still cheeks, rub baby oil into dry hair so that it could be smoothed and brushed, gently slip limp arms into a favorite dress or shirt. There would be no baby for her to tend to, but she'd settle for a corpse.

sweetie, please text me back

Her throat tightened and she turned off her phone. Then a session she hadn't seen before caught her eye.

'The Most Important Job in the World' was its title. 'It's never too late to fix things. Join us to gain the tools you need to turn yourself around. We can help you.'

Normally she would have laughed. That just about took the cake for bland conference vagueness. She'd circled a few other options that had looked interesting yesterday – one about social media and another about aftercare. She closed her eyes. She was so tired. The cramps were nearly gone, though the blood was now steady, black and slimy with stringy clots and a rich earthy smell that turned her stomach. She needed to go home.

But Jonathan would know as soon as she walked in the door, and if he didn't, she would have to tell him. She imagined his face crumpling.

"We can help you."

She wanted to know what it meant. Forty-five more minutes couldn't make things any worse, could it?

* * *

She drifted down the conference halls looking for the Daffodil Room. She found Magnolia, Peony, Snapdragon, Rose, Iris, and Begonia, but no daffodils.

"Excuse me," she said, flagging down a conference volunteer. "Where's the Daffodil Room?" She pointed at her program.

The volunteer squinted at it. "There isn't one," she said and gave Mallory a strange look.

"It says right here," Mallory insisted, thrusting the program at her.

"That's an ad for cremains keepsakes." The volunteer was inching away from her.

"No," Mallory started to argue, but then looked at her program again. Sure enough, there was nothing at the bottom of the page but a pixelated logo of a company selling custom paperweights and pendants made with cremation ash.

"You're looking for the Daffodil Room?" A woman asked behind her.

Mallory turned. The speaker was a nondescript middle aged woman in a conservative skirt suit and tasteful pumps. But when Mallory tried to focus on her face, the woman's features seemed to blur. Mallory had an uncomfortable feeling that she would never be able to point this woman out in a crowd, but then she found herself pulled under by the sound of the woman's low, resonant voice. "I'm headed that way. I can show you."

"Okay," Mallory said, forgetting the shifting conference program, the nonexistent Daffodil Room, the look the volunteer had given her. The woman smelled like cloves and camp fires. Mallory realized she was inching closer to her, waiting for her to speak again.

"I saw you on the conference shuttle," the woman continued as they walked. "You looked like you were hurting."

Mallory shook her head. "Cramps," she said and laughed nervously.

The woman nodded seriously. "I see," she said. "Let us talk to you. We can help. And we need you."

They were now at the end of a long hallway she hadn't been down before, but the walls were the same aggressively neutral shade of blue gray. Mallory had a fizzy feeling in her head, like she was on the verge of panicked laughter at a frightening joke she couldn't understand.

"Who do you work for?" Mallory asked.

The woman took her hand. Mallory, who generally wasn't a touchy feely person, didn't mind in the slightest. "Someone powerful," the woman answered.

Mallory obediently followed her into the Daffodil Room and took a seat in the last row near the doors. There were a handful of other attendees, but they all sat alone, facing forward, backs to Mallory. No one spoke.

She was starting to feel a little lightheaded. Maybe she needed to leave, to go to an urgent care clinic. She wondered if she was losing more blood than she thought. She felt herself slowing down, a heavy liquid calm coagulating in her veins. Her eyelids were heavy.

I need to go home. The thought was a flash of animal instinct, and she started to stand up. But then the woman who had walked her into the room tapped the mic.

"Welcome," she said, spreading her hands. "Thank you for choosing to spend your time here, with us. We're here to help you."

She seemed to be whispering directly in Mallory's ear.

"You feel lost," the presenter continued. "Broken. But don't worry. We can show you how to make a correction, to get back on track. It's never too late. Everything is negotiable. But in the end, it will be up to you to use the tools we give you. We can only nudge you in the right direction. Will you let us?"

Yes, Mallory nodded. Yes. A distant part of her saw that the mic was unplugged, and saw that there was something unnatural about the stillness of the other attendees. That part of her frantically tried to flood her body with adrenalin, to make her stand up and run, screaming for help. But it was such a small part of her, and it was so far away.

"You have lost something," the woman said, her voice a snake coiling itself around Mallory's brain. "So have we. We need your help, too. Together, we can turn back the order of things."

Mallory smiled sleepily. The presenter launched into her slide deck.

* * *

When the session was over, Mallory felt warm, content, and prepared. She reached under her chair and wrapped her fingers around the swag underneath it. An oversized tote bag. A large plastic case containing a cordless oscillating sternum saw. A newspaper clipping.

Missing Infant Last Seen Near River.

Her breath caught at the sight of the little boy's grinning face. Her little boy's grinning face.

* * *

The drive back home took about an hour and a half. Oklahoma slipped past her like a vague dream. *How long was I in that presentation?* She steered her car into town, toward work. It was nearly midnight, but Laura's Civic was parked outside, as Mallory knew it would be. She'd seen it on one of the presentation's slides.

Her college boyfriend had gotten ahold of pure dextromethorphan powder once, and they'd administered heroic doses to themselves. It had resulted in an odd, floating state where Mallory had experienced her mind tethered to her body by the slightest spider thread. She'd thought she was going to die, and it had been the gentlest, lightest feeling she'd ever had.

When she greeted Laura, she felt something similar. Laura was shaken, as Mallory had been told she would be.

"Good, you got my message," Laura said, steering her toward the prep room. "This one… this is bad, I don't know what else to say."

Laura hoarsely explained that their guest's age was eighteen months, that he'd been alone in a dark, floating world for four days. Drowned. Decomp minimal, but skin damage and discoloration significant (it was this word that broke Laura's voice). Laura possessed infinite depths of compassion for her families, but Mallory had never seen her lose her composure over a corpse before.

The family wanted a closed casket service and wouldn't be persuaded otherwise. Mallory gathered that Laura, for once, hadn't even attempted to sell them on it.

"Mal, can you finish this one for me?" Laura asked. "I'm sorry. I just…I knew him. I knew his parents. This one is too much."

"Of course," Mallory said. "Why don't you go home, get some sleep? I'll take good care of him."

"Are you sure?" Laura asked.

The gratitude in her voice stirred something in Mallory. She tried to make her mouth form the words – HELP ME – but they stuck in her throat.

"Thank you," Laura murmured. "I'll check in with you tomorrow morning, okay?"

* * *

Mallory made sure Laura had gone before she approached the small shape on the gurney. The air was heavy with a briny smell.

She gently peeled the sheet back.

His face, blackish green and puffy as it was, was beautiful. His open mouth was frozen in a gasp of wonder, his black lips forming a perfectly round 'oh'.

She took his small hand, feeling his chubby fingers. She imagined them in embryo, floating, slowly curling and uncurling.

Laura had already started the embalming process, which had removed some of the fluid, but there was only so much that could be done in a case with this much water damage.

He was fragile. He needed her.

She gathered his little body to her and sang into the cold green seashell of his ear.

"Hush, little baby, don't say a word."

She kissed his head.

His eyes were a muddy sea green when he opened them.

* * *

When they arrived at her house, she assembled the oscillating saw. From somewhere deep and inescapable, Mallory shrieked and hurled the full weight of her soul against what was about to happen, to no effect. Her mind felt as though it had been trapped under ice, and she rushed up at it and screamed a choking underwater scream.

Jonathan threw open the door. "Thank god," he yelped. "Where the hell have you been, Mal?"

"I'm sorry," Mallory managed to choke as she depressed the trigger and plunged the whirring saw into his sternum.

Jonathan screamed and tried to wrench the saw out of her hands, reflexively twisting away from her.

"He has to eat!" she sobbed. "I'm so sorry, but he has to eat!" She lunged at him again.

Jonathan pushed her away and tried to run, thick black blood oozing between his fingers, but the ragged opening in his chest brought him to his knees. He collapsed.

Mallory leaped to her feet and ran to the car, helping her baby boy out of the enormous tote bag. She brought him to Jonathan. She pushed her husband over on his side.

He tried to speak, or more likely to scream, but nothing came out except bubbling wheezing gasps and pink froth. Her baby boy toddled toward him, his muddy eyes curious and excited.

Mallory sobbed, struggling to crack open Jonathan's rib cage. He was slipping away quickly; she'd damaged his lungs. Her mind felt cruelly clear but unable to control her own hands. Unable to stop. She dug into Jonathan's center. His heart was still beating, weakly.

Her baby boy sat down next to her and grinned up at her.

Mallory's mind stilled, her own thoughts and self pushed under the surface again.

"That's my boy," she cooed. "Eat up."

His little face disappeared inside Jonathan's chest. Jonathan slipped away forever a moment later.

* * *

She dragged Jonathan's body into the guest room and closed the door. Her little boy followed her inside. She lifted him up and he wrapped his pudgy little arms around her neck. He leaned his cold face against her shoulder, his tiny weight collapsing against her, puffy, waterlogged skin soft and pungent.

She held him all night. He never cried, though he sucked his thumb occasionally. His mud colored eyes never closed.

* * *

Laura was next.

She came to Mallory's house the next morning. "Mal!" she yelled, pounding on the door. "I know you're in there, open up! Please, the police will be here soon. I want to talk to you first. Let me in. We know you took him."

Mallory slid the saw into its battery base. Her baby boy, who'd grown (so fast, they grow so fast), watched quietly from the corner.

"Please," Mallory whispered. "Please don't make me do this." Sparks showered her vision at the effort of wrenching the words out from the dark and watery place she watched herself from.

But then he smiled at her. "Mama," he said. Mallory stared at him, and then her mind slipped out of her grasp again.

"Baby," she said, running over to kiss his cheek.

"Hungee," he said next, rubbing his round little belly.

"Of course, sweetheart. Of course."

* * *

Laura's funeral parlor nose recognized the thick, heavy scent of Jonathan's putrefaction as soon as Mallory opened the door. The older woman's eyes flew open, but Mallory grabbed her by the wrist and pulled her inside with one hand. With the other, she slit her throat.

Laura gurgled confusedly. It hadn't been a perfect cut, but the blood spurted vigorously enough. Laura staggered backwards, clutching her neck, and Mallory reached for the saw.

This time, though, her baby boy flew at Laura. How did he get so strong, Mallory thought bemusedly as he tore open her mentor's chest and sank his teeth into the slick fist of her heart. He was just a little baby only moments ago, and now look at him. All grown up.

* * *

When he'd finished his slurpy meal and Mallory had wiped off his cheeks and hands for him, she dragged the body to the guest room. She looked at Jonathan's corpse, which had begun to bloat.

This was wrong. Laura would be furious if she could see this scene. This was not how the dead should be treated.

And just like that, she was herself again. The act of caring for her dead jolted her back into a universe with its own logic of birth and death, insensate to the forces of will, human and otherwise, that tried so desperately to overturn its trajectory. A universe that she had violated.

She dropped the saw.

While her baby boy greeted the two police officers that had arrived at her house, she carefully arranged Jonathan and Laura on the guest bed, putting pillows under both of their heads and folding their hands. She drew the blanket up over the ragged holes in their chests. She held their hands. This much she could do.

"I'm so sorry," Mallory choked softly to Jonathan and Laura, though she doubted the thing wearing the flesh of a dead child could hear her over the screams of the police officers in the living room. "God, Jonathan, I'm so sorry." She started to shake violently and turned away from the corpses and dry heaved in huge shuddering convulsions.

But then she heard the silence in the living room. She squeezed Jonathan's hand one last time. She'd made a terrible, terrible mistake, and she understood that with each victim, the thing was growing stronger and harder to stop.

She'd have to stop its borrowed heart from beating with the borrowed blood of the people she loved. She picked the saw up again and took a deep breath.

* * *

But she froze at the sight in her living room.

A little boy, with Jonathan's curly hair and her blue eyes, sat on his play mat in the living room, wearing nothing but a diaper and giggling uncontrollably at the sight of himself in the hallway mirror. His belly was round and soft and his skin pink and smelling of baby lotion.

When he saw Mallory, his face brightened, a goofy, impossibly sincere smile breaking out across his face. He waved both hands at her. "Mamamamama!" he yelled in his sweet little voice. He wobbled as he stood up, but then he ran toward her on his pudgy little legs, hollering "Up up up up up!"

Mallory laughed and set down the handheld mixer she was carrying, ignoring the splatters of red velvet cake batter it shed on the linoleum.

Her head felt a little fuzzy, like she'd just woken up from a nap in the middle of a sleep cycle. Jonathan would be home soon, and they'd all three eat dinner together, afterwards maybe cheat a little bit and plonk Benjamin down in front of *Sesame Street* to give them a minute to reconnect, just the two of them.

What had she been dreaming about that had made her so sweaty? Why was her heart pounding so hard?

She glanced at the hallway mirror. Had she seen huge splatters of dark red meat in its surface? Two blue uniformed shapes in broken heaps on the floor? A malevolent black shape just behind them, waiting patiently for its next meal? Where were these thoughts even coming from?

She shook her head to clear it. She needed to get dinner on the table, and she'd need to do something about that smell. What was that smell? And when was the last time Benji ate? Maybe she needed to give him a snack.

God please no, please no, somebody help me. HELP ME.

She swept Benji up in her arms and rubbed her nose against his.

He giggled again.

She could drown in that sound.

Thalassa's Pool

Sara M. Harvey

THE HARDEST PART is when I think they'll make it.

Logically, I know that's impossible, because otherwise they would not have been sent here. But sometimes they are still warm, still twitching, and there's always a moment of hopeless hope. Especially when they're little.

When the first one came, it was a mess here. We thought it was a suicide. But who would come all the way to this tiny little island with its nearly forgotten little resort just to drown in our pool?

We didn't know her. So we knew she wasn't from here.

It was the off-season, although, to be frank, even during the on-season no one hardly comes here anymore. Our rugged, hilly island with the whitewashed walls that gleam like gold in the sunset and fresh cheese and homebrewed beer and our salt-water swimming pool used to be a big draw and we'd spend the summers hip-deep in tourists from all over the world. But those days are gone, replaced with austerity and war all around us. And now we are only hip-deep in corpses.

Because the girl in the pool was only the first.

The resort's owner, usually a cheap bastard who squeezes every penny he has, had a big fence built. We had a little one before, but it was low enough to step over. This new one all made of black wrought iron was tall and majestic and expensive and, ultimately, useless.

We spent weeks trying to locate the girl's family. But no one reported her missing. She had nothing but the clothes on her back. So we buried her on the western hillside, overlooking the sea.

She couldn't have been more than fourteen. I remember fourteen. That's how old I was when I came to work at this place for a summer job. For fun. But I ended up staying because there were no other jobs and no reason for me to go back to school. Living in a hotel was fun for a little while, but it's become so tiresome, especially with so little to do. But we have beds and meals, which is better than what I'd get at home. So I stay. And think of that song about the Hotel California where you can check out any time you'd like, but you can never leave.

Neither can the ones that appear in our pool.

I have stayed up all night with a few of the other women here, keeping vigil.

As the first light of day touches the still, cool water they appear. Indistinct shadows that resolve into human shapes, like turning the focus on a lens. Filmy, incorporeal figures that fill out, become real people. Dead people. Wearing whatever clothes they had on, sometimes carrying whatever they clutched in their hands. It happens so quickly. One moment, the pool is empty and the next it is not. Some still float, while others lie along the bottom like rocks.

The gate is always still locked.

The first girl was found at the bottom. I remember the desperate swim and my uniform pinafore tangling up in her clothes as I hauled her up to the surface. I rolled her onto my chest and breathed into her mouth. She was cold, her lips firm and her jaw unyielding, but I kept at it until one of the maintenance men dragged us both onto the concrete deck. He took one look at her ashen skin and shook his head, then went to find the owner.

I have waited in the pool, teeth chattering and flesh waterlogged, hoping to catch them as they come, hoping to maybe pluck them out and back into the living air before it is too late. But that hope is always dashed and shattered. By the time they come to us, it is always too late to save them. Always.

No one looks for them, these anonymous dead.

Many of them are poor. Bad teeth, malnourished bodies, improperly healed injuries, gnarled and calloused feet and hands all tell sad tales of hard work, long journeys, and never enough food to go around.

But some are not. Their faces show a recent gauntness, stress and hunger etched into comfortable plumpness, manicured nails freshly chipped and broken, expensive clothes just beginning to fray at the cuffs and the collars.

Sometimes they wear layers of clothes, to keep warm maybe or to save them from carrying a suitcase. Whatever use they thought this would be to them, it only accelerated their death as the water weighed down every fiber and dragged them down more quickly. Perhaps it was a mercy.

I don't know where these people came from or where they had hoped to go.

Not here to this forgotten place. To this forsaken swimming pool.

The water for our pool had been drawn from the sea, filtered and cleaned, and poured into the basin that had been cut into the bedrock of the island and lined with handmade tiles. It had been the thing for which our little island was most famous for generations.

Salt water was thought to be a curative. There was once a cruise ship I read about that had hot and cold running salt water taps for their baths. People came here to soak in our pool. They sought to be cured of whatever ailed them: arthritis, asthma, pain, skin problems. The brochures, now yellowed and faded in the hotel's lobby, extol the virtues of our amazing pool.

I asked the owner once and he said he thought there was something to it. There was always someone who came here and made some miraculous recovery.

Word got around.

The little island with its little resort housed what came to be known as Thalassa's Pool, a sacred place.

It's a nearly-forgotten place now. But sacred, once bestowed, cannot be undone.

Personally, I think that's why they came. Or were sent.

I think the lady of the seas sends these lost souls to us. I only wish I knew why.

The impromptu cemetery on the hillside fills with graves. All overlooking the sea.

We mark them with stones, flowers when we have them. We do our best.

* * *

A few weeks passed with no one. I thought maybe they had stopped. Prayed fervently that it was true.

But this morning, I wake early, before dawn.

I go down to the garden, to the garden to gather flowers, not to the pool, although they are situated beside one another. Once, this seemed like a marvelous idea.

The light has not even yet touched the water, but already I know that something is not right. The water is dark, too dark.

But it isn't dawn, yet.

Without conscious thought, my hand is on the gate to the pool, fiddling with the complicated latch meant to deter children. The gate swings open, it usually creaks but I don't hear it. I don't hear anything because the sight before me overwhelms every other sense in my body.

Something terrible has happened.

The woman's body is shrouded in yards and yards of black fabric and it billows from her, as if the ocean's currents still hold sway here.

There are children all around her. I know they must be hers. Something about the way her arms, weightless and lifeless, still reach towards them.

There are others, as well.

But the baby.

She is dressed in yellow, yellow like sunshine. And she holds a small stuffed toy in her plump fist. It sways in a rhythm too perfect to be waves.

I don't remember jumping into the water, but I am there and I catch her up in my arms. She is warm and she is moving. I raise her flushed, puckered face into the air. Her tiny fingers reflexively curl around my hand.

Her belly is taut and filled with seawater. On the edge of the pool, I press gently, turning her over to let the liquid flow freely from her mouth and nose. She spasms, hiccupping. Watery snot gushes from her nose and I wipe her face with my wet sleeve.

And, damn my heart, I have a name for her in my mind and a life and a future. I keep her head elevated, pitching her body a little bit forward, singing and cooing to her as I pound gently on her back.

She snuffles and her swollen eyes flicker open for a moment, but they see nothing. They roll back without the eyelids closing.

I breathe into her tiny, perfect mouth again and again. With each breath, more water pours out of her, as if the whole ocean were emptying itself through the orifice of this infant in my lap. And then it isn't water anymore, but bubbles and then foam and I know I have failed.

Her body, so small and so exhausted, cools immediately. She drops the little stuffed toy into my lap.

I hold them both and cry.

The morning light breaks cool and gray, illuminating the swimming pool full of the doomed.

My compatriot coworkers arrive. Every morning we always come to check the pool at dawn. They are hopeful as they approach, I can hear it in their voices. Hoping that perhaps this curse we bear has at last been lifted. It's been so long, after all, since anyone has appeared in the pool.

Their chatter falls to silence as they near the gate.

The silence turns to sounds of sorrow as they see me. Me and this woman's baby daughter, who could have been mine. I would have taken her away from this place, this island of never-ending death. Taken her to a place filled with joy and life. There is nothing I would not have done for her, nothing I would not have sacrificed.

I hold her as long as I can. Long after her kin have all been laid to rest on the hillside overlooking the sea.

Before they pour the dirt over her mother, I am finally convinced to let her go. I nestle her back into the arms that gave her comfort and solace in all the days of her too-short life. They look surreal, laying in the dark earth, the baby's head against the woman's shoulder. They should be but sleeping, not dead.

I lay the mother's arm across the baby's body. Her fingers are stiffening, they clench and curl around the child beside her.

I know it is a natural and normal thing that happens to the dead, but it gives me pause. I feel like I have been rebuked for coveting this child that was never destined to be mine.

My arms ache at the memory of the weight of her, the warmth of her.

The dirt goes into the grave, covering the sunshine yellow dress, committing it to the world of the dead.

I hold the stuffed toy. Some bear or mouse or dog that once was white but is no longer any color recognizable. I cradle it in the crook of my arm.

The sun is setting again.

I wonder how many this hillside can hold. And if they will keep coming when we run out of space.

I wonder if there is a piece missing from the ocean, a hole that these lost travelers fall through to end up here.

I wonder if Thalassa's Pool might work in the other direction, that if I could somehow swim deep enough into it, that I would find myself at the mercy of the sea. Instead of at the mercy of this island.

Or if would I simply end up back here, dead among the dead, buried on a hillside overlooking the ocean with the golden sunlight shining down on my grave.

I sit down among them, these unknown dead who feel more like kin to me than my own faraway family, and watch the long, evening sunbeams gild the little mounds of earth with which we have covered their bodies. On the older ones there is grass growing, the blades rippling in undulating shadows like waves.

The Beast with Five Fingers

W.F. Harvey

WHEN I WAS a little boy I once went with my father to call on Adrian Borlsover. I played on the floor with a black spaniel while my father appealed for a subscription. Just before we left my father said, "Mr. Borlsover, may my son here shake hands with you? It will be a thing to look back upon with pride when he grows to be a man."

I came up to the bed on which the old man was lying and put my hand in his, awed by the still beauty of his face. He spoke to me kindly, and hoped that I should always try to please my father. Then he placed his right hand on my head and asked for a blessing to rest upon me. "Amen!" said my father, and I followed him out of the room, feeling as if I wanted to cry. But my father was in excellent spirits.

"That old gentleman, Jim," said he, "is the most wonderful man in the whole town. For ten years he has been quite blind."

"But I saw his eyes," I said. "They were ever so black and shiny; they weren't shut up like Nora's puppies. Can't he see at all?"

And so I learnt for the first time that a man might have eyes that looked dark and beautiful and shining without being able to see.

"Just like Mrs. Tomlinson has big ears," I said, "and can't hear at all except when Mr. Tomlinson shouts."

"Jim," said my father, "it's not right to talk about a lady's ears. Remember what Mr. Borlsover said about pleasing me and being a good boy."

That was the only time I saw Adrian Borlsover. I soon forgot about him and the hand which he laid in blessing on my head. But for a week I prayed that those dark tender eyes might see.

"His spaniel may have puppies," I said in my prayers, "and he will never be able to know how funny they look with their eyes all closed up. Please let old Mr. Borlsover see."

* * *

Adrian Borlsover, as my father had said, was a wonderful man. He came of an eccentric family. Borlsovers' sons, for some reason, always seemed to marry very ordinary women, which perhaps accounted for the fact that no Borlsover had been a genius, and only one Borlsover had been mad. But they were great champions of little causes, generous patrons of odd sciences, founders of querulous sects, trustworthy guides to the bypath meadows of erudition.

Adrian was an authority on the fertilization of orchids. He had held at one time the family living at Borlsover Conyers, until a congenital weakness of the lungs obliged him to seek a less rigorous climate in the sunny south coast watering-place where I had seen him. Occasionally he would relieve one or other of the local clergy. My father described him as a fine preacher, who gave long and inspiring sermons from what many men would have considered unprofitable texts. "An excellent proof," he would add, "of the truth of the doctrine of direct verbal inspiration."

Adrian Borlsover was exceedingly clever with his hands. His penmanship was exquisite. He illustrated all his scientific papers, made his own woodcuts, and carved the reredos that is at present the chief feature of interest in the church at Borlsover Conyers. He had an exceedingly clever knack in cutting silhouettes for young ladies and paper pigs and cows for little children, and made more than one complicated wind instrument of his own devising.

When he was fifty years old Adrian Borlsover lost his sight. In a wonderfully short time he had adapted himself to the new conditions of life. He quickly learned to read Braille. So marvelous indeed was his sense of touch that he was still able to maintain his interest in botany. The mere passing of his long supple fingers over a flower was sufficient means for its identification, though occasionally he would use his lips. I have found several letters of his among my father's correspondence. In no case was there anything to show that he was afflicted with blindness and this in spite of the fact that he exercised undue economy in the spacing of lines. Towards the close of his life the old man was credited with powers of touch that seemed almost uncanny: it has been said that he could tell at once the color of a ribbon placed between his fingers. My father would neither confirm nor deny the story.

I

ADRIAN BORLSOVER was a bachelor. His elder brother George had married late in life, leaving one son, Eustace, who lived in the gloomy Georgian mansion at Borlsover Conyers, where he could work undisturbed in collecting material for his great book on heredity.

Like his uncle, he was a remarkable man. The Borlsovers had always been born naturalists, but Eustace possessed in a special degree the power of systematizing his knowledge. He had received his university education in Germany, and then, after post-graduate work in Vienna and Naples, had traveled for four years in South America and the East, getting together a huge store of material for a new study into the processes of variation.

He lived alone at Borlsover Conyers with Saunders his secretary, a man who bore a somewhat dubious reputation in the district, but whose powers as a mathematician, combined with his business abilities, were invaluable to Eustace.

Uncle and nephew saw little of each other. The visits of Eustace were confined to a week in the summer or autumn: long weeks, that dragged almost as slowly as the bath-chair in which the old man was drawn along the sunny sea front. In their way the two men were fond of each other, though their intimacy would doubtless have been greater had they shared the same religious views. Adrian held to the old-fashioned evangelical dogmas of his early manhood; his nephew for many years had been thinking of embracing Buddhism. Both men possessed, too, the reticence the Borlsovers had always shown, and which their enemies sometimes called hypocrisy. With Adrian it was a reticence as to the things he had left undone; but with Eustace it seemed that the curtain which he was so careful to leave undrawn hid something more than a half-empty chamber.

* * *

Two years before his death Adrian Borlsover developed, unknown to himself, the not uncommon power of automatic writing. Eustace made the discovery by accident. Adrian was sitting reading in bed, the forefinger of his left hand tracing the Braille characters, when his nephew noticed that a pencil the old man held in his right hand was moving slowly along the opposite page. He left his seat in the window and sat down beside the bed. The right hand continued to move, and now he could see plainly that they were letters and words which it was forming.

'Adrian Borlsover,' wrote the hand, 'Eustace Borlsover, George Borlsover, Francis Borlsover Sigismund Borlsover, Adrian Borlsover, Eustace Borlsover, Saville Borlsover. B, for Borlsover. Honesty is the Best Policy. Beautiful Belinda Borlsover.'

"What curious nonsense!" said Eustace to himself.

'King George the Third ascended the throne in 1760,' wrote the hand. 'Crowd, a noun of multitude; a collection of individual – Adrian Borlsover, Eustace Borlsover.'

"It seems to me," said his uncle, closing the book, "that you had much better make the most of the afternoon sunshine and take your walk now."
"I think perhaps I will," Eustace answered as he picked up the volume. "I won't go far, and when I come back I can read to you those articles in *Nature* about which we were speaking."
He went along the promenade, but stopped at the first shelter, and seating himself in the corner best protected from the wind, he examined the book at leisure. Nearly every page was scored with a meaningless jungle of pencil marks: rows of capital letters, short words, long words, complete sentences, copy-book tags. The whole thing, in fact, had the appearance of a copy-book, and on a more careful scrutiny Eustace thought that there was ample evidence to show that the handwriting at the beginning of the book good, though it was not nearly so good as the handwriting at the end.
He left his uncle at the end of October, with a promise to return early in December. It seemed to him quite clear that the old man's power of automatic writing was developing rapidly, and for the first time he looked forward to a visit that combined duty with interest.
But on his return he was at first disappointed. His uncle, he thought, looked older. He was listless too, preferring others to read to him and dictating nearly all his letters. Not until the day before he left had Eustace an opportunity of observing Adrian Borlsover's new-found faculty.
The old man, propped up in bed with pillows, had sunk into a light sleep. His two hands lay on the coverlet, his left hand tightly clasping his right. Eustace took an empty manuscript book and placed a pencil within reach of the fingers of the right hand. They snatched at it eagerly; then dropped the pencil to unloose the left hand from its restraining grasp.
"Perhaps to prevent interference I had better hold that hand," said Eustace to himself, as he watched the pencil. Almost immediately it began to write.

'Blundering Borlsovers, unnecessarily unnatural, extraordinarily eccentric, culpably curious.'
"Who are you?" asked Eustace, in a low voice.
'Never you mind,' wrote the hand of Adrian.
"Is it my uncle who is writing?"
'Oh, my prophetic soul, mine uncle.'
"Is it anyone I know?"
'Silly Eustace, you'll see me very soon.'
"When shall I see you?"
'When poor old Adrian's dead.'
"Where shall I see you?"

'Where shall you not?'
Instead of speaking his next question, Borlsover wrote it. 'What is the time?'
The fingers dropped the pencil and moved three or four times across the paper. Then, picking up the pencil, they wrote:
'Ten minutes before four. Put your book away, Eustace. Adrian mustn't find us working at this sort of thing. He doesn't know what to make of it, and I won't have poor old Adrian disturbed. Au revoir.'

Adrian Borlsover awoke with a start.
"I've been dreaming again," he said; "such queer dreams of leaguered cities and forgotten towns. You were mixed up in this one, Eustace, though I can't remember how. Eustace, I want to warn you. Don't walk in doubtful paths. Choose your friends well. Your poor grandfather –"
A fit of coughing put an end to what he was saying, but Eustace saw that the hand was still writing. He managed unnoticed to draw the book away. "I'll light the gas," he said, "and ring for tea." On the other side of the bed curtain he saw the last sentences that had been written.
"It's too late, Adrian," he read. "We're friends already; aren't we, Eustace Borlsover?"
On the following day Eustace Borlsover left. He thought his uncle looked ill when he said goodbye, and the old man spoke despondently of the failure his life had been.
"Nonsense, uncle!" said his nephew. "You have got over your difficulties in a way not one in a hundred thousand would have done. Everyone marvels at your splendid perseverance in teaching your hand to take the place of your lost sight. To me it's been a revelation of the possibilities of education."
"Education," said his uncle dreamily, as if the word had started a new train of thought, "education is good so long as you know to whom and for what purpose you give it. But with the lower orders of men, the base and more sordid spirits, I have grave doubts as to its results. Well, goodbye, Eustace, I may not see you again. You are a true Borlsover, with all the Borlsover faults. Marry, Eustace. Marry some good, sensible girl. And if by any chance I don't see you again, my will is at my solicitor's. I've not left you any legacy, because I know you're well provided for, but I thought you might like to have my books. Oh, and there's just one other thing. You know, before the end people often lose control over themselves and make absurd requests. Don't pay any attention to them, Eustace. Goodbye!" and he held out his hand. Eustace took it. It remained in his a fraction of a second longer than he had expected, and gripped him with a virility that was surprising. There was, too, in its touch a subtle sense of intimacy.
"Why, uncle!" he said, "I shall see you alive and well for many long years to come."
Two months later Adrian Borlsover died.

II

EUSTACE BORLSOVER was in Naples at the time. He read the obituary notice in the *Morning Post* on the day announced for the funeral.
"Poor old fellow!" he said. "I wonder where I shall find room for all his books."
The question occurred to him again with greater force when three days later he found himself standing in the library at Borlsover Conyers, a huge room built for use, and not for beauty, in the year of Waterloo by a Borlsover who was an ardent admirer of the great Napoleon. It was arranged on the plan of many college libraries, with tall, projecting bookcases forming deep recesses of dusty silence, fit graves for the old hates of forgotten controversy, the dead passions of forgotten lives. At the end of the room, behind the bust of some unknown

eighteenth-century divine, an ugly iron corkscrew stair led to a shelf-lined gallery. Nearly every shelf was full.

"I must talk to Saunders about it," said Eustace. "I suppose that it will be necessary to have the billiard-room fitted up with book cases."

The two men met for the first time after many weeks in the dining-room that evening.

"Hullo!" said Eustace, standing before the fire with his hands in his pockets. "How goes the world, Saunders? Why these dress togs?" He himself was wearing an old shooting-jacket. He did not believe in mourning, as he had told his uncle on his last visit; and though he usually went in for quiet-colored ties, he wore this evening one of an ugly red, in order to shock Morton the butler, and to make them thrash out the whole question of mourning for themselves in the servants' hall. Eustace was a true Borlsover. "The world," said Saunders, "goes the same as usual, confoundedly slow. The dress togs are accounted for by an invitation from Captain Lockwood to bridge."

"How are you getting there?"

"I've told your coachman to drive me in your carriage. Any objection?"

"Oh, dear me, no! We've had all things in common for far too many years for me to raise objections at this hour of the day."

"You'll find your correspondence in the library," went on Saunders. "Most of it I've seen to. There are a few private letters I haven't opened. There's also a box with a rat, or something, inside it that came by the evening post. Very likely it's the six-toed albino. I didn't look, because I didn't want to mess up my things but I should gather from the way it's jumping about that it's pretty hungry."

"Oh, I'll see to it," said Eustace, "while you and the Captain earn an honest penny."

Dinner over and Saunders gone, Eustace went into the library. Though the fire had been lit the room was by no means cheerful.

"We'll have all the lights on at any rate," he said, as he turned the switches. "And, Morton," he added, when the butler brought the coffee, "get me a screwdriver or something to undo this box. Whatever the animal is, he's kicking up the deuce of a row. What is it? Why are you dawdling?"

"If you please, sir, when the postman brought it he told me that they'd bored the holes in the lid at the post-office. There were no breathin' holes in the lid, sir, and they didn't want the animal to die. That is all, sir."

"It's culpably careless of the man, whoever he was," said Eustace, as he removed the screws, "packing an animal like this in a wooden box with no means of getting air. Confound it all! I meant to ask Morton to bring me a cage to put it in. Now I suppose I shall have to get one myself."

He placed a heavy book on the lid from which the screws had been removed, and went into the billiard-room. As he came back into the library with an empty cage in his hand he heard the sound of something falling, and then of something scuttling along the floor.

"Bother it! The beast's got out. How in the world am I to find it again in this library!"

To search for it did indeed seem hopeless. He tried to follow the sound of the scuttling in one of the recesses where the animal seemed to be running behind the books in the shelves, but it was impossible to locate it. Eustace resolved to go on quietly reading. Very likely the animal might gain confidence and show itself. Saunders seemed to have dealt in his usual methodical manner with most of the correspondence. There were still the private letters.

What was that? Two sharp clicks and the lights in the hideous candelabra that hung from the ceiling suddenly went out.

"I wonder if something has gone wrong with the fuse," said Eustace, as he went to the switches by the door. Then he stopped. There was a noise at the other end of the room, as if something was crawling up the iron corkscrew stair. "If it's gone into the gallery," he said, "well and good." He hastily turned on the lights, crossed the room, and climbed up the stair. But he could see nothing. His grandfather had placed a little gate at the top of the stair, so that children could run and romp in the gallery without fear of accident. This Eustace closed, and having considerably narrowed the circle of his search, returned to his desk by the fire.

How gloomy the library was! There was no sense of intimacy about the room. The few busts that an eighteenth-century Borlsover had brought back from the grand tour, might have been in keeping in the old library. Here they seemed out of place. They made the room feel cold, in spite of the heavy red damask curtains and great gilt cornices.

With a crash two heavy books fell from the gallery to the floor; then, as Borlsover looked, another and yet another.

"Very well; you'll starve for this, my beauty!" he said. "We'll do some little experiments on the metabolism of rats deprived of water. Go on! Chuck them down! I think I've got the upper hand." He turned once again to his correspondence. The letter was from the family solicitor. It spoke of his uncle's death and of the valuable collection of books that had been left to him in the will.

"There was one request," he read, "which certainly came as a surprise to me. As you know, Mr. Adrian Borlsover had left instructions that his body was to be buried in as simple a manner as possible at Eastbourne. He expressed a desire that there should be neither wreaths nor flowers of any kind, and hoped that his friends and relatives would not consider it necessary to wear mourning. The day before his death we received a letter canceling these instructions. He wished his body to be embalmed (he gave us the address of the man we were to employ – Pennifer, Ludgate Hill), with orders that his right hand was to be sent to you, stating that it was at your special request. The other arrangements as to the funeral remained unaltered."

"Good Lord!" said Eustace; "What in the world was the old boy driving at? And what in the name of all that's holy is that?"

Someone was in the gallery. Someone had pulled the cord attached to one of the blinds, and it had rolled up with a snap. Someone must be in the gallery, for a second blind did the same. Someone must be walking round the gallery, for one after the other the blinds sprang up, letting in the moonlight.

"I haven't got to the bottom of this yet," said Eustace, "but I will do before the night is very much older," and he hurried up the corkscrew stair. He had just got to the top when the lights went out a second time, and he heard again the scuttling along the floor. Quickly he stole on tiptoe in the dim moonshine in the direction of the noise, feeling as he went for one of the switches. His fingers touched the metal knob at last. He turned on the electric light.

About ten yards in front of him, crawling along the floor, was a man's hand. Eustace stared at it in utter astonishment. It was moving quickly, in the manner of a geometer caterpillar, the fingers humped up one moment, flattened out the next; the thumb appeared to give a crab-like motion to the whole. While he was looking, too surprised to stir, the hand disappeared round the corner Eustace ran forward. He no longer saw it, but he could hear it as it squeezed its way behind the books on one of the shelves. A heavy volume had been displaced. There was a gap in the row of books where it had got in. In his fear lest it should escape him again, he seized the first book that came to his hand and plugged it into the hole. Then, emptying two shelves of their contents, he took the wooden boards and propped them up in front to make his barrier doubly sure.

"I wish Saunders was back," he said; "one can't tackle this sort of thing alone." It was after eleven, and there seemed little likelihood of Saunders returning before twelve. He did not dare to leave the shelf unwatched, even to run downstairs to ring the bell. Morton the butler often used to come round about eleven to see that the windows were fastened, but he might not come. Eustace was thoroughly unstrung. At last he heard steps down below.

"Morton!" he shouted; "Morton!"

"Sir?"

"Has Mr. Saunders got back yet?"

"Not yet, sir."

"Well, bring me some brandy, and hurry up about it. I'm up here in the gallery, you duffer."

"Thanks," said Eustace, as he emptied the glass. "Don't go to bed yet, Morton. There are a lot of books that have fallen down by accident; bring them up and put them back in their shelves."

Morton had never seen Borlsover in so talkative a mood as on that night. "Here," said Eustace, when the books had been put back and dusted, "you might hold up these boards for me, Morton. That beast in the box got out, and I've been chasing it all over the place."

"I think I can hear it chawing at the books, sir. They're not valuable, I hope? I think that's the carriage, sir; I'll go and call Mr. Saunders."

It seemed to Eustace that he was away for five minutes, but it could hardly have been more than one when he returned with Saunders. "All right, Morton, you can go now. I'm up here, Saunders."

"What's all the row?" asked Saunders, as he lounged forward with his hands in his pockets. The luck had been with him all the evening. He was completely satisfied, both with himself and with Captain Lockwood's taste in wines. "What's the matter? You look to me to be in an absolute blue funk."

"That old devil of an uncle of mine," began Eustace – "oh, I can't explain it all. It's his hand that's been playing old Harry all the evening. But I've got it cornered behind these books. You've got to help me catch it."

"What's up with you, Eustace? What's the game?"

"It's no game, you silly idiot! If you don't believe me take out one of those books and put your hand in and feel."

"All right," said Saunders; "but wait till I've rolled up my sleeve. The accumulated dust of centuries, eh?" He took off his coat, knelt down, and thrust his arm along the shelf.

"There's something there right enough," he said. "It's got a funny stumpy end to it, whatever it is, and nips like a crab. Ah, no, you don't!" He pulled his hand out in a flash. "Shove in a book quickly. Now it can't get out."

"What was it?" asked Eustace.

"It was something that wanted very much to get hold of me. I felt what seemed like a thumb and forefinger. Give me some brandy."

"How are we to get it out of there?"

"What about a landing net?"

"No good. It would be too smart for us. I tell you, Saunders, it can cover the ground far faster than I can walk. But I think I see how we can manage it. The two books at the end of the shelf are big ones that go right back against the wall. The others are very thin. I'll take out one at a time, and you slide the rest along until we have it squashed between the end two."

It certainly seemed to be the best plan. One by one, as they took out the books, the space behind grew smaller and smaller. There was something in it that was certainly very much alive. Once they caught sight of fingers pressing outward for a way of escape. At last they had it pressed between the two big books.

"There's muscle there, if there isn't flesh and blood," said Saunders, as he held them together. "It seems to be a hand right enough, too. I suppose this is a sort of infectious hallucination. I've read about such cases before."

"Infectious fiddlesticks!" said Eustace, his face white with anger; "Bring the thing downstairs. We'll get it back into the box."

It was not altogether easy, but they were successful at last. "Drive in the screws," said Eustace, "we won't run any risks. Put the box in this old desk of mine. There's nothing in it that I want. Here's the key. Thank goodness, there's nothing wrong with the lock."

"Quite a lively evening," said Saunders. "Now let's hear more about your uncle."

They sat up together until early morning. Saunders had no desire for sleep. Eustace was trying to explain and to forget: to conceal from himself a fear that he had never felt before – the fear of walking alone down the long corridor to his bedroom.

III

"WHATEVER IT WAS," said Eustace to Saunders on the following morning, "I propose that we drop the subject. There's nothing to keep us here for the next ten days. We'll motor up to the Lakes and get some climbing."

"And see nobody all day, and sit bored to death with each other every night. Not for me thanks. Why not run up to town? Run's the exact word in this case, isn't it? We're both in such a blessed funk. Pull yourself together Eustace, and let's have another look at the hand."

"As you like," said Eustace; "there's the key." They went into the library and opened the desk. The box was as they had left it on the previous night.

"What are you waiting for?" asked Eustace.

"I am waiting for you to volunteer to open the lid. However, since you seem to funk it, allow me. There doesn't seem to be the likelihood of any rumpus this morning, at all events." He opened the lid and picked out the hand.

"Cold?" asked Eustace.

"Tepid. A bit below blood-heat by the feel. Soft and supple too. If it's the embalming, it's a sort of embalming I've never seen before. Is it your uncle's hand?"

"Oh, yes, it's his all right," said Eustace. "I should know those long thin fingers anywhere. Put it back in the box, Saunders. Never mind about the screws. I'll lock the desk, so that there'll be no chance of its getting out. We'll compromise by motoring up to town for a week. If we get off soon after lunch we ought to be at Grantham or Stamford by night."

"Right," said Saunders; "and tomorrow – oh, well, by tomorrow we shall have forgotten all about this beastly thing."

If when the morrow came they had not forgotten, it was certainly true that at the end of the week they were able to tell a very vivid ghost story at the little supper Eustace gave on Hallowe'en.

"You don't want us to believe that it's true, Mr. Borlsover? How perfectly awful!"

"I'll take my oath on it, and so would Saunders here; wouldn't you, old chap?"

"Any number of oaths," said Saunders. "It was a long thin hand, you know, and it gripped me just like that."

"Don't Mr. Saunders! Don't! How perfectly horrid! Now tell us another one, do. Only a really creepy one, please!"

* * *

"Here's a pretty mess!" said Eustace on the following day as he threw a letter across the table to Saunders. "It's your affair, though. Mrs. Merrit, if I understand it, gives a month's notice."

"Oh, that's quite absurd on Mrs. Merrit's part," Saunders replied. "She doesn't know what she's talking about. Let's see what she says."

"Dear Sir," he read, "this is to let you know that I must give you a month's notice as from Tuesday the 13th. For a long time I've felt the place too big for me, but when Jane Parfit, and Emma Laidlaw go off with scarcely as much as an 'if you please,' after frightening the wits out of the other girls, so that they can't turn out a room by themselves or walk alone down the stairs for fear of treading on half-frozen toads or hearing it run along the passages at night, all I can say is that it's no place for me. So I must ask you, Mr. Borlsover, sir, to find a new housekeeper that has no objection to large and lonely houses, which some people do say, not that I believe them for a minute, my poor mother always having been a Wesleyan, are haunted.

"Yours faithfully,
Elizabeth Merrit.

"P.S. – I should be obliged if you would give my respects to Mr. Saunders. I hope that he won't run no risks with his cold."

"Saunders," said Eustace, "you've always had a wonderful way with you in dealing with servants. You mustn't let poor old Merrit go."

"Of course she shan't go," said Saunders. "She's probably only angling for a rise in salary. I'll write to her this morning."

"No; there's nothing like a personal interview. We've had enough of town. We'll go back tomorrow, and you must work your cold for all it's worth. Don't forget that it's got on to the chest, and will require weeks of feeding up and nursing."

"All right. I think I can manage Mrs. Merrit."

But Mrs. Merrit was more obstinate than he had thought. She was very sorry to hear of Mr. Saunders's cold, and how he lay awake all night in London coughing; very sorry indeed. She'd change his room for him gladly, and get the south room aired. And wouldn't he have a basin of hot bread and milk last thing at night? But she was afraid that she would have to leave at the end of the month.

"Try her with an increase of salary," was the advice of Eustace.

It was no use. Mrs. Merrit was obdurate, though she knew of a Mrs. Handyside who had been housekeeper to Lord Gargrave, who might be glad to come at the salary mentioned.

"What's the matter with the servants, Morton?" asked Eustace that evening when he brought the coffee into the library. "What's all this about Mrs. Merrit wanting to leave?"

"If you please, sir, I was going to mention it myself. I have a confession to make, sir. When I found your note asking me to open that desk and take out the box with the rat, I broke the lock as you told me, and was glad to do it, because I could hear the animal in the box making a great noise, and I thought it wanted food. So I took out the box, sir, and got a cage, and was going to transfer it, when the animal got away."

"What in the world are you talking about? I never wrote any such note."

"Excuse me, sir, it was the note I picked up here on the floor on the day you and Mr. Saunders left. I have it in my pocket now."

It certainly seemed to be in Eustace's handwriting. It was written in pencil, and began somewhat abruptly.

"Get a hammer, Morton," he read, "or some other tool, and break open the lock in the old desk in the library. Take out the box that is inside. You need not do anything else. The lid is already open. Eustace Borlsover."

"And you opened the desk?"

"Yes, sir; and as I was getting the cage ready the animal hopped out."

"What animal?"

"The animal inside the box, sir."

"What did it look like?"

"Well, sir, I couldn't tell you," said Morton nervously; "my back was turned, and it was halfway down the room when I looked up."

"What was its color?" asked Saunders; "black?"

"Oh, no, sir, a grayish white. It crept along in a very funny way, sir. I don't think it had a tail."

"What did you do then?"

"I tried to catch it, but it was no use. So I set the rat-traps and kept the library shut. Then that girl Emma Laidlaw left the door open when she was cleaning, and I think it must have escaped."

"And you think it was the animal that's been frightening the maids?"

"Well, no, sir, not quite. They said it was – you'll excuse me, sir – a hand that they saw. Emma trod on it once at the bottom of the stairs. She thought then it was a half-frozen toad, only white. And then Parfit was washing up the dishes in the scullery. She wasn't thinking about anything in particular. It was close on dusk. She took her hands out of the water and was drying them absent-minded like on the roller towel, when she found that she was drying someone else's hand as well, only colder than hers."

"What nonsense!" exclaimed Saunders.

"Exactly, sir; that's what I told her; but we couldn't get her to stop."

"You don't believe all this?" said Eustace, turning suddenly towards the butler.

"Me, sir? Oh, no, sir! I've not seen anything."

"Nor heard anything?"

"Well, sir, if you must know, the bells do ring at odd times, and there's nobody there when we go; and when we go round to draw the blinds of a night, as often as not somebody's been there before us. But as I says to Mrs. Merrit, a young monkey might do wonderful things, and we all know that Mr. Borlsover has had some strange animals about the place."

"Very well, Morton, that will do."

"What do you make of it?" asked Saunders when they were alone. "I mean of the letter he said you wrote."

"Oh, that's simple enough," said Eustace. "See the paper it's written on? I stopped using that years ago, but there were a few odd sheets and envelopes left in the old desk. We never fastened up the lid of the box before locking it in. The hand got out, found a pencil, wrote this note, and shoved it through a crack on to the floor where Morton found it. That's plain as daylight."

"But the hand couldn't write?"

"Couldn't it? You've not seen it do the things I've seen," and he told Saunders more of what had happened at Eastbourne.

"Well," said Saunders, "in that case we have at least an explanation of the legacy. It was the hand which wrote unknown to your uncle that letter to your solicitor, bequeathing itself to you. Your uncle had no more to do with that request than I. In fact, it would seem that he had some idea of this automatic writing, and feared it."

"Then if it's not my uncle, what is it?"

"I suppose some people might say that a disembodied spirit had got your uncle to educate and prepare a little body for it. Now it's got into that little body and is off on its own."

"Well, what are we to do?"

"We'll keep our eyes open," said Saunders, "and try to catch it. If we can't do that, we shall have to wait till the bally clockwork runs down. After all, if it's flesh and blood, it can't live for ever."

For two days nothing happened. Then Saunders saw it sliding down the banister in the hall. He was taken unawares, and lost a full second before he started in pursuit, only to find that the thing had escaped him. Three days later, Eustace, writing alone in the library at night, saw it sitting on an open book at the other end of the room. The fingers crept over the page, feeling the print as if it were reading; but before he had time to get up from his seat, it had taken the alarm and was pulling itself up the curtains. Eustace watched it grimly as it hung on to the cornice with three fingers, flicking thumb and forefinger at him in an expression of scornful derision.

"I know what I'll do," he said. "If I only get it into the open I'll set the dogs on to it."

He spoke to Saunders of the suggestion.

"It's jolly good idea," he said; "only we won't wait till we find it out of doors. We'll get the dogs. There are the two terriers and the under-keeper's Irish mongrel that's on to rats like a flash. Your spaniel has not got spirit enough for this sort of game." They brought the dogs into the house, and the keeper's Irish mongrel chewed up the slippers, and the terriers tripped up Morton as he waited at table; but all three were welcome. Even false security is better than no security at all.

For a fortnight nothing happened. Then the hand was caught, not by the dogs, but by Mrs. Merrit's gray parrot. The bird was in the habit of periodically removing the pins that kept its seed and water tins in place, and of escaping through the holes in the side of the cage. When once at liberty Peter would show no inclination to return, and would often be about the house for days. Now, after six consecutive weeks of captivity, Peter had again discovered a new means of unloosing his bolts and was at large, exploring the tapestried forests of the curtains and singing songs in praise of liberty from cornice and picture rail.

"It's no use your trying to catch him," said Eustace to Mrs. Merrit, as she came into the study one afternoon towards dusk with a step-ladder. "You'd much better leave Peter alone. Starve him into surrender, Mrs. Merrit, and don't leave bananas and seed about for him to peck at when he fancies he's hungry. You're far too softhearted."

"Well, sir, I see he's right out of reach now on that picture rail, so if you wouldn't mind closing the door, sir, when you leave the room, I'll bring his cage in tonight and put some meat inside it. He's that fond of meat, though it does make him pull out his feathers to suck the quills. They *do* say that if you cook –"

"Never mind, Mrs. Merrit," said Eustace, who was busy writing. "That will do; I'll keep an eye on the bird."

There was silence in the room, unbroken but for the continuous whisper of his pen.

"Scratch poor Peter," said the bird. "Scratch poor old Peter!"

"Be quiet, you beastly bird!"

"Poor old Peter! Scratch poor Peter, do."

"I'm more likely to wring your neck if I get hold of you." He looked up at the picture rail, and there was the hand holding on to a hook with three fingers, and slowly scratching the head of the parrot with the fourth. Eustace ran to the bell and pressed it hard; then across to the window, which he closed with a bang. Frightened by the noise the parrot shook its wings preparatory to flight, and as it did so the fingers of the hand got hold of it by the throat. There was a shrill scream from Peter as he fluttered across the room, wheeling round in circles that ever descended, borne down under the weight that clung to him. The bird dropped at last quite suddenly, and Eustace saw fingers and feathers rolled into an inextricable mass on the floor. The struggle abruptly ceased as finger and thumb squeezed the neck; the bird's eyes rolled up to show the whites, and there was a faint, half-choked gurgle. But before the fingers had time to loose their hold, Eustace had them in his own.

"Send Mr. Saunders here at once," he said to the maid who came in answer to the bell. "Tell him I want him immediately."

Then he went with the hand to the fire. There was a ragged gash across the back where the bird's beak had torn it, but no blood oozed from the wound. He noticed with disgust that the nails had grown long and discolored.

"I'll burn the beastly thing," he said. But he could not burn it. He tried to throw it into the flames, but his own hands, as if restrained by some old primitive feeling, would not let him. And so Saunders found him pale and irresolute, with the hand still clasped tightly in his fingers.

"I've got it at last," he said in a tone of triumph.

"Good; let's have a look at it."

"Not when it's loose. Get me some nails and a hammer and a board of some sort."

"Can you hold it all right?"

"Yes, the thing's quite limp; tired out with throttling poor old Peter, I should say."

"And now," said Saunders when he returned with the things, "what are we going to do?"

"Drive a nail through it first, so that it can't get away; then we can take our time over examining it."

"Do it yourself," said Saunders. "I don't mind helping you with guinea-pigs occasionally when there's something to be learned; partly because I don't fear a guinea-pig's revenge. This thing's different."

"All right, you miserable skunk. I won't forget the way you've stood by me."

He took up a nail, and before Saunders had realised what he was doing had driven it through the hand, deep into the board.

"Oh, my aunt," he giggled hysterically, "look at it now," for the hand was writhing in agonized contortions, squirming and wriggling upon the nail like a worm upon the hook.

"Well," said Saunders, "you've done it now. I'll leave you to examine it."

"Don't go, in heaven's name. Cover it up, man, cover it up! Shove a cloth over it! Here!" and he pulled off the antimacassar from the back of a chair and wrapped the board in it. "Now get the keys from my pocket and open the safe. Chuck the other things out. Oh, Lord, it's getting itself into frightful knots! And open it quick!" He threw the thing in and banged the door.

"We'll keep it there till it dies," he said. "May I burn in hell if I ever open the door of that safe again."

* * *

Mrs. Merrit departed at the end of the month. Her successor certainly was more successful in the management of the servants. Early in her rule she declared that she would stand no nonsense, and gossip soon withered and died. Eustace Borlsover went back to his old way of life. Old habits crept over and covered his new experience. He was, if anything, less morose, and showed a greater inclination to take his natural part in country society.

"I shouldn't be surprised if he marries one of these days," said Saunders. "Well, I'm in no hurry for such an event. I know Eustace far too well for the future Mrs. Borlsover to like me. It will be the same old story again: a long friendship slowly made – marriage – and a long friendship quickly forgotten."

IV

BUT EUSTACE BORLSOVER did not follow the advice of his uncle and marry. He was too fond of old slippers and tobacco. The cooking, too, under Mrs. Handyside's management was excellent, and she seemed, too, to have a heaven-sent faculty in knowing when to stop dusting.

Little by little the old life resumed its old power. Then came the burglary. The men, it was said, broke into the house by way of the conservatory. It was really little more than an attempt, for they only succeeded in carrying away a few pieces of plate from the pantry. The safe in the study was certainly found open and empty, but, as Mr. Borlsover informed the police inspector, he had kept nothing of value in it during the last six months.

"Then you're lucky in getting off so easily, sir," the man replied. "By the way they have gone about their business, I should say they were experienced cracksmen. They must have caught the alarm when they were just beginning their evening's work."

"Yes," said Eustace, "I suppose I am lucky."

"I've no doubt," said the inspector, "that we shall be able to trace the men. I've said that they must have been old hands at the game. The way they got in and opened the safe shows that. But there's one little thing that puzzles me. One of them was careless enough not to wear gloves, and I'm bothered if I know what he was trying to do. I've traced his finger-marks on the new varnish on the window sashes in every one of the downstairs rooms. They are very distinct ones too."

"Right hand or left, or both?" asked Eustace.

"Oh, right every time. That's the funny thing. He must have been a foolhardy fellow, and I rather think it was him that wrote that." He took out a slip of paper from his pocket. "That's what he wrote, sir. 'I've got out, Eustace Borlsover, but I'll be back before long.' Some gaol bird just escaped, I suppose. It will make it all the easier for us to trace him. Do you know the writing, sir?"

"No," said Eustace; "it's not the writing of anyone I know."

"I'm not going to stay here any longer," said Eustace to Saunders at luncheon. "I've got on far better during the last six months than ever I expected, but I'm not going to run the risk of seeing that thing again. I shall go up to town this afternoon. Get Morton to put my things together, and join me with the car at Brighton on the day after tomorrow. And bring the proofs of those two papers with you. We'll run over them together."

"How long are you going to be away?"

"I can't say for certain, but be prepared to stay for some time. We've stuck to work pretty closely through the summer, and I for one need a holiday. I'll engage the rooms at Brighton. You'll find it best to break the journey at Hitchin. I'll wire to you there at the Crown to tell you the Brighton address."

The house he chose at Brighton was in a terrace. He had been there before. It was kept by his old college gyp, a man of discreet silence, who was admirably partnered by an excellent cook. The rooms were on the first floor. The two bedrooms were at the back, and opened out of each other. "Saunders can have the smaller one, though it is the only one with a fireplace," he said. "I'll stick to the larger of the two, since it's got a bathroom adjoining. I wonder what time he'll arrive with the car."

Saunders came about seven, cold and cross and dirty. "We'll light the fire in the dining-room," said Eustace, "and get Prince to unpack some of the things while we are at dinner. What were the roads like?"

"Rotten; swimming with mud, and a beastly cold wind against us all day. And this is July. Dear old England!"

"Yes," said Eustace, "I think we might do worse than leave dear old England for a few months."

They turned in soon after twelve.

"You oughtn't to feel cold, Saunders," said Eustace, "when you can afford to sport a great cat-skin lined coat like this. You do yourself very well, all things considered. Look at those gloves, for instance. Who could possibly feel cold when wearing them?"

"They are far too clumsy though for driving. Try them on and see," and he tossed them through the door on to Eustace's bed, and went on with his unpacking. A minute later he heard a shrill cry of terror. "Oh, Lord," he heard, "it's in the glove! Quick, Saunders, quick!" Then came a smacking thud. Eustace had thrown it from him. "I've chucked it into the bathroom," he gasped, "it's hit the wall and fallen into the bath. Come now if you want to help." Saunders, with a lighted candle in his hand, looked over the edge of the bath. There it was, old and maimed, dumb and blind, with a ragged hole in the middle, crawling, staggering, trying to creep up the slippery sides, only to fall back helpless.

"Stay there," said Saunders. "I'll empty a collar box or something, and we'll jam it in. It can't get out while I'm away."

"Yes, it can," shouted Eustace. "It's getting out now. It's climbing up the plug chain. No, you brute, you filthy brute, you don't! Come back, Saunders, it's getting away from me. I can't hold it; it's all slippery. Curse its claw! Shut the window, you idiot! The top too, as well as the bottom. You utter idiot! It's got out!" There was the sound of something dropping on to the hard flagstones below, and Eustace fell back fainting.

* * *

For a fortnight he was ill.

"I don't know what to make of it," the doctor said to Saunders. "I can only suppose that Mr. Borlsover has suffered some great emotional shock. You had better let me send someone to help you nurse him. And by all means indulge that whim of his never to be left alone in the dark. I would keep a light burning all night if I were you. But he *must* have more fresh air. It's perfectly absurd this hatred of open windows."

Eustace, however, would have no one with him but Saunders. "I don't want the other men," he said. "They'd smuggle it in somehow. I know they would."

"Don't worry about it, old chap. This sort of thing can't go on indefinitely. You know I saw it this time as well as you. It wasn't half so active. It won't go on living much longer, especially after that fall. I heard it hit the flags myself. As soon as you're a bit stronger we'll leave this place; not bag and baggage, but with only the clothes on our backs, so that it won't be able to hide anywhere. We'll escape it that way. We won't give any address, and we won't have any parcels sent after us. Cheer up, Eustace! You'll be well enough to leave in a day or two. The doctor says I can take you out in a chair tomorrow."

"What have I done?" asked Eustace. "Why does it come after me? I'm no worse than other men. I'm no worse than you, Saunders; you know I'm not. It was you who were at the bottom of that dirty business in San Diego, and that was fifteen years ago."

"It's not that, of course," said Saunders. "We are in the twentieth century, and even the parsons have dropped the idea of your old sins finding you out. Before you caught the hand in the library it was filled with pure malevolence – to you and all mankind. After you spiked it through with that nail it naturally forgot about other people, and concentrated its attention on you. It was shut up in the safe, you know, for nearly six months. That gives plenty of time for thinking of revenge."

Eustace Borlsover would not leave his room, but he thought that there might be something in Saunders's suggestion to leave Brighton without notice. He began rapidly to regain his strength.

"We'll go on the first of September," he said.

* * *

The evening of August 31st was oppressively warm. Though at midday the windows had been wide open, they had been shut an hour or so before dusk. Mrs. Prince had long since ceased to wonder at the strange habits of the gentlemen on the first floor. Soon after their arrival she had been told to take down the heavy window curtains in the two bedrooms, and day by day the rooms had seemed to grow more bare. Nothing was left lying about.

"Mr. Borlsover doesn't like to have any place where dirt can collect," Saunders had said as an excuse. "He likes to see into all the corners of the room."

"Couldn't I open the window just a little?" he said to Eustace that evening. "We're simply roasting in here, you know."

"No, leave well alone. We're not a couple of boarding-school misses fresh from a course of hygiene lectures. Get the chessboard out."

They sat down and played. At ten o'clock Mrs. Prince came to the door with a note. "I am sorry I didn't bring it before," she said, "but it was left in the letter-box."

"Open it, Saunders, and see if it wants answering."

It was very brief. There was neither address nor signature.

"Will eleven o'clock tonight be suitable for our last appointment?"

"Who is it from?" asked Borlsover.

"It was meant for me," said Saunders. "There's no answer, Mrs. Prince," and he put the paper into his pocket. "A dunning letter from a tailor; I suppose he must have got wind of our leaving."

It was a clever lie, and Eustace asked no more questions. They went on with their game.

On the landing outside Saunders could hear the grandfather's clock whispering the seconds, blurting out the quarter-hours.

"Check!" said Eustace. The clock struck eleven. At the same time there was a gentle knocking on the door; it seemed to come from the bottom panel.

"Who's there?" asked Eustace.

There was no answer.

"Mrs. Prince, is that you?"

"She is up above," said Saunders; "I can hear her walking about the room."

"Then lock the door; bolt it too. Your move, Saunders."

While Saunders sat with his eyes on the chessboard, Eustace walked over to the window and examined the fastenings. He did the same in Saunders's room and the bathroom. There were no doors between the three rooms, or he would have shut and locked them too.

"Now, Saunders," he said, "don't stay all night over your move. I've had time to smoke one cigarette already. It's bad to keep an invalid waiting. There's only one possible thing for you to do. What was that?"

"The ivy blowing against the window. There, it's your move now, Eustace."

"It wasn't the ivy, you idiot. It was someone tapping at the window," and he pulled up the blind. On the outer side of the window, clinging to the sash, was the hand.

"What is it that it's holding?"

"It's a pocket-knife. It's going to try to open the window by pushing back the fastener with the blade."

"Well, let it try," said Eustace. "Those fasteners screw down; they can't be opened that way. Anyhow, we'll close the shutters. It's your move, Saunders. I've played."

But Saunders found it impossible to fix his attention on the game. He could not understand Eustace, who seemed all at once to have lost his fear. "What do you say to some wine?" he asked. "You seem to be taking things coolly, but I don't mind confessing that I'm in a blessed funk."

"You've no need to be. There's nothing supernatural about that hand, Saunders. I mean it seems to be governed by the laws of time and space. It's not the sort of thing that vanishes into thin air or slides through oaken doors. And since that's so, I defy it to get in here. We'll leave the place in the morning. I for one have bottomed the depths of fear. Fill your glass, man! The windows are all shuttered, the door is locked and bolted. Pledge me my uncle Adrian! Drink, man! What are you waiting for?"

Saunders was standing with his glass half raised. "It can get in," he said hoarsely; "it can get in! We've forgotten. There's the fireplace in my bedroom. It will come down the chimney."

"Quick!" said Eustace, as he rushed into the other room; "we haven't a minute to lose. What can we do? Light the fire, Saunders. Give me a match, quick!"

"They must be all in the other room. I'll get them."

"Hurry, man, for goodness' sake! Look in the bookcase! Look in the bathroom! Here, come and stand here; I'll look."

"Be quick!" shouted Saunders. "I can hear something!"

"Then plug a sheet from your bed up the chimney. No, here's a match." He had found one at last that had slipped into a crack in the floor.

"Is the fire laid? Good, but it may not burn. I know – the oil from that old reading-lamp and this cotton-wool. Now the match, quick! Pull the sheet away, you fool! We don't want it now."

There was a great roar from the grate as the flames shot up. Saunders had been a fraction of a second too late with the sheet. The oil had fallen on to it. It, too, was burning.

"The whole place will be on fire!" cried Eustace, as he tried to beat out the flames with a blanket. "It's no good! I can't manage it. You must open the door, Saunders, and get help."

Saunders ran to the door and fumbled with the bolts. The key was stiff in the lock.

"Hurry!" shouted Eustace; "the whole place is ablaze!"

The key turned in the lock at last. For half a second Saunders stopped to look back. Afterwards he could never be quite sure as to what he had seen, but at the time he thought that something black and charred was creeping slowly, very slowly, from the mass of flames towards Eustace Borlsover. For a moment he thought of returning to his friend, but the noise and the smell of the burning sent him running down the passage crying, "Fire! Fire!" He rushed to the telephone to summon help, and then back to the bathroom – he should have thought of that before – for water. As he burst open the bedroom door there came a scream of terror which ended suddenly, and then the sound of a heavy fall.

The Searcher of the End House

William Hope Hodgson

IT WAS STILL EVENING, as I remember, and the four of us, Jessop, Arkright, Taylor and I, looked disappointedly at Carnacki, where he sat silent in his great chair.

We had come in response to the usual card of invitation, which – as you know – we have come to consider as a sure prelude to a good story; and now, after telling us the short incident of the Three Straw Platters, he had lapsed into a contented silence, and the night not half gone, as I have hinted.

However, as it chanced, some pitying fate jogged Carnacki's elbow, or his memory, and he began again, in his queer level way:

"The 'Straw Platters' business reminds me of the 'Searcher' Case, which I have sometimes thought might interest you. It was some time ago, in fact a deuce of a long time ago, that the thing happened; and my experience of what I might term 'curious' things was very small at that time.

"I was living with my mother when it occurred, in a small house just outside of Appledorn, on the South Coast. The house was the last of a row of detached cottage villas, each house standing in its own garden; and very dainty little places they were, very old, and most of them smothered in roses; and all with those quaint old leaded windows, and doors of genuine oak. You must try to picture them for the sake of their complete niceness.

"Now I must remind you at the beginning that my mother and I had lived in that little house for two years; and in the whole of that time there had not been a single peculiar happening to worry us.

"And then, something happened.

"It was about two o'clock one morning, as I was finishing some letters, that I heard the door of my mother's bedroom open, and she came to the top of the stairs, and knocked on the banisters.

"'All right, dear,' I called; for I suppose she was merely reminding me that I should have been in bed long ago; then I heard her go back to her room, and I hurried my work, for fear she should lie awake, until she heard me safe up to my room.

"When I was finished, I lit my candle, put out the lamp, and went upstairs. As I came opposite the door of my mother's room, I saw that it was open, called good night to her, very softly, and asked whether I should close the door. As there was no answer, I knew that she had dropped off to sleep again, and I closed the door very gently, and turned into my room, just across the passage. As I did so, I experienced a momentary, half-aware sense of a faint, peculiar, disagreeable odour in the passage; but it was not until the following night that I *realized* I had noticed a smell that offended me. You follow me? It is so often like that – one suddenly knows a thing that really recorded itself on one's consciousness, perhaps a year before.

"The next morning at breakfast, I mentioned casually to my mother that she had 'dropped off', and I had shut the door for her. To my surprise, she assured me she had never been out of her room. I reminded her about the two raps she had given upon the banister; but she still was certain I must be mistaken; and in the end I teased her, saying she had grown so accustomed to my bad habit of sitting up late, that she had come to call me in her sleep. Of course, she denied this, and I let the matter drop; but I was more than a little puzzled, and did not know whether to believe my own explanation, or to take the mater's, which was to put the noises down to the mice, and the open door to the fact that she couldn't have properly latched it, when she went to bed. I suppose, away in the subconscious part of me, I had a stirring of less reasonable thoughts; but certainly, I had no real uneasiness at that time.

"The next night there came a further development. About two thirty a.m., I heard my mother's door open, just as on the previous night, and immediately afterward she rapped sharply, on the banister, as it seemed to me. I stopped my work and called up that I would not be long. As she made no reply, and I did not hear her go back to bed, I had a quick sense of wonder whether she might not be doing it in her sleep, after all, just as I had said.

"With the thought, I stood up, and taking the lamp from the table, began to go toward the door, which was open into the passage. It was then I got a sudden nasty sort of thrill; for it came to me, all at once, that my mother never knocked, when I sat up too late; she always called. You will understand I was not really frightened in any way; only vaguely uneasy, and pretty sure she must really be doing the thing in her sleep.

"I went quickly up the stairs, and when I came to the top, my mother was not there; but her door was open. I had a bewildered sense though believing she must have gone quietly back to bed, without my hearing her. I entered her room and found her sleeping quietly and naturally; for the vague sense of trouble in me was sufficiently strong to make me go over to look at her.

"When I was sure that she was perfectly right in every way, I was still a little bothered; but much more inclined to think my suspicion correct and that she had gone quietly back to bed in her sleep, without knowing what she had been doing. This was the most reasonable thing to think, as you must see.

"And then it came to me, suddenly, that vague, queer, mildewy smell in the room; and it was in that instant I became aware I had smelt the same strange, uncertain smell the night before in the passage.

"I was definitely uneasy now, and began to search my mother's room; though with no aim or clear thought of anything, except to assure myself that there was nothing in the room. All the time, you know, I never *expected really* to find anything; only my uneasiness had to be assured.

"In the middle of my search my mother woke up, and of course I had to explain. I told her about her door opening, and the knocks on the banister, and that I had come up and found her asleep. I said nothing about the smell, which was not very distinct; but told her that the thing happening twice had made me a bit nervous, and possibly fanciful, and I thought I would take a look 'round, just to feel satisfied.

"I have thought since that the reason I made no mention of the smell, was not only that I did not want to frighten my mother, for I was scarcely that myself; but because I had only a vague half-knowledge that I associated the smell with fancies too indefinite and peculiar to bear talking about. You will understand that I am able *now* to analyse and put the thing into words; but *then* I did not even know my chief reason for saying nothing; let alone appreciate its possible significance.

"It was my mother, after all, who put part of my vague sensations into words:

"'What a disagreeable smell!' she exclaimed, and was silent a moment, looking at me. Then: 'You feel there's something wrong?' still looking at me, very quietly but with a little, nervous note of questioning expectancy.

"'I don't know,' I said. 'I can't understand it, unless you've really been walking about in your sleep.'

"'The smell,' she said.

"'Yes,' I replied. 'That's what puzzles me too. I'll take a walk through the house; but I don't suppose it's anything.'

"I lit her candle, and taking the lamp, I went through the other bedrooms, and afterward all over the house, including the three underground cellars, which was a little trying to the nerves, seeing that I was more nervous than I would admit.

"Then I went back to my mother, and told her there was really nothing to bother about; and, you know, in the end, we talked ourselves into believing it was nothing. My mother would not agree that she might have been sleepwalking; but she was ready to put the door opening down to the fault of the latch, which certainly snicked very lightly. As for the knocks, they might be the old warped woodwork of the house cracking a bit, or a mouse rattling a piece of loose plaster. The smell was more difficult to explain; but finally we agreed that it might easily be the queer night smell of the moist earth, coming in through the open window of my mother's room, from the back garden, or – for that matter – from the little churchyard beyond the big wall at the bottom of the garden.

"And so we quieted down, and finally I went to bed, and to sleep.

"I think this is certainly a lesson on the way we humans can delude ourselves; for there was not one of these explanations that my reason could really accept. Try to imagine yourself in the same circumstances, and you will see how absurd our attempts to explain the happenings really were.

"In the morning, when I came down to breakfast, we talked it all over again, and whilst we agreed that it was strange, we also agreed that we had begun to imagine funny things in the backs of our minds, which now we felt half ashamed to admit. This is very strange when you come to look into it; but very human.

"And then that night again my mother's door was slammed once more just after midnight. I caught up the lamp, and when I reached her door, I found it shut. I opened it quickly, and went in, to find my mother lying with her eyes open, and rather nervous; having been waked by the bang of the door. But what upset me more than anything, was the fact that there was a disgusting smell in the passage and in her room.

"Whilst I was asking her whether she was all right, a door slammed twice downstairs; and you can imagine how it made me feel. My mother and I looked at one another; and then I lit her candle, and taking the poker from the fender, went downstairs with the lamp, beginning to feel really nervous. The cumulative effect of so many queer happenings was getting hold of me; and all the *apparently* reasonable explanations seemed futile.

"The horrible smell seemed to be very strong in the downstairs passage; also in the front room and the cellars; but chiefly in the passage. I made a very thorough search of the house, and when I had finished, I knew that all the lower windows and doors were properly shut and fastened, and that there was no living thing in the house, beyond our two selves. Then I went up to my mother's room again, and we talked the thing over for an hour or more, and in the end came to the conclusion that we might, after all, be reading too much into a number of little things; but, you know, inside of us, we did not believe this.

"Later, when we had talked ourselves into a more comfortable state of mind, I said good night, and went off to bed; and presently managed to get to sleep.

"In the early hours of the morning, whilst it was still dark, I was waked by a loud noise. I sat up in bed, and listened. And from downstairs, I heard: bang, bang, bang, one door after another being slammed; at least, that is the impression the sounds gave to me.

"I jumped out of bed, with the tingle and shiver of sudden fright on me; and at the same moment, as I lit my candle, my door was pushed slowly open; I had left it unlatched, so as not to feel that my mother was quite shut off from me.

"'Who's there?' I shouted out, in a voice twice as deep as my natural one, and with a queer breathlessness, that sudden fright so often gives one. 'Who's there?'

"Then I heard my mother saying:

"'It's me, Thomas. Whatever is happening downstairs?'

"She was in the room by this, and I saw she had her bedroom poker in one hand, and her candle in the other. I could have smiled at her, had it not been for the extraordinary sounds downstairs.

"I got into my slippers, and reached down an old sword bayonet from the wall; then I picked up my candle, and begged my mother not to come; but I knew it would be little use, if she had made up her mind; and she had, with the result that she acted as a sort of rearguard for me, during our search. I know, in some ways, I was very glad to have her with me, as you will understand.

"By this time, the door slamming had ceased, and there seemed, probably because of the contrast, to be an appalling silence in the house. However, I led the way, holding my candle high, and keeping the sword bayonet very handy. Downstairs we found all the doors wide open; although the outer doors and the windows were closed all right. I began to wonder whether the noises had been made by the doors after all. Of one thing only were we sure, and that was, there was no living thing in the house, beside ourselves, while everywhere throughout the house, there was the taint of that disgusting odour.

"Of course it was absurd to try to make believe any longer. There was something strange about the house; and as soon as it was daylight, I set my mother to packing; and soon after breakfast, I saw her off by train.

"Then I set to work to try to clear up the mystery. I went first to the landlord, and told him all the circumstances. From him, I found that twelve or fifteen years back, the house had got rather a curious name from three or four tenants; with the result that it had remained empty a long while; in the end he had let it at a low rent to a Captain Tobias, on the one condition that he should hold his tongue, if he saw anything peculiar. The landlord's idea – as he told me frankly – was to free the house from these tales of 'something queer', by keeping a tenant in it, and then to sell it for the best price he could get.

"However, when Captain Tobias left, after a ten years' tenancy, there was no longer any talk about the house; so when I offered to take it on a five years' lease, he had jumped at the offer. This was the whole story; so he gave me to understand. When I pressed him for details of the supposed peculiar happenings in the house, all those years back, he said the tenants had talked about a woman who always moved about the house at night. Some tenants never saw anything; but others would not stay out the first month's tenancy.

"One thing the landlord was particular to point out, that no tenant had ever complained about knockings, or door slamming. As for the smell, he seemed positively indignant about it; but why, I don't suppose he knew himself, except that he probably had some vague feeling that it was an indirect accusation on my part that the drains were not right.

"In the end, I suggested that he should come down and spend the night with me. He agreed at once, especially as I told him I intended to keep the whole business quiet, and try to get to the bottom of the curious affair; for he was anxious to keep the rumour of the haunting from getting about.

"About three o'clock that afternoon, he came down, and we made a thorough search of the house, which, however, revealed nothing unusual. Afterward, the landlord made one or two tests, which showed him the drainage was in perfect order; after that we made our preparations for sitting up all night.

"First, we borrowed two policemen's dark lanterns from the station nearby, and where the superintendent and I were friendly, and as soon as it was really dusk, the landlord went up to his house for his gun. I had the sword bayonet I have told you about; and when the landlord got back, we sat talking in my study until nearly midnight.

"Then we lit the lanterns and went upstairs. We placed the lanterns, gun and bayonet handy on the table; then I shut and sealed the bedroom doors; afterward we took our seats, and turned off the lights.

"From then until two o'clock, nothing happened; but a little after two, as I found by holding my watch near the faint glow of the closed lanterns, I had a time of extraordinary nervousness; and I bent toward the landlord, and whispered to him that I had a queer feeling something was about to happen, and to be ready with his lantern; at the same time I reached out toward mine. In the very instant I made this movement, the darkness which filled the passage seemed to become suddenly of a dull violet colour; not, as if a light had been shone; but as if the natural blackness of the night had changed colour. And then, coming through this violet night, through this violet-coloured gloom, came a little naked Child, running. In an extraordinary way, the Child seemed not to be distinct from the surrounding gloom; but almost as if it were a concentration of that extraordinary atmosphere; as if that gloomy colour which had changed the night, came from the Child. It seems impossible to make clear to you; but try to understand it.

"The Child went past me, running, with the natural movement of the legs of a chubby human child, but in an absolute and inconceivable silence. It was a very small Child, and must have passed under the table; but I saw the Child through the table, as if it had been only a slightly darker shadow than the coloured gloom. In the same instant, I saw that a fluctuating glimmer of violet light outlined the metal of the gun-barrels and the blade of the sword bayonet, making them seem like faint shapes of glimmering light, floating unsupported where the tabletop should have shown solid.

"Now, curiously, as I saw these things, I was subconsciously aware that I heard the anxious breathing of the landlord, quite clear and laboured, close to my elbow, where he waited nervously with his hands on the lantern. I realized in that moment that he saw nothing; but waited in the darkness, for my warning to come true.

"Even as I took heed of these minor things, I saw the Child jump to one side, and hide behind some half-seen object that was certainly nothing belonging to the passage. I stared, intently, with a most extraordinary thrill of expectant wonder, with fright making goose flesh of my back. And even as I stared, I solved for myself the less important problem of what the two black clouds were that hung over a part of the table. I think it very curious and interesting, the double working of the mind, often so much more apparent during times of stress. The two clouds came from two faintly shining shapes, which I knew must be the metal of the lanterns; and the things that looked black to the sight with which I was then seeing, could be nothing else but what to normal human sight is known as light. This phenomenon I have always remembered. I have twice seen a somewhat similar thing; in the Dark Light Case and in that trouble of Maetheson's, which you know about.

"Even as I understood this matter of the lights, I was looking to my left, to understand why the Child was hiding. And suddenly, I heard the landlord shout out: 'The Woman!' But I saw nothing. I had a disagreeable sense that something repugnant was near to me, and I was aware in the same moment that the landlord was gripping my arm in a hard, frightened grip. Then I was looking back to where the Child had hidden. I saw the Child peeping out from behind its hiding place, seeming to be looking up the passage; but whether in fear I could not tell. Then it came out, and ran headlong away, through the place where should have been the wall of my mother's bedroom; but the Sense with which I was seeing these things, showed me the wall only as a vague, upright shadow, unsubstantial. And immediately the child was lost to me, in the dull violet gloom. At the same time, I felt the landlord press back against me, as if something had passed close to him; and he called out again, a hoarse sort of cry: 'The Woman! The Woman!' and turned the shade clumsily from off his lantern. But I had seen no Woman; and the passage showed empty, as he shone the beam of his light jerkily to and fro; but chiefly in the direction of the doorway of my mother's room.

"He was still clutching my arm, and had risen to his feet; and now, mechanically and almost slowly, I picked up my lantern and turned on the light. I shone it, a little dazedly, at the seals upon the doors; but none were broken; then I sent the light to and fro, up and down the passage; but there was nothing; and I turned to the landlord, who was saying something in a rather incoherent fashion. As my light passed over his face, I noted, in a dull sort of way, that he was drenched with sweat.

"Then my wits became more handleable, and I began to catch the drift of his words: 'Did you see her? Did you see her?' he was saying, over and over again; and then I found myself telling him, in quite a level voice, that I had not seen any Woman. He became more coherent then, and I found that he had seen a Woman come from the end of the passage, and go past us; but he could not describe her, except that she kept stopping and looking about her, and had even peered at the wall, close beside him, as if looking for something. But what seemed to trouble him most, was that she had not seemed to see him at all. He repeated this so often, that in the end I told him, in an absurd sort of way, that he ought to be very glad she had not. 'What did it all mean?' was the question; somehow I was not so frightened, as utterly bewildered. I had seen less then, than since; but what I had seen, had made me feel adrift from my anchorage of Reason.

"What did it mean? He had seen a Woman, searching for something. *I* had not seen this Woman. *I* had seen a Child, running away, and hiding from Something or Someone. *He* had not seen the Child, or the other things – only the Woman. And *I* had not seen her. What did it all mean?

"I had said nothing to the landlord about the Child. I had been too bewildered, and I realized that it would be futile to attempt an explanation. He was already stupid with the thing he had seen; and not the kind of man to understand. All this went through my mind as we stood there, shining the lanterns to and fro. All the time, intermingled with a streak of practical reasoning, I was questioning myself, what did it all mean? What was the Woman searching for; what was the Child running from?

"Suddenly, as I stood there, bewildered and nervous, making random answers to the landlord, a door below was violently slammed, and directly I caught the horrible reek of which I have told you.

"'There!' I said to the landlord, and caught his arm, in my turn. 'The Smell! Do *you* smell it?'

"He looked at me so stupidly that in a sort of nervous anger, I shook him.

"'Yes,' he said, in a queer voice, trying to shine the light from his shaking lantern at the stair head.

"'Come on!' I said, and picked up my bayonet; and he came, carrying his gun awkwardly. I think he came, more because he was afraid to be left alone, than because he had any pluck left, poor beggar. I never sneer at that kind of funk, at least very seldom; for when it takes hold of you, it makes rags of your courage.

"I led the way downstairs, shining my light into the lower passage, and afterward at the doors to see whether they were shut; for I had closed and latched them, placing a corner of a mat against each door, so I should know which had been opened.

"I saw at once that none of the doors had been opened; then I threw the beam of my light down alongside the stairway, in order to see the mat I had placed against the door at the top of the cellar stairs. I got a horrid thrill; for the mat was flat! I paused a couple of seconds, shining my light to and fro in the passage, and holding fast to my courage, I went down the stairs.

"As I came to the bottom step, I saw patches of wet all up and down the passage. I shone my lantern on them. It was the imprint of a wet foot on the oilcloth of the passage; not an ordinary footprint, but a queer, soft, flabby, spreading imprint, that gave me a feeling of extraordinary horror.

"Backward and forward I flashed the light over the impossible marks and saw them everywhere. Suddenly I noticed that they led to each of the closed doors. I felt something touch my back, and glanced 'round swiftly, to find the landlord had come close to me, almost pressing against me, in his fear.

"'It's all right,' I said, but in a rather breathless whisper, meaning to put a little courage into him; for I could feel that he was shaking through all his body. Even then as I tried to get him steadied enough to be of some use, his gun went off with a tremendous bang. He jumped, and yelled with sheer terror; and I swore because of the shock.

"'Give it to me, for God's sake!' I said, and slipped the gun from his hand; and in the same instant there was a sound of running steps up the garden path, and immediately the flash of a bull's-eye lantern upon the fan light over the front door. Then the door was tried, and directly afterward there came a thunderous knocking, which told me a policeman had heard the shot.

"I went to the door, and opened it. Fortunately the constable knew me, and when I had beckoned him in, I was able to explain matters in a very short time. While doing this, Inspector Johnstone came up the path, having missed the officer, and seeing lights and the open door. I told him as briefly as possible what had occurred, and did not mention the Child or the Woman; for it would have seemed too fantastic for him to notice. I showed him the queer, wet footprints and how they went toward the closed doors. I explained quickly about the mats, and how that the one against the cellar door was flat, which showed the door had been opened.

"The inspector nodded, and told the constable to guard the door at the top of the cellar stairs. He then asked the hall lamp to be lit, after which he took the policeman's lantern, and led the way into the front room. He paused with the door wide open, and threw the light all 'round; then he jumped into the room, and looked behind the door; there was no one there; but all over the polished oak floor, between the scattered rugs, went the marks of those horrible spreading footprints; and the room permeated with the horrible odour.

"The inspector searched the room carefully, and then went into the middle room, using the same precautions. There was nothing in the middle room, or in the kitchen or pantry; but everywhere went the wet footmarks through all the rooms, showing plainly wherever there were woodwork or oilcloth; and always there was the smell.

"The inspector ceased from his search of the rooms, and spent a minute in trying whether the mats would really fall flat when the doors were open, or merely ruckle up in a way as to appear they had been untouched; but in each case, the mats fell flat, and remained so.

"'Extraordinary!' I heard Johnstone mutter to himself. And then he went toward the cellar door. He had inquired at first whether there were windows to the cellar, and when he learned there was no way out, except by the door, he had left this part of the search to the last.

"As Johnstone came up to the door, the policeman made a motion of salute, and said something in a low voice; and something in the tone made me flick my light across him. I saw then that the man was very white, and he looked strange and bewildered.

"'What?' said Johnstone impatiently. 'Speak up!'

"'A woman come along 'ere, sir, and went through this 'ere door,' said the constable, clearly, but with a curious monotonous intonation that is sometimes heard from an unintelligent man.

"'Speak up!' shouted the inspector.

"'A woman come along and went through this 'ere door,' repeated the man, monotonously.

"The inspector caught the man by the shoulder, and deliberately sniffed his breath.

"'No!' he said. And then sarcastically: 'I hope you held the door open politely for the lady.'

"'The door weren't opened, sir,' said the man, simply.

"'Are you mad –' began Johnstone.

"'No,' broke in the landlord's voice from the back. Speaking steadily enough. 'I saw the Woman upstairs.' It was evident that he had got back his control again.

"'I'm afraid, Inspector Johnstone,' I said, 'that there's more in this than you think. I certainly saw some very extraordinary things upstairs.'

"The inspector seemed about to say something; but instead, he turned again to the door, and flashed his light down and 'round about the mat. I saw then that the strange, horrible footmarks came straight up to the cellar door; and the last print showed *under* the door; yet the policeman said the door had not been opened.

"And suddenly, without any intention, or realization of what I was saying, I asked the landlord:

"'What were the feet like?'

"I received no answer; for the inspector was ordering the constable to open the cellar door, and the man was not obeying. Johnstone repeated the order, and at last, in a queer automatic way, the man obeyed, and pushed the door open. The loathsome smell beat up at us, in a great wave of horror, and the inspector came backward a step.

"'My God!' he said, and went forward again, and shone his light down the steps; but there was nothing visible, only that on each step showed the unnatural footprints.

"The inspector brought the beam of the light vividly on the top step; and there, clear in the light, there was something small, moving. The inspector bent to look, and the policeman and I with him. I don't want to disgust you; but the thing we looked at was a maggot. The policeman backed suddenly out of the doorway:

"'The churchyard,' he said, '... at the back of the 'ouse.'

"'Silence!' said Johnstone, with a queer break in the word, and I knew that at last he was frightened. He put his lantern into the doorway, and shone it from step to step, following the footprints down into the darkness; then he stepped back from the open doorway, and we all gave back with him. He looked 'round, and I had a feeling that he was looking for a weapon of some kind.

"'Your gun,' I said to the landlord, and he brought it from the front hall, and passed it over to the inspector, who took it and ejected the empty shell from the right barrel. He held out his hand for a live cartridge, which the landlord brought from his pocket. He loaded the gun and snapped the breech. He turned to the constable:

"'Come on,' he said, and moved toward the cellar doorway.

"'I ain't comin', sir,' said the policeman, very white in the face.

"With a sudden blaze of passion, the inspector took the man by the scruff and hove him bodily down into the darkness, and he went downward, screaming. The inspector followed him instantly, with his lantern and the gun; and I after the inspector, with the bayonet ready. Behind me, I heard the landlord.

"At the bottom of the stairs, the inspector was helping the policeman to his feet, where he stood swaying a moment, in a bewildered fashion; then the inspector went into the front cellar, and his man followed him in stupid fashion; but evidently no longer with any thought of running away from the horror.

"We all crowded into the front cellar, flashing our lights to and fro. Inspector Johnstone was examining the floor, and I saw that the footmarks went all 'round the cellar, into all the corners, and across the floor. I thought suddenly of the Child that was running away from Something. Do you see the thing that I was seeing vaguely?

"We went out of the cellar in a body, for there was nothing to be found. In the next cellar, the footprints went everywhere in that queer erratic fashion, as of someone searching for something, or following some blind scent.

"In the third cellar the prints ended at the shallow well that had been the old water supply of the house. The well was full to the brim, and the water so clear that the pebbly bottom was plainly to be seen, as we shone the lights into the water. The search came to an abrupt end, and we stood about the well, looking at one another, in an absolute, horrible silence.

"Johnstone made another examination of the footprints; then he shone his light again into the clear shallow water, searching each inch of the plainly seen bottom; but there was nothing there. The cellar was full of the dreadful smell; and everyone stood silent, except for the constant turning of the lamps to and fro around the cellar.

"The inspector looked up from his search of the well, and nodded quietly across at me, with his sudden acknowledgment that our belief was now his belief, the smell in the cellar seemed to grow more dreadful, and to be, as it were, a menace – the material expression that some monstrous thing was there with us, invisible.

"'I think –' began the inspector, and shone his light toward the stairway; and at this the constable's restraint went utterly, and he ran for the stairs, making a queer sound in his throat.

"The landlord followed, at a quick walk, and then the inspector and I. He waited a single instant for me, and we went up together, treading on the same steps, and with our lights held backward. At the top, I slammed and locked the stair door, and wiped my forehead, and my hands were shaking.

"The inspector asked me to give his man a glass of whisky, and then he sent him on his beat. He stayed a short while with the landlord and me, and it was arranged that he would join us again the following night and watch the Well with us from midnight until daylight. Then he left us, just as the dawn was coming in. The landlord and I locked up the house, and went over to his place for a sleep.

"In the afternoon, the landlord and I returned to the house, to make arrangements for the night. He was very quiet, and I felt he was to be relied on, now that he had been 'salted', as it were, with his fright of the previous night.

"We opened all the doors and windows, and blew the house through very thoroughly; and in the meanwhile, we lit the lamps in the house, and took them into the cellars, where we set them all about, so as to have light everywhere. Then we carried down three chairs and a table, and set them in the cellar where the well was sunk. After that, we stretched thin piano wire across the cellar, about nine inches from the floor, at such a height that it should catch anything moving about in the dark.

"When this was done, I went through the house with the landlord, and sealed every window and door in the place, excepting only the front door and the door at the top of the cellar stairs.

"Meanwhile, a local wire-smith was making something to my order; and when the landlord and I had finished tea at his house, we went down to see how the smith was getting on. We found the thing complete. It looked rather like a huge parrot's cage, without any bottom, of very heavy gage wire, and stood about seven feet high and was four feet in diameter. Fortunately, I remembered to have it made longitudinally in two halves, or else we should never have got it through the doorways and down the cellar stairs.

"I told the wire-smith to bring the cage up to the house so he could fit the two halves rigidly together. As we returned, I called in at an ironmonger's, where I bought some thin hemp rope and an iron rack pulley, like those used in Lancashire for hauling up the ceiling clothes racks, which you will find in every cottage. I bought also a couple of pitchforks.

"'We shan't want to touch it,' I said to the landlord; and he nodded, rather white all at once.

"As soon as the cage arrived and had been fitted together in the cellar, I sent away the smith; and the landlord and I suspended it over the well, into which it fitted easily. After a lot of trouble, we managed to hang it so perfectly central from the rope over the iron pulley, that when hoisted to the ceiling and dropped, it went every time plunk into the well, like a candle-extinguisher. When we had it finally arranged, I hoisted it up once more, to the ready position, and made the rope fast to a heavy wooden pillar, which stood in the middle of the cellar.

"By ten o'clock, I had everything arranged, with the two pitchforks and the two police lanterns; also some whisky and sandwiches. Underneath the table I had several buckets full of disinfectant.

"A little after eleven o'clock, there was a knock at the front door, and when I went, I found Inspector Johnstone had arrived, and brought with him one of his plainclothes men. You will understand how pleased I was to see there would be this addition to our watch; for he looked a tough, nerveless man, brainy and collected; and one I should have picked to help us with the horrible job I felt pretty sure we should have to do that night.

"When the inspector and the detective had entered, I shut and locked the front door; then, while the inspector held the light, I sealed the door carefully, with tape and wax. At the head of the cellar stairs, I shut and locked that door also, and sealed it in the same way.

"As we entered the cellar, I warned Johnstone and his man to be careful not to fall over the wires; and then, as I saw his surprise at my arrangements, I began to explain my ideas and intentions, to all of which he listened with strong approval. I was pleased to see also that the detective was nodding his head, as I talked, in a way that showed he appreciated all my precautions.

"As he put his lantern down, the inspector picked up one of the pitchforks, and balanced it in his hand; he looked at me, and nodded.

"'The best thing,' he said. 'I only wish you'd got two more.'

"Then we all took our seats, the detective getting a washing stool from the corner of the cellar. From then, until a quarter to twelve, we talked quietly, whilst we made a light supper of whisky and sandwiches; after which, we cleared everything off the table, excepting the lanterns and the pitchforks. One of the latter, I handed to the inspector; the other I took myself, and then, having set my chair so as to be handy to the rope which lowered the cage into the well, I went 'round the cellar and put out every lamp.

"I groped my way to my chair, and arranged the pitchfork and the dark lantern ready to my hand; after which I suggested that everyone should keep an absolute silence throughout the watch. I asked, also, that no lantern should be turned on, until I gave the word.

"I put my watch on the table, where a faint glow from my lantern made me able to see the time. For an hour nothing happened, and everyone kept an absolute silence, except for an occasional uneasy movement.

"About half-past one, however, I was conscious again of the same extraordinary and peculiar nervousness, which I had felt on the previous night. I put my hand out quickly, and eased the hitched rope from around the pillar. The inspector seemed aware of the movement; for I saw the faint light from his lantern, move a little, as if he had suddenly taken hold of it, in readiness.

"A minute later, I noticed there was a change in the colour of the night in the cellar, and it grew slowly violet tinted upon my eyes. I glanced to and fro, quickly, in the new darkness, and even as I looked, I was conscious that the violet colour deepened. In the direction of the well, but seeming to be at a great distance, there was, as it were, a nucleus to the change; and the nucleus came swiftly toward us, appearing to come from a great space, almost in a single moment. It came near, and I saw again that it was a little naked Child, running, and seeming to be of the violet night in which it ran.

"The Child came with a natural running movement, exactly as I described it before; but in a silence so peculiarly intense, that it was as if it brought the silence with it. About half-way between the well and the table, the Child turned swiftly, and looked back at something invisible to me; and suddenly it went down into a crouching attitude, and seemed to be hiding behind something that showed vaguely; but there was nothing there, except the bare floor of the cellar; nothing, I mean, of our world.

"I could hear the breathing of the three other men, with a wonderful distinctness; and also the tick of my watch upon the table seemed to sound as loud and as slow as the tick of an old grandfather's clock. Someway I knew that none of the others saw what I was seeing.

"Abruptly, the landlord, who was next to me, let out his breath with a little hissing sound; I knew then that something was visible to him. There came a creak from the table, and I had a feeling that the inspector was leaning forward, looking at something that I could not see. The landlord reached out his hand through the darkness, and fumbled a moment to catch my arm:

"'The Woman!' he whispered, close to my ear. 'Over by the well.'

"I stared hard in that direction; but saw nothing, except that the violet colour of the cellar seemed a little duller just there.

"I looked back quickly to the vague place where the Child was hiding. I saw it was peering back from its hiding place. Suddenly it rose and ran straight for the middle of the table, which showed only as vague shadow half-way between my eyes and the unseen floor. As the Child ran under the table, the steel prongs of my pitchfork glimmered with a violet, fluctuating light. A little way off, there showed high up in the gloom, the vaguely shining outline of the other fork, so I knew the inspector had it raised in his hand, ready. There was no doubt but that he saw something. On the table, the metal of the five lanterns shone with the same strange glow; and about each lantern there was a little cloud of absolute blackness, where the phenomenon that is light to our natural eyes, came through the fittings; and in this complete darkness, the metal of each lantern showed plain, as might a cat's-eye in a nest of black cotton wool.

"Just beyond the table, the Child paused again, and stood, seeming to oscillate a little upon its feet, which gave the impression that it was lighter and vaguer than a thistle-down; and yet, in the same moment, another part of me seemed to know that it was to me, as something that might be beyond thick, invisible glass, and subject to conditions and forces that I was unable to comprehend.

"The Child was looking back again, and my gaze went the same way. I stared across the cellar, and saw the cage hanging clear in the violet light, every wire and tie outlined with its glimmering; above it there was a little space of gloom, and then the dull shining of the iron pulley which I had screwed into the ceiling.

"I stared in a bewildered way 'round the cellar; there were thin lines of vague fire crossing the floor in all directions; and suddenly I remembered the piano wire that the landlord and I had stretched. But there was nothing else to be seen, except that near the table there were indistinct glimmerings of light, and at the far end the outline of a dull glowing revolver, evidently in the detective's pocket. I remember a sort of subconscious satisfaction, as I settled the point in a queer automatic fashion. On the table, near to me, there was a little shapeless collection of the light; and this I knew, after an instant's consideration, to be the steel portions of my watch.

"I had looked several times at the Child, and 'round at the cellar, whilst I was decided these trifles; and had found it still in that attitude of hiding from something. But now, suddenly, it ran clear away into the distance, and was nothing more than a slightly deeper coloured nucleus far away in the strange coloured atmosphere.

"The landlord gave out a queer little cry, and twisted over against me, as if to avoid something. From the inspector there came a sharp breathing sound, as if he had been suddenly drenched with cold water. Then suddenly the violet colour went out of the night, and I was conscious of the nearness of something monstrous and repugnant.

"There was a tense silence, and the blackness of the cellar seemed absolute, with only the faint glow about each of the lanterns on the table. Then, in the darkness and the silence, there came a faint tinkle of water from the well, as if something were rising noiselessly out of it, and the water running back with a gentle tinkling. In the same instant, there came to me a sudden waft of the awful smell.

"I gave a sharp cry of warning to the inspector, and loosed the rope. There came instantly the sharp splash of the cage entering the water; and then, with a stiff, frightened movement, I opened the shutter of my lantern, and shone the light at the cage, shouting to the others to do the same.

"As my light struck the cage, I saw that about two feet of it projected from the top of the well, and there was something protruding up out of the water, into the cage. I stared, with a feeling that I recognized the thing; and then, as the other lanterns were opened, I saw that it was a leg of mutton. The thing was held by a brawny fist and arm, that rose out of the water. I stood utterly bewildered, watching to see what was coming. In a moment there rose into view a great bearded face, that I felt for one quick instant was the face of a drowned man, long dead. Then the face opened at the mouth part, and spluttered and coughed. Another big hand came into view, and wiped the water from the eyes, which blinked rapidly, and then fixed themselves into a stare at the lights.

"From the detective there came a sudden shout:

"'Captain Tobias!' he shouted, and the inspector echoed him; and instantly burst into loud roars of laughter.

"The inspector and the detective ran across the cellar to the cage; and I followed, still bewildered. The man in the cage was holding the leg of mutton as far away from him as possible, and holding his nose.

"'Lift thig dam trap, quig!' he shouted in a stifled voice; but the inspector and the detective simply doubled before him, and tried to hold their noses, whilst they laughed, and the light from their lanterns went dancing all over the place.

"'Quig! Quig!' said the man in the cage, still holding his nose, and trying to speak plainly.

"Then Johnstone and the detective stopped laughing, and lifted the cage. The man in the well threw the leg across the cellar, and turned swiftly to go down into the well; but the officers were too quick for him, and had him out in a twinkling. Whilst they held him, dripping upon the floor, the inspector jerked his thumb in the direction of the offending leg, and the landlord, having harpooned it with one of the pitchforks, ran with it upstairs and so into the open air.

"Meanwhile, I had given the man from the well a stiff tot of whisky; for which he thanked me with a cheerful nod, and having emptied the glass at a draft, held his hand for the bottle, which he finished, as if it had been so much water.

"As you will remember, it was a Captain Tobias who had been the previous tenant; and this was the very man, who had appeared from the well. In the course of the talk that followed, I learned the reason for Captain Tobias leaving the house; he had been wanted by the police for smuggling. He had undergone imprisonment; and had been released only a couple of weeks earlier.

"He had returned to find new tenants in his old home. He had entered the house through the well, the walls of which were not continued to the bottom (this I will deal with later); and gone up by a little stairway in the cellar wall, which opened at the top through a panel beside my mother's bedroom. This panel was opened, by revolving the left doorpost of the bedroom door, with the result that the bedroom door always became unlatched, in the process of opening the panel.

"The captain complained, without any bitterness, that the panel had warped, and that each time he opened it, it made a cracking noise. This had been evidently what I mistook for raps. He would not give his reason for entering the house; but it was pretty obvious that he had hidden something, which he wanted to get. However, as he found it impossible to get into the house without the risk of being caught, he decided to try to drive us out, relying on the bad reputation of the house, and his own artistic efforts as a ghost. I must say he succeeded. He intended then to rent the house again, as before; and would then, of course have plenty of time to get whatever he had hidden. The house suited him admirably; for there was a passage – as he showed me afterward – connecting the dummy well with the crypt of the church beyond the garden wall; and these, in turn, were connected with certain caves in the cliffs, which went down to the beach beyond the church.

"In the course of his talk, Captain Tobias offered to take the house off my hands; and as this suited me perfectly, for I was about stalled with it, and the plan also suited the landlord, it was decided that no steps should be taken against him; and that the whole business should be hushed up.

"I asked the captain whether there was really anything queer about the house; whether he had ever seen anything. He said yes, that he had twice seen a Woman going about the house. We all looked at one another, when the captain said that. He told us she never bothered him, and that he had only seen her twice, and on each occasion it had followed a narrow escape from the Revenue people.

"Captain Tobias was an observant man; he had seen how I had placed the mats against the doors; and after entering the rooms, and walking all about them, so as to leave the foot-marks of an old pair of wet woollen slippers everywhere, he had deliberately put the mats back as he found them.

"The maggot which had dropped from his disgusting leg of mutton had been an accident, and beyond even his horrible planning. He was hugely delighted to learn how it had affected us.

"The mouldy smell I had noticed was from the little closed stairway, when the captain opened the panel. The door slamming was also another of his contributions.

"I come now to the end of the captain's ghost play; and to the difficulty of trying to explain the other peculiar things. In the first place, it was obvious there was something genuinely strange in the house; which made itself manifest as a Woman. Many different people had seen this Woman, under differing circumstances, so it is impossible to put the thing down to fancy; at the same time it must seem extraordinary that I should have lived two years in the house, and seen nothing; whilst the policeman saw the Woman, before he had been there twenty minutes; the landlord, the detective, and the inspector all saw her.

"I can only surmise that *fear* was in every case the key, as I might say, which opened the senses to the presence of the Woman. The policeman was a highly-strung man, and when he became frightened, was able to see the Woman. The same reasoning applies all 'round. *I* saw nothing, until I became really frightened; then I saw, not the Woman; but a Child, running away from Something or Someone. However, I will touch on that later. In short, until a very strong degree of fear was present, no one was affected by the Force which made Itself evident, as a Woman. My theory explains why some tenants were never aware of anything strange in the house, whilst others left immediately. The more sensitive they were, the less would be the degree of fear necessary to make them aware of the Force present in the house.

"The peculiar shining of all the metal objects in the cellar, had been visible only to me. The cause, naturally I do not know; neither do I know why I, alone, was able to see the shining."

"The Child," I asked. "Can you explain that part at all? Why *you* didn't see the Woman, and why *they* didn't see the Child. Was it merely the same Force, appearing differently to different people?"

"No," said Carnacki, "I can't explain that. But I am quite sure that the Woman and the Child were not only two complete and different entities; but even they were each not in quite the same planes of existence.

"To give you a root idea, however, it is held in the Sigsand MS. that a child 'stillborn' is 'Snatyched back bye thee Haggs.' This is crude; but may yet contain an elemental truth. Yet, before I make this clearer, let me tell you a thought that has often been made. It may be that physical birth is but a secondary process; and that prior to the possibility, the Mother Spirit searches for, until it finds, the small Element – the primal Ego or child's soul. It may be that a certain waywardness would cause such to strive to evade capture by the Mother Spirit. It may have been such a thing as this, that I saw. I have always tried to think so; but it is impossible to ignore the sense of repulsion that I felt when the unseen Woman went past me. This repulsion carries forward the idea suggested in the Sigsand MS., that a stillborn child is thus, because its ego or spirit has been snatched back by the 'Hags'. In other words, by certain of the Monstrosities of the Outer Circle. The thought is inconceivably terrible, and probably the more so because it is so fragmentary. It leaves us with the conception of a child's soul adrift half-way between two lives, and running through Eternity from Something incredible and inconceivable (because not understood) to our senses.

"The thing is beyond further discussion; for it is futile to attempt to discuss a thing, to any purpose, of which one has a knowledge so fragmentary as this. There is one thought, which is often mine. Perhaps there is a Mother Spirit –"

"And the well?" said Arkwright. "How did the captain get in from the other side?"

"As I said before," answered Carnacki. "The side walls of the well did not reach to the bottom; so that you had only to dip down into the water, and come up again on the other side of the wall, under the cellar floor, and so climb into the passage. Of course, the water was the same height on both sides of the walls. Don't ask me who made the well entrance or the little stairway; for I don't know. The house was very old, as I have told you; and that sort of thing was useful in the old days."

"And the Child," I said, coming back to the thing which chiefly interested me. "You would say that the birth must have occurred in that house; and in this way, one might suppose that the house to have become *en rapport*, if I can use the word in that way, with the Forces that produced the tragedy?"

"Yes," replied Carnacki. "This is, supposing we take the suggestion of the Sigsand MS., to account for the phenomenon."

"There may be other houses –" I began.

"There are," said Carnacki; and stood up.

"Out you go," he said, genially, using the recognized formula. And in five minutes we were on the Embankment, going thoughtfully to our various homes.

The Elementary Spirit

E.T.A. Hoffmann

ON THE 20TH of November, 1815, Albert von B—, lieutenant-colonel in the Prussian service, found himself on the road from Liège to Aix-la-Chapelle. The corps to which he belonged was on its return from France to march to Liège to head-quarters on that very day, and was to remain there for two or three days more. Albert had arrived the evening before; but in the morning he felt himself attacked by a strange restlessness, and – as he would hardly have confessed to himself – an obscure dream, which had haunted him all night, and had foretold that a very pleasant adventure awaited him at Aix-la-Chapelle, was the only cause of his sudden departure. Much surprised even at his own proceeding, he was sitting on the swift horse, which would, he hoped, take him to the city before nightfall.

A severe cutting autumn wind roared over the bare fields, and awakened the voices of the leafless wood in the distance, which united their groans to its howling. Birds of prey came croaking, and followed in flocks the thick clouds which gathered more and more, until the last ray of sunlight had vanished, and a faint dull gray had overspread the entire sky. Albert wrapped his mantle more closely about him, and while he trotted on along the broad road, the picture of the last eventful time unfolded itself to his imagination. He thought how, a few months before, he had travelled on the same road, in an opposite direction, and during the loveliest season of the year. The fields then bloomed forth luxuriantly, the fragrant meadows resembled variegated carpets, and the bushes in which the birds joyously chirped and sung, shone in the fair light of golden sunbeams. The earth, like a longing bride, had richly adorned herself to receive in her dark nuptial chamber, the victims consecrated to death – the heroes who fell in the sanguinary battles.

Albert had reached the corps to which he was appointed, when the cannon had already begun to thunder by the Sambre, though he was in time enough to take part in the bloody battles of Charleroi, Gilly, and Gosselins. Indeed, chance seemed to wish that Albert should be present just when anything decided took place. Thus he was at the last storming of the village Planchenoit, which caused the victory in the most remarkable of all battles – Waterloo. He was in the last engagement of the campaign, when the final effort of rage and fierce despair on the part of the enemy wreaked itself on the immoveable courage of the heroes, who having a fine position in the village of Issy, drove back the foe as they sought, amid the most furious discharge of grape, to scatter death and destruction in the ranks; and indeed drove them back so far, that the sharp-shooters pursued them almost to the barriers of Paris. The night afterwards (that of the 3rd and 4th of July), was, as is well known, that on which the military convention for the surrender of the metropolis was settled at St. Cloud.

The battle of Issy now rose brightly before Albert's soul; he thought of things, which as it seemed, he had not observed, nay, had not been able to observe during the fight. Thus the faces of many individual officers and men appeared before his eyes, depicted in the most lively manner, and his heart was struck by the inexplicable expression, not of proud or unfeeling contempt of death, but of really divine inspiration, which beamed from many an eye. Thus he heard sounds, now exhorting to fight, now uttered with the last sigh of death, which deserved to be treasured up for posterity like the animating utterances of the heroes of antiquity.

"Do I not," thought Albert, "almost feel like one who has a notion of his dream when he wakes, but who does not recollect all its single features till several days afterwards? Ay, a dream, and only a dream, one would think, by flying over time and space, with its mighty wings, could render possible, the gigantic, monstrous, unheard-of events, that took place during the eighteen eventful days of a campaign, which mocks the boldest thoughts, the most daring combinations of the speculative mind. Indeed the human mind does not know its own greatness; the act surpasses the thought. For it is not rude physical force, no! It is the mind, which creates deeds as they have happened, and it is the psychic power of every single person, really inspired, which attaches itself to the wisdom and genius of the general, and helps to accomplish the monstrous and the unexpected."

Albert was disturbed in these meditations by his groom, who kept about twenty paces behind him, and whom he heard cry out, "Eh! Paul Talkebarth, where the deuce do you come from?" He turned his horse, and perceived that a horseman, who had just trotted past him, and whom he had not particularly observed, was standing still with his groom, beating out the cheeks of the large fox-fur cap with which his head was covered, so that soon the well-known face of Paul Talkebarth, Colonel Victor von S—'s old groom, was made manifest, glowing with the finest vermilion.

Now Albert knew at once what it was that impelled him so irresistibly from Liège to Aix-la-Chapelle, and he could not comprehend how the thought of Victor, his most intimate and dearest friend, whom he had every reason to suppose at Aix, merely lay dimly in his soul, and attained nothing like distinctness. He now also cried out, "Eh! Paul Talkebarth, whence do you come? Where is your master?"

Paul curvetted up to him very gracefully, and said, holding the palm of his hand against the far-too-large cockade of his cap, by way of military salutation: "Yes, 'faith, I am Paul Talkebarth indeed, gracious lieutenant-colonel. We've bad weather here, Zermannöre (*sur mon honneur*). But the groundsel brings that about. Old Lizzy always used to say so. I cannot say, gracious lieutenant-colonel, if you know Lizzy: she lives at Genthin, but if one has been at Paris, and has seen the wild goat in the Schartinpland (*Jardin des Plantes*). Now, what one seeks for one finds near, and here I am in the presence of the gracious lieutenant-colonel, whom I was to seek at Liège. The spirus familis (*spiritus familiaris*), whispered yesterday evening into my master's ear, that the gracious lieutenant-colonel had come to Liège. Zackermannthö (*sacré mon de Dieu*), there was delight! It may be as it will, but I have never put any faith in the cream-colour. A fine beast, Zermannöre, but a mere childish thing, and the baronness did her utmost – that is true! There are decent sort of people here, but the wine is good for nothing – and when one has been in Paris –! Now, the colonel might have marched in, like one through the Argen trumph (*Arc de triomphe*), and I should have put the new shabrach on the white horse; gad, how he would have pricked up his ears! But old Lizzy – she was my aunt, at Genthin, was always accustomed to say – I don't know, gracious lieutenant-colonel, whether you –"

"May your tongue be lamed," said Albert, interrupting the incorrigible babbler. "If your master is at Aix, we must make haste, for we have still above five leagues to go."

"Stop," cried Paul Talkebarth, with all his might; "stop, stop, gracious lieutenant-colonel, the weather is bad here; but for fodder – those who have eyes like us, that shine in the fog."

"Paul," cried Albert, "do not wear out my patience. Where is your master? Is he not in Aix?"

Paul Talkebarth smiled with such delight, that his whole countenance puckered up into a thousand folds, like a wet glove, and then stretching out his arm he pointed to the building, which might be seen behind the wood, upon a gentle declivity, and said, "Yonder, in the castle!" Without waiting for what Paul might have to prattle further, Albert struck into the path that led from the high road, and hurried on in a rapid trot. After the little that he has said, honest Paul Talkebarth must appear to the gracious reader as an odd sort of fellow. We have only to say, that he being an heir-loom of the family, served Colonel Victor von S— from the moment when the latter first put on his officer's sword, after having been the intendent-general and *maître des plaisirs* of all the sports and mad pranks of his childhood. An old and very odd *magister*, who had been tutor to the family through two generations, completed, with the amount of education which he allowed to flow to honest Paul, those happy talents for extraordinary confusion and strange Eulenspiegelei with which nature had by no means scantily endued him. At the same time he was the most faithful soul that could possibly exist. Ready every moment to sacrifice his life for his master, neither his advanced age nor any other consideration could prevent the good Paul from following him to the field in the year 1813. His own nature rendered him superior to every hardship; but less strong than his corporeal was his spiritual nature, which seemed to have received a strange shock, or at any rate some extraordinary impulse during his residence in France, especially in Paris. Then, for the first time, did he properly feel that Magister Spreugepileus had been perfectly right when he called him a great light, that would one day shine forth brightly. This shining quality Paul had discovered by the aptness with which he had accommodated himself to the manners of a foreign people, and had learned their language. Therefore, he boasted not a little, and ascribed it to his extraordinary talent alone, that he could often, in respect to quarters and provisions, obtain that which seemed unattainable. Talkebarth's fine French phrases, the gentle reader has already been made acquainted with some pleasant curses – were current, if not through the whole army, at any rate through the corps to which his master was attached. Every trooper who came to quarters in a village, cried to the peasant with Paul's words, "Pisang! De lavendel pur di schevals!" (*Paysan, de l'avoine pour les chevaux.*)

Paul, as is generally the case with eccentric natures, did not like things to happen in the ordinary manner. He was particularly fond of surprises, and sought to prepare them in every possible manner for his master, who was certainly often surprised, though in quite another manner than was designed by honest Talkebarth, whose happy schemes generally failed in their execution. Thus, he now entreated Lieutenant-colonel von B—, when the latter was riding straight up to the principal entrance of the house, to take a circuitous course and enter the court-yard by the back way, that his master might not see him before he entered the room. To meet this view, Albert was obliged to ride over a marshy meadow, where he was grievously splashed by the mud, and then he had to go over a fragile bridge on a ditch. Paul Talkebarth wished to show off his horsemanship by jumping cleverly over; but he fell in with his horse up to the belly, and was with difficulty brought back to firm ground by Albert's groom. Now, in high spirits, he put spurs to his horse, and with a wild huzza leaped into the court-yard. As all the geese, ducks, turkeys, and poultry of the household were gathered together here to rest; while from the one side a flock of sheep, and from the other side a flock of pigs, had been driven in, we may easily imagine that Paul Talkebarth, who not being perfect master of his horse, galloped about the court in large circles, without any will of his own, produced no little devastation in the domestic economy. Amid the fearful noise of squeaking, cackling, bleating, grunting animals, the barking of the dogs, and the scolding of the servants, Albert made his glorious entrance, wishing honest Paul Talkebarth at all the devils, with his project of surprise.

At last Albert leaped from his horse, and entered the house, which, without any claim to beauty or elegance, looked roomy and convenient enough. On the steps he was met by a well-fed, not very tall man, in a short, gray, hunting-jacket, who, with a half-sour smile, said: "Quartered?" By the tone in which the man asked this question, Albert perceived at once that the master of the house, Baron von E— (as he had learned from Paul) was before him. He assured him that he was not quartered, but merely purposed to visit his intimate friend, Colonel Victor von S—, who was, he was told, residing there, and that he only required the baron's hospitality for that evening and the night, as he intended to start very early on the following morning.

The baron's face visibly cleared up, and the full sun-shine, which ordinarily seemed to play upon his good-humoured, but somewhat too broad, countenance, returned completely, when Albert as he ascended the stairs with him remarked, that in all probability no division of the army now marching would touch this spot.

The baron opened a door, Albert entered a cheerful-looking parlour, and perceived Victor, who sat with his back towards him. At the sound of his entrance Victor turned round, and with a loud exclamation of joy fell into the arms of the lieutenant. "Is it not true, Albert, you thought of me last night? I knew it, my inner sense told me that you were in Liège at the very moment when you first entered the place. I fixed all my thoughts upon you, my spiritual arms embraced you; you could not escape me."

Albert confessed that – as the gentle reader already knows – dark dreams which came to no clear shape had driven him from Liège.

"Yes," cried Victor, with transport, "yes, it is no fancy, no idle notion; the divine power is given to us, which, ruling space and time, manifests the supersensual in the world of sense."

Albert did not know what Victor meant. Indeed the whole behaviour of his friend, so different from his usual manner, seemed to denote an over-excited state. In the meanwhile the lady, who had been sitting before the fire near Victor, arose and approached the stranger. Albert bowed to her, casting an inquiring glance at Victor. "This is the Baroness Aurora von E—," said Victor, "my hospitable hostess, who tends me ever carefully and faithfully in sickness and in trouble!"

Albert as he looked at the baroness felt quite convinced that the little plump woman had not yet attained her fortieth year, and that she would have been very well made had not the nutritious food of the country, together with much sunshine, caused her shape to deviate a little from the line of beauty. This counteracted the favourable effect of her pretty, fresh-coloured face, the dark blue eyes of which might otherwise have beamed somewhat dangerously for the heart. Albert considered the attire of the baroness almost too homely, for the material of her dress, which was of a dazzling whiteness, while it showed the excellence of the washing and bleaching department, also showed the great distance at which the domestic spinning and weaving stood from perfection. A cotton kerchief, of a very glaring pattern, thrown negligently about the neck, so that its whiteness was visible enough, did not at all increase the brilliant effect of the costume. The oddest thing of all was that the baroness wore on her little feet the most elegant silken shoes, and on her head the most charming lace cap, after the newest Parisian fashion. This head-dress, it is true, reminded the lieutenant-colonel of a pretty grisette, with whom chance had made him acquainted at Paris, but for this very reason a quantity of uncommonly gallant things flowed from his lips, while he apologised for his sudden appearance. The baroness did not fail to reply to these prettinesses in the proper style, and having once opened her mouth the stream of her discourse flowed on uninterruptedly, till she at last went so far as to say, that it would be impossible to show sufficient attention to such an amiable guest, the friend of the colonel, who was so dear to the family. At the sudden ring of the bell, and the shrill cry: "Mariane, Mariane!" a peevish old woman made her appearance, who, by the bunch of keys which hung from her waist, seemed to be the housekeeper. A consultation was now held with this lady and the husband, as to what nice things could be got ready. It was soon found, however, that all the delicacies, such as venison and the like, were either already consumed, or could only be got the next day. Albert, with difficulty suppressing his displeasure, said that they would force him to quit immediately in the night, if on his account they disturbed the arrangements of the house in the slightest degree. A little cold meat, nay, some bread and butter, would be sufficient for his supper. The baroness replied by protesting that it was impossible for the lieutenant-colonel to do without something warm, after his ride in the rough, bleak weather, and after a long consultation with Mariane, the preparation of some mulled wine was found to be possible and decided on. Mariane vanished through the door-way, rattling as she went, but at the very moment when they were about to take their seats, the baroness was called out by an amazed maid-servant. Albert overheard that the baroness was being informed at the door of the frightful devastations of Paul Talkebarth, with a list – no inconsiderable one – of the dead, wounded, and missing. The baron ran out after his wife, and while she was scolding he was wishing honest Paul Talkebarth at Jericho, and the servants were uttering general lamentations. Albert briefly told his friend of Paul's exploit in the yard. "That old Eulenspiegel is always playing such tricks," said Victor, angrily, "and yet the rascal means so well from the very bottom of his heart, that one cannot attack him."

At that moment all became quiet without; the chief maid-servant had brought the glad intelligence that Hans Gucklick had been frightened indeed, but had come off free from other harm, and was now eating with a good appetite.

The baron entered with a cheerful mien, and repeated, in a tone of satisfaction, that Hans Gucklick had been spared from that wild, life-disregarding Paul Talkebarth. At the same time he took occasion to expatiate at great length, and from an agricultural point of view, the utility of extending the breeding of poultry. This Hans Gucklick, who had only been very frightened, and had not been otherwise hurt, was the old cock, who was highly prized, and had been for years the pride and ornament of the whole poultry-yard.

The baroness now made her re-appearance, but it was only to arm herself with a great bunch of keys, which she took out of a cupboard. Quickly she hurried off, and Albert could hear both her and the housekeeper clattering and rattling upstairs and downstairs, accompanied by the shrill voices of the maid-servants who were called, and the pleasant music of pestles and mortars and graters, which ascended from the kitchen. "Good heavens!" thought Albert. "If the general had marched in with the whole of the head-quarters, there could not have been more noise than has been occasioned by my unlucky cup of mulled wine."

The baron, who had wandered from the breeding of poultry to hunting, had not quite got to the end of a very complicated story of a fine deer which he had seen, and had not shot, when the baroness entered the room, followed by no less a person than Paul Talkebarth, who bore the mulled wine in a handsome porcelain vessel. "Bring it all here, good Paul," said the baroness, very kindly. Whereupon Paul replied, with an indescribably sweet, "A fu zerpir (*à vous servir*), madame." The manes of the victims in the yard seemed to be appeased, and all seemed forgiven.

Now, at last, they all sat down quietly together. The baroness, after she had handed the cup to the visitor, began to knit a monstrous worsted stocking, and the baron took occasion to enlarge upon the species of knitting which was designed to be worn while hunting. During his discourse he seized the vessel, that he also might take a cup. "Ernest!" cried the baroness to him, in an angry tone. He at once desisted from his purpose, and slunk to the cupboard, where he quietly refreshed himself with a glass of Schnapps. Albert availed himself of the moment to put a stop to the baron's tedious disquisitions, by urgently asking his friend how he was going on. Victor was of opinion that there was plenty of time to say, in two words, what had happened to him since their separation, and that he could not expect to hear from Albert's lips all the mighty occurrences of the late portentous period. The baroness assured him, with a smile, that there was nothing prettier than tales of war and murder; while the baron, who had rejoined the party, said that he liked amazingly to hear of battles, when they were very bloody, as they always reminded him of his hunting-parties. He was upon the point of returning to the story of the stag that he did not shoot, but Albert cut him short, and laughing out loud, though with increased displeasure, remarked that, though there was, to be sure, some smart shooting in the chase, it was a comfortable arrangement that the stags, hares, etc., whose blood was at stake, could not return the fire.

Albert felt thoroughly warmed by the beverage which he had drunk, and which he found was excellently made of splendid wine, and his comfortable state of body had a good effect on his mind, completely overcoming the ill-humour which had taken possession of him in this uncomfortable society. He unfolded before Victor's eyes the whole sublime and fearful picture of the awful battle, that at once annihilated all the hopes of the fancied ruler of the world. With the most glowing imagination, he described the invincible, lion-like courage of those battalions who at last stormed the village of Planchenoit, and concluded with the words: "Oh! Victor, Victor! Would you had been there, and fought with me!"

Victor had moved close to the baroness's chair, and having picked up the large ball of worsted, which had rolled down from her lap, was playing with it in his hands, so that the industrious knitter was compelled to draw the threads through his fingers, and often could not avoid touching his arm with her long needle.

At the words, which Albert uttered with an elevated voice, Victor appeared suddenly to wake as from a dream. He eyed his friend with a singular smile, and said, in a half-suppressed tone: "Yes, dear Albert, what you say is but too true! Man often implicates himself early in snares, the gordian knot of which death alone forcibly sunders! As for what concerns the raising of the devil in general, the audacious invocation of one's own fearful spirit is the most perilous thing possible. But here everything sleeps!"

Victor's dark, unintelligible words were a sufficient proof that he had not heard a syllable of all that Albert had said, but had been occupied all the time with dreams, which must have been of a very singular kind.

Albert, as may be supposed, was dumb with amazement. Looking around him he perceived, for the first time, that the master of the house, who with hands folded before him, had sunk against the back of a chair, had dropped his weary head upon his breast, and that the baroness with closed eyes continued to knit mechanically like a piece of clock-work wound up.

Albert sprung up quickly, making a noise as he rose, but at the very same moment the baroness rose also, and approached him with an air, so free, noble, and graceful, that he saw no more of the little, plump, almost comical figure, but thought that the baroness was transformed to another creature. "Pardon the housewife who is employed from break of day, lieutenant-colonel," said she, in a sweet voice, as she grasped Albert's hand, "if in the evening she is unable to resist the effects of fatigue, even though she hears the greatest events recorded in the finest manner. This you must also pardon in the active sportsman. You must certainly be anxious to be alone with your friend and to open your heart to him, and under such circumstances every witness is an incumberance. It will certainly be agreeable to you to take, alone with your friend, the supper which I have served in his apartment."

No proposal could have been more opportune to Albert. He immediately in the most courteous language wished a good night to his kind hostess, whom he now heartily forgave for the bunch of keys, and the grief about frightened Hans Gucklick, as well as for the stocking-knitting and the nodding.

"Dear Ernest!" cried the baroness, as the friends wished to bid good night to the baron; but as the latter, instead of answering only cried out very plainly: "Huss! Huss! Tyrus! Waldmann! Allons!" and let his head hang on the other side, they tried no more to arouse him from his pleasant dreams.

"Now," said Albert, finding himself alone with Victor for the first time, "tell me how you have fared. But, however, first let us eat a bit, for I am very hungry, and it appears there is something more here than the bread and butter."

The lieutenant-colonel was right, for he found a table elegantly set out with the choicest cold delicacies, the chief ornament of which was a Bayonne ham, and a pasty of red partridges. Paul Talkebarth, when Albert expressed his satisfaction, said, waggishly smiling, that if he had not been present, and had not given Mariane a hint of what it was that the lieutenant-colonel liked, as suppenfink (*super-fine*) – but that, nevertheless, he could not forget his aunt Lizzy, who had burned the rice-pudding on his wedding-day, and that he had now been a widower for thirty years, and one could not tell, since marriages were made in heaven, and that Mariane – but that it was the gracious baroness who had given him the best herself, namely, a whole basket of celery for the gentleman. Albert did not know why such an unreasonable quantity of vegetable food should be served, and was highly delighted, when Paul Talkebarth brought the basket, which contained – not celery – but six bottles of the finest *vin de Sillery*.

While Albert was enjoying himself, Victor narrated how he had come to the estate of the Baron von E—.

The fatigues of the first campaign (1813), which had often proved too much for the strongest constitutions, had ruined Victor's health. The waters at Aix-la-Chapelle would, he hoped, restore him, and he was residing there when Bonaparte's flight from Elba gave the signal for a new and sanguinary contest. When preparations were making for the campaign, Victor received orders from the *Residence* to join the army on the Lower Rhine, if his health permitted; but fate allowed him no more than a ride of four or five leagues. Just before the gate of the house in which the friends now were, Victor's horse, which had usually been the surest and most fearless animal in the world, and had been tried in the wildest tumults of battle, suddenly took fright, and reared, and Victor fell – to use his own words – like a schoolboy who has mounted a horse for the first time. He lay insensible, while the blood flowed from a severe wound in his head, which he had struck against a sharp stone. He was carried into the house, and here, as removal seemed dangerous, he was forced to remain till the time of his recovery, which did not yet seem complete, since, although the wound had been long healed, he was weakened by the attacks of fever. Victor spoke of the care and attention which the baroness had bestowed upon him in terms of the warmest gratitude.

"Well," cried Albert, laughing aloud, "for this I was not prepared. I thought you were going to tell me something very extraordinary, and now, lo, and behold – don't be offended – the whole affair seems to turn out a silly sort of story, like those that have been so worn out in a hundred stupid novels, that nobody with decency can have anything to do with such adventures. The wounded knight is borne into the castle, the mistress of the house tends him, and he becomes a tender *Amoroso*. For, Victor, that you, in spite of your good taste hitherto, in spite of your whole mode of life, should all of a sudden fall in love with a plump elderly woman, who is homely and domestic to the last degree, that you should play the pining lack-a-daisical youth, who, as somebody says, 'sighs like an oven, and makes songs on his mistress's tears,' – that, I say, I can only look upon as a sort of disease! The only thing that could excuse you in any way, and put you in a poetical light, would be the Spanish Infanta in the 'Physician of his Honour', who, meeting a fate similar to yours, fell upon his nose before Donna Menzia's gate, and at last found the beloved one, who unconsciously –"

"Stop!" interrupted Victor, "Stop! Don't you think that I see clearly enough, that you take me for a silly dolt? No, no, there is something else – something more mysterious at work. Let us drink!"

The wine, and Albert's lively talk, had produced a wholesome excitement in Victor, who seemed aroused from a gloomy dream. But when, at last, Albert, raising his full glass, said, "Now, Victor, my dear Infanta, here's a health to Donna Menzia, and may she look like our little pet hostess." – Victor cried, laughing, "No, no, I cannot bear that you should take me for a fool. I feel quite cheerful, and ready to make a confession to you of everything! You must, however, submit to hear an entire youthful period of my life, and it is possible that half the night will be taken up by the narrative."

"Begin!" replied Albert, "For I see we have enough wine to cheer up our somewhat sinking spirits. I only wish it was not so confoundedly cold, nor a crime to wake up the good folks of the house."

"Perhaps," said Victor, "Paul Talkebarth may have made some provision." And, indeed, the said Paul, cursing in his well-known French dialect, courteously assured them, that he had cut small and kept excellent wood for firing, which he was ready to kindle at once. "Fortunately," said Victor, "the same thing cannot happen to me here, that happened at a drysalter's at Meaux, where honest Paul lit me a fire that cost, at least, 1200 francs. The good fellow had got hold of Brazilian sandal-wood, hacked it to pieces, and put it on the hearth, so that I looked almost like Andolosia, the famous son of the celebrated Fortunatus, whose cook had to light a fire of spices, because the king forbade him to buy wood.

"You know," continued Victor, as the fire merrily crackled and flamed up, and Paul Talkebarth had left the room, "you know, my dear friend, Albert, that I began my military career in the guards, at Potsdam; indeed, that is nearly all you know of my younger days, because I never had a special opportunity to talk about them – and, still more, because the picture of those years has been represented to my soul in dim outlines, and did not, until I came here, flame up again in bright colours. My first education, in my father's house, does not even deserve the name of a bad one. I had, in fact, no education at all, but was left entirely to my own inclinations, and these indicated anything rather than a call to the profession of arms. I felt manifestly impelled towards a scientific culture, which the old magister, who was my appointed tutor, and who only liked to be left in quiet, could not give me. At Potsdam I gained with facility a knowledge of modern languages, while I zealously and successfully pursued those studies that are requisite for an officer. I read, besides, with a kind of mania, all that fell into my hands, without selection or regard to utility; however, as my memory was excellent, I had acquired a mass of historical knowledge, I scarcely knew how. People have since done me the honour to assure me that a poetical spirit dwelled in me, which I myself would not rightly appreciate. Certain it is that the *chefs-d'oeuvre* of the great poets, of that period, raised me to a state of inspiration of which I had previously no notion. I appeared to myself as another being, developed for the first time into active life. I will only name the *Sorrows of Werther*, and, more especially, Schiller's *Robbers*.

"My fancy received an impulse quite of a different sort from a book, which, for the very reason that it is not finished, gives the mind an impetus that keeps it swinging like a pendulum in constant motion. I mean Schiller's *Ghostseer*. It may be that the inclination to the mystical and marvellous, which is generally deep-rooted in human nature, was particularly prevalent in me; – whatever was the cause, it is sufficient for me to say that, when I read that book, which seems to contain the exorcising formula belonging to the mightiest black art, a magical kingdom, full of super-terrestrial, or, rather, sub-terrestrial marvels, was opened to me, in which I moved about as a dreamer. Once given to this mood, I eagerly swallowed all that would accord with it, and even works of far less worth did not fail in their effect upon me. Thus the *Genius*, by Grosse, made a deep impression upon me, and I have the less reason to feel ashamed of this, since the first part, at least, on account of the liveliness of the style and the clear treatment of the subject, produced a sensation through the whole literary world. Many an arrest I was obliged to endure, when upon guard, for being absorbed in such a book, or perhaps only in mystic dreams, I did not hear the call, and was forced to be fetched by the inferior officer.

"Just at this time chance made me acquainted with a very extraordinary man. It happened on a fine summer evening, when the sun had already sunk, and twilight had already begun, that, according to my custom, I was walking alone in a pleasure ground near Potsdam. I fancied that, from the thicket of a little wood, which lay by the road-side, I could hear plaintive sounds, and some words uttered with energy in a language unknown to me. I thought someone wanted assistance, so I hastened to the spot whence the sounds seemed to proceed, and soon, in the red glimmer of the evening, discovered a large, broad-shouldered figure, enveloped in a common military mantle, and stretched upon the ground. Approaching nearer I recognised, to my astonishment, Major O'Malley of the grenadiers. 'Good heavens!' I exclaimed, 'Is this you, major? In this situation? Are you ill? Can I help you?' The major looked at me with a fixed, wild stare, and then said, in a harsh voice, 'What the devil brings you here, lieutenant? What does it matter to you whether I lie here or not? Go back to the town!'

"Nevertheless, the deadly paleness of O'Malley's face made me suspect that there was something wrong, and I declared that I would not leave him, but would only return to the town in his company. 'Good!' said the major, quite coldly and deliberately, after he had remained silent for some moments, and had endeavoured to raise himself, in which attempt, as it appeared to be attended with difficulty, I assisted him. I perceived now that – as was frequently the case when he went out in the evening – he had nothing but a shirt under the cloak, which was a common *commis-mantel* as they call it, that he had put on his boots, and that he wore upon his bald head his officer's hat, with broad gold lace. A pistol, which lay on the ground near him, he caught up hastily, and, to conceal it from me, put it into the pocket of his cloak. During the whole way to the town he did not speak a syllable to me, but now and then uttered disjointed phrases in his own language – he was an Irishman by birth – which I did not understand. When he had reached his quarters he pressed my hand, and said, in a tone in which there was something indescribable – something that had never been heard before, and which still echoes in my soul: 'Good night, lieutenant! Heaven guard you, and give you good dreams!'

"This Major O'Malley was one of the strangest men possible, and if, perhaps, I except a few somewhat eccentric Englishmen, whom I have met, I know no officer in the whole great army to compare in outward appearance with O'Malley. If it be true – as some travellers affirm – that nature nowhere produces such peculiarities as in Ireland, and that, therefore, every family can exhibit the prettiest cabinet pictures, Major O'Malley would justly serve as a prototype for all his nation. Imagine a man strong as a tree, six feet high, whose build could scarcely be called awkward, but none of whose limbs fitted the rest, so that his whole figure seemed huddled together, as in that game where figures are composed of single parts, the numbers on which are decided by the throw of the dice. An aquiline nose, and delicately formed lips would have given a noble appearance to his countenance, but his prominent glassy eyes were almost repulsive, and his black bushy eyebrows had the character of a comic mask. Strangely enough there was something lachrymose in the major's face whenever he laughed, which, by the way, seldom happened, while he seemed to laugh whenever the wildest passion mastered him, and in this laugh there was something so terrific, that the oldest and most stout-hearted fellows would shudder at it.

"But, however, seldom as Major O'Malley laughed, it was just as seldom that he allowed himself to be carried away by passion. That the major should ever have a uniform to fit him seemed an utter impossibility. The best tailors in the regiment failed utterly when they applied their art to the formless figure of the major; his coat, though cut according to the most accurate measure, fell into unseemly folds, and hung on his body as if placed there to be brushed, while his sword dangled against his legs, and his hat sat upon his head in such a queer fashion that the military schismatic might be recognised a hundred paces off. A thing quite unheard of in those days in which there was so much pedantry in matters of form – O'Malley wore no tail! To be sure a tail could scarcely have been fastened to the few gray locks that curled at the back of his head, and, with the exception of these, he was perfectly bald. When the major rode, people expected every moment to see him tumble from his horse, when he fought they expected to see him beaten; and yet he was the very best rider and fencer – in a word, the very best *Gymnastiker* that could exist.

"This will suffice to give you the picture of a man, whose whole mode of life might be called mysterious, as he now threw away large sums, now seemed in want of assistance, and removed from all the control of superiors, and every restraint of service, could do exactly as he liked. And even that which he did like was so eccentric, or rather so splenetically mad, that one felt uneasy about his sanity. They said that the major, at a certain period, when Potsdam and its environs was the scene of a strange mystification, that even found a place in the history of the day, had played an important part, and still stood in certain relations, which caused the incomprehensibility of his position. A book of very ill-repute, which appeared at the time – it was called 'Excorporations', if I mistake not, – and which contained the portrait of a man very like the major, increased that belief, and I, struck by the mysterious contents of this book, felt the more inclined to consider O'Malley a sort of Arminian, the more I observed his chimerical, I may almost say supernatural proceedings. He himself gave me additional opportunity to make such observations, for since the evening on which I found him ill, or otherwise overcome, in the wood, he had taken an especial fancy to me, so that it seemed absolutely necessary for him to see me every day. To describe to you the whole peculiarity of this intercourse with the major, to tell you a great deal that seemed to confirm the judgment of the men, who boldly maintained that he had second-sight, and was in compact with the devil, would be superfluous, as you will soon have sufficient knowledge of the awful spirit that was destined to disturb the peace of my life.

"I was on guard at the castle, and there received a visit from my cousin, Captain von T—, who had come with a young officer from Berlin to Potsdam. We were indulging in friendly converse over our wine, when, towards midnight, Major O'Malley entered. 'I thought to find you alone, lieutenant,' said he, casting glances of displeasure at my guests, and he wished to depart at once. The captain then reminded him that they were old acquaintance, and at my request he consented to remain.

"'Your wine,' exclaimed O'Malley, as he tossed down a bumper, after his usual manner; 'your wine, lieutenant, is the vilest stuff that ever tortured an honest fellow's bowels. Let us see if this is of a better sort.'

"He then took a bottle from the pocket of the cloak which he had drawn over his shirt, and filled the glasses. We pronounced the wine excellent, and considered it to be very fiery Hungarian.

"Somehow or other, I cannot say how, conversation turned upon magical operations, and particularly upon the book of ill report, to which I have already alluded. The captain, especially when he had drunk wine, had a certain scoffing tone, which everyone could not endure, and in this tone he began to talk about military exorcisors and wizards, who had done very pretty things at that time, so that even at the present time people revered their power, and made offerings to it. 'Whom do you mean?' cried O'Malley, in a threatening tone; 'whom do you mean, captain? If you mean me, we will put the subject of raising spirits aside; I can show you that I understand the art of conjuring the soul out of the body, and for that art I require no talisman but my sword or a good pistol-barrel.'

"There was nothing the captain desired less than a quarrel with O'Malley. He therefore gave a neat turn to the subject, asserting that he did indeed mean the major, but intended nothing but a jest, which was, perhaps, an ill-timed one. Now, however, he would ask the major in earnest, whether he would not do well by contradicting the silly rumour that he commanded mysterious powers, and thus, in his own person, check the foolish superstition, which by no means accorded with an age so enlightened. The major leaned completely across the table, rested his head on both his fists, so that his nose was scarcely a span removed from the captain's face, and then said very calmly, staring at him with his prominent eyes: 'Even, friend, if Heaven has not blessed you with a very penetrating intellect, I hope you will be able to see, that it is the silliest conceit, nay, I may say, the most atrocious presumption to believe that with our own spiritual existence everything is concluded, and that there are no spiritual beings, which, differently endowed from ourselves, often from their own nature alone, make themselves temporary forms, manifest themselves in space and time, and further, aiming at a sort of reaction, can take refuge in the mass of clay, which we call a body. I do not reproach you, captain, for not having read, and for being ignorant of everything that cannot be learned at a review or on parade, but this I will tell you, that if you had peeped now and then into clever books, and knew Cardanus, Justin Martyr, Lactantius, Cyprian, Clement of Alexandria, Macrobius, Trismegistus, Nollius, Dorneus, Theophrastus, Fludd, William Postel, Mirandola; nay, even the cabalistic Jews, Josephus and Philo, you might have had an inkling of things which are at present above your horizon, and of which you therefore have no right to talk.'

"With these words O'Malley sprang up, and walked up and down with heavy steps, so that the windows and glasses vibrated.

"The captain, somewhat astonished, assured the major, that although he had the highest esteem for his learning, and did not wish to deny that there were, nay, must be, higher spiritual natures, he was firmly convinced that any communication with an unknown spiritual world was contrary to the very conditions of humanity, and therefore impossible, and that anything advanced as a proof of the contrary, was based on self-delusion or imposture.

"After the captain had been silent for a few seconds, O'Malley suddenly stood still, and began, 'Captain, or,' – turning to me – 'lieutenant, do me the favour to sit down and write an epic as noble and as superhumanly great as the *Iliad*.'

"We both answered that neither of us would succeed, as neither of us had the Homeric genius. 'Ha! Ha!' cried the major, 'Mark that, captain! Because your mind is incapable of conceiving and bringing forth the divine; nay, because your nature is not so constituted, that it can even kindle into the knowledge of it, you presume to deny that such things are possible with anyone. I tell you, the intercourse with higher spiritual natures depends on a particular *psychic* organisation. That organisation, like the creative power of poetry, is a gift which the spirit of the universe bestows upon its favourites.'

"I read in the captain's face, that he was on the point of making some satirical reply to the major. To stop this, I took up the conversation myself, and remarked to the major that, as far as I had any knowledge of the subject, the cabalists prescribed certain rules and forms, that intercourse with unknown spiritual beings might be attained. Before the major could reply, the captain, who was heated with wine, sprang from his seat, and said bitterly, 'What is the use of all this talking? You give yourself out as a superior being, major, and want to believe, that because you are made of better stuff than any of us, you command spirits! You must allow me to believe that you are nothing but a besotted dreamer, until you give us some ocular demonstration of your *psychic* power.'

"The major laughed wildly, and said, 'So, captain, you take me for a common necromancer, a miserable juggler, do you? That accords with your limited view! However, you shall be permitted to take a peep into a dark region of which you have no notion, and which may, perhaps, have a destructive effect upon you. I warn you against it, and would have you reflect, that your mind may not be strong enough to bear many things, which to me would be no more than agreeable pastime.'

"The captain protested that he was quite ready to cope with all the spirits and devils that O'Malley could raise, and we were obliged to give our word of honour to the major that we would meet him at ten o'clock on the night of the autumnal equinox, at the inn near the gate, when we should learn more.

"In the meanwhile it had become clear daylight; the sun was shining through the window. The major then placed himself in the middle of the room, and cried with a voice of thunder, 'Incubus! Incubus! Nehmahmihah Scedim!' He then threw off his cloak, which he had not yet laid aside, and stood in full uniform.

"At that moment I was obliged to leave the room as the guard was getting under arms. When I returned, the major and the captain had both vanished.

"'I only stayed behind,' said the young officer, a good, amiable youth, whom I found alone. 'I only stayed behind to warn you against this major, this fearful man! I will have nothing to do with his fearful secrets, and I only regret that I have given my word to be present at a deed, which will be destructive, perhaps, to us all, and certainly to the captain. You may depend upon it that I am not inclined to believe in the tales that old nurses tell to children; but did you observe that the major successively took eight bottles from his pocket, that seemed scarcely large enough to hold one? That at last, although he wore nothing but his shirt under his cloak, he suddenly stood attired by invisible hands?' It was, indeed, as the lieutenant had said, and I felt an icy shudder come over me.

"On the appointed day the captain called upon me with my young friend, and at the stroke of ten we were at the inn as we had promised the major. The lieutenant was silent and reserved, but the captain was so much the louder and in high spirits. 'Indeed!' he cried, when it was already half-past ten, and no O'Malley had made his appearance, 'Indeed I believe that the conjuror has left us in the lurch with all his spirits and devils!' 'That he has not,' said a voice close behind the captain, and O'Malley was among us without anyone having seen how he entered. The laugh, into which the captain was about to break, died away.

"The major, who was dressed as usual in his military cloak, thought that there was time to drink a few glasses of punch before he took us to the place where he designed to fulfill his promise. It would do us good as the night was cold and rough, and we had a tolerably long way to go. We sat down at a table, on which the major had laid some links bound together, and a book.

"'Ho ho!' cried the captain, 'This is your conjuring book is it, major?'

"'Most assuredly,' replied O'Malley, drily.

"The captain seized the book, opened it, and at that moment laughed so immoderately, that we did not know what could have struck him, as being so very ridiculous.

"'Come,' said he, recovering himself with difficulty, 'come, this is too bad! What the devil, major – oh, you want to play your tricks upon us, or have you made some mistake? Only look here, comrades!'

"You may conceive our astonishment, friend Albert, when we saw that the book which the captain held before our eyes, was no other than 'Peplier's French Grammar'. O'Malley took the book out of the captain's hand, put it into the pocket in his cloak, and then said very quietly – indeed his whole demeanour was quiet and milder than usual – 'It must be very immaterial to you, captain, of what instruments I make use to fulfill my promise, which only binds me to give you a sensible demonstration of my intercourse with the world of spirits which surrounds us, and which, in fact, comprises the condition of our higher being. Do you think that my power requires such paltry crutches as especial mystical forms, choice of a particular time, a remote awful spot – things which paltry cabalists are in the habit of employing for their useless experiments? In the open market-place, at every hour, I could show you my power; and when, after you had presumptuously enough challenged me to enter the lists, I chose a particular time, and, as you will perceive, a place that you may think rather awful, I only wished to show a civility to him, who, on this occasion, is to be in some sort your guest. One likes to receive guests in one's best room, and at the most suitable hour.'

"It struck eleven, the major took up the torches, and desired us to follow him.

"He strode so quickly along the high road that we had a difficulty in following him, and when we had reached the toll-house, turned into a footpath on the right, that led to a thick wood of firs. After we had run for nearly an hour, the major stood still, and told us to keep close behind him, as we might otherwise lose ourselves in the thicket of the wood that we now had to enter. We went through the densest bushes, so that one or the other of us was constantly caught by the uniform or the sword, so as to extricate himself with difficulty, until at last we came to an open space. The moonbeams were breaking through the dark clouds, and I perceived the ruins of a large building, into which the major strode. It grew darker and darker; the major desired us to stand still, as he wished to conduct every one of us down singly. He began with the captain, and my turn came next. The major clasped me round, and I was more carried by him than I walked into the depth. 'Stop here,' whispered the major, 'stop here quietly till I have fetched the lieutenant, then my work shall begin.'

"Amid the impenetrable darkness I heard the breathing of a person who stood close by me. 'Is that you, captain?' I exclaimed. 'Certainly it is,' replied the captain, 'have a care, cousin; this will all end in foolish jugglery, but it is a cursed place to which the major has brought us, and I wish we were sitting at a bowl of punch, for my limbs are all trembling with cold, and, if you will have it so, with a certain childish apprehension.'

"It was no better with me than with the captain. The boisterous autumn wind whistled and howled through the walls, and a strange groaning and whispering answered it from below. Scared night birds swept fluttering by us, while a low whining noise seemed to be gliding away close to the ground. Truly both the captain and myself might say of the horrors of our situation the same thing that Cervantes says of Don Quixote, when he passes the portentous night before the adventure with the fulling-mills: 'One less courageous would have lost his presence of mind altogether.' The splashing of some water in the vicinity, and the barking of dogs, showed that we were not far from the leather-manufactory, which is by the river in the neighbourhood of Potsdam. We at last heard some dully sounding steps, which became nearer and nearer until the major cried out close to us: 'Now we are together, and that which we have begun can be completed.' By means of a chemical fire-box he kindled the torches which he had brought with him and stuck them in the ground. They were seven in number. We found that we were in the ruined vault of a cellar. O'Malley ranged us in a half-circle, threw off his cloak and shirt, so that he remained naked to the waist, and opening the book began to read as follows, in a voice that more resembled the dull roaring of a distant beast of prey than the sound of a human being: *Monsieur, pretez moi un peu, s'il vous plâit, votre canif. – Oui, Monsieur, d'abord – le voilà, je vous le rendrai.*'

"Come," said Albert, here interrupting his friend, "this is indeed too bad! The dialogue 'On writing', from *Peplier's Grammar*, as a formula for exorcism! And you did not laugh out and bring the whole thing to an end at once?"

"I am now," continued Victor, "coming to a moment which I doubt whether I shall succeed in describing. May your fancy only give animation to my words! The major's voice grew more awful, while the wind howled more loudly, and the flickering light of the torches covered the walls with strange forms, that changed as they flitted by. I felt the cold perspiration dripping on my forehead, and forcibly succeeded in preserving my presence of mind, when a cutting tone whistled through the vault, and close before my eyes stood something –"

"How?" cried Albert. "Something! What do you mean, Victor? A frightful form?"

"It sounds absurd," continued Victor, "to talk of 'a formless form', but I can find no other word to express the hideous something that I saw. It is enough to say that at that moment the horror of hell thrust its pointed ice-dagger into my heart, and I became insensible. At broad mid-day I found myself undressed and lying upon my couch. All the horrors of the night had passed, and I felt quite well and easy. My young friend, the lieutenant, was asleep in the arm-chair. As soon as I stirred he awoke, and testified the greatest joy at finding me in perfect health. From him I learned that as soon as the major had begun his gloomy work, he had closed his eyes, and had endeavoured closely to follow the dialogue from *Peplier's Grammar*, without regarding anything else. Notwithstanding all his efforts, a fearful apprehension, hitherto unknown, had gained the mastery over him, though he preserved his consciousness. The frightful whistle, was, he said, followed by wild laughter. He had once involuntarily opened his eyes, and perceived the major, who had again thrown his mantle round him, and was upon the point of taking upon his shoulders the captain, who lay senseless on the ground. 'Take care of your friend,' cried O'Malley to the lieutenant, and giving him a torch, he went up with the captain. The lieutenant then spoke to me, as I stood there immoveable, but it was to no purpose. I seemed quite paralysed, and he had the greatest difficulty in bringing me into the open air. Suddenly the major returned, took me on his shoulders, and carried me away as he had carried the captain before. But what was the horror of the lieutenant, when on leaving the wood, he saw a second O'Malley who was carrying the captain along the broad path! However, silently praying to himself, he got the better of his horror, and followed me, firmly resolved not to quit me, happen what might, till we reached my quarters, where O'Malley set me down and left me, without speaking a word. With the help of my servant – who even then, was my honest Eulenspiegel, Paul Talkebarth; the lieutenant had brought me into my room, and put me to bed.

"Having concluded this narrative, my young friend implored me, in the most touching manner, to shun all association with the terrible O'Malley. The physician, who had been called in, found the captain in the inn by the gate, where we had assembled, struck speechless by apoplexy. He recovered, indeed, but remained unfit for the service, and was forced to quit it. The major had vanished, having, as the officers said, obtained leave of absence. I was glad that I did not see him again, for a deep indignation had mingled itself with the horror which his dark mode of life occasioned. My cousin's misfortune was the work of O'Malley, and it seemed my duty to take a sanguinary revenge.

"A considerable time had elapsed, and the remembrance of that fatal night grew faint. The occupations required by the service overcame my propensity to mystical dreaming. A book then fell into my hands, the effect of which, on my whole being, seemed perfectly inexplicable, even to myself. I mean that strange story of Cazotte's, which is known in a German translation as 'Teufel Amor' (The Devil Love). My natural bashfulness, nay, a kind of childish timidity, had kept me from the society of ladies, while the particular direction of my mind resisted every ebullition of rude passion. Now, for the first time, was a sensual tendency revealed in me which I had never suspected. My pulse beat high, a consuming fire coursed through nerves and veins, as I went through those scenes of the most dangerous, nay, most horrible love, which the poet had described in the most glowing colours. I saw, I heard, I was sensible to nothing but the charming Biondetta. I sank under the pleasing torments, like Alvarez –"

"Stop, stop!" interrupted Albert, "I have no very clear remembrance of Cazotte's 'Diable Amoureux'; but, so far as I recollect, the whole story turns upon the circumstance that a young officer of the guards, in the service of the King of Naples, is tempted by a mystical comrade to raise the devil in the ruins of Portici. When he has uttered the formula of exorcism, a hideous camel's head, with a long neck, thrust itself towards him out of a window, and cries, in a horrible voice, '*Che vuoi.*' Alvarez – so is the young officer named – commands the spectre to appear in the shape of a spaniel, and then in that of a page. This happens; but the page soon becomes a most charming, amorous girl, and completely entangles the enchanter. How Cazotte's pretty story concludes has quite escaped me."

"That is at present quite immaterial," said Victor; "but you will perhaps be reminded of it by the conclusion to my story. Attribute it to my propensity to the wonderful, and also to something mysterious which I experienced, that Cazotte's tale soon appeared to me a magic mirror, in which I could discern my own fate. Was not O'Malley to me that mystical Dutchman who decoyed Alvarez by his arts?

"The desire which glowed in my heart, of achieving the terrible adventure of Alvarez, filled me with horror; but even this horror made me tremble with unspeakable delight, such as I had never before known. Often did a wish arise within me, that O'Malley would return and place in my arms the hell-birth, to which my entire self was abandoned, and I could not kill the sinful hope and deep abhorrence which again darted through my heart like a dagger. The strange mood produced by my excited condition remained a mystery to all; they thought I suffered from some morbid state of mind, and sought to cheer me and dissipate my gloomy thoughts.

"Under the pretext of some service, they sent me to the *Residence*, where the most brilliant circle was open to me. But if I had always been shy and bashful, society – especially the approach of ladies – now produced in me absolute repugnance. The most charming only seemed to scoff at Biondetta's image which I bore within me. When I returned to Potsdam, I shunned all association with my comrades, and my favourite abode was the wood – the scene of those frightful events that had nearly cost my poor cousin his life. I stood close by the ruins, and, being impelled by an undefined desire, was on the point of making my way in, through the thick brushwood, when I suddenly saw O'Malley, who walked slowly out, and did not seem to perceive me. My long repressed anger boiled up instantly, I darted upon the major, and told him in few words, that he must fight with me on account of my cousin. 'Be it so at once,' said the major, coldly and gravely, and he threw off his mantle, drew his sword, and at the very first pass struck mine out of my hand with irresistible force and dexterity. 'We will fight with pistols,' cried I, wild with rage, and was about to pick up my sword, when O'Malley held me fast, and said, in a calm mild tone, such as I had scarcely ever heard from him before: 'Do not be a fool, my son! You see that I am your superior in fighting; you could sooner wound the air than me, and I could never prevail on myself to stand in a hostile position to you, to whom I owe my life, and indeed something more.'

"The major then took me by the arm, and gently drawing me along, proved to me that the captain alone had been the cause of his own misfortune, since, in spite of every warning, he had ventured on things to which he was unequal, and had forced the major to do what he did, by his ill-timed and insulting raillery. I myself cannot tell what a singular magic there was in O'Malley's words, nay, in his whole manner. He not only succeeded in quieting me, but had such an effect upon me, that I involuntarily revealed to him the secret of my internal condition – of the destructive warfare that was carried on within my soul. 'The particular constellation,' said O'Malley, when I had finished, 'which rules over you, my son, has now ordained that a silly book should make you attentive to your own internal being. I call the book silly, because it treats of a goblin that is at once repulsive and without character. What you ascribe to the effect of these licentious images of the poet is nothing but an impulse towards a union with a spiritual being of another region, which results from your happily constituted organisation. If you had shown more confidence in me, you would have been on a higher grade long ago. However, I will take you as my scholar.'

"O'Malley now began to make me acquainted with the nature of elementary spirits. I understood little that he said, but all referred to the doctrine of sylphs, undines, salamanders, and gnomes, such as you may find in the dialogues of the Comte de Cabalis. He concluded by prescribing me a particular course of life, and thought that in the course of a year I might obtain my Biondetta, who would certainly not do me the wrong of changing into the incarnate Satan in my arms. With the same ardour as Alvarez, I thought that I should die of impatience in so long a time, and would venture anything to attain my end sooner. The major remained reflecting in silence for some moments, and then said: 'It is certain that an elementary spirit is seeking your good graces. This may enable you to obtain that in a short time, for which others strive during whole years. I will cast your horoscope. Perhaps your mistress will reveal herself to me. In nine days you shall hear more.' I actually counted the hours, feeling now penetrated by a mysterious delightful hope, and now as if I had involved myself in a dangerous affair.

"Late in the evening of the ninth day, the major at last entered my room, and desired me to follow him. 'Are we to go to the ruins?' I asked. 'Certainly not,' replied O'Malley, smiling, 'for the work which we now have in hand, we want neither a remote awful spot, nor a terrible exorcism out of Peplier's grammar. Besides, my incubus can have no part in today's experiment, which, properly speaking, you undertake, not I.' The major conducted me to his quarters, and there explained to me that the matter was to procure something by means of which my own self might be opened to the elementary spirit, and the latter might have the power of revealing itself to me in the invisible world, and holding intercourse with me. This *something* was what the Jewish cabalists called 'Teraphim'. He now pushed aside a bookcase, opened the door concealed behind it, and we entered a little vaulted cabinet, in which, besides all sorts of strange unknown utensils, I saw a complete apparatus for chemical – or, as I might almost believe – alchemical experiments. From the glaring charcoal on a small hearth were darting forth little blue flames.

"Before this hearth I had to sit opposite the major, and to uncover my bosom. I had no sooner done this, than the major, before I was aware of it, scratched me with a lancet under the left breast, and caught in a little vial the few drops of blood that flowed from the slight wound, which I could scarcely feel. He next took a bright plate of metal, polished like a mirror, poured upon it first another vial that contained a reddish liquid, and afterwards the one filled with my blood, and then held the plate close over the charcoal fire. I was seized with deep horror, when I thought I saw a long, pointed, glaring tongue rise serpent-like upon the coals, and greedily lick away the blood from the metallic mirror. The major now told me to look into the fire with a mind firmly fixed. I did so, and soon I seemed to behold, as in a dream, a number of confused forms, flashing through one another on the metal, which the major still held over the charcoal. Suddenly, I felt in my breast, where the major had scratched my skin, such a strong, piercing pain, that I involuntarily shrieked aloud. 'Won! Won!' cried O'Malley at that instant, and, rising from his seat, he placed before me on the hearth a little doll, about two inches long, into which the metal seemed to have formed itself. 'That,' said the major, 'is your Teraphim. The favours of the elementary spirit towards you seem to be more than ordinary. You may now venture on the utmost.'

"At the major's bidding, I took the little figure, from which, though it looked red-hot, only a genial warmth was streaming, pressed it to the wound, and placed myself before a round mirror, from which the major had withdrawn the covering. 'Force your wishes,' said O'Malley, 'to the greatest intensity, which will not be difficult, as the Teraphim is operating, and utter in the sweetest tone of which you are capable, the word —.' To tell you the truth, I have forgotten the strange-sounding word, which was spoken by O'Malley. Scarcely had half the syllables passed my lips, than an ugly, madly-distorted face grinned at me spitefully from the mirror. 'In the name of all the devils, whence come you, you accursed dog?' yelled O'Malley behind me. I turned round, and saw my Paul Talkebarth, who was standing in the door-way, and whose handsome face was reflected in the magic mirror. The major, wild with rage, flew at honest Paul; yet, before I could get between them, O'Malley stood close to him, perfectly motionless, and Paul availed himself of the opportunity to make a prolix apology; saying, how he had looked for me, how he had found the door open, how he had walked in, etc. 'Begone, rascal,' said O'Malley at last, in a quieter tone, and when I added, 'Go, good Paul, I will return home directly'; the Eulenspiegel departed quite terrified and confounded.

"I had held the doll fast in my hand, and O'Malley assured me that it was owing to this circumstance alone that all our labour had not been in vain. Talkebarth's ill-timed intrusion had, however, delayed the completion of the work for a long time. He advised me to turn off that faithful servant, but this I had not the heart to do. Moreover, he assured me that the elementary spirit which had shown me such favour, was nothing less than a salamander, as indeed, he suspected, when he cast my horoscope and found that Mars stood in the first house. I now come again to moments of which you can have but a slight notion, as words are incapable of describing them. The Devil Amor, Biondetta – all was forgotten; I thought only of my Teraphim. For whole hours I could look at the doll, as it lay on the table before me, and the glow of love that streamed through my veins seemed then, like the heavenly fire of Prometheus, to animate the little figure which grew up as in ardent longing. But this form vanished as soon as I had thought it, and the unspeakable anguish which cut through my heart, was associated with a strange indignation, that impelled me to fling the doll away from me as a miserable ridiculous toy. Yet when I grasped it, an electric shock seemed to dart through all my limbs, and I felt as if a separation from the talisman of love would annihilate me.

"I will openly confess to you that my passion, although the proper object of it was an elementary spirit, was directed among all sorts of equivocal dreams towards objects in the miserable world that surrounded me, so that my excited fancy made now this, now that lady, the representative of the coy salamander that eluded my embrace. I confessed my wrong, indeed, and entreated my little mystery to pardon my infidelity; but by the declining power of that strange crisis, which had ordinarily moved my inmost soul with glowing love; nay, by a certain unpleasant void, I could plainly feel that I was receding from my object rather than approaching it. And yet the passions of a youth, blooming in full vigour, seemed to deride my mystery and my repugnance. I trembled at the slightest touch of a charming woman, though I found myself red with blushes. Chance conducted me again to the *Residence*. I saw the Countess von L—, the most charming woman, and the greatest lover of conquests that then shone in the first circles of Berlin. She cast her glances upon me, and the mood in which I then was naturally rendered it very easy for her to lure me completely into her toils. Nay, she at last induced me to reveal my whole soul, without reserve, to discover my secret, and even to show her the mysterious image that I wore upon my breast."

"And," interrupted Albert, "did she not laugh at you heartily, and call you a besotted youth?"

"Nothing of the sort," continued Victor; "she listened to me with a seriousness which she had not shown on any other occasion, and when I had finished, she implored me, with tears in her eyes, to renounce the diabolical arts of the infamous O'Malley. Taking me by both my hands, and looking at me with an expression of the tenderest love, she spoke of the dark practices of the cabalistic art in a manner so learned and so profound, that I was not a little surprised. But my astonishment reached the highest point when she called the major the most abandoned, abominable traitor, for trying to lure me into destruction by his black art, when I had saved his life. Weary of existence, and in danger of being crushed to the earth by the deepest ignominy, O'Malley was, it seems, on the point of shooting himself, when I stepped in and prevented the suicide, for which he no longer felt any inclination, as the evil that oppressed him had been averted. The countess concluded by assuring me, that if the major had plunged me into a state of psychic distemper, she would save me, and that the first step to that end would consist in my delivering the little image into her hands. This I did readily, for thus I thought I should, in the most beautiful manner, be freed from a useless torment. The countess would not have been what she really was had she not let a lover pine a long time in vain – and this course she pursued with me. At last, however, my passion was to be requited. At midnight a confidential servant waited for me at the back door of the palace, and led me through distant passages into an apartment which the god of love seemed to have decorated. There I was to expect the countess. Half overcome by the fumes of the fine scents that wound through the chamber, trembling with love and expectation, I stood in the midst of the room. All at once a glance darted through my soul like a flash of lightning –"

"How!" cried Albert, "a glance, and no eyes! And you saw nothing? Another formless form!"

"You may find it incomprehensible," said Victor, "but so it was; I could see no form – nothing, and yet I felt the glance deep in my bosom, and a sudden pain quivered at the spot which O'Malley had wounded. At the same moment I perceived upon the chimney-piece my little image, grasped it, darted from the room, commanded the terrified servant, with a threatening gesture, to lead me down, ran home, awakened my man Paul, and had all my things packed up. At the earliest hour of morning I was already on my way back to Potsdam. I had passed several months at the *Residence*, my comrades were delighted at my unexpected return, and kept me fast the whole day, so that I did not return to my quarters till late at night. I placed the darling image I had recovered upon the table, and, no longer able to resist the effects of fatigue, threw myself on my couch without undressing. Soon a dreamy feeling came over me, as if I were surrounded by a beaming light; – I awoke; – I opened my eyes, and the room was indeed gleaming with magical radiance. But – Oh, Heavens! – on the same table on which I had laid the doll, I perceived a female figure, who, resting her head on her hand, appeared to slumber. I can only tell you that I never dreamed of a more delicate or graceful form – a more lovely face. To give you a notion in words of the strange mysterious magic, which beamed from this lovely figure, I am not able. She wore a silken flame-coloured dress, which, fitting tight to the waist and bosom, reached only to the ancles, exhibiting her delicately formed feet; the lovely arms, which were bare to the shoulders, and seemed both from their colour and form to have been breathed by Titian, were adorned with bracelets; in her brown, somewhat reddish hair, a diamond sparkled."

"Oh!" said Albert, smiling, "Thy salamandrine has no very exquisite taste. With reddish brown hair, she dresses in flame-coloured silk."

"Do not jest," continued Victor, "do not jest. I repeat to you that under the influence of a mysterious magic, my breath was stopped. At last a deep sigh escaped my oppressed bosom. She then opened her eyes, raised herself, approached me, and grasped my hand. All the glow of the most ardent love darted like a flash of lightning through my soul, when she gently pressed my hand, and whispered with the sweetest voice – 'Yes, thou hast conquered – thou art my ruler – I am thine!' – 'Oh, thou child of the Gods – thou heavenly being!' I cried aloud; and embracing her, I pressed her close to my bosom. But at that instant the creature melted away in my arms."

"How!" said Albert, interrupting his friend, "In Heaven's name, melted away?"

"Melted away," continued Victor, "in my arms. In no other manner can I describe to you my sensation of the incomprehensible disappearance of that lovely being. At the same time the glittering light was extinguished, and I fell, I do not know how, into a profound sleep. When I awoke I held the doll in my hand. I should weary you if I were to tell you more of my strange intercourse with that mysterious being, which now began and lasted for several weeks, than by saying that the visit was repeated every night in the same manner. Much as I strove against it, I could not resist the dreamy situation which came over me, and from which the lovely being awoke me with a kiss. She remained with me longer and longer on every occasion. She said much concerning mysterious things, but I listened more to the sweet melody of her voice, than to the words themselves. Even by day-time I often seemed to feel the warm breath of some being near me; nay, I often heard a whispering, a sighing close by me in society, especially when I spoke with any lady, so that all my thoughts were directed to my lovely mysterious mistress, and I was dumb and lifeless for all surrounding objects.

"It once happened at a party that a lady bashfully approached me to give me the kiss which I had won at a game of forfeits. But when I bent to her I felt – before my lips had touched hers – a loud kiss upon my mouth, and a soft voice whispered at the same time, 'To me alone do your kisses belong.' Both I and the lady were somewhat alarmed, while the rest of the party thought we had kissed in reality. This kiss I held to be a sign that Aurora – so I called my mysterious mistress – would now for good and all take some living shape, and no more leave me. When the lovely one again appeared to me on the following night, I entreated her in the usual manner, and in the most touching words, such as the ardour of love inspired to complete my happiness, and to be mine for ever in a visible form. She gently extricated herself from my arms, and then said with mild earnestness, 'You know in what manner you became my master. My happiest wish was to belong to you entirely; but the fetters that bind me to the throne to which the race, of which I am one, is subjected, are only half-broken. The stronger, the more potent your sway, so much the freer do I feel from tormenting slavery. Our intercourse will become more and more intimate, and perhaps the goal may be reached before a year has elapsed. Would you, beloved, anticipate the destiny that presides over us, many a sacrifice, many a step, apparently doubtful, might be necessary.' – 'No!' I exclaimed, 'for me nothing will be a sacrifice, no step will appear doubtful to obtain thee entirely. I cannot live longer without thee, I am dying of impatience – of unspeakable pain!' Then Aurora embraced me, and whispered in a scarcely audible voice, 'Art thou happy in my arms?' – 'There is no other happiness,' I exclaimed, and glowing with love even to madness, I pressed the charming creature to my bosom. I felt living kisses upon my lips, and these very kisses were melodies of heaven, through which I heard the words, 'Couldst thou, to possess me, renounce the happiness of an unknown hereafter?' An icy cold shudder trembled through me, but in the midst of this shudder passion raged still more furiously, and I cried in the involuntary madness of love, 'Without thee there is no happiness! – I renounce –'

"I still believe that I stopped here. 'Tomorrow night our compact will be concluded,' whispered Aurora, and I felt that she was about to vanish from my arms. I pressed her to me with greater force, she seemed to struggle in vain, when suddenly – I awoke from deep slumber, thinking of the Devil Amor, and the seductive Biondetta. What I had done in that fatal night fell heavily upon my soul. I thought of that unholy invocation by the horrible O'Malley, of the warnings of my pious young friend. I believed that I was in the toils of the evil one – that I was lost. Torn to the very depth of my soul, I sprang up and hastened into the open air. In the street I was met by the major, who held me fast while he said: 'I congratulate you, lieutenant! To tell you the truth, I scarcely gave you credit for so much courage and resolution; you outstrip your master.' Glowing with rage and shame, incapable of uttering a single word, I freed myself from his grasp and pursued my way. The major laughed behind me, and I could detect the scornful laughter of Satan. In the road near those fatal ruins, I perceived a veiled female form, who, lying under a tree, seemed absorbed in a soliloquy. I approached her cautiously, and overheard the words: 'He is mine, he is mine – oh! Bliss of heaven! Even the last trial he has withstood. If men are capable of such love, what is our wretched existence without it?' You may guess that it was Aurora whom I found. She threw back her veil, and love itself cannot be more charming. The delicate paleness of her cheeks, the glance that was sublimed into the sweetest melancholy, made me tremble with unspeakable pleasure. I felt ashamed of my dark thoughts; yet at the very moment when I wished to throw myself at her feet, she had vanished like a form of mist. At the same time I heard a sound in the hedges, as of one clearing one's throat, and out stepped my honest Eulenspiegel, Paul Talkebarth. 'Whence did the devil bring you, fellow?' I began.

"'No, no,' said he, with that queer smile which you know, 'the devil did not bring me here, but very likely he met me. You went out so early, gracious lieutenant, and had forgotten your pipe and tobacco, and I thought so early in the morning, in the damp air – for my aunt at Genthin used to say –'

"'Hold your tongue, prattle, and give me that,' cried I, as I made him hand me the lighted pipe. Scarcely, however, had we proceeded a few paces, than Paul began again very softly, 'My aunt at Genthin used to say, the Root-mannikin (*Wurzelmännlein*) was not to be trusted; indeed, such a chap was no better than an incubus or a chezim, and ended by breaking one's heart. Old coffee Lizzy here in the suburbs – ah, gracious sir, you should only see what fine flowers, and men, and animals she can pour out. Man should help himself as he can, my aunt at Genthin used to say. I was yesterday with Lizzy and took her a little fine mocha. One of us has a heart as well as the rest – Becker's Dolly is a pretty thing, but then there is something so odd about her eyes, so salamander-like –'

"'What is that you say, fellow?' I exclaimed, hastily. Paul was silent, but began again in a few seconds: 'Yes, Lizzy is a good woman after all; she said, after she had looked at the coffee grounds, that there was nothing the matter with Dolly, and that the salamander look about the eyes came from cracknel-baking or the dancing-room; but, at the same time, she advised me to remain single, and told me that a certain good gentleman was in great danger. These salamanders, she said, are the worst sort of things that the devil employs to lure a poor human soul to destruction, because they have certain passions – ah, one must only stand firm and keep God in one's heart – then I myself saw in the coffee grounds Major O'Malley quite like and natural.'

"I bid the fellow hold his tongue, but you may conceive the feelings that were awakened in me at this strange discourse of Paul's, whom I suddenly found initiated into my dark secret, and who so unexpectedly displayed a knowledge of cabalistic matters, for which he was probably indebted to the coffee-prophetess. I passed the most uneasy day I ever had in my life. Paul was not to be got out of the room all that evening, but was constantly returning and finding something to do. When it was near midnight, and he was at last obliged to go, he said softly, as if praying to himself: 'Bear God in thy heart – think of the salvation of thy soul – and thou wilt resist the enticements of Satan.'

"I cannot describe the manner – I may almost say, the fearful manner – in which my soul was moved at these simple words of my servant. All my endeavours to keep myself awake were in vain. I fell into that state of confused dreaming, which I could not look upon as natural, but as the operation of some foreign principle. The magical beaming woke me as usual. Aurora in the full lustre of supernatural beauty, stood before me, and passionately stretched her arms towards me. Nevertheless, Paul's pious words shone in my soul as if written there with letters of fire. 'Depart, thou seductive birth of hell!' I cried, when the terrible O'Malley, now of a gigantic stature, rose before me, and piercing me with eyes, from which an infernal fire was flashing, howled out: 'Resist not – poor atom of humanity. Thou hast become ours!' My courage could have withstood the frightful aspect of the most hideous spectre, but I lost my senses at the sight of O'Malley, and fell to the ground.

"A loud report awoke me from this state of stupefaction. I felt myself held by the arms of a man, and struggled with all the force of despair, to free myself. 'Gracious lieutenant, it is I,' said a voice in my ears. It was honest Paul who endeavoured to raise me from the ground. I let him have his own way. He would not at first tell me plainly how all had happened, but he at last assured me, with a mysterious smile, that he knew better to what unholy acquaintance the major had lured me, than I could suspect. The old pious Lizzy had revealed everything to him. He had not gone to sleep the night before, but had well loaded his gun, and had watched at the door. When he had heard me cry aloud and fall to the ground, he had, although his courage failed him a little, burst open the door and entered. 'There,' he continued in his mad way, 'there stood Major O'Malley before me, as frightful to look upon as in the cup of coffee. He grinned at me hideously, but I did not allow myself to be stirred from my purpose and said: 'If, gracious major, you are the devil, pardon me for stepping boldly up to you as a pious Christian and saying to you: 'Avaunt, thou cursed Satan-Major, I command thee in the name of the Lord. Begone, or I will fire!' The major would not give way, but kept on grinning at me, and began to abuse me. I then cried, 'Shall I fire? – shall I fire? And when he persisted in keeping his place I fired in reality. But all had vanished – both Major Satan and Mam'sell Belzebub had departed through the wall!'

"The continued strain upon the mind during the period that had just passed, together with the last frightful moments, threw me upon a tedious sick-bed. When I recovered I left Potsdam, without seeing any more of O'Malley, whose further fate has remained unknown to me. The image of those portentous days grew fainter and fainter, and at last vanished all together, so that I recovered perfect freedom of mind, until here –"

"Well," asked Albert, with the greatest curiosity and astonishment, "do you mean to say you have lost your freedom again here? I cannot conceive, why here –"

"Oh," said Victor, interrupting his friend, while his tone became somewhat solemn, "I can explain all in two words. In the sleepless nights of the illness, I endured here, all the dreams of that noblest and most terrible period of my life were revived. It was my glowing passion itself, that assumed a form – Aurora – she again appeared to me – glorified – purified in the fire of Heaven; – no devilish O'Malley has further power over her – Aurora is – the baroness!"

"How! What!" cried Albert, shrinking with horror. Then he muttered to himself, "The little plump housewife with the great bunch of keys – she an elementary spirit! – she a salamander!" – and he felt a difficulty in suppressing his laughter.

"In the figure," continued Victor, "there is no longer any trace of resemblance to be found, that is to say, in ordinary life; but the mysterious fire that flashes from her eyes – the pressure of her hand."

"You have been very ill," said Albert, gravely, "for the wound you received in your head was serious enough to put your life in peril; but now I find you are so far recovered that you will be able to go with me. From the very bottom of my heart I implore you, my dear – my beloved friend, to leave this place, and accompany me tomorrow to Aix-la-Chapelle."

"I certainly do not intend to remain here any longer," replied Victor. "so I will go with you; however, let this matter first be cleared up."

The next morning, when Albert woke, Victor told him that a strange, ghostly sort of dream had revealed to him the mysterious word, which O'Malley had taught him, when they prepared the Teraphim. He thought that he would make use of it for the last time. Albert shook his head doubtfully, and caused every thing to be got ready for a speedy departure, while Paul Talkebarth evinced the most joyful activity by all sorts of mad expressions. "Zackermanthö," he muttered to himself in Albert's hearing, "It is a good thing that the devil Bear fetched the Irish devil Foot long ago, otherwise there would have been something wrong now."

Victor, as he had wished, found the baroness alone in her room, occupied with some domestic work. He told her that he was now at last about to quit the house, where he had enjoyed such noble hospitality. The baroness assured him that she had never entertained a friend more dear to her. Victor then took her hand, and asked her if she were ever at Potsdam, and knew a certain Irish Major. "Victor," said the baroness interrupting him hastily, "we shall part today, we shall never see each other again; nay, we must not. A dark veil hangs over my life. Let it suffice if I tell you that a fearful destiny condemns me always to appear a different being from the one which I really am. In the hateful position in which you have found me, and which causes me spiritual torments, which my bodily health seems to belie, I am atoning for a heavy fault – yet no more – farewell!" Upon this, Victor cried with a loud voice: "Nehelmiahmiheal!" and the baroness, with a shriek of horror, fell senseless to the ground. Victor under the influence of a storm of strange feelings, and quite beside himself could scarcely summon resolution enough to ring the bell. However, having done this, he rushed from the chamber. "At once – let us leave at once!" he cried to his friend, and told him in a few words what had happened. Both leaped upon the horses that had been brought for them, and rode off without waiting for the return of the baron, who had gone out hunting.

Albert's reflections on the ride from Liège to Aix-la-Chapelle have already shown, with what profound earnestness, with what noble feeling, he had appreciated the events of that fatal period. On the journey to the Residence, whither the two friends now returned, he succeeded in completely delivering Victor from the dreamy condition into which he had sunk, and while Albert brought to his friend's mind, depicted in the most lively colours, all the monstrous occurrences which the days of the last campaign had brought forth, the latter felt himself animated by the same spirit as that which dwelt in Albert. And although Albert never ventured upon long contradictions or doubts, Victor himself now seemed to look upon his mystical adventure as nothing but a bad dream.

In the Residence it was natural that the ladies were favourably disposed to the colonel, who was rich, of noble figure, young for the high rank which he held, and who, moreover, was amiability itself. Albert looked upon him as a lucky man, who might choose the fairest for a wife, but Victor observed, very seriously: "Whether it was, that I had been mystified, and, by wicked means, made to serve some unknown end, or whether an evil power really tried to tempt me, this much is certain, that though the past has not cost me my happiness, it has deprived me of the paradise of love. Never can that time return, when I felt the highest earthly felicity, when the ideal of my sweetest, most transporting dreams, nay, love itself, was in my arms. Love and pleasure have vanished, since a horrible mystery deprived me of her, who to my inmost heart was really a higher being, such as I shall not again find upon earth!"

The colonel remained unmarried.

J.O.

Mary Burnet

James Hogg

THE FOLLOWING INCIDENTS are related as having occurred at a shepherd's house, not a hundred miles from St Mary's Loch; but, as the descendants of one of the families still reside in the vicinity, I deem it requisite to use names which cannot be recognised, save by those who have heard the story.

John Allanson, the farmer's son of Inverlawn, was a handsome, roving, and incautious young man, enthusiastic, amorous, and fond of adventure, and one who could hardly be said to fear the face of either man, woman, or spirit. Among other love adventures, he fell a-courting Mary Burnet, of Kirkstyle, a most beautiful and innocent maiden, and one who had been bred up in rural simplicity. She loved him, but yet she was afraid of him; and though she had no objection to meeting with him among others, yet she carefully avoided meeting him alone, though often and earnestly urged to it. One day, the young man, finding an opportunity, at Our Lady's Chapel, after mass, urged his suit for a private meeting so ardently, and with so many vows of love and sacred esteem, that Mary was so far won, as to promise, that *perhaps* she would come and meet him.

The trysting place was a little green sequestered spot, on the very verge of the lake, well known to many an angler, and to none better than the writer of this old tale; and the hour appointed, the time when the King's Elwand (now foolishly termed the Belt of Orion) set his first golden knob above the hill. Allanson came too early; and he watched the sky with such eagerness and devotion, that he thought every little star that arose in the south-east the top knob of the King's Elwand. At last the Elwand did arise in good earnest, and then the youth, with a heart palpitating with agitation, had nothing for it but to watch the heathery brow by which bonny Mary Burnet was to descend. No Mary Burnet made her appearance, even although the King's Elwand had now measured its own equivocal length five or six times up the lift.

Young Allanson now felt all the most poignant miseries of disappointment; and, as the story goes, uttered in his heart an unhallowed wish – he wished that some witch or fairy would influence his Mary to come to him in spite of her maidenly scruples. This wish was thrice repeated with all the energy of disappointed love. It was thrice repeated, and no more, when, behold, Mary appeared on the brae, with wild and eccentric motions, speeding to the appointed place. Allanson's excitement seems to have been more than he was able to bear, as he instantly became delirious with joy, and always professed that he could remember nothing of their first meeting, save that Mary remained silent, and spoke not a word, neither good nor bad. In a short time she fell a-sobbing and weeping, refusing to be comforted, and then, uttering a piercing shriek, sprung up, and ran from him with amazing speed.

At this part of the loch, which, as I said, is well known to many, the shore is overhung by a precipitous cliff, of no great height, but still inaccessible, either from above or below. Save in a great drought, the water comes to within a yard of the bottom of this cliff, and the intermediate space is filled with rough unshapely pieces of rock fallen from above. Along this narrow and rude space, hardly passable by the angler at noon, did Mary bound with the swiftness of a kid, although surrounded with darkness. Her lover, pursuing with all his energy, called out, "Mary! Mary! My dear Mary, stop and speak with me. I'll conduct you home, or anywhere you please, but do not run from me. Stop, my dearest Mary – stop!"

Mary would not stop; but ran on, till, coming to a little cliff that jutted into the lake, round which there was no passage, and, perceiving that her lover would there overtake her, she uttered another shriek, and plunged into the lake. The loud sound of her fall into the still water rung in the young man's ears like the knell of death; and if before he was crazed with love, he was now as much so with despair. He saw her floating lightly away from the shore towards the deepest part of the loch; but, in a short time, she began to sink, and gradually disappeared, without uttering a throb or a cry. A good while previous to this, Allanson had flung off his bonnet, shoes, and coat, and plunged in. He swam to the place where Mary disappeared; but there was neither boil nor gurgle on the water, nor even a bell of departing breath, to mark the place where his beloved had sunk. Being strangely impressed, at that trying moment, with a determination to live or die with her, he tried to dive, in hopes either to bring her up or to die in her arms; and he thought of their being so found on the shore of the lake, with a melancholy satisfaction; but by no effort of his could he reach the bottom, nor knew he what distance he was still from it. With an exhausted frame, and a despairing heart, he was obliged again to seek the shore, and, dripping wet as he was, and half naked, he ran to her father's house with the woeful tidings. Everything there was quiet. The old shepherd's family, of whom Mary was the youngest, and sole daughter, were all sunk in silent repose; and oh how the distracted lover wept at the thoughts of wakening them to hear the doleful tidings! But waken them he must; so, going to the little window close by the goodman's bed, he called, in a melancholy tone, "Andrew! Andrew Burnet, are you waking?"

"Troth, man, I think I be: or, at least, I'm half-and-half. What hast thou to say to auld Andrew Burnet at this time o' night?"

"Are you waking, I say?"

"Gudewife, am I waking? Because if I be, tell that stravaiger sae. He'll maybe tak your word for it, for mine he winna tak."

"O Andrew, none of your humour tonight; – I bring you tidings the most woful, the most dismal, the most heart-rending, that ever were brought to an honest man's door."

"To his window, you mean," cried Andrew, bolting out of bed, and proceeding to the door. "Gude sauff us, man, come in, whaever you be, and tell us your tidings face to face; and then we'll can better judge of the truth of them. If they be in concord wi' your voice, they are melancholy indeed. Have the reavers come, and are our kye driven?"

"Oh, alas! Waur than that – a thousand times waur than that! Your daughter – your dear beloved and only daughter, Mary –"

"What of Mary?" cried the goodman. "What of Mary?" cried her mother, shuddering and groaning with terror; and at the same time she kindled a light.

The sight of their neighbour, half-naked, and dripping with wet, and madness and despair in his looks, sent a chillness to their hearts, that held them in silence, and they were unable to utter a word, till he went on thus – "Mary is gone; your darling and mine is lost, and sleeps this night in a watery grave – and I have been her destroyer!"

"Thou art mad, John Allanson," said the old man, vehemently, "raving mad; at least I hope so. Wicked as thou art, thou hadst not the heart to kill my dear child, O yes, you are mad – God be thanked, you are mad. I see it in your looks and demeanour. Heaven be praised, you are mad! You *are* mad; but you'll get better again. But what do I say?" continued he, as recollecting himself, "We can soon convince our own senses. Wife, lead the way to our daughter's bed."

With a heart throbbing with terror and dismay, old Jean Linton led the way to Mary's chamber, followed by the two men, who were eagerly gazing, one over each of her shoulders. Mary's little apartment was in the farther end of the long narrow cottage; and as soon as they entered it, they perceived a form lying on the bed, with the bed-clothes drawn over its head; and on the lid of Mary's little chest, that stood at the bedside, her clothes were lying neatly folded, as they wont to be. Hope seemed to dawn on the faces of the two old people when they beheld this, but the lover's heart sunk still deeper in despair. The father called her name, but the form on the bed returned no answer; however, they all heard distinctly sobs, as of one weeping. The old man then ventured to pull down the clothes from her face; and, strange to say, there indeed lay Mary Burnet, drowned in tears, yet apparently nowise surprised at the ghastly appearance of the three naked figures. Allanson gasped for breath, for he remained still incredulous. He touched her clothes – he lifted her robes one by one – and all of them were dry, neat, and clean, and had no appearance of having sunk in the lake.

There can be no doubt that Allanson was confounded by the strange event that had befallen him, and felt like one struggling with a frightful vision, or some energy beyond the power of man to comprehend. Nevertheless, the assurance that Mary was there in life, weeping although she was, put him once more beside himself with joy; and he kneeled at her bedside, beseeching permission but to kiss her hand. She, however, repulsed him with disdain, saying, with great emphasis – "You are a bad man, John Allanson, and I entreat you to go out of my sight. The sufferings that I have undergone this night, have been beyond the power of flesh and blood to endure; and by some cursed agency of yours have these sufferings been brought about. I therefore pray you, in His name, whose law you have transgressed, to depart out of my sight."

Wholly overcome by conflicting passions, by circumstances so contrary to one another, and so discordant with everything either in the works of Nature or Providence, the young man could do nothing but stand like a rigid statue, with his hands lifted up, and his visage like that of a corpse, until led away by the two old people from their daughter's apartment. They then lighted up a fire to dry him, and began to question him with the most intense curiosity; but they could elicit nothing from him, but the most disjointed exclamations – such as, "Lord in Heaven, what can be the meaning of this!" And at other times – "It is all the enchantment of the devil; the evil spirits have got dominion over me!"

Finding they could make nothing of him, they began to form conjectures of their own. Jean affirmed that it had been the Mermaid of the loch that had come to him in Mary's shape, to allure him to his destruction; but Andrew Burnet, setting his bonnet to one side, and raising his left hand to a level with it, so that he might have full scope to motion and flourish, suiting his action to his words, thus began, with a face of sapience never to be excelled:

"Gudewife, it doth strike me that thou art very wide of the mark. It must have been a spirit of a great deal higher quality than a meer-maiden, who played this extraordinary prank. The meer-maiden is not a spirit, but a beastly sensitive creature, with a malicious spirit within it. Now, what influence could a cauld clatch of a creature like that, wi' a tail like a great saumont-fish, hae ower our bairn, either to make her happy or unhappy? Or where could it borrow her claes, Jean? Tell me that. Na, na, Jean Linton, depend on it, the spirit that courtit wi' poor sinfu' Jock there, has been a fairy; but whether a good ane or an ill ane, it is hard to determine."

Andrew's disquisition was interrupted by the young man falling into a fit of trembling that was fearful to look at, and threatened soon to terminate his existence. Jean ran for the family cordial, observing, by the way, that "though he was a wicked person, he was still a fellow-creature, and might live to repent;" and influenced by this spark of genuine humanity, she made him swallow two horn-spoonfuls of strong aquavitæ. Andrew then put a piece of scarlet thread round each wrist, and taking a strong rowan-tree staff in his hand, he conveyed his trembling and astonished guest home, giving him at parting this sage advice:

"I'll tell you what it is, Jock Allanson – ye hae run a near risk o' perdition, and, escaping that for the present, o' losing your right reason. But tak an auld man's advice – never gang again out by night to beguile ony honest man's daughter, lest a worse thing befall thee."

Next morning Mary dressed herself more neatly than usual, but there was manifestly a deep melancholy settled on her lovely face, and at times the unbidden tear would start into her eye. She spoke no word, either good or bad, that ever her mother could recollect, that whole morning; but she once or twice observed her daughter gazing at her, as with an intense and melancholy interest. About nine o'clock in the morning, she took a hay-raik over her shoulder, and went down to a meadow at the east end of the loch, to coil a part of her father's hay, her father and brother engaging to join her about noon, when they came from the sheep-fold. As soon as old Andrew came home, his wife and he, as was natural, instantly began to converse on the events of the preceding night; and in the course of their conversation, Andrew said, "Gudeness be about us, Jean, was not yon an awfu' speech o' our bairn's to young Jock Allanson last night?"

"Ay, it was a downsetter, gudeman, and spoken like a good Christian lass."

"I'm no sae sure o' that, Jean Linton. My good woman, Jean Linton, I'm no sae sure o' that. Yon speech has gi'en me a great deal o' trouble o' heart; for d'ye ken, an take my life, – ay, an take your life, Jean – nane o' us can tell whether it was in the Almighty's name, or the devil's, that she discharged her lover."

"O fy, Andrew, how can ye say sae? How can ye doubt that it was in the Almighty's name?"

"Couldna she have said sae then, and that wad hae put it beyond a' doubt? And that wad hae been the natural way too; but instead of that, she says, 'I pray you, in the name of him whose law you have transgressed, to depart out o' my sight.' I confess I'm terrified when I think about yon speech, Jean Linton. Didna she say, too, that 'her sufferings had been beyond what flesh and blood could have endured?' What was she but flesh and blood? Didna that remark infer that she was something mair than a mortal creature? Jean Linton, Jean Linton! what will you say, if it should turn out that our daughter *is* drowned, and that yon was the fairy we had in the house a' the night and this morning?"

"O haud your tongue, Andrew Burnet, and dinna make my heart cauld within me. We hae aye trusted in the Lord yet, and he has never forsaken us, nor will he yet gie the Wicked One power ower us or ours."

"Ye say very weel, Jean, and we maun e'en hope for the best," quoth old Andrew; and away he went, accompanied by his son Alexander, to assist their beloved Mary on the meadow.

No sooner had Andrew set his head over the bents and come in view of the meadow, than he said to his son, "I wish Jock Allanson maunna hae been east-the-loch fishing for geds the day, for I think my Mary has made very little progress in the meadow."

"She's ower muckle ta'en up about other things this while, to mind her wark," said Alexander: "I wadna wonder, father, if that lassie gangs a black gate yet."

Andrew uttered a long and a deep sigh, that seemed to ruffle the very fountains of life, and, without speaking another word, walked on to the hay field. It was three hours since Mary had left home, and she ought at least to have put up a dozen coils of hay each hour. But, in place of that, she had put up only seven altogether, and the last was unfinished. Her own hay-raik, that had an M and a B neatly cut on the head of it, was leaning on the unfinished coil, and Mary was wanting. Her brother, thinking she had hid herself from them in sport, ran from one coil to another, calling her many bad names, playfully; but, after he had turned them all up, and several deep swathes besides, she was not to be found. This young man, who slept in the byre, knew nothing of the events of the foregoing night, the old people and Allanson having mutually engaged to keep them a profound secret, and he had therefore less reason than his father to be seriously alarmed. When they began to work at the hay, Andrew could work none; he looked this way and that way, but in no way could he see Mary approaching: so he put on his coat, and went away home, to pour his sorrows into the bosom of his wife; and in the meantime, he desired his son to run to all the neighbouring farming-houses and cots, every one, and make inquiries if anybody had seen Mary.

When Andrew went home and informed his wife that their darling was missing, the grief and astonishment of the aged couple knew no bounds. They sat down, and wept together, and declared, over and over, that this act of Providence was too strange for them, and too high to be understood. Jean besought her husband to kneel instantly, and pray urgently to God to restore their child to them; but he declined it, on account of the wrong frame of his mind, for he declared, that his rage against John Allanson was so extreme, as to unfit him for approaching the throne of his Maker. "But if the profligate refuses to listen to the entreaties of an injured parent," added he, "he shall feel the weight of an injured father's arm."

Andrew went straight away to Inverlawn, though without the least hope of finding young Allanson at home; but, on reaching the place, to his amazement, he found the young man lying ill of a burning fever, raving incessantly of witches, spirits, and Mary Burnet. To such a height had his frenzy arrived, that when Andrew went there, it required three men to hold him in the bed. Both his parents testified their opinions openly, that their son was bewitched, or possessed of a demon, and the whole family was thrown into the greatest consternation. The good old shepherd, finding enough of grief there already, was obliged to confine his to his own bosom, and return disconsolate to his little family circle, in which there was a woeful blank that night.

His son returned also from a fruitless search. No one had seen any traces of his sister, but an old crazy woman, at a place called Oxcleuch, said that she had seen her go by in a grand chariot with young Jock Allanson, toward the Birkhill Path, and by that time they were at the Cross of Dumgree. The young man said he asked her what sort of a chariot it was, as there was never such a thing in that country as a chariot, nor yet a road for one. But she replied that he was widely mistaken, for that a great number of chariots sometimes passed that way, though never any of them returned. These words appearing to be merely the ravings of superannuation, they were not regarded; but when no other traces of Mary could be found, old Andrew went up to consult this crazy dame once more, but he was not able to bring any such thing to her recollection. She spoke only in parables, which to him were incomprehensible.

Bonny Mary Burnet was lost. She left her father's house at nine o'clock on a Wednesday morning, the 17th of September, neatly dressed in a white jerkin and green bonnet, with her hay-raik over her shoulder; and that was the last sight she was doomed ever to see of her native cottage. She seemed to have had some presentiment of this, as appeared from her demeanour that morning before she left it. Mary Burnet of Kirkstyle was lost, and great was the sensation produced over the whole country by the mysterious event. There was a long ballad extant at one period on the melancholy catastrophe, which was supposed to have been composed by the chaplain of St Mary's; but I have only heard tell of it, without ever hearing it sung or recited. Many of the verses concluded thus:

*But Bonny Mary Burnet
We will never see again.*

The story soon got abroad, with all its horrid circumstances (and there is little doubt that it was grievously exaggerated), and there was no obloquy that was not thrown on the survivor, who certainly in some degree deserved it, for, instead of growing better, he grew ten times more wicked than he was before. In one thing the whole country agreed, that it had been the real Mary Burnet who was drowned in the loch, and that the being which was found in her bed, lying weeping and complaining of suffering, and which vanished the next day, had been a fairy, an evil spirit, or a changeling of some sort, for that it never spoke save once, and that in a mysterious manner; nor did it partake of any food with the rest of the family. Her father and mother knew not what to say or what to think, but they wandered through this weary world like people wandering in a dream. Everything that belonged to Mary Burnet was kept by her parents as the most sacred relics, and many a tear did her aged mother shed over them. Every article of her dress brought the once comely wearer to mind. Andrew often said, "That to have lost the darling child of their old age in any way would have been a great trial, but to lose her in the way that they had done, was really mair than human frailty could endure."

Many a weary day did he walk by the shores of the loch, looking eagerly for some vestige of her garments, and though he trembled at every appearance, yet did he continue to search on. He had a number of small bones collected, that had belonged to lambs and other minor animals, and, haply, some of them to fishes, from a fond supposition that they might once have formed joints of her toes or fingers. These he kept concealed in a little bag, in order, as he said, "to let the doctors see them." But no relic, besides these, could he ever discover of Mary's body.

Young Allanson recovered from his raging fever scarcely in the manner of other men, for he recovered all at once, after a few days raving and madness. Mary Burnet, it appeared, was by him no more remembered. He grew ten times more wicked than before, and hesitated at no means of accomplishing his unhallowed purposes. The devout shepherds and cottagers around detested him; and, both in their families and in the wild, when there was no ear to hear but that of Heaven, they prayed protection from his devices, as if he had been the Wicked One; and they all prophesied that he would make a bad end.

One fine day about the middle of October, when the days begin to get very short, and the nights long and dark, on a Friday morning, the next year but one after Mary Burnet was lost, a memorable day in the fairy annals, John Allanson, younger of Inverlawn, went to a great hiring fair at a village called Moffat in Annandale, in order to hire a house-maid. His character was so notorious, that not one young woman in the district would serve in his father's house; so away he went to the fair at Moffat, to hire the prettiest and loveliest girl he could there find, with the intention of ruining her as soon as she came home. This is no supposititious accusation, for he acknowledged his plan to Mr. David Welch of Cariferan, who rode down to the market with him, and seemed to boast of it, and dwell on it with delight. But the maidens of Annandale had a guardian angel in the fair that day, of which neither he nor they were aware.

Allanson looked through the hiring market, and through the hiring market, and at length fixed on one young woman, which indeed was not difficult to do, for there was no such form there for elegance and beauty. Mr. Welch stood still and eyed him. He took the beauty aside. She was clothed in green, and as lovely as a new-blown rose.

"Are you to hire, pretty maiden?"

"Yes, sir."

"Will you hire with me?"

"I care not though I do. But if I hire with you, it must be for the long term."

"Certainly. The longer the better. What are your wages to be?"

"You know, if I hire, I must be paid in kind. I must have the first living creature that I see about Inverlawn to myself."

"I wish it may be me, then. But what do you know about Inverlawn?"

"I think I *should* know about it."

"Bless me! I know the face as well as I know my own, and better. But the name has somehow escaped me. Pray, may I ask your name?"

"Hush! Hush!" said she solemnly, and holding up her hand at the same time; "Hush, hush, you had better say nothing about that here."

"I am in utter amazement!" he exclaimed. "What is the meaning of this? I conjure you to tell me your name?"

"It is Mary Burnet," said she, in a soft whisper; and at the same time she let down a green veil over her face.

If Allanson's death-warrant had been announced to him at that moment, it could not have deprived him so completely of sense and motion. His visage changed into that of a corpse, his jaws fell down, and his eyes became glazed, so as apparently to throw no reflection inwardly. Mr. Welch, who had kept his eye steadily on them all the while, perceived his comrade's dilemma, and went up to him. "Allanson? – Mr. Allanson? What is the matter with you, man?" said he. "Why, the girl has bewitched you, and turned you into a statue!"

Allanson made some sound in his throat, as if attempting to speak, but his tongue refused its office, and he only jabbered. Mr. Welch, conceiving that he was seized with some fit, or about to faint, supported him into the Johnston Arms; but he either could not, or would not, grant him any explanation. Welch being, however, resolved to see the maiden in green once more, persuaded Allanson, after causing him to drink a good deal, to go out into the hiring-market again, in search of her. They ranged the market through and through, but the maiden in green was gone, and not to be found. She had vanished in the crowd the moment she divulged her name, and even though Welch had his eye fixed on her, he could not discover which way she went. Allanson appeared to be in a kind of stupor as well as terror, but when he found that she had left the market, he began to recover himself, and to look out again for the top of the market.

He soon found one more beautiful than the last. She was like a sylph, clothed in robes of pure snowy white, with green ribbons. Again he pointed this new flower out to Mr. David Welch, who declared that such a perfect model of beauty he had never in his life seen. Allanson, being resolved to have this one at any wages, took her aside, and put the usual question: "Do you wish to hire, pretty maiden?"

"Yes, sir."

"Will you hire with me?"

"I care not though I do."

"What, then, are your wages to be? Come – say? And be reasonable; I am determined not to part with you for a trifle."

"My wages must be in kind; I work on no other conditions. Pray, how are all the good people about Inverlawn?"

Allanson's breath began to cut, and a chillness to creep through his whole frame, and he answered, with a faltering tongue – "I thank you – much in their ordinary way."

"And your aged neighbours," rejoined she, "are they still alive and well?"

"I – I – I think they are," said he, panting for breath. "But I am at a loss to know whom I am indebted to for these kind recollections."

"What," said she, "have you so soon forgot Mary Burnet of Kirkstyle?"

Allanson started as if a bullet had gone through his heart. The lovely sylph-like form glided into the crowd, and left the astounded libertine once more standing like a rigid statue, until aroused by his friend, Mr. Welch. He tried a third fair one, and got the same answers, and the same name given. Indeed, the first time ever I heard the tale, it bore that he tried *seven*, who all turned out to be Mary Burnets of Kirkstyle; but I think it unlikely that he would try so many, as he must long ere that time have been sensible that he laboured under some power of enchantment. However, when nothing else would do, he helped himself to a good proportion of strong drink. While he was thus engaged, a phenomenon of beauty and grandeur came into the fair, that caught the sole attention of all present. This was a lovely dame, riding in a gilded chariot, with two livery-men before, and two behind, clothed in green and gold; and never sure was there so splendid a meteor seen in a Moffat fair. The word instantly circulated in the market, that this was the Lady Elizabeth Douglas, eldest daughter to the Earl of Morton, who then sojourned at Auchincastle, in the vicinity of Moffat, and which lady at that time was celebrated as a great beauty all over Scotland. She was afterwards Lady Keith; and the mention of this name in the tale, as it were by mere accident, fixes the era of it in the reign of James the Fourth, at the very time that fairies, brownies, and witches, were at the rifest in Scotland.

Everyone in the market believed the lady to be the daughter of the Earl of Morton; and when she came to the Johnston Arms, a gentleman in green came out bareheaded, and received her out of the carriage. All the crowd gazed at such unparalleled beauty and grandeur, but none was half so much overcome as Allanson. He had never conceived aught half so lovely either in earth, or heaven, or fairyland; and while he stood in a burning fever of admiration, think of his astonishment, and the astonishment of the countless crowd that looked on, when this brilliant and matchless beauty beckoned him towards her! He could not believe his senses, but looked this way and that to see how others regarded the affair; but she beckoned him a second time, with such a winning courtesy and smile, that immediately he pulled off his beaver cap and hasted up to her; and without more ado she gave him her arm, and the two walked into the hostel.

Allanson conceived that he was thus distinguished by Lady Elizabeth Douglas, the flower of the land, and so did all the people of the market; and greatly they wondered who the young farmer could be that was thus particularly favoured; for it ought to have been mentioned that he had not one personal acquaintance in the fair save Mr. David Welch of Carifran. The first thing the lady did was to inquire kindly after his health. Allanson thanked her ladyship with all the courtesy he was master of; and being by this time persuaded that she was in love with him, he became as light as if treading on the air. She next inquired after his father and mother. Oho! Thought he to himself, poor creature, she is terribly in for it! But her love shall not be thrown away upon a backward or ungrateful object. He answered her with great politeness, and at length began to talk of her noble father and young Lord William, but she cut him short by asking if he did not recognise her.

"Oh, yes! He knew who her ladyship was, and remembered that he had seen her comely face often before, although he could not, at that particular moment, recall to his memory the precise time or places of their meeting."

She next asked for his old neighbours of Kirkstyle, and if they were still in life and health!

Allanson felt as if his heart were a piece of ice. A chillness spread over his whole frame; he sank back on a seat, and remained motionless; but the beautiful and adorable creature soothed him with kind words, till he again gathered courage to speak.

"What!" said he; "and has it been your own lovely self who has been playing tricks on me this whole day?"

"A first love is not easily extinguished, Mr. Allanson," said she. "You may guess from my appearance, that I have been fortunate in life; but, for all that, my first love for you has continued the same, unaltered and unchanged, and you must forgive the little freedoms I used today to try your affections, and the effects my appearance would have on you."

"It argues something for my good taste, however, that I never pitched on any face for beauty today but your own," said he. "But now that we have met once more, we shall not so easily part again. I will devote the rest of my life to you, only let me know the place of your abode."

"It is hard by," said she, "only a very little space from this; and happy, happy, would I be to see you there tonight, were it proper or convenient. But my lord is at present from home, and in a distant country."

"I should not conceive that any particular hinderance to my visit," said he.

With great apparent reluctance she at length consented to admit of his visit, and offered to leave one of her gentlemen, whom she could trust, to be his conductor; but this he positively refused. It was his desire, he said, that no eye of man should see him enter or leave her happy dwelling. She said he was a self-willed man, but should have his own way; and after giving him such directions as would infallibly lead him to her mansion, she mounted her chariot and was driven away.

Allanson was uplifted above every sublunary concern. Seeking out his friend, David Welch, he imparted to him his extraordinary good fortune, but he did not tell him that she was not the Lady Elizabeth Douglas. Welch insisted on accompanying him on the way, and refused to turn back till he came to the very point of the road next to the lady's splendid mansion; and in spite of all that Allanson could say, Welch remained there till he saw his comrade enter the court gate, which glowed with lights as innumerable as the stars of the firmament.

Allanson had promised to his father and mother to be home on the morning after the fair to breakfast. He came not either that day or the next; and the third day the old man mounted his white pony, and rode away towards Moffat in search of his son. He called at Cariferan on his way, and made inquiries at Mr. Welch. The latter manifested some astonishment that the young man had not returned; nevertheless he assured his father of his safety, and desired him to return home; and then with reluctance confessed that the young man was engaged in an amour with the Earl of Morton's beautiful daughter; that he had gone to the castle by appointment, and that he, David Welch, had accompanied him to the gate, and seen him enter, and it was apparent that his reception had been a kind one, since he had tarried so long.

Mr. Welch, seeing the old man greatly distressed, was persuaded to accompany him on his journey, as the last who had seen his son, and seen him enter the castle. On reaching Moffat they found his steed standing at the hostel, whither it had returned on the night of the fair, before the company broke up; but the owner had not been heard of since seen in company with Lady Elizabeth Douglas. The old man set out for Auchincastle, taking Mr. David Welch along with him; but long ere they reached the place, Mr. Welch assured him he would not find his son there, as it was nearly in a different direction that they rode on the evening of the fair. However, to the castle they went, and were admitted to the Earl, who, after hearing the old man's tale, seemed to consider him in a state of derangement. He sent for his daughter Elizabeth, and questioned her concerning her meeting with the son of the old respectable countryman – of her appointment with him on the night of the preceding Friday, and concluded by saying he hoped she had him still in some safe concealment about the castle.

The lady, hearing her father talk in this manner, and seeing the serious and dejected looks of the old man, knew not what to say, and asked an explanation. But Mr. Welch put a stop to it by declaring to old Allanson that the Lady Elizabeth was not the lady with whom his son made the appointment, for he had seen her, and would engage to know her again among ten thousand; nor was that the castle towards which he had accompanied his son, nor any thing like it. "But go with me," continued he, "and, though I am a stranger in this district, I think I can take you to the very place."

They set out again; and Mr. Welch traced the road from Moffat, by which young Allanson and he had gone, until, after travelling several miles, they came to a place where a road struck off to the right at an angle. "Now I know we are right," said Welch; "for here we stopped, and your son intreated me to return, which I refused, and accompanied him to yon large tree, and a little way beyond it, from whence I saw him received in at the splendid gate. We shall be in sight of the mansion in three minutes."

They passed on to the tree, and a space beyond it; but then Mr. Welch lost the use of his speech, as he perceived that there was neither palace nor gate there, but a tremendous gulf, fifty fathoms deep, and a dark stream foaming and boiling below.

"How is this?" said old Allanson. "There is neither mansion nor habitation of man here!"

Welch's tongue for a long time refused its office, and he stood like a statue, gazing on the altered and awful scene. "He only, who made the spirits of men," said he, at last, "and all the spirits that sojourn in the earth and air, can tell how this is. We are wandering in a world of enchantment, and have been influenced by some agencies above human nature, or without its pale; for here of a certainty did I take leave of your son – and there, in that direction, and apparently either on the verge of that gulf, or the space above it, did I see him received in at the court gate of a mansion, splendid beyond all conception. How can human comprehension make anything of this?"

They went forward to the verge, Mr. Welch leading the way to the very spot on which he saw the gate opened, and there they found marks where a horse had been plunging. Its feet had been over the brink, but it seemed to have recovered itself, and deep, deep down, and far within, lay the mangled corpse of John Allanson; and in this manner, mysterious beyond all example, terminated the career of that wicked and flagitious young man. What a beautiful moral may be extracted from this fairy tale!

But among all these turnings and windings, there is no account given, you will say, of the fate of Mary Burnet; for this last appearance of hers at Moffat seems to have been altogether a phantom or illusion. Gentle and kind reader, I can give you no account of the fate of that maiden; for though the ancient fairy tale proceeds, it seems to me to involve her fate in ten times more mystery than what we have hitherto seen of it.

The yearly return of the day on which Mary was lost, was observed as a day of mourning by her aged and disconsolate parents – a day of sorrow, of fasting, and humiliation. Seven years came and passed away, and the seventh returning day of fasting and prayer was at hand. On the evening previous to it, old Andrew was moving along the sands of the loch, still looking for some relic of his beloved Mary, when he was aware of a little shrivelled old man, who came posting towards him. The creature was not above five spans in height, and had a face scarcely like that of a human creature; but he was, nevertheless, civil in his deportment, and sensible in speech. He bade Andrew a good evening, and asked him what he was looking for. Andrew answered that he was looking for that which he should never find.

"Pray, what is your name, ancient shepherd?" said the stranger; "for methinks I should know something of you, and perhaps have a commission to you."

"Alas! Why should you ask after my name?" said Andrew. "My name is now nothing to anyone."

"Had not you once a beautiful daughter, named Mary?" said the stranger.

"It is a heart-rending question, man," said Andrew; "but certes, I had once a beloved daughter named Mary."

"What became of her?" asked the stranger.

Andrew shook his head, turned round, and began to move away; it was a theme that his heart could not brook. He sauntered along the loch sands, his dim eye scanning every white pebble as he passed along. There was a hopelessness in his stooping form, his gait, his eye, his features – in every step that he took there was a hopeless apathy. The dwarf followed him, and began to expostulate with him. "Old man, I see you are pining under some real or fancied affliction," said he. "But in continuing to do so, you are neither acting according to the dictates of reason nor true religion. What is man that he should fret, or the son of man that he should repine, under the chastening hand of his Maker?"

"I am far frae justifying mysell," returned Andrew, surveying his shrivelled monitor with some degree of astonishment. "But there are some feelings that neither reason nor religion can o'ermaster; and there are some that a parent may cherish without sin."

"I deny the position," said the stranger, "taken either absolutely or relatively. All repining under the Supreme decree is leavened with unrighteousness. But, subtleties aside, I ask you, as I did before: What became of your daughter?"

"Ask the Father of her spirit, and the framer of her body," said Andrew, solemnly; "ask Him into whose hands I committed her from childhood. He alone knows what became of her, but I do not."

"How long is it since you lost her?"

"It is seven years tomorrow."

"Ay! You remember the time well. And have you mourned for her all that while?"

"Yes; and I will go down to the grave mourning for my only daughter, the child of my age, and of all my affection. O, thou unearthly-looking monitor, knowest thou aught of my darling child? For if thou dost, thou wilt know that she was not like other women. There was a simplicity and a purity about my Mary, that was hardly consistent with our frail nature."

"Wouldst thou like to see her again?" said the dwarf.

Andrew turned round, his whole frame shaking as with a palsy, and gazed on the audacious imp. "See her again, creature!" cried he vehemently – "Would I like to see her again, say'st thou?"

"I said so," said the dwarf, "and I say farther, dost thou know this token? Look, and see if thou dost?"

Andrew took the token, and looked at it, then at the shrivelled stranger, and then at the token again; and at length he burst into tears, and wept aloud; but they were tears of joy, and his weeping seemed to have some breathings of laughter intermingled in it. And still as he kissed the token, he called out in broken and convulsive sentences – "Yes, auld body, I *do* know it! – I *do* know it! – I *do* know it! It is indeed the same golden Edward, with three holes in it, with which I presented my Mary on her birthday, in her eighteenth year, to buy a new suit for the holidays. But when she took it she said – ay, I mind weel what my bonny woman said – 'It is sae bonny and sae kenspeckle,' said she, 'that I think I'll keep it for the sake of the giver.' O dear, dear! – Blessed little creature, tell me how she is, and where she is? Is she living, or is she dead?"

"She is living, and in good health," said the dwarf; "and better, and braver, and happier, and lovelier than ever; and if you make haste, you will see her and her family at Moffat tomorrow afternoon. They are to pass there on a journey, but it is an express one, and I am sent to you with that token, to inform you of the circumstance, that you may have it in your power to see and embrace your beloved daughter once before you die."

"And am I to meet my Mary at Moffat? Come away, little, dear, welcome body, thou blessed of heaven, come away, and taste of an auld shepherd's best cheer, and I'll gang foot for foot with you to Moffat, and my auld wife shall gang foot for foot with us too. I tell you, little, blessed, and welcome crile, come along with me."

"I may not tarry to enter your house, or taste of your cheer, good shepherd," said the being. "May plenty still be within your walls, and a thankful heart to enjoy it! But my directions are neither to taste meat nor drink in this country, but to haste back to her that sent me. Go – haste, and make ready, for you have no time to lose."

"At what time will she be there?" cried Andrew, flinging the plaid from him to run home with the tidings.

"Precisely when the shadow of the Holy Cross falls due east," cried the dwarf; and turning round, he hasted on his way.

When old Jean Linton saw her husband coming hobbling and running home without his plaid, and having his doublet flying wide open, she had no doubt that he had lost his wits; and, full of anxiety, she met him at the side of the kail-yard. "Gudeness preserve us a' in our right senses, Andrew Burnet, what's the matter wi' you, Andrew Burnet?"

"Stand out o' my gate, wife, for, d'ye see, I'm rather in a haste, Jean Linton."

"I see that indeed, gudeman; but stand still, and tell me what has putten you *in* sic a haste. Ir ye dementit?"

"Na, na; gudewife, Jean Linton, I'm no dementit – I'm only gaun away till Moffat."

"O, gudeness pity the poor auld body! How can ye gang to Moffat, man? Or what have ye to do at Moffat? Dinna ye mind that the morn is the day o' our solemnity?"

"Haud out o' my gate, auld wife, and dinna speak o' solemnities to me. I'll keep it at Moffat the morn. Ay, gudewife, and ye shall keep it at Moffat, too. What d'ye think o' that, woman? Too-whoo! Ye dinna ken the metal that's in an auld body till it be tried."

"Andrew – Andrew Burnet!"

"Get away wi' your frightened looks, woman; and haste ye, gang and fling me out my Sabbath-day claes. And, Jean Linton, my woman, d'ye hear, gang and pit on your bridal gown, and your silk hood, for ye maun be at Moffat the morn too; and it is mair nor time we were away. Dinna look sae surprised, woman, till I tell ye, that our ain Mary is to meet us at Moffat the morn."

"O, Andrew! Dinna sport wi' the feelings of an auld forsaken heart!"

"Gude forbid, my auld wife, that I should ever sport wi' feeling o' yours," cried Andrew, bursting into tears; "they are a' as saacred to me as breathings frae the Throne o' Grace. But it is true that I tell ye; our dear bairn is to meet us at Moffat the morn, wi' a son in every hand; and we maun e'en gang and see her aince again, and kiss her and bless her afore we dee."

The tears now rushed from the old woman's eyes like fountains, and dropped from her sorrow-worn cheeks to the earth, and then, as with a spontaneous movement, she threw her skirt over her head, kneeled down at her husband's feet, and poured out her soul in thanksgiving to her Maker. She then rose up, quite deprived of her senses through joy, and ran crouching away on the road towards Moffat, as if hasting beyond her power to be at it. But Andrew brought her back; and they prepared themselves for their journey.

Kirkstyle being twenty miles from Moffat, they set out on the afternoon of Tuesday, the 16th of September; slept that night at a place called Turnberry Sheil, and were in Moffat next day by noon. Wearisome was the remainder of the day to that aged couple; they wandered about conjecturing by what road their daughter would come, and how she would come attended. "I have made up my mind on baith these matters," said Andrew; "at first I thought it was likely that she would come out of the east, because a' our blessings come frae that airt; but finding now that would be o'er near to the very road we hae come oursells, I now take it for granted she'll come frae the south; and I just think I see her leading a bonny boy in every hand, and a servant lass carrying a bit bundle ahint her."

The two now walked out on all the southern roads, in hopes to meet their Mary, but always returned to watch the shadow of the Holy Cross; and, by the time it fell due east, they could do nothing but stand in the middle of the street, and look round them in all directions. At length, about half a mile out on the Dumfries road, they perceived a poor beggar woman approaching with two children following close to her, and another beggar a good way behind. Their eyes were instantly riveted on these objects; for Andrew thought he perceived his friend the dwarf in the one that was behind; and now all other earthly objects were to them nothing, save these approaching beggars. At that moment a gilded chariot entered the village from the south, and drove by them at full speed, having two livery-men before, and two behind, clothed in green and gold. "Ach-wow! The vanity of worldly grandeur!" ejaculated Andrew, as the splendid vehicle went thundering by; but neither he nor his wife deigned to look at it farther, their whole attention being fixed on the group of beggars. "Ay, it is just my woman," said Andrew, "it is just hersell; I ken her gang yet, sair pressed down wi' poortith although she be. But I dinna care how poor she be, for baith her and hers sall be welcome to my fireside as lang as I hae ane."

While their eyes were thus strained, and their hearts melting with tenderness and pity, Andrew felt something embracing his knees, and, on looking down, there was his Mary, blooming in splendour and beauty, kneeling at his feet. Andrew uttered a loud hysterical scream of joy, and clasped her to his bosom; and old Jean Linton stood trembling, with her arms spread, but durst not close them on so splendid a creature, till her daughter first enfolded her in a fond embrace, and then she hung upon her and wept. It was a wonderful event – a restoration without a parallel. They indeed beheld their Mary, their long-lost darling; they held her in their embraces, believed in her identity, and were satisfied. Satisfied, did I say? They were happy beyond the lot of mortals. She had just alighted from her chariot; and, perceiving her aged parents standing together, she ran and kneeled at their feet. They now retired into the hostel, where Mary presented her two sons to her father and mother. They spent the evening in every social endearment; and Mary loaded the good old couple with rich presents, watched over them till midnight, when they both fell into a deep and happy sleep, and then she remounted her chariot, and was driven away. If she was any more seen in Scotland, I never heard of it; but her parents rejoiced in the thoughts of her happiness till the day of their death.

Only Bella

Kurt Hunt

BELLA WAS BORN in a hollow wych elm, alone, and came forth from a fracture in the bark during the first thunderstorm of the first spring after the War.

I know this because she told me. Her soft, bare feet made catpaw sounds on the wide-planked floor of my bedroom, her hair grown around her like a shroud, her fingernails curved downward into claws, thick and sharp, *tick-tick-tick*ing across the seams of the floorboards. Each time: "I was born in a hollow wych elm, alone, and came forth from a fracture in the bark during the first thunderstorm of the first spring after the War."

* * *

I'd seen many things in the war, but the first time I saw her, I yelled and jumped out of bed and made an ass of myself in my surprise, and she disappeared down the stairs like flowing water.

The second time I blanched but managed to stammer out questions. Bella slowly cocked her head until it was almost upside-down like an owl's, and when I turned on the lamp, my hair standing on end, she was gone.

The third night, I stayed silent and refused to look directly at her – whatever she was – and prayed she would leave. Beneath the blanket, I gripped a bayonet so tightly that my hand was curled the entire next day.

By the following evening, my mind had finally worked through the impossible situation. So that night, I said only "do you need help?" and shut my mouth and listened.

She smiled, and her teeth were white as the moon.

* * *

She was a pretty girl, I think, but so young. Even with shadows obscuring her, I could see the smooth curves of her face, and her skinny body wrapped in a tattered dress beneath that tangle of ever-growing hair.

She had a wedding ring, too, above those shining claws, and said she remembered some things from before. Running, and hard breath. People, not like her but like me. Warm and solid. And hands. In a sudden rush she asked me, her lungs making a sound like the crinkling of paper, if I had big hands. I simply held them up, palms toward her, and she stared from across the room, her head weaving in the air as if tracing every curve and whorl of my fingerprints.

After several minutes of quiet, she said "you have no ring," and continued her list of memories. Frost. Ripping. Leaf spirals. Stars behind trees, so many stars.

She said there were no stars now. I could see them out my window, but I said nothing.

There was no hope for conversation. Questions stormed in me – but whenever I asked them she went silent and gray and curled up on the floor until morning. Perhaps something about my voice. The timbre…

* * *

Town seemed less friendly after Bella started visiting. Maybe it was the mystery staining every interaction with suspicion, or maybe I just talked too much – all the questions I had for Bella got redirected to storekeepers, neighbors, and children. They stared and shrugged, and looked uncomfortable when I described her, detailing the wave of her hair, the glaze of her eyes, how she smelled like the rot of wood and sometimes spit small pieces of taffeta onto my floor. They looked away when I asked, "do you know who put her there?"

People started whispering and asking questions about my questions…so I stopped. And anyway, it was no use.

Nobody remembered Bella.

* * *

But Bella kept coming. I told her no one knew anything, no one would talk, no one would help. She nodded and still she came, so I had no choice. I searched by myself.

Trees groaned while I stumbled through the woods, looking for the elm and for Bella, always at night in case she saw fit to guide me. But she didn't. If I tried instead to follow her, she slipped away like an eel with a flick of darkness around a corner.

Each night I wandered without direction, but never found the tree.

Never found her.

But still I heard her talons each sundown, scraping on the stairs, getting sharper with each *tick*, and saw her in the corner. Entire nights passed without a word between us, but we looked at each other. Night after night, I grew angrier. Who was it? Who condemned her to haunt?

Someone knew. Someone must know.

* * *

Minds don't work properly without sleep. Memories, neither.

I see the frost now, as she did, and the spiral of late-autumn leaves. And big hands, too, and behind them a face, a face, but whose?

I have to help her, and I cannot find her.

But she understands me and one night holds out a piece of charcoal and allows me to approach to take it. And I understand her.

And so.

I will plant a question deep within the townspeople, and it will spread like a contagion. It will infect their children, and their children's children.

"Who put Bella down the wych elm?"

They'll ask it on monuments, on fences, on buildings: 'Who put Bella down the wych elm?' 'Who put Bella down the wych elm?' 'Who put Bella down the wych elm?'

They will think of her and remember her – and others like her, at the mercy of the merciless – even without ever laying eyes on her.

And someone, someday, will see the question and it will draw out of them like snake poison the chill of a dark night in the wood near Hagley, and the brush of their fingers against her corset – and others, even years later, will chill over and remember other terrible things done in quiet places – and their remembrances will be a beacon.

Clouds race tonight, free from the burden of rain. Charcoal shakes in my hand as I scrawl the words on a wall and spread the disease of curiosity.

I will never see the beacons that go up.

But Bella will, and she will follow them.

I will never find the men that see the message and startle in recognition.

But Bella will. And the men will have no warning except the *tick-tick-tick* of her claws on the stairs.

The Adventure of the German Student

Washington Irving

ON A STORMY NIGHT, in the tempestuous times of the French Revolution, a young German was returning to his lodgings, at a late hour, across the old part of Paris. The lightning gleamed, and the loud claps of thunder rattled through the lofty narrow streets – but I should first tell you something about this young German.

Gottfried Wolfgang was a young man of good family. He had studied for some time at Göttingen, but being of a visionary and enthusiastic character, he had wandered into those wild and speculative doctrines which have so often bewildered German students. His secluded life, his intense application, and the singular nature of his studies, had an effect on both mind and body. His health was impaired; his imagination diseased. He had been indulging in fanciful speculations on spiritual essences, until, like Swedenborg, he had an ideal world of his own around him. He took up a notion, I do not know from what cause, that there was an evil influence hanging over him; an evil genius or spirit seeking to ensnare him and ensure his perdition. Such an idea working on his melancholy temperament produced the most gloomy effects. He became haggard and desponding. His friends discovered the mental malady preying upon him, and determined that the best cure was a change of scene; he was sent, therefore, to finish his studies amidst the splendors and gayeties of Paris.

Wolfgang arrived at Paris at the breaking out of the revolution. The popular delirium at first caught his enthusiastic mind, and he was captivated by the political and philosophical theories of the day: but the scenes of blood which followed shocked his sensitive nature, disgusted him with society and the world, and made him more than ever a recluse. He shut himself up in a solitary apartment in the Pays Latin, the quarter of students. There, in a gloomy street not far from the monastic walls of the Sorbonne, he pursued his favorite speculations. Sometimes he spend hours together in the great libraries of Paris, those catacombs of departed authors, rummaging among their hoards of dusty and obsolete works in quest of food for his unhealthy appetite. He was, in a manner, a literary ghoul, feeding in the charnel-house of decayed literature.

Wolfgang, thought solitary and recluse, was of an ardent temperament, but for a time it operated merely upon his imagination. He was too shy and ignorant of the world to make any advances to the fair, but he was a passionate admirer of female beauty, and in his lonely chamber would often lose himself in reveries on forms and faces which he had seen, and his fancy would deck out images of loveliness far surpassing the reality.

While his mind was in this excited and sublimated state, a dream produced an extraordinary effect upon him. It was of a female face of transcendent beauty. So strong was the impression made, that he dreamt of it again and again. It haunted his thoughts by day, his slumbers by night; in fine, he became passionately enamored of this shadow of a dream. This lasted so long that it became one of those fixed ideas which haunt the minds of melancholy men, and are at times mistaken for madness.

Such was Gottfried Wolfgang, and such his situation at the time I mentioned. He was returning home late on stormy night, through some of the old and gloomy streets of the Marais, the ancient part of Paris. The loud claps of thunder rattled among the high houses of the narrow streets. He came to the Place de Grève, the square, where public executions are performed. The lightning quivered about the pinnacles of the ancient Hôtel de Ville, and shed flickering gleams over the open space in front. As Wolfgang was crossing the square, he shrank back with horror at finding himself close by the guillotine. It was the height of the reign of terror, when this dreadful instrument of death stood ever ready, and its scaffold was continually running with the blood of the virtuous and the brave. It had that very day been actively employed in the work of carnage, and there it stood in grim array, amidst a silent and sleeping city, waiting for fresh victims.

Wolfgang's heart sickened within him, and he was turning shuddering from the horrible engine, when he beheld a shadowy form, cowering as it were at the foot of the steps which led up to the scaffold. A succession of vivid flashes of lightning revealed it more distinctly. It was a female figure, dressed in black. She was seated on one of the lower steps of the scaffold, leaning forward, her face hid in her lap; and her long dishevelled tresses hanging to the ground, streaming with the rain which fell in torrents. Wolfgang paused. There was something awful in this solitary monument of woe. The female had the appearance of being above the common order. He knew the times to be full of vicissitude, and that many a fair head, which had once been pillowed on down, now wandered houseless. Perhaps this was some poor mourner whom the dreadful axe had rendered desolate, and who sat here heart-broken on the strand of existence, from which all that was dear to her had been launched into eternity.

He approached, and addressed her in the accents of sympathy. She raised her head and gazed wildly at him. What was his astonishment at beholding, by the bright glare of the lighting, the very face which had haunted him in his dreams. It was pale and disconsolate, but ravishingly beautiful.

Trembling with violent and conflicting emotions, Wolfgang again accosted her. He spoke something of her being exposed at such an hour of the night, and to the fury of such a storm, and offered to conduct her to her friends. She pointed to the guillotine with a gesture of dreadful signification.

"I have no friend on earth!" said she.

"But you have a home," said Wolfgang.

"Yes – in the grave!"

The heart of the student melted at the words.

"If a stranger dare make an offer," said he, "without danger of being misunderstood, I would offer my humble dwelling as a shelter; myself as a devoted friend. I am friendless myself in Paris, and a stranger in the land; but if my life could be of service, it is at your disposal, and should be sacrificed before harm or indignity should come to you."

There was an honest earnestness in the young man's manner that had its effect. His foreign accent, too, was in his favor; it showed him not to be a hackneyed inhabitant of Paris. Indeed, there is an eloquence in true enthusiasm that is not to be doubted. The homeless stranger confided herself implicitly to the protection of the student.

He supported her faltering steps across the Pont Neuf, and by the place where the statue of Henry the Fourth had been overthrown by the populace. The storm had abated, and the thunder rumbled at a distance. All Paris was quiet; that great volcano of human passion slumbered for a while, to gather fresh strength for the next day's eruption. The student conducted his charge through the ancient streets of the Pays Latin, and by the dusky walls of the Sorbonne, to the great dingy hotel which he inhabited. The old portress who admitted them stared with surprise at the unusual sight of the melancholy Wolfgang with a female companion.

On entering his apartment, the student, for the first time, blushed at the scantiness and indifference of his dwelling. He had but one chamber – an old-fashioned saloon – heavily carved, and fantastically furnished with the remains of former magnificence, for it was one of those hotels in the quarter nobility. It was lumbered with books and papers, and all the usual apparatus of a student, and his bed stood in a recess at one end.

When lights were brought, and Wolfgang had a better opportunity of contemplating the stranger, he was more than ever intoxicated by her beauty. Her face was pale, but of a dazzling fairness, set off by a profusion of raven hair that hung clustering about it. Her eyes were large and brilliant, with a singular expression approaching almost to wildness. As far as her black dress permitted her shape to be seen, it was of perfect symmetry. Her whole appearance was highly striking, though she was dressed in the simplest style. The only thing approaching to an ornament which she wore was a broad black band round her neck, clasped by diamonds.

The perplexity now commenced with the student how to dispose of the helpless being thus thrown upon his protection. He thought of abandoning his chamber to her, and seeking shelter for himself elsewhere. Still he was so fascinate by her charms, there seemed to be such a spell upon his thoughts and senses, that he could not tear himself from her presence. Her manner, too, was singular and unaccountable. She spoke no more of the guillotine. Her grief had abated. The attentions of the student had first won her confidence, and then, apparently, her heart. She was evidently an enthusiast like himself, and enthusiasts soon understand each other.

In the infatuation of the moment, Wolfgang avowed his passion for her. He told her the story of his mysterious dream, and how she had possessed his heart before he had even seen her. She was strangely affected by his recital, and acknowledged to have felt an impulse towards him equally unaccountable. It was the time for wild theory and wild actions. Old prejudices and superstitions were done away; everything was under the sway of the 'Goddess of Reason'. Among other rubbish of the old times, the forms and ceremonies of marriage began to be considered superfluous bonds for honorable minds. Social compact were the vogue. Wolfgang was too much of theorist not to be tainted by the liberal doctrines of the day.

"Why should we separate?" said he: "our heart are united; in the eye of reason and honor we are as one. What need is there of sordid forms to bind high soul together?"

The stranger listened with emotion: she had evidently received illumination at the same school.

"You have no home nor family," continued he: "Let me be everything to you, or rather let us be everything to one another. If form is necessary, form shall be observed – there is my hand. I pledge myself to you forever."

"Forever?" said the stranger, solemnly.

"Forever!" repeated Wolfgang.

The stranger clasped the hand extended to her: "Then I am yours," murmured she, and sank upon his bosom.

The next morning the student left his bride sleeping, and sallied forth at an early hour to seek more spacious apartments suitable to the change in his situation. When he returned, he found the stranger lying with her head hanging over the bed, and one arm thrown over it. He spoke to her, but received no reply. He advanced to awaken her from her uneasy posture. On taking her hand, it was cold – there was no pulsation – her face was pallid and ghastly. In a word, she was a corpse.

Horrified and frantic, he alarmed the house. A scene of confusion ensued. The police was summoned. As the officer of police entered the room, he started back on beholding the corpse.

"Great heaven!" cried he, "How did this woman come here?"

"Do you know anything about her?" said Wolfgang eagerly.

"Do I?" exclaimed the officer: "she was guillotined yesterday."

He stepped forward; undid the black collar round the neck of the corpse, and the head rolled on the floor!

The student burst into a frenzy. "The fiend! The fiend has gained possession of me!" shrieked he; "I am lost forever."

They tried to soothe him, but in vain. He was possessed with the frightful belief that an evil spirit had reanimated the dead body to ensnare him. He went distracted, and died in a mad-house.

Here the old gentleman with the haunted head finished his narrative.

"And is this really a fact?" said the inquisitive gentleman.

"A fact not to be doubted," replied the other. "I had it it from the best authority. The student told it me himself. I saw him in a mad-house in Paris."

The Jolly Corner

Henry James

Chapter I

"EVERYONE ASKS ME what I 'think' of everything," said Spencer Brydon; "and I make answer as I can – begging or dodging the question, putting them off with any nonsense. It wouldn't matter to any of them really," he went on, "for, even were it possible to meet in that stand-and-deliver way so silly a demand on so big a subject, my 'thoughts' would still be almost altogether about something that concerns only myself." He was talking to Miss Staverton, with whom for a couple of months now he had availed himself of every possible occasion to talk; this disposition and this resource, this comfort and support, as the situation in fact presented itself, having promptly enough taken the first place in the considerable array of rather unattenuated surprises attending his so strangely belated return to America. Everything was somehow a surprise; and that might be natural when one had so long and so consistently neglected everything, taken pains to give surprises so much margin for play. He had given them more than thirty years – thirty-three, to be exact; and they now seemed to him to have organised their performance quite on the scale of that licence. He had been twenty-three on leaving New York – he was fifty-six today; unless indeed he were to reckon as he had sometimes, since his repatriation, found himself feeling; in which case he would have lived longer than is often allotted to man. It would have taken a century, he repeatedly said to himself, and said also to Alice Staverton, it would have taken a longer absence and a more averted mind than those even of which he had been guilty, to pile up the differences, the newnesses, the queernesses, above all the bignesses, for the better or the worse, that at present assaulted his vision wherever he looked.

The great fact all the while, however, had been the incalculability; since he *had* supposed himself, from decade to decade, to be allowing, and in the most liberal and intelligent manner, for brilliancy of change. He actually saw that he had allowed for nothing; he missed what he would have been sure of finding, he found what he would never have imagined. Proportions and values were upside-down; the ugly things he had expected, the ugly things of his far-away youth, when he had too promptly waked up to a sense of the ugly – these uncanny phenomena placed him rather, as it happened, under the charm; whereas the 'swagger' things, the modern, the monstrous, the famous things, those he had more particularly, like thousands of ingenuous enquirers every year, come over to see, were exactly his sources of dismay. They were as so many set traps for displeasure, above all for reaction, of which his restless tread was constantly pressing the spring. It was interesting, doubtless, the whole show, but it would have been too disconcerting hadn't a certain finer truth saved the situation. He had distinctly not, in this steadier light, come over *all* for the monstrosities; he had come, not only in the last analysis but quite on the face of the act, under an impulse with which they had nothing to do. He had come – putting the thing pompously – to look at his 'property', which he had thus for a third of a century not been within four thousand miles of; or, expressing it less sordidly, he had yielded to the humour of seeing again his house on the jolly corner, as he usually, and quite fondly, described it – the one in which he had first seen the light, in which various members of his family had lived and had died, in which the holidays of his overschooled boyhood had been passed and the few social flowers of his chilled adolescence gathered, and which, alienated then for so long a period, had, through the successive deaths of his two brothers and the termination of old arrangements, come wholly into his hands. He was the owner of another, not quite so 'good' – the jolly corner having been, from far back, superlatively extended and consecrated; and the value of the pair represented his main capital, with an income consisting, in these later years, of their respective rents which (thanks precisely to their original excellent type) had never been depressingly low. He could live in 'Europe', as he had been in the habit of living, on the product of these flourishing New York leases, and all the better since, that of the second structure, the mere number in its long row, having within a twelvemonth fallen in, renovation at a high advance had proved beautifully possible.

These were items of property indeed, but he had found himself since his arrival distinguishing more than ever between them. The house within the street, two bristling blocks westward, was already in course of reconstruction as a tall mass of flats; he had acceded, some time before, to overtures for this conversion – in which, now that it was going forward, it had been not the least of his astonishments to find himself able, on the spot, and though without a previous ounce of such experience, to participate with a certain intelligence, almost with a certain authority. He had lived his life with his back so turned to such concerns and his face addressed to those of so different an order that he scarce knew what to make of this lively stir, in a compartment of his mind never yet penetrated, of a capacity for business and a sense for construction. These virtues, so common all round him now, had been dormant in his own organism – where it might be said of them perhaps that they had slept the sleep of the just. At present, in the splendid autumn weather – the autumn at least was a pure boon in the terrible place – he loafed about his 'work' undeterred, secretly agitated; not in the least 'minding' that the whole proposition, as they said, was vulgar and sordid, and ready to climb ladders, to walk the plank, to handle materials and look wise about them, to ask questions, in fine, and challenge explanations and really 'go into' figures.

It amused, it verily quite charmed him; and, by the same stroke, it amused, and even more, Alice Staverton, though perhaps charming her perceptibly less. She wasn't, however, going to be better-off for it, as *he* was – and so astonishingly much: nothing was now likely, he knew, ever to make her better-off than she found herself, in the afternoon of life, as the delicately frugal possessor and tenant of the small house in Irving Place to which she had subtly managed to cling through her almost unbroken New York career. If he knew the way to it now better than to any other address among the dreadful multiplied numberings which seemed to him to reduce the whole place to some vast ledger-page, overgrown, fantastic, of ruled and criss-crossed lines and figures – if he had formed, for his consolation, that habit, it was really not a little because of the charm of his having encountered and recognised, in the vast wilderness of the wholesale, breaking through the mere gross generalisation of wealth and force and success, a small still scene where items and shades, all delicate things, kept the sharpness of the notes of a high voice perfectly trained, and where economy hung about like the scent of a garden. His old friend lived with one maid and herself dusted her relics and trimmed her lamps and polished her silver; she stood oft, in the awful modern crush, when she could, but she sallied forth and did battle when the challenge was really to 'spirit', the spirit she after all confessed to, proudly and a little shyly, as to that of the better time, that of *their* common, their quite far-away and antediluvian social period and order. She made use of the street-cars when need be, the terrible things that people scrambled for as the panic-stricken at sea scramble for the boats; she affronted, inscrutably, under stress, all the public concussions and ordeals; and yet, with that slim mystifying grace of her appearance, which defied you to say if she were a fair young woman who looked older through trouble, or a fine smooth older one who looked young through successful indifference with her precious reference, above all, to memories and histories into which he could enter, she was as exquisite for him as some pale pressed flower (a rarity to begin with), and, failing other sweetnesses, she was a sufficient reward of his effort. They had communities of knowledge, 'their' knowledge (this discriminating possessive was always on her lips) of presences of the other age, presences all overlaid, in his case, by the experience of a man and the freedom of a wanderer, overlaid by pleasure, by infidelity, by passages of life that were strange and dim to her, just by 'Europe' in short, but still unobscured, still exposed and cherished, under that pious visitation of the spirit from which she had never been diverted.

She had come with him one day to see how his 'apartment-house' was rising; he had helped her over gaps and explained to her plans, and while they were there had happened to have, before her, a brief but lively discussion with the man in charge, the representative of the building firm that had undertaken his work. He had found himself quite 'standing up' to this personage over a failure on the latter's part to observe some detail of one of their noted conditions, and had so lucidly argued his case that, besides ever so prettily flushing, at the time, for sympathy in his triumph, she had afterwards said to him (though to a slightly greater effect of irony) that he had clearly for too many years neglected a real gift. If he had but stayed at home he would have anticipated the inventor of the sky-scraper. If he had but stayed at home he would have discovered his genius in time really to start some new variety of awful architectural hare and run it till it burrowed in a gold mine. He was to remember these words, while the weeks elapsed, for the small silver ring they had sounded over the queerest and deepest of his own lately most disguised and most muffled vibrations.

It had begun to be present to him after the first fortnight, it had broken out with the oddest abruptness, this particular wanton wonderment: it met him there – and this was the image under which he himself judged the matter, or at least, not a little, thrilled and flushed with it – very much as he might have been met by some strange figure, some unexpected occupant, at a turn of one of the dim passages of an empty house. The quaint analogy quite hauntingly remained with him, when he didn't indeed rather improve it by a still intenser form: that of his opening a door behind which he would have made sure of finding nothing, a door into a room shuttered and void, and yet so coming, with a great suppressed start, on some quite erect confronting presence, something planted in the middle of the place and facing him through the dusk. After that visit to the house in construction he walked with his companion to see the other and always so much the better one, which in the eastward direction formed one of the corners – the 'jolly' one precisely, of the street now so generally dishonoured and disfigured in its westward reaches, and of the comparatively conservative Avenue. The Avenue still had pretensions, as Miss Staverton said, to decency; the old people had mostly gone, the old names were unknown, and here and there an old association seemed to stray, all vaguely, like some very aged person, out too late, whom you might meet and feel the impulse to watch or follow, in kindness, for safe restoration to shelter.

They went in together, our friends; he admitted himself with his key, as he kept no one there, he explained, preferring, for his reasons, to leave the place empty, under a simple arrangement with a good woman living in the neighbourhood and who came for a daily hour to open windows and dust and sweep. Spencer Brydon had his reasons and was growingly aware of them; they seemed to him better each time he was there, though he didn't name them all to his companion, any more than he told her as yet how often, how quite absurdly often, he himself came. He only let her see for the present, while they walked through the great blank rooms, that absolute vacancy reigned and that, from top to bottom, there was nothing but Mrs. Muldoon's broomstick, in a corner, to tempt the burglar. Mrs. Muldoon was then on the premises, and she loquaciously attended the visitors, preceding them from room to room and pushing back shutters and throwing up sashes – all to show them, as she remarked, how little there was to see. There was little indeed to see in the great gaunt shell where the main dispositions and the general apportionment of space, the style of an age of ampler allowances, had nevertheless for its master their honest pleading message, affecting him as some good old servant's, some lifelong retainer's appeal for a character, or even for a retiring-pension; yet it was also a remark of Mrs. Muldoon's that, glad as she was to oblige him by her noonday round, there was a request she greatly hoped he would never make of her. If he should wish her for any reason to come in after dark she would just tell him, if he 'pleased', that he must ask it of somebody else.

The fact that there was nothing to see didn't militate for the worthy woman against what one *might* see, and she put it frankly to Miss Staverton that no lady could be expected to like, could she? "Craping up to thim top storeys in the ayvil hours." The gas and the electric light were off the house, and she fairly evoked a gruesome vision of her march through the great grey rooms – so many of them as there were too! – with her glimmering taper. Miss Staverton met her honest glare with a smile and the profession that she herself certainly would recoil from such an adventure. Spencer Brydon meanwhile held his peace – for the moment; the question of the 'evil' hours in his old home had already become too grave for him. He had begun some time since to 'crape', and he knew just why a packet of candles addressed to that pursuit had been stowed by his own hand, three weeks before, at the back of a drawer of the fine old sideboard that occupied, as a 'fixture', the deep recess in the dining-room. Just now he laughed at his companions – quickly however changing the subject; for the reason that, in the first place, his laugh struck him even at that moment as starting the odd echo, the conscious human resonance (he scarce knew how to qualify it) that sounds made while he was there alone sent back to his ear or his fancy; and that, in the second, he imagined Alice Staverton for the instant on the point of asking him, with a divination, if he ever so prowled. There were divinations he was unprepared for, and he had at all events averted enquiry by the time Mrs. Muldoon had left them, passing on to other parts.

There was happily enough to say, on so consecrated a spot, that could be said freely and fairly; so that a whole train of declarations was precipitated by his friend's having herself broken out, after a yearning look round: "But I hope you don't mean they want you to pull *this* to pieces!" His answer came, promptly, with his re-awakened wrath: it was of course exactly what they wanted, and what they were 'at' him for, daily, with the iteration of people who couldn't for their life understand a man's liability to decent feelings. He had found the place, just as it stood and beyond what he could express, an interest and a joy. There were values other than the beastly rent-values, and in short, in short –! But it was thus Miss Staverton took him up. "In short you're to make so good a thing of your sky-scraper that, living in luxury on *those* ill-gotten gains, you can afford for a while to be sentimental here!" Her smile had for him, with the words, the particular mild irony with which he found half her talk suffused; an irony without bitterness and that came, exactly, from her having so much imagination – not, like the cheap sarcasms with which one heard most people, about the world of 'society', bid for the reputation of cleverness, from nobody's really having any. It was agreeable to him at this very moment to be sure that when he had answered, after a brief demur, "Well, yes; so, precisely, you may put it!" her imagination would still do him justice. He explained that even if never a dollar were to come to him from the other house he would nevertheless cherish this one; and he dwelt, further, while they lingered and wandered, on the fact of the stupefaction he was already exciting, the positive mystification he felt himself create.

He spoke of the value of all he read into it, into the mere sight of the walls, mere shapes of the rooms, mere sound of the floors, mere feel, in his hand, of the old silver-plated knobs of the several mahogany doors, which suggested the pressure of the palms of the dead the seventy years of the past in fine that these things represented, the annals of nearly three generations, counting his grandfather's, the one that had ended there, and the impalpable ashes of his long-extinct youth, afloat in the very air like microscopic motes. She listened to everything; she was a woman who answered intimately but who utterly didn't chatter. She scattered abroad therefore no cloud of words; she could assent, she could agree, above all she could encourage, without doing that. Only at the last she went a little further than he had done himself. "And then how do you know? You may still, after all, want to live here." It rather indeed pulled him up, for it wasn't what he had been thinking, at least in her sense of the words, "You mean I may decide to stay on for the sake of it?"

"Well, *with* such a home –!" But, quite beautifully, she had too much tact to dot so monstrous an *i*, and it was precisely an illustration of the way she didn't rattle. How could anyone – of any wit – insist on anyone else's 'wanting' to live in New York?

"Oh," he said, "I *might* have lived here (since I had my opportunity early in life); I might have put in here all these years. Then everything would have been different enough – and, I dare say, 'funny' enough. But that's another matter. And then the beauty of it – I mean of my perversity, of my refusal to agree to a 'deal' – is just in the total absence of a reason. Don't you see that if I had a reason about the matter at all it would *have* to be the other way, and would then be inevitably a reason of dollars? There are no reasons here *but* of dollars. Let us therefore have none whatever – not the ghost of one."

They were back in the hall then for departure, but from where they stood the vista was large, through an open door, into the great square main saloon, with its almost antique felicity of brave spaces between windows. Her eyes came back from that reach and met his own a moment. "Are you very sure the 'ghost' of one doesn't, much rather, serve –?"

He had a positive sense of turning pale. But it was as near as they were then to come. For he made answer, he believed, between a glare and a grin: "Oh ghosts – of course the place must swarm with them! I should be ashamed of it if it didn't. Poor Mrs. Muldoon's right, and it's why I haven't asked her to do more than look in."

Miss Staverton's gaze again lost itself, and things she didn't utter, it was clear, came and went in her mind. She might even for the minute, off there in the fine room, have imagined some element dimly gathering. Simplified like the death-mask of a handsome face, it perhaps produced for her just then an effect akin to the stir of an expression in the 'set' commemorative plaster. Yet whatever her impression may have been she produced instead a vague platitude. "Well, if it were only furnished and lived in –!"

She appeared to imply that in case of its being still furnished he might have been a little less opposed to the idea of a return. But she passed straight into the vestibule, as if to leave her words behind her, and the next moment he had opened the house-door and was standing with her on the steps. He closed the door and, while he re-pocketed his key, looking up and down, they took in the comparatively harsh actuality of the Avenue, which reminded him of the assault of the outer light of the Desert on the traveller emerging from an Egyptian tomb. But he risked before they stepped into the street his gathered answer to her speech. "For me it *is* lived in. For me it is furnished." At which it was easy for her to sigh "Ah yes!" all vaguely and discreetly; since his parents and his favourite sister, to say nothing of other kin, in numbers, had run their course and met their end there. That represented, within the walls, ineffaceable life.

It was a few days after this that, during an hour passed with her again, he had expressed his impatience of the too flattering curiosity – among the people he met – about his appreciation of New York. He had arrived at none at all that was socially producible, and as for that matter of his 'thinking' (thinking the better or the worse of anything there) he was wholly taken up with one subject of thought. It was mere vain egoism, and it was moreover, if she liked, a morbid obsession. He found all things come back to the question of what he personally might have been, how he might have led his life and 'turned out', if he had not so, at the outset, given it up. And confessing for the first time to the intensity within him of this absurd speculation – which but proved also, no doubt, the habit of too selfishly thinking – he affirmed the impotence there of any other source of interest, any other native appeal. "What would it have made of me, what would it have made of me? I keep for ever wondering, all idiotically; as if I could possibly know! I see what it has made of dozens of others, those I meet, and it positively aches within me, to the point of exasperation, that it would have made something of me as well. Only I can't make out what, and the worry of it, the small rage of curiosity never to be satisfied, brings back what I remember to have felt, once or twice, after judging best, for reasons, to burn some important letter unopened. I've been sorry, I've hated it – I've never known what was in the letter. You may, of course, say it's a trifle –!"

"I don't say it's a trifle," Miss Staverton gravely interrupted.

She was seated by her fire, and before her, on his feet and restless, he turned to and fro between this intensity of his idea and a fitful and unseeing inspection, through his single eye-glass, of the dear little old objects on her chimney-piece. Her interruption made him for an instant look at her harder. "I shouldn't care if you did!" he laughed, however; "And it's only a figure, at any rate, for the way I now feel. *Not* to have followed my perverse young course – and almost in the teeth of my father's curse, as I may say; not to have kept it up, so, 'over there,' from that day to this, without a doubt or a pang; not, above all, to have liked it, to have loved it, so much, loved it, no doubt, with such an abysmal conceit of my own preference; some variation from *that*, I say, must have produced some different effect for my life and for my 'form'. I should have stuck here – if it had been possible; and I was too young, at twenty-three, to judge, *pour deux sous*, whether it *were* possible. If I had waited I might have seen it was, and then I might have been, by staying here, something nearer to one of these types who have been hammered so hard and made so keen by their conditions. It isn't that I admire them so much – the question of any charm in them, or of any charm, beyond that of the rank money-passion, exerted by their conditions *for* them, has nothing to do with the matter: it's only a question of what fantastic, yet perfectly possible, development of my own nature I mayn't have missed. It comes over me that I had then a strange *alter ego* deep down somewhere within me, as the full-blown flower is in the small tight bud, and that I just took the course, I just transferred him to the climate, that blighted him for once and for ever."

"And you wonder about the flower," Miss Staverton said. "So do I, if you want to know; and so I've been wondering these several weeks. I believe in the flower," she continued, "I feel it would have been quite splendid, quite huge and monstrous."

"Monstrous above all!" her visitor echoed; "And I imagine, by the same stroke, quite hideous and offensive."

"You don't believe that," she returned; "if you did you wouldn't wonder. You'd know, and that would be enough for you. What you feel – and what I feel *for* you – is that you'd have had power."

"You'd have liked me that way?" he asked.

She barely hung fire. "How should I not have liked you?"

"I see. You'd have liked me, have preferred me, a billionaire!"

"How should I not have liked you?" she simply again asked.

He stood before her still – her question kept him motionless. He took it in, so much there was of it; and indeed his not otherwise meeting it testified to that. "I know at least what I am," he simply went on; "the other side of the medal's clear enough. I've not been edifying – I believe I'm thought in a hundred quarters to have been barely decent. I've followed strange paths and worshipped strange gods; it must have come to you again and again – in fact you've admitted to me as much – that I was leading, at any time these thirty years, a selfish frivolous scandalous life. And you see what it has made of me."

She just waited, smiling at him. "You see what it has made of *me*."

"Oh you're a person whom nothing can have altered. You were born to be what you are, anywhere, anyway: you've the perfection nothing else could have blighted. And don't you see how, without my exile, I shouldn't have been waiting till now –?" But he pulled up for the strange pang.

"The great thing to see," she presently said, "seems to me to be that it has spoiled nothing. It hasn't spoiled your being here at last. It hasn't spoiled this. It hasn't spoiled your speaking –" She also however faltered.

He wondered at everything her controlled emotion might mean. "Do you believe then – too dreadfully! – that I *am* as good as I might ever have been?"

"Oh no! Far from it!" With which she got up from her chair and was nearer to him. "But I don't care," she smiled.

"You mean I'm good enough?"

She considered a little. "Will you believe it if I say so? I mean will you let that settle your question for you?" And then as if making out in his face that he drew back from this, that he had some idea which, however absurd, he couldn't yet bargain away: "Oh you don't care either – but very differently: you don't care for anything but yourself."

Spencer Brydon recognised it – it was in fact what he had absolutely professed. Yet he importantly qualified. "*He* isn't myself. He's the just so totally other person. But I do want to see him," he added. "And I can. And I shall."

Their eyes met for a minute while he guessed from something in hers that she divined his strange sense. But neither of them otherwise expressed it, and her apparent understanding, with no protesting shock, no easy derision, touched him more deeply than anything yet, constituting for his stifled perversity, on the spot, an element that was like breatheable air. What she said however was unexpected. "Well, *I've* seen him."

"You –?"

"I've seen him in a dream."

"Oh a 'dream' –!" It let him down.

"But twice over," she continued. "I saw him as I see you now."

"You've dreamed the same dream –?"

"Twice over," she repeated. "The very same."

This did somehow a little speak to him, as it also gratified him. "You dream about me at that rate?"

"Ah about *him*!" she smiled.

His eyes again sounded her. "Then you know all about him." And as she said nothing more: "What's the wretch like?"

She hesitated, and it was as if he were pressing her so hard that, resisting for reasons of her own, she had to turn away. "I'll tell you some other time!"

Chapter II

IT WAS AFTER THIS that there was most of a virtue for him, most of a cultivated charm, most of a preposterous secret thrill, in the particular form of surrender to his obsession and of address to what he more and more believed to be his privilege. It was what in these weeks he was living for – since he really felt life to begin but after Mrs. Muldoon had retired from the scene and, visiting the ample house from attic to cellar, making sure he was alone, he knew himself in safe possession and, as he tacitly expressed it, let himself go. He sometimes came twice in the twenty-four hours; the moments he liked best were those of gathering dusk, of the short autumn twilight; this was the time of which, again and again, he found himself hoping most. Then he could, as seemed to him, most intimately wander and wait, linger and listen, feel his fine attention, never in his life before so fine, on the pulse of the great vague place: he preferred the lampless hour and only wished he might have prolonged each day the deep crepuscular spell. Later – rarely much before midnight, but then for a considerable vigil – he watched with his glimmering light; moving slowly, holding it high, playing it far, rejoicing above all, as much as he might, in open vistas, reaches of communication between rooms and by passages; the long straight chance or show, as he would have called it, for the revelation he pretended to invite. It was a practice he found he could perfectly 'work' without exciting remark; no one was in the least the wiser for it; even Alice Staverton, who was moreover a well of discretion, didn't quite fully imagine.

He let himself in and let himself out with the assurance of calm proprietorship; and accident so far favoured him that, if a fat Avenue 'officer' had happened on occasion to see him entering at eleven-thirty, he had never yet, to the best of his belief, been noticed as emerging at two. He walked there on the crisp November nights, arrived regularly at the evening's end; it was as easy to do this after dining out as to take his way to a club or to his hotel. When he left his club, if he hadn't been dining out, it was ostensibly to go to his hotel; and when he left his hotel, if he had spent a part of the evening there, it was ostensibly to go to his club. Everything was easy in fine; everything conspired and promoted: there was truly even in the strain of his experience something that glossed over, something that salved and simplified, all the rest of consciousness. He circulated, talked, renewed, loosely and pleasantly, old relations – met indeed, so far as he could, new expectations and seemed to make out on the whole that in spite of the career, of such different contacts, which he had spoken of to Miss Staverton as ministering so little, for those who might have watched it, to edification, he was positively rather liked than not. He was a dim secondary social success – and all with people who had truly not an idea of him. It was all mere surface sound, this murmur of their welcome, this popping of their corks – just as his gestures of response were the extravagant shadows, emphatic in proportion as they meant little, of some game of *ombres chinoises*. He projected himself all day, in thought, straight over the bristling line of hard unconscious heads and into the other, the real, the waiting life; the life that, as soon as he had heard behind him the click of his great house-door, began for him, on the jolly corner, as beguilingly as the slow opening bars of some rich music follows the tap of the conductor's wand.

He always caught the first effect of the steel point of his stick on the old marble of the hall pavement, large black-and-white squares that he remembered as the admiration of his childhood and that had then made in him, as he now saw, for the growth of an early conception of style. This effect was the dim reverberating tinkle as of some far-off bell hung who should say where? – In the depths of the house, of the past, of that mystical other world that might have flourished for him had he not, for weal or woe, abandoned it. On this impression he did ever the same thing; he put his stick noiselessly away in a corner – feeling the place once more in the likeness of some great glass bowl, all precious concave crystal, set delicately humming by the play of a moist finger round its edge. The concave crystal held, as it were, this mystical other world, and the indescribably fine murmur of its rim was the sigh there, the scarce audible pathetic wail to his strained ear, of all the old baffled forsworn possibilities. What he did therefore by this appeal of his hushed presence was to wake them into such measure of ghostly life as they might still enjoy. They were shy, all but unappeasably shy, but they weren't really sinister; at least they weren't as he had hitherto felt them – before they had taken the Form he so yearned to make them take, the Form he at moments saw himself in the light of fairly hunting on tiptoe, the points of his evening shoes, from room to room and from storey to storey.

That was the essence of his vision – which was all rank folly, if one would, while he was out of the house and otherwise occupied, but which took on the last verisimilitude as soon as he was placed and posted. He knew what he meant and what he wanted; it was as clear as the figure on a cheque presented in demand for cash. His *alter ego* 'walked' – that was the note of his image of him, while his image of his motive for his own odd pastime was the desire to waylay him and meet him. He roamed, slowly, warily, but all restlessly, he himself did – Mrs. Muldoon had been right, absolutely, with her figure of their 'craping'; and the presence he watched for would roam restlessly too. But it would be as cautious and as shifty; the conviction of its probable, in fact its already quite sensible, quite audible evasion of pursuit grew for him from night to night, laying on him finally a rigour to which nothing in his life had been comparable. It had been the theory of many superficially-judging persons, he knew, that he was wasting that life in a surrender to sensations, but he had tasted of no pleasure so fine as his actual tension, had been introduced to no sport that demanded at once the patience and the nerve of this stalking of a creature more subtle, yet at bay perhaps more formidable, than any beast of the forest. The terms, the comparisons, the very practices of the chase positively came again into play; there were even moments when passages of his occasional experience as a sportsman, stirred memories, from his younger time, of moor and mountain and desert, revived for him – and to the increase of his keenness – by the tremendous force of analogy. He found himself at moments – once he had placed his single light on some mantel-shelf or in some recess – stepping back into shelter or shade, effacing himself behind a door or in an embrasure, as he had sought of old the vantage of rock and tree; he found himself holding his breath and living in the joy of the instant, the supreme suspense created by big game alone.

He wasn't afraid (though putting himself the question as he believed gentlemen on Bengal tiger-shoots or in close quarters with the great bear of the Rockies had been known to confess to having put it); and this indeed – since here at least he might be frank! – because of the impression, so intimate and so strange, that he himself produced as yet a dread, produced certainly a strain, beyond the liveliest he was likely to feel. They fell for him into categories, they fairly became familiar, the signs, for his own perception, of the alarm his presence and his vigilance created; though leaving him always to remark, portentously, on his probably having formed a relation, his probably enjoying a consciousness, unique in the experience of man.

People enough, first and last, had been in terror of apparitions, but who had ever before so turned the tables and become himself, in the apparitional world, an incalculable terror? He might have found this sublime had he quite dared to think of it; but he didn't too much insist, truly, on that side of his privilege. With habit and repetition he gained to an extraordinary degree the power to penetrate the dusk of distances and the darkness of corners, to resolve back into their innocence the treacheries of uncertain light, the evil-looking forms taken in the gloom by mere shadows, by accidents of the air, by shifting effects of perspective; putting down his dim luminary he could still wander on without it, pass into other rooms and, only knowing it was there behind him in case of need, see his way about, visually project for his purpose a comparative clearness. It made him feel, this acquired faculty, like some monstrous stealthy cat; he wondered if he would have glared at these moments with large shining yellow eyes, and what it mightn't verily be, for the poor hard-pressed *alter ego*, to be confronted with such a type.

He liked however the open shutters; he opened everywhere those Mrs. Muldoon had closed, closing them as carefully afterwards, so that she shouldn't notice: he liked – oh this he did like, and above all in the upper rooms! – the sense of the hard silver of the autumn stars through the window-panes, and scarcely less the flare of the street-lamps below, the white electric lustre which it would have taken curtains to keep out. This was human actual social; this was of the world he had lived in, and he was more at his ease certainly for the countenance, coldly general and impersonal, that all the while and in spite of his detachment it seemed to give him. He had support of course mostly in the rooms at the wide front and the prolonged side; it failed him considerably in the central shades and the parts at the back. But if he sometimes, on his rounds, was glad of his optical reach, so none the less often the rear of the house affected him as the very jungle of his prey. The place was there more subdivided; a large 'extension' in particular, where small rooms for servants had been multiplied, abounded in nooks and corners, in closets and passages, in the ramifications especially of an ample back staircase over which he leaned, many a time, to look far down – not deterred from his gravity even while aware that he might, for a spectator, have figured some solemn simpleton playing at hide-and-seek. Outside in fact he might himself make that ironic *rapprochement*; but within the walls, and in spite of the clear windows, his consistency was proof against the cynical light of New York.

It had belonged to that idea of the exasperated consciousness of his victim to become a real test for him; since he had quite put it to himself from the first that, oh distinctly! He could 'cultivate' his whole perception. He had felt it as above all open to cultivation – which indeed was but another name for his manner of spending his time. He was bringing it on, bringing it to perfection, by practice; in consequence of which it had grown so fine that he was now aware of impressions, attestations of his general postulate, that couldn't have broken upon him at once. This was the case more specifically with a phenomenon at last quite frequent for him in the upper rooms, the recognition – absolutely unmistakeable, and by a turn dating from a particular hour, his resumption of his campaign after a diplomatic drop, a calculated absence of three nights – of his being definitely followed, tracked at a distance carefully taken and to the express end that he should the less confidently, less arrogantly, appear to himself merely to pursue. It worried, it finally quite broke him up, for it proved, of all the conceivable impressions, the one least suited to his book. He was kept in sight while remaining himself – as regards the essence of his position – sightless, and his only recourse then was in abrupt turns, rapid recoveries of ground. He wheeled about, retracing his steps, as if he might so catch in his face at least the stirred air of some other quick revolution. It was indeed true that his fully dislocalised thought of these manoeuvres recalled to him Pantaloon, at the Christmas farce buffeted and tricked from behind by ubiquitous Harlequin; but it left intact the influence of the conditions themselves each time he was re-exposed to them, so that in fact this association had he suffered it to become constant, would on a certain side have but ministered to his intenser gravity. He had made, as I have said, to create on the premises the baseless sense of a reprieve, his three absences; and the result of the third was to confirm the after-effect of the second.

On his return that night – the night succeeding his last intermission – he stood in the hall and looked up the staircase with a certainty more intimate than any he had yet known. "He's *there*, at the top, and waiting – not, as in general, falling back for disappearance. He's holding his ground, and it's the first time – which is a proof, isn't it? That something has happened for him." So Brydon argued with his hand on the banister and his foot on the lowest stair; in which position he felt as never before the air chilled by his logic. He himself turned cold in it, for he seemed of a sudden to know what now was involved. "Harder pressed? – Yes, he takes it in, with its thus making clear to him that I've come, as they say, 'to stay'. He finally doesn't like and can't bear it, in the sense, I mean, that his wrath, his menaced interest now balances with his dread. I've hunted him till he has 'turned'; that, up there, is what has happened – he's the fanged or the antlered animal brought at last to bay." There came to him as I say – but determined by an influence beyond my notation! – the acuteness of this certainty under which however the next moment he had broken into a sweat that he would as little have consented to attribute to fear as he would have dared immediately to act upon it for enterprise. It marked none the less a prodigious thrill, a thrill that represented sudden dismay, no doubt, but also represented, and with the selfsame throb, the strangest, the most joyous, possibly the next minute almost the proudest, duplication of consciousness.

"He has been dodging, retreating, hiding, but now, worked up to anger, he'll fight!" – This intense impression made a single mouthful, as it were, of terror and applause. But what was wondrous was that the applause, for the felt fact, was so eager, since, if it was his other self he was running to earth, this ineffable identity was thus in the last resort not unworthy of him. It bristled there – somewhere near at hand, however unseen still – as the hunted thing, even as the trodden worm of the adage must at last bristle; and Brydon at this instant tasted probably of a sensation more complex than had ever before found itself consistent with sanity. It was as if it would have shamed him that a character so associated with his own should triumphantly succeed in just skulking, should to the end not risk the open; so that the drop of this danger was, on the spot, a great lift of the whole situation. Yet with another rare shift of the same subtlety he was already trying to measure by how much more he himself might now be in peril of fear; so rejoicing that he could, in another form, actively inspire that fear, and simultaneously quaking for the form in which he might passively know it.

The apprehension of knowing it must after a little have grown in him, and the strangest moment of his adventure perhaps, the most memorable or really most interesting, afterwards of his crisis, was the lapse of certain instants of concentrated conscious *combat*, the sense of a need to hold on to something, even after the manner of a man slipping and slipping on some awful incline; the vivid impulse, above all, to move, to act, to charge, somehow and upon something – to show himself, in a word, that he wasn't afraid. The state of 'holding on' was thus the state to which he was momentarily reduced; if there had been anything, in the great vacancy, to seize, he would presently have been aware of having clutched it as he might under a shock at home have clutched the nearest chair-back. He had been surprised at any rate – of this he *was* aware – into something unprecedented since his original appropriation of the place; he had closed his eyes, held them tight, for a long minute, as with that instinct of dismay and that terror of vision. When he opened them the room, the other contiguous rooms, extraordinarily, seemed lighter – so light, almost, that at first he took the change for day. He stood firm, however that might be, just where he had paused; his resistance had helped him – it was as if there were something he had tided over. He knew after a little what this was – it had been in the imminent danger of flight. He had stiffened his will against going; without this he would have made for the stairs, and it seemed to him that, still with his eyes closed, he would have descended them, would have known how, straight and swiftly, to the bottom.

Well, as he had held out, here he was – still at the top, among the more intricate upper rooms and with the gauntlet of the others, of all the rest of the house, still to run when it should be his time to go. He would go at his time – only at his time: didn't he go every night very much at the same hour? He took out his watch – there was light for that: it was scarcely a quarter past one, and he had never withdrawn so soon. He reached his lodgings for the most part at two – with his walk of a quarter of an hour. He would wait for the last quarter – he wouldn't stir till then; and he kept his watch there with his eyes on it, reflecting while he held it that this deliberate wait, a wait with an effort, which he recognised, would serve perfectly for the attestation he desired to make. It would prove his courage – unless indeed the latter might most be proved by his budging at last from his place. What he mainly felt now was that, since he hadn't originally scuttled, he had his dignities – which had never in his life seemed so many – all to preserve and to carry aloft. This was before him in truth as a physical image, an image almost worthy of an age of greater romance. That remark indeed glimmered for him only to glow the next instant with a finer light; since what age of romance, after all, could have matched either the state of his mind or, 'objectively', as they said, the wonder of his situation? The only difference would have been that, brandishing his dignities over his head as in a parchment scroll, he might then – that is in the heroic time – have proceeded downstairs with a drawn sword in his other grasp.

At present, really, the light he had set down on the mantel of the next room would have to figure his sword; which utensil, in the course of a minute, he had taken the requisite number of steps to possess himself of. The door between the rooms was open, and from the second another door opened to a third. These rooms, as he remembered, gave all three upon a common corridor as well, but there was a fourth, beyond them, without issue save through the preceding. To have moved, to have heard his step again, was appreciably a help; though even in recognising this he lingered once more a little by the chimney-piece on which his light had rested. When he next moved, just hesitating where to turn, he found himself considering a circumstance that, after his first and comparatively vague apprehension of it, produced in him the start that often attends some pang of recollection, the violent shock of having ceased happily to forget. He had come into sight of the door in which the brief chain of communication ended and which he now surveyed from the nearer threshold, the one not directly facing it. Placed at some distance to the left of this point, it would have admitted him to the last room of the four, the room without other approach or egress, had it not, to his intimate conviction, been closed *since* his former visitation, the matter probably of a quarter of an hour before. He stared with all his eyes at the wonder of the fact, arrested again where he stood and again holding his breath while he sounded his sense. Surely it had been *subsequently* closed – that is it had been on his previous passage indubitably open!

He took it full in the face that something had happened between – that he couldn't have noticed before (by which he meant on his original tour of all the rooms that evening) that such a barrier had exceptionally presented itself. He had indeed since that moment undergone an agitation so extraordinary that it might have muddled for him any earlier view; and he tried to convince himself that he might perhaps then have gone into the room and, inadvertently, automatically, on coming out, have drawn the door after him. The difficulty was that this exactly was what he never did; it was against his whole policy, as he might have said, the essence of which was to keep vistas clear. He had them from the first, as he was well aware, quite on the brain: the strange apparition, at the far end of one of them, of his baffled 'prey' (which had become by so sharp an irony so little the term now to apply!) was the form of success his imagination had most cherished, projecting into it always a refinement of beauty. He had known fifty times the start of perception that had afterwards dropped; had fifty times gasped to himself "There!" under some fond brief hallucination. The house, as the case stood, admirably lent itself; he might wonder at the taste, the native architecture of the particular time, which could rejoice so in the multiplication of doors – the opposite extreme to the modern, the actual almost complete proscription of them; but it had fairly contributed to provoke this obsession of the presence encountered telescopically, as he might say, focused and studied in diminishing perspective and as by a rest for the elbow.

It was with these considerations that his present attention was charged – they perfectly availed to make what he saw portentous. He *couldn't*, by any lapse, have blocked that aperture; and if he hadn't, if it was unthinkable, why what else was clear but that there had been another agent? Another agent? He had been catching, as he felt, a moment back, the very breath of him; but when had he been so close as in this simple, this logical, this completely personal act? It was so logical, that is, that one might have *taken* it for personal; yet for what did Brydon take it, he asked himself, while, softly panting, he felt his eyes almost leave their sockets. Ah this time at last they *were*, the two, the opposed projections of him, in presence; and this time, as much as one would, the question of danger loomed. With it rose, as not before, the question of courage – for what he knew the blank face of the door to say to him was "Show us how much you have!" It stared, it glared back at him with that challenge; it put to him the two alternatives: should he just push it open or not? Oh to have this consciousness was to *think* – and to think, Brydon knew, as he stood there, was, with the lapsing moments, not to have acted! Not to have acted – that was the misery and the pang – was even still not to act; was in fact *all* to feel the thing in another, in a new and terrible way. How long did he pause and how long did he debate? There was presently nothing to measure it; for his vibration had already changed – as just by the effect of its intensity. Shut up there, at bay, defiant, and with the prodigy of the thing palpably proveably *done*, thus giving notice like some stark signboard – under that accession of accent the situation itself had turned; and Brydon at last remarkably made up his mind on what it had turned to.

It had turned altogether to a different admonition; to a supreme hint, for him, of the value of Discretion! This slowly dawned, no doubt – for it could take its time; so perfectly, on his threshold, had he been stayed, so little as yet had he either advanced or retreated. It was the strangest of all things that now when, by his taking ten steps and applying his hand to a latch, or even his shoulder and his knee, if necessary, to a panel, all the hunger of his prime need might have been met, his high curiosity crowned, his unrest assuaged – it was amazing, but it was also exquisite and rare, that insistence should have, at a touch, quite dropped from him. Discretion – he jumped at that; and yet not, verily, at such a pitch, because it saved his nerves or his skin, but because, much more valuably, it saved the situation. When I say he 'jumped' at it I feel the consonance of this term with the fact that – at the end indeed of I know not how long – he did move again, he crossed straight to the door. He wouldn't touch it – it seemed now that he might if he would: he would only just wait there a little, to show, to prove, that he wouldn't. He had thus another station, close to the thin partition by which revelation was denied him; but with his eyes bent and his hands held off in a mere intensity of stillness. He listened as if there had been something to hear, but this attitude, while it lasted, was his own communication. "If you won't then – good: I spare you and I give up. You affect me as by the appeal positively for pity: you convince me that for reasons rigid and sublime – what do I know? We both of us should have suffered. I respect them then, and, though moved and privileged as, I believe, it has never been given to man, I retire, I renounce – never, on my honour, to try again. So rest for ever – and let *me*!"

That, for Brydon, was the deep sense of this last demonstration – solemn, measured, directed, as he felt it to be. He brought it to a close, he turned away; and now verily he knew how deeply he had been stirred. He retraced his steps, taking up his candle, burnt, he observed, well-nigh to the socket, and marking again, lighten it as he would, the distinctness of his footfall; after which, in a moment, he knew himself at the other side of the house. He did here what he had not yet done at these hours – he opened half a casement, one of those in the front, and let in the air of the night; a thing he would have taken at any time previous for a sharp rupture of his spell. His spell was broken now, and it didn't matter – broken by his concession and his surrender, which made it idle henceforth that he should ever come back. The empty street – its other life so marked even by great lamp-lit vacancy – was within call, within touch; he stayed there as to be in it again, high above it though he was still perched; he watched as for some comforting common fact, some vulgar human note, the passage of a scavenger or a thief, some night-bird however base. He would have blessed that sign of life; he would have welcomed positively the slow approach of his friend the policeman, whom he had hitherto only sought to avoid, and was not sure that if the patrol had come into sight he mightn't have felt the impulse to get into relation with it, to hail it, on some pretext, from his fourth floor.

The pretext that wouldn't have been too silly or too compromising, the explanation that would have saved his dignity and kept his name, in such a case, out of the papers, was not definite to him: he was so occupied with the thought of recording his Discretion – as an effect of the vow he had just uttered to his intimate adversary – that the importance of this loomed large and something had overtaken all ironically his sense of proportion. If there had been a ladder applied to the front of the house, even one of the vertiginous perpendiculars employed by painters and roofers and sometimes left standing overnight, he would have managed somehow, astride of the window-sill, to compass by outstretched leg and arm that mode of descent. If there had been some such uncanny thing as he had found in his room at hotels, a workable fire-escape in the form of notched cable or a canvas shoot, he would have availed himself of it as a proof – well, of his present delicacy. He nursed that sentiment, as the question stood, a little in vain, and even – at the end of he scarce knew, once more, how long – found it, as by the action on his mind of the failure of response of the outer world, sinking back to vague anguish. It seemed to him he had waited an age for some stir of the great grim hush; the life of the town was itself under a spell – so unnaturally, up and down the whole prospect of known and rather ugly objects, the blankness and the silence lasted. Had they ever, he asked himself, the hard-faced houses, which had begun to look livid in the dim dawn, had they ever spoken so little to any need of his spirit? Great builded voids, great crowded stillnesses put on, often, in the heart of cities, for the small hours, a sort of sinister mask, and it was of this large collective negation that Brydon presently became conscious – all the more that the break of day was, almost incredibly, now at hand, proving to him what a night he had made of it.

He looked again at his watch, saw what had become of his time-values (he had taken hours for minutes – not, as in other tense situations, minutes for hours) and the strange air of the streets was but the weak, the sullen flush of a dawn in which everything was still locked up. His choked appeal from his own open window had been the sole note of life, and he could but break off at last as for a worse despair. Yet while so deeply demoralised he was capable again of an impulse denoting – at least by his present measure – extraordinary resolution; of retracing his steps to the spot where he had turned cold with the extinction of his last pulse of doubt as to there being in the place another presence than his own. This required an effort strong enough to sicken him; but he had his reason, which over-mastered for the moment everything else. There was the whole of the rest of the house to traverse, and how should he screw himself to that if the door he had seen closed were at present open? He could hold to the idea that the closing had practically been for him an act of mercy, a chance offered him to descend, depart, get off the ground and never again profane it. This conception held together, it worked; but what it meant for him depended now clearly on the amount of forbearance his recent action, or rather his recent inaction, had engendered. The image of the 'presence' whatever it was, waiting there for him to go – this image had not yet been so concrete for his nerves as when he stopped short of the point at which certainty would have come to him. For, with all his resolution, or more exactly with all his dread, he did stop short – he hung back from really seeing. The risk was too great and his fear too definite: it took at this moment an awful specific form.

He knew – yes, as he had never known anything – that, *should* he see the door open, it would all too abjectly be the end of him. It would mean that the agent of his shame – for his shame was the deep abjection – was once more at large and in general possession; and what glared him thus in the face was the act that this would determine for him. It would send him straight about to the window he had left open, and by that window, be long ladder and dangling rope as absent as they would, he saw himself uncontrollably insanely fatally take his way to the street. The hideous chance of this he at least could avert; but he could only avert it by recoiling in time from assurance. He had the whole house to deal with, this fact was still there; only he now knew that uncertainty alone could start him. He stole back from where he had checked himself – merely to do so was suddenly like safety – and, making blindly for the greater staircase, left gaping rooms and sounding passages behind. Here was the top of the stairs, with a fine large dim descent and three spacious landings to mark off. His instinct was all for mildness, but his feet were harsh on the floors, and, strangely, when he had in a couple of minutes become aware of this, it counted somehow for help. He couldn't have spoken, the tone of his voice would have scared him, and the common conceit or resource of 'whistling in the dark' (whether literally or figuratively) have appeared basely vulgar; yet he liked none the less to hear himself go, and when he had reached his first landing – taking it all with no rush, but quite steadily – that stage of success drew from him a gasp of relief.

The house, withal, seemed immense, the scale of space again inordinate; the open rooms, to no one of which his eyes deflected, gloomed in their shuttered state like mouths of caverns; only the high skylight that formed the crown of the deep well created for him a medium in which he could advance, but which might have been, for queerness of colour, some watery under-world. He tried to think of something noble, as that his property was really grand, a splendid possession; but this nobleness took the form too of the clear delight with which he was finally to sacrifice it. They might come in now, the builders, the destroyers – they might come as soon as they would. At the end of two flights he had dropped to another zone, and from the middle of the third, with only one more left, he recognised the influence of the lower windows, of half-drawn blinds, of the occasional gleam of street-lamps, of the glazed spaces of the vestibule. This was the bottom of the sea, which showed an illumination of its own and which he even saw paved – when at a given moment he drew up to sink a long look over the banisters – with the marble squares of his childhood. By that time indubitably he felt, as he might have said in a commoner cause, better; it had allowed him to stop and draw breath, and the case increased with the sight of the old black-and-white slabs. But what he most felt was that now surely, with the element of impunity pulling him as by hard firm hands, the case was settled for what he might have seen above had he dared that last look. The closed door, blessedly remote now, was still closed – and he had only in short to reach that of the house.

He came down further, he crossed the passage forming the access to the last flight and if here again he stopped an instant it was almost for the sharpness of the thrill of assured escape. It made him shut his eyes – which opened again to the straight slope of the remainder of the stairs. Here was impunity still, but impunity almost excessive; inasmuch as the side-lights and the high fantracery of the entrance were glimmering straight into the hall; an appearance produced, he the next instant saw, by the fact that the vestibule gaped wide, that the hinged halves of the inner door had been thrown far back. Out of that again the *question* sprang at him, making his eyes, as he felt, half-start from his head, as they had done, at the top of the house, before the sign of the other door. If he had left that one open, hadn't he left this one closed, and wasn't he now in *most* immediate presence of some inconceivable occult activity? It was as sharp, the question, as a knife in his side, but the answer hung fire still and seemed to lose itself in the vague darkness to which the thin admitted dawn, glimmering archwise over the whole outer door, made a semicircular margin, a cold silvery nimbus that seemed to play a little as he looked – to shift and expand and contract.

It was as if there had been something within it, protected by indistinctness and corresponding in extent with the opaque surface behind, the painted panels of the last barrier to his escape, of which the key was in his pocket. The indistinctness mocked him even while he stared, affected him as somehow shrouding or challenging certitude, so that after faltering an instant on his step he let himself go with the sense that here *was* at last something to meet, to touch, to take, to know – something all unnatural and dreadful, but to advance upon which was the condition for him either of liberation or of supreme defeat. The penumbra, dense and dark, was the virtual screen of a figure which stood in it as still as some image erect in a niche or as some black-vizored sentinel guarding a treasure. Brydon was to know afterwards, was to recall and make out, the particular thing he had believed during the rest of his descent. He saw, in its great grey glimmering margin, the central vagueness diminish, and he felt it to be taking the very form toward which, for so many days, the passion of his curiosity had yearned. It gloomed, it loomed, it was something, it was somebody, the prodigy of a personal presence.

Rigid and conscious, spectral yet human, a man of his own substance and stature waited there to measure himself with his power to dismay. This only could it be – this only till he recognised, with his advance, that what made the face dim was the pair of raised hands that covered it and in which, so far from being offered in defiance, it was buried, as for dark deprecation. So Brydon, before him, took him in; with every fact of him now, in the higher light, hard and acute – his planted stillness, his vivid truth, his grizzled bent head and white masking hands, his queer actuality of evening-dress, of dangling double eye-glass, of gleaming silk lappet and white linen, of pearl button and gold watch-guard and polished shoe. No portrait by a great modern master could have presented him with more intensity, thrust him out of his frame with more art, as if there had been 'treatment', of the consummate sort, in his every shade and salience. The revulsion, for our friend, had become, before he knew it, immense – this drop, in the act of apprehension, to the sense of his adversary's inscrutable manoeuvre. That meaning at least, while he gaped, it offered him; for he could but gape at his other self in this other anguish, gape as a proof that *he*, standing there for the achieved, the enjoyed, the triumphant life, couldn't be faced in his triumph. Wasn't the proof in the splendid covering hands, strong and completely spread? – So spread and so intentional that, in spite of a special verity that surpassed every other, the fact that one of these hands had lost two fingers, which were reduced to stumps, as if accidentally shot away, the face was effectually guarded and saved.

'Saved', though, *would* it be? – Brydon breathed his wonder till the very impunity of his attitude and the very insistence of his eyes produced, as he felt, a sudden stir which showed the next instant as a deeper portent, while the head raised itself, the betrayal of a braver purpose. The hands, as he looked, began to move, to open; then, as if deciding in a flash, dropped from the face and left it uncovered and presented. Horror, with the sight, had leaped into Brydon's throat, gasping there in a sound he couldn't utter; for the bared identity was too hideous as *his*, and his glare was the passion of his protest. The face, *that* face, Spencer Brydon's? – He searched it still, but looking away from it in dismay and denial, falling straight from his height of sublimity. It was unknown, inconceivable, awful, disconnected from any possibility! – He had been 'sold', he inwardly moaned, stalking such game as this: the presence before him was a presence, the horror within him a horror, but the waste of his nights had been only grotesque and the success of his adventure an irony. Such an identity fitted his at *no* point, made its alternative monstrous. A thousand times yes, as it came upon him nearer now, the face was the face of a stranger. It came upon him nearer now, quite as one of those expanding fantastic images projected by the magic lantern of childhood; for the stranger, whoever he might be, evil, odious, blatant, vulgar, had advanced as for aggression, and he knew himself give ground. Then harder pressed still, sick with the force of his shock, and falling back as under the hot breath and the roused passion of a life larger than his own, a rage of personality before which his own collapsed, he felt the whole vision turn to darkness and his very feet give way. His head went round; he was going; he had gone.

Chapter III

WHAT HAD NEXT brought him back, clearly – though after how long? – was Mrs. Muldoon's voice, coming to him from quite near, from so near that he seemed presently to see her as kneeling on the ground before him while he lay looking up at her; himself not wholly on the ground, but half-raised and upheld – conscious, yes, of tenderness of support and, more particularly, of a head pillowed in extraordinary softness and faintly refreshing fragrance. He considered, he wondered, his wit but half at his service; then another face intervened, bending more directly over him, and he finally knew that Alice Staverton had made her lap an ample and perfect cushion to him, and that she had to this end seated herself on the lowest degree of the staircase, the rest of his long person remaining stretched on his old black-and-white slabs. They were cold, these marble squares of his youth; but *he* somehow was not, in this rich return of consciousness – the most wonderful hour, little by little, that he had ever known, leaving him, as it did, so gratefully, so abysmally passive, and yet as with a treasure of intelligence waiting all round him for quiet appropriation; dissolved, he might call it, in the air of the place and producing the golden glow of a late autumn afternoon. He had come back, yes – come back from further away than any man but himself had ever travelled; but it was strange how with this sense what he had come back *to* seemed really the great thing, and as if his prodigious journey had been all for the sake of it. Slowly but surely his consciousness grew, his vision of his state thus completing itself; he had been miraculously *carried* back – lifted and carefully borne as from where he had been picked up, the uttermost end of an interminable grey passage. Even with this he was suffered to rest, and what had now brought him to knowledge was the break in the long mild motion.

It had brought him to knowledge, to knowledge – yes, this was the beauty of his state; which came to resemble more and more that of a man who has gone to sleep on some news of a great inheritance, and then, after dreaming it away, after profaning it with matters strange to it, has waked up again to serenity of certitude and has only to lie and watch it grow. This was the drift of his patience – that he had only to let it shine on him. He must moreover, with intermissions, still have been lifted and borne; since why and how else should he have known himself, later on, with the afternoon glow intenser, no longer at the foot of his stairs – situated as these now seemed at that dark other end of his tunnel – but on a deep window-bench of his high saloon, over which had been spread, couch-fashion, a mantle of soft stuff lined with grey fur that was familiar to his eyes and that one of his hands kept fondly feeling as for its pledge of truth. Mrs. Muldoon's face had gone, but the other, the second he had recognised, hung over him in a way that showed how he was still propped and pillowed. He took it all in, and the more he took it the more it seemed to suffice: he was as much at peace as if he had had food and drink. It was the two women who had found him, on Mrs. Muldoon's having plied, at her usual hour, her latch-key – and on her having above all arrived while Miss Staverton still lingered near the house. She had been turning away, all anxiety, from worrying the vain bell-handle – her calculation having been of the hour of the good woman's visit; but the latter, blessedly, had come up while she was still there, and they had entered together. He had then lain, beyond the vestibule, very much as he was lying now – quite, that is, as he appeared to have fallen, but all so wondrously without bruise or gash; only in a depth of stupor. What he most took in, however, at present, with the steadier clearance, was that Alice Staverton had for a long unspeakable moment not doubted he was dead.

"It must have been that I *was*." He made it out as she held him. "Yes – I can only have died. You brought me literally to life. Only," he wondered, his eyes rising to her, "only, in the name of all the benedictions, how?"

It took her but an instant to bend her face and kiss him, and something in the manner of it, and in the way her hands clasped and locked his head while he felt the cool charity and virtue of her lips, something in all this beatitude somehow answered everything.

"And now I keep you," she said.

"Oh keep me, keep me!" he pleaded while her face still hung over him: in response to which it dropped again and stayed close, clingingly close. It was the seal of their situation – of which he tasted the impress for a long blissful moment in silence. But he came back. "Yet how did you know –?"

"I was uneasy. You were to have come, you remember – and you had sent no word."

"Yes, I remember – I was to have gone to you at one today." It caught on to their 'old' life and relation – which were so near and so far. "I was still out there in my strange darkness – where was it, what was it? I must have stayed there so long." He could but wonder at the depth and the duration of his swoon.

"Since last night?" she asked with a shade of fear for her possible indiscretion.

"Since this morning – it must have been: the cold dim dawn of today. Where have I been," he vaguely wailed, "where have I been?" He felt her hold him close, and it was as if this helped him now to make in all security his mild moan. "What a long dark day!"

All in her tenderness she had waited a moment. "In the cold dim dawn?" she quavered.

But he had already gone on piecing together the parts of the whole prodigy. "As I didn't turn up you came straight –?"

She barely cast about. "I went first to your hotel – where they told me of your absence. You had dined out last evening and hadn't been back since. But they appeared to know you had been at your club."

"So you had the idea of *this* –?"

"Of what?" she asked in a moment.

"Well – of what has happened."

"I believed at least you'd have been here. I've known, all along," she said, "that you've been coming."

"'Known' it –?"

"Well, I've believed it. I said nothing to you after that talk we had a month ago – but I felt sure. I knew you *would*," she declared.

"That I'd persist, you mean?"

"That you'd see him."

"Ah but I didn't!" cried Brydon with his long wail. "There's somebody – an awful beast; whom I brought, too horribly, to bay. But it's not me."

At this she bent over him again, and her eyes were in his eyes. "No – it's not you." And it was as if, while her face hovered, he might have made out in it, hadn't it been so near, some particular meaning blurred by a smile. "No, thank heaven," she repeated, "it's not you! Of course it wasn't to have been."

"Ah but it *was*," he gently insisted. And he stared before him now as he had been staring for so many weeks. "I was to have known myself."

"You couldn't!" she returned consolingly. And then reverting, and as if to account further for what she had herself done, "But it wasn't only *that*, that you hadn't been at home," she went on. "I waited till the hour at which we had found Mrs. Muldoon that day of my going with you; and she arrived, as I've told you, while, failing to bring anyone to the door, I lingered in my despair on the steps. After a little, if she hadn't come, by such a mercy, I should have found means to hunt her up. But it wasn't," said Alice Staverton, as if once more with her fine intentions – "it wasn't only that."

His eyes, as he lay, turned back to her. "What more then?"

She met it, the wonder she had stirred. "In the cold dim dawn, you say? Well, in the cold dim dawn of this morning I too saw you."

"Saw *me* –?"

"Saw *him*," said Alice Staverton. "It must have been at the same moment."

He lay an instant taking it in – as if he wished to be quite reasonable. "At the same moment?"

"Yes – in my dream again, the same one I've named to you. He came back to me. Then I knew it for a sign. He had come to you."

At this Brydon raised himself; he had to see her better. She helped him when she understood his movement, and he sat up, steadying himself beside her there on the window-bench and with his right hand grasping her left. "*He* didn't come to me."

"You came to yourself," she beautifully smiled.

"Ah I've come to myself now – thanks to you, dearest. But this brute, with his awful face – this brute's a black stranger. He's none of *me*, even as I *might* have been," Brydon sturdily declared.

But she kept the clearness that was like the breath of infallibility. "Isn't the whole point that you'd have been different?"

He almost scowled for it. "As different as *that* –?"

Her look again was more beautiful to him than the things of this world. "Haven't you exactly wanted to know *how* different? So this morning," she said, "you appeared to me."

"Like *him*?"

"A black stranger!"

"Then how did you know it was I?"

"Because, as I told you weeks ago, my mind, my imagination, has worked so over what you might, what you mightn't have been – to show you, you see, how I've thought of you. In the midst of that you came to me – that my wonder might be answered. So I knew," she went on; "and believed that, since the question held you too so fast, as you told me that day, you too would see for yourself. And when this morning I again saw I knew it would be because you had – and also then, from the first moment, because you somehow wanted me. *He* seemed to tell me of that. So why," she strangely smiled, "shouldn't I like him?"

It brought Spencer Brydon to his feet. "You 'like' that horror –?"

"I *could* have liked him. And to me," she said, "he was no horror. I had accepted him."

"'Accepted' –?" Brydon oddly sounded.

"Before, for the interest of his difference – yes. And as *I* didn't disown him, as *I* knew him – which you at last, confronted with him in his difference, so cruelly didn't, my dear – well, he must have been, you see, less dreadful to me. And it may have pleased him that I pitied him."

She was beside him on her feet, but still holding his hand – still with her arm supporting him. But though it all brought for him thus a dim light, "You 'pitied' him?" he grudgingly, resentfully asked.

"He has been unhappy, he has been ravaged," she said.

"And haven't I been unhappy? Am not I – you've only to look at me! – ravaged?"

"Ah I don't say I like him *better*," she granted after a thought. "But he's grim, he's worn – and things have happened to him. He doesn't make shift, for sight, with your charming monocle."

"No" – it struck Brydon; "I couldn't have sported mine 'down-town'. They'd have guyed me there."

"His great convex pince-nez – I saw it, I recognised the kind – is for his poor ruined sight. And his poor right hand –!"

"Ah!" Brydon winced – whether for his proved identity or for his lost fingers. Then, "He has a million a year," he lucidly added. "But he hasn't you."

"And he isn't – no, he isn't – *you*!" she murmured, as he drew her to his breast.

The Haunted Dolls' House

M.R. James

"I SUPPOSE you get stuff of that kind through your hands pretty often?" said Mr. Dillet, as he pointed with his stick to an object which shall be described when the time comes: and when he said it, he lied in his throat, and knew that he lied. Not once in twenty years – perhaps not once in a lifetime – could Mr. Chittenden, skilled as he was in ferreting out the forgotten treasures of half a dozen counties, expect to handle such a specimen. It was collectors' palaver, and Mr. Chittenden recognized it as such.

"Stuff of that kind, Mr. Dillet! It's a museum piece, that is."

"Well, I suppose there are museums that'll take anything."

"I've seen one, not as good as that, years back," said Mr. Chittenden thoughtfully. "But that's not likely to come into the market: and I'm told they 'ave some fine ones of the period over the water. No: I'm only telling you the truth, Mr. Dillet, when I was to say that if you was to place an unlimited order with me for the very best that could be got – and you know I 'ave facilities for getting to know of such things, and a reputation to maintain – well, all I can say is, I should lead you straight up to that one and say, 'I can't do no better for you than that, sir.'"

"Hear, hear!" said Mr. Dillet, applauding ironically with the end of his stick on the floor of the shop. "How much are you sticking the innocent American buyer for it, eh?"

"Oh, I shan't be over hard on the buyer, American or otherwise. You see, it stands this way, Mr. Dillet – if I knew just a bit more about the pedigree –"

"Or just a bit less," Mr. Dillet put in.

"Ha, ha! You will have your joke, sir. No, but as I was saying, if I knew just a little more than what I do about the piece – though anyone can see for themselves it's a genuine thing, every last corner of it, and there's not been one of my men allowed to so much as touch it since it came into the shop – there'd be another figure in the price I'm asking."

"And what's that: five and twenty?"

"Multiply that by three and you've got it, sir. Seventy-five's my price."

"And fifty's mine," said Mr. Dillet. The point of agreement was, of course, somewhere between the two, it does not matter exactly where – I think sixty guineas. But half an hour later the object was being packed, and within an hour Mr. Dillet had called for it in his car and driven away. Mr. Chittenden, holding the cheque in his hand, saw him off from the door with smiles, and returned, still smiling, into the parlour where his wife was making the tea. He stopped at the door.

"It's gone," he said. "Thank God for that!" said Mrs. Chittenden, putting down the teapot. "Mr. Dillet, was it?"

"Yes, it was."

"Well, I'd sooner it was him than another." "Oh, I don't know; he ain't a bad feller, my dear."

"Maybe not, but in my opinion he'd be none the worse for a bit of a shake up."

"Well, if that's your opinion, it's my opinion he's put himself into the way of getting one. Anyhow, we shan't have no more of it, and that's something to be thankful for." And so Mr. and Mrs. Chittenden sat down to tea.

And what of Mr. Dillet and his new acquisition? What it was, the title of this story will have told you. What it was like, I shall have to indicate as well as I can.

There was only just enough room for it in the car, and Mr. Dillet had to sit with the driver: he had also to go slow, for though the rooms of the Dolls' House had all been stuffed carefully with soft cottonwool, jolting was to be avoided, in view of the immense number of small objects which thronged them; and the ten-mile drive was an anxious time for him, in spite of all the precautions he insisted upon. At last his front door was reached, and Collins, the butler, came out.

"Look here, Collins, you must help me with this thing – it's a delicate job. We must get it out upright, see? It's full of little things that mustn't be displaced more than we can help. Let's see, where shall we have it? (After a pause for consideration.) Really, I think I shall have to put it in my own room, to begin with at any rate. On the big table – that's it."

It was conveyed – with much talking – to Mr. Dillet's spacious room on the first floor, looking out on the drive. The sheeting was unwound from it, and the front thrown open, and for the next hour or two Mr. Dillet was fully occupied in extracting the padding and setting in order the contents of the rooms.

When this thoroughly congenial task was finished, I must say that it would have been difficult to find a more perfect and attractive specimen of a Dolls' House in Strawberry Hill Gothic than that which now stood on Mr. Dillet's large kneehole table, lighted up by the evening sun which came slanting through three tall slash-windows.

It was quite six feet long, including the Chapel or Oratory which flanked the front on the left as you faced it, and the stable on the right. The main block of the house was, as I have said, in the Gothic manner: that is to say, the windows had pointed arches and were surmounted by what are called ogival hoods, with crockets and finials such as we see on the canopies of tombs built into church walls. At the angles were absurd turrets covered with arched panels. The Chapel had pinnacles and buttresses, and a bell in the turret and coloured glass in the windows. When the front of the house was open you saw four large rooms, bedroom, dining-room, drawing-room and kitchen, each with its appropriate furniture in a very complete state.

The stable on the right was in two storeys, with its proper complement of horses, coaches and grooms, and with its clock and Gothic cupola for the clock bell.

Pages, of course, might be written on the outfit of the mansion – how many frying-pans, how many gilt chairs, what pictures, carpets, chandeliers, four-posters, table linen, glass, crockery and plate it possessed; but all this must be left to the imagination. I will only say that the base or plinth on which the house stood (for it was fitted with one of some depth which allowed of a flight of steps to the front door and a terrace, partly balustraded) contained a shallow drawer or drawers in which were neatly stored sets of embroidered curtains, changes of raiment for the inmates, and, in short, all the materials for an infinite series of variations and refittings of the most absorbing and delightful kind.

"Quintessence of Horace Walpole, that's what it is: he must have had something to do with the making of it." Such was Mr. Dillet's murmured reflection as he knelt before it in a reverent ecstasy. "Simply wonderful! This is my day and no mistake. Five hundred pounds coming in this morning for that cabinet which I never cared about, and now this tumbling into my hands for a tenth, at the very most, of what it would fetch in town. Well, well! It almost makes one afraid something'll happen to counter it. Let's have a look at the population, anyhow."

Accordingly, he set them before him in a row. Again, here is an opportunity, which some would snatch at, of making an inventory of costume: I am incapable of it.

There were a gentleman and lady, in blue satin and brocade respectively. There were two children, a boy and a girl. There was a cook, a nurse, a footman, and there were the stable servants, two postilions, a coachman, two grooms.

"Anyone else? Yes, possibly."

The curtains of the four-poster in the bedroom were closely drawn round all four sides of it, and he put his finger in between them and felt in the bed. He drew the finger back hastily, for it almost seemed to him as if something had – not stirred, perhaps, but yielded – in an odd live way as he pressed it. Then he put back the curtains, which ran on rods in the proper manner, and extracted from the bed a white-haired old gentleman in a long linen night-dress and cap, and laid him down by the rest. The tale was complete.

Dinner-time was now near, so Mr. Dillet spent but five minutes in putting the lady and children into the drawing-room, the gentleman into the dining-room, the servants into the kitchen and stables, and the old man back into his bed. He retired into his dressing-room next door, and we see and hear no more of him until something like eleven o'clock at night.

His whim was to sleep surrounded by some of the gems of his collection. The big room in which we have seen him contained his bed: bath, wardrobe, and all the appliances of dressing were in a commodious room adjoining: but his four-poster, which itself was a valued treasure, stood in the large room where he sometimes wrote, and often sat, and even received visitors. Tonight he repaired to it in a highly complacent frame of mind.

There was no striking clock within earshot – none on the staircase, none in the stable, none in the distant church tower. Yet it is indubitable that Mr. Dillet was started out of a very pleasant slumber by a bell tolling One.

He was so much startled that he did not merely lie breathless with wide-open eyes, but actually sat up in his bed.

He never asked himself, till the morning hours, how it was that, though there was no light at all in the room, the Dolls' House on the kneehole table stood out with complete clearness. But it was so. The effect was that of a bright harvest moon shining full on the front of a big white stone mansion – a quarter of a mile away it might be, and yet every detail was photographically sharp. There were trees about it, too – trees rising behind the chapel and the house. He seemed to be conscious of the scent of a cool still September night. He thought he could hear an occasional stamp and clink from the stables, as of horses stirring. And with another shock he realized that, above the house, he was looking, not at the wall of his room with its pictures, but into the profound blue of a night sky.

There were lights, more than one, in the windows, and he quickly saw that this was no four-roomed house with a movable front, but one of many rooms and staircases – a real house, but seen as if through the wrong end of a telescope.

"You mean to show me something," he muttered to himself, and he gazed earnestly on the lighted windows. They would in real life have been shuttered or curtained, no doubt, he thought; but, as it was, there was nothing to intercept his view of what was being transacted inside the rooms.

Two rooms were lighted – one on the ground floor to the right of the door, one upstairs, on the left – the first brightly enough, the other rather dimly. The lower room was the dining-room: a table was laid, but the meal was over, and only wine and glasses were left on the table. The man of the blue satin and the woman of the brocade were alone in the room, and they were talking very earnestly, seated close together at the table, their elbows on it: every now and again stopping to listen, as it seemed. Once he rose, came to the window and opened it and put his head out and his hand to his ear. There was a lighted taper in a silver candlestick on a sideboard. When the man left the window he seemed to leave the room also; and the lady, taper in hand, remained standing and listening. The expression on her face was that of one striving her utmost to keep down a fear that threatened to master her – and succeeding. It was a hateful face, too; broad, flat and sly. Now the man came back and she took some small thing from him and hurried out of the room. He, too, disappeared, but only for a moment or two. The front door slowly opened and he stepped out and stood on the top of the perron, looking this way and that; then turned towards the upper window that was lighted, and shook his fist.

It was time to look at that upper window. Through it was seen a four-post bed: a nurse or other servant in an arm-chair, evidently sound asleep; in the bed an old man lying: awake, and, one would say, anxious, from the way in which he shifted about and moved his fingers, beating tunes on the coverlet. Beyond the bed a door opened. Light was seen on the ceiling, and the lady came in: she set down her candle on a table, came to the fireside and roused the nurse. In her hand she had an old-fashioned wine bottle, ready uncorked. The nurse took it, poured some of the contents into a little silver saucepan, added some spice and sugar from casters on the table, and set it to warm on the fire. Meanwhile the old man in the bed beckoned feebly to the lady, who came to him, smiling, took his wrist as if to feel his pulse, and bit her lip as if in consternation. He looked at her anxiously, and then pointed to the window, and spoke. She nodded, and did as the man below had done; opened the casement and listened – perhaps rather ostentatiously: then drew in her head and shook it, looking at the old man, who seemed to sigh.

By this time the posset on the fire was steaming, and the nurse poured it into a small two-handled silver bowl and brought it to the bedside. The old man seemed disinclined for it and was waving it away, but the lady and the nurse together bent over him and evidently pressed it upon him. He must have yielded, for they supported him into a sitting position, and put it to his lips. He drank most of it, in several draughts, and they laid him down. The lady left the room, smiling good night to him, and took the bowl, the bottle and the silver saucepan with her. The nurse returned to the chair, and there was an interval of complete quiet.

Suddenly the old man started up in his bed – and he must have uttered some cry, for the nurse started out of her chair and made but one step of it to the bedside. He was a sad and terrible sight – flushed in the face, almost to blackness, the eyes glaring whitely, both hands clutching at his heart, foam at his lips. For a moment the nurse left him, ran to the door, flung it wide open, and, one supposes, screamed aloud for help, then darted back to the bed and seemed to try feverishly to soothe him – to lay him down – anything. But as the lady, her husband, and several servants, rushed into the room with horrified faces, the old man collapsed under the nurse's hands and lay back, and his features, contorted with agony and rage, relaxed slowly into calm.

A few moments later, lights showed out to the left of the house, and a coach with flambeaux drove up to the door. A white-wigged man in black got nimbly out and ran up the steps, carrying a small leather trunk-shaped box. He was met in the doorway by the man and his wife, she with her handkerchief clutched between her hands, he with a tragic face, but retaining his self-control. They led the new-comer into the dining-room, where he set his box of papers on the table, and, turning to them, listened with a face of consternation at what they had to tell. He nodded his head again and again, threw out his hands slightly, declined, it seemed, offers of refreshment and lodging for the night, and within a few minutes came slowly down the steps, entering the coach and driving off the way he had come. As the man in blue watched him from the top of the steps, a smile not pleasant to see stole slowly over his fat white face. Darkness fell over the whole scene as the lights of the coach disappeared.

But Mr. Dillet remained sitting up in the bed: he had rightly guessed that there would be a sequel. The house front glimmered out again before long. But now there was a difference. The lights were in other windows, one at the top of the house, the other illuminating the range of coloured windows of the chapel. How he saw through these is not quite obvious, but he did. The interior was as carefully furnished as the rest of the establishment, with its minute red cushions on the desks, its Gothic stall-canopies, and its western gallery and pinnacled organ with gold pipes. On the centre of the black and white pavement was a bier: four tall candles burned at the corners. On the bier was a coffin covered with a pall of black velvet.

As he looked the folds of the pall stirred. It seemed to rise at one end: it slid downwards: it fell away, exposing the black coffin with its silver handles and name-plate. One of the tall candlesticks swayed and toppled over. Ask no more, but turn, as Mr. Dillet hastily did, and look in at the lighted window at the top of the house, where a boy and girl lay in two truckle-beds, and a four-poster for the nurse rose above them. The nurse was not visible for the moment; but the father and mother were there, dressed now in mourning, but with very little sign of mourning in their demeanour. Indeed, they were laughing and talking with a good deal of animation, sometimes to each other, and sometimes throwing a remark to one or other of the children, and again laughing at the answers. Then the father was seen to go on tiptoe out of the room, taking with him as he went a white garment that hung on a peg near the door. He shut the door after him. A minute or two later it was slowly opened again, and a muffled head poked round it. A bent form of sinister shape stepped across to the truckle-beds, and suddenly stopped, threw up its arms and revealed, of course, the father, laughing. The children were in agonies of terror, the boy with the bedclothes over his head, the girl throwing herself out of bed into her mother's arms. Attempts at consolation followed – the parents took the children on their laps, patted them, picked up the white gown and showed there was no harm in it, and so forth; and at last putting the children back into bed, left the room with encouraging waves of the hand. As they left it, the nurse came in, and soon the light died down.

Still Mr. Dillet watched immovable.

A new sort of light – not of lamp or candle – a pale ugly light, began to dawn around the door-case at the back of the room. The door was opening again. The seer does not like to dwell upon what he saw entering the room: he says it might be described as a frog – the size of a man – but it had scanty white hair about its head. It was busy about the truckle-beds, but not for long. The sound of cries – faint, as if coming out of a vast distance – but, even so, infinitely appalling, reached the ear.

There were signs of a hideous commotion all over the house: lights moved along and up, and doors opened and shut, and running figures passed within the windows. The clock in the stable turret tolled one, and darkness fell again.

It was only dispelled once more, to show the house front. At the bottom of the steps dark figures were drawn up in two lines, holding flaming torches. More dark figures came down the steps, bearing, first one, then another small coffin. And the lines of torch-bearers with the coffins between them moved silently onward to the left.

The hours of night passed on – never so slowly, Mr. Dillet thought. Gradually he sank down from sitting to lying in his bed – but he did not close an eye: and early next morning he sent for the doctor.

The doctor found him in a disquieting state of nerves, and recommended sea-air. To a quiet place on the East Coast he accordingly repaired by easy stages in his car.

One of the first people he met on the sea front was Mr. Chittenden, who, it appeared, had likewise been advised to take his wife away for a bit of a change.

Mr. Chittenden looked somewhat askance upon him when they met: and not without cause. "Well, I don't wonder at you being a bit upset, Mr. Dillet. What? Yes, well, I might say 'orrible upset, to be sure, seeing what me and my poor wife went through ourselves. But I put it to you, Mr. Dillet, one of two things: was I going to scrap a lovely piece like that on the one 'and, or was I going to tell customers: 'I'm selling you a regular picture-palace-dramar in reel life of the olden time, billed to perform regular at one o'clock a.m.?' Why, what would you 'ave said yourself? And next thing you know, two Justices of the Peace in the back parlour, and pore Mr. and Mrs. Chittenden off in a spring cart to the County Asylum and everyone in the street saying, 'Ah, I thought it 'ud come to that. Look at the way the man drank!' – and me next door, or next door but one, to a total abstainer, as you know. Well, there was my position. What? Me 'ave it back in the shop? Well, what do you think? No, but I'll tell you what I will do. You shall have your money back, bar the ten pound I paid for it, and you make what you can."

Later in the day, in what is offensively called the 'smoke-room' of the hotel, a murmured conversation between the two went on for some time.

"How much do you really know about that thing, and where it came from?"

"Honest, Mr. Dillet, I don't know the 'ouse. Of course, it came out of the lumber room of a country 'ouse – that anyone could guess. But I'll go as far as say this, that I believe it's not a hundred miles from this place. Which direction and how far I've no notion. I'm only judging by guess-work. The man as I actually paid the cheque to ain't one of my regular men, and I've lost sight of him; but I 'ave the idea that this part of the country was his beat, and that's every word I can tell you. But now, Mr. Dillet, there's one thing that rather physicks me. That old chap – I suppose you saw him drive up to the door – I thought so: now, would he have been the medical man, do you take it? My wife would have it so, but I stuck to it that was the lawyer, because he had papers with him, and one he took out was folded up."

"I agree," said Mr. Dillet. "Thinking it over, I came to the conclusion that was the old man's will, ready to be signed."

"Just what I thought," said Mr. Chittenden, "and I took it that will would have cut out the young people, eh? Well, well! It's been a lesson to me, I know that. I shan't buy no more dolls' houses, nor waste no more money on the pictures – and as to this business of poisonin' grandpa, well, if I know myself, I never 'ad much of a turn for that. Live and let live: that's bin my motto throughout life, and I ain't found it a bad one."

Filled with these elevated sentiments, Mr. Chittenden retired to his lodgings. Mr. Dillet next day repaired to the local Institute, where he hoped to find some clue to the riddle that absorbed him. He gazed in despair at a long file of the Canterbury and York Society's publications of the Parish Registers of the District. No print resembling the house of his nightmare was among those that hung on the staircase and in the passages. Disconsolate, he found himself at last in a derelict room, staring at a dusty model of a church in a dusty glass case:

Model of St. Stephen's Church, Coxham. Presented by J. Merewether, Esq., of Ilbridge House, 1877. The work of his ancestor James Merewether, d. 1786.

There was something in the fashion of it that reminded him dimly of his horror. He retraced his steps to a wall map he had noticed, and made out that Ilbridge House was in Coxham Parish. Coxham was, as it happened, one of the parishes of which he had retained the name when he glanced over the file of printed registers, and it was not long before he found in them the record of the burial of Roger Milford, aged 76, on the 11th of September, 1757, and of Roger and Elizabeth Merewether, aged 9 and 7, on the 19th of the same month. It seemed worthwhile to follow up this clue, frail as it was; and in the afternoon he drove out to Coxham. The east end of the north aisle of the church is a Milford chapel, and on its north wall are tablets to the same persons; Roger, the elder, it seems, was distinguished by all the qualities which adorn 'the Father, the Magistrate and the Man': the memorial was erected by his attached daughter Elizabeth, 'who did not long survive the loss of a parent ever solicitous for her welfare, and of two amiable children'. The last sentence was plainly an addition to the original inscription.

A yet later slab told of James Merewether, husband of Elizabeth, "who in the dawn of life practised, not without success, those arts which, had he continued their exercise, might in the opinion of the most competent judges have earned for him the name of the British Vitruvius: but who, overwhelmed by the visitation which deprived him of an affectionate partner and a blooming offspring, passed his Prime and Age in a secluded yet elegant Retirement: his grateful Nephew and Heir indulges a pious sorrow by this too brief recital of his excellences."

The children were more simply commemorated. Both died on the night of the 12th of September.

Mr. Dillet felt sure that in Ilbridge House he had found the scene of his drama. In some old sketchbook, possibly in some old print, he may yet find convincing evidence that he is right. But the Ilbridge House of today is not that which he sought; it is an Elizabethan erection of the forties, in red brick with stone quoins and dressings. A quarter of a mile from it, in a low part of the park, backed by ancient, staghorned, ivy-strangled trees and thick undergrowth, are marks of a terraced platform overgrown with rough grass. A few stone balusters lie here and there, and a heap or two, covered with nettles and ivy, of wrought stones with badly-carved crockets. This, someone told Mr. Dillet, was the site of an older house.

As he drove out of the village, the hall clock struck four, and Mr. Dillet started up and clapped his hands to his ears. It was not the first time he had heard that bell.

Awaiting an offer from the other side of the Atlantic, the dolls' house still reposes, carefully sheeted, in a loft over Mr. Dillet's stables, whither Collins conveyed it on the day when Mr. Dillet started for the sea coast.

The Man of Science

Jerome K. Jerome

I MET A MAN in the Strand one day that I knew very well, as I thought, though I had not seen him for years. We walked together to Charing Cross, and there we shook hands and parted. Next morning, I spoke of this meeting to a mutual friend, and then I learnt, for the first time, that the man had died six months before.

The natural inference was that I had mistaken one man for another, an error that, not having a good memory for faces, I frequently fall into. What was remarkable about the matter, however, was that throughout our walk I had conversed with the man under the impression that he was that other dead man, and, whether by coincidence or not, his replies had never once suggested to me my mistake.

As soon as I finished, Jephson, who had been listening very thoughtfully, asked me if I believed in spiritualism 'to its fullest extent'.

"That is rather a large question," I answered. "What do you mean by 'spiritualism to its fullest extent'?"

"Well, do you believe that the spirits of the dead have not only the power of revisiting this earth at their will, but that, when here, they have the power of action, or rather, of exciting to action? Let me put a definite case. A spiritualist friend of mine, a sensible and by no means imaginative man, once told me that a table, through the medium of which the spirit of a friend had been in the habit of communicating with him, came slowly across the room towards him, of its own accord, one night as he sat alone, and pinioned him against the wall. Now can any of you believe that, or can't you?"

"I could," Brown took it upon himself to reply; "but, before doing so, I should wish for an introduction to the friend who told you the story. Speaking generally," he continued, "it seems to me that the difference between what we call the natural and the supernatural is merely the difference between frequency and rarity of occurrence. Having regard to the phenomena we are compelled to admit, I think it illogical to disbelieve anything we are unable to disprove."

"For my part," remarked MacShaughnassy, "I can believe in the ability of our spirit friends to give the quaint entertainments credited to them much easier than I can in their desire to do so."

"You mean," added Jephson, "that you cannot understand why a spirit, not compelled as we are by the exigencies of society, should care to spend its evenings carrying on a laboured and childish conversation with a room full of abnormally uninteresting people."

"That is precisely what I cannot understand," MacShaughnassy agreed.

"Nor I, either," said Jephson. "But I was thinking of something very different altogether. Suppose a man died with the dearest wish of his heart unfulfilled, do you believe that his spirit might have power to return to earth and complete the interrupted work?"

"Well," answered MacShaughnassy, "if one admits the possibility of spirits retaining any interest in the affairs of this world at all, it is certainly more reasonable to imagine them engaged upon a task such as you suggest, than to believe that they occupy themselves with the performance of mere drawing-room tricks. But what are you leading up to?"

"Why, to this," replied Jephson, seating himself straddle-legged across his chair, and leaning his arms upon the back. "I was told a story this morning at the hospital by an old French doctor. The actual facts are few and simple; all that is known can be read in the Paris police records of sixty-two years ago.

"The most important part of the case, however, is the part that is not known, and that never will be known.

"The story begins with a great wrong done by one man unto another man. What the wrong was I do not know. I am inclined to think, however, it was connected with a woman. I think that, because he who had been wronged hated him who had wronged him with a hate such as does not often burn in a man's brain, unless it be fanned by the memory of a woman's breath.

"Still that is only conjecture, and the point is immaterial. The man who had done the wrong fled, and the other man followed him. It became a point-to-point race, the first man having the advantage of a day's start. The course was the whole world, and the stakes were the first man's life.

"Travellers were few and far between in those days, and this made the trail easy to follow. The first man, never knowing how far or how near the other was behind him, and hoping now and again that he might have baffled him, would rest for a while. The second man, knowing always just how far the first one was before him, never paused, and thus each day the man who was spurred by Hate drew nearer to the man who was spurred by Fear.

"At this town the answer to the never-varied question would be:

"'At seven o'clock last evening, M'sieur.'

"'Seven – ah; eighteen hours. Give me something to eat, quick, while the horses are being put to.'

"At the next the calculation would be sixteen hours.

"Passing a lonely châlet, Monsieur puts his head out of the window:

"'How long since a carriage passed this way, with a tall, fair man inside?'

"'Such a one passed early this morning, M'sieur.'

"'Thanks, drive on, a hundred francs apiece if you are through the pass before daybreak.'

"'And what for dead horses, M'sieur?'

"'Twice their value when living.'

"One day the man who was ridden by Fear looked up, and saw before him the open door of a cathedral, and, passing in, knelt down and prayed. He prayed long and fervently, for men, when they are in sore straits, clutch eagerly at the straws of faith. He prayed that he might be forgiven his sin, and, more important still, that he might be pardoned the consequences of his sin, and be delivered from his adversary; and a few chairs from him, facing him, knelt his enemy, praying also.

"But the second man's prayer, being a thanksgiving merely, was short, so that when the first man raised his eyes, he saw the face of his enemy gazing at him across the chair-tops, with a mocking smile upon it.

"He made no attempt to rise, but remained kneeling, fascinated by the look of joy that shone out of the other man's eyes. And the other man moved the high-backed chairs one by one, and came towards him softly.

"Then, just as the man who had been wronged stood beside the man who had wronged him, full of gladness that his opportunity had come, there burst from the cathedral tower a sudden clash of bells, and the man, whose opportunity had come, broke his heart and fell back dead, with that mocking smile still playing round his mouth.

"And so he lay there.

"Then the man who had done the wrong rose up and passed out, praising God.

"What became of the body of the other man is not known. It was the body of a stranger who had died suddenly in the cathedral. There was none to identify it, none to claim it.

"Years passed away, and the survivor in the tragedy became a worthy and useful citizen, and a noted man of science.

"In his laboratory were many objects necessary to him in his researches, and, prominent among them, stood in a certain corner a human skeleton. It was a very old and much-mended skeleton, and one day the long-expected end arrived, and it tumbled to pieces.

"Thus it became necessary to purchase another.

"The man of science visited a dealer he well knew – a little parchment-faced old man who kept a dingy shop, where nothing was ever sold, within the shadow of the towers of Notre Dame.

"The little parchment-faced old man had just the very thing that Monsieur wanted – a singularly fine and well-proportioned 'study'. It should be sent round and set up in Monsieur's laboratory that very afternoon.

"The dealer was as good as his word. When Monsieur entered his laboratory that evening, the thing was in its place.

"Monsieur seated himself in his high-backed chair, and tried to collect his thoughts. But Monsieur's thoughts were unruly, and inclined to wander, and to wander always in one direction.

"Monsieur opened a large volume and commenced to read. He read of a man who had wronged another and fled from him, the other man following. Finding himself reading this, he closed the book angrily, and went and stood by the window and looked out. He saw before him the sun-pierced nave of a great cathedral, and on the stones lay a dead man with a mocking smile upon his face.

"Cursing himself for a fool, he turned away with a laugh. But his laugh was short-lived, for it seemed to him that something else in the room was laughing also. Struck suddenly still, with his feet glued to the ground, he stood listening for a while: then sought with starting eyes the corner from where the sound had seemed to come. But the white thing standing there was only grinning.

"Monsieur wiped the damp sweat from his head and hands, and stole out.

"For a couple of days he did not enter the room again. On the third, telling himself that his fears were those of a hysterical girl, he opened the door and went in. To shame himself, he took his lamp in his hand, and crossing over to the far corner where the skeleton stood, examined it. A set of bones bought for three hundred francs. Was he a child, to be scared by such a bogey!

"He held his lamp up in front of the thing's grinning head. The flame of the lamp flickered as though a faint breath had passed over it.

"The man explained this to himself by saying that the walls of the house were old and cracked, and that the wind might creep in anywhere. He repeated this explanation to himself as he recrossed the room, walking backwards, with his eyes fixed on the thing. When he reached his desk, he sat down and gripped the arms of his chair till his fingers turned white.

"He tried to work, but the empty sockets in that grinning head seemed to be drawing him towards them. He rose and battled with his inclination to fly screaming from the room. Glancing fearfully about him, his eye fell upon a high screen, standing before the door. He dragged it forward, and placed it between himself and the thing, so that he could not see it – nor it see him. Then he sat down again to his work. For a while he forced himself to look at the book in front of him, but at last, unable to control himself any longer, he suffered his eyes to follow their own bent.

"It may have been an hallucination. He may have accidentally placed the screen so as to favour such an illusion. But what he saw was a bony hand coming round the corner of the screen, and, with a cry, he fell to the floor in a swoon.

"The people of the house came running in, and lifting him up, carried him out, and laid him upon his bed. As soon as he recovered, his first question was, where had they found the thing – where was it when they entered the room? And when they told him they had seen it standing where it always stood, and had gone down into the room to look again, because of his frenzied entreaties, and returned trying to hide their smiles, he listened to their talk about overwork, and the necessity for change and rest, and said they might do with him as they would.

"So for many months the laboratory door remained locked. Then there came a chill autumn evening when the man of science opened it again, and closed it behind him.

"He lighted his lamp, and gathered his instruments and books around him, and sat down before them in his high-backed chair. And the old terror returned to him.

"But this time he meant to conquer himself. His nerves were stronger now, and his brain clearer; he would fight his unreasoning fear. He crossed to the door and locked himself in, and flung the key to the other end of the room, where it fell among jars and bottles with an echoing clatter.

"Later on, his old housekeeper, going her final round, tapped at his door and wished him goodnight, as was her custom. She received no response, at first, and, growing nervous, tapped louder and called again; and at length an answering 'goodnight' came back to her.

"She thought little about it at the time, but afterwards she remembered that the voice that had replied to her had been strangely grating and mechanical. Trying to describe it, she likened it to such a voice as she would imagine coming from a statue.

"Next morning his door remained still locked. It was no unusual thing for him to work all night and far into the next day, so no one thought to be surprised. When, however, evening came, and yet he did not appear, his servants gathered outside the room and whispered, remembering what had happened once before.

"They listened, but could hear no sound. They shook the door and called to him, then beat with their fists upon the wooden panels. But still no sound came from the room.

"Becoming alarmed, they decided to burst open the door, and, after many blows, it gave way, and they crowded in.

"He sat bolt upright in his high-backed chair. They thought at first he had died in his sleep. But when they drew nearer and the light fell upon him, they saw the livid marks of bony fingers round his throat; and in his eyes there was a terror such as is not often seen in human eyes."

* * *

Brown was the first to break the silence that followed. He asked me if I had any brandy on board. He said he felt he should like just a nip of brandy before going to bed. That is one of the chief charms of Jephson's stories: they always make you feel you want a little brandy.

Thurnley Abbey

Perceval Landon

THREE YEARS AGO I was on my way out to the East, and as an extra day in London was of some importance, I took the Friday evening mail-train to Brindisi instead of the usual Thursday morning Marseilles express. Many people shrink from the long forty-eight-hour train journey through Europe, and the subsequent rush across the Mediterranean on the nineteen-knot *Isis* or *Osiris*; but there is really very little discomfort on either the train or the mail-boat, and unless there is actually nothing for me to do, I always like to save the extra day and a half in London before I say goodbye to her for one of my longer tramps. This time – it was early, I remember, in the shipping season, probably about the beginning of September – there were few passengers, and I had a compartment in the P&O Indian express to myself all the way from Calais. All Sunday I watched the blue waves dimpling the Adriatic, and the pale rosemary along the cuttings; the plain white towns, with their flat roofs and their bold 'duomos', and the grey-green gnarled olive orchards of Apulia. The journey was just like any other. We ate in the dining-car as often and as long as we decently could. We slept after luncheon; we dawdled the afternoon away with yellow-backed novels; sometimes we exchanged platitudes in the smoking-room, and it was there that I met Alastair Colvin.

Colvin was a man of middle height, with a resolute, well-cut jaw; his hair was turning grey; his moustache was sun-whitened, otherwise he was clean-shaven – obviously a gentleman, and obviously also a preoccupied man. He had no great wit. When spoken to, he made the usual remarks in the right way, and I dare say he refrained from banalities only because he spoke less than the rest of us; most of the time he buried himself in the Wagon-lit Company's time-table, but seemed unable to concentrate his attention on any one page of it. He found that I had been over the Siberian railway, and for a quarter of an hour he discussed it with me. Then he lost interest in it, and rose to go to his compartment. But he came back again very soon, and seemed glad to pick up the conversation again.

Of course this did not seem to me to be of any importance. Most travellers by train become a trifle infirm of purpose after thirty-six hours' rattling. But Colvin's restless way I noticed in somewhat marked contrast with the man's personal importance and dignity; especially ill suited was it to his finely made large hand with strong, broad, regular nails and its few lines. As I looked at his hand I noticed a long, deep, and recent scar of ragged shape. However, it is absurd to pretend that I thought anything was unusual. I went off at five o'clock on Sunday afternoon to sleep away the hour or two that had still to be got through before we arrived at Brindisi.

Once there, we few passengers transhipped our hand baggage, verified our berths – there were only a score of us in all – and then, after an aimless ramble of half an hour in Brindisi, we returned to dinner at the Hotel International, not wholly surprised that the town had been the death of Virgil. If I remember rightly, there is a gaily painted hall at the International – I do not wish to advertise am-thine, but there is no other place in Brindisi at which to await the coming of the mails – and after dinner I was looking with awe at a trellis overgrown with blue vines, when Colvin moved across the room to my table. He picked up *Il Secolo*, but almost immediately gave up the pretence of reading it. He turned squarely to me and said:

"Would you do me a favour?"

One doesn't do favours to stray acquaintances on Continental expresses without knowing something more of them than I knew of Colvin. But I smiled in a noncommittal way, and asked him what he wanted. I wasn't wrong in part of my estimate of him; he said bluntly:

"Will you let me sleep in your cabin on the *Osiris*?" And he coloured a little as he said it.

Now, there is nothing more tiresome than having to put up with a stable-companion at sea, and I asked him rather pointedly:

"Surely there is room for all of us?" I thought that perhaps he had been partnered off with some mangy Levantine, and wanted to escape from him at all hazards.

Colvin, still somewhat confused, said: "Yes; I am in a cabin by myself. But you would do me the greatest favour if you would allow me to share yours."

This was all very well, but, besides the fact that I always sleep better when alone, there had been some recent thefts on board English liners, and I hesitated, frank and honest and self-conscious as Colvin was. Just then the mail-train came in with a clatter and a rush of escaping steam, and I asked him to see me again about it on the boat when we started. He answered me curtly – I suppose he saw the mistrust in my manner – "I am a member of White's. I smiled to myself as he said it, but I remembered in a moment that the man – if he were really what he claimed to be, and I make no doubt that he was – must have been sorely put to it before he urged the fact as a guarantee of his respectability to a total stranger at a Brindisi hotel.

That evening, as we cleared the red and green harbour-lights of Brindisi, Colvin explained. This is his story in his own words.

"When I was travelling in India some years ago, I made the acquaintance of a youngish man in the Woods and Forests. We camped out together for a week, and I found him a pleasant companion. John Broughton was a light-hearted soul when off duty, but a steady and capable man in any of the small emergencies that continually arise in that department. He was liked and trusted by the natives, and though a trifle over-pleased with himself when he escaped to civilization at Simla or Calcutta, Broughton's future was well assured in Government service, when a fair-sized estate was unexpectedly left to him, and he joyfully shook the dust of the Indian plains from his feet and returned to England. For five years he drifted about London. I saw him now and then. We dined together about every eighteen months, and I could trace pretty exactly the gradual sickening of Broughton with a merely idle life. He then set out on a couple of long voyages, returned as restless as before, and at last told me that he had decided to marry and settle down at his place, Thurnley Abbey, which had long been empty. He spoke about looking after the property and standing for his constituency in the usual way. Vivien Wilde, his fiancée, had, I suppose, begun to take him in hand. She was a pretty girl with a deal of fair hair and rather an exclusive manner; deeply religious in a narrow school, she was still kindly and high-spirited, and I thought that Broughton was in luck. He was quite happy and full of information about his future.

"Among other things, I asked him about Thurnley Abbey. He confessed that he hardly knew the place. The last tenant, a man called Clarke, had lived in one wing for fifteen years and seen no one. He had been a miser and a hermit. It was the rarest thing for a light to be seen at the Abbey after dark. Only the barest necessities of life were ordered, and the tenant himself received them at the side-door. His one half-caste manservant, after a month's stay in the house, had abruptly left without warning, and had returned to the Southern States. One thing Broughton complained bitterly about: Clarke had wilfully spread the rumour among the villagers that the Abbey was haunted, and had even condescended to play childish tricks with spirit-lamps and salt in order to scare trespassers away at night. He had been detected in the act of this tomfoolery, but the story spread, and no one, said Broughton, would venture near the house except in broad daylight. The hauntedness of Thurnley Abbey was now, he said with a grin, part of the gospel of the countryside, but he and his young wife were going to change all that. Would I propose myself anytime I liked? I, of course, said I would, and equally, of course, intended to do nothing of the sort without a definite invitation.

"The house was put in thorough repair, though not a stick of the old furniture and tapestry were removed. Floors and ceilings were relaid: the roof was made watertight again, and the dust of half a century was scoured out. He showed me some photographs of the place. It was called an Abbey, though as a matter of fact it had been only the infirmary of the long-vanished Abbey of Closter some five miles away. The larger part of this building remained as it had been in pre-Reformation days, but a wing had been added in Jacobean times, and that part of the house had been kept in something like repair by Mr. Clarke. He had in both the ground and first floors set a heavy timber door, strongly barred with iron, in the passage between the earlier and the Jacobean parts of the house, and had entirely neglected the former. So there had been a good deal of work to be done.

"Broughton, whom I saw in London two or three times about this period, made a deal of fun over the positive refusal of the workmen to remain after sundown. Even after the electric light had been put into every room, nothing would induce them to remain, though, as Broughton observed, electric light was death on ghosts. The legend of the Abbey's ghosts had gone far and wide, and the men would take no risks. They went home in batches of five and six, and even during the daylight hours there was an inordinate amount of talking between one and another, if either happened to be out of sight of his companion. On the whole, though nothing of any sort or kind had been conjured up even by their heated imaginations during their five months' work upon the Abbey, the belief in the ghosts was rather strengthened than otherwise in Thurnley because of the men's confessed nervousness, and local tradition declared itself in favour of the ghost of an immured nun.

"Good old nun!" said Broughton.

"I asked him whether in general he believed in the possibility of ghosts, and, rather to my surprise, he said that he couldn't say he entirely disbelieved in them. A man in India had told him one morning in camp that he believed that his mother was dead in England, as her vision had come to his tent the night before. He had not been alarmed, but had said nothing, and the figure vanished again. As a matter of fact, the next possible dak-walla brought on a telegram announcing the mother's death. 'There the thing was,' said Broughton. But at Thurnley he was practical enough. He roundly cursed the idiotic selfishness of Clarke, whose silly antics had caused all the inconvenience. At the same time, he couldn't refuse to sympathize to some extent with the ignorant workmen. 'My own idea,' said he, 'is that if a ghost ever does come in one's way, one ought to speak to it.'

"I agreed. Little as I knew of the ghost world and its conventions, I had always remembered that a spook was in honour bound to wait to be spoken to. It didn't seem much to do, and I felt that the sound of one's own voice would at any rate reassure oneself as to one's wakefulness. But there are few ghosts outside Europe – few, that is, that a white man can see – and I had never been troubled with any. However, as I have said, I told Broughton that I agreed.

"So the wedding took place, and I went to it in a tall hat which I bought for the occasion, and the new Mrs. Broughton smiled very nicely at me afterwards. As it had to happen, I took the Orient Express that evening and was not in England again for nearly six months. Just before

I came back I got a letter from Broughton. He asked if I could see him in London or come to Thurnley, as he thought I should be better able to help him than anyone else he knew. His wife sent a nice message to me at the end, so I was reassured about at least one thing. I wrote from Budapest that I would come and see him at Thurnley two days after my arrival in London, and as I sauntered out of the Pannonia into the Kerepesi Utcza to post my letters, I wondered of what earthly service I could be to Broughton. I had been out with him after tiger on foot, and I could imagine few men better able at a pinch to manage their own business. However, I had nothing to do, so after dealing with some small accumulations of business during my absence, I packed a kit-bag and departed to Euston.

"I was met by Broughton's great limousine at Thurnley Road station, and after a drive of nearly seven miles we echoed through the sleepy streets of Thurnley village, into which the main gates of the park thrust themselves, splendid with pillars and spreadeagles and tom-cats rampant atop of them. I never was a herald, but I know that the Broughtons have the right to supporters – Heaven knows why! From the gates a quadruple avenue of beech-trees led inwards for a quarter of a mile. Beneath them a neat strip of fine turf edged the road and ran back until the poison of the dead beech-leaves killed it under the trees. There were many wheel-tracks on the road, and a comfortable little pony trap jogged past me laden with a country parson and his wife and daughter. Evidently there was some garden party going on at the Abbey. The road dropped away to the right at the end of the avenue, and I could see the Abbey across a wide pasturage and a broad lawn thickly dotted with guests.

"The end of the building was plain. It must have been almost mercilessly austere when it was first built, but time had crumbled the edges and toned the stone down to an orange-lichened grey wherever it showed behind its curtain of magnolia, jasmine, and ivy. Further on was the three-storied Jacobean house, tall and handsome. There had not been the slightest attempt to adapt the one to the other, but the kindly ivy had glossed over the touching-point. There was a tall flèche in the middle of the building, surmounting a small bell tower. Behind the house there rose the mountainous verdure of Spanish chestnuts all the way up the hill.

"Broughton had seen me coming from afar, and walked across from his other guests to welcome me before turning me over to the butler's care. This man was sandy-haired and rather inclined to be talkative. He could, however, answer hardly any questions about the house; he had, he said, only been there three weeks. Mindful of what Broughton had told me, I made no enquiries about ghosts, though the room into which I was shown might have justified anything. It was a very large low room with oak beams projecting from the white ceiling. Every inch of the walls, including the doors, was covered with tapestry, and a remarkably fine Italian fourpost bedstead, heavily draped, added to the darkness and dignity of the place. All the furniture was old, well made and dark. Underfoot there was a plain green pile carpet, the only new thing about the room except the electric light fittings and the jugs and basins. Even the looking-glass on the dressing-table was an old pyramidal Venetian glass set in heavy repoussé frame of tarnished silver.

"After a few minutes' cleaning up, I went downstairs and out upon the lawn, where I greeted my hostess. The people gathered there were of the usual country type, all anxious to be pleased and roundly curious as to the new master of the Abbey. Rather to my surprise, and quite to my pleasure, I rediscovered Glenham, whom I had known well in old days in Barotseland: he lived quite close, as he remarked with a grin. I ought to have known. 'But,' he added, 'I don't live in a place like this.' He swept his hand to the long, low lines of the Abbey in obvious admiration, and then, to my intense interest, muttered beneath his breath, 'Thank

God!' He saw that I had overheard him, and turning to me said decidedly, 'Yes, thank God I said, and I meant it. I wouldn't live at the Abbey for all Broughton's money.'

"'But surely,' I demurred, 'you know that old Clarke was discovered in the very act of setting light to his bug-a-boos?'

"Glenham shrugged his shoulders. 'Yes, I know about that. But there is something wrong with the place still. All I can say is that Broughton is a different man since he has lived here. I don't believe that he will remain much longer. But – you're staying here? – well, you'll hear all about it tonight. There's a big dinner, I understand." The conversation turned off to old reminiscences, and Glenham soon after had to go.

"Before I went to dress that evening I had twenty minutes' talk with Broughton in his library. There was no doubt that the man was altered, gravely altered. He was nervous and fidgety, and I found him looking at me only when my eye was off him. I naturally asked him what he wanted of me. I told him I would do anything I could, but that I couldn't conceive what he lacked that I could provide. He said with a lustreless smile that there was, however, something, and that he would tell me the following morning. It struck me that he was somehow ashamed of himself and perhaps ashamed of the part he was asking me to play. However, I dismissed the subject from my mind and went up to dress in my palatial room. As I shut the door a draught blew out the Queen of Sheba from the wall, and I noticed that the tapestries were not fastened to the wall at the bottom. I have always held very practical views about spooks, and it has often seemed to me that the slow waving in firelight of loose tapestry upon a wall would account for ninety-nine per cent of the stories one hears. Certainly the dignified undulation of this lady with her attendants and huntsmen – one of whom was untidily cutting the throat of a fallow deer upon the very steps on which King Solomon, a grey-faced Flemish nobleman with the order of the Golden Fleece, awaited his fair visitor – gave colour to my hypothesis.

"Nothing much happened at dinner. The people were very much like those of the garden party. A young woman next to me seemed anxious to know what was being read in London. As she was far more familiar than I with the most recent magazines and literary supplements, I found salvation in being myself instructed in the tendencies of modern fiction. All true art, she said, was shot through and through with melancholy. How vulgar were the attempts at wit that marked so many modern books! From the beginning of literature it had always been tragedy that embodied the highest attainment of every age. To call such works morbid merely begged the question. No thoughtful man – she looked sternly at me through the steel rim of her glasses – could fail to agree with me. Of course, as one would, I immediately and properly said that I slept with Pett Ridge and Jacobs under my pillow at night, and that if *Jorrocks* weren't quite so large and cornery, I would add him to the company. She hadn't read any of them, so I was saved – for a time. But I remember grimly that she said that the dearest wish of her life was to be in some awful and soul-freezing situation of horror, and I remember that she dealt hardly with the hero of Nat Paynter's vampire story, between nibbles at her brown-bread ice. She was a cheerless soul, and I couldn't help thinking that if there were many such in the neighbourhood, it was not surprising that old Glenham had been stuffed with some nonsense or other about the Abbey. Yet nothing could well have been less creeps than the glitter of silver and glass, and the subdued lights and cackle of conversation all round the dinner-table.

"After the ladies had gone I found myself talking to the rural dean. He was a thin, earnest man, who at once turned the conversation to old Clarke's buffooneries. But, he said, Mr. Broughton had introduced such a new and cheerful spirit, not only into the Abbey, but, he might say, into the whole neighbourhood, that he had great hopes that the ignorant superstitions of the past were from henceforth destined to oblivion. Thereupon his other neighbour, a portly gentleman of independent means and position, audibly remarked 'Amen', which damped the rural dean, and we talked of partridges past, partridges present, and pheasants to come. At the other end of the table Broughton sat with a couple of his friends, red-faced hunting men. Once I noticed that they were discussing me, but I paid no attention to it at the time. I remembered it a few hours later.

"By eleven all the guests were gone, and Broughton, his wife, and I were alone together under the fine plaster ceiling of the Jacobean drawing-room. Mrs. Broughton talked about one or two of the neighbours, and then, with a smile, said that she knew I would excuse her, shook hands with me, and went off to bed. I am not very good at analysing things, but I felt that she talked a little uncomfortably and with a suspicion of effort, smiled rather conventionally, and was obviously glad to go. These things seem trifling enough to repeat, but I had throughout the faint feeling that everything was not square. Under the circumstances, this was enough to set me wondering what on earth the service could be that I was to render – wondering also whether the whole business were not some ill-advised jest in order to make me come down from London for a mere shooting-party.

"Broughton said little after she had gone. But he was evidently labouring to bring the conversation round to the so-called haunting of the Abbey. As soon as I saw this, of course I asked him directly about it. He then seemed at once to lose interest in the matter. There was no doubt about it: Broughton was somehow a changed man, and to my mind he had changed in no way for the better. Mrs. Broughton seemed no sufficient cause. He was clearly very fond of her, and she of him. I reminded him that he was going to tell me what I could do for him in the morning, pleaded my journey, lighted a candle, and went upstairs with him. At the end of the passage leading into the old house he grinned weakly and said, 'Mind, if you see a ghost, do talk to it; you said you would.' He stood irresolutely a moment and then turned away. At the door of his dressing-room he paused once more: 'I'm here,' he called out, 'if you should want anything. Good night,' and he shut his door.

"I went along the passage to my room, undressed, switched on a lamp beside my bed, read a few pages of *The Jungle Book*, and then, more than ready for sleep, turned the light off and went fast asleep.

"Three hours later I woke up. There was not a breath of wind outside. There was not even a flicker of light from the fireplace. As I lay there, an ash tinkled slightly as it cooled, but there was hardly a gleam of the dullest red in the grate. An owl cried among the silent Spanish chestnuts on the slope outside. I idly reviewed the events of the day, hoping that I should fall off to sleep again before I reached dinner. But at the end I seemed as wakeful as ever. There was no help for it. I must read my Jungle Book again till I felt ready to go off, so I fumbled for the pear at the end of the cord that hung down inside the bed, and I switched on the bedside lamp. The sudden glory dazzled me for a moment. I felt under my pillow for my hook with half-shut eyes. Then, growing used to the light, I happened to look down to the foot of my bed.

"I can never tell you really what happened then. Nothing I could ever confess in the most abject words could even faintly picture to you what I felt. I know that my heart stopped dead, and my throat shut automatically. In one instinctive movement I crouched back up against the head-boards of the bed, staring at the horror. The movement set my heart going again, and the sweat dripped from every pore. I am not a particularly religious man, but I had always believed that God would never allow any supernatural appearance to present itself to man in such a guise and in such circumstances that harm, either bodily or mental, could result to him. I can only tell you that at that moment both my life and my reason rocked unsteadily on their seats."

The other *Osiris* passengers had gone to bed. Only he and I remained leaning over the starboard railing, which rattled uneasily now and then under the fierce vibration of the over-engined mail-boat. Far over, there were the lights of a few fishing-smacks riding out the night, and a great rush of white combing and seething water fell out and away from us overside.

At last Colvin went on:

"Leaning over the foot of my bed, looking at me, was a figure swathed in a rotten and tattered veiling. This shroud passed over the head, but left both eyes and the right side of the face bare. It then followed the line of the arm down to where the hand grasped the bed-end. The face was not entirely that of a skull, though the eyes and the flesh of the face were totally gone. There was a thin, dry skin drawn tightly over the features, and there was some skin left on the hand. One wisp of hair crossed the forehead. It was perfectly still. I looked at it, and it looked at me, and my brains turned dry and hot in my head. I had still got the pear of the electric lamp in my hand, and I played idly with it; only I dared not turn the light out again. I shut my eyes, only to open them in a hideous terror the same second. The thing had not moved. My heart was thumping, and the sweat cooled me as it evaporated. Another cinder tinkled in the grate, and a panel creaked in the wall.

"My reason failed me. For twenty minutes, or twenty seconds. I was able to think of nothing else but this awful figure, till there came, hurtling through the empty channels of my senses, the remembrance that Broughton and his friends had discussed me furtively at dinner. The dim possibility of its being a hoax stole gratefully into my unhappy mind, and once there, one's pluck came creeping back along a thousand tiny veins. My first sensation was one of blind unreasoning thankfulness that my brain was going to stand the trial. I am not a timid man, but the best of us needs some human handle to steady him in time of extremity, and in this faint but growing hope that after all it might be only a brutal hoax, I found the fulcrum that I needed. At last I moved.

"How I managed to do it I cannot tell you, but with one spring towards the foot of the bed I got within arm's-length and struck out one fearful blow with my fist at the thing. It crumbled under it, and my hand was cut to the bone. With a sickening revulsion after my terror, I dropped half-fainting across the end of the bed. So it was merely a foul trick after all. No doubt the trick had been played many a time before: no doubt Broughton and his friends had had some large bet among themselves as to what I should do when I discovered the gruesome thing. From my state of abject terror I found myself transported into an insensate anger. I shouted curses upon Broughton. I dived rather than climbed over the bed-end on to the sofa. I tore at the robed skeleton – how well the whole thing had been carried out, I thought – I broke the skull against the floor, and stamped upon its dry bones. I flung the head away under the bed, and rent the brittle bones of the trunk in pieces. I snapped the thin thigh-bones across my knee, and flung them in different directions. The shin-bones I set up against a stool and broke with my heel. I raged like a Berserker against the loathly thing, and stripped the ribs from the backbone and slung the breastbone against the cupboard. My fury increased as the work of destruction went on. I tore the frail rotten veil into twenty pieces, and the dust went up over everything, over the clean blotting-paper and the silver inkstand. At last my work was done. There was but a raffle of broken bones and strips of parchment and crumbling wool. Then, picking up a piece of the skull – it was the check and temple bone of the right side, I remember – I opened the door and went down the passage to Broughton's dressing-room. I remember still how my sweat-dripping pyjamas clung to me as I walked. At the door I kicked and entered.

"Broughton was in bed. He had already turned the light on and seemed shrunken and horrified. For a moment he could hardly pull himself together. Then I spoke. I don't know what I said. Only I know that from a heart full and over-full with hatred and contempt, spurred on by shame of my own recent cowardice, I let my tongue run on. He answered nothing. I was amazed at my own fluency. My hair still clung lankily to my wet temples, my hand was bleeding profusely, and I must have looked a strange sight. Broughton huddled himself up at the head of the bed just as I had. Still he made no answer, no defence. He seemed preoccupied with something besides my reproaches, and once or twice moistened his lips with his tongue. But he could say nothing though he moved his hands now and then, just as a baby who cannot speak moves its hands.

"At last the door into Mrs. Broughton's room opened and she came in, white and terrified. 'What is it? What is it? Oh, in God's name! What is it?' she cried again and again, and then she went up to her husband and sat on the bed in her night-dress, and the two faced me. I told her what the matter was. I spared her husband not a word for her presence there. Yet he seemed hardly to understand. I told the pair that I had spoiled their cowardly joke for them. Broughton looked up.

"'I have smashed the foul thing into a hundred pieces,' I said. Broughton licked his lips again and his mouth worked. 'By God!' I shouted, 'it would serve you right if I thrashed you within an inch of your life. I will take care that not a decent man or woman of my acquaintance ever speaks to you again. And there,' I added, throwing the broken piece of the skull upon the floor beside his bed, 'there is a souvenir for you, of your damned work tonight!'

"Broughton saw the bone, and in a moment it was his turn to frighten me. He squealed like a hare caught in a trap. He screamed and screamed till Mrs. Broughton, almost as bewildered as myself, held on to him and coaxed him like a child to be quiet. But Broughton – and as he moved I thought that ten minutes ago I perhaps looked as terribly ill as he did – thrust her from him, and scrambled out of the bed on to the floor, and still screaming put out his hand to the bone. It had blood on it from my hand. He paid no attention to me whatever. In truth I said nothing. This was a new turn indeed to the horrors of the evening. He rose from the floor with the bone in his hand and stood silent. He seemed to be listening. 'Time, time, perhaps,' he muttered, and almost at the same moment fell at full length on the carpet, cutting his head against the fender. The bone flew from his hand and came to rest near the door. I picked Broughton up, haggard and broken, with blood over his face. He whispered hoarsely and quickly, 'Listen. Listen!' We listened.

"After ten seconds' utter quiet, I seemed to hear something. I could not be sure, but at last there was no doubt. There was a quiet sound as of one moving along the passage. Little regular steps came towards us over the hard oak flooring. Broughton moved to where his wife sat, white and speechless, on the bed, and pressed her face into his shoulder.

"Then, the last thing that I could see as he turned the light out, he fell forward with his own head pressed into the pillow of the bed. Something in their company, something in their cowardice, helped me, and I faced the open doorway of the room, which was outlined fairly clearly against the dimly lighted passage. I put out one hand and touched Mrs. Broughton's shoulder in the darkness. But at the last moment I too failed. I sank on my knees and put my face in the bed. Only we all heard. The footsteps came to the door, and there they stopped. The piece of bone was lying a yard inside the door. There was a rustle of moving stuff, and the thing was in the room. Mrs. Broughton was silent: I could hear Broughton's voice praying, muffled in the pillow: I was cursing my own cowardice. Then the steps moved out again on the oak boards of the passage, and I heard the sounds dying away. In a flash of remorse I went to the door and looked out. At the end of the corridor I thought I saw something that moved away. A moment later the passage was empty. I stood with my forehead against the jamb of the door almost physically sick.

"'You can turn the light on,' I said, and there was an answering flare. There was no bone at my feet. Mrs. Broughton had fainted. Broughton was almost useless, and it took me ten minutes to bring her to. Broughton only said one thing worth remembering. For the most part he went on muttering prayers. But I was glad afterwards to recollect that he had said that thing. He said in a colourless voice, half as a question, half as a reproach, 'You didn't speak to her.'

"We spent the remainder of the night together. Mrs. Broughton actually fell off into in a kind of sleep before dawn, but she suffered so horribly in her dreams that I shook her into consciousness again. Never was dawn so long in coming. Three or four times Broughton spoke to himself. Mrs. Broughton would then just tighten her hold on his arm, but she could say nothing. As for me, I can honestly say that I grew worse as the hours passed and the light strengthened. The two violent reactions had battered down my steadiness of view, and I felt that the foundations of my life had been built upon the sand. I said nothing, and after binding up my hand with a towel, I did not move. It was better so. They helped me and I helped them, and we all three knew that our reason had gone very near to ruin that night. At last, when the light came in pretty strongly, and the birds outside were chattering and singing, we felt that we must do something. Yet we never moved. You might have thought that we should particularly dislike being found as we were by the servants: yet nothing of that kind mattered a straw, and an overpowering listlessness bound us as we sat, until Chapman, Broughton's man, actually knocked and opened the door. None of us moved. Broughton, speaking hardly and stiffly, said, 'Chapman you can come back in five minutes.' Chapman was a discreet man, but it would have made no difference to us if he had carried his news to the 'room' at once.

"We looked at each other and I said I must go back. I meant to wait outside till Chapman returned. I simply dared not re-enter my bedroom alone. Broughton roused himself and said that he would come with me. Mrs. Broughton agreed to remain in her own room for five minutes if the blinds were drawn up and all the doors left open.

"So Broughton and I, leaning stiffly one against the other, went down to my room. By the morning light that filtered past the blinds we could see our way, and I released the blinds. There was nothing wrong in the room from end to end, except smears of my own blood on the end of the bed, on the sofa, and on the carpet where I had torn the thing to pieces."

Colvin had finished his story. There was nothing to say. Seven bells stuttered out from the fo'c'sle, and the answering cry wailed through the darkness. I took him downstairs.

"Of course I am much better now, but it is a kindness of you to let me sleep in your cabin."

The Death-Bride
Friedrich Laun

*– She shall be such
As walk'd your first queen's ghost –*
Shakespeare

THE SUMMER had been uncommonly fine, and the baths crowded with company beyond all comparison: but still the public rooms were scarce ever filled, and never gay. The nobility and military associated only with those of their own rank, and the citizens contented themselves by slandering both parties. So many partial divisions necessarily proved an obstacle to a general and united assembly.

Even the public balls did not draw the *beau-monde* together, because the proprietor of the baths appeared there bedizened with insignia of knighthood; and this glitter, added to the stiff manners of this great man's family, and the tribe of lackeys in splendid liveries who constantly attended him, compelled the greater part of the company assembled, silently to observe the rules prescribed to them according to their different ranks.

For these reasons the balls became gradually less numerously attended. Private parties were formed, in which it was endeavoured to preserve the charms that were daily diminishing in the public assemblies.

One of these societies met generally twice a week in a room which at that time was usually unoccupied. There they supped, and afterwards enjoyed, either in a walk abroad, or remaining in the room, the charms of unrestrained conversation.

The members of this society were already acquainted, at least by name; but an Italian marquis, who had lately joined their party, was unknown to them, and indeed to everyone assembled at the baths.

The title of *Italian* marquis appeared the more singular, as his name, according to the entry of it in the general list, seemed to denote him of Northern extraction, and was composed of so great a number of consonants, that no one could pronounce it without difficulty.

His physiognomy and manners likewise presented many singularities. His long and wan visage, his black eyes, his imperious look, had so little of attraction in them, that everyone would certainly have avoided him, had he not possessed a fund of entertaining stories, the relation of which proved an excellent antidote to *ennui*: the only drawback against them was that in general they required rather too great a share of credulity on the part of his auditors.

The party had one day just risen from table, and found themselves but ill inclined for gaiety. They were still too much fatigued from the ball of the preceding evening to enjoy the recreation of walking, although invited so to do by the bright light of the moon. They were even unable to keep up any conversation; therefore it is not to be wondered at that they were more than usually anxious for the marquis to arrive.

"Where can he be?" exclaimed the countess in an impatient tone.

"Doubtless still at the faro-table, to the no small grief of the bankers," replied Florentine. "This very morning he has occasioned the sudden departure of two of these gentlemen."

"No great loss," answered another.

"To us –" replied Florentine; "but it is to the proprietor of the baths, who only prohibited gambling, that it might be pursued with greater avidity."

"The marquis ought to abstain from such achievements," said the chevalier with an air of mystery. "Gamblers are revengeful, and have generally advantageous connections. If what is whispered be correct, that the marquis is unfortunately implicated in political affairs –."

"But," demanded the countess, "what then has the marquis done to the bankers of the gaming-table?"

"Nothing; except that he betted on cards which almost invariably won. And what renders it rather singular, he scarcely derived any advantage from it himself, for he always adhered to the weakest party. But the other punters were not so scrupulous; for they charged their cards in such a manner that the bank broke before the deal had gone round."

The countess was on the point of asking other questions, when the marquis coming in changed the conversation.

"Here you are at last!" exclaimed several persons at the same moment.

"We have," said the countess, "been most anxious for your society; and just on this day you have been longer than usual absent."

"I have projected an important expedition; and it has succeeded to my wishes. I hope by tomorrow there will not be a single gaming-table left here. I have been from one gambling-room to another; and there are not sufficient post-horses to carry off the ruined bankers."

"And cannot you," asked the countess, "teach us your wonderful art of always winning?"

"It would be a difficult task, my fair lady; and in order to do it, one must ensure a fortunate hand, for without that nothing could be done."

"Nay," replied the chevalier, laughing, "never did I see so fortunate a one as yours."

"As you are still very young, my dear chevalier, you have many novelties to witness."

Saying these words, the marquis threw on the chevalier so piercing a look that the latter cried:

"Will you then cast my nativity?"

"Provided that it is not done today," said the countess; "for who knows whether your future destiny will afford us so amusing a history as that which the marquis two days since promised we should enjoy?"

"I did not exactly say *amusing.*"

"But at least full of extraordinary events: and we require some such, to draw us from the lethargy which has overwhelmed us all day."

"Most willingly: but first I am anxious to learn whether any of you know aught of the surprising things related of the *Death-Bride.*"

No one remembered to have heard speak of her.

The marquis appeared anxious to add something more by way of preface; but the countess and the rest of the party so openly manifested their impatience, that the marquis began his narration as follows:

"I had for a long time projected a visit to the count Lieppa, at his estates in Bohemia. We had met each other in almost every country in Europe: attracted *hither* by the frivolity of youth to partake of every pleasure which presented itself, but led *thither* when years of discretion had rendered us more sedate and steady. At length, in our more advanced age, we ardently desired, ere the close of life, once again to enjoy, by the charms of recollection, the moments of delight which we had passed together. For my part, I was anxious to see the castle of my friend, which was, according to his description, in an extremely romantic district. It was built some hundred years back by his ancestors; and their successors had preserved it with so much care, that it still maintained its imposing appearance, at the same time it afforded a comfortable abode. The count generally passed the greater part of the year at it with his family, and only returned to the capital at the approach of winter. Being well acquainted with his movements, I did not think it needful to announce my visit; and I arrived at the castle one evening precisely at the time when I knew he would be there; and as I approached it, could not but admire the variety and beauty of the scenery which surrounded it.

"The hearty welcome which I received could not, however, entirely conceal from my observation the secret grief depicted on the countenances of the count, his wife, and their daughter, the lovely Ida. In a short time I discovered that they still mourned the loss of Ida's twin-sister, who had died about a year before. Ida and Hildegarde resembled each other so much, that they were only to be distinguished from each other by a slight mark of a strawberry visible on Hildegarde's neck. Her room, and everything in it, was left precisely in the same state as when she was alive, and the family were in the habit of visiting it whenever they wished to indulge the sad satisfaction of meditating on the loss of this beloved child. The two sisters had but one heart, one mind: and the parents could not but apprehend that their separation would be but of short duration; they dreaded lest Ida should also be taken from them.

"I did everything in my power to amuse this excellent family, by entertaining them with laughable anecdotes of my younger days, and by directing their thoughts to less melancholy subjects than that which now wholly occupied them. I had the satisfaction of discovering that my efforts were not ineffectual. Sometimes we walked in the canton round the castle, which was decked with all the beauties of summer; at other times we took a survey of the different apartments of the castle, and were astonished at their wonderful state of preservation, whilst we amused ourselves by talking over the actions of the past generation, whose portraits hung in a long gallery.

"One evening the count had been speaking to me in confidence, on the subject of his future plans: among other subjects he expressed his anxiety, that Ida (who had already, though only in her sixteenth year, refused several offers) should be happily married; when suddenly the gardener, quite out of breath, came to tell us he had seen the ghost (as he believed, the old chaplain belonging to the castle), who had appeared a century back. Several of the servants followed the gardener, and their pallid countenances confirmed the alarming tidings he had brought.

"'I believe you will shortly be afraid of your own shadow,' said the count to them. He then sent them off, desiring them not again to trouble him with the like fooleries.

"'It is really terrible,' said he to me, 'to see to what lengths superstition will carry persons of that rank of life; and it is impossible wholly to undeceive them. From one generation to another an absurd report has from time to time been spread abroad, of an old chaplain's ghost wandering in the environs of the castle; and that he says mass in the chapel, with other idle stories of a similar nature. This report has greatly died away since I came into possession of the castle; but it now appears to me, it will never be altogether forgotten.'

"At this moment the duke de Marino was announced. The count did not recollect ever having heard of him.

"I told him that I was tolerably well acquainted with his family; and that I had lately been present, in Venice, at the betrothing of a young man of that name.

"The very same young man came in while I was speaking. I should have felt very glad at seeing him, had I not perceived that my presence caused him evident uneasiness.

"'Ah,' said he in a tolerably gay tone, after the customary forms of politeness had passed between us; 'the finding you here, my dear marquis, explains to me an occurrence, which with shame I own caused me a sensation of fear. To my no small surprise, they knew my name in the adjacent district; and as I came up the hill which leads to the castle, I heard it pronounced three times in a voice wholly unknown to me: and in a still more audible tone this strange voice bade me welcome. I now, however, conclude it was yours.'

"I assured him, (and with truth,) that till his name was announced the minute before, I was ignorant of his arrival, and that none of my servants knew him; for that the valet who accompanied me into Italy was not now with me.

"'And above all,' added I, 'it would be impossible to discover any equipage, however well known to one, in so dark an evening.'

"'That is what astonishes me,' exclaimed the duke, a little amazed.

"The incredulous count very politely added, 'that the voice which had told the duke he was welcome, had at least expressed the sentiments of all the family.'

"Marino, ere he said a word relative to the motive of his visit, asked a private audience of me; and confided in me, by telling me that he was come with the intention of obtaining the lovely Ida's hand; and that if he was able to procure her consent, he should demand her of her father.

"'The countess Apollonia, your bride elect, is then no longer living?' asked I.

"'We will talk on that subject hereafter,' answered he.

"The deep sigh which accompanied these words led me to conclude that Apollonia had been guilty of infidelity or some other crime towards the duke; and consequently I thought that I ought to abstain from any further questions, which appeared to rend his heart, already so sensibly wounded.

"Yet, as he begged me to become his mediator with the count, in order to obtain from him his consent to the match, I painted in glowing colours the danger of an alliance, which he had no other motive for contracting, than the wish to obliterate the remembrance of a dearly, and without doubt, still more tenderly, beloved object. But he assured me that he was far from thinking of the lovely Ida from so blameable a motive, and that he should be the happiest of men if she but proved propitious to his wishes.

"His expressive and penetrating tone of voice, while he said this, lulled the uneasiness that I was beginning to feel; and I promised him I would prepare the count Lieppa to listen to his entreaties, and would give him the necessary information relative to the fortune and family of Marino. But I declared to him at the same time that I should by no means hurry the conclusion of the affair by my advice, as I was not in the habit of taking upon myself so great a charge as the uncertain issue of a marriage.

"The duke signified his satisfaction at what I said, and made me give (what then appeared to me of no consequence) a promise, that I would not make mention of the former marriage he was on the point of contracting, as it would necessarily bring on a train of unpleasant explanations.

"The duke's views succeeded with a promptitude beyond his most sanguine hopes. His well-proportioned form and sparkling eyes smoothed the paths of love, and introduced him to the heart of Ida. His agreeable conversation promised to the mother an amiable son-in-law; and the knowledge in rural economy, which he evinced as occasions offered, made the count hope for a useful helpmate in his usual occupations; for since the first day of the duke's arrival he had been prevented from pursuing them.

"Marino followed up these advantages with great ardour; and I was one evening much surprised by the intelligence of his being betrothed, as I did not dream of matters drawing so near a conclusion. They spoke at table of some bridal preparations of which I had made mention just before the duke's arrival at the castle; and the countess asked me whether that young Marino was a near relation of the one who was that very day betrothed to her daughter.'

"'Near enough,' I answered, recollecting my promise. Marino looked at me with an air of embarrassment.

"'But, my dear duke,' continued I, 'tell me who mentioned the amiable Ida to you; or was it a portrait, or what else, which caused you to think of looking for a beauty, the selection of whom does so much honour to your taste, in this remote corner; for, if I am not mistaken, you said but yesterday that you had purposed travelling about for another six months; when all at once (I believe while in Paris) you changed your plan, and projected a journey wholly and solely to see the charming Ida?'

"'Yes, it was at Paris,' replied the duke; 'you are very rightly informed. I went there to see and admire the superb gallery of pictures at the Museum; but I had scarcely entered it, when my eyes turned from the inanimate beauties, and were riveted on a lady whose incomparable features were heightened by an air of melancholy. With fear and trembling I approached her, and only ventured to follow without speaking to her. I still followed her after she quitted the gallery; and I drew her servant aside to learn the name of his mistress. He told it me: but when I expressed a wish to become acquainted with the father of this beauty, he said that was next to impossible while at Paris, as the family were on the point of quitting that city; nay, of quitting France altogether.

"'Possibly, however,' said I, 'some opportunity may present itself.' And I looked everywhere for the lady: but she, probably imagining that her servant was following her closely, had continued to walk on, and was entirely out of sight. While I was looking around for her, the servant had likewise vanished from my view.'

"'Who was this beautiful lady?' asked Ida, in a tone of astonishment.

"'What! You really did not then perceive me in the gallery?'

"'Me!' – 'My daughter –!' exclaimed at the same moment Ida and her parents.

"'Yes, you yourself, mademoiselle. The servant, whom fortunately for me you left at Paris, and whom I met the same evening unexpectedly, as my guardian angel, informed me of all; so that after a short rest at home, I was able to come straight hither.'

"'What a fable!' said the count to his daughter, who was mute with astonishment.

"'Ida,' he added, turning to me, 'has never yet been out of her native country; and for myself, I have not been in Paris these seventeen years.'

"The duke looked at the count and his daughter with similar marks of astonishment visible in their countenances; and conversation would have been entirely at an end, if I had not taken care to introduce other topics: but I had it nearly all to myself.

"The repast was no sooner over, than the count took the duke into the recess of a window; and although I was at a considerable distance, and appeared wholly to fix my attention on a new chandelier, I overheard all their conversation.

"'What motive,' demanded the count with a serious and dissatisfied air, 'could have induced you to invent that singular scene in the gallery of the Museum at Paris? For according to my judgment, it could in no way benefit you. Since you are anxious to conceal the cause which brought you to ask my daughter in marriage, at least you might have plainly said as much; and though possibly you might have felt repugnance at making such a declaration, there were a thousand ways of framing your answer, without its being needful thus to offend probability.'

"'Monsieur le comte,' replied the duke much piqued; 'I held my peace at table, thinking that possibly you had reasons for wishing to keep secret your and your daughter's journey to Paris. I was silent merely from motives of discretion; but the singularity of your reproaches compels me to maintain what I have said; and, notwithstanding your reluctance to believe the truth, to declare before all the world, that the capital of France was the spot where I first saw your daughter Ida.'

"'But what if I prove to you, not only by the witness of my servants, but also by that of all my tenants, that my daughter has never quitted her native place?'

"'I shall still believe the evidence of my own eyes and ears, which have as great authority over me.'

"'What you say is really enigmatical,' answered the count in a graver tone: 'your serious manner convinces me you have been the dupe of some illusion; and that you have seen some other person, whom you have taken for my daughter. Excuse me, therefore, for having taken up the thing so warmly.'

"'Another person! What then, I not only mistook another person for your daughter; but the very servant of whom I made mention, and who gave me so exact a description of this castle, was, according to what you say, some other person!'

"'My dear Marino, that servant was some cheat who knew this castle, and who, God only knows for what motive, spoke to you of my daughter as resembling the lady.'

"''Tis certainly no wish of mine to contradict you; but Ida's features are precisely the same as those which made so deep an impression on me at Paris, and which my imagination has preserved with such scrupulous fidelity.'

"The count shook his head; and Marino continued:

"'What is still more – (but pray pardon me for mentioning a little particularity, which nothing short of necessity would have drawn from me) – while in the gallery, I was standing behind the lady, and the handkerchief that covered her neck was a little disarranged, which occasioned me distinctly to perceive the mark of a small strawberry.'

"'Another strange mystery!' exclaimed the count, turning pale: 'it appears you are determined to make me believe wonderful stories.'

"'I have only one question to ask: Has Ida such a mark on her neck?'

"'No, monsieur,' replied the count, looking steadfastly at Marino.

"'No!' exclaimed the latter, in the utmost astonishment.

"'No, I tell you: but Ida's twin-sister, who resembled her in the most surprising manner, had the mark you mention on her neck, and a year since carried it with her into the grave.'

"'And yet 'tis only within the last few months that I saw this person in Paris!'

"At this moment the countess and Ida, who had kept aside, a prey to uneasiness, not knowing what to think of the conversation, which appeared of so very important a nature, approached; but the count in a commanding tone ordered them to retire immediately. He then led the duke entirely away into a retired corner of the window, and continued the conversation in so low a voice that I could hear nothing further.

"My astonishment was extreme when, that very same evening, the count gave orders to have Hildegarde's tomb opened in his presence: but he beforehand related briefly what I have just told you, and proposed my assisting the duke and him in opening the grave. The duke excused himself, by saying that the very idea made him tremble with horror; for he could not overcome, especially at night, his fear of a corpse.

"The count begged he would not mention the gallery scene to anyone; and above all, to spare the extreme sensibility of the affianced bride from a recital of the conversation they had just had, even if she should request to be informed of it.

"In the meantime the sexton arrived with his lantern. The count and I followed him.

"'It is morally impossible,' said the count to me, as we walked together, 'that any trick can have been played respecting my daughter's death: the circumstances attendant thereon are but too well known to me. You may readily believe also, that the affection we bore our poor girl would prevent our running any risk of burying her too soon: but suppose even the possibility of that, and that the tomb had been opened by some avaricious persons, who found, on opening the coffin, that the body became re-animated; no one can believe for a moment that my daughter would not have instantly returned to her parents, who doted on her, rather than have fled to a distant country. This last circumstance puts the matter beyond doubt: for even should it be admitted as a truth, that she was carried by force to some distant part of the world, she would have found a thousand ways of returning. My eyes are, however, about to be convinced, that the sacred remains of my Hildegarde really repose in the grave.

"'To convince myself!' cried he again, in a tone of voice so melancholy yet loud that the sexton turned his head.

"This movement rendered the count more circumspect; and he continued in a lower tone of voice:

"'How should I for a moment believe it possible that the slightest trace of my daughter's features should be still in existence, or that the destructive hand of time should have spared her beauty? Let us return, marquis; for who could tell, even were I to see the skeleton, that I should know it from that of an entire stranger, whom they may have placed in the tomb to fill her place?'

"He was even about to give orders not to open the door of the chapel (at which we were just arrived), when I represented to him, that were I in his place I should have found it extremely difficult to determine on such a measure; but that having gone thus far, it was requisite to complete the task, by examining whether some of the jewels buried with Hildegarde's corpse were not wanting. I added that judging by a number of well-known facts, all bodies were not destroyed equally soon.

"My representations had the desired effect: the count squeezed my hand; and we followed the sexton, who, by his pallid countenance and trembling limbs, evidently showed that he was unaccustomed to nocturnal employments of this nature.

"I know not whether any of this present company were ever in a chapel at midnight, before the iron doors of a vault, about to examine the succession of leaden coffins enclosing the remains of an illustrious family. Certain it is, that at such a moment the noise of bolts and bars produces such a remarkable sensation, that one is led to dread the sound of the door grating on its hinges; and when the vault is opened, one cannot help hesitating for an instant to enter it.

"The count was evidently seized with these sensations of terror, which I discovered by a stifled sigh; but he concealed his feelings: notwithstanding, I remarked that he dared not trust himself to look on any other coffin than the one containing his daughter's remains. He opened it himself.

"'Did I not say so?' cried he, seeing that the features of the corpse bore a perfect resemblance to those of Ida. I was obliged to prevent the count, who was seized with astonishment, from kissing the forehead of the inanimate body.

"'Do not,' I added, 'disturb the peace of those who repose in death.' And I used my utmost efforts to withdraw the count immediately from this dismal abode.

"On our return to the castle, we found those persons whom we had left there, in an anxious state of suspense. The two ladies had closely questioned the duke on what had passed; and would not admit as a valid excuse the promise he had made of secrecy. They entreated us also, but in vain, to satisfy their curiosity.

"They succeeded better the following day with the sexton, whom they sent for privately, and who told them all he knew: but it only tended to excite their anxious wish to learn the subject of the conversation which had occasioned this nocturnal visit to the sepulchral vault.

"As for myself, I dreamt the whole of the following night of the apparition Marino had seen at Paris; I conjectured many things which I did not think fit to communicate to the count, because he absolutely questioned the connection of a superior world with ours. At this juncture of affairs, I with pleasure saw that this singular circumstance, if not entirely forgotten, was at least but rarely and slightly mentioned.

"But I now began to find another cause for anxious solicitude. The duke constantly persisted in refusing to explain himself on the subject of his previous engagement, even when we were alone: and the embarrassment he could not conceal, whenever I made mention of the good qualities that I believed his intended to have possessed, as well as several other little singularities, led me to conclude that Marino's attachment for Apollonia had been first shaken at the picture gallery, at sight of the lovely incognita; and that Apollonia had been forsaken, owing to his yielding to temptations; and that doubtless she could never have been guilty of breaking off an alliance so solemnly contracted.

Foreseeing from this that the charming Ida could never hope to find much happiness in a union with Marino, and knowing that the wedding-day was nigh at hand, I resolved to unmask the perfidious deceiver as quickly as possible, and to make him repent his infidelity. An excellent occasion presented itself one day for me to accomplish my designs. Having finished supper, we were still sitting at table; and someone said that iniquity is frequently punished in this world: upon which I observed, that I myself had witnessed striking proofs of the truth of this remark; when Ida and her mother entreated me to name one of these examples.

"'Under these circumstances, ladies,' answered I, 'permit me to relate a history to you, which, according to my opinion, will particularly interest you.'

"'Us!' they both exclaimed. At the same time I fixed my eyes on the duke, who for several days past had evidently distrusted me; and I saw that his conscience had rendered him pale.

"'That at least is *my* opinion,' replied I: 'But, my dear count, will you pardon me, if the supernatural is sometimes interwoven with my narration?'

"'Very willingly,' answered he smiling: 'and I will content myself with expressing my surprise at so many things of this sort having happened to you, as I have never experienced any of them myself.'

"I plainly perceived that the duke made signs of approval at what he said: but I took no notice of it, and answered the count by saying that "all the world have not probably the use of their eyes".

"'That may be,' replied he, still smiling.

"'But,' said I to him in a low and expressive voice, 'think you an uncorrupted body in the vault is a *common* phenomenon?'

"He appeared staggered: and I thus continued in an undertone of voice:

"'For that matter, 'tis very possible to account for it naturally, and therefore it would be useless to contest the subject with you.'

"'We are wandering from the point,' said the countess a little angrily; and she made me a sign to begin, which I accordingly did, in the following words:

"'The scene of my anecdote lies in Venice.'

"'I possibly then may know something of it,' cried the duke, who entertained some suspicions.

"'Possibly so,' replied I; 'but there were reasons for keeping the event secret: it happened somewhere about eighteen months since, at the period you first set out on your travels.

"The son of an extremely wealthy nobleman, whom I shall designate by the name of Filippo, being attracted to Leghorn by the affairs consequent on his succession to an inheritance, had won the heart of an amiable and lovely girl, called Clara. He promised her, as well as her parents, that ere his return to Venice he would come back and marry her. The moment for his departure was preceded by certain ceremonies, which in their termination were terrible: for after the two lovers had exhausted every protestation of reciprocal affection, Filippo invoked the aid of the spirit of vengeance, in case of infidelity: they prayed even that whichever of the lovers should prove faithful might not be permitted to repose quietly in the grave, but should haunt the perjured one, and force the inconstant party to come amongst the dead, and to share in the grave those sentiments which on earth had been forgotten.

"The parents, who were seated by them at table, remembered their youthful days, and permitted the overheated and romantic imagination of the young people to take its free course. The lovers finished by making punctures in their arms, and letting their blood run into a glass filled with white champagne.

"'Our souls shall be inseparable as our blood!' exclaimed Filippo; and drinking half the contents of the glass, he gave the rest to Clara."

At this moment the duke experienced a violent degree of agitation, and from time to time darted such menacing looks at me, that I was led to conclude, that in *his* adventure some scene of a similar nature had taken place. I can however affirm that I related the details respecting Filippo's departure as they were represented in a letter written by the mother of Clara.

"Who," continued I, "after so many demonstrations of such a violent passion, could have expected the denouement? Filippo's return to Venice happened precisely at the period at which a young beauty, hitherto educated in a distant convent, made her first appearance in the great world: she on a sudden exhibited herself as an angel whom a cloud had till then concealed, and excited universal admiration. Filippo's parents had heard frequent mention of Clara, and of the projected alliance between her and their son; but they thought that this alliance was like many others, contracted one day without the parties knowing why, and broken off the next with equal want of thought; and influenced by this idea, they presented their son to the parents of Camilla (which was the name of the young beauty), whose family were of the highest rank.

"They represented to Filippo the great advantages he would obtain by an alliance with her. The Carnival happening just at this period completed the business, by affording him so many favourable opportunities of being with Camilla; and in the end, the remembrance of Leghorn held but very little place in his mind. His letters became colder and colder each succeeding day; and on Clara expressing how sensibly she felt the change, he ceased writing to her altogether, and did everything in his power to hasten his union with Camilla, who was, without compare, much the handsomer and more wealthy. The agonies poor Clara endured were manifest in her illegible writing, and by the tears which were but too evidently shed over her letters: but neither the one nor the other had any more influence over the fickle heart of Filippo than the prayers of the unfortunate girl. Even the menace of coming, according to their solemn agreement, from the tomb to haunt him, and carry him with her to that grave which threatened so soon to enclose her, had but little effect on his mind, which was entirely engrossed by the idea of the happiness he should enjoy in the arms of Camilla.

"The father of the latter (who was my intimate friend) invited me before-hand to the wedding. And although numerous affairs detained him that summer in the city, so that he could not as usual enjoy the pleasures of the country, yet we sometimes went to his pretty villa, situated on the banks of the Brenta; where his daughter's marriage was to be celebrated with all possible splendour.

"A particular circumstance, however, occasioned the ceremony to be deferred for some weeks. The parents of Camilla having been very happy in their own union, were anxious that the same priest who married them should pronounce the nuptial benediction on their daughter. This priest, who, notwithstanding his great age, had the appearance of vigorous health, was seized with a slow fever which confined him to his bed: however, in time it abated, he became gradually better and better, and the wedding-day was at length fixed. But, as if some secret power was at work to prevent this union, the worthy priest was, on the very day destined for the celebration of their marriage, seized with a feverish shivering of so alarming a nature that he dared not stir out of the house, and he strongly advised the young couple to select another priest to marry them.

"The parents still persisted in their design of the nuptial benediction being given to their children by the respectable old man who had married *them*. They would have certainly spared themselves a great deal of grief if they had never swerved from their determination. Very grand preparations had been made in honour of the day; and as they could no longer be deferred, it was decided that they should consider it as a ceremony of solemn affiance. At noon the bargemen attired in their splendid garb awaited the company's arrival on the banks of the canal: their joyous song was soon distinguished, while conducting to the villa, now decorated with flowers, the numerous gondolas containing parties of the best company.

"During the dinner, which lasted till evening, the betrothed couple exchanged rings. At the very moment of their so doing, a piercing shriek was heard, which struck terror into the breasts of all the company, and absolutely struck Filippo with horror. Everyone ran to the windows: for although it was becoming dark, each object was visible; but no one was to be seen."

"Stop an instant," said the duke to me, with a fierce smile. His countenance, which had frequently changed colour during the recital, evinced strong marks of the torments of a wicked conscience. "I am also acquainted with that story, of a voice being heard in the air; it is borrowed from the 'Memoirs of Mademoiselle Clairon'; a deceased lover tormented *her* in this completely original manner. The shriek in her case was followed by a clapping of hands: I hope, monsieur le marquis, that you will not omit that particular in your story."

"And why," replied I, "should you imagine that nothing of a similar nature could occur to any one besides that actress? Your incredulity appears to me so much the more extraordinary, as it seems to rest on facts which may lay claim to belief."

The countess made me a sign to continue; and I pursued my narrative as follows:

"A short time after they had heard this inexplicable shriek, I begged Camilla, facing whom I was sitting, to permit me to look at her ring once more, the exquisite workmanship of which had already been much admired. But it was not on her finger: a general search was made, but not the slightest trace of the ring could be discovered. The company even rose from their seats to look for it, but all in vain.

"Meanwhile, the time for the evening's amusements approached: fire-works were exhibited on the Brenta preceding the ball; the company were masked and got into the gondolas; but nothing was so striking as the silence which reigned during this *fête*; no one seemed inclined to open their mouth; and scarcely was heard a faint exclamation of *Bravo*, at sight of the fire-works.

"The ball was one of the most brilliant I ever witnessed: the precious stones and jewels with which the ladies of the party were covered reflected the lights in the chandeliers with redoubled lustre. The most splendidly attired of the whole was Camilla. Her father, who was fond of pomp, rejoiced in the idea that no one in the assembly was equal to his daughter in splendour or beauty.

"Possibly to satisfy himself of this fact, he made a tour of the room; and returned loudly expressing his surprise, at having perceived on another lady precisely the same jewels which adorned Camilla. He was even weak enough to express a slight degree of chagrin. However, he consoled himself with the idea that a bouquet of diamonds which was destined for Camilla to wear at supper would alone in value be greater than all she then had on.

"But as they were on the point of sitting down to table, and the anxious father again threw a look around him, he discovered that the same lady had also a bouquet which appeared to the full as valuable as Camilla's.

"My friend's curiosity could no longer be restrained; he approached, and asked whether it would be too great a liberty to learn the name of the fair mask? But to his great surprise, the lady shook her head, and turned away from him.

"At the same instant the steward came in, to ask whether since dinner there had been any addition to the party, as the covers were not sufficient.

"His master answered, with rather a dissatisfied air, that there were only the same number, and accused his servants of negligence; but the steward still persisted in what he had said.

"An additional cover was placed: the master counted them himself, and discovered that there really was one more in number than he had invited. As he had recently, on account of some inconsiderate expressions, had a dispute with government, he was apprehensive that some spy had contrived to slip in with the company: but as he had no reason to believe, that on such a day as that, anything of a suspicious nature would be uttered, he resolved, in order to be satisfied respecting so indiscreet a procedure as the introduction of such a person in a family *fête*, to beg everyone present to unmask; but in order to avoid the inconvenience likely to arise from such a request, he determined not to propose it till the very last thing.

"Everyone present expressed their surprise at the luxuries and delicacies of the table, for it far surpassed everything of the sort seen in that country, especially with respect to the wines. Still, however, the father of Camilla was not satisfied, and loudly lamented that an accident had happened to his capital red champagne, which prevented his being able to offer his guests a single glass of it.

"The company seemed anxious to become gay, for the whole of the day nothing like gaiety had been visible among them; but no one around where I sat partook of this inclination, for curiosity alone appeared to occupy their whole attention. I was sitting near the lady who was so splendidly attired; and I remarked that she neither ate nor drank anything; that she neither addressed nor answered a word to her neighbours, and that she appeared to have her eyes constantly fixed on the affianced couple.

"The rumour of this singularity gradually spread round the room, and again disturbed the mirth which had become pretty general. Each whispered to the other a thousand conjectures on this mysterious personage. But the general opinion was that some unhappy passion for Filippo was the cause of this extaordinary conduct. Those sitting next the unknown were the first to rise from table, in order to find more cheerful associates, and their places were filled by others who hoped to discover some acquaintance in this silent lady, and obtain from her a more welcome reception; but their hopes were equally futile.

"At the time the champagne was handed round, Filippo also brought a chair and sat by the unknown. She then became somewhat more animated, and turned towards Filippo, which was more than she had done to anyone else; and she offered him her glass, as if wishing him to drink out of it.

"A violent trembling seized Filippo, when she looked at him steadfastly.

"'The wine is red!' cried he, holding up the glass; 'I thought there had been no *red* champagne.'

"'Red!' said the father of Camilla, with an air of extreme surprise, approaching him from curiosity.

"'Look at the lady's glass,' replied Filippo.

"'The wine in it is as white as all the rest,' answered Camilla's father; and he called all present to witness it. They everyone unanimously declared that the wine was white.

"Filippo drank it not, but quitted his seat; for a second look from his neighbour had caused him extreme agitation. He took the father of Camilla aside, and whispered something to him. The latter returned to the company, saying:

"'Ladies and gentlemen, I entreat you, for reasons which I will tell you presently, instantly to unmask.'

"As in this request he but expressed in a degree the general wish, everyone's mask was off as quick as thought, and each face uncovered, excepting that of the silent lady, on whom every look was fixed, and whose face they were the most anxious to see.

"'You alone keep on your mask,' said Camilla's father to her, after a short silence: 'May I hope you will also remove yours?'

"She obstinately persisted in her determination of remaining unknown.

"This strange conduct affected the father of Camilla the more sensibly, as he recognised in the others all those whom he had invited to the *fête*, and found beyond doubt that the mute lady was the one exceeding the number invited. He was, however, unwilling to force her to unmask; because the uncommon splendour of her dress did not permit him any longer to harbour the idea that this additional guest was a spy; and thinking her also a person of distinction, he did not wish to be deficient in good manners. He thought possibly she might be some friend of the family, who, not residing at Venice, but finding on her arrival in that city that he was to give this *fête*, had conceived this innocent frolic.

"It was thought right, however, at all events to obtain all the information that could be gained from the servants: but none of them knew anything of this lady; there were no servants of hers there; and those belonging to Camilla's father did not recollect having seen any who appeared to appertain to her.

"What rendered this circumstance doubly strange was that, as I before mentioned, this lady only put the magnificent bouquet into her bosom the instant previous to her sitting down to supper.

"The whispering, which had generally usurped the place of all conversation, gained each moment more and more ascendancy; when on a sudden the masked lady arose, and walking towards the door, beckoned Filippo to follow her; but Camilla hindered him from obeying her signal, for she had a long time observed with what fixed attention the mysterious lady looked at her intended husband; and she had also remarked that the latter had quitted the stranger in violent agitation; and from all this she apprehended that love had caused him to be guilty of some folly or other. The master of the house, turning a deaf ear to all his daughter's remonstrances, and a prey to the most terrible fears, followed the unknown (at a distance, it is true); but she was no sooner out of the room than he returned. At this moment, the shriek which they had heard at noon was repeated, but seemed louder from the silence of night, and communicated anew affright to all present. By the time the father of Camilla had returned from the first movement which his fear had occasioned him to make, the unknown was nowhere to be found.

"The servants in waiting outside the house had no knowledge whatever of the masked lady. In every direction around there were crowds of persons; the river was lined with gondolas; and yet not an individual among them had seen the mysterious female.

"All these circumstances had occasioned so much uneasiness to the whole party, that everyone was anxious to return home; and the master of the house was obliged to permit the departure of the gondolas much earlier than he had intended.

"The return home was, as might naturally be expected, very melancholy.

"On the following day the betrothed couple were, however, pretty composed. Filippo had even adopted Camilla's idea of the unknown being someone whom love had deprived of reason; and as for the horrible shriek twice repeated, they were willing to attribute it to some people who were diverting themselves; and they decided, that inattention on the part of the servants was the sole cause of the unknown absenting herself without being perceived; and they even at last persuaded themselves that the sudden disappearance of the ring, which they had not been able to find, was owing to the malice of some one of the servants who had pilfered it.

"In a word, they banished everything that could tend to weaken these explanations; and only one thing remained to harass them. The old priest, who was to bestow on them the nuptial benediction, had yielded up his last breath; and the friendship which had so intimately subsisted between him and the parents of Camilla, did not permit them in decency to think of marriage and amusements the week following his death.

"The day this venerable priest was buried, Filippo's gaiety received a severe shock; for he learned, in a letter from Clara's mother, the death of that lovely girl. Sinking under the grief occasioned her by the infidelity of the man she had never ceased to love, she died: but to her latest hour she declared she should never rest quietly in her grave, until the perjured man had fulfilled the promise he had made to her.

"This circumstance produced a stronger effect on him than all the imprecations of the unhappy mother; for he recollected that the first shriek (the cause of which they had never been able to ascertain) was heard at the precise moment of Clara's death; which convinced him that the unknown mask could only have been the spirit of Clara.

"This idea deprived him at intervals of his senses.

"He constantly carried this letter about him; and with an air of wandering would sometimes draw it from his pocket, in order to reconsider it attentively: even Camilla's presence did not deter him.

"As it was natural to conclude this letter contained the cause of the extraordinary change which had taken place in Filippo, she one day gladly seized the opportunity of reading it, when in one of his absent fits he let it fall from his hands.

"Filippo, struck by the death-like paleness and faintness which overcame Camilla, as she returned him the letter, knew instantly that she had read it. In the deepest affliction he threw himself at her feet, and conjured her to tell him how he must act.

"'Love *me* with greater constancy than you did her,' replied Camilla mournfully.

"With transport he promised to do so. But his agitation became greater and greater, and increased to a most extraordinary pitch the morning of the day fixed for the wedding. As he was going to the house of Camilla's father before it became dark (from whence he was to take his bride at dawn of day to the church, according to the custom of the country), he fancied he saw Clara's spirit walking constantly at his side.

"Never was seen a couple about to receive the nuptial benediction with so mournful an aspect. I accompanied the parents of Camilla, who had requested me to be a witness: and the sequel has made an indelible impression on my mind of the events of that dismal morning.

"We were proceeding silently to the church of the Salutation; when Filippo, in our way thither, frequently requested me to remove the stranger from Camilla's side, for she had evil designs against her.

"'What stranger?' I asked him.

"'In God's name, don't speak so loud,' replied he; 'for you cannot but see how anxious she is to force herself between Camilla and me.'

"'Mere chimera, my friend; there are none but yourself and Camilla.'

"'Would to Heaven my eyes did not deceive me!' – 'Take care that she does not enter the church,' added he, as we arrived at the door.

"'She will not enter it, rest assured,' said I: and to the great astonishment of Camilla's parents I made a motion as if to drive someone away.

"We found Filippo's father already in the church; and as soon as his son perceived him, he took leave of him as if he was going to die. Camilla sobbed; and Filippo exclaimed:

"'There's the stranger; she has then got in.'

"The parents of Camilla doubted whether under such circumstances the marriage ceremony ought to be begun.

"But Camilla, entirely devoted to her love, cried: 'These chimeras of fancy render my care and attention the more necessary.'

"They approached the altar. At that moment a sudden gust of wind blew out the wax-tapers. The priest appeared displeased at their not having shut the windows more securely; but Filippo exclaimed: 'The windows! See you not, then, that there is one here who blew out the wax-tapers purposely?'

"Everyone looked astonished: and Filippo cried, as he hastily disengaged his hand from that of Camilla, 'Don't you see, also, that she is tearing me away from my intended bride?'

"Camilla fell fainting into the arms of her parents; and the priest declared that under such peculiar circumstances it was impossible to proceed with the ceremony.

"The parents of both attributed Filippo's state to mental derangement. They even supposed he had been poisoned; for an instant after, the unfortunate man expired in most violent convulsions. The surgeons who opened his body could not, however, discover any grounds for this suspicion.

"The parents, who as well as myself were informed by Camilla of the subject of these supposed horrors of Filippo, did everything in their power to conceal this adventure: yet, on talking over all the circumstances, they could never satisfactorily explain the apparition of the mysterious mask at the time of the wedding *fête*. And what still appeared very surprising was that the ring lost at the country villa was found amongst Camilla's other jewels, at the time of their return from church."

"'This is, indeed, a wonderful history!' said the count. His wife uttered a deep sigh: and Ida exclaimed:

"'It has really made *me* shudder.'

"'That is precisely what every betrothed person ought to feel who listens to such recitals,' answered I, looking steadfastly at the duke, who, while I was talking, had risen and sat down again several times; and who, from his troubled look, plainly showed that he feared I should counteract his wishes.

"'A word with you!' he whispered me, as we were retiring to rest: and he accompanied me to my room. 'I plainly perceive your generous intentions; this history invented for the occasion –"

"'Hold!' said I to him in an irritated tone of voice: 'I was eye-witness to what you have just heard. How then can you doubt its authenticity, without accusing a man of honour of uttering a falsehood?'

"'We will talk on this subject presently,' replied he in a tone of raillery. 'But tell me truly from whence you learnt the anecdote relative to mixing the blood with wine? – I know the person from whose life you borrowed this idea.'

"'I do assure you that I have taken it from no one's life but Filippo's; and yet there may be similar stories – as of the shriek, for instance. But even this singular manner of irrevocably affiancing themselves may have presented itself to *any* two lovers.'

"'Perhaps so! Yet one could trace in your narration many traits resembling another history.'

"'That is very possible: all love-stories are founded on the same stock, and cannot deny their parentage.'

"'No matter,' replied Marino; 'but I desire that from henceforth you do not permit yourself to make any allusion to my past life; and still less that you relate certain anecdotes to the count. On these conditions, and only on these conditions, do I pardon your former very ingenious fiction.'

"'Conditions! – Forgiveness! – And do you dare thus to talk to *me?* – This is rather too much. Now take my answer: tomorrow morning the count shall know that you have been already affianced, and what you now exact.'

"'Marquis, if you dare –'

"Oh! Oh! – Yes, I dare do it; and I owe it to an old friend. The impostor who dares accuse me of falsehood shall no longer wear his deceitful mask in this house.'

"Passion had, spite of my endeavours, carried me so far, that a duel became inevitable. The duke challenged me. And we agreed, at parting, to meet the following morning in a neighbouring wood with pistols.

"In effect, before day-light we each took our servant and went into the forest. Marino, remarking that I had not given any orders in case of my being killed, undertook to do so for me; and accordingly he told my servant what to do with my body, as if everything was already decided. He again addressed me ere we shook hands:

"'For,' said he, 'the combat between us must be very unequal. I am young,' added he; 'but in many instances my hand has proved a steady one. I have not, it is true, absolutely killed any man; but I have invariably hit my adversary precisely on the part I intended. In this instance, however, I must, for the first time, *kill* my man, as it is the only effectual method of preventing your annoying me further; unless you will give me your word of honour not to discover any occurrences of my past life to the count, in which case I consent to consider the affair as terminated here.'

"As you may naturally believe, I rejected his proposition.

"'As it must be so,' replied he, 'recommend your soul to God.' We prepared accordingly.

"'It is your first fire,' he said to me.

"'I yield it to you,' answered I.

"He refused to fire first. I then drew the trigger, and caused the pistol to drop from his hand. He appeared surprised: but his astonishment was great indeed, when, after taking up another pistol, he found he had missed me. He pretended to have aimed at my heart; and had not even the possibility of an excuse; for he could not but acknowledge that no sensation of fear on my part had induced me to move, and baulk his aim.

"At his request I fired a second time; and again aimed at his pistol which he held in his left hand: and to his great astonishment it dropped also; but the ball had passed so near his hand, that it was a good deal bruised.

"His second fire having passed me, I told him I would not fire again; but that, as it was possible the extreme agitation of his mind had occasioned him to miss me twice, I proposed adjusting matters.

"Before he had time to refuse my offer, the count, who had suspicions that all was not right, was between us, with his daughter. He complained loudly of such conduct on the part of his guests; and demanded some explanation on the cause of our dispute. I then developed the whole business in presence of Marino, whose evident embarrassment convinced the count and Ida of the truth of the reproaches his conscience made him.

"But the duke soon availed himself of Ida's affection, and created an entire change in the count's mind; who that very evening said to me:

"'You are right; I certainly ought to take some decided step, and send the duke from my house: but what could win the Apollonia whom he has abandoned, and whom he will never see again? Added to which, he is the only man for whom my daughter has ever felt a sincere attachment. Let us leave the young people to follow their own inclinations: the countess perfectly coincides in this opinion; and adds, that it would hurt her much were this handsome Venetian to be driven from our house. How many little infidelities and indiscretions are committed in the world and excused, owing to particular circumstances?'

"'But it appears to me, that in the case in point, these particular circumstances are wanting,' answered I. However, finding the count persisted in his opinion, I said no more.

"The marriage took place without any interruption: but still there was very little of gaiety at the feast, which usually on these occasions is of so splendid and jocund a nature. The ball in the evening was dull; and Marino alone danced with most extraordinary glee.

"'Fortunately, monsieur le marquis,' said he in my ear, quitting the dance for an instant and laughing aloud, "there are no ghosts or spirits here, as at your Venetian wedding.'

"'Don't,' I answered, putting up my finger to him, 'rejoice too soon: misery is slow in its operations; and often is not perceived by us blind mortals till it treads on our heels.'

"Contrary to my intention, this conversation rendered him quite silent; and what convinced me the more strongly of the effect it had made on him, was the redoubled vehemence with which the duke again began dancing.

"The countess in vain entreated him to be careful of his health: and all Ida's supplications were able to obtain was a few minutes' rest to take breath when he could no longer go on.

"A few minutes after, I saw Ida in tears, which did not appear as if occasioned by joy; and she quitted the ball-room. I was standing as close to the door as I am to you at this moment; so that I could not for an instant doubt its being really Ida: but what appeared to me very strange was that in a few seconds I saw her come in again with a countenance as calm as possible. I followed her, and remarked that she asked the duke to dance; and was so far from moderating his violence, that she partook of and even increased it by her own example. I also remarked that as soon as the dance was over the duke took leave of the parents of Ida, and with her vanished through a small door leading to the nuptial apartment.

"While I was endeavouring to account in my own mind how it was possible for Ida so suddenly to change her sentiments, a conference in an undertone took place at the door of the room, between the count and his valet.

"The subject was evidently a very important one, as the greatly incensed looks of the count towards his gardener evinced, while *he* confirmed, as it appeared, what the valet had before said.

"I drew near the trio, and heard, that at a particular time the church organ was heard to play, and that the whole edifice had been illuminated within, until twelve o'clock, which had just struck.

"The count was very angry at their troubling him with so silly a tale, and asked why they did not sooner inform him of it. They answered that everyone was anxious to see how it would end. The gardener added that the old chaplain had been seen again; and the peasantry who lived near the forest, even pretended that they had seen the summit of the mountain which overhung their valley illuminated, and spirits dance around it.

"'Very well!' exclaimed the count with a gloomy air; 'So all the old idle trash is resumed: the *Death-Bride* is also, I hope, going to play her part.'

"The valet having pushed aside the gardener, that he might not still further enrage the count, I put in my word; and said to the count, 'You might at least listen to what they have to say, and learn what it is they pretend to have seen.'

"'What is said about the *Death-Bride?*' said I to the gardener.

"He shrugged up his shoulders.

"'Was I not right?' cried the count: 'Here we are then, and must listen to this ridiculous tale. All these things are treasured in the memory of these people, and constantly afford subjects and phantoms to their imaginations. Is it permitted to ask under what form?'

"'Pray pardon me,' replied the gardener; 'but it resembled the deceased mademoiselle Hildegarde. She passed close to me in the garden, and then came into the castle.'

"'O!' said the count to him, 'I beg, in future you will be a little more circumspect in your fancies, and leave my daughter to rest quietly in the tomb – 'Tis well –'

"He then made a signal to his servants, who went out.

"'Well! My dear marquis!' said he to me.

"'Well?'

"'Your belief in stories will not, surely, carry you so far as to give credence to my Hildegarde's spirit appearing?'

"'At least it may have appeared to the gardener only – do you recollect the adventure in the Museum at Paris?'

"'You are right: that again was a pretty invention, which to this moment I cannot fathom. Believe me, I should sooner have refused my daughter to the duke for his having been the fabricator of so gross a story, than for his having forsaken his first love.'

"'I see very plainly that we shall not easily accord on this point; for if my ready belief appears strange to you, your doubts seem to me incomprehensible.'

"The company assembled at the castle, retired by degrees; and *I alone* was left with the count and his lady, when Ida came to the room-door, clothed in her ball-dress, and appeared astonished at finding the company had left.

"'What can this mean?' demanded the countess. Her husband could not find words to express his astonishment.

"'Where is Marino?' exclaimed Ida.

"'Do *you* ask us where he is?' replied her mother; 'did we not see you go out with him through that small door?'

"'That could not be – you mistake.'

"'No, no; my dear child! A very short time since you were dancing with singular vehemence; and then you both went out together.'

"'*Me!* My mother?'

"'Yes, my dear Ida: how is it possible you should have forgotten all this?'

"'I have forgotten nothing, believe me.'

"'Where then have you been all this time?'

"'In my sister's chamber,' said Ida.

"I remarked that at these words the count became somewhat pale; and his fearful eye caught mine: he however said nothing. The countess, fearing that her daughter was deceiving her, said to her in an afflicted tone of voice:

"'How could so singular a fancy possess you on a day like this?'

"'I cannot account for it; and only know that all on a sudden I felt an oppression at my heart, and fancied that all I wanted was Hildegarde. At the same time I felt a firm belief that I should find her in her room playing on her guitar; for which reason I crept thither softly.'

"'And did you find her there?'

"'Alas! No: but the eager desire that I felt to see her, added to the fatigue of dancing, so entirely overpowered me, that I seated myself on a chair, where I fell fast asleep.'

"'How long since did you quit the room?'

"'The clock in the tower struck the three-quarters past eleven just as I entered my sister's room.'

"'What does all this mean?' said the countess to her husband in a low voice: 'she talks in a connected manner; and yet I know, that as the clock struck three-quarters past eleven, I entreated Ida on this very spot to dance more moderately.'

"'And Marino?' – asked the count.

"'I thought, as I before said, that I should find him here.'

"'Good God!' exclaimed the mother, 'She raves: but the duke – where is he then?'

"'What then, my good mother?' said Ida with an air of great disquiet, while leaning on the countess.

"Meanwhile the count took a wax-taper, and made a sign for me to follow him. A horrible spectacle awaited us in the bridal-chamber, whither he conducted me. We there found the duke extended on the floor. There did not appear the slightest signs of life in him; and his features were distorted in the most frightful manner.

"Imagine the extreme affliction Ida endured when she heard this recital, and found that all the resources of the medical attendants were employed in vain.

"The count and his family could not be roused from the deep consternation which threatened to overwhelm them. A short time after this event, some business of importance occasioned me to quit their castle; and certainly I was not sorry for the excuse to get away.

"But ere I left that county, I did not fail to collect in the village every possible information relative to the *Death-Bride;* whose history unfortunately, in passing from one mouth to another, experienced many alterations. It appeared to me, however, upon the whole, that this affianced bride lived in this district, about the fourteenth or fifteenth century. She was a young lady of noble family, and she had conducted herself with so much perfidy and ingratitude towards her lover, that he died of grief; but afterwards, when she was about to marry, he appeared to her the night of her intended wedding, and she died in consequence. And it is said, that since that time, the spirit of this unfortunate creature wanders on earth in every possible shape; particularly in that of lovely females, to render their lovers inconstant.

"As it was not permitted for her to appear in the form of any living being, she always chose amongst the dead those who the most strongly resembled them. It was for this reason she voluntarily frequented the galleries in which were hung family portraits. It is even reported that she has been seen in galleries of pictures open to public inspection. Finally, it is said, that, as a punishment for her perfidy, she will wander till she finds a man whom she will in vain endeavour to make swerve from his engagement; and it appears, they added, that as yet she had not succeeded.

"Having inquired what connection subsisted between this spirit and the old chaplain (of whom also I had heard mention), they informed me that the fate of the last depended on the young lady, because he had assisted her in her criminal conduct. But no one was able to give me any satisfactory information concerning the voice which had called the duke by his name, nor on the meaning of the church being illuminated at night; and why the grand mass was chanted. No one either knows how to account for the dance on the mountain's top in the forest.

"For the rest," added the marquis, "you will own, that the traditions are admirably adapted to my story, and may, to a certain degree, serve to fill up the gaps; but I am not enabled to give a more satisfactory explanation. I reserve for another time a second history of this same *Death-Bride;* I only heard it a few weeks since: it appears to me interesting; but it is too late to begin today, and indeed, even now, I fear that I have intruded too long on the leisure of the company present by my narrative."

He had just finished these words, and some of his auditors (though all thanked him for the trouble he had taken) were expressing their disbelief of the story, when a person of his acquaintance came into the room in a hurried manner, and whispered something in his ear. Nothing could be more striking than the contrast presented by the bustling and uneasy air of the newly arrived person while speaking to the marquis, and the calm air of the latter while listening to him.

"Haste, I pray you," said the first (who appeared quite out of patience at the marquis's *sang-froid*): "In a few moments you will have cause to repent this delay."

"I am obliged to you for your affecting solicitude," replied the marquis; who in taking up his hat, appeared more to do, as all the rest of the party were doing, in preparing to return home, than from any anxiety of hastening away.

"You are lost," said the other, as he saw an officer enter the room at the head of a detachment of military, who inquired for the marquis. The latter instantly made himself known to him.

"You are my prisoner," said the officer. The marquis followed him, after saying Adieu with a smiling air to all the party, and begging they would not feel any anxiety concerning him.

"Not feel anxiety!" replied he whose advice he had neglected. "I must inform you that they have discovered that the marquis has been detected in a connection with very suspicious characters; and his death-warrant may be considered as signed. I came in pity to warn him of his danger, for possibly he might then have escaped; but from his conduct since, I can scarcely imagine he is in his proper senses."

The party, who were singularly affected by this event, were conjecturing a thousand things, when the officer returned, and again asked for the marquis.

"He just now left the room with you," answered some one of the company.

"But he came in again."

"We have seen no one."

"He has then disappeared," replied the officer, smiling: he searched every corner for the marquis, but in vain. The house was thoroughly examined, but without success; and the following day the officer quitted the baths with his soldiers, without his prisoner, and very much dissatisfied.

The Strange High House in the Mist

H.P. Lovecraft

IN THE MORNING, mist comes up from the sea by the cliffs beyond Kingsport. White and feathery it comes from the deep to its brothers the clouds, full of dreams of dank pastures and caves of leviathan. And later, in still summer rains on the steep roofs of poets, the clouds scatter bits of those dreams, that men shall not live without rumor of old strange secrets, and wonders that planets tell planets alone in the night. When tales fly thick in the grottoes of tritons, and conchs in seaweed cities blow wild tunes learned from the Elder Ones, then great eager mists flock to heaven laden with lore, and oceanward eyes on tile rocks see only a mystic whiteness, as if the cliff's rim were the rim of all earth, and the solemn bells of buoys tolled free in the aether of faery.

Now north of archaic Kingsport the crags climb lofty and curious, terrace on terrace, till the northernmost hangs in the sky like a gray frozen wind-cloud. Alone it is, a bleak point jutting in limitless space, for there the coast turns sharp where the great Miskatonic pours out of the plains past Arkham, bringing woodland legends and little quaint memories of New England's hills. The sea-folk of Kingsport look up at that cliff as other sea-folk look up at the pole-star, and time the night's watches by the way it hides or shows the Great Bear, Cassiopeia and the Dragon. Among them it is one with the firmament, and truly, it is hidden from them when the mist hides the stars or the sun.

Some of the cliffs they love, as that whose grotesque profile they call Father Neptune, or that whose pillared steps they term 'The Causeway'; but this one they fear because it is so near the sky. The Portuguese sailors coming in from a voyage cross themselves when they first see it, and the old Yankees believe it would be a much graver matter than death to climb it, if indeed that were possible. Nevertheless there is an ancient house on that cliff, and at evening men see lights in the small-paned windows.

The ancient house has always been there, and people say One dwells within who talks with the morning mists that come up from the deep, and perhaps sees singular things oceanward at those times when the cliff's rim becomes the rim of all earth, and solemn buoys toll free in the white aether of faery. This they tell from hearsay, for that forbidding crag is always unvisited, and natives dislike to train telescopes on it. Summer boarders have indeed scanned it with jaunty binoculars, but have never seen more than the gray primeval roof, peaked and shingled, whose eaves come nearly to the gray foundations, and the dim yellow light of the little windows peeping out from under those eaves in the dusk. These summer people do not believe that the same One has lived in the ancient house for hundreds of years, but cannot prove their heresy to any real Kingsporter. Even the Terrible Old Man who talks to leaden pendulums in bottles, buys groceries with centuried Spanish gold, and keeps stone idols in the yard of his antediluvian cottage in Water Street can only say these things were the same when his grandfather was a boy, and that must have been inconceivable ages ago, when Belcher or Shirley or Pownall or Bernard was Governor of His Majesty's Province of the Massachusetts-Bay.

Then one summer there came a philosopher into Kingsport. His name was Thomas Olney, and he taught ponderous things in a college by Narragansett Bay. With stout wife and romping children he came, and his eyes were weary with seeing the same things for many years, and thinking the same well-disciplined thoughts. He looked at the mists from the diadem of Father Neptune, and tried to walk into their white world of mystery along the titan steps of The Causeway. Morning after morning he would lie on the cliffs and look over the world's rim at the cryptical aether beyond, listening to spectral bells and the wild cries of what might have been gulls. Then, when the mist would lift and the sea stand out prosy with the smoke of steamers, he would sigh and descend to the town, where he loved to thread the narrow olden lanes up and down hill, and study the crazy tottering gables and odd-pillared doorways which had sheltered so many generations of sturdy sea-folk. And he even talked with the Terrible Old Man, who was not fond of strangers, and was invited into his fearsomely archaic cottage where low ceilings and wormy panelling hear the echoes of disquieting soliloquies in the dark small hours.

Of course it was inevitable that Olney should mark the gray unvisited cottage in the sky, on that sinister northward crag which is one with the mists and the firmament. Always over Kingsport it hung, and always its mystery sounded in whispers through Kingsport's crooked alleys. The Terrible Old Man wheezed a tale that his father had told him, of lightning that shot one night up from that peaked cottage to the clouds of higher heaven; and Granny Orne, whose tiny gambrel-roofed abode in Ship Street is all covered with moss and ivy, croaked over something her grandmother had heard at second-hand, about shapes that flapped out of the eastern mists straight into the narrow single door of that unreachable place – for the door is set close to the edge of the crag toward the ocean, and glimpsed only from ships at sea.

At length, being avid for new strange things and held back by neither the Kingsporter's fear nor the summer boarder's usual indolence, Olney made a very terrible resolve. Despite a conservative training – or because of it, for humdrum lives breed wistful longings of the unknown – he swore a great oath to scale that avoided northern cliff and visit the abnormally antique gray cottage in the sky. Very plausibly his saner self argued that the place must be tenanted by people who reached it from inland along the easier ridge beside the Miskatonic's estuary. Probably they traded in Arkham, knowing how little Kingsport liked their habitation or perhaps being unable to climb down the cliff on the Kingsport side. Olney walked out along the lesser cliffs to where the great crag leaped insolently up to consort with celestial things, and became very sure that no human feet could mount it or descend it on that beetling southern slope. East and north it rose thousands of feet perpendicular from the water so only the western side, inland and toward Arkham, remained.

One early morning in August Olney set out to find a path to the inaccessible pinnacle. He worked northwest along pleasant back roads, past Hooper's Pond and the old brick powderhouse to where the pastures slope up to the ridge above the Miskatonic and give a lovely vista of Arkham's white Georgian steeples across leagues of river and meadow. Here he found a shady road to Arkham, but no trail at all in the seaward direction he wished. Woods and fields crowded up to the high bank of the river's mouth, and bore not a sign of man's presence; not even a stone wall or a straying cow, but only the tall grass and giant trees and tangles of briars that the first Indian might have seen. As he climbed slowly east, higher and higher above the estuary on his left and nearer and nearer the sea, he found the way growing in difficulty till he wondered how ever the dwellers in that disliked place managed to reach the world outside, and whether they came often to market in Arkham.

Then the trees thinned, and far below him on his right he saw the hills and antique roofs and spires of Kingsport. Even Central Hill was a dwarf from this height, and he could just make out the ancient graveyard by the Congregational Hospital beneath which rumor said some terrible caves or burrows lurked. Ahead lay sparse grass and scrub blueberry bushes, and beyond them the naked rock of the crag and the thin peak of the dreaded gray cottage. Now the ridge narrowed, and Olney grew dizzy at his loneliness in the sky, south of him the frightful precipice above Kingsport, north of him the vertical drop of nearly a mile to the river's mouth. Suddenly a great chasm opened before him, ten feet deep, so that he had to let himself down by his hands and drop to a slanting floor, and then crawl perilously up a natural defile in the opposite wall. So this was the way the folk of the uncanny house journeyed betwixt earth and sky!

When he climbed out of the chasm a morning mist was gathering, but he clearly saw the lofty and unhallowed cottage ahead; walls as gray as the rock, and high peak standing bold against the milky white of the seaward vapors. And he perceived that there was no door on this landward end, but only a couple of small lattice windows with dingy bull's-eye panes leaded in seventeenth century fashion. All around him was cloud and chaos, and he could see nothing below the whiteness of illimitable space. He was alone in the sky with this queer and very disturbing house; and when he sidled around to the front and saw that the wall stood flush with the cliff's edge, so that the single narrow door was not to be reached save from the empty aether, he felt a distinct terror that altitude could not wholly explain. And it was very odd that shingles so worm-eaten could survive, or bricks so crumbled still form a standing chimney.

As the mist thickened, Olney crept around to the windows on the north and west and south sides, trying them but finding them all locked. He was vaguely glad they were locked, because the more he saw of that house the less he wished to get in. Then a sound halted him. He heard a lock rattle and a bolt shoot, and a long creaking follow as if a heavy door were slowly and cautiously opened. This was on the oceanward side that he could not see, where the narrow portal opened on blank space thousands of feet in the misty sky above the waves.

Then there was heavy, deliberate tramping in the cottage, and Olney heard the windows opening, first on the north side opposite him, and then on the west just around the corner. Next would come the south windows, under the great low eaves on the side where he stood; and it must be said that he was more than uncomfortable as he thought of the detestable house on one side and the vacancy of upper air on the other. When a fumbling came in the nearer casements he crept around to the west again, flattening himself against the wall beside the now opened windows. It was plain that the owner had come home; but he had not come from the land, nor from any balloon or airship that could be imagined. Steps sounded again, and Olney edged round to the north; but before he could find a haven a voice called softly, and he knew he must confront his host.

Stuck out of the west window was a great black-bearded face whose eyes were phosphorescent with the imprint of unheard-of sights. But the voice was gentle, and of a quaint olden kind, so that Olney did not shudder when a brown hand reached out to help him over the sill and into that low room of black oak wainscots and carved Tudor furnishings. The man was clad in very ancient garments, and had about him an unplaceable nimbus of sea-lore and dreams of tall galleons. Olney does not recall many of the wonders he told, or even who he was; but says that he was strange and kindly, and filled with the magic of unfathomed voids of time and space. The small room seemed green with a dim aqueous light, and Olney saw that the far windows to the east were not open, but shut against the misty aether with dull panes like the bottoms of old bottles.

That bearded host seemed young, yet looked out of eyes steeped in the elder mysteries; and from the tales of marvelous ancient things he related, it must be guessed that the village folk were right in saying he had communed with the mists of the sea and the clouds of the sky ever since there was any village to watch his taciturn dwelling from the plain below. And the day wore on, and still Olney listened to rumors of old times and far places, and heard how the kings of Atlantis fought with the slippery blasphemies that wriggled out of rifts in ocean's floor, and how the pillared and weedy temple of Poseidon is still glimpsed at midnight by lost ships, who knew by its sight that they are lost. Years of the Titans were recalled, but the host grew timid when he spoke of the dim first age of chaos before the gods or even the Elder Ones were born, and when the other gods came to dance on the peak of Hatheg-Kla in the stony desert near Ulthar, beyond the River Skai.

It was at this point that there came a knocking on the door; that ancient door of nail-studded oak beyond which lay only the abyss of white cloud. Olney started in fright, but the bearded man motioned him to be still, and tiptoed to the door to look out through a very small peephole. What he saw he did not like, so pressed his fingers to his lips and tiptoed around to shut and lock all the windows before returning to the ancient settle beside his guest. Then Olney saw lingering against the translucent squares of each of the little dim windows in succession a queer black outline as the caller moved inquisitively about before leaving; and he was glad his host had not answered the knocking. For there are strange objects in the great abyss, and the seeker of dreams must take care not to stir up or meet the wrong ones.

Then the shadows began to gather; first little furtive ones under the table, and then bolder ones in the dark panelled corners. And the bearded man made enigmatical gestures of prayer, and lit tall candles in curiously wrought brass candle-sticks. Frequently he would glance at the door as if he expected someone, and at length his glance seemed answered by a singular rapping which must have followed some very ancient and secret code. This time he did not even glance through the peep-hole, but swung the great oak bar and shot the bolt, unlatching the heavy door and flinging it wide to the stars and the mist.

And then to the sound of obscure harmonies there floated into that room from the deep all the dreams and memories of earth's sunken Mighty Ones. And golden flames played about weedy locks, so that Olney was dazzled as he did them homage. Trident-bearing Neptune was there, and sportive tritons and fantastic nereids, and upon dolphins' backs was balanced a vast crenulate shell wherein rode the gay and awful form of primal Nodens, Lord of the Great Abyss. And the conchs of the tritons gave weird blasts, and the nereids made strange sounds by striking on the grotesque resonant shells of unknown lurkers in black seacaves. Then hoary Nodens reached forth a wizened hand and helped Olney and his host into the vast shell, whereat the conchs and the gongs set up a wild and awesome clamor. And out into the limitless aether reeled that fabulous train, the noise of whose shouting was lost in the echoes of thunder.

All night in Kingsport they watched that lofty cliff when the storm and the mists gave them glimpses of it, and when toward the small hours the little dim windows went dark they whispered of dread and disaster. And Olney's children and stout wife prayed to the bland proper god of Baptists, and hoped that the traveller would borrow an umbrella and rubbers unless the rain stopped by morning. Then dawn swam dripping and mist-wreathed out of the sea, and the buoys tolled solemn in vortices of white aether. And at noon elfin horns rang over the ocean as Olney, dry and lightfooted, climbed down from the cliffs to antique Kingsport with the look of far places in his eyes. He could not recall what he had dreamed in the skyperched hut of that still nameless hermit, or say how he had crept down that crag untraversed by other feet. Nor could he talk of these matters at all save with the Terrible Old Man, who afterward mumbled queer things in his long white beard; vowing that the man who came down from that crag was not wholly the man who went up, and that somewhere under that gray peaked roof, or amidst inconceivable reaches of that sinister white mist, there lingered still the lost spirit of him who was Thomas Olney.

And ever since that hour, through dull dragging years of grayness and weariness, the philosopher has labored and eaten and slept and done uncomplaining the suitable deeds of a citizen. Not anymore does he long for the magic of farther hills, or sigh for secrets that peer like green reefs from a bottomless sea. The sameness of his days no longer gives him sorrow and well-disciplined thoughts have grown enough for his imagination. His good wife waxes stouter and his children older and prosier and more useful, and he never fails to smile correctly with pride when the occasion calls for it. In his glance there is not any restless light, and if he ever listens for solemn bells or far elfin horns it is only at night when old dreams are wandering. He has never seen Kingsport again, for his family disliked the funny old houses and complained that the drains were impossibly bad. They have a trim bungalow now at Bristol Highlands, where no tall crags tower, and the neighbors are urban and modern.

But in Kingsport strange tales are abroad, and even the Terrible Old Man admits a thing untold by his grandfather. For now, when the wind sweeps boisterous out of the north past the high ancient house that is one with the firmament, there is broken at last that ominous, brooding silence ever before the bane of Kingsport's maritime cotters. And old folk tell of pleasing voices heard singing there, and of laughter that swells with joys beyond earth's joys; and say that at evening the little low windows are brighter than formerly. They say, too, that the fierce aurora comes oftener to that spot, shining blue in the north with visions of frozen worlds while the crag and the cottage hang black and fantastic against wild coruscations. And the mists of the dawn are thicker, and sailors are not quite so sure that all the muffled seaward ringing is that of the solemn buoys.

Worst of all, though, is the shrivelling of old fears in the hearts of Kingsport's young men, who grow prone to listen at night to the north wind's faint distant sounds. They swear no harm or pain can inhabit that high peaked cottage, for in the new voices gladness beats, and with them the tinkle of laughter and music. What tales the sea-mists may bring to that haunted and northernmost pinnacle they do not know, but they long to extract some hint of the wonders that knock at the cliff-yawning door when clouds are thickest. And patriarchs dread lest some day one by one they seek out that inaccessible peak in the sky, and learn what centuried secrets hide beneath the steep shingled roof which is part of the rocks and the stars and the ancient fears of Kingsport. That those venturesome youths will come back they do not doubt, but they think a light may be gone from their eyes, and a will from their hearts. And they do not wish quaint Kingsport with its climbing lanes and archaic gables to drag listless down the years while voice by voice the laughing chorus grows stronger and wilder in that unknown and terrible eyrie where mists and the dreams of mists stop to rest on their way from the sea to the skies.

They do not wish the souls of their young men to leave the pleasant hearths and gambrel-roofed taverns of old Kingsport, nor do they wish the laughter and song in that high rocky place to grow louder. For as the voice which has come has brought fresh mists from the sea and from the north fresh lights, so do they say that still other voices will bring more mists and more lights, till perhaps the olden gods (whose existence they hint only in whispers for fear the Congregational parson shall hear) may come out of the deep and from unknown Kadath in the cold waste and make their dwelling on that evilly appropriate crag so close to the gentle hills and valleys of quiet, simple fisher folk. This they do not wish, for to plain people things not of earth are unwelcome; and besides, the Terrible Old Man often recalls what Olney said about a knock that the lone dweller feared, and a shape seen black and inquisitive against the mist through those queer translucent windows of leaded bull's-eyes.

All these things, however, the Elder Ones only may decide; and meanwhile the morning mist still comes up by that lovely vertiginous peak with the steep ancient house, that gray, low-eaved house where none is seen but where evening brings furtive lights while the north wind tells of strange revels. White and feathery it comes from the deep to its brothers the clouds, full of dreams of dank pastures and caves of leviathan. And when tales fly thick in the grottoes of tritons, and conchs in seaweed cities blow wild tunes learned from the Elder Ones, then great eager vapors flock to heaven laden with lore; and Kingsport, nestling uneasy in its lesser cliffs below that awesome hanging sentinel of rock, sees oceanward only a mystic whiteness, as if the cliff's rim were the rim of all earth, and the solemn bells of the buoys tolled free in the aether of faery.

The Inmost Light

Arthur Machen

I

ONE EVENING in autumn, when the deformities of London were veiled in faint blue mist, and its vistas and far-reaching streets seemed splendid, Mr. Charles Salisbury was slowly pacing down Rupert Street, drawing nearer to his favourite restaurant by slow degrees. His eyes were downcast in study of the pavement, and thus it was that as he passed in at the narrow door a man who had come up from the lower end of the street jostled against him.

"I beg your pardon – wasn't looking where I was going. Why, it's Dyson!"

"Yes, quite so. How are you, Salisbury?"

"Quite well. But where have you been, Dyson? I don't think I can have seen you for the last five years?"

"No; I dare say not. You remember I was getting rather hard up when you came to my place at Charlotte Street?"

"Perfectly. I think I remember your telling me that you owed five weeks' rent, and that you had parted with your watch for a comparatively small sum."

"My dear Salisbury, your memory is admirable. Yes, I was hard up. But the curious thing is that soon after you saw me I became harder up. My financial state was described by a friend as 'stone broke'. I don't approve of slang, mind you, but such was my condition. But suppose we go in; there might be other people who would like to dine – it's a human weakness, Salisbury."

"Certainly; come along. I was wondering as I walked down whether the corner table were taken. It has a velvet back, you know."

"I know the spot; it's vacant. Yes, as I was saying, I became even harder up."

"What did you do then?" asked Salisbury, disposing of his hat, and settling down in the corner of the seat, with a glance of fond anticipation at the menu.

"What did I do? Why, I sat down and reflected. I had a good classical education, and a positive distaste for business of any kind: that was the capital with which I faced the world. Do you know, I have heard people describe olives as nasty! What lamentable Philistinism! I have often thought, Salisbury, that I could write genuine poetry under the influence of olives and red wine. Let us have Chianti; it may not be very good, but the flasks are simply charming."

"It is pretty good here. We may as well have a big flask."

"Very good. I reflected, then, on my want of prospects, and I determined to embark in literature."

"Really; that was strange. You seem in pretty comfortable circumstances, though."

"Though! What a satire upon a noble profession. I am afraid, Salisbury, you haven't a proper idea of the dignity of an artist. You see me sitting at my desk – or at least you can see me if you care to call – with pen and ink, and simple nothingness before me, and if you come again in a few hours you will (in all probability) find a creation!"

"Yes, quite so. I had an idea that literature was not remunerative."

"You are mistaken; its rewards are great. I may mention, by the way, that shortly after you saw me I succeeded to a small income. An uncle died, and proved unexpectedly generous."

"Ah, I see. That must have been convenient."

"It was pleasant – undeniably pleasant. I have always considered it in the light of an endowment of my researches. I told you I was a man of letters; it would, perhaps, be more correct to describe myself as a man of science."

"Dear me, Dyson, you have really changed very much in the last few years. I had a notion, don't you know, that you were a sort of idler about town, the kind of man one might meet on the north side of Piccadilly every day from May to July."

"Exactly. I was even then forming myself, though all unconsciously. You know my poor father could not afford to send me to the University. I used to grumble in my ignorance at not having completed my education. That was the folly of youth, Salisbury; my University was Piccadilly. There I began to study the great science which still occupies me."

"What science do you mean?"

"The science of the great city; the physiology of London; literally and metaphysically the greatest subject that the mind of man can conceive. What an admirable *salmi* this is; undoubtedly the final end of the pheasant. Yet I feel sometimes positively overwhelmed with the thought of the vastness and complexity of London. Paris a man may get to understand thoroughly with a reasonable amount of study; but London is always a mystery. In Paris you may say: 'Here live the actresses, here the Bohemians, and the *Ratés*'; but it is different in London. You may point out a street, correctly enough, as the abode of washerwomen; but, in that second floor, a man may be studying Chaldee roots, and in the garret over the way a forgotten artist is dying by inches."

"I see you are Dyson, unchanged and unchangeable," said Salisbury, slowly sipping his Chianti. "I think you are misled by a too fervid imagination; the mystery of London exists only in your fancy. It seems to me a dull place enough. We seldom hear of a really artistic crime in London, whereas I believe Paris abounds in that sort of thing."

"Give me some more wine. Thanks. You are mistaken, my dear fellow, you are really mistaken. London has nothing to be ashamed of in the way of crime. Where we fail is for want of Homers, not Agamemnons. *Carent quia vate sacro*, you know."

"I recall the quotation. But I don't think I quite follow you."

"Well, in plain language, we have no good writers in London who make a speciality of that kind of thing. Our common reporter is a dull dog; every story that he has to tell is spoilt in the telling. His idea of horror and of what excites horror is so lamentably deficient. Nothing will content the fellow but blood, vulgar red blood, and when he can get it he lays it on thick, and considers that he has produced a telling article. It's a poor notion. And, by some curious fatality, it is the most commonplace and brutal murders which always attract the most attention and get written up the most. For instance, I dare say that you never heard of the Harlesden case?"

"No; no, I don't remember anything about it."

"Of course not. And yet the story is a curious one. I will tell it you over our coffee. Harlesden, you know, or I expect you don't know, is quite on the out-quarters of London; something curiously different from your fine old crusted suburb like Norwood or Hampstead, different as each of these is from the other. Hampstead, I mean, is where you look for the head of your great China house with his three acres of land and pine-houses, though of late there is the artistic substratum; while Norwood is the home of the prosperous middle-class family who took the house 'because it was near the Palace', and sickened of the Palace six months afterwards; but Harlesden is a place of no character. It's too new to have any character as yet. There are the rows of red houses and the rows of white houses and the bright green Venetians, and the blistering doorways, and the little backyards they call gardens, and a few feeble shops, and then, just as you think you're going to grasp the physiognomy of the settlement, it all melts away."

"How the dickens is that? The houses don't tumble down before one's eyes, I suppose!"

"Well, no, not exactly that. But Harlesden as an entity disappears. Your street turns into a quiet lane, and your staring houses into elm trees, and the back-gardens into green meadows. You pass instantly from town to country; there is no transition as in a small country town, no soft gradations of wider lawns and orchards, with houses gradually becoming less dense, but a dead stop. I believe the people who live there mostly go into the City. I have seen once or twice a laden bus bound thitherwards. But however that may be, I can't conceive a greater loneliness in a desert at midnight than there is there at midday. It is like a city of the dead; the streets are glaring and desolate, and as you pass it suddenly strikes you that this too is part of London.

"Well, a year or two ago there was a doctor living there; he had set up his brass plate and his red lamp at the very end of one of those shining streets, and from the back of the house, the fields stretched away to the north. I don't know what his reason was in settling down in such an out-of-the-way place, perhaps Dr. Black, as we will call him, was a far-seeing man and looked ahead. His relations, so it appeared afterwards, had lost sight of him for many years and didn't even know he was a doctor, much less where he lived. However, there he was settled in Harlesden, with some fragments of a practice, and an uncommonly pretty wife. People used to see them walking out together in the summer evenings soon after they came to Harlesden, and, so far as could be observed, they seemed a very affectionate couple. These walks went on through the autumn, and then ceased; but, of course, as the days grew dark and the weather cold, the lanes near Harlesden might be expected to lose many of their attractions. All through the winter nobody saw anything of Mrs. Black; the doctor used to reply to his patients' inquiries that she was a 'little out of sorts, would be better, no doubt, in the spring.' But the spring came, and the summer, and no Mrs. Black appeared, and at last people began to rumour and talk amongst themselves, and all sorts of queer things were said at 'high teas', which you may possibly have heard are the only form of entertainment known in such suburbs. Dr. Black began to surprise some very odd looks cast in his direction, and the practice, such as it was, fell off before his eyes. In short, when the neighbours whispered about the matter, they whispered that Mrs. Black was dead, and that the doctor had made away with her.

"But this wasn't the case; Mrs. Black was seen alive in June. It was a Sunday afternoon, one of those few exquisite days that an English climate offers, and half London had strayed out into the fields, north, south, east, and west to smell the scent of the white May, and to see if the wild roses were yet in blossom in the hedges. I had gone out myself early in the morning, and had had a long ramble, and somehow or other as I was steering homeward I found myself in this very Harlesden we have been talking about. To be exact, I had a glass of beer in the 'General Gordon', the most flourishing house in the neighbourhood, and as I was wandering rather aimlessly about, I saw an uncommonly tempting gap in a hedgerow, and resolved to explore the meadow beyond. Soft grass is very grateful to the feet after the infernal grit strewn on suburban sidewalks, and after walking about for some time I thought I should like to sit down on a bank and have a smoke.

"While I was getting out my pouch, I looked up in the direction of the houses, and as I looked I felt my breath caught back, and my teeth began to chatter, and the stick I had in one hand snapped in two with the grip I gave it. It was as if I had had an electric current down my spine, and yet for some moment of time which seemed long, but which must have been very short, I caught myself wondering what on earth was the matter. Then I knew what had made my very heart shudder and my bones grind together in an agony. As I glanced up I had looked straight towards the last house in the row before me, and in an upper window of that house I had seen for some short fraction of a second a face. It was the face of a woman, and yet it was not human. You and I, Salisbury, have heard in our time, as we sat in our seats in church in sober English fashion, of a lust that cannot be satiated and of a fire that is unquenchable, but few of us have any notion what these words mean. I hope you never may, for as I saw that face at the window, with the blue sky above me and the warm air playing in gusts about me, I knew I had looked into another world – looked through the window of a commonplace, brand-new house, and seen hell open before me.

"When the first shock was over, I thought once or twice that I should have fainted; my face streamed with a cold sweat, and my breath came and went in sobs, as if I had been half drowned. I managed to get up at last, and walked round to the street, and there I saw the name 'Dr. Black' on the post by the front gate. As fate or my luck would have it, the door opened and a man came down the steps as I passed by. I had no doubt it was the doctor himself. He was of a type rather common in London; long and thin, with a pasty face and a dull black moustache. He gave me a look as we passed each other on the pavement, and though it was merely the casual glance which one foot-passenger bestows on another, I felt convinced in my mind that here was an ugly customer to deal with. As you may imagine, I went my way a good deal puzzled and horrified too by what I had seen; for I had paid another visit to the 'General Gordon', and had got together a good deal of the common gossip of the place about the Blacks. I didn't mention the fact that I had seen a woman's face in the window; but I heard that Mrs. Black had been much admired for her beautiful golden hair, and round what had struck me with such a nameless terror, there was a mist of flowing yellow hair, as it were an aureole of glory round the visage of a satyr. The whole thing bothered me in an indescribable manner; and when I got home I tried my best to think of the impression I had received as an illusion, but it was no use. I knew very well I had seen what I have tried to describe to you, and I was morally certain that I had seen Mrs. Black. And then there was the gossip of the place, the suspicion of foul play, which I knew to be false, and my own conviction that there was some deadly mischief or other going on in that bright red house at the corner of Devon Road: how to construct a theory of a reasonable kind out of these two elements.

"In short, I found myself in a world of mystery; I puzzled my head over it and filled up my leisure moments by gathering together odd threads of speculation, but I never moved a step towards any real solution, and as the summer days went on the matter seemed to grow misty and indistinct, shadowing some vague terror, like a nightmare of last month. I suppose it would before long have faded into the background of my brain – I should not have forgotten it, for such a thing could never be forgotten – but one morning as I was looking over the paper my eye was caught by a heading over some two dozen lines of small type. The words I had seen were simply 'the Harlesden Case', and I knew what I was going to read. Mrs. Black was dead. Black had called in another medical man to certify as to cause of death, and something or other had aroused the strange doctor's suspicions and there had been an inquest and post-mortem. And the result? That, I will confess, did astonish me considerably; it was the triumph of the unexpected. The two doctors who made the autopsy were obliged to confess that they could not discover the faintest trace of any kind of foul play; their most exquisite tests and reagents failed to detect the presence of poison in the most infinitesimal quantity. Death, they found, had been caused by a somewhat obscure and scientifically interesting form of brain disease. The tissue of the brain and the molecules of the grey matter had undergone a most extraordinary series of changes; and the younger of the two doctors, who has some reputation, I believe, as a specialist in brain trouble, made some remarks in giving his evidence which struck me deeply at the time, though I did not then grasp their full significance. He said: 'At the commencement of the examination I was astonished to find appearances of a character entirely new to me, notwithstanding my somewhat large experience. I need not specify these appearances at present, it will be sufficient for me to state that as I proceeded in my task I could scarcely believe that the brain before me was that of a human being at all.' There was some surprise at this statement, as you may imagine, and the coroner asked the doctor if he meant to say that the brain resembled that of an animal. 'No,' he replied, 'I should not put it in that way. Some of the appearances I noticed seemed to point in that direction, but others, and these were the more surprising, indicated a nervous organization of a wholly different character from that either of man or the lower animals.' It was a curious thing to say, but of course the jury brought in a verdict of death from natural causes, and, so far as the public was concerned, the case came to an end. But after I had read what the doctor said I made up my mind that I should like to know a good deal more, and I set to work on what seemed likely to prove an interesting investigation. I had really a good deal of trouble, but I was successful in a measure. Though why – my dear fellow, I had no notion at the time. Are you aware that we have been here nearly four hours? The waiters are staring at us. Let's have the bill and be gone."

The two men went out in silence, and stood a moment in the cool air, watching the hurrying traffic of Coventry Street pass before them to the accompaniment of the ringing bells of hansoms and the cries of the newsboys; the deep far murmur of London surging up ever and again from beneath these louder noises.

"It is a strange case, isn't it?" said Dyson at length. "What do you think of it?"

"My dear fellow, I haven't heard the end, so I will reserve my opinion. When will you give me the sequel?"

"Come to my rooms some evening; say next Thursday. Here's the address. Goodnight; I want to get down to the Strand." Dyson hailed a passing hansom, and Salisbury turned northward to walk home to his lodgings.

II

MR. SALISBURY, as may have been gathered from the few remarks which he had found it possible to introduce in the course of the evening, was a young gentleman of a peculiarly solid form of intellect, coy and retiring before the mysterious and the uncommon, with a constitutional dislike of paradox. During the restaurant dinner he had been forced to listen in almost absolute silence to a strange tissue of improbabilities strung together with the ingenuity of a born meddler in plots and mysteries, and it was with a feeling of weariness that he crossed Shaftesbury Avenue, and dived into the recesses of Soho, for his lodgings were in a modest neighbourhood to the north of Oxford Street.

As he walked he speculated on the probable fate of Dyson, relying on literature, unbefriended by a thoughtful relative, and could not help concluding that so much subtlety united to a too vivid imagination would in all likelihood have been rewarded with a pair of sandwich-boards or a super's banner. Absorbed in this train of thought, and admiring the perverse dexterity which could transmute the face of a sickly woman and a case of brain disease into the crude elements of romance, Salisbury strayed on through the dimly-lighted streets, not noticing the gusty wind which drove sharply round corners and whirled the stray rubbish of the pavement into the air in eddies, while black clouds gathered over the sickly yellow moon. Even a stray drop or two of rain blown into his face did not rouse him from his meditations, and it was only when with a sudden rush the storm tore down upon the street that he began to consider the expediency of finding some shelter. The rain, driven by the wind, pelted down with the violence of a thunderstorm, dashing up from the stones and hissing through the air, and soon a perfect torrent of water coursed along the kennels and accumulated in pools over the choked-up drains.

The few stray passengers who had been loafing rather than walking about the street had scuttered away, like frightened rabbits, to some invisible places of refuge, and though Salisbury whistled loud and long for a hansom, no hansom appeared. He looked about him, as if to discover how far he might be from the haven of Oxford Street, but strolling carelessly along, he had turned out of his way, and found himself in an unknown region, and one to all appearance devoid even of a public-house where shelter could be bought for the modest sum of twopence. The street lamps were few and at long intervals, and burned behind grimy glasses with the sickly light of oil, and by this wavering glimmer Salisbury could make out the shadowy and vast old houses of which the street was composed.

As he passed along, hurrying, and shrinking from the full sweep of the rain, he noticed the innumerable bell-handles, with names that seemed about to vanish of old age graven on brass plates beneath them, and here and there a richly carved penthouse overhung the door, blackening with the grime of fifty years. The storm seemed to grow more and more furious; he was wet through, and a new hat had become a ruin, and still Oxford Street seemed as far off as ever; it was with deep relief that the dripping man caught sight of a dark archway which seemed to promise shelter from the rain if not from the wind. Salisbury took up his position in the driest corner and looked about him; he was standing in a kind of passage contrived under part of a house, and behind him stretched a narrow footway leading between blank walls to regions unknown.

He had stood there for some time, vainly endeavouring to rid himself of some of his superfluous moisture, and listening for the passing wheel of a hansom, when his attention was aroused by a loud noise coming from the direction of the passage behind, and growing louder as it drew nearer. In a couple of minutes he could make out the shrill, raucous voice of a woman, threatening and renouncing, and making the very stones echo with her accents, while now and then a man grumbled and expostulated. Though to all appearance devoid of romance, Salisbury had some relish for street rows, and was, indeed, somewhat of an amateur in the more amusing phases of drunkenness; he therefore composed himself to listen and observe with something of the air of a subscriber to grand opera. To his annoyance, however, the tempest seemed suddenly to be composed, and he could hear nothing but the impatient steps of the woman and the slow lurch of the man as they came towards him. Keeping back in the shadow of the wall, he could see the two drawing nearer; the man was evidently drunk, and had much ado to avoid frequent collision with the wall as he tacked across from one side to the other, like some bark beating up against a wind. The woman was looking straight in front of her, with tears streaming from her eyes, but suddenly as they went by the flame blazed up again, and she burst forth into a torrent of abuse, facing round upon her companion.

"You low rascal, you mean, contemptible cur," she went on, after an incoherent storm of curses, "you think I'm to work and slave for you always, I suppose, while you're after that Green Street girl and drinking every penny you've got? But you're mistaken, Sam – indeed, I'll bear it no longer. Damn you, you dirty thief, I've done with you and your master too, so you can go your own errands, and I only hope they'll get you into trouble."

The woman tore at the bosom of her dress, and taking something out that looked like paper, crumpled it up and flung it away. It fell at Salisbury's feet. She ran out and disappeared in the darkness, while the man lurched slowly into the street, grumbling indistinctly to himself in a perplexed tone of voice. Salisbury looked out after him and saw him maundering along the pavement, halting now and then and swaying indecisively, and then starting off at some fresh tangent. The sky had cleared, and white fleecy clouds were fleeting across the moon, high in the heaven. The light came and went by turns, as the clouds passed by, and, turning round as the clear, white rays shone into the passage, Salisbury saw the little ball of crumpled paper which the woman had cast down. Oddly curious to know what it might contain, he picked it up and put it in his pocket, and set out afresh on his journey.

III

SALISBURY WAS a man of habit. When he got home, drenched to the skin, his clothes hanging lank about him, and a ghastly dew besmearing his hat, his only thought was of his health, of which he took studious care. So, after changing his clothes and encasing himself in a warm dressing-gown, he proceeded to prepare a sudorific in the shape of a hot gin and water, warming the latter over one of those spirit-lamps which mitigate the austerities of the modern hermit's life. By the time this preparation had been exhibited, and Salisbury's disturbed feelings had been soothed by a pipe of tobacco, he was able to get into bed in a happy state of vacancy, without a thought of his adventure in the dark archway, or of the weird fancies with which Dyson had seasoned his dinner.

It was the same at breakfast the next morning, for Salisbury made a point of not thinking of anything until that meal was over; but when the cup and saucer were cleared away, and the morning pipe was lit, he remembered the little ball of paper, and began fumbling in the pockets of his wet coat. He did not remember into which pocket he had put it, and as he dived now into one and now into another, he experienced a strange feeling of apprehension lest it should not be there at all, though he could not for the life of him have explained the importance he attached to what was in all probability mere rubbish. But he sighed with relief when his fingers touched the crumpled surface in an inside pocket, and he drew it out gently and laid it on the little desk by his easy-chair with as much care as if it had been some rare jewel. Salisbury sat smoking and staring at his find for a few minutes, an odd temptation to throw the thing in the fire and have done with it struggling with as odd a speculation as to its possible contents, and as to the reason why the infuriated woman should have flung a bit of paper from her with such vehemence. As might be expected, it was the latter feeling that conquered in the end, and yet it was with something like repugnance that he at last took the paper and unrolled it, and laid it out before him. It was a piece of common dirty paper, to all appearance torn out of a cheap exercise-book, and in the middle were a few lines written in a queer cramped hand. Salisbury bent his head and stared eagerly at it for a moment, drawing a long breath, and then fell back in his chair gazing blankly before him, till at last with a sudden revulsion he burst into a peal of laughter, so long and loud and uproarious that the landlady's baby on the floor below awoke from sleep and echoed his mirth with hideous yells. But he laughed again and again, and took the paper up to read a second time what seemed such meaningless nonsense.

Q. has had to go and see his friends in Paris, it began. *Traverse Handle S.* 'Once around the grass, and twice around the lass, and thrice around the maple tree.'

Salisbury took up the paper and crumpled it as the angry woman had done, and aimed it at the fire. He did not throw it there, however, but tossed it carelessly into the well of the desk, and laughed again. The sheer folly of the thing offended him, and he was ashamed of his own eager speculation, as one who pores over the high-sounding announcements in the agony column of the daily paper, and finds nothing but advertisement and triviality. He walked to the window, and stared out at the languid morning life of his quarter; the maids in slatternly print dresses washing door-steps, the fish-monger and the butcher on their rounds, and the tradesmen standing at the doors of their small shops, drooping for lack of trade and excitement. In the distance a blue haze gave some grandeur to the prospect, but the view as a whole was depressing, and would only have interested a student of the life of London, who finds something rare and choice in its very aspect. Salisbury turned away in disgust, and settled himself in the easy-chair, upholstered in a bright shade of green, and decked with yellow gimp, which was the pride and attraction of the apartments.

Here he composed himself to his morning's occupation – the perusal of a novel that dealt with sport and love in a manner that suggested the collaboration of a stud-groom and a ladies' college. In an ordinary way, however, Salisbury would have been carried on by the interest of the story up to lunch-time, but this morning he fidgeted in and out of his chair, took the book up and laid it down again, and swore at last to himself and at himself in mere irritation. In point of fact the jingle of the paper found in the archway had 'got into his head', and do what he would he could not help muttering over and over, "Once around the grass, and twice around the lass, and thrice around the maple tree." It became a positive pain, like the foolish burden of a music-hall song, everlastingly quoted, and sung at all hours of the day and night, and treasured by the street-boys as an unfailing resource for six months together.

He went out into the streets, and tried to forget his enemy in the jostling of the crowds and the roar and clatter of the traffic, but presently he would find himself stealing quietly aside, and pacing some deserted byway, vainly puzzling his brains, and trying to fix some meaning to phrases that were meaningless. It was a positive relief when Thursday came, and he remembered that he had made an appointment to go and see Dyson; the flimsy reveries of the self-styled man of letters appeared entertaining when compared with this ceaseless iteration, this maze of thought from which there seemed no possibility of escape. Dyson's abode was in one of the quietest of the quiet streets that led down from the Strand to the river, and when Salisbury passed from the narrow stairway into his friend's room, he saw that the uncle had been beneficent indeed. The floor glowed and flamed with all the colours of the East; it was, as Dyson pompously remarked, 'a sunset in a dream', and the lamplight, the twilight of London streets, was shut out with strangely worked curtains, glittering here and there with threads of gold. In the shelves of an oak armoire stood jars and plates of old French china, and the black and white of etchings not to be found in the Haymarket or in Bond Street, stood out against the splendour of a Japanese paper. Salisbury sat down on the settle by the hearth, and sniffed the mingled fumes of incense and tobacco, wondering and dumb before all this splendour after the green rep and the oleographs, the gilt-framed mirror, and the lustres of his own apartment.

"I am glad you have come," said Dyson. "Comfortable little room, isn't it? But you don't look very well, Salisbury. Nothing disagreed with you, has it?"

"No; but I have been a good deal bothered for the last few days. The fact is I had an odd kind of – of – adventure, I suppose I may call it, that night I saw you, and it has worried me a good deal. And the provoking part of it is that it's the merest nonsense – but, however, I will tell you all about it, by and by. You were going to let me have the rest of that odd story you began at the restaurant."

"Yes. But I am afraid, Salisbury, you are incorrigible. You are a slave to what you call matter of fact. You know perfectly well that in your heart you think the oddness in that case is of my making, and that it is all really as plain as the police reports. However, as I have begun, I will go on. But first we will have something to drink, and you may as well light your pipe."

Dyson went up to the oak cupboard, and drew from its depths a rotund bottle and two little glasses, quaintly gilded.

"It's Benedictine," he said. "You'll have some, won't you?"

Salisbury assented, and the two men sat sipping and smoking reflectively for some minutes before Dyson began.

"Let me see," he said at last, "we were at the inquest, weren't we? No, we had done with that. Ah, I remember. I was telling you that on the whole I had been successful in my inquiries, investigation, or whatever you like to call it, into the matter. Wasn't that where I left off?"

"Yes, that was it. To be precise, I think 'though' was the last word you said on the matter."

"Exactly. I have been thinking it all over since the other night, and I have come to the conclusion that that 'though' is a very big 'though' indeed. Not to put too fine a point on it, I have had to confess that what I found out, or thought I found out, amounts in reality to nothing. I am as far away from the heart of the case as ever. However, I may as well tell you what I do know. You may remember my saying that I was impressed a good deal by some remarks of one of the doctors who gave evidence at the inquest. Well, I determined that my first step must be to try if I could get something more definite and intelligible out of that doctor. Somehow or other I managed to get an introduction to the man, and he gave me an appointment to come and see him. He turned out to be a pleasant, genial fellow; rather young and not in the least like the typical medical man, and he began the conference by offering me whisky and cigars. I didn't think it worthwhile to beat about the bush, so I began by saying that part of his evidence at the Harlesden Inquest struck me as very peculiar, and I gave him the printed report, with the sentences in question underlined. He just glanced at the slip, and gave me a queer look. 'It struck you as peculiar, did it?' said he. 'Well, you must remember that the Harlesden case was very peculiar. In fact, I think I may safely say that in some features it was unique – quite unique.' 'Quite so,' I replied, 'and that's exactly why it interests me, and why I want to know more about it. And I thought that if anybody could give me any information it would be you. What is your opinion of the matter?'

"It was a pretty downright sort of question, and my doctor looked rather taken aback.

"'Well,' he said, 'as I fancy your motive in inquiring into the question must be mere curiosity, I think I may tell you my opinion with tolerable freedom. So, Mr., Mr. Dyson? if you want to know my theory, it is this: I believe that Dr. Black killed his wife.'

"'But the verdict,' I answered, 'the verdict was given from your own evidence.'

"'Quite so; the verdict was given in accordance with the evidence of my colleague and myself, and, under the circumstances, I think the jury acted very sensibly. In fact, I don't see what else they could have done. But I stick to my opinion, mind you, and I say this also. I don't wonder at Black's doing what I firmly believe he did. I think he was justified.'

"'Justified! How could that be?' I asked. I was astonished, as you may imagine, at the answer I had got. The doctor wheeled round his chair and looked steadily at me for a moment before he answered.

"'I suppose you are not a man of science yourself? No; then it would be of no use my going into detail. I have always been firmly opposed myself to any partnership between physiology and psychology. I believe that both are bound to suffer. No one recognizes more decidedly than I do the impassable gulf, the fathomless abyss that separates the world of consciousness from the sphere of matter. We know that every change of consciousness is accompanied by a rearrangement of the molecules in the grey matter; and that is all. What the link between them is, or why they occur together, we do not know, and most authorities believe that we never can know. Yet, I will tell you that as I did my work, the knife in my hand, I felt convinced, in spite of all theories, that what lay before me was not the brain of a dead woman – not the brain of a human being at all. Of course I saw the face; but it was quite placid, devoid of all expression. It must have been a beautiful face, no doubt, but I can honestly say that I would not have looked in that face when there was life behind it for a thousand guineas, no, nor for twice that sum.'

"'My dear sir,' I said, 'you surprise me extremely. You say that it was not the brain of a human being. What was it then?'

"'The brain of a devil.' He spoke quite coolly, and never moved a muscle. 'The brain of a devil,' he repeated, 'and I have no doubt that Black found some way of putting an end to it. I don't blame him if he did. Whatever Mrs. Black was, she was not fit to stay in this world. Will you have anything more? No? Goodnight, goodnight.'

"It was a queer sort of opinion to get from a man of science, wasn't it? When he was saying that he would not have looked on that face when alive for a thousand guineas, or two thousand guineas, I was thinking of the face I had seen, but I said nothing. I went again to Harlesden, and passed from one shop to another, making small purchases, and trying to find out whether there was anything about the Blacks which was not already common property, but there was very little to hear. One of the tradesmen to whom I spoke said he had known the dead woman well; she used to buy of him such quantities of grocery as were required for their small household, for they never kept a servant, but had a charwoman in occasionally, and she had not seen Mrs. Black for months before she died. According to this man Mrs. Black was 'a nice lady', always kind and considerate, and so fond of her husband and he of her, as everyone thought. And yet, to put the doctor's opinion on one side, I knew what I had seen.

"And then after thinking it all over, and putting one thing with another, it seemed to me that the only person likely to give me much assistance would be Black himself, and I made up my mind to find him. Of course he wasn't to be found in Harlesden; he had left, I was told, directly after the funeral. Everything in the house had been sold, and one fine day Black got into the train with a small portmanteau, and went, nobody knew where. It was a chance if he were ever heard of again, and it was by a mere chance that I came across him at last. I was walking one day along Gray's Inn Road, not bound for anywhere in particular, but looking about me, as usual, and holding on to my hat, for it was a gusty day in early March, and the wind was making the treetops in the Inn rock and quiver.

"I had come up from the Holborn end, and I had almost got to Theobald's Road when I noticed a man walking in front of me, leaning on a stick, and to all appearance very feeble. There was something about his look that made me curious, I don't know why, and I began to walk briskly with the idea of overtaking him, when of a sudden his hat blew off and came bounding along the pavement to my feet. Of course I rescued the hat, and gave it a glance as I went towards its owner. It was a biography in itself; a Piccadilly maker's name in the inside, but I don't think a beggar would have picked it out of the gutter. Then I looked up and saw Dr. Black of Harlesden waiting for me. A queer thing, wasn't it? But, Salisbury, what a change! When I saw Dr. Black come down the steps of his house at Harlesden he was an upright man, walking firmly with well-built limbs; a man, I should say, in the prime of his life. And now before me there crouched this wretched creature, bent and feeble, with shrunken cheeks, and hair that was whitening fast, and limbs that trembled and shook together, and misery in his eyes. He thanked me for bringing him his hat, saying, 'I don't think I should ever have got it, I can't run much now. A gusty day, sir, isn't it?' and with this he was turning away, but by little and little I contrived to draw him into the current of conversation, and we walked together eastward. I think the man would have been glad to get rid of me; but I didn't intend to let him go, and he stopped at last in front of a miserable house in a miserable street. It was, I verily believe, one of the most wretched quarters I have ever seen: houses that must have been sordid and hideous enough when new, that had gathered foulness with every year, and now seemed to lean and totter to their fall. 'I live up there,' said Black, pointing to the tiles, 'not in the front – in the back. I am very quiet there. I won't ask you to come in now, but perhaps some other day –' I caught him up at that, and told him I should be only too glad to come and see him. He gave me an odd sort of glance, as if he were wondering what on earth I or anybody else could care about him, and I left him fumbling with his latch-key.

I think you will say I did pretty well when I tell you that within a few weeks I had made myself an intimate friend of Black's. I shall never forget the first time I went to his room; I hope I shall never see such abject, squalid misery again. The foul paper, from which all pattern or trace of a pattern had long vanished, subdued and penetrated with the grime of the evil street, was hanging in mouldering pennons from the wall. Only at the end of the room was it possible to stand upright, and the sight of the wretched bed and the odour of corruption that pervaded the place made me turn faint and sick. Here I found him munching a piece of bread; he seemed surprised to find that I had kept my promise, but he gave me his chair and sat on the bed while we talked. I used to go to see him often, and we had long conversations together, but he never mentioned Harlesden or his wife. I fancy that he supposed me ignorant of the matter, or thought that if I had heard of it, I should never connect the respectable Dr. Black of Harlesden with a poor garreteer in the backwoods of London. He was a strange man, and as we sat together smoking, I often wondered whether he were mad or sane, for I think the wildest dreams of Paracelsus and the Rosicrucians would appear plain and sober fact compared with the theories I have heard him earnestly advance in that grimy den of his. I once ventured to hint something of the sort to him. I suggested that something he had said was in flat contradiction to all science and all experience. 'No,' he answered, 'not all experience, for mine counts for something. I am no dealer in unproved theories; what I say I have proved for myself, and at a terrible cost. There is a region of knowledge which you will never know, which wise men seeing from afar off shun like the plague, as well they may, but into that region I have gone. If you knew, if you could even dream of what may be done, of what one or two men have done in this quiet world of ours, your very soul would shudder and faint within you. What you have heard from me has been but the merest husk and outer covering of true science – that science which means death, and that which is more awful than death, to those who gain it. No, when men say that there are strange things in the world, they little know the awe and the terror that dwell always with them and about them.' There was a sort of fascination about the man that drew me to him, and I was quite sorry to have to leave London for a month or two; I missed his odd talk.

A few days after I came back to town I thought I would look him up, but when I gave the two rings at the bell that used to summon him, there was no answer. I rang and rang again, and was just turning to go away, when the door opened and a dirty woman asked me what I wanted. From her look I fancy she took me for a plain-clothes officer after one of her lodgers, but when I inquired if Mr. Black were in, she gave me a stare of another kind. 'There's no Mr. Black lives here,' she said. 'He's gone. He's dead this six weeks. I always thought he was a bit queer in his head, or else had been and got into some trouble or other. He used to go out every morning from ten till one, and one Monday morning we heard him come in, and go into his room and shut the door, and a few minutes after, just as we was a-sitting down to our dinner, there was such a scream that I thought I should have gone right off. And then we heard a stamping, and down he came, raging and cursing most dreadful, swearing he had been robbed of something that was worth millions. And then he just dropped down in the passage, and we thought he was dead. We got him up to his room, and put him on his bed, and I just sat there and waited, while my 'usband he went for the doctor. And there was the winder wide open, and a little tin box he had lying on the floor open and empty, but of course nobody could possible have got in at the winder, and as for him having anything that was worth anything, it's nonsense, for he was often weeks and weeks behind with his rent, and my 'usband he threatened often and often to turn him into the street, for, as he said, we've got a living to myke like other people – and, of course, that's true; but, somehow, I didn't like to do it, though he was an odd kind of a man, and I fancy had been better off. And then the doctor came and looked at him, and said as he couldn't do nothing, and that night he died as I was a-sitting by his bed; and I can tell you that, with one thing and another, we lost money by him, for the few bits of clothes as he had were worth next to nothing when they came to be sold.'

"I gave the woman half a sovereign for her trouble, and went home thinking of Dr. Black and the epitaph she had made him, and wondering at his strange fancy that he had been robbed. I take it that he had very little to fear on that score, poor fellow; but I suppose that he was really mad, and died in a sudden access of his mania. His landlady said that once or twice when she had had occasion to go into his room (to dun the poor wretch for his rent, most likely), he would keep her at the door for about a minute, and that when she came in she would find him putting away his tin box in the corner by the window; I suppose he had become possessed with the idea of some great treasure, and fancied himself a wealthy man in the midst of all his misery. *Explicit*, my tale is ended, and you see that though I knew Black, I know nothing of his wife or of the history of her death. – That's the Harlesden case, Salisbury, and I think it interests me all the more deeply because there does not seem the shadow of a possibility that I or anyone else will ever know more about it. What do you think of it?"

"Well, Dyson, I must say that I think you have contrived to surround the whole thing with a mystery of your own making. I go for the doctor's solution: Black murdered his wife, being himself in all probability an undeveloped lunatic."

"What? Do you believe, then, that this woman was something too awful, too terrible to be allowed to remain on the earth? You will remember that the doctor said it was the brain of a devil?"

"Yes, yes, but he was speaking, of course, metaphorically. It's really quite a simple matter if you only look at it like that."

"Ah, well, you may be right; but yet I am sure you are not. Well, well, it's no good discussing it anymore. A little more Benedictine? That's right; try some of this tobacco. Didn't you say that you had been bothered by something – something which happened that night we dined together?"

"Yes, I have been worried, Dyson, worried a great deal. I – but it's such a trivial matter – indeed, such an absurdity – that I feel ashamed to trouble you with it."

"Never mind, let's have it, absurd or not."

With many hesitations, and with much inward resentment of the folly of the thing, Salisbury told his tale, and repeated reluctantly the absurd intelligence and the absurder doggerel of the scrap of paper, expecting to hear Dyson burst out into a roar of laughter.

"Isn't it too bad that I should let myself be bothered by such stuff as that?" he asked, when he had stuttered out the jingle of once, and twice, and thrice.

Dyson listened to it all gravely, even to the end, and meditated for a few minutes in silence.

"Yes," he said at length, "it was a curious chance, your taking shelter in that archway just as those two went by. But I don't know that I should call what was written on the paper nonsense; it is bizarre certainly, but I expect it has a meaning for somebody. Just repeat it again, will you, and I will write it down. Perhaps we might find a cipher of some sort, though I hardly think we shall."

Again had the reluctant lips of Salisbury slowly to stammer out the rubbish that he abhorred, while Dyson jotted it down on a slip of paper.

"Look over it, will you?" he said, when it was done; "It may be important that I should have every word in its place. Is that all right?"

"Yes; that is an accurate copy. But I don't think you will get much out of it. Depend upon it, it is mere nonsense, a wanton scribble. I must be going now, Dyson. No, no more; that stuff of yours is pretty strong. Goodnight."

"I suppose you would like to hear from me, if I did find out anything?"

"No, not I; I don't want to hear about the thing again. You may regard the discovery, if it is one, as your own."

"Very well. Goodnight."

IV

A GOOD MANY HOURS after Salisbury had returned to the company of the green rep chairs, Dyson still sat at his desk, itself a Japanese romance, smoking many pipes, and meditating over his friend's story. The bizarre quality of the inscription which had annoyed Salisbury was to him an attraction, and now and again he took it up and scanned thoughtfully what he had written, especially the quaint jingle at the end. It was a token, a symbol, he decided, and not a cipher, and the woman who had flung it away was in all probability entirely ignorant of its meaning; she was but the agent of the 'Sam' she had abused and discarded, and he too was again the agent of someone unknown, possibly of the individual styled Q, who had been forced to visit his French friends. But what to make of 'traverse Handle S.' Here was the root and source of the enigma, and not all the tobacco of Virginia seemed likely to suggest any clue here. It seemed almost hopeless, but Dyson regarded himself as the Wellington of mysteries, and went to bed feeling assured that sooner or later he would hit upon the right track.

For the next few days he was deeply engaged in his literary labours, labours which were a profound mystery even to the most intimate of his friends, who searched the railway bookstalls in vain for the result of so many hours spent at the Japanese bureau in company with strong tobacco and black tea. On this occasion Dyson confined himself to his room for four days, and it was with genuine relief that he laid down his pen and went out into the streets in quest of relaxation and fresh air. The gas-lamps were being lighted, and the fifth edition of the evening papers was being howled through the streets, and Dyson, feeling that he wanted quiet, turned away from the clamorous Strand, and began to trend away to the north-west. Soon he found himself in streets that echoed to his footsteps, and crossing a broad new thoroughfare, and verging still to the west, Dyson discovered that he had penetrated to the depths of Soho. Here again was life; rare vintages of France and Italy, at prices which seemed contemptibly small, allured the passer-by; here were cheeses, vast and rich, here olive oil, and here a grove of Rabelaisian sausages; while in a neighbouring shop the whole Press of Paris appeared to be on sale. In the middle of the roadway a strange miscellany of nations sauntered to and fro, for there cab and hansom rarely ventured; and from window over window the inhabitants looked forth in pleased contemplation of the scene.

Dyson made his way slowly along, mingling with the crowd on the cobble-stones, listening to the queer babel of French and German, and Italian and English, glancing now and again at the shop-windows with their levelled batteries of bottles, and had almost gained the end of the street, when his attention was arrested by a small shop at the corner, a vivid contrast to its neighbours. It was the typical shop of the poor quarter; a shop entirely English. Here were vended tobacco and sweets, cheap pipes of clay and cherry-wood; penny exercise-books and penholders jostled for precedence with comic songs, and story papers with appalling cuts showed that romance claimed its place beside the actualities of the evening paper, the bills of which fluttered at the doorway. Dyson glanced up at the name above the door, and stood by the kennel trembling, for a sharp pang, the pang of one who has made a discovery, had for a moment left him incapable of motion. The name over the shop was Travers. Dyson looked up again, this time at the corner of the wall above the lamp-post, and read in white letters on a blue ground the words 'Handel Street, W.C.', and the legend was repeated in fainter letters just below. He gave a little sigh of satisfaction, and without more ado walked boldly into the shop, and stared full in the face the fat man who was sitting behind the counter. The fellow rose to his feet, and returned the stare a little curiously, and then began in stereotyped phrase:

"What can I do for you, sir?"

Dyson enjoyed the situation and a dawning perplexity on the man's face. He propped his stick carefully against the counter and leaning over it, said slowly and impressively:

"Once around the grass, and twice around the lass, and thrice around the maple-tree."

Dyson had calculated on his words producing an effect, and he was not disappointed. The vendor of miscellanies gasped, open-mouthed like a fish, and steadied himself against the counter. When he spoke, after a short interval, it was in a hoarse mutter, tremulous and unsteady.

"Would you mind saying that again, sir? I didn't quite catch it."

"My good man, I shall most certainly do nothing of the kind. You heard what I said perfectly well. You have got a clock in your shop, I see; an admirable timekeeper, I have no doubt. Well, I give you a minute by your own clock."

The man looked about him in a perplexed indecision, and Dyson felt that it was time to be bold.

"Look here, Travers, the time is nearly up. You have heard of Q, I think. Remember, I hold your life in my hands. Now!"

Dyson was shocked at the result of his own audacity. The man shrank and shrivelled in terror, the sweat poured down a face of ashy white, and he held up his hands before him.

"Mr. Davies, Mr. Davies, don't say that – don't for Heaven's sake. I didn't know you at first, I didn't indeed. Good God! Mr. Davies, you wouldn't ruin me? I'll get it in a moment."

"You had better not lose any more time."

The man slunk piteously out of his own shop, and went into a back parlour. Dyson heard his trembling fingers fumbling with a bunch of keys, and the creak of an opening box. He came back presently with a small package neatly tied up in brown paper in his hands, and, still full of terror, handed it to Dyson.

"I'm glad to be rid of it," he said. "I'll take no more jobs of this sort."

Dyson took the parcel and his stick, and walked out of the shop with a nod, turning round as he passed the door. Travers had sunk into his seat, his face still white with terror, with one hand over his eyes, and Dyson speculated a good deal as he walked rapidly away as to what queer chords those could be on which he had played so roughly. He hailed the first hansom he could see and drove home, and when he had lit his hanging lamp, and laid his parcel on the table, he paused for a moment, wondering on what strange thing the lamplight would soon shine. He locked his door, and cut the strings, and unfolded the paper layer after layer, and came at last to a small wooden box, simply but solidly made. There was no lock, and Dyson had simply to raise the lid, and as he did so he drew a long breath and started back. The lamp seemed to glimmer feebly like a single candle, but the whole room blazed with light – and not with light alone, but with a thousand colours, with all the glories of some painted window; and upon the walls of his room and on the familiar furniture, the glow flamed back and seemed to flow again to its source, the little wooden box.

For there upon a bed of soft wool lay the most splendid jewel, a jewel such as Dyson had never dreamed of, and within it shone the blue of far skies, and the green of the sea by the shore, and the red of the ruby, and deep violet rays, and in the middle of all it seemed aflame as if a fountain of fire rose up, and fell, and rose again with sparks like stars for drops. Dyson gave a long deep sigh, and dropped into his chair, and put his hands over his eyes to think. The jewel was like an opal, but from a long experience of the shop-windows he knew there was no such thing as an opal one-quarter or one-eighth of its size. He looked at the stone again, with a feeling that was almost awe, and placed it gently on the table under the lamp, and watched the wonderful flame that shone and sparkled in its centre, and then turned to the box, curious to know whether it might contain other marvels. He lifted the bed of wool on which the opal had reclined, and saw beneath, no more jewels, but a little old pocket-book, worn and shabby with use. Dyson opened it at the first leaf, and dropped the book again appalled. He had read the name of the owner, neatly written in blue ink:

Steven Black, M.D., Oranmore, Devon Road, Harlesden.

It was several minutes before Dyson could bring himself to open the book a second time; he remembered the wretched exile in his garret; and his strange talk, and the memory too of the face he had seen at the window, and of what the specialist had said, surged up in his mind, and as he held his finger on the cover, he shivered, dreading what might be written within. When at last he held it in his hand, and turned the pages, he found that the first two leaves were blank, but the third was covered with clear, minute writing, and Dyson began to read with the light of the opal flaming in his eyes.

V

EVER SINCE I was a young man – the record began – I devoted all my leisure and a good deal of time that ought to have been given to other studies to the investigation of curious and obscure branches of knowledge. What are commonly called the pleasures of life had never any attractions for me, and I lived alone in London, avoiding my fellow-students, and in my turn avoided by them as a man self-absorbed and unsympathetic. So long as I could gratify my desire of knowledge of a peculiar kind, knowledge of which the very existence is a profound secret to most men, I was intensely happy, and I have often spent whole nights sitting in the darkness of my room, and thinking of the strange world on the brink of which I trod.

My professional studies, however, and the necessity of obtaining a degree, for some time forced my more obscure employment into the background, and soon after I had qualified I met Agnes, who became my wife. We took a new house in this remote suburb, and I began the regular routine of a sober practice, and for some months lived happily enough, sharing in the life about me, and only thinking at odd intervals of that occult science which had once fascinated my whole being. I had learnt enough of the paths I had begun to tread to know that they were beyond all expression difficult and dangerous, that to persevere meant in all probability the wreck of a life, and that they led to regions so terrible, that the mind of man shrinks appalled at the very thought. Moreover, the quiet and the peace I had enjoyed since my marriage had wiled me away to a great extent from places where I knew no peace could dwell.

But suddenly – I think indeed it was the work of a single night, as I lay awake on my bed gazing into the darkness – suddenly, I say, the old desire, the former longing, returned, and returned with a force that had been intensified ten times by its absence; and when the day dawned and I looked out of the window, and saw with haggard eyes the sunrise in the east, I knew that my doom had been pronounced; that as I had gone far, so now I must go farther with unfaltering steps. I turned to the bed where my wife was sleeping peacefully, and lay down again, weeping bitter tears, for the sun had set on our happy life and had risen with a dawn of terror to us both.

I will not set down here in minute detail what followed; outwardly I went about the day's labour as before, saying nothing to my wife. But she soon saw that I had changed; I spent my spare time in a room which I had fitted up as a laboratory, and often I crept upstairs in the grey dawn of the morning, when the light of many lamps still glowed over London; and each night I had stolen a step nearer to that great abyss which I was to bridge over, the gulf between the world of consciousness and the world of matter. My experiments were many and complicated in their nature, and it was some months before I realized whither they all pointed, and when this was borne in upon me in a moment's time, I felt my face whiten and my heart still within me.

But the power to draw back, the power to stand before the doors that now opened wide before me and not to enter in, had long ago been absent; the way was closed, and I could only pass onward. My position was as utterly hopeless as that of the prisoner in an utter dungeon, whose only light is that of the dungeon above him; the doors were shut and escape was impossible. Experiment after experiment gave the same result, and I knew, and shrank even as the thought passed through my mind, that in the work I had to do there must be elements which no laboratory could furnish, which no scales could ever measure. In that work, from which even I doubted to escape with life, life itself must enter; from some human being there must be drawn that essence which men call the soul, and in its place (for in the scheme of the world there is no vacant chamber) – in its place would enter in what the lips can hardly utter, what the mind cannot conceive without a horror more awful than the horror of death itself.

And when I knew this, I knew also on whom this fate would fall; I looked into my wife's eyes. Even at that hour, if I had gone out and taken a rope and hanged myself, I might have escaped, and she also, but in no other way. At last I told her all.

She shuddered, and wept, and called on her dead mother for help, and asked me if I had no mercy, and I could only sigh. I concealed nothing from her; I told her what she would become, and what would enter in where her life had been; I told her of all the shame and of all the horror.

You who will read this when I am dead – if indeed I allow this record to survive – you who have opened the box and have seen what lies there, if you could understand what lies hidden in that opal! For one night my wife consented to what I asked of her, consented with the tears running down her beautiful face, and hot shame flushing red over her neck and breast, consented to undergo this for me. I threw open the window, and we looked together at the sky and the dark earth for the last time; it was a fine star-light night, and there was a pleasant breeze blowing, and I kissed her on her lips, and her tears ran down upon my face. That night she came down to my laboratory, and there, with shutters bolted and barred down, with curtains drawn thick and close, so that the very stars might be shut out from the sight of that room, while the crucible hissed and boiled over the lamp, I did what had to be done, and led out what was no longer a woman. But on the table the opal flamed and sparkled with such light as no eyes of man have ever gazed on, and the rays of the flame that was within it flashed and glittered, and shone even to my heart. My wife had only asked one thing of me; that when there came at last what I had told her, I would kill her. I have kept that promise.

* * *

There was nothing more. Dyson let the little pocket-book fall, and turned and looked again at the opal with its flaming inmost light, and then with unutterable irresistible horror surging up in his heart, grasped the jewel, and flung it on the ground, and trampled it beneath his heel. His face was white with terror as he turned away, and for a moment stood sick and trembling, and then with a start he leapt across the room and steadied himself against the door. There was an angry hiss, as of steam escaping under great pressure, and as he gazed, motionless, a volume of heavy yellow smoke was slowly issuing from the very centre of the jewel, and wreathing itself in snake-like coils above it. And then a thin white flame burst forth from the smoke, and shot up into the air and vanished; and on the ground there lay a thing like a cinder, black and crumbling to the touch.

The Bowmen

Arthur Machen

IT WAS DURING the Retreat of the Eighty Thousand, and the authority of the Censorship is sufficient excuse for not being more explicit. But it was on the most awful day of that awful time, on the day when ruin and disaster came so near that their shadow fell over London far away; and, without any certain news, the hearts of men failed within them and grew faint; as if the agony of the army in the battlefield had entered into their souls.

On this dreadful day, then, when three hundred thousand men in arms with all their artillery swelled like a flood against the little English company, there was one point above all other points in our battle line that was for a time in awful danger, not merely of defeat, but of utter annihilation. With the permission of the Censorship and of the military expert, this corner may, perhaps, be described as a salient, and if this angle were crushed and broken, then the English force as a whole would be shattered, the Allied left would be turned, and Sedan would inevitably follow.

All the morning the German guns had thundered and shrieked against this corner, and against the thousand or so of men who held it. The men joked at the shells, and found funny names for them, and had bets about them, and greeted them with scraps of music-hall songs. But the shells came on and burst, and tore good Englishmen limb from limb, and tore brother from brother, and as the heat of the day increased so did the fury of that terrific cannonade. There was no help, it seemed. The English artillery was good, but there was not nearly enough of it; it was being steadily battered into scrap iron.

There comes a moment in a storm at sea when people say to one another, "It is at its worst; it can blow no harder," and then there is a blast ten times more fierce than any before it. So it was in these British trenches.

There were no stouter hearts in the whole world than the hearts of these men; but even they were appalled as this seven-times-heated hell of the German cannonade fell upon them and overwhelmed them and destroyed them. And at this very moment they saw from their trenches that a tremendous host was moving against their lines. Five hundred of the thousand remained, and as far as they could see the German infantry was pressing on against them, column upon column, a gray world of men, ten thousand of them, as it appeared afterwards.

There was no hope at all. They shook hands, some of them. One man improvised a new version of the battle-song "Good-by, good-by to Tipperary", ending with "And we shan't get there." And they all went on firing steadily. The officer pointed out that such an opportunity for high-class fancy shooting might never occur again; the Tipperary humorist asked, "What price Sidney Street?" And the few machine guns did their best. But everybody knew it was of no use. The dead gray bodies lay in companies and battalions, as others came on and on and on, and they swarmed and stirred, and advanced from beyond and beyond.

"World without end. Amen," said one of the British soldiers with some irrelevance as he took aim and fired. And then he remembered – he says he cannot think why or wherefore – a queer vegetarian restaurant in London where he had once or twice eaten eccentric dishes of cutlets made of lentils and nuts that pretended to be steak. On all the plates in this restaurant there was printed a figure of St. George in blue, with the motto, 'Adsit Anglis Sanctus Georgius' – 'May St. George be a present help to the English.' This soldier happened to know Latin and other useless things, and now, as he fired at his man in the gray advancing mass – three hundred yards away – he uttered the pious vegetarian motto. He went on firing to the end, and at last Bill on his right had to clout him cheerfully over the head to make him stop, pointing out as he did so that the King's ammunition cost money and was not lightly to be wasted in drilling funny patterns into dead Germans.

For as the Latin scholar uttered his invocation he felt something between a shudder and an electric shock pass through his body. The roar of the battle died down in his ears to a gentle murmur; instead of it, he says, he heard a great voice and a shout louder than a thunder-peal crying, "Array, array, array!"

His heart grew hot as a burning coal, it grew cold as ice within him, as it seemed to him that a tumult of voices answered to his summons. He heard, or seemed to hear, thousands shouting: "St. George! St. George!"

"Ha! Messire, ha! Sweet Saint, grant us good deliverance!"

"St. George for merry England!"

"Harow! Harow! Monseigneur St. George, succor us!"

"Ha! St. George! Ha! St. George! A long bow and a strong bow."

"Heaven's Knight, aid us!"

And as the soldier heard these voices he saw before him, beyond the trench, a long line of shapes, with a shining about them. They were like men who drew the bow, and with another shout, their cloud of arrows flew singing and tingling through the air towards the German hosts.

The other men in the trench were firing all the while. They had no hope; but they aimed just as if they had been shooting at Bisley.

Suddenly one of them lifted up his voice in the plainest English.

"Gawd help us!" he bellowed to the man next to him, "but we're blooming marvels! Look at those gray...gentlemen, look at them! D'ye see them? They're not going down in dozens nor in 'undreds; it's thousands, it is. Look! Look! there's a regiment gone while I'm talking to ye."

"Shut it!" the other soldier bellowed, taking aim, "What are ye gassing about?"

But he gulped with astonishment even as he spoke, for, indeed, the gray men were falling by the thousands. The English could hear the guttural scream of the German officers, the crackle of their revolvers as they shot the reluctant; and still line after line crashed to the earth.

All the while the Latin-bred soldier heard the cry:

"Harow! Harow! Monseigneur, dear Saint, quick to our aid! St. George help us!"

"High Chevalier, defend us!"

The singing arrows fled so swift and thick that they darkened the air, the heathen horde melted from before them.

"More machine guns!" Bill yelled to Tom.

"Don't hear them," Tom yelled back.

"But, thank God, anyway; they've got it in the neck."

In fact, there were ten thousand dead German soldiers left before that salient of the English army, and consequently there was no Sedan. In Germany, a country ruled by scientific principles, the Great General Staff decided that the contemptible English must have employed shells containing an unknown gas of a poisonous nature, as no wounds were discernible on the bodies of the dead German soldiers. But the man who knew what nuts tasted like when they called themselves steak knew also that St. George had brought his Agincourt Bowmen to help the English.

Until There Is Only Hunger

Michael Matheson

BONES COME UNDONE at the Magician's touch. Wind themselves up like silver and dance into the air. Strung like copper wire. Their fire a shimmering, living thing.

She's all smiles for the crowd.

And, of course, they are never *her* bones. That's not the trick.

The trick is to keep the audience from noticing how much lighter they all feel. They'll notice a twinge, an emptiness later, deep in the night, when the carnival is done and home and the softness of white-sheeted beds have called. When sweet-souled revenants beckon, and the witching hour is but a memory.

Everyone gives something for the magic. That's how it works. You are not spectator. You are participant. Always.

The Magician in the too-tall top hat has no assistant. Her great-tailed coat keeps time with her spidery limbs as she sways: limbs and torso too long, wild hair a knotted, tangled halo. Her shadow spans double her height, twelve feet easy. It swallows the stage around it, outstretched arms like wings unfolding up to the star-flecked sky. Hungry. But patient. Always patient.

The bones pinwheel before her. The audience applauds, eyes transfixed on light and colour and fire.

Later, when the last show is done and the carnival an hour from closing, only stragglers wandering the midway, she smokes behind the three-ring tent. Her shadow curled back inside her greatcoat. Drawn tight like the warm arms of a lover, stroking her chest, its chin resting on her shoulder. The Magician draws the cigarette from her lips and lets the smoke billow up to the night sky to coil. She stands outlined in castoff light from the dusky glow of carnival lamps, brown skin glowing gold with the fire. Takes another drag before examining the night's take.

Rib bones, tiny finger bones, cochlear bones. Always the bones whose loss sneaks up on you. The ones whose lack you doubt, until the absence of them is a pit in you, gnawing. Fingers finding the hole and probing, curious, at new-made rawness.

They are so easily missed. At first.

The Magician examines each carefully. Polishes their slicked surfaces, and stuffs them in the bag at her belt that is not a bag. The Tattooed Lady and the Lizard Woman, hand in hand, nod at her as they pass. She returns a salute and a smile after the couple, the cigarette making a tiny, smoldering arc.

"You look cold," says the Ringmaster from behind her, slipping through the fabric of the tent as if it weren't there to lay a lazy arm over her shoulder.

"I'm always cold," whispers the Magician over her shoulder.

The Ringmaster presses in against the Magician's back and angles her head up to breathe into the Magician's ear: "We could go somewhere warmer."

The Magician's smile is a mirror of the moon's sliver.

* * *

She pins down the Ringmaster's legs to bury her tongue deep in her lover as the Ringmaster moans. The taste of the Ringmaster salty-sweet, like the sea. *The ever-present sea. The endless weight of it crushing down on her. The nudge and graze of deep-diving sharks. The caress of deep-dweller squid, tentacles curious as they shoot past.*

And hunger. So much hunger.

The Ringmaster throws back her head as she comes, and the Magician drinks down her bucking and her heat. Drinks it down deep. Lets the heat and weight of it fill the emptiness in her. Lets it fill the hole where her heart should be.

* * *

Wrapped in a tangle of limbs, the Ringmaster's head on her chest, the Magician dreams.

Bones wash out of the sea to deposit on the sandy shore – white contours oil-slicked, upended. Way markers leading in from the swell and crash. Great sleek bodies drag themselves out of the sea after the charnel – sharks blackened from fire where there should be no fire, oil coating the surface of the sea, lit and burning. They beach and falter in swift measure, gasping for air, gills flapping. Hundreds of them, until the beach is a scour of bloodied foam and effluvia.

Out in the water, the behemoth wades closer to shore. Powerful strokes take her in. Her long arms slicing through the water, legs kicking up long waves. She draws in a lungful of air and dives deep again.

Rises, sluicing water, silent at the beach's edge. One long hand after the other gripping mud and propelling her up the long, slow incline, every line a perfect angle, every edge scalpel-cut. Kinked black hair drips down her dark chest as she wades through the sharks, cartilage crushing unheeded beneath massive feet.

In her wake there is only thrashing and moon-kissed sharkskin, razor-sharp like teeth.

She turns. Features contorted in sleep. Fingers clasping for something impossibly far.

In her dreaming, the Magician remembers walking the face of the world as cloud and ash cover the sun. Cities burning. Her body a towering monolith, impervious. Or it might be what's coming.

Time out of joint. Cracked and broken. Always.

* * *

The Magician wakes with no memory of her dreams. Just fleeting images. And a pain behind her eyes. The same one that's always there on waking. Too much of her for this skin to contain. Her shadow beats against the cage of her bones. Unheeded.

The Ringmaster stirs beside her. Throws a long-fingered, ebony hand across the Magician's stomach. For a moment she can't tell which limbs belong to whom. Takes comfort in it. "Whass wrong?" the Ringmaster slurs, still half-asleep.

"Nothing," says the Magician. Kisses the Ringmaster's lips. Morning breath mingling. Leans in to breathe the shea butter scent of her lover's plaited hair, and slips from the bed. Dresses and rises while the Ringmaster wraps herself deeper under the covers against the morning chill.

The Magician glances back at her lover, tent flap raised, before slipping quietly out into the midway.

Pale sky shadows her steps. The roar of nightfires slowly extinguished. Ghostly memories of children, unfleshed, testing the borders of their guard fires by the dark of the moon. They get closer every night.

Come a few more nights even the Ringmaster's magic may not be enough to keep them at bay.

They need to move on. Soon.

The smell of baking bread and a soup pot pulls her to the makeshift cookhouse, open to the air. White-bellied sand much-scuffled under the pale sun at the centre of the tiny tent city hidden behind colourful tents and concession stands.

The Twins are the first to greet her, bending at their shared hip. She returns their bow with a flourish, setting the young girls giggling. Her shadow lingers a moment too long after them, and she snaps it taut again with a crook of her finger. She's learned not to feed on her fellows. It never goes well.

And this isn't the first carnival that's hidden her.

She finds her usual place with the Lizard Woman and the Tattooed Lady. Drinks in the scent of their breakfast, but takes none for herself. Just draws her coat tighter around her shoulders.

"Aren't you going to at least pretend to eat something?" asks the Lizard Woman, her scales glittering like black lotus petals in the sun. The Tattooed Lady nudges her, and shakes her head at her lover. Laughter dancing at the edges of their lips.

They don't know her secret. But the Magician's sure they'll guess it eventually. Some of it, perhaps.

"They're getting closer," says the Magician. Gaze drifting to the banked fires.

"A day, two days, we'll be ready to move on," shrugs the Tattooed Lady. "Ringmaster's not done here yet."

"This one should know," says the Lizard Woman into her bowl. Licks her grinning lips with her forked tongue. The motion lascivious. Slow.

The Magician smiles. Ignores their play. Other things on her mind this morning. "I've never seen this many at once. It doesn't take many to overrun a city. Or us."

The Tattooed Lady shrugs. "They're shadows. Disorganized. The fires will hold."

"Will they?"

"You afraid of them?" asks the Lizard Woman, putting down her bowl.

The Magician shakes her head. Stands up and stretches. Filling more space than her slender body should. Turns to leave and stops. "I'll probably be missing breakfast tomorrow."

* * *

There are ages. There are days. There are tides. All burning down from an empty sky. All beating like the thing in place of her heart. The weight there. The one that doesn't go away.

She coils her hand around it. Hand buried deep in her ribcage, slipped like twine between her bones. Squeezes and lets the liquid darkness there seep between her crushing fingers.

"Excuse me," calls a young woman, a townie, from the edge of her tent. It pulls her from her reverie.

The Magician pinches the bridge of her nose against the pain. "Can I help you?"

"You're the Magician?"

She nods. Waiting. The townie hesitates, and the woman with her lays a hand on her shoulder, matching rings on their hands. Wives then.

"The barkers told me you find things?"

The Magician draws up to her full height. Lets her raised eyebrow answer for her.

"My daughter…"

The Magician shakes her head. Turns away. "No."

"*Please*. I can feel her. Every night. Little hands beating at the walls of our house. Begging to be let in." Her wife takes her hand. Clasps it tight.

The Magician doesn't fail to notice. Sighs and crumples in. Her shadow tries to warn her. Reminds her what happens when she helps. But they both know she will anyway. She always does.

"How old is she?"

Both women look up. So much hope in their eyes. The Magician steels herself against it. "Eight. So little when we lost her."

"You live in town?"

Both women nod.

"How deep do your roots go?"

"Back to the founding, and further still," says the other woman, breaking her silence. Squeezes her wife's hand. "Our foremothers came across the sea. Built the boats that brought us here. They fled the burning and the end of the world."

The Magician stares at their hands. Intertwined like unbroken roots, rich and brown as watered earth. She aches, remembering. Longs for the touch of the Ringmaster's skin to quiet memory. Her shadow shakes its head at the Magician's weakness. Whispers words she doesn't listen to.

"How long ago did your daughter disappear?"

"A year. We thought her gone. Until the noises started – the scratching at our door; the tiny beating at the walls. Please. Can you bring her back to us?"

"You're sure you want her back?"

"Of course."

"You know what she's become." It's not a question. The Magician's sure they know. And they don't disappoint.

"It doesn't matter. She's our *daughter*."

The Magician swallows. Doesn't even bother trying to dissuade them. A conversation she's had so many times before. No one ever listens. "Yes. I can bring her back."

Both women draw in sharp breaths. The townie who first made their request buries her face in her wife's chest, tears streaming down her face. Her wife holding back her own.

When the townies have paid her – a meagre collection of coins; not that she needs them, but there are proprieties to be maintained; and the tiny bones they don't yet know they're missing – and plans have been made, the women leave. The Magician watches them go from the edge of her tent, shadow coiling around her arms and slipping home into the hole where her heart should be.

"You won't want what comes back," the Magician whispers after them. They don't hear her. No one ever does.

* * *

The Ringmaster finds her while she's packing her bags. "Are you leaving us?"

"No."

The Ringmaster lays a hand on her arm. "Another request?" The Magician doesn't look at her. Just keeps stuffing what she'll need into the weathered bags. "You can't make them whole again."

"No, I can't." The Magician's smile doesn't reach her eyes. She kisses her lover, hand on the back of The Ringmaster's neck to draw her in. Rests her forehead against her lover's. "That's not what they want."

"You'll be back tomorrow?"

"Yes. Keep the fires banked high after sundown. There are more of them every night."

"We'll be fine. Just another day or two and we can move on. I need to finish laying the groundwork or it won't hold when we leave."

The Magician nods. Thinking. "Don't let the others exorcise any of them. It'll set the rest of them off."

"You'd think I was new to this the way you worry." The Ringmaster cups the Magician's cheek. "Don't make me leave without you."

The Magician hoists her bags over her shoulder. "Not yet, no."

* * *

The Geek, the Twins, and the other carnies lingering at the edge of the makeshift midway cleaning up the damage done to their defences in the night watch her go. Watch her head past the banked train, coal-stained engine cool and quiet in the early morning sun, iron tracks gleaming off into the distance.

Out across the sea of waving grass, trampled by hundreds of tiny feet. Across the path made smooth by larger feet, booted and shod carnival customers coming to see the attractions: the freak show, the thrill acts, and the ten-in-ones. Or to watch the concession women conjure food from thin air. The kind that leaves a customer emptier than before; the lie of it the need. And the thrill of the big top and the high wire acts. The iron jaw their greatest draw, her dagger teeth necessitating a new bar every night.

It's not a long walk to the town. They've set up as close as the town council will allow. The Magician doesn't know the exact deal the Ringmaster made with the councilwomen, but she can feel their welcome wearing thin. It's in the eyes of the guardswomen at the edge of town. In the looks of the women coming off shift at the foundries, black skin coated grey from the ash and coal dust powering the furnaces. It's in the wide berth the merchants give her as she makes her way through narrow, cobbled lanes. The black stone of the town, its high towers and sloped, gabling roofs and crooked sprawl at odds with the soft, waving grass just beyond their borders. The rail station rising dug out of the earth beyond the town's edge a concession to both worlds, the stockyards at its edge straddling the wall half-in, half-out. The smell of the abattoirs drowned out by the soot from the foundry district. The town a small city, walled off from the world falling apart around it.

The Magician doesn't know its name. Doesn't care to know. They're all alike to her. And she never lingers long.

The only reason she can see that this town hasn't been overrun yet is the height of its walls, and the stone of its heavy gates. But it's just a matter of time.

* * *

She shares a midday meal with the wives who've contracted her services. Eats though it does her no good. The weight of it settles in her stomach like iron.

They ask her so many questions. Her answers are short. Easy lies, rolling off her tongue with the weight of long practice.

The Magician tells them she needs the entire day to prepare. The only truth she's spoken since she crossed their threshold. And they leave her to it. Trying so hard not to let their excitement, their hope, show.

They leave her in the daughter's room. Untouched since the night she disappeared. Her mother's cleaning it, keeping it woodshine bright, but it's a shrine. As if they expect her to return with the break of every dawn.

The Magician sits down on the floor in the middle of the girl's room and closes her eyes, getting the scent of her. She lays out her tools. Empties her bags. And begins arranging the bones she's scattered before her. All the things she'll need to call their daughter back from spirit to flesh.

When the circles are arranged around her, sanctified with her own blood, she closes her eyes and seeks the emptiness where her heart should be. And waits, asleep in the arms of her cradling shadow as it rocks her softly.

* * *

It comes in the long, slow hours after midnight. When the night is deepest, and the moon hidden by passing cloud.

The thing that was once the girl.

The Magician can hear it long before the scratching at the door begins. Long before a small child's hand knocks against wood. Plaintive. Quiet. So soft you'd swear it wasn't there if you weren't already listening for it.

She opens her eyes at the sound. Drawn up from dreams of depth, and water, and hunger. From dreams of stalking through fire and blood.

The wives linger at the edge of their daughter's bedroom. Waiting for the Magician to guide them.

"Answer it," says the Magician.

She's not sure which woman answers the door, her back to them as she rises to her feet. The latch unlocks and the Magician draws her coat tighter around her against the sudden cold that fills the house.

"Child, is that you?" asks the mother further from the door, her voice choked with need. Tiny feet enter, and the door shuts behind them. The Magician closes her ears to what follows. The sound of bones breaking. Of bodies flung against wood and rent open by tiny hands. The screaming. It takes forever for the screaming to stop.

When the Magician turns, the thing that was their daughter is there, at the threshold of what was once her room. It stares at the designs the Magician has drawn on the floor. Its body an absence of light in the shape of a small girl, about eight. More presence than body there. Blood and gore trailing from little fingers. Its eyes points of white light in negative space, its features lines traced in charcoal across a mostly hollow frame.

It mimics breathing, remembering.

The Magician watches it. Coat held tight around her, her own features drawn tight, straining against the bonds of her flesh.

The revenant crosses the threshold, one tentative foot laid into her old world. Into the space she left behind, the room oppressively full with the memory of her.

The Magician's hands unclench, and her features soften. "I'm sorry." The ghost locks eyes with her, no understanding there.

She opens herself wide, lets her shadow unfurl. Shapeless. Dark. Hungry. It floods back against the walls of the room, blots out what moonlight comes through the room's lone window, and sloshes across the length of the wood. A flood of oil and motion and teeth.

It falls on the revenant. Tears the embodied ghost limb from limb to get at precious bone. Splattering second-hand gore across shadowed walls and windowpane.

When it's done, the Magician rises from the floor where she's fallen. Body shaking, the hole in her so full she can barely stand, she gathers up her things and erases any trace of her presence.

She waits until the cool breezes of dawn are blowing before she leaves town. She passes through the black gates as the rising sun lights their edges in pale fire. Different guardswomen than the day before eyeing her back as she makes for the carnival grounds, distant pennants crowning big top tent poles waving in the wind.

* * *

When she gets back to her tent the Ringmaster's waiting for her. "Did you give them what they wanted?"

"Yes," says the Magician, and drops her bags on the only table in the room. "They came in the night?"

"They came. The fires held them at bay. But they won't for another night. You're right: their numbers are higher every time. What happened in this place that so many linger?"

"Same thing that happens everywhere. Children die." The Ringmaster casts down her eyes. "Are we ready to leave?"

"Yes, I've laid down the cage. All the revenants are forever bound to this place; to the city. You know, the city council wanted them bound to the tracks – wanted them scattered along the rails as we left. As if secrets can be kept from coming home."

"It'll be a slaughter," says the Magician.

The Ringmaster shrugs. "They brought it on themselves. Whatever they did to have so many dead children to shift. We need to move on anyway, the numbers were down while you were away; this town's had its fill of freaks and magic. The advance sent back word of a contract down the line. Another binding. I've closed the show for the day to tear down. We'll be gone before we're missed."

"Always a binding," says the Magician. Throws off her coat and tosses it across the table.

"Better than nothing. Can you imagine trying to support this place with ticket sales alone?"

The Magician's reply is slow to come. "I'm so tired."

"I know," says the Ringmaster, and strokes her lover's face. "But the moving on is all there is."

* * *

It's twilight by the time the carnival train gets up a full head of steam and pulls away from the former midway. The sun riding low along the horizon, aching to kiss the ground, as the Magician watches the town whose name she couldn't be bothered to learn fall into long shadow.

The ghosts of the town's dead children glimmer along the edges of the fields. In gulleys and long stretches of waving grass, bent low in soft wind.

The Magician watches them mass. Watches an army of them drawn toward the town by the Ringmaster's binding. Watches it call them home.

The first alarm bells sounding from behind the walls as the guardswomen catch sight of the revenants on their doorstep. The sound faint and already growing fainter.

The Magician's alone on the caboose as the town grows smaller in the distance. Just her and the cold of the rail under her fingers, the wind carrying the scent of dry creekbeds and the stink of the abattoir. And even that fades as they start their curve south along the rail lines, steam dispersing into the sky. The engine's lonely, whistling scream their only goodbye.

When the town is out of sight and dusk has almost given way to night, the Magician heads inside.

Her shadow rumbles from deep inside her chest. Still sated from their last meal. It's sleepy. Contented, nestled in her breast, in the hole where her heart should be. Its warmth the stroking of a lover's hand along the inside of her ribcage.

She catches her reflection in the edge of a silvered windowpane. Kinked, hopelessly tangled hair wild and windblown, threatening to come free of the tie she's used to bind it. Every line of her face as flawless as cut stone. Her body a carved statue, cast in flesh. No sign of her age, even if she knew how old she is.

The Magician studies her reflection. Runs a too-smooth hand along the edge of her jaw. Along the line of her neck. Takes up her top hat, tamps it down smartly, and completes her costume.

Another name. Another role. Another mantle to wander the world with, in a body too small to hold all of her forever.

But she's fed. And she has the Ringmaster. And there's always somewhere else down the line.

It's not enough. But it'll do.

She smiles at her reflection, and goes to find the Ringmaster. The rumble of the train under her feet, and the roar of the engine in her ears.

The whole world waiting for them to bring a little magic into their lives.

Melmoth the Wanderer
Abridged Version
Charles Maturin

JOHN MELMOTH, student at Trinity College, Dublin, having journeyed to County Wicklow for attendance at the deathbed of his miserly uncle, finds the old man, even in his last moments, tortured by avarice, and by suspicion of all around him. He whispers to John:

"I want a glass of wine, it would keep me alive for some hours, but there is not one I can trust to get it for me – they'd steal a bottle, and ruin me." John was greatly shocked. "Sir, for God's sake, let *me* get a glass of wine for you."

"Do you know where?" said the old man, with an expression in his face John could not understand. "No, Sir; you know I have been rather a stranger here, Sir."

"Take this key," said old Melmoth, after a violent spasm; "take this key, there is wine in that closet – Madeira. I always told them there was nothing there, but they did not believe me, or I should not have been robbed as I have been. At one time I said it was whisky, and then I fared worse than ever, for they drank twice as much of it."

John took the key from his uncle's hand; the dying man pressed it as he did so, and John, interpreting this as a mark of kindness, returned the pressure. He was undeceived by the whisper that followed – "John, my lad, don't drink any of that wine while you are there."

"Good God!" said John, indignantly throwing the key on the bed; then, recollecting that the miserable being before him was no object of resentment, he gave the promise required, and entered the closet, which no foot but that of old Melmoth had entered for nearly sixty years. He had some difficulty in finding out the wine, and indeed stayed long enough to justify his uncle's suspicions – but his mind was agitated, and his hand unsteady. He could not but remark his uncle's extraordinary look, that had the ghastliness of fear superadded to that of death, as he gave him permission to enter his closet. He could not but see the looks of horror which the women exchanged as he approached it. And, finally, when he was in it, his memory was malicious enough to suggest some faint traces of a story, too horrible for imagination, connected with it. He remembered in one moment most distinctly, that no one but his uncle had ever been known to enter it for many years.

Before he quitted it, he held up the dim light, and looked around him with a mixture of terror and curiosity. There was a great deal of decayed and useless lumber, such as might be supposed to be heaped up to rot in a miser's closet; but John's eyes were in a moment, and as if by magic, riveted on a portrait that hung on the wall, and appeared, even to his untaught eye, far superior to the tribe of family pictures that are left to molder on the walls of a family mansion. It represented a man of middle age. There was nothing remarkable in the costume, or in the countenance, but *the eyes*, John felt, were such as one feels they wish they had never seen, and feels they can never forget. Had he been acquainted with the poetry of Southey, he might have often exclaimed in his after-life:

> *"Only the eyes had life,*
> *They gleamed with demon light."*
> **Thalaba**

From an impulse equally resistless and painful, he approached the portrait, held the candle toward it, and could distinguish the words on the border of the painting – 'Jno. Melmoth, anno 1646'. John was neither timid by nature, nor nervous by constitution, nor superstitious from habit, yet he continued to gaze in stupid horror on this singular picture, till, aroused by his uncle's cough, he hurried into his room. The old man swallowed the wine. He appeared a little revived; it was long since he had tasted such a cordial – his heart appeared to expand to a momentary confidence. "John, what did you see in that room?"

"Nothing, Sir."

"That's a lie; everyone wants to cheat or to rob me."

"Sir, I don't want to do either."

"Well, what did you see that you – you took notice of?"

"Only a picture, Sir."

"A picture, Sir! – The original is still alive." John, though under the impression of his recent feelings, could not but look incredulous. "John," whispered his uncle; – "John, they say I am dying of this and that; and one says it is for want of nourishment, and one says it is for want of medicine – but, John," and his face looked hideously ghastly, "I am dying of a fright. That man," and he extended his meager arm toward the closet, as if he was pointing to a living being; "that man, I have good reason to know, is alive still."

"How is that possible, Sir?" said John involuntarily, "the date on the picture is 1646." "You have seen it – you have noticed it," said his uncle. "Well," – he rocked and nodded on his bolster for a moment, then, grasping John's hand with an unutterable look, he exclaimed, "You will see him again, he is alive." Then, sinking back on his bolster, he fell into a kind of sleep or stupor, his eyes still open, and fixed on John.

The house was now perfectly silent, and John had time and space for reflection. More thoughts came crowding on him than he wished to welcome, but they would not be repulsed. He thought of his uncle's habits and character, turned the matter over and over again in his mind, and he said to himself, "The last man on earth to be superstitious. He never thought of anything but the price of stocks, and the rate of exchange, and my college expenses, that hung heavier at his heart than all; and such a man to die of a fright – a ridiculous fright, that a man living 150 years ago is alive still, and yet – he is dying." John paused, for facts will confute the most stubborn logician. "With all his hardness of mind, and of heart, he is dying of a fright. I heard it in the kitchen, I have heard it from himself – he could not be deceived. If I had ever heard he was nervous, or fanciful, or superstitious, but a character so contrary to all these impressions – a man that, as poor Butler says, in his 'Remains of the Antiquarian', would have 'sold Christ over again for the numerical piece of silver which Judas got for him,' – such a man to die of fear! Yet he *is* dying," said John, glancing his fearful eye on the contracted nostril, the glazed eye, the drooping jaw, the whole horrible apparatus of the facies Hippocraticae displayed, and soon to cease its display.

Old Melmoth at this moment seemed to be in a deep stupor; his eyes lost that little expression they had before, and his hands, that had convulsively been catching at the blankets, let go their short and quivering grasp, and lay extended on the bed like the claws of some bird that had died of hunger – so meager, so yellow, so spread. John, unaccustomed to the sight of death, believed this to be only a sign that he was going to sleep; and, urged by an impulse for which he did not attempt to account to himself, caught up the miserable light, and once more ventured into the forbidden room – the *Blue Chamber* of the dwelling. The motion roused the dying man; he sat bolt upright in his bed. This John could not see, for he was now in the closet; but he heard the groan, or rather the choked and gurgling rattle of the throat, that announces the horrible conflict between muscular and mental convulsion. He started, turned away; but, as he turned away, he thought he saw the eyes of the portrait, on which his own was fixed, *move*, and hurried back to his uncle's bedside.

Old Melmoth died in the course of that night, and died as he had lived, in a kind of avaricious delirium. John could not have imagined a scene so horrible as his last hours presented. He cursed and blasphemed about three halfpence, missing, as he said, some weeks before, in an account of change with his groom, about hay to a starved horse that he kept. Then he grasped John's hand, and asked him to give him the sacrament. "If I send to the clergyman, he will charge me something for it, which I cannot pay – I cannot. They say I am rich – look at this blanket – but I would not mind that, if I could save my soul." And, raving, he added, "Indeed, Doctor, I am a very poor man. I never troubled a clergyman before, and all I want is, that you will grant me two trifling requests, very little matters in your way – save my soul, and (whispering) make interest to get me a parish coffin – I have not enough left to bury me. I always told everyone I was poor, but the more I told them so, the less they believed me."

John, greatly shocked, retired from the bedside, and sat down in a distant corner of the room. The women were again in the room, which was very dark. Melmoth was silent from exhaustion, and there was a deathlike pause for some time. At this moment John saw the door open, and a figure appear at it, who looked round the room, and then quietly and deliberately retired, but not before John had discovered in his face the living original of the portrait. His first impulse was to utter an exclamation of terror, but his breath felt stopped. He was then rising to pursue the figure, but a moment's reflection checked him. What could be more absurd, than to be alarmed or amazed at a resemblance between a living man and the portrait of a dead one! The likeness was doubtless strong enough to strike him even in that darkened room, but it was doubtless only a likeness; and though it might be imposing enough to terrify an old man of gloomy and retired habits, and with a broken constitution, John resolved it should not produce the same effect on him.

But while he was applauding himself for this resolution, the door opened, and the figure appeared at it, beckoning and nodding to him, with a familiarity somewhat terrifying. John now started up, determined to pursue it; but the pursuit was stopped by the weak but shrill cries of his uncle, who was struggling at once with the agonies of death and his housekeeper. The poor woman, anxious for her master's reputation and her own, was trying to put on him a clean shirt and nightcap, and Melmoth, who had just sensation enough to perceive they were taking something from him, continued exclaiming feebly, "They are robbing me – robbing me in my last moments – robbing a dying man. John, won't you assist me – I shall die a beggar; they are taking my last shirt – I shall die a beggar." – And the miser died.

* * *

A few days after the funeral, the will was opened before proper witnesses, and John was found to be left sole heir to his uncle's property, which, though originally moderate, had, by his grasping habits, and parsimonious life, become very considerable.

As the attorney who read the will concluded, he added, "There are some words here, at the corner of the parchment, which do not appear to be part of the will, as they are neither in the form of a codicil, nor is the signature of the testator affixed to them; but, to the best of my belief, they are in the handwriting of the deceased." As he spoke he showed the lines to Melmoth, who immediately recognized his uncle's hand (that perpendicular and penurious hand, that seems determined to make the most of the very paper, thriftily abridging every word, and leaving scarce an atom of margin), and read, not without some emotion, the following words:

I enjoin my nephew and heir, John Melmoth, to remove, destroy, or cause to be destroyed, the portrait inscribed 'J. Melmoth, 1646', hanging in my closet. I also enjoin him to search for a manuscript, which I think he will find in the third and lowest left-hand drawer of the mahogany chest standing under that portrait – it is among some papers of no value, such as manuscript sermons, and pamphlets on the improvement of Ireland, and such stuff; he will distinguish it by its being tied round with a black tape, and the paper being very moldy and discolored. He may read it if he will; – I think he had better not. At all events, I adjure him, if there be any power in the adjuration of a dying man, to burn it.

After reading this singular memorandum, the business of the meeting was again resumed; and as old Melmoth's will was very clear and legally worded, all was soon settled, the party dispersed, and John Melmoth was left alone.

* * *

He resolutely entered the closet, shut the door, and proceeded to search for the manuscript. It was soon found, for the directions of old Melmoth were forcibly written, and strongly remembered. The manuscript, old, tattered, and discolored, was taken from the very drawer in which it was mentioned to be laid. Melmoth's hands felt as cold as those of his dead uncle, when he drew the blotted pages from their nook. He sat down to read – there was a dead silence through the house. Melmoth looked wistfully at the candles, snuffed them, and still thought they looked dim, (perchance he thought they burned blue, but such thought he kept to himself). Certain it is, he often changed his posture, and would have changed his chair, had there been more than one in the apartment.

He sank for a few moments into a fit of gloomy abstraction, till the sound of the clock striking twelve made him start – it was the only sound he had heard for some hours, and the sounds produced by inanimate things, while all living beings around are as dead, have at such an hour an effect indescribably awful. John looked at his manuscript with some reluctance, opened it, paused over the first lines, and as the wind sighed round the desolate apartment, and the rain pattered with a mournful sound against the dismantled window, wished – what did he wish for? – he wished the sound of the wind less dismal, and the dash of the rain less monotonous. He may be forgiven, it was past midnight, and there was not a human being awake but himself within ten miles when he began to read.

* * *

The manuscript was discolored, obliterated, and mutilated beyond any that had ever before exercised the patience of a reader. Michaelis himself, scrutinizing into the pretended autograph of St. Mark at Venice, never had a harder time of it. Melmoth could make out only a sentence here and there. The writer, it appeared, was an Englishman of the name of Stanton, who had traveled abroad shortly after the Restoration. Traveling was not then attended with the facilities which modern improvement has introduced, and scholars and literati, the intelligent, the idle, and the curious, wandered over the Continent for years, like Tom Corvat, though they had the modesty, on their return, to entitle the result of their multiplied observations and labors only 'crudities'.

Stanton, about the year 1676, was in Spain; he was, like most of the travelers of that age, a man of literature, intelligence, and curiosity, but ignorant of the language of the country, and fighting his way at times from convent to convent, in quest of what was called 'Hospitality', that is, obtaining board and lodging on the condition of holding a debate in Latin, on some point theological or metaphysical, with any monk who would become the champion of the strife. Now, as the theology was Catholic, and the metaphysics Aristotelian, Stanton sometimes wished himself at the miserable Posada from whose filth and famine he had been fighting his escape; but though his reverend antagonists always denounced his creed, and comforted themselves, even in defeat, with the assurance that he must be damned, on the double score of his being a heretic and an Englishman, they were obliged to confess that his Latin was good, and his logic unanswerable; and he was allowed, in most cases, to sup and sleep in peace. This was not doomed to be his fate on the night of the 17th August 1677, when he found himself in the plains of Valencia, deserted by a cowardly guide, who had been terrified by the sight of a cross erected as a memorial of a murder, had slipped off his mule unperceived, crossing himself every step he took on his retreat from the heretic, and left Stanton amid the terrors of an approaching storm, and the dangers of an unknown country. The sublime and yet softened beauty of the scenery around had filled the soul of Stanton with delight, and he enjoyed that delight as Englishmen generally do, silently.

The magnificent remains of two dynasties that had passed away, the ruins of Roman palaces, and of Moorish fortresses, were around and above him; the dark and heavy thunder clouds that advanced slowly seemed like the shrouds of these specters of departed greatness; they approached, but did not yet overwhelm or conceal them, as if Nature herself was for once awed by the power of man; and far below, the lovely valley of Valencia blushed and burned in all the glory of sunset, like a bride receiving the last glowing kiss of the bridegroom before the approach of night. Stanton gazed around. The difference between the architecture of the Roman and Moorish ruins struck him. Among the former are the remains of a theater, and something like a public place; the latter present only the remains of fortresses, embattled, castellated, and fortified from top to bottom – not a loophole for pleasure to get in by – the loopholes were only for arrows; all denoted military power and despotic subjugation a l'outrance. The contrast might have pleased a philosopher, and he might have indulged in the reflection, that though the ancient Greeks and Romans were savages (as Dr. Johnson says all people who want a press must be, and he says truly), yet they were wonderful savages for their time, for they alone have left traces of their taste for pleasure in the countries they conquered, in their superb theaters, temples (which were also dedicated to pleasure one way or another), and baths, while other conquering bands of savages never left anything behind them but traces of their rage for power. So thought Stanton, as he still saw strongly defined, though darkened by the darkening clouds, the huge skeleton of a Roman amphitheater, its arched and gigantic colonnades now admitting a gleam of light, and now commingling with the purple thunder cloud; and now the solid and heavy mass of a Moorish fortress, no light playing between its impermeable walls

– the image of power, dark, isolated, impenetrable. Stanton forgot his cowardly guide, his loneliness, his danger amid an approaching storm and an inhospitable country, where his name and country would shut every door against him, and every peal of thunder would be supposed justified by the daring intrusion of a heretic in the dwelling of an old Christian, as the Spanish Catholics absurdly term themselves, to mark the distinction between them and the baptized Moors.

All this was forgot in contemplating the glorious and awful scenery before him – light struggling with darkness – and darkness menacing a light still more terrible, and announcing its menace in the blue and livid mass of cloud that hovered like a destroying angel in the air, its arrows aimed, but their direction awfully indefinite. But he ceased to forget these local and petty dangers, as the sublimity of romance would term them, when he saw the first flash of the lightning, broad and red as the banners of an insulting army whose motto is *Vae victis*, shatter to atoms the remains of a Roman tower; the rifted stones rolled down the hill, and fell at the feet of Stanton. He stood appalled, and, awaiting his summons from the Power in whose eye pyramids, palaces, and the worms whose toil has formed them, and the worms who toil out their existence under their shadow or their pressure, are perhaps all alike contemptible, he stood collected, and for a moment felt that defiance of danger which danger itself excites, and we love to encounter it as a physical enemy, to bid it 'do its worst', and feel that its worst will perhaps be ultimately its best for us. He stood and saw another flash dart its bright, brief, and malignant glance over the ruins of ancient power, and the luxuriance of recent fertility. Singular contrast! The relics of art forever decaying – the productions of nature forever renewed. (Alas! For what purpose are they renewed, better than to mock at the perishable monuments which men try in vain to rival them by.) The pyramids themselves must perish, but the grass that grows between their disjointed stones will be renewed from year to year.

Stanton was thinking thus, when all power of thought was suspended, by seeing two persons bearing between them the body of a young, and apparently very lovely girl, who had been struck dead by the lightning. Stanton approached, and heard the voices of the bearers repeating, "There is none who will mourn for her!" "There is none who will mourn for her!" said other voices, as two more bore in their arms the blasted and blackened figure of what had once been a man, comely and graceful; – "there is not *one* to mourn for her now!" They were lovers, and he had been consumed by the flash that had destroyed her, while in the act of endeavoring to defend her. As they were about to remove the bodies, a person approached with a calmness of step and demeanor, as if he were alone unconscious of danger, and incapable of fear; and after looking on them for some time, burst into a laugh so loud, wild, and protracted, that the peasants, starting with as much horror at the sound as at that of the storm, hurried away, bearing the corpses with them. Even Stanton's fears were subdued by his astonishment, and, turning to the stranger, who remained standing on the same spot, he asked the reason of such an outrage on humanity. The stranger, slowly turning round, and disclosing a countenance which – (Here the manuscript was illegible for a few lines), said in English – (A long hiatus followed here, and the next passage that was legible, though it proved to be a continuation of the narrative, was but a fragment.)

* * *

The terrors of the night rendered Stanton a sturdy and unappeasable applicant; and the shrill voice of the old woman, repeating, "no heretic – no English – Mother of God protect us – avaunt Satan!" – combined with the clatter of the wooden casement (peculiar to the houses in Valencia) which she opened to discharge her volley of anathematization, and shut again as the lightning glanced through the aperture, were unable to repel his importunate request for admittance, in a night whose terrors ought to soften all the miserable petty local passions into one awful feeling of fear for the Power who caused it, and compassion for those who were exposed to it. But Stanton felt there was something more than national bigotry in the exclamations of the old woman; there was a peculiar and personal horror of the English. And he was right; but this did not diminish the eagerness of his....

* * *

The house was handsome and spacious, but the melancholy appearance of desertion....

* * *

The benches were by the wall, but there were none to sit there; the tables were spread in what had been the hall, but it seemed as if none had gathered round them for many years; the clock struck audibly, there was no voice of mirth or of occupation to drown its sound; time told his awful lesson to silence alone; the hearths were black with fuel long since consumed; the family portraits looked as if they were the only tenants of the mansion; they seemed to say, from their moldering frames, "there are none to gaze on us"; and the echo of the steps of Stanton and his feeble guide was the only sound audible between the peals of thunder that rolled still awfully, but more distantly – every peal like the exhausted murmurs of a spent heart. As they passed on, a shriek was heard. Stanton paused, and fearful images of the dangers to which travelers on the Continent are exposed in deserted and remote habitations, came into his mind. "Don't heed it," said the old woman, lighting him on with a miserable lamp – "it is only he....

* * *

The old woman having now satisfied herself, by ocular demonstration, that her English guest, even if he was the devil, had neither horn, hoof, nor tail, that he could bear the sign of the cross without changing his form, and that, when he spoke, not a puff of sulphur came out of his mouth, began to take courage, and at length commenced her story, which, weary and comfortless as Stanton was....

* * *

Every obstacle was now removed; parents and relations at last gave up all opposition, and the young pair were united. Never was there a lovelier – they seemed like angels who had only anticipated by a few years their celestial and eternal union. The marriage was solemnized with much pomp, and a few days after there was a feast in that very wainscoted chamber which you paused to remark was so gloomy. It was that night hung with rich tapestry, representing the exploits of the Cid, particularly that of his burning a few Moors who refused to renounce their accursed religion. They were represented beautifully tortured, writhing and howling, and "Mahomet! Mahomet!" issuing out of their mouths, as they called on him in their burning agonies – you could almost hear them scream. At the upper end of the room, under a splendid estrade, over which was an image of the blessed Virgin, sat Donna Isabella de Cardoza, mother to the bride, and near her Donna Ines, the bride, on rich almohadas; the bridegroom sat opposite to her, and though they never spoke to each other, their eyes, slowly raised, but suddenly withdrawn (those eyes that blushed), told to each other the delicious secret of their happiness. Don Pedro de Cardoza had assembled a large party in honor of his daughter's nuptials; among them was an Englishman of the name of *Melmoth*, a traveler; no one knew who had brought him there. He sat silent like the rest, while the iced waters and the sugared wafers were presented to the company. The night was intensely hot, and the moon glowed like a sun over the ruins of Saguntum; the embroidered blinds flapped heavily, as if the wind made an effort to raise them in vain, and then desisted.

(Another defect in the manuscript occurred here, but it was soon supplied.)

* * *

The company were dispersed through various alleys of the garden; the bridegroom and bride wandered through one where the delicious perfume of the orange trees mingled itself with that of the myrtles in blow. On their return to the ball, both of them asked, Had the company heard the exquisite sounds that floated through the garden just before they quitted it? No one had heard them. They expressed their surprise. The Englishman had never quitted the hall; it was said he smiled with a most particular and extraordinary expression as the remark was made. His silence had been noticed before, but it was ascribed to his ignorance of the Spanish language, an ignorance that Spaniards are not anxious either to expose or remove by speaking to a stranger. The subject of the music was not again reverted to till the guests were seated at supper, when Donna Ines and her young husband, exchanging a smile of delighted surprise, exclaimed they heard the same delicious sounds floating round them. The guests listened, but no one else could hear it; everyone felt there was something extraordinary in this. Hush! was uttered by every voice almost at the same moment. A dead silence followed – you would think, from their intent looks, that they listened with their very eyes. This deep silence, contrasted with the splendor of the feast, and the light effused from torches held by the domestics, produced a singular effect – it seemed for some moments like an assembly of the dead. The silence was interrupted, though the cause of wonder had not ceased, by the entrance of Father Olavida, the Confessor of Donna Isabella, who had been called away previous to the feast, to administer extreme unction to a dying man in the neighborhood. He was a priest of uncommon sanctity, beloved in the family, and respected in the neighborhood, where he had displayed uncommon taste and talents for exorcism – in fact, this was the good Father's forte, and he piqued himself on it accordingly. The devil never fell into worse hands than Father Olavida's, for when he was so contumacious as to resist Latin, and even the first verses of the Gospel of St. John in Greek, which the good Father never had recourse to but in cases of extreme stubbornness and difficulty – (here Stanton recollected the English story of the Boy of Bilson, and blushed even in Spain for his countrymen) – then he always applied to the Inquisition; and if the devils were ever so obstinate before, they were always seen to fly out of the possessed, just as, in the midst of their cries (no doubt of blasphemy), they were tied to the stake. Some held out even till the flames surrounded them; but even the most stubborn must have been dislodged when the operation was over, for the devil himself could no longer tenant a crisp and glutinous lump of cinders. Thus Father Olavida's fame spread far and wide, and the Cardoza family had made uncommon interest to procure him for a Confessor, and happily succeeded. The ceremony he had just been performing had cast a shade over the good Father's countenance, but it dispersed as he mingled among the guests, and was introduced to them. Room was soon made for him, and he happened accidentally to be seated opposite the Englishman. As the wine was presented to him, Father Olavida (who, as I observed, was a man of singular sanctity) prepared to utter a short internal prayer. He hesitated – trembled – desisted; and, putting down the wine, wiped the drops from his forehead with the sleeve of his habit. Donna Isabella gave a sign to a domestic, and other wine of a higher quality was offered to him. His lips moved, as if in the effort to pronounce a benediction on it and the company, but the effort again failed; and the change in his countenance was so extraordinary, that it was perceived by all the guests. He felt the sensation that his extraordinary appearance excited, and attempted to remove it by again endeavoring to lift the cup to his lips. So strong was the anxiety with which the company watched him, that the only sound heard in that spacious and crowded hall was the rustling of his habit as he attempted to lift the cup to his lips once more – in vain. The guests sat in astonished silence. Father Olavida alone remained standing; but at that moment the Englishman rose, and appeared determined to fix Olavida's regards by a gaze like that of fascination. Olavida rocked, reeled, grasped the arm of a page, and at last, closing his eyes for a moment, as if to escape the horrible fascination of that unearthly glare (the Englishman's eyes were observed by all the guests, from the moment of his entrance, to effuse a most fearful and preternatural luster), exclaimed, "Who is among us? – Who? – I cannot utter a blessing while he is here. I cannot feel one. Where he treads, the earth is parched! – Where he breathes, the air is fire! – Where he feeds, the food is poison! – Where he turns his glance is lightning! – *Who is among us? – Who?*" repeated the priest in the agony of adjuration, while his cowl fallen back, his few thin hairs around the scalp instinct and alive with terrible emotion, his outspread arms protruded from the sleeves of his habit, and extended toward the awful stranger, suggested the idea of an inspired being in the dreadful rapture of prophetic denunciation. He stood – still stood, and the Englishman stood calmly opposite to him. There was an agitated irregularity in the attitudes of those around them, which contrasted strongly the fixed and stern postures of those two, who remained gazing silently at each other. "Who knows him?" exclaimed Olavida, starting apparently from a trance; "Who knows him? Who brought him here?"

The guests severally disclaimed all knowledge of the Englishman, and each asked the other in whispers, "who *had* brought him there?" Father Olavida then pointed his arm to each of the company, and asked each individually, "Do you know him?"

"No! No! No!" was uttered with vehement emphasis by every individual. "But I know him," said Olavida, "by these cold drops!" and he wiped them off; "by these convulsed joints!" and he attempted to sign the cross, but could not. He raised his voice, and evidently speaking with increased difficulty – "By this bread and wine, which the faithful receive as the body and blood of Christ, but which *his* presence converts into matter as viperous as the suicide foam of the dying Judas – by all these – I know him, and command him to be gone! – He is – he is –" and he bent forward as he spoke, and gazed on the Englishman with an expression which the mixture of rage, hatred, and fear rendered terrible. All the guests rose at these words – the whole company now presented two singular groups, that of the amazed guests all collected together, and repeating, "Who, what is he?" and that of the Englishman, who stood unmoved, and Olavida, who dropped dead in the attitude of pointing to him.

* * *

The body was removed into another room, and the departure of the Englishman was not noticed till the company returned to the hall. They sat late together, conversing on this extraordinary circumstance, and finally agreed to remain in the house, lest the evil spirit (for they believed the Englishman no better) should take certain liberties with the corpse by no means agreeable to a Catholic, particularly as he had manifestly died without the benefit of the last sacraments. Just as this laudable resolution was formed, they were roused by cries of horror and agony from the bridal chamber, where the young pair had retired.

They hurried to the door, but the father was first. They burst it open, and found the bride a corpse in the arms of her husband.

* * *

He never recovered his reason; the family deserted the mansion rendered terrible by so many misfortunes. One apartment is still tenanted by the unhappy maniac; his were the cries you heard as you traversed the deserted rooms. He is for the most part silent during the day, but at midnight he always exclaims, in a voice frightfully piercing, and hardly human, "They are coming! They are coming!" and relapses into profound silence.

The funeral of Father Olavida was attended by an extraordinary circumstance. He was interred in a neighboring convent; and the reputation of his sanctity, joined to the interest caused by his extraordinary death, collected vast numbers at the ceremony. His funeral sermon was preached by a monk of distinguished eloquence, appointed for the purpose. To render the effect of his discourse more powerful, the corpse, extended on a bier, with its face uncovered, was placed in the aisle. The monk took his text from one of the prophets – "Death is gone up into our palaces." He expatiated on mortality, whose approach, whether abrupt or lingering, is alike awful to man. He spoke of the vicissitudes of empires with much eloquence and learning, but his audience were not observed to be much affected. He cited various passages from the lives of the saints, descriptive of the glories of martyrdom, and the heroism of those who had bled and blazed for Christ and his blessed mother, but they appeared still waiting for something to touch them more deeply. When he inveighed against the tyrants under whose bloody persecution those holy men suffered, his hearers were roused for a moment, for it is always easier to excite a passion than a moral feeling. But when he spoke of the dead, and pointed with emphatic gesture to the corpse, as it lay before them cold and motionless, every eye was fixed, and every ear became attentive. Even the lovers, who, under pretense of dipping their fingers into the holy water, were contriving to exchange amorous billets, forbore for one moment this interesting intercourse, to listen to the preacher. He dwelt with much energy on the virtues of the deceased, whom he declared to be a particular favorite of the Virgin; and enumerating the various losses that would be caused by his departure to the community to which he belonged, to society, and to religion at large; he at last worked up himself to a vehement expostulation with the Deity on the occasion. "Why hast thou," he exclaimed, "why hast thou, Oh God! thus dealt with us? Why hast thou snatched from our sight this glorious saint, whose merits, if properly applied, doubtless would have been sufficient to atone for the apostasy of St. Peter, the opposition of St. Paul (previous to his conversion), and even the treachery of Judas himself? Why hast thou, Oh God! snatched him from us?" – and a deep and hollow voice from among the congregation answered – "Because he deserved his fate." The murmurs of approbation with which the congregation honored this apostrophe half drowned this extraordinary interruption; and though there was some little commotion in the immediate vicinity of the speaker, the rest of the audience continued to listen intently. "What," proceeded the preacher, pointing to the corpse, "what hath laid thee there, servant of God?" – "Pride, ignorance, and fear," answered the same voice, in accents still more thrilling. The disturbance now became universal. The preacher paused, and a circle opening, disclosed the figure of a monk belonging to the convent, who stood among them.

* * *

After all the usual modes of admonition, exhortation, and discipline had been employed, and the bishop of the diocese, who, under the report of these extraordinary circumstances, had visited the convent in person to obtain some explanation from the contumacious monk in vain, it was agreed, in a chapter extraordinary, to surrender him to the power of the Inquisition. He testified great horror when this determination was made known to him – and offered to tell over and over again all that he *could* relate of the cause of Father Olavida's death. His humiliation, and repeated offers of confession, came too late. He was conveyed to the Inquisition. The proceedings of that tribunal are rarely disclosed, but there is a secret report (I cannot answer for its truth) of what he said and suffered there. On his first examination, he said he would relate all he *could*. He was told that was not enough, he must relate all he knew.

* * *

"Why did you testify such horror at the funeral of Father Olavida?" – "Everyone testified horror and grief at the death of that venerable ecclesiastic, who died in the odor of sanctity. Had I done otherwise, it might have been reckoned a proof of my guilt."

"Why did you interrupt the preacher with such extraordinary exclamations?" – To this no answer. "Why do you refuse to explain the meaning of those exclamations?" – No answer. "Why do you persist in this obstinate and dangerous silence? Look, I beseech you, brother, at the cross that is suspended against this wall," and the Inquisitor pointed to the large black crucifix at the back of the chair where he sat; "one drop of the blood shed there can purify you from all the sin you have ever committed; but all that blood, combined with the intercession of the Queen of Heaven, and the merits of all its martyrs, nay, even the absolution of the Pope, cannot deliver you from the curse of dying in unrepented sin." – "What sin, then, have I committed?" – "The greatest of all possible sins; you refuse answering the questions put to you at the tribunal of the most holy and merciful Inquisition; – you will not tell us what you know concerning the death of Father Olavida." – "I have told you that I believe he perished in consequence of his ignorance and presumption." – "What proof can you produce of that?" – "He sought the knowledge of a secret withheld from man." – "What was that?" – "The secret of discovering the presence or agency of the evil power." – "Do you possess that secret?" – After much agitation on the part of the prisoner, he said distinctly, but very faintly, "My master forbids me to disclose it." – "If your master were Jesus Christ, he would not forbid you to obey the commands, or answer the questions of the Inquisition." – "I am not sure of that." There was a general outcry of horror at these words. The examination then went on. "If you believed Olavida to be guilty of any pursuits or studies condemned by our mother the church, why did you not denounce him to the Inquisition?" – "Because I believed him not likely to be injured by such pursuits; his mind was too weak – he died in the struggle," said the prisoner with great emphasis. "You believe, then, it requires strength of mind to keep those abominable secrets, when examined as to their nature and tendency?" – "No, I rather imagine strength of body." – "We shall try that presently," said an Inquisitor, giving a signal for the torture.

* * *

The prisoner underwent the first and second applications with unshrinking courage, but on the infliction of the water-torture, which is indeed insupportable to humanity, either to suffer or relate, he exclaimed in the gasping interval, he would disclose everything. He was released, refreshed, restored, and the following day uttered the following remarkable confession....

* * *

The old Spanish woman further confessed to Stanton, that...and that the Englishman certainly had been seen in the neighborhood since – seen, as she had heard, that very night. "Great G—d!" exclaimed Stanton, as he recollected the stranger whose demoniac laugh had so appalled him, while gazing on the lifeless bodies of the lovers, whom the lightning had struck and blasted.

As the manuscript, after a few blotted and illegible pages, became more distinct, Melmoth read on, perplexed and unsatisfied, not knowing what connection this Spanish story could have with his ancestor, whom, however, he recognized under the title of the Englishman; and wondering how Stanton could have thought it worth his while to follow him to Ireland, write a long manuscript about an event that occurred in Spain, and leave it in the hands of his family, to 'verify untrue things', in the language of Dogberry – his wonder was diminished, though his curiosity was still more inflamed, by the perusal of the next lines, which he made out with some difficulty. It seems Stanton was now in England.

* * *

About the year 1677, Stanton was in London, his mind still full of his mysterious countryman. This constant subject of his contemplations had produced a visible change in his exterior – his walk was what Sallust tells us of Catiline's – his were, too, the *'faedi oculi'*. He said to himself every moment, "If I could but trace that being, I will not call him man," – and the next moment he said, "and what if I could?" In this state of mind, it is singular enough that he mixed constantly in public amusements, but it is true. When one fierce passion is devouring the soul, we feel more than ever the necessity of external excitement; and our dependence on the world for temporary relief increases in direct proportion to our contempt of the world and all its works. He went frequently to the theaters, *then* fashionable, when:

> *The fair sat panting at a courtier's play,*
> *And not a mask went unimproved away.*

* * *

It was that memorable night, when, according to the history of the veteran Betterton, Mrs. Barry, who personated Roxana, had a green-room squabble with Mrs. Bowtell, the representative of Statira, about a veil, which the partiality of the property man adjudged to the latter. Roxana suppressed her rage till the fifth act, when, stabbing Statira, she aimed the blow with such force as to pierce through her stays, and inflict a severe though not dangerous wound. Mrs. Bowtell fainted, the performance was suspended, and, in the commotion which this incident caused in the house, many of the audience rose, and Stanton among them. It was at this moment that, in a seat opposite to him, he discovered the object of his search for four years – the Englishman whom he had met in the plains of Valencia, and whom he believed the same with the subject of the extraordinary narrative he had heard there.

He was standing up. There was nothing particular or remarkable in his appearance, but the expression of his eyes could never be mistaken or forgotten. The heart of Stanton palpitated with violence – a mist overspread his eye – a nameless and deadly sickness, accompanied with a creeping sensation in every pore, from which cold drops were gushing, announced the....

* * *

Before he had well recovered, a strain of music, soft, solemn, and delicious, breathed round him, audibly ascending from the ground, and increasing in sweetness and power till it seemed to fill the whole building. Under the sudden impulse of amazement and pleasure, he inquired of some around him from whence those exquisite sounds arose. But, by the manner in which he was answered, it was plain that those he addressed considered him insane; and, indeed, the remarkable change in his expression might well justify the suspicion. He then remembered that night in Spain, when the same sweet and mysterious sounds were heard only by the young bridegroom and bride, of whom the latter perished on that very night. "And am I then to be the next victim?" thought Stanton; "and are those celestial sounds, that seem to prepare us for heaven, only intended to announce the presence of an incarnate fiend, who mocks the devoted with 'airs from heaven', while he prepares to surround them with 'blasts from hell'?" It is very singular that at this moment, when his imagination had reached its highest pitch of elevation – when the object he had pursued so long and fruitlessly, had in one moment become as it were tangible to the grasp both of mind and body – when this spirit, with whom he had wrestled in darkness, was at last about to declare its name, that Stanton began to feel a kind of disappointment at the futility of his pursuits, like Bruce at discovering the source of the Nile, or Gibbon on concluding his History. The feeling which he had dwelt on so long, that he had actually converted it into a duty, was after all mere curiosity; but what passion is more insatiable, or more capable of giving a kind of romantic grandeur to all its wanderings and eccentricities? Curiosity is in one respect like love, it always compromises between the object and the feeling; and provided the latter possesses sufficient energy, no matter how contemptible the former may be. A child might have smiled at the agitation of Stanton, caused as it was by the accidental appearance of a stranger; but no man, in the full energy of his passions, was there, but must have trembled at the horrible agony of emotion with which he felt approaching, with sudden and irresistible velocity, the crisis of his destiny.

When the play was over, he stood for some moments in the deserted streets. It was a beautiful moonlight night, and he saw near him a figure, whose shadow, projected half across the street (there were no flagged ways then, chains and posts were the only defense of the foot passenger), appeared to him of gigantic magnitude. He had been so long accustomed to contend with these phantoms of the imagination, that he took a kind of stubborn delight in subduing them. He walked up to the object, and observing the shadow only was magnified, and the figure was the ordinary height of man, he approached it, and discovered the very object of his search – the man whom he had seen for a moment in Valencia, and, after a search of four years, recognized at the theater.

* * *

"You were in quest of me?" – "I was." "Have you anything to inquire of me?" – "Much." – "Speak, then." – "This is no place." – "No place! Poor wretch, I am independent of time and place. Speak, if you have anything to ask or to learn." – "I have many things to ask, but nothing to learn, I hope, from you." "You deceive yourself, but you will be undeceived when next we meet." – "And when shall that be?" said Stanton, grasping his arm; "Name your hour and your place." – "The hour shall be midday," answered the stranger, with a horrid and unintelligible smile; "and the place shall be the bare walls of a madhouse, where you shall rise rattling in your chains, and rustling from your straw, to greet me – yet still you shall have *The Curse of Sanity*, and of memory. My voice shall ring in your ears till then, and the glance of these eyes shall be reflected from every object, animate or inanimate, till you behold them again." – "Is it under circumstances so horrible we are to meet again?" said Stanton, shrinking under the full-lighted blaze of those demon eyes. "I never," said the stranger, in an emphatic tone – "I never desert my friends in misfortune. When they are plunged in the lowest abyss of human calamity, they are sure to be visited by me."

* * *

The narrative, when Melmoth was again able to trace its continuation, described Stanton, some years after, plunged in a state the most deplorable.

He had been always reckoned of a singular turn of mind, and the belief of this, aggravated by his constant talk of Melmoth, his wild pursuit of him, his strange behavior at the theater, and his dwelling on the various particulars of their extraordinary meetings, with all the intensity of the deepest conviction (while he never could impress them on anyone's conviction but his own), suggested to some prudent people the idea that he was deranged. Their malignity probably took part with their prudence. The selfish Frenchman [Rochefoucauld] says, we feel a pleasure even in the misfortunes of our friends – a *plus forte* in those of our enemies; and as everyone is an enemy to a man of genius of course, the report of Stanton's malady was propagated with infernal and successful industry. Stanton's next relative, a needy unprincipled man, watched the report in its circulation, and saw the snares closing round his victim. He waited on him one morning, accompanied by a person of a grave, though somewhat repulsive appearance. Stanton was as usual abstracted and restless, and, after a few moments' conversation, he proposed a drive a few miles out of London, which he said would revive and refresh him. Stanton objected, on account of the difficulty of getting a hackney coach (for it is singular that at this period the number of private equipages, though infinitely fewer than they are now, exceeded the number of hired ones), and proposed going by water. This, however, did not suit the kinsman's views; and, after pretending to send for a carriage (which was in waiting at the end of the street), Stanton and his companions entered it, and drove about two miles out of London.

The carriage then stopped. "Come, Cousin," said the younger Stanton – "come and view a purchase I have made." Stanton absently alighted, and followed him across a small paved court; the other person followed. "In troth, Cousin," said Stanton, "your choice appears not to have been discreetly made; your house has somewhat of a gloomy aspect." – "Hold you content, Cousin," replied the other; "I shall take order that you like it better, when you have been some time a dweller therein." Some attendants of a mean appearance, and with most suspicious visages, awaited them on their entrance, and they ascended a narrow staircase, which led to a room meanly furnished. "Wait here," said the kinsman, to the man who accompanied them, "till I go for company to divertise my cousin in his loneliness." They were left alone. Stanton took no notice of his companion, but as usual seized the first book near him, and began to read. It was a volume in manuscript – they were then much more common than now.

The first lines struck him as indicating insanity in the writer. It was a wild proposal (written apparently after the great fire of London) to rebuild it with stone, and attempting to prove, on a calculation wild, false, and yet sometimes plausible, that this could be done out of the colossal fragments of Stonehenge, which the writer proposed to remove for that purpose. Subjoined were several grotesque drawings of engines designed to remove those massive blocks, and in a corner of the page was a note:

I would have drawn these more accurately, but was not allowed a knife to mend my pen.

The next was entitled, 'A modest proposal for the spreading of Christianity in foreign parts, whereby it is hoped its entertainment will become general all over the world.' This modest proposal was, to convert the Turkish ambassadors (who had been in London a few years before), by offering them their choice of being strangled on the spot, or becoming Christians. Of course the writer reckoned on their embracing the easier alternative, but even this was to be clogged with a heavy condition – namely, that they must be bound before a magistrate to convert twenty Mussulmans a day, on their return to Turkey. The rest of the pamphlet was reasoned very much in the conclusive style of Captain Bobadil – these twenty will convert twenty more apiece, and these two hundred converts, converting their due number in the same time, all Turkey would be converted before the Grand Signior knew where he was. Then comes the coup d'eclat – one fine morning, every minaret in Constantinople was to ring out with bells, instead of the cry of the Muezzins; and the Imaum, coming out to see what was the matter, was to be encountered by the Archbishop of Canterbury, in pontificalibus, performing Cathedral service in the church of St. Sophia, which was to finish the business. Here an objection appeared to arise, which the ingenuity of the writer had anticipated. – "It may be redargued," saith he, "by those who have more spleen than brain, that forasmuch as the Archbishop preacheth in English, he will not thereby much edify the Turkish folk, who do altogether hold in a vain gabble of their own." But this (to use his own language) he 'evites', by judiciously observing, that where service was performed in an unknown tongue, the devotion of the people was always observed to be much increased thereby; as, for instance, in the church of Rome – that St. Augustine, with his monks, advanced to meet King Ethelbert singing litanies (in a language his majesty could not possibly have understood), and converted him and his whole court on the spot; that the sybilline books....

* * *

Cum multis aliis.

Between the pages were cut most exquisitely in paper the likenesses of some of these Turkish ambassadors; the hair of the beards, in particular, was feathered with a delicacy of touch that seemed the work of fairy fingers – but the pages ended with a complaint of the operator, that his scissors had been taken from him. However, he consoled himself and the reader with the assurance, that he would that night catch a moonbeam as it entered through the grating, and, when he had whetted it on the iron knobs of his door, would do wonders with it. In the next page was found a melancholy proof of powerful but prostrated intellect. It contained some insane lines, ascribed to Lee the dramatic poet, commencing:

O that my lungs could bleat like buttered pease, etc.

There is no proof whatever that these miserable lines were really written by Lee, except that the measure is the fashionable quatrain of the period. It is singular that Stanton read on without suspicion of his own danger, quite absorbed in the album of a madhouse, without ever reflecting on the place where he was, and which such compositions too manifestly designated.

It was after a long interval that he looked round, and perceived that his companion was gone. Bells were unusual then. He proceeded to the door – it was fastened. He called aloud – his voice was echoed in a moment by many others, but in tones so wild and discordant, that he desisted in involuntary terror. As the day advanced, and no one approached, he tried the window, and then perceived for the first time it was grated. It looked out on the narrow flagged yard, in which no human being was; and if there had, from such a being no human feeling could have been extracted.

Sickening with unspeakable horror, he sunk rather than sat down beside the miserable window, and 'wished for day'.

* * *

At midnight he started from a doze, half a swoon, half a sleep, which probably the hardness of his seat, and of the deal table on which he leaned, had not contributed to prolong.

He was in complete darkness; the horror of his situation struck him at once, and for a moment he was indeed almost qualified for an inmate of that dreadful mansion. He felt his way to the door, shook it with desperate strength, and uttered the most frightful cries, mixed with expostulations and commands. His cries were in a moment echoed by a hundred voices. In maniacs there is a peculiar malignity, accompanied by an extraordinary acuteness of some of the senses, particularly in distinguishing the voice of a stranger. The cries that he heard on every side seemed like a wild and infernal yell of joy, that their mansion of misery had obtained another tenant.

He paused, exhausted – a quick and thundering step was heard in the passage. The door was opened, and a man of savage appearance stood at the entrance – two more were seen indistinctly in the passage. "Release me, villain!" – "Stop, my fine fellow, what's all this noise for?" – "Where am I?" – "Where you ought to be." – "Will you dare to detain me?" – "Yes, and a little more than that," answered the ruffian, applying a loaded horsewhip to his back and shoulders, till the patient soon fell to the ground convulsed with rage and pain. "Now you see you are where you ought to be," repeated the ruffian, brandishing the horsewhip over him, "and now take the advice of a friend, and make no more noise. The lads are ready for you with the darbies, and they'll clink them on in the crack of this whip, unless you prefer another touch of it first." They then were advancing into the room as he spoke, with fetters in their hands (strait waistcoats being then little known or used), and showed, by their frightful countenances and gestures, no unwillingness to apply them. Their harsh rattle on the stone pavement made Stanton's blood run cold; the effect, however, was useful. He had the presence of mind to acknowledge his (supposed) miserable condition, to supplicate the forbearance of the ruthless keeper, and promise complete submission to his orders. This pacified the ruffian, and he retired.

Stanton collected all his resolution to encounter the horrible night; he saw all that was before him, and summoned himself to meet it. After much agitated deliberation, he conceived it best to continue the same appearance of submission and tranquillity, hoping that thus he might in time either propitiate the wretches in whose hands he was, or, by his apparent inoffensiveness, procure such opportunities of indulgence, as might perhaps ultimately facilitate his escape. He therefore determined to conduct himself with the utmost tranquillity, and never to let his voice be heard in the house; and he laid down several other resolutions with a degree of prudence which he already shuddered to think might be the cunning of incipient madness, or the beginning result of the horrid habits of the place.

These resolutions were put to desperate trial that very night. Just next to Stanton's apartment were lodged two most uncongenial neighbors. One of them was a puritanical weaver, who had been driven mad by a single sermon from the celebrated Hugh Peters, and was sent to the madhouse as full of election and reprobation as he could hold – and fuller. He regularly repeated over the five points while daylight lasted, and imagined himself preaching in a conventicle with distinguished success; toward twilight his visions were more gloomy, and at midnight his blasphemies became horrible. In the opposite cell was lodged a loyalist tailor, who had been ruined by giving credit to the cavaliers and their ladies – (for at this time, and much later, down to the reign of Anne, tailors were employed by females even to make and fit on their stays) – who had run mad with drink and loyalty on the burning of the Rump, and ever since had made the cells of the madhouse echo with fragments of the ill-fated Colonel Lovelace's song, scraps from Cowley's 'Cutter of Coleman street', and some curious specimens from Mrs. Aphra Behn's plays, where the cavaliers are denominated the heroicks, and Lady Lambert and Lady Desborough represented as going to meeting, their large Bibles carried before them by their pages, and falling in love with two banished cavaliers by the way. The voice in which he shrieked out such words was powerfully horrible, but it was like the moan of an infant compared to the voice which took up and reechoed the cry, in a tone that made the building shake. It was the voice of a maniac, who had lost her husband, children, subsistence, and finally her reason, in the dreadful fire of London. The cry of fire never failed to operate with terrible punctuality on her associations. She had been in a disturbed sleep, and now started from it as suddenly as on that dreadful night. It was Saturday night too, and she was always observed to be particularly violent on that night – it was the terrible weekly festival of insanity with her. She was awake, and busy in a moment escaping from the flames; and she dramatized the whole scene with such hideous fidelity, that Stanton's resolution was far more in danger from her than from the battle between his neighbors Testimony and Hothead. She began exclaiming she was suffocated by the smoke; then she sprung from her bed, calling for a light, and appeared to be struck by the sudden glare that burst through her casement. "The last day," she shrieked, "The last day! The very heavens are on fire!" – "That will not come till the Man of Sin be first destroyed," cried the weaver; "thou ravest of light and fire, and yet thou art in utter darkness – I pity thee, poor mad soul, I pity thee!" The maniac never heeded him; she appeared to be scrambling up a staircase to her children's room. She exclaimed she was scorched, singed, suffocated; her courage appeared to fail, and she retreated. "But my children are there!" she cried in a voice of unspeakable agony, as she seemed to make another effort; "here I am – here I am come to save you. – Oh God! They are all blazing! – Take this arm – no, not that, it is scorched and disabled – well, any arm – take hold of my clothes – no, they are blazing too! – Well, take me all on fire as I am! – And their hair, how it hisses! – Water, one drop of water for my youngest – he is but an infant – for my youngest, and let me burn!" She paused in horrid silence, to watch the fall of a blazing rafter that was about to shatter the staircase on which she stood. "The roof has fallen on my head!" she exclaimed. "The earth is weak, and all the inhabitants thereof," chanted the weaver; "I bear up the pillars of it."

The maniac marked the destruction of the spot where she thought she stood by one desperate bound, accompanied by a wild shriek, and then calmly gazed on her infants as they rolled over the scorching fragments, and sunk into the abyss of fire below. "There they go – one – two – three – all!" and her voice sunk into low mutterings, and her convulsions into faint, cold shudderings, like the sobbings of a spent storm, as she imagined herself to 'stand in safety and despair', amid the thousand houseless wretches assembled in the suburbs of London on the dreadful nights after the fire, without food, roof, or raiment, all gazing on the burning ruins of their dwellings and their property. She seemed to listen to their complaints, and even repeated some of them very affectingly, but invariably answered them with the same words, "But I have lost all my children – all!" It was remarkable, that when this sufferer began to rave, all the others became silent. The cry of nature hushed every other cry – she was the only patient in the house who was not mad from politics, religion, ebriety, or some perverted passion; and terrifying as the outbreak of her frenzy always was, Stanton used to await it as a kind of relief from the dissonant, melancholy, and ludicrous ravings of the others.

But the utmost efforts of his resolution began to sink under the continued horrors of the place. The impression on his senses began to defy the power of reason to resist them. He could not shut out these frightful cries nightly repeated, nor the frightful sound of the whip employed to still them. Hope began to fail him, as he observed, that the submissive tranquillity (which he had imagined, by obtaining increased indulgence, might contribute to his escape, or perhaps convince the keeper of his sanity) was interpreted by the callous ruffian, who was acquainted only with the varieties of *madness*, as a more refined species of that cunning which he was well accustomed to watch and baffle.

On his first discovery of his situation, he had determined to take the utmost care of his health and intellect that the place allowed, as the sole basis of his hope of deliverance. But as that hope declined, he neglected the means of realizing it. He had at first risen early, walked incessantly about his cell, and availed himself of every opportunity of being in the open air. He took the strictest care of his person in point of cleanliness, and with or without appetite, regularly forced down his miserable meals; and all these efforts were even pleasant, as long as hope prompted them. But now he began to relax them all. He passed half the day in his wretched bed, in which he frequently took his meals, declined shaving or changing his linen, and, when the sun shone into his cell, he turned from it on his straw with a sigh of heartbroken despondency. Formerly, when the air breathed through his grating, he used to say, "Blessed air of heaven, I shall breathe you once more in freedom! – Reserve all your freshness for that delicious evening when I shall inhale you, and be as free as you myself." Now when he felt it, he sighed and said nothing. The twitter of the sparrows, the pattering of rain, or the moan of the wind, sounds that he used to sit up in his bed to catch with delight, as reminding him of nature, were now unheeded.

He began at times to listen with sullen and horrible pleasure to the cries of his miserable companions. He became squalid, listless, torpid, and disgusting in his appearance.

* * *

It was one of those dismal nights, that, as he tossed on his loathsome bed – more loathsome from the impossibility to quit it without feeling more 'unrest', – he perceived the miserable light that burned in the hearth was obscured by the intervention of some dark object. He turned feebly toward the light, without curiosity, without excitement, but with a wish to diversify the monotony of his misery, by observing the slightest change made even accidentally in the dusky atmosphere of his cell. Between him and the light stood the figure of Melmoth, just as he had seen him from the first; the figure was the same; the expression of the face was the same – cold, stony, and rigid; the eyes, with their infernal and dazzling luster, were still the same.

Stanton's ruling passion rushed on his soul; he felt this apparition like a summons to a high and fearful encounter. He heard his heart beat audibly, and could have exclaimed with Lee's unfortunate heroine – "It pants as cowards do before a battle; oh the great march has sounded!"

Melmoth approached him with that frightful calmness that mocks the terror it excites. "My prophecy has been fulfilled; you rise to meet me rattling from your chains, and rustling from your straw – am I not a true prophet?" Stanton was silent. "Is not your situation very miserable?" – Still Stanton was silent; for he was beginning to believe this an illusion of madness. He thought to himself, "How could he have gained entrance here?" – "Would you not wish to be delivered from it?" Stanton tossed on his straw, and its rustling seemed to answer the question. "I have the power to deliver you from it." Melmoth spoke very slowly and very softly, and the melodious smoothness of his voice made a frightful contrast to the stony rigor of his features, and the fiendlike brilliancy of his eyes. "Who are you, and whence come you?" said Stanton, in a tone that was meant to be interrogatory and imperative, but which, from his habits of squalid debility, was at once feeble and querulous. His intellect had become affected by the gloom of his miserable habitation, as the wretched inmate of a similar mansion, when produced before a medical examiner, was reported to be a complete Albino. – His skin was bleached, his eyes turned white; he could not bear the light; and, when exposed to it, he turned away with a mixture of weakness and restlessness, more like the writhings of a sick infant than the struggles of a man.

Such was Stanton's situation. He was enfeebled now, and the power of the enemy seemed without a possibility of opposition from either his intellectual or corporeal powers.

* * *

Of all their horrible dialogue, only these words were legible in the manuscript, "You know me now." – "I always knew you." – "That is false; you imagined you did, and that has been the cause of all the wild…of the…of your finally being lodged in this mansion of misery, where only I would seek, where only I can succor you." – "You, demon!" – "Demon! – Harsh words! – Was it a demon or a human being placed you here? – Listen to me, Stanton; nay, wrap not yourself in that miserable blanket – that cannot shut out my words. Believe me, were you folded in thunder clouds, you must hear *me*! Stanton, think of your misery. These bare walls – what do they present to the intellect or to the senses? – Whitewash, diversified with the scrawls of charcoal or red chalk, that your happy predecessors have left for you to trace over. You have a taste for drawing – I trust it will improve. And here's a grating, through which the sun squints on you like a stepdame, and the breeze blows, as if it meant to tantalize you with a sigh from that sweet mouth, whose kiss you must never enjoy. And where's your library – intellectual man – traveled man?" he repeated in a tone of bitter derision; "where be your companions, your peaked men of countries, as your favorite Shakespeare has it? You must be content with the spider and the rat, to crawl and scratch round your flock bed! I have known prisoners in the Bastille to feed them for companions – why don't you begin your task? I have known a spider to descend at the tap of a finger, and a rat to come forth when the daily meal was brought, to share it with his fellow prisoner! – How delightful to have vermin for your guests! Aye, and when the feast fails them, they make a meal of their entertainer! You shudder. Are you, then, the first prisoner who has been devoured alive by the vermin that infested his cell? – Delightful banquet, not 'where you eat, but where you are eaten'! Your guests, however, will give you one token of repentance while they feed; there will be gnashing of teeth, and you shall hear it, and feel it too perchance! – And then for meals – Oh you are daintily off! – The soup that the cat has lapped; and (as her progeny has probably contributed to the hell broth) why not? Then your hours of solitude, deliciously diversified by the yell of famine, the howl of madness, the crash of whips, and the broken-hearted sob of those who, like you, are supposed, or *driven* mad by the crimes of others! – Stanton, do you imagine your reason can possibly hold out amid such scenes? – Supposing your reason was unimpaired, your health not destroyed – suppose all this, which is, after all, more than fair supposition can grant, guess the effect of the continuance of these scenes on your senses alone. A time will come, and soon, when, from mere habit, you will echo the scream of every delirious wretch that harbors near you; then you will pause, clasp your hands on your throbbing head, and listen with horrible anxiety whether the scream proceeded from *you* or *them*. The time will come, when, from the want of occupation, the listless and horrible vacancy of your hours, you will feel as anxious to hear those shrieks, as you were at first terrified to hear them – when you will watch for the ravings of your next neighbor, as you would for a scene on the stage. All humanity will be extinguished in you. The ravings of these wretches will become at once your sport and your torture. You will watch for the sounds, to mock them with the grimaces and bellowings of a fiend. The mind has a power of accommodating itself to its situation, that you will experience in its most frightful and deplorable efficacy. Then comes the dreadful doubt of one's own sanity, the terrible announcer that *that* doubt will soon become fear, and *that* fear certainty. Perhaps (still more dreadful) the *fear* will at last become a *hope* – shut out from society, watched by a brutal keeper, writhing with all the impotent agony of an incarcerated mind, without communication and without sympathy, unable to exchange ideas but with those whose ideas are only the hideous specters of departed intellect, or even to hear the welcome sound of the human voice, except to mistake it for the howl of a fiend, and stop the ear desecrated by its intrusion – then at last your fear will become a more fearful hope; you will wish to become one of them, to escape the agony of consciousness. As those who have long leaned over a precipice, have at last felt a desire to plunge below, to relieve the intolerable temptation of their giddiness, you will hear them laugh amid their wildest paroxysms; you will say, 'Doubtless those wretches have some consolation, but I have none; my sanity is my greatest curse in this abode of horrors. They greedily devour their miserable meals, while I loathe mine. They sleep sometimes soundly, while my sleep is – worse than their waking. They are revived every morning by some delicious illusion of cunning madness, soothing them with the hope of escaping, baffling or tormenting their keeper; my sanity precludes all such hope. *I know I never can escape*, and the preservation of my faculties is only an aggravation of my sufferings. I have all their miseries – I have none of their consolations. They laugh – I hear them; would I could laugh like them.' You will try, and the very effort will be an invocation to the demon of insanity to come and take full possession of you from that moment forever."

(There were other details, both of the menaces and temptations employed by Melmoth, which are too horrible for insertion. One of them may serve for an instance.)

"You think that the intellectual power is something distinct from the vitality of the soul, or, in other words, that if even your reason should be destroyed (which it nearly is), your soul might yet enjoy beatitude in the full exercise of its enlarged and exalted faculties, and all the clouds which obscured them be dispelled by the Sun of Righteousness, in whose beams you hope to bask forever and ever. Now, without going into any metaphysical subtleties about the distinction between mind and soul, experience must teach you, that there can be no crime into which madmen would not, and do not, precipitate themselves; mischief is their occupation, malice their habit, murder their sport, and blasphemy their delight. Whether a soul in this state can be in a hopeful one, it is for you to judge; but it seems to me, that with the loss of reason (and reason cannot long be retained in this place) you lose also the hope of immortality. – Listen," said the tempter, pausing, "listen to the wretch who is raving near you, and whose blasphemies might make a demon start. – He was once an eminent puritanical preacher. Half the day he imagines himself in a pulpit, denouncing damnation against Papists, Arminians, and even Sublapsarians (he being a Supra-lapsarian himself). He foams, he writhes, he gnashes his teeth; you would imagine him in the hell he was painting, and that the fire and brimstone he is so lavish of were actually exhaling from his jaws. At night his creed retaliates on him; he believes himself one of the reprobates he has been all day denouncing, and curses God for the very decree he has all day been glorifying Him for.

"He, whom he has for twelve hours been vociferating 'is the loveliest among ten thousand', becomes the object of demoniac hostility and execration. He grapples with the iron posts of his bed, and says he is rooting out the cross from the very foundations of Calvary; and it is remarkable, that in proportion as his morning exercises are intense, vivid, and eloquent, his nightly blasphemies are outrageous and horrible. Hark! Now he believes himself a demon; listen to his diabolical eloquence of horror!"

Stanton listened, and shuddered....

* * *

"Escape – escape for your life," cried the tempter; "break forth into life, liberty, and sanity. Your social happiness, your intellectual powers, your immortal interests, perhaps, depend on the choice of this moment. – There is the door, and the key is in my hand. – Choose – choose!" – "And how comes the key in your hand? and what is the condition of my liberation?" said Stanton.

* * *

The explanation occupied several pages, which, to the torture of young Melmoth, were wholly illegible. It seemed, however, to have been rejected by Stanton with the utmost rage and horror, for Melmoth at last made out – "Begone, monster, demon! – Begone to your native place. Even this mansion of horror trembles to contain you; its walls sweat, and its floors quiver, while you tread them."

* * *

The conclusion of this extraordinary manuscript was in such a state, that, in fifteen moldy and crumbling pages, Melmoth could hardly make out that number of lines. No antiquarian, unfolding with trembling hand the calcined leaves of a Herculaneum manuscript, and hoping to discover some lost lines of the *Aeneid* in Virgil's own autograph, or at least some unutterable abomination of Petronius or Martial, happily elucidatory of the mysteries of the Spintriae, or the orgies of the Phallic worshipers, ever pored with more luckless diligence, or shook a head of more hopeless despondency over his task. He could but just make out what tended rather to excite than assuage that feverish thirst of curiosity which was consuming his inmost soul. The manuscript told no more of Melmoth, but mentioned that Stanton was finally liberated from his confinement – that his pursuit of Melmoth was incessant and indefatigable – that he himself allowed it to be a species of insanity – that while he acknowledged it to be the master passion, he also felt it the master torment of his life. He again visited the Continent, returned to England – pursued, inquired, traced, bribed, but in vain. The being whom he had met thrice, under circumstances so extraordinary, he was fated never to encounter again *in his lifetime*. At length, discovering that he had been born in Ireland, he resolved to go there – went, and found his pursuit again fruitless, and his inquiries unanswered. The family knew nothing of him, or at least what they knew or imagined, they prudently refused to disclose to a stranger, and Stanton departed unsatisfied. It is remarkable, that he too, as appeared from many half-obliterated pages of the manuscript, never disclosed to mortal the particulars of their conversation in the madhouse; and the slightest allusion to it threw him into fits of rage and gloom equally singular and alarming. He left the manuscript, however, in the hands of the family, possibly deeming, from their incuriosity, their apparent indifference to their relative, or their obvious unacquaintance with reading of any kind, manuscript or books, his deposit would be safe. He seems, in fact, to have acted like men, who, in distress at sea, intrust their letters and dispatches to a bottle sealed, and commit it to the waves. The last lines of the manuscript that were legible, were sufficiently extraordinary....

* * *

"I have sought him everywhere. The desire of meeting him once more is become as a burning fire within me – it is the necessary condition of my existence. I have vainly sought him at last in Ireland, of which I find he is a native. Perhaps our final meeting will be in....

* * *

Such was the conclusion of the manuscript which Melmoth found in his uncle's closet. When he had finished it, he sunk down on the table near which he had been reading it, his face hid in his folded arms, his senses reeling, his mind in a mingled state of stupor and excitement. After a few moments, he raised himself with an involuntary start, and saw the picture gazing at him from its canvas. He was within ten inches of it as he sat, and the proximity appeared increased by the strong light that was accidentally thrown on it, and its being the only representation of a human figure in the room. Melmoth felt for a moment as if he were about to receive an explanation from its lips.

He gazed on it in return – all was silent in the house – they were alone together. The illusion subsided at length: and as the mind rapidly passes to opposite extremes, he remembered the injunction of his uncle to destroy the portrait. He seized it – his hand shook at first, but the moldering canvas appeared to assist him in the effort. He tore it from the frame with a cry half terrific, half triumphant – it fell at his feet, and he shuddered as it fell. He expected to hear some fearful sounds, some unimaginable breathings of prophetic horror, follow this act of sacrilege, for such he felt it, to tear the portrait of his ancestor from his native walls. He paused and listened: – "There was no voice, nor any that answered" – but as the wrinkled and torn canvas fell to the floor, its undulations gave the portrait the appearance of smiling. Melmoth felt horror indescribable at this transient and imaginary resuscitation of the figure. He caught it up, rushed into the next room, tore, cut, and hacked it in every direction, and eagerly watched the fragments that burned like tinder in the turf fire which had been lit in his room. As Melmoth saw the last blaze, he threw himself into bed, in hope of a deep and intense sleep. He had done what was required of him, and felt exhausted both in mind and body; but his slumber was not so sound as he had hoped for. The sullen light of the turf fire, burning but never blazing, disturbed him every moment. He turned and turned, but still there was the same red light glaring on, but not illuminating, the dusky furniture of the apartment. The wind was high that night, and as the creaking door swung on its hinges, every noise seemed like the sound of a hand struggling with the lock, or of a foot pausing on the threshold. But (for Melmoth never could decide) was it in a dream or not, that he saw the figure of his ancestor appear at the door? Hesitatingly as he saw him at first on the night of his uncle's death – saw him enter the room, approach his bed, and heard him whisper, "You have burned me, then; but those are flames I can survive. – I am alive – I am beside you." Melmoth started, sprung from his bed – it was broad daylight. He looked round – there was no human being in the room but himself. He felt a slight pain in the wrist of his right arm. He looked at it, it was black and blue, as from the recent gripe of a strong hand.

Every Time She Kills Him

J.A.W. McCarthy

I PUT THE NOSE down the garbage disposal. It's a futile act, of course, but I always do that with the first parts, the soft parts. It's how I let him know I'm in control.

When the fingers appear next, I bury those in the backyard. In the shady part between the camellias I nestle an index finger, two pinkies and a thumb in the grainy earth, atop the previous fingers that now look like nothing more than chicken bones. Sometimes the possums get to them if I don't dig deep enough, but there isn't much else I can do. Can't put bones down the garbage disposal.

By the time the eye arrives, though, I have officially given up.

He's getting smarter this time. Usually the parts appear in the same room where I keep the bandaid tin – a nose under the desk, an ear in the closet – but last week I found the nose in a saucepan in the kitchen cabinet. Two of the fingers were in my right rain boot; the thumb surprised me in a jar of cotton swabs. The eye I stepped on because it was on the floor between the couch and the coffee table. He's spreading out, both hiding from me and taunting me, buying time.

Nina comes over while I'm checking the tin.

"What are you doing?"

Startled, I drop the bandaid tin back onto the desk, its metal lid clacking like an antique chattering toy.

"Your back door was open," she explains, straightening in the doorway.

I had just buried the eye with the fingers; I didn't like the way it was staring up at me from between the garbage disposal's rubber flaps.

"Huh. That's not like me."

Nina's eyebrows draw together as she parses my expression. "What do you mean? You always kept your back door unlocked. We used to joke about making one big house out of our two." She starts to move towards me. "Grace, are you okay?"

"I'm fine. Busy." I pick up the bandaid tin again, comforted by its hollow weight in my hand. "Why are you here?"

"I have those shears you wanted." She holds out a plastic bag as she crosses the short distance between us, gobbling up what little buffer I have. "Seriously, Grace, are you –"

The tin clatters to the floor and slides across the hardwood, stopping when it hits the pointed toe of Nina's shoe. This is the only time I've ever been glad to find it empty.

* * *

The man first appeared to Grace when she was seven years old. Actually, he appeared in pieces: lips under her bed, loose toes in her shoe, a pale blue eye in her toy box. Her parents didn't believe her when she told them; she was afraid to touch the pieces and they were always gone when she brought her mother or father to look. She began to think she had imagined them, like her parents insisted. Then, in a matter of days, the pieces started to knit together out of Grace's sight until one day she discovered half of a man's face and the entirety of his right foot behind her sleeping bag in her closet. She wore the same clothes to school three days in a row and cried until her parents let her sleep in their bed with them. When they made her go back to her room, she put a chair in front of her closet door and piled it high with all of her stuffed animals.

Grace hardly slept at night for weeks, always keeping her heavy eyes trained on the barrier between her bed and the closet door, waiting for one of her stuffed animals to twitch or fall out of place. In the morning her mother would scold Grace while dismantling her furry army, lecturing her about how it was time to grow out of these silly nightmares as she rifled through the closet for that day's outfit. Her mother never saw the man pressed against the wall behind those hanging sweaters and skirts, not even when he grew a torso and both arms.

The man became complete as Grace lay paralyzed under her quilt. She knew it had taken about six weeks because she'd been marking the days in pencil on the wall behind her bed. As the toys she'd neatly stacked yet again that night came tumbling down, she squeezed her eyes shut and counted backwards from ten as her father had taught her ("When you get to one, you'll see there's no monster – I promise."). At *eight* she heard the soft click of plastic eyes hitting the floor. On *four* the chair scooted across the hardwood and tipped over. The footsteps came just as she got to *one*.

"It's okay, little girl. I won't hurt you."

Grace pushed her fingers into her ears. She tightened her whole face as if she could make her eyes disappear, folded her limbs in and curled her body into a knot so that he wouldn't see her. The bed protected her from the bottom, the quilt from the top. Nothing was showing for him to touch or pull or bite. She would be so tiny that he would give up and go away.

"Show yourself, little girl," the man said, ripping the quilt from her body.

He was tall with shaggy dark hair and a very wide, thin mouth. As he pulled the sheet down to her toes, she noticed his gnarled fingers, the joints swollen and the skin too weathered for a man who otherwise looked younger than her father. He wore a very fitted dark suit, and the shirt underneath was the same dingy hue as his teeth. When he leaned over her, his tie came loose and swung in her face, the edges of the brown fabric frayed like torn burlap.

"Go away," Grace hissed.

The man lowered his lanky frame onto the edge of the bed. He cupped his hand around her bare foot so that she had to unfurl herself to push him away.

"Too young," he said after a long moment of observing the girl. He leaned closer as she scurried up against the headboard, making herself small again by yanking the hem of her nightgown over her curled toes. "You don't have to be afraid," the man continued, his eyes tracing the outline of her face. "I would never hurt you. You're perfect."

"What do you want?" Grace demanded. She tried to sound big and strong, but she was still afraid to wake her parents.

The man smiled. "My wife."

"She's not here."

"I know. She can't come back like I can. She can't make her own body."

"Go away."

The man laughed. "Don't worry, I will. You're no use to me now anyway." He brought one of his gnarled fingers to her face and gently pushed a lock of her brown hair across her cheek. "I'll come back later. Take care of yourself."

He kept his finger pressed to the fattest part of her cheek, his rough skin so hot she thought he was burning her. So she bit him and started to scream.

At the sound of stirrings down the hall, the man calmly rose from Grace's bed and walked out of her room, his dress shoes clacking rhythmically against the wood floor. She kept screaming – only an abrupt "Mommy!" or "Daddy!" puncturing the constant wail – until the man was out of her sight and both of her parents were in her doorway looking bleary-eyed and shaken.

"Down the stairs!" Grace cried, now standing on her bed and pointing. "There's a man!"

"I heard someone on the stairs," her mother acknowledged, looking at her father.

Grace and her mother hovered at the top of the stairs while her father grabbed his shotgun and headed down. They heard the shuffle of slippers and dress shoes, of racing and ambling, then the unexpected relief of Grace's father's voice as he ordered the intruder to stop. The blast of the shotgun rattled the entire house beneath their feet.

The man lay slumped against the kitchen cabinets, a big meaty hole in the center of his chest, his limbs splayed as if he was still falling. Grace wasn't supposed to see this, but her mother hadn't been thinking when they both hurtled into the room. As both parents stood frozen and staring, her father still pointing the gun at the man as if he might rise from the dead, a fascinated Grace watched the blood run down the man's suit and pool in twin lakes at his sides. It was so dark and shiny, almost as black as the stripes on her school bus. The same dark blood dripped from the man's nostrils and mouth, making lines down his face and shirt and meeting up with the twin lakes like tributaries. A part of her wanted to touch it, but she didn't seriously consider it until she saw a strange viscous blob slip from between his lips and onto his chest.

While her father stood immobilized and her mother dialed 911, Grace crept to the body and scooped up the small, gelatinous mass. No bigger than a silver dollar, it fit comfortably in the palm of her hand, cooling quickly in the air as it jiggled slightly under her breath. The pearlized blob looked like the phlegm she coughed up when she was sick, except it didn't stick to her fingers when she touched it. She knew it was important, though, not just some loose bodily fluid expelled in death. When her father finally placed the shotgun on the table, she saw the bandaid tin next to the napkin holder. No one noticed as she dumped out all of the bandages and slid the man's soul into the empty tin.

* * *

I use Nina's heavy-duty gardening shears to cut the mouth and nose from the swath of face that has formed; even though I have given up at this point, I still can't resist slowing him down a bit. Right now there is a thigh and a knee in my coat closet, and a right foot growing cramped and twisted in one my favorite pumps. I won't be able to disarticulate and chop and bury for much longer. One day I would like to smell green grass and regular old rotting food in the garbage instead of the constant odors of blood and bleach.

After I put what I can down the garbage disposal and my whole house once again reeks of bleach, I grab the blue tarps from the garage and lay them out all around my bed. Up the walls to the windows, over furniture legs and to the closet door, I tape down my plastic wall-to-wall carpeting. Under my pillow there's the knife I can't sleep without, and between the mattress and box spring I've wedged a length of metal pipe. I think of his rough, skeletal fingers touching my face, how I have to let him do it every time so he will get close enough.

He left a scratch one time. His ragged, yellowed fingernail tore a line from the corner of my mouth almost to my ear lobe, a puffy pink abrasion that never bled but grew a dotted line of scabs like stitches across my cheek. It was enough to catch the eyes of bartenders and grocery store cashiers, and even a layer of concealer didn't keep Nina from calling me 'honey' and asking questions. I told her it was nothing – scratched myself in my sleep, I said, hiding my stubby, bitten-to-the-quick fingernails behind my back – because I couldn't tell her about all the other times that were so much worse. I couldn't let slip about the time he threw me down the stairs, or broke both my wrists, or punched me so hard he shattered my eye socket and cheek, making me wish for a new face he would never recognize.

Once I finish in the bedroom, I go back to the little room I have turned into an office. Every time I enter this room my eyes are drawn to the bandaid tin, flanked by a box of tissues and a stack of dust-covered paperbacks like soldiers keeping it in place on the end of my desk. There's always been a comfort in seeing it there, knowing where he is even if I can't do anything to stop him from escaping and gathering and growing again. It's so strange that a man like him is content to bide his time in an object no larger than a deck of cards, to let his very essence rub up against rusty seams when he used to shower three times a day and made me launder his suit if so much as a flake of dandruff defiled it. I bought a lockbox once, when it became clear that he would keep coming back, but his slimy little soul always found a way out from under locks and stacks of books and furniture that should have crushed it. And every time I kill him, no matter what I do, his soul never fails to crawl home to the bandaid tin.

I found another use for that lockbox, though. Like I do almost daily, I go to the closet and pull it out from behind the sweaters on the top shelf. It was meant for important papers that fit in #10 envelopes and ring boxes and maybe a little bit of cash, but I think it's roomy enough, a mansion compared to the bandaid tin. Holding it in both hands, I tip the metal box ever so gently until I feel that little bit of weight settle above my left hand. I imagine it sliding against the red silk lining I fashioned, how luxurious it must feel, how much I used to enjoy silk unfurling over my skin when I was younger. I think of how it is so different for everyone, how that little distillation can look like nothing more than the contents of a tissue or seem to glow, shimmering with a clear pure light that defines the person that used to be. As a twinge of guilt ripples through me, I right the lockbox until I feel the weight settle in the center. It shivers in my hands, but I don't open the box. I never open the box.

* * *

Grace never forgot the man, which was why she wasn't that surprised when the ear appeared in her jewelry box two days before her sixteenth birthday. Her family lived in a different house in a different town now, but the bandaid tin had travelled with them in the bottom of her backpack before coming to rest inside a shoebox in the very back corner of her closet shelf, out of sight but always close. Though she didn't know what she would do with it, Grace liked knowing that she was in possession of another person's soul.

So when the ear appeared, the raw edge gooey as if it was already preparing for its head, Grace immediately pulled the shoebox from her closet and opened the tin. She had tentatively checked the little container a few times over the years and always found that viscid mass exactly as she had left it, never smaller or larger or dried out. This time, though, she found the bandaid tin empty.

On the morning of her sixteenth birthday she discovered a nipple and a bit of skin in the kangaroo pocket of her favorite hoodie. Like she had done with the ear, she tossed the nipple and the empty tin in the Dumpster behind the Arby's.

The other parts came fast after that. Grace searched every inch of the house for the man's soul, but only found two molars under her desk and a small scrap of scalp, a few long greasy black hairs attached, tucked into her precalculus textbook. There was a jumble of fingers and toes in her wool beanie, then two watery blue eyeballs under the rug at the foot of her bed. She scattered the parts in random garbage cans and buried them in overgrown fields all over the city, but the man just kept making more and hiding them better around her room. Still, she told no one and started sleeping with a kitchen knife under her pillow.

"Young woman," she heard one night as she was finally drifting off to sleep. "Young woman...."

Grace kept her eyes closed, pretended to be asleep until she felt the man pull the sheets from her body.

"Still too young," he sighed, dropping to a crouch in front of her.

Grace was lying on her stomach. She opened her eyes slowly, careful to keep her arms under her pillow. The man wore the same dark suit and frayed tie as when she first saw him nine years ago. His hair was still black and stringy, not even a fleck of grey at the temples like her father had developed. This time she noticed a mildewy smell all around the man, especially when he opened his mouth, and a yellowish film coating his tongue when he spoke. His gnarled fingers were exactly as she remembered as he brushed a fawn-colored curl from her cheek.

"You are perfect," he marveled, shaking his head. "But your parents.... And people would stare."

Under her pillow Grace's fingers curled around the knife's handle. For days now she had been practicing whipping the knife out, one swift, smooth motion at the hinge of her elbow, over and over again until she didn't hesitate and the tip of the blade didn't catch on the sheets. She had practiced driving the knife into countless honeydews and watermelons as they wobbled on the kitchen counter. Each time she had enjoyed the initial *thwack*, that little bit of suction as she cleaved the tough rind of the fruit.

"My wife can't wait long, though. I'll have to come back when you are alone," the man said, drawing his face close to hers.

Grace willed herself to relax, started to rise up onto her elbows. "I'm not your wife," she seethed, driving the knife into the side of his neck.

The man's pale eyes were huge – seemingly bugged and exposed like when she found them under her rug – as he clutched his throat and fell back onto his heels. Grace jumped off her bed when the blood sprayed once he pulled the knife from his neck. It was the worst thing she had ever seen, worse than lips under her bed and a piece of scalp in her book, worse than when her father blew a hole through the man's middle with a shotgun. It was the most exhilarated she had ever felt in her life.

This time, when the man's soul slipped from his nostril as he laid lifeless in a big dark pool on her bedroom floor, Grace stomped the gelatinous blob twice with her slipper then slid it up his sleeve. She made sure it was still there when the coroner came to take him away.

* * *

It's hard to sleep at night. I lie awake, wrapped tightly in my cocoon of sheets and blankets as if I am a child afraid of the dark, refusing to get out of bed because I know he is somewhere in this house linking all of the pieces together. I think of the feet in my closet, the face forming again under the kitchen sink, the hands growing so fast they look like scorpions scuttling across the far end of the room just as my eyes are getting heavy. At every groan and creak of the house I pray for a burglar, or an animal in my room – something that I don't have to keep a secret. Sometimes, when I finally do sleep, I wake up in the morning with my hand wrapped around the metal pipe beneath my mattress.

Last time it took him only ten days to fully form. Before that, it was exactly two weeks between the first ear in the pantry and his finger on my cheek as I stiffened in my bed. I hadn't laid the tarps out yet that time, so I spent days scrubbing the walls and floor, haunted by how he fights a little less each time, how he has made me complicit in this same useless cycle. My eyes burning and my fingers puckered even inside the gloves, I realized then that I enjoy the ritual, perhaps as much as he does.

I wish I could tell Nina. There was a time when I would have – when I almost did – and she often alludes to moments when we sat in her backyard under fairy lights and a too-bright moon not so long ago, my face still puffy and red as an errant "I can't keep doing this" slipped from my mouth after one too many beers. I shook my head as she asked me if I was talking about my job or a man or life in general. *A man*, I remember thinking as she leaned in close and pulled my hand into hers. *Does it always have to be a fucking man?* There are still times she looks at me with such deep, naked concern when I can't recall a favorite movie or private joke or some strangely gilded road trip memory we're supposed to share. If I tell her the truth now it will all make sense to her, but she won't understand. Then I won't have anyone.

I figure I have no more than three days until he returns fully-formed to take me for his wife. I have to be weightless in my conversations with Nina, and keep up with texts, and go home right after happy hour, insisting that I am nothing more than simply tired from a long day at work. She can't be worried enough to come by after a tearful phone call, bottle of wine in hand as I am driving a metal pipe over and over again into the man's skull.

* * *

When the man found Grace at twenty-three, there were two things she knew for sure: that he could find her anywhere, and that she was now the right age to be his wife.

By this time she had moved six hundred miles away from her parents and the people who had grown up with her but never really knew her. She never had a roommate, or a boyfriend who could spend the night. She changed her hair color, the perfume she wore, even the way she walked. She would have changed her name too, had the man ever bothered to ask it.

It was a Tuesday when the bandaid tin appeared. Resurrected from the Arby's Dumpster, it sat smugly atop a pile of unopened mail on her coffee table, willing her to look inside, to check for rusty edges and the same faded print she had memorized in the nine year span between when she first and last saw the man. Despite the respite of the last seven years, she had always known it wasn't over. Even at sixteen as she had scattered the pieces of the man all over town, Grace had suspected that he would be back. Like a hand pushing down on the top of her head, the resignation to this cycle – destroy, kill, destroy, run – ground her down to the soles of her feet as she scoured her apartment for an eye, an ear, a tongue, and fingers that would soon scrape across her face.

This time she knew to prepare her room for him. Plastic sheeting over every surface so that it was like rummaging around in a garbage bag to find her bleating alarm clock every morning. A kitchen knife under her pillow again when she had to reject the idea of a gun because her neighbors would hear. More plastic in the bathtub and the kind of thoughts that made her retch because she couldn't call the police again, because three dead men in sixteen years of one woman's life was too suspicious.

So when the man was fully-formed and standing over her bed eighteen days later, Grace was ready. At the sound of his voice, she turned slowly onto her side and faced the familiar pale eyes and garishly wide mouth as he crouched in front of her.

"Who are you? What's your name?"

"It doesn't matter," the man said, his diluted blue eyes slowly outlining her from her forehead to her shape under the sheets.

"It matters to me," she told him, sliding her hand under her pillow. "Don't you want to know my name?"

The man's eyes returned to Grace's face, lingered on her lips. "I only want your body."

"Why me? If your wife needs a body, why don't you choose someone else, someone who won't know how to fight back?"

The man didn't answer.

"You know I'm going to kill you," Grace said. "Every time you come back, I'll kill you."

The man nodded, and Grace thrust the knife into his throat.

* * *

He's drawing it out, teasing me, making me wait. One day late, one day outside of the pattern, and I'm sleep-deprived and raw all over just like he wants me. Like he used to keep me: on my knees, perfecting, redoing, apologizing through gritted teeth. The back of his hand, a pillow over my face as I slept, store clerks and friends refusing to meet my black eye – over and over again because he could. Now I see why he likes the ritual.

When he calls me, I play along. It's exhausting being two different women, the one who answers and the one who prepares. He doesn't start calling until he's very close to being complete, so when I finally hear my name, it's a relief. I answer like I always do and let him know that I'm ready. Then, in the morning when he's busy growing skin and drawing his limbs together, I check the tarp. I consider pissing in the bandaid tin. I practice swinging the metal pipe.

Nina calls too. She tries to convince me to get a drink with her tonight. A new bar she wants to try, some coworker's cute brother is the bartender, *It would be good to meet new people, don't you think, Grace?* I promise her tomorrow night, because I need her, because she sees. If I'd known her back then – back when I needed my hand held, back when I needed someone to ask me if I was okay – maybe I wouldn't be this woman now. So I make her believe there will be a tomorrow night. There has to be a tomorrow night.

Tonight, as I am getting into bed, I will hear him in my closet. I will listen for that little sigh as the last pieces click into place. He'll barely remember what happened last time, the routine outweighing the anomalies in his slumber-rumpled memory. I'm hoping he'll see it in my eyes, though. I hope he feels the same fear I always did as he watches the pipe come down.

* * *

As she had been the many times before, Grace was prepared the last time the man came. Her only mistake was the pepper spray.

When he crouched down to greet her, she pulled the canister from underneath her pillow and unleashed the toxic mist in his face. She waited for him to fall backwards, blind and choking, but he didn't react. While the man did nothing more than grin, the residual mist blanketed the air between them, seeping into Grace's eyes, nose and mouth before she realized what was happening.

"Woman," the man said, grasping her shoulders as she flailed on the bed. "I am stronger than you this time."

Grace felt him pull her flat onto her back, straddling her on the uneven wood of the bedroom floor. With every truncated, jagged breath she managed to take, her throat burned down to her lungs and she felt like her nose was bleeding. She bucked beneath him and swung her arms, desperately grabbing at any bit of flesh or hair she could feel, the hottest tears burning her swollen-shut eyes. Her fingers clumsily found the edge of the mattress, but the man pinned her arms down at her sides before she could grab the knife.

"What are you doing?" she managed to choke out between coughs, the words catching like cactus burrs in her throat. "What are you going to do to me?"

"It won't hurt," the man said, the weight of the room gathering tightly around him. "My wife will be gentle."

His wife was a specter. That was the best way Grace could describe the form that pushed its way towards her as she opened her still stinging eyes. The specter seemed to split the air, reshaping it into a swirl of dirty grey and black, leaving in her wake a swollen seam that showed the path she'd cut in the dark bedroom. As the specter neared, Grace's fear was tempered with an unexpected surge of relief. She had feared another viscous mass like the man's soul, a piece of himself that he had squirreled away while he was forming, a corporeal invader like components of a disease slithering into her nose or mouth. This specter – like smoke, just a little burn – might be painless as he had promised.

This knowledge didn't keep Grace from fighting, though.

She kicked and bucked and hammered her fists against the floor. She called for a neighbor, no longer caring about the police's questions. When the man leaned in close to muffle her screams, she slammed her forehead into his until he fell backwards.

Grace was able to get up onto her hands and knees, but the man grabbed her legs and pulled her back before she could get to the bed. On her stomach now, she saw the specter wind across the floor, leaving a trail that blurred the air like steam. It parted the hair over her face and seemed to stop there, taking a moment to assess its new host. Instinctively, Grace pressed her lips together and held her breath. As she squeezed her eyes shut, she felt the wife slip through her hair and into her ear.

"It's too late," the man said, his voice distant and muffled as Grace's head filled.

The wife was like warm whisky filling Grace's mouth and sliding down her throat and blooming across her chest. She tunneled through arms and legs and pooled in fingers and toes. She snaked between heart and lungs and nestled against intestines, made herself known as a heavy weight blanketing kidneys, swelling vessels, replacing blood. As Grace managed to inch towards the bed, she felt the room tightening around a body that she was losing, inside and outside squeezing out what little was left of her. On her tongue a warm mass gathered, swelling quickly against her teeth.

"I'll kill you," Grace managed, rolling the mass under her tongue. The man turned her onto her back, hovering with his face just inches from hers. "You can't have me," she told him, her fingers finding the boxspring.

When her hand finally met the knife's handle, it was easy again like it had been three years ago and five before that, though the man's face was different in this moment. With the first plunge of the blade his cloudy blue eyes went clear and wide with shock as if he hadn't remembered all of the other times he died just like this. Hands to his throat, he jerked violently and tipped backwards. He tried to speak, tried to say her name, but only dark blood came from his mouth. At this she smiled and spit the viscid mass she'd been keeping under her tongue onto the floor.

"I'll burn you this time," she said, letting the sudden weight of her body sink into the hardwood. She shoved the still-sputtering man off of her, causing a spray of blood across her face that felt hot and strange and exciting all at once. "I'll burn what's left of you," she swore.

* * *

Once he's stunned and on his back, I sit astride him and bring the pipe down again just hard enough to make his hands slide from my thighs and his legs stop kicking. I hate this intimacy, the feeling of his muscles tensing against my own; I find it worse than disarticulating his body or cutting up the stray pieces as they appear.

"Is it really worth it to you?" I ask, pinning his arms to the floor while he's still too dazed to struggle. "You want to control me so badly that it's worth being alive for only five fucking minutes every few years? It's worth getting killed over and over again?"

I watch his eyes roll upwards then down as he struggles to focus on my face. "You wouldn't understand," he hisses through pink teeth.

"Oh, I do understand."

"My wife will be gentle," he promises with a treacly little grin.

"I wasn't gentle," I say. "I just wanted a body."

At that the grin flattens on his mouth and I can see the slightest tremor rippling under his skin, tightening his face from his jaw upwards. His eyes seem to grow even cloudier, as if he is receding to the last time, two years ago, when I killed him. I am a little insulted that he doesn't remember how different the blade felt that time.

"I'll take your friend. I'll make her mine," he threatens, his arms pushing up against my hands as he starts to buck beneath me again. Blood streams from his hairline and down his temples, tracing mazes along both ears.

"I'll kill you first."

"You'll grow weak and you'll make a mistake. The day will come when you tire of this."

"That's what I used to say to you," I recall, letting go of one of his arms just long enough to grab the pipe.

The room fills with the sickly-sweet odor of the inside turning out, my husband's dark, murky blood heavy across my eyelids and cheeks and chest. He remains looking at me – just as I want – even as his gaze sinks behind all of that viscera and his whole body seems to deflate under my own. As I break him into pieces, I think of these same parts returning in a few years and how one day I will break them again. He and Grace and I are the same in that respect: our need for ritual, our commitment despite the outcome, the strange comfort we find in futility. The satisfaction is fleeting, though. Once his soul slips from his ear, I grind my heel into the gelatinous mass then scoop it up with the end of the metal pipe and drop it into the bandaid tin.

In the closet she is waiting for me. Still sticky with his foul blood, I pull the metal lockbox from the top shelf, careful to keep it level. I feel the little weight in the center roll and stretch, waking up. This time, for the first time in two years, I open the box.

"It's done, Grace," I tell the opalescent form inside. The red silk cradles her soul, giving it a pink halo. "Just give me one more day," I say, and I mean it this time, I really do. "I promised Nina I would go out with her tomorrow night. I want to say goodbye."

Grace does the only thing she can and shivers in response.

The Price of Forever

John M. McIlveen

HENDERSON SILENTLY SMILES as he approaches the immense stairway. Slabs of stacked dark granite loom before him, seeming to expand and steepen as he gets closer. He sprints up the stairs, accidentally spilling some ale from a bottle he carries. He mechanically mouths *thirty-six* as his foot settles on the landing. He wasn't aware that he had counted the treads, and he's a little surprised by the height from the top. A part of him wants to double check the number of steps, but he's in a hurry. He is late for his appointment.

Although he is a tall man, rugged and athletic, the huge granite landing and the massive set of heavy oak doors make him feel irrelevant. It is a sensation that is uncommon to him. Gothic sconces of hammered iron are mounted on either side of the doors, slanted forward like medieval leering condors. A subdued orange glow oozes through narrow slots in the lamps, contributing too little lighting to the murky surroundings.

The forged iron door handles are cold, weighty, and solid, with a flowing curve that fails to add delicacy. Simple engravings of fish, crosses, and doves adorn the handles and back-plates; iconic symbols of Christianity. They seem a product of the same mind that created the sconces. Henderson pulls open the weighty door to the cathedral and enters a silent antechamber that offers entry to the inner cathedral through a set of sturdy interior doors. A large bulletin board mounted to the dark mahogany walls looms to the left. It is riddled with computer printouts of benefit drives and from parishioners promoting goods or services; blood drive Saturday/Sunday, babysitter available nights and weekends – call Jenny, Dell laptop for sale – software included. They're as conspicuous as weeds in a rose garden; an obscene testament to a contemporary age. The antechamber is otherwise empty and has the gloomy and cold atmosphere common to churches...especially older ones. It humors him that Christianity, a faith that regularly refers to the light, is represented by so much darkness. *I am the light, walk in the light, the Lord is my light, let there be light. We'll leave the light on for you,* Henderson thinks and chuckles.

He pours his remaining ale into the stoup mounted beside the doorway to the main worship hall. Challenged as to where to put the empty bottle, he sets it in the stoup as well and then strides through the doorway and along the nave, his footsteps ringing hollow and as loud as hoof beats in the vast emptiness of the cathedral.

A solitary figure sits alone in the dusky distance of the front row of pews. As Henderson approaches, the silhouette becomes man, and then even more distinguishable as his black shirt and white clerical collar becomes visible. The young priest crosses himself and looks up as Henderson reaches the first row. He is handsome in an earthy, country boy way, with curly light-brown hair, ruddy cheeks, and a fresh complexion. A baby-face, some would say.

"Father Lowery?" asks Henderson.

The priest stands up and extends a compact hand. "Ah yes, you must be Patrick White. How can I help you, Mr. White?"

The priest motions for Henderson to have a seat. He obliges and sits hunkered forward, nervously kneading his hands.

"Thank you for agreeing to see me on such short notice, Father," Henderson says.

"Nonsense. It's what I'm here for, Patrick."

Nonsense is what I'm here for, Henderson nearly chuckles. It's amusing how the smallest of tweaks can completely alter the meaning of words…like in the bible. He smiles appreciatively and offers a contemplative look.

"I hear you're a healer," says Henderson.

"Not me, I am simply a vessel through which our Lord God works." Father Lowery says and smiles humbly.

"Ahhh, yes. Of course you are." Henderson hesitates and considers his words. "You see, Father. I'm having a little bit of…trouble. I need to know, Father Lowery. Are you an honorable man? I mean, do you live for and by the cloth?"

Father Lowery's brow furrows, a little surprised by the question. He says, "I've always tried to serve our Lord with supreme devotion. I believe in my heart that he is pleased with my service to him."

"In your heart. Good…good. Dedication is very important." Henderson looks at the young priest. "You see, I've got this…predicament." He repositions himself, turning more to face the priest. "You might think this is crazy, but there's this ancient shrine tucked away in an Egyptian village that I've recently visited, and it seems there's a queen who is mummified and entombed there. The locals believe she's a real high maintenance sort of gal, but the story goes that whoever pleases her most will be rewarded with great wealth and immortality."

Father Lowery sighs deeply and rests a comforting hand on Henderson's shoulder. "Patrick, the scriptures teach us that we are all immortal, and those who aspire to heaven will reap the wealth of Paradise for eternity. God has promised this to us all. We don't need to seek other… *pagan* means to obtain these rewards."

Henderson says, "Well, that's all well and dandy, Father, but that's not where my problem lies. What I need to know for certain is whether you are a truly holy man or not. The last priest I relied on wasn't. He was crooked as a bobby pin, and I think maybe he had a taste for the little boys, which seems a common quandary among your sort, am I wrong?"

Skepticism clouds Father Lowery's face. "I fail to see where…" he starts saying, but Henderson interrupts.

"Father, you're missing the point. The last priest, he put on a good show, but underneath it all he was a dirt bag; had a soiled heart. Naunet will only accept a holy man with a truly pure heart." Henderson draws a large blade from within his blazer and drives it upward, beneath the priest's ribs. He leans forward and whispers into the Father Lowery's ear. "It pisses me off when people waste my time. I hope you're not wasting my time, Father."

The priest's body twitches as his blood runs over the knife handle and into his attacker's hand. Henderson reaches into his left pocket and retrieves two matching emeralds. He rubs his hands together coating the gems with the still-warm fluid and drops them into a small pouch.

* * *

Utter darkness. All is silent except for the sound of slow, tortured breaths rattling damply with illness. The air is fetid and damp, and reeks of moss and disease.

A heavy, metallic clack breaks the silence. It is distant, but echoes loudly throughout the vast chamber, startling the sickly breather. A great latch activates, followed by the distinct sound of a heavy door opening laboriously on ancient hinges, the stubborn scraping of stones and primeval rust. An unsteady yellow light is born into the stale vault as the door is wrestled open. A figure enters carrying an excruciatingly bright lamp, though a candle would glare like the sun to the breather, who hasn't seen light in what feels like eternities.

The light-bearer moves slowly forward, exposing a great granite crypt, eighty feet long by twenty feet wide with a comparatively low stone ceiling twelve feet overhead. Passing primordial stone pillars lined up like soldiers every fifteen feet, the light-bearer comes to a halt before a ten-by-ten-foot cage, constructed of thick gold bars.

At the center of the prison an old man drifts slowly in small arcs, suspended six inches above the floor by a thick rope tethered to the top of the cage. He is naked and ghastly thin, his knees prominent knobs that bisect the thin bones of his legs. Long yellowed and crusted whiskers fall from his skeletal face, washing over ribs that protrude through translucent flesh like surfacing tree roots and ending whip-like at his waist. His mouth is a gaping oval revealing sparse and rotted teeth. The hanging man partially averts his head from the brilliance of the light as the stranger cautiously approaches him, yet he is interested. His head twitches in birdlike jerks as he follows the new man's movement.

"Ah, a guest," the hanging man says in a tongue redolent of old Latin. His voice is gravelly and weedy from long abandonment and the constriction of the rope. Each breath is dragged in and forced out, scraping from his throat like stone upon stone.

"That's Greek to me, comrade! No comprende. Capice?" Henderson says. He stops two feet from the cage.

"Please *(hiss),* come forward," says the hanging man, switching to a proper English dialect. His limited breath nearly whistles from him. "What is your name?" He tries raising his head to confront the tall stranger, but it remains awkwardly canted to the left at an impossible angle.

"That doesn't concern you old man, but you certainly *are* the guy I'm looking for," Henderson replies.

He approaches the cage warily, an expression of disgust overwriting his unease as the hanging man comes fully into his view. Still disturbed by the light, the ancient man focuses his odd, pale eyes on Henderson. The baby-blue, nearly white irises are not reminiscent of summer skies, but of the blubbery, albino creatures that reside in the deepest part of the ocean.

"On the contrary my greedy seeker *(hiss).* You have come here with a wish that *(hiss)* I cannot fulfill without your name."

"Okay. Call me Ken Smith."

"I call you a liar, Mr. William James Henderson *(hiss)* of Norton, Ohio."

Surprise crosses Henderson's face, but he quickly tethers it. "Alright, then," he says, regaining composure. I'm looking for…"

"Wealth and immortality," completes the caged man. He wrestles another breath in. "It's what they all seek."

"Who're you talking about when you say *all*?" Henderson asks.

"Only a fool would believe *(hiss)* that he is the only one who seeks wealth (hiss) and immortality."

Henderson walks the perimeter of the cage, feeling uncomfortable with the hanging man's sickly eyes on him. "How many have come knocking?" he asks.

"Scores." The hanging man offers a shrewd grin. "Legions."

"And?"

"They leave with nothing," he promises. "They have all (hiss) come up short…as will you."

Henderson reaches deep into the pocket of his cargo pants and retracts a small pink pouch. He displays it to the hanging man, yet holds it well out of his reach. The old man inhales a slow and savoring breath through his nostrils and closes his eyes in reverence.

"The flesh of a virgin child (hiss). Admirable, but you are not the first."

Henderson opens the bag and dumps its contents into his left hand and displays it to the caged man.

"You bluff! Those are clearly not Naunet's amulets *(hiss)*," the hanging man rasps. The task seems too extreme, yet he persists. There is a pronounced change in his demeanor. "They are the wrong hue."

"Who's the liar now?" asks Henderson. "What other color do emeralds come in? I've done all the work with my own hands, and you know it, pal!"

"I know I smell the blood of a saint on your hands *(hiss)*. You reek of blasphemy."

"Which means I did what had to be done," Henderson stresses with a hiss.

The hanging man locks onto Henderson with his sickly insipid eyes. "Then you would know *(hiss)* what you must do next," he says.

"I have to hold these amulets to your eyes."

"And try to steal from me *(hiss)* as all the others have tried to steal, yet failed."

Henderson smiles derisively. "What good is wealth to you when you're chained up in there?" he asks. "And why in the *hell* would you want immortality?"

"You could free me *(hiss)* if your heart is good, but forfeit your *(hiss)* prize," says the old man.

Henderson laughs mockingly and moves cautiously to the bars of the cage.

"Ah, I thought not," says the hanging man, forcing a horrific smile. "What is it you fear? I am bound and decrepit *(hiss)*. What harm can I possibly present to you?"

"None whatsoever. I'm not afraid of you. I'm disgusted by you. You're a fucking mess. Lean your head over here," Henderson demands, stepping closer to the cage.

The hanging man bows his head and waits for the kiss of the amulets to his eyes. Henderson reaches into the cage and presses the gems to the ancient fellow's eyes. The emeralds immediately heat like coals as they sear into the old man's eyelids, and the smell of burnt flesh fills the space between them. The old man rears his head back in pain and grabs Henderson's arms with amazing speed. He pulls himself against the bars, jabs his legs through and locks them around Henderson's legs, trapping Henderson's arms between his body and the bars of his prison.

Shock and disgust paralyze Henderson as the hanging man closes in on him face to face, as if to kiss him. His breath if fetid and vile and Henderson fights to settle his rising gorge as the squalid lips brush against his. The hanging man inhales a deep and tortured breath, and Henderson feels something large and serpentine being drawn from deep within. It struggles to remain within Henderson, clinging inside of him but failing. It pulls free of him with the rending of a hundred talons, carries with it all that is Henderson; his health, his desires, and his sanity. The hanging man takes another deep breath and exhales a fetid smoke into Henderson's mouth in a trade of breaths that tastes of death and rancid meat and jars Henderson to his core, forcing him to collapse weakly against the bars.

The hanging man reels backwards as if propelled by a huge blow. He strikes against the far bars of the cage and swings back on the rope, to and fro in gliding arcs, slowing to finally center in the cage. Absolute and abject terror radiates from his hazel eyes, and is etched into his wizened features. He claws at his throat, digging for release from the constricting rope.

Henderson smirks at the old man, winking at him with his new baby blues.

"Don't look so surprised, my friend," he says, exhaling his words freely for the first time in centuries…millennia, neither strangled nor constricted. "You have what you came for. Your wishes are granted. You wanted wealth? These gold bars weigh tons…a fortune, and they are yours. You are sole heir to this priceless cage." He taps the bars with long sturdy fingers…

Henderson's long, sturdy fingers. He pauses and a slight and contented smile forms on his healthy lips. "And you have your immortality, though I suspect you will opt to trade it in once… make that *if* the next greedy soul finds the keys and meets the demands."

Henderson's form bends over to pick up the amulets from the floor. "I will do my best to hide these well, but it could make for interesting sport, a little game of hide and seek? Naunet does love her games."

He pauses and stares at the decrepit old man swinging in wide arcs within the cage, digging at the rope encircling his neck.

"Well, Mr. Henderson. Oh, that's right…I'm Mr. Henderson, now. Nonetheless, as I was saying…it's not all bad. This is not your average prison, though there are *some* forgiving attributes. For one, you don't have to stew in your own waste, because the cursed and the dead do not require food, just an inclusive memory of our transgressions and a full acknowledgement of pain…we feed well on those."

He walks for the doorway, tossing the amulets playfully in the air and catching them like dice. He pauses when the swinging form in the cage rasps.

"No *(hiss)*! Wait!"

He pauses and chuckles softly. "I think not. I have waited eternities, and I feel no remorse… concerning you, that is. I know what you've done to get inside these wretched cavern walls, beneath that wretched holy city."

Panicking, the hanging man jerks violently and retches as the rope bites harder into his neck.

You might want to mind that," says the man wearing Henderson's body. He points to the collar on his neck. "It only gets tighter, but *never* tight enough. No. Never tight enough."

He tosses the amulets up in the air and catches them and says, "You know, I once sold a pure and holy man for thirty pieces of silver. That was my sin. Maybe your eternity will be shorter than mine, but I doubt it." He grabs the door handle, smiles, winks at the prisoner and says, "Hey! See you later."

He closes the door. The room sinks into blackness as the latch engages with deafening finality.

Man-Size in Marble

E. Nesbit

ALTHOUGH EVERY WORD of this story is as true as despair, I do not expect people to believe it. Nowadays a 'rational explanation' is required before belief is possible. Let me then, at once, offer the 'rational explanation' which finds most favour among those who have heard the tale of my life's tragedy. It is held that we were 'under a delusion', Laura and I, on that 31st of October; and that this supposition places the whole matter on a satisfactory and believable basis. The reader can judge, when he, too, has heard my story, how far this is an 'explanation', and in what sense it is 'rational'. There were three who took part in this: Laura and I and another man. The other man still lives, and can speak to the truth of the least credible part of my story.

* * *

I never in my life knew what it was to have as much money as I required to supply the most ordinary needs – good colours, books, and cab-fares – and when we were married we knew quite well that we should only be able to live at all by 'strict punctuality and attention to business'. I used to paint in those days, and Laura used to write, and we felt sure we could keep the pot at least simmering. Living in town was out of the question, so we went to look for a cottage in the country, which should be at once sanitary and picturesque. So rarely do these two qualities meet in one cottage that our search was for some time quite fruitless. We tried advertisements, but most of the desirable rural residences which we did look at proved to be lacking in both essentials, and when a cottage chanced to have drains it always had stucco as well and was shaped like a tea-caddy. And if we found a vine or rose-covered porch, corruption invariably lurked within. Our minds got so befogged by the eloquence of house-agents and the rival disadvantages of the fever-traps and outrages to beauty which we had seen and scorned, that I very much doubt whether either of us, on our wedding morning, knew the difference between a house and a haystack. But when we got away from friends and house-agents, on our honeymoon, our wits grew clear again, and we knew a pretty cottage when at last we saw one. It was at Brenzett – a little village set on a hill over against the southern marshes. We had gone there, from the seaside village where we were staying, to see the church, and two fields from the church we found this cottage. It stood quite by itself, about two miles from the village. It was a long, low building, with rooms sticking out in unexpected places. There was a bit of stone-work – ivy-covered and moss-grown, just two old rooms, all that was left of a big house that had once stood there – and round this stone-work the house had grown up. Stripped of its roses and jasmine it would have been hideous. As it stood it was charming, and after a brief examination we took it. It was absurdly cheap. The rest of our honeymoon we spent in grubbing about in second-hand shops in the county town, picking up bits of old oak and Chippendale chairs for our furnishing. We wound up with a run up to town and a visit to Liberty's, and soon the low oak-beamed lattice-windowed rooms began to be home. There was a jolly old-fashioned garden, with grass paths, and no end of hollyhocks and sunflowers, and big lilies. From the window you could see the marsh-pastures, and beyond them the blue, thin line of the sea. We were as happy as the summer was glorious, and settled down into work sooner than we ourselves expected. I was never tired of sketching the view and the wonderful cloud effects from the open lattice, and Laura would sit at the table and write verses about them, in which I mostly played the part of foreground.

We got a tall old peasant woman to do for us. Her face and figure were good, though her cooking was of the homeliest; but she understood all about gardening, and told us all the old names of the coppices and cornfields, and the stories of the smugglers and highwaymen, and, better still, of the 'things that walked', and of the 'sights' which met one in lonely glens of a starlight night. She was a great comfort to us, because Laura hated housekeeping as much as I loved folklore, and we soon came to leave all the domestic business to Mrs. Dorman, and to use her legends in little magazine stories which brought in the jingling guinea.

We had three months of married happiness, and did not have a single quarrel. One October evening I had been down to smoke a pipe with the doctor – our only neighbour – a pleasant young Irishman. Laura had stayed at home to finish a comic sketch of a village episode for the *Monthly Marplot*. I left her laughing over her own jokes, and came in to find her a crumpled heap of pale muslin weeping on the window seat.

"Good heavens, my darling, what's the matter?" I cried, taking her in my arms. She leaned her little dark head against my shoulder and went on crying. I had never seen her cry before – we had always been so happy, you see – and I felt sure some frightful misfortune had happened.

"What *is* the matter? Do speak."

"It's Mrs. Dorman," she sobbed.

"What has she done?" I inquired, immensely relieved.

"She says she must go before the end of the month, and she says her niece is ill; she's gone down to see her now, but I don't believe that's the reason, because her niece is always ill. I believe someone has been setting her against us. Her manner was so queer –"

"Never mind, Pussy," I said; "whatever you do, don't cry, or I shall have to cry too, to keep you in countenance, and then you'll never respect your man again!"

She dried her eyes obediently on my handkerchief, and even smiled faintly.

"But you see," she went on, "it is really serious, because these village people are so sheepy, and if one won't do a thing you may be quite sure none of the others will. And I shall have to cook the dinners, and wash up the hateful greasy plates; and you'll have to carry cans of water about, and clean the boots and knives – and we shall never have any time for work, or earn any money, or anything. We shall have to work all day, and only be able to rest when we are waiting for the kettle to boil!"

I represented to her that even if we had to perform these duties, the day would still present some margin for other toils and recreations. But she refused to see the matter in any but the greyest light. She was very unreasonable, my Laura, but I could not have loved her any more if she had been as reasonable as Whately.

"I'll speak to Mrs. Dorman when she comes back, and see if I can't come to terms with her," I said. "Perhaps she wants a rise in her screw. It will be all right. Let's walk up to the church."

The church was a large and lonely one, and we loved to go there, especially upon bright nights. The path skirted a wood, cut through it once, and ran along the crest of the hill through two meadows, and round the churchyard wall, over which the old yews loomed in black masses of shadow. This path, which was partly paved, was called 'the bier-balk', for it had long been the way by which the corpses had been carried to burial. The churchyard was richly treed, and was shaded by great elms which stood just outside and stretched their majestic arms in benediction over the happy dead. A large, low porch let one into the building by a Norman doorway and a heavy oak door studded with iron. Inside, the arches rose into darkness, and between them the reticulated windows, which stood out white in the moonlight. In the chancel, the windows were of rich glass, which showed in faint light their noble colouring, and made the black oak of the choir pews hardly more solid than the shadows. But on each side of the altar lay a grey marble figure of a knight in full plate armour lying upon a low slab, with hands held up in everlasting prayer, and these figures, oddly enough, were always to be seen if there was any glimmer of light in the church. Their names were lost, but the peasants told of them that they had been fierce and wicked men, marauders by land and sea, who had been the scourge of their time, and had been guilty of deeds so foul that the house they had lived in – the big house, by the way, that had stood on the site of our cottage – had been stricken by lightning and the vengeance of Heaven. But for all that, the gold of their heirs had bought them a place in the church. Looking at the bad hard faces reproduced in the marble, this story was easily believed.

The church looked at its best and weirdest on that night, for the shadows of the yew trees fell through the windows upon the floor of the nave and touched the pillars with tattered shade. We sat down together without speaking, and watched the solemn beauty of the old church, with some of that awe which inspired its early builders. We walked to the chancel and looked at the sleeping warriors. Then we rested some time on the stone seat in the porch, looking out over the stretch of quiet moonlit meadows, feeling in every fibre of our being the peace of the night and of our happy love; and came away at last with a sense that even scrubbing and blackleading were but small troubles at their worst.

Mrs. Dorman had come back from the village, and I at once invited her to a *tête-à-tête*.

"Now, Mrs. Dorman," I said, when I had got her into my painting room, "what's all this about your not staying with us?"

"I should be glad to get away, sir, before the end of the month," she answered, with her usual placid dignity.

"Have you any fault to find, Mrs. Dorman?"

"None at all, sir; you and your lady have always been most kind, I'm sure –"

"Well, what is it? Are your wages not high enough?"

"No, sir, I gets quite enough."

"Then why not stay?"

"I'd rather not" – with some hesitation – "my niece is ill."

"But your niece has been ill ever since we came."

No answer. There was a long and awkward silence. I broke it.

"Can't you stay for another month?" I asked.

"No, sir. I'm bound to go by Thursday."

And this was Monday!

"Well, I must say, I think you might have let us know before. There's no time now to get anyone else, and your mistress is not fit to do heavy housework. Can't you stay till next week?"

"I might be able to come back next week."

I was now convinced that all she wanted was a brief holiday, which we should have been willing enough to let her have, as soon as we could get a substitute.

"But why must you go this week?" I persisted. "Come, out with it."

Mrs. Dorman drew the little shawl, which she always wore, tightly across her bosom, as though she were cold. Then she said, with a sort of effort:

"They say, sir, as this was a big house in Catholic times, and there was a many deeds done here."

The nature of the 'deeds' might be vaguely inferred from the inflection of Mrs. Dorman's voice – which was enough to make one's blood run cold. I was glad that Laura was not in the room. She was always nervous, as highly-strung natures are, and I felt that these tales about our house, told by this old peasant woman, with her impressive manner and contagious credulity, might have made our home less dear to my wife.

"Tell me all about it, Mrs. Dorman," I said; "you needn't mind about telling me. I'm not like the young people who make fun of such things."

Which was partly true.

"Well, sir" – she sank her voice – "you may have seen in the church, beside the altar, two shapes."

"You mean the effigies of the knights in armour," I said cheerfully.

"I mean them two bodies, drawed out man-size in marble," she returned, and I had to admit that her description was a thousand times more graphic than mine, to say nothing of a certain weird force and uncanniness about the phrase 'drawed out man-size in marble'.

"They do say, as on All Saints' Eve them two bodies sits up on their slabs, and gets off of them, and then walks down the aisle, *in their marble*" – (another good phrase, Mrs. Dorman) – "and as the church clock strikes eleven they walks out of the church door, and over the graves, and along the bier-balk, and if it's a wet night there's the marks of their feet in the morning."

"And where do they go?" I asked, rather fascinated.

"They comes back here to their home, sir, and if anyone meets them –"

"Well, what then?" I asked.

But no – not another word could I get from her, save that her niece was ill and she must go. After what I had heard I scorned to discuss the niece, and tried to get from Mrs. Dorman more details of the legend. I could get nothing but warnings.

"Whatever you do, sir, lock the door early on All Saints' Eve, and make the cross-sign over the doorstep and on the windows."

"But has anyone ever seen these things?" I persisted.

"That's not for me to say. I know what I know, sir."

"Well, who was here last year?"

"No one, sir; the lady as owned the house only stayed here in summer, and she always went to London a full month afore *the* night. And I'm sorry to inconvenience you and your lady, but my niece is ill and I must go on Thursday."

I could have shaken her for her absurd reiteration of that obvious fiction, after she had told me her real reasons.

She was determined to go, nor could our united entreaties move her in the least.

I did not tell Laura the legend of the shapes that 'walked in their marble', partly because a legend concerning our house might perhaps trouble my wife, and partly, I think, from some more occult reason. This was not quite the same to me as any other story, and I did not want to talk about it till the day was over. I had very soon ceased to think of the legend, however. I was painting a portrait of Laura, against the lattice window, and I could not think of much else. I had got a splendid background of yellow and grey sunset, and was working away with enthusiasm at her face. On Thursday Mrs. Dorman went. She relented, at parting, so far as to say:

"Don't you put yourself about too much, ma'am, and if there's any little thing I can do next week, I'm sure I shan't mind."

From which I inferred that she wished to come back to us after Halloween. Up to the last she adhered to the fiction of the niece with touching fidelity.

Thursday passed off pretty well. Laura showed marked ability in the matter of steak and potatoes, and I confess that my knives, and the plates, which I insisted upon washing, were better done than I had dared to expect.

Friday came. It is about what happened on that Friday that this is written. I wonder if I should have believed it, if anyone had told it to me. I will write the story of it as quickly and plainly as I can. Everything that happened on that day is burnt into my brain. I shall not forget anything, nor leave anything out.

I got up early, I remember, and lighted the kitchen fire, and had just achieved a smoky success, when my little wife came running down, as sunny and sweet as the clear October morning itself. We prepared breakfast together, and found it very good fun. The housework was soon done, and when brushes and brooms and pails were quiet again, the house was still indeed. It is wonderful what a difference one makes in a house. We really missed Mrs. Dorman, quite apart from considerations concerning pots and pans. We spent the day in dusting our books and putting them straight, and dined gaily on cold steak and coffee. Laura was, if possible, brighter and gayer and sweeter than usual, and I began to think that a little domestic toil was really good for her. We had never been so merry since we were married, and the walk we had that afternoon was, I think, the happiest time of all my life. When we had watched the deep scarlet clouds slowly pale into leaden grey against a pale-green sky, and saw the white mists curl up along the hedgerows in the distant marsh, we came back to the house, silently, hand in hand.

"You are sad, my darling," I said, half-jestingly, as we sat down together in our little parlour. I expected a disclaimer, for my own silence had been the silence of complete happiness. To my surprise she said –

"Yes. I think I am sad, or rather I am uneasy. I don't think I'm very well. I have shivered three or four times since we came in, and it is not cold, is it?"

"No," I said, and hoped it was not a chill caught from the treacherous mists that roll up from the marshes in the dying light. No – she said, she did not think so. Then, after a silence, she spoke suddenly –

"Do you ever have presentiments of evil?"

"No," I said, smiling, "and I shouldn't believe in them if I had."

"I do," she went on; "the night my father died I knew it, though he was right away in the north of Scotland." I did not answer in words.

She sat looking at the fire for some time in silence, gently stroking my hand. At last she sprang up, came behind me, and, drawing my head back, kissed me.

"There, it's over now," she said. "What a baby I am! Come, light the candles, and we'll have some of these new Rubinstein duets."

And we spent a happy hour or two at the piano.

At about half-past ten I began to long for the good-night pipe, but Laura looked so white that I felt it would be brutal of me to fill our sitting-room with the fumes of strong cavendish.

"I'll take my pipe outside," I said.

"Let me come, too."

"No, sweetheart, not tonight; you're much too tired. I shan't be long. Get to bed, or I shall have an invalid to nurse tomorrow as well as the boots to clean."

I kissed her and was turning to go, when she flung her arms round my neck, and held me as if she would never let me go again. I stroked her hair.

"Come, Pussy, you're over-tired. The housework has been too much for you."

She loosened her clasp a little and drew a deep breath.

"No. We've been very happy today, Jack, haven't we? Don't stay out too long."

"I won't, my dearie."

I strolled out of the front door, leaving it unlatched. What a night it was! The jagged masses of heavy dark cloud were rolling at intervals from horizon to horizon, and thin white wreaths covered the stars. Through all the rush of the cloud river, the moon swam, breasting the waves and disappearing again in the darkness. When now and again her light reached the woodlands they seemed to be slowly and noiselessly waving in time to the swing of the clouds above them. There was a strange grey light over all the earth; the fields had that shadowy bloom over them which only comes from the marriage of dew and moonshine, or frost and starlight.

I walked up and down, drinking in the beauty of the quiet earth and the changing sky. The night was absolutely silent. Nothing seemed to be abroad. There was no skurrying of rabbits, or twitter of the half-asleep birds. And though the clouds went sailing across the sky, the wind that drove them never came low enough to rustle the dead leaves in the woodland paths. Across the meadows I could see the church tower standing out black and grey against the sky. I walked there thinking over our three months of happiness – and of my wife, her dear eyes, her loving ways. Oh, my little girl! My own little girl; what a vision came then of a long, glad life for you and me together!

I heard a bell-beat from the church. Eleven already! I turned to go in, but the night held me. I could not go back into our little warm rooms yet. I would go up to the church. I felt vaguely that it would be good to carry my love and thankfulness to the sanctuary whither so many loads of sorrow and gladness had been borne by the men and women of the dead years.

I looked in at the low window as I went by. Laura was half lying on her chair in front of the fire. I could not see her face, only her little head showed dark against the pale blue wall. She was quite still. Asleep, no doubt. My heart reached out to her, as I went on. There must be a God, I thought, and a God who was good. How otherwise could anything so sweet and dear as she have ever been imagined?

I walked slowly along the edge of the wood. A sound broke the stillness of the night, it was a rustling in the wood. I stopped and listened. The sound stopped too. I went on, and now distinctly heard another step than mine answer mine like an echo. It was a poacher or a wood-stealer, most likely, for these were not unknown in our Arcadian neighbourhood. But whoever it was, he was a fool not to step more lightly. I turned into the wood, and now the footstep seemed to come from the path I had just left. It must be an echo, I thought. The wood looked perfect in the moonlight. The large dying ferns and the brushwood showed where through thinning foliage the pale light came down. The tree trunks stood up like Gothic columns all around me. They reminded me of the church, and I turned into the bier-balk, and passed through the corpse-gate between the graves to the low porch. I paused for a moment on the stone seat where Laura and I had watched the fading landscape. Then I noticed that the door of the church was open, and I blamed myself for having left it unlatched the other night. We were the only people who ever cared to come to the church except on Sundays, and I was vexed to think that through our carelessness the damp autumn airs had had a chance of getting in and injuring the old fabric. I went in. It will seem strange, perhaps, that I should have gone half-way up the aisle before I remembered – with a sudden chill, followed by as sudden a rush of self-contempt – that this was the very day and hour when, according to tradition, the 'shapes drawed out man-size in marble' began to walk.

Having thus remembered the legend, and remembered it with a shiver, of which I was ashamed, I could not do otherwise than walk up towards the altar, just to look at the figures – as I said to myself; really what I wanted was to assure myself, first, that I did not believe the legend, and, secondly, that it was not true. I was rather glad that I had come. I thought now I could tell Mrs. Dorman how vain her fancies were, and how peacefully the marble figures slept on through the ghastly hour. With my hands in my pockets I passed up the aisle. In the grey dim light the eastern end of the church looked larger than usual, and the arches above the two tombs looked larger too. The moon came out and showed me the reason. I stopped short, my heart gave a leap that nearly choked me, and then sank sickeningly.

The 'bodies drawed out man-size' *were gone*, and their marble slabs lay wide and bare in the vague moonlight that slanted through the east window.

Were they really gone? Or was I mad? Clenching my nerves, I stooped and passed my hand over the smooth slabs, and felt their flat unbroken surface. Had someone taken the things away? Was it some vile practical joke? I would make sure, anyway. In an instant I had made a torch of a newspaper, which happened to be in my pocket, and lighting it held it high above my head. Its yellow glare illuminated the dark arches and those slabs. The figures were gone. And I was alone in the church; or was I alone?

And then a horror seized me, a horror indefinable and indescribable – an overwhelming certainty of supreme and accomplished calamity. I flung down the torch and tore along the aisle and out through the porch, biting my lips as I ran to keep myself from shrieking aloud. Oh, was I mad – or what was this that possessed me? I leaped the churchyard wall and took the straight cut across the fields, led by the light from our windows. Just as I got over the first stile, a dark figure seemed to spring out of the ground. Mad still with that certainty of misfortune, I made for the thing that stood in my path, shouting, "Get out of the way, can't you!"

But my push met with a more vigorous resistance than I had expected. My arms were caught just above the elbow and held as in a vice, and the raw-boned Irish doctor actually shook me.

"Would ye?" he cried, in his own unmistakable accents – "Would ye, then?"

"Let me go, you fool," I gasped. "The marble figures have gone from the church; I tell you they've gone."

He broke into a ringing laugh. "I'll have to give ye a draught tomorrow, I see. Ye've bin smoking too much and listening to old wives' tales."

"I tell you, I've seen the bare slabs."

"Well, come back with me. I'm going up to old Palmer's – his daughter's ill; we'll look in at the church and let me see the bare slabs."

"You go, if you like," I said, a little less frantic for his laughter; "I'm going home to my wife."

"Rubbish, man," said he; "d'ye think I'll permit of that? Are ye to go saying all yer life that ye've seen solid marble endowed with vitality, and me to go all me life saying ye were a coward? No, sir – ye shan't do ut."

The night air – a human voice – and I think also the physical contact with this six feet of solid common sense, brought me back a little to my ordinary self, and the word 'coward' was a mental shower-bath.

"Come on, then," I said sullenly; "perhaps you're right."

He still held my arm tightly. We got over the stile and back to the church. All was still as death. The place smelt very damp and earthy. We walked up the aisle. I am not ashamed to confess that I shut my eyes: I knew the figures would not be there. I heard Kelly strike a match.

"Here they are, ye see, right enough; ye've been dreaming or drinking, asking yer pardon for the imputation."

I opened my eyes. By Kelly's expiring vesta I saw two shapes lying 'in their marble' on their slabs. I drew a deep breath, and caught his hand.

"I'm awfully indebted to you," I said. "It must have been some trick of light, or I have been working rather hard, perhaps that's it. Do you know, I was quite convinced they were gone."

"I'm aware of that," he answered rather grimly; "ye'll have to be careful of that brain of yours, my friend, I assure ye."

He was leaning over and looking at the right-hand figure, whose stony face was the most villainous and deadly in expression.

"By Jove," he said, "something has been afoot here – this hand is broken."

And so it was. I was certain that it had been perfect the last time Laura and I had been there.

"Perhaps someone has *tried* to remove them," said the young doctor.

"That won't account for my impression," I objected.

"Too much painting and tobacco will account for that, well enough."

"Come along," I said, "or my wife will be getting anxious. You'll come in and have a drop of whisky and drink confusion to ghosts and better sense to me."

"I ought to go up to Palmer's, but it's so late now I'd best leave it till the morning," he replied. "I was kept late at the Union, and I've had to see a lot of people since. All right, I'll come back with ye."

I think he fancied I needed him more than did Palmer's girl, so, discussing how such an illusion could have been possible, and deducing from this experience large generalities concerning ghostly apparitions, we walked up to our cottage. We saw, as we walked up the garden-path, that bright light streamed out of the front door, and presently saw that the parlour door was open too. Had she gone out?

"Come in," I said, and Dr. Kelly followed me into the parlour. It was all ablaze with candles, not only the wax ones, but at least a dozen guttering, glaring tallow dips, stuck in vases and ornaments in unlikely places. Light, I knew, was Laura's remedy for nervousness. Poor child! Why had I left her? Brute that I was.

We glanced round the room, and at first we did not see her. The window was open, and the draught set all the candles flaring one way. Her chair was empty and her handkerchief and book lay on the floor. I turned to the window. There, in the recess of the window, I saw her. Oh, my child, my love, had she gone to that window to watch for me? And what had come into the room behind her? To what had she turned with that look of frantic fear and horror? Oh, my little one, had she thought that it was I whose step she heard, and turned to meet – what?

She had fallen back across a table in the window, and her body lay half on it and half on the window-seat, and her head hung down over the table, the brown hair loosened and fallen to the carpet. Her lips were drawn back, and her eyes wide, wide open. They saw nothing now. What had they seen last?

The doctor moved towards her, but I pushed him aside and sprang to her; caught her in my arms and cried:

"It's all right, Laura! I've got you safe, wifie."

She fell into my arms in a heap. I clasped her and kissed her, and called her by all her pet names, but I think I knew all the time that she was dead. Her hands were tightly clenched. In one of them she held something fast. When I was quite sure that she was dead, and that nothing mattered at all anymore, I let him open her hand to see what she held.

It was a grey marble finger.

The Obstinate One

Jessica Nickelsen

THEY ARE MOVING into the house today, the house that has been my family's for so many generations. I watch from the topmost window as they pull up the shell drive, littered with leaves. The woman gets out first, and I immediately dislike her. She wears too much make-up, and there's a hard look about her face. And then he steps from the car.

He is tall – so tall! Sandy brown hair that lifts a little in the breeze. Eyes that dart from the old tree out front, up to the weather-vane at the top of the house, and back down to the sagging front steps. His gaze passes over me, where I am pressed to the attic window. His mouth twists into a grim smile when she speaks sharply to him.

She takes the keys from him and steps carefully up towards the front door. I hear the key in the lock (I know everything that happens inside my house) and her step as she crosses the threshold. My threshold.

A terrible wrath rises up in me then, like the tantrums of my youth. My hands clench into fists and I hold my breath. The glass in the window pane, sensing my anger, contracts with a sound like someone dragging an iron nail across it.

She is in my house, but he is still out in the garden, with the sunlight on his hair. I watch him examine the old rose beds, and my mood dissipates like a stone thrown into a pond. I again press myself to the window. But it is too much, after so long spent alone in these dusty rooms, in this lonely house. I am unable to bear looking at him for too long, and I hear a wail rise up inside me. I turn from the window, like smoke, like mist, like air, and I flow down to the other end of the attic, to the other window that looks out over the sea. But his face is still there before my eyes, handsome and angry, just like my bonny Will's.

None of my ancestors became ghosts – none that I know of, anyway. They had quietly died and gone on, like meek white mice, all off to the hereafter. I was always the obstinate one. But the attic is still crammed with all of their things, which is almost like being haunted: piles of sheet music, instruments, books, silver baby rattles, and fine knitted clothes for newborns. Looking at it all, heaped in dusty piles that I can do nothing with, makes me cross.

The door to the attic is locked. All the same, I do not like to think of the woman getting her hands on my things.

* * *

They are fighting again, the couple. I hate it when they fight. The whole house soaks up their anger, like a tree bringing water up to its very topmost leaves. The frustration and resentment that rises up from the couple in the downstairs parlour makes the doorknobs get hot, and the curtains flutter, as if they are aflame, and even the weather vane has to keep spinning just to cool down.

The man sits on the couch, looking at his hands, while the woman walks around the house, opening and closing cupboard doors, doing chores angrily. "Is this what you mean when you say I don't do anything around here?" she screeches.

It hurts my poor ears to have to listen to her.

Eventually she gives up. She looks over at the man, still on the couch. She curses and goes up to the second floor to start getting ready for bed. He sighs and finally lifts his head. I want to go to him, to cool his forehead with my kisses, and to blow gently on his hair.

He sighs.

I will go to him. I slip quickly down through the walls, which I usually hate doing because of all the spiders and cobwebs, and the smell of mouse. But I am soon in the parlour, slightly hidden behind a large wing-backed chair.

He looks up then, fingers pressed tight to his temples, and sees me. His hands drop to his lap. "I knew it," he says, his eyes suddenly bright. "Hello – can you hear me?"

He isn't afraid!

"I can hear you," I say. I stay behind the chair, my hands resting on the old red damask. We look at each other. I am suddenly dumbstruck. All the things I had wanted to say, that made so much sense when I'd spoken them aloud in the attic, have evaporated from my tongue. He stands up, wobbling, and knocks over an empty bottle that rolls noisily along the wooden floor and hits the leg of the couch. His face is slack and numb but his eyes are shining.

He looks like Will, how he was at the end. My heart lurches in different directions.

I flee.

* * *

Most days, the woman gets up early, puts on makeup and perfume, and dresses in a suit. She gets into the car and drives away. He wakes up late (later and later now), and goes to the kitchen. He drinks endless cups of coffee, from a small machine that gurgles away beside the sink.

He knows I am there, knows I follow him around the house, and that I watch everything he does. He talks to me sometimes; calls me his 'little friend'. He tells me about his marriage, about their life, about the baby that died. I tell him things too: who I was, the life I used to lead. I don't know if he really hears me but he seems to understand.

I take him to the painting of my family that used to hang in the hall, but now is wrapped in mouse-nibbled paper in the cellar. Tucked in beside it is a miniature portrait of me, with my name on it. I look young and beautiful. I want to prove to him that I was alive, once. He holds the portrait in his hands and speaks my name aloud. Hearing it on his warm lips makes my hair stand on end. I show him the key to the attic, behind a loose board on the second floor landing. He promises to keep the woman away.

I am glad he talks to me, but I still end up feeling sad and alone, with his stories sitting like a hard little nut in my belly. The woman comes home late, usually after dark. She smells of alcohol, and so does he. He drinks it all night long. Most nights end in an argument. I go up to the widow's walk, where I wail, and pull my hair. What can we do to be together, this passionate man and I?

One night she comes home very late. She staggers up the steps that still need to be fixed, giggling and singing to herself. He has gone to bed and locked the door, so she pounds and pounds on it with the flat of her hand, then the side of her fist, until he gets out of bed. I curl up in the cupola, in the dusty blue glass like a sea shell, and listen to them fight. She smells like sex, he says. She slaps his face. He hits her, hard, and she falls over, falls backwards down the sagging front steps, and lands down on the crushed shells of the drive.

I gasp at the sound of fist against flesh, and press my hand hard to my stomach. Will he go to her now? Lower himself down on her, digging her harder into the sharp shells as he presses his forearm across her throat? He must. It is what should be done.

But he is not Will, and I am not the woman on the ground, now raising herself up on scraped elbows.

I follow him as he turns and runs back through the house, right up to the top floor. He kicks the attic door and falls to the ground. His body trembles. I hover over him, as close as I can get.

Come up into the attic, I say. *She will leave now and we can be together.* I will him to take the key from behind the board. *We can lie together on the small bed upstairs.* But it's like he doesn't hear me, just curls up tight into a ball and shakes.

* * *

The woman doesn't leave, like she should. Instead, she stays home from work for a week, and spends the time lying on the couch, pressing iced peas, and then warm cloths, to her cheek. A yellow bruise has blossomed over one side of her face. He is chastised, and hovers over her, making sure she is comfortable, making sure she has everything she needs. She stands at the window and looks out to the garden, where he is digging weeds, trimming the roses and spreading fresh bark over the rose beds. She smiles, and draws the ends of the quilt closer over her shoulders. Then she goes outside.

I am unable to follow; surely he knows this! I watch from the window, standing where she stood moments before. She walks over, says something – a joke – and then he laughs and pulls her to him. They embrace, his hands hard against her. I see him look up over her shoulder. He sees me and frowns.

The wrath is upon me again, I cannot stop it. I go to their bedroom, one of the smaller ones on the second floor, and in my anger I force open the chest of drawers and pull out its contents; underthings by the look of them. Hers. Things of the like I never saw before, all gossamer and lace. I make them float in the air, and then I rend through them with my anger. They fall to the bed like bits of burned feather.

The blankets, the pillows. The bed. I race back up to the attic. I block my ears against the awful sounds that are starting to seep out of me like water.

* * *

She has gone. They argued long into the night after I ruined their bedroom, and though I felt bad afterward, I would do it again in a heartbeat if it meant she would go. I am so happy I let myself float up through the roof, and I lie with my back on the tiles, and look up at the stars. It has happened. He is mine.

I want him to come to me, to say my name again. But he is restless tonight, and he moves from room to room, looking for something else. It is a lovely warm night, and I think I can almost feel the caress of the wind. Will used to stroke my hair, when we'd sit down by the garden together.

I get distracted, thinking about the past, and when I come back to myself I realise that the man has moved to the bathroom, and is standing before the sink. He has done something. There is crimson everywhere; it hurts my eyes.

He is slipping away from me, too fast.

I hurry down to the bathroom, pass through walls and come out through the mirror where he is standing.

His eyes take a moment to focus on me. "I'm sorry," he whispers.

He reaches a hand out to me, and touches my hair. Actually touches it. I reach up and feel the wetness there.

I want him to stay.

I want him to die!

To die, and then be with me forever.

Gently, I lay him down on the yellow tiles, and I stroke his head while he looks up at me. He looks up at me, and it all feels familiar.

It feels right.

* * *

It is nearly morning and I am waiting. I think of all the things I want to show him, like the tiny bird skeletons in the nest up the very top of the chimney, and the mouse family that has settled in a chest of silks.

But he has not come.

The house is all a-flutter, what with my nerves. I move from room to room, imagining how we will share the space together. I will show him the top of the roof, where you can sit and watch the sky slowly turn pink, and listen to the lowing of the cows in the neighbouring pasture. We will lie, upside down, in the sky-blue cupola painted with gold stars, and we will curl together like kittens.

I'm sure of it, he will come.

The Open Door

Margaret Oliphant

I TOOK the house of Brentwood on my return from India in 18—, for the temporary accommodation of my family, until I could find a permanent home for them. It had many advantages which made it peculiarly appropriate. It was within reach of Edinburgh; and my boy Roland, whose education had been considerably neglected, could ride in and out to school; which was thought to be better for him than either leaving home altogether or staying there always with a tutor. The lad was doubly precious to us, being the only one left to us of many; and he was fragile in body, we believed, and deeply sensitive in mind. The two girls also found at Brentwood everything they wanted. They were near enough to Edinburgh to have masters and lessons as many as they required for completing that never-ending education which the young people seem to require nowadays.

Brentwood stands on that fine and wealthy slope of country – one of the richest in Scotland – which lies between the Pentland Hills and the Firth. In clear weather you could see the blue gleam of the great estuary on one side of you; and on the other the blue heights. Edinburgh – with its two lesser heights, the Castle and the Calton Hill, its spires and towers piercing through the smoke, and Arthur's Seat lying crouched behind, like a guardian no longer very needful, taking his repose beside the well-beloved charge, which is now, so to speak, able to take care of itself without him – lay at our right hand.

The village of Brentwood, with its prosaic houses, lay in a hollow almost under our house. Village architecture does not flourish in Scotland. Still a cluster of houses on different elevations, with scraps of garden coming in between, a hedgerow with clothes laid out to dry, the opening of a street with its rural sociability, the women at their doors, the slow wagon lumbering along, gives a centre to the landscape. In the park which surrounded the house were the ruins of the former mansion of Brentwood – a much smaller and less important house than the solid Georgian edifice which we inhabited. The ruins were picturesque, however, and gave importance to the place. Even we, who were but temporary tenants, felt a vague pride in them, as if they somehow reflected a certain consequence upon ourselves. The old building had the remains of a tower – an indistinguishable mass of masonwork, overgrown with ivy; and the shells of the walls attached to this were half filled up with soil. At a little distance were some very commonplace and disjointed fragments of buildings, one of them suggesting a certain pathos by its very commonness and the complete wreck which it showed. This was the end of a low gable, a bit of grey wall, all incrusted with lichens, in which was a common door-way. Probably it had been a servants' entrance, a backdoor, or opening into what are called 'the offices' in Scotland. No offices remained to be entered – pantry and kitchen had all been swept out of being; but there stood the door-way open and vacant, free to all the winds, to the rabbits, and every wild creature. It struck my eye, the first time I went to Brentwood, like a melancholy comment upon a life that was over. A door that led to nothing – closed once, perhaps, with anxious care, bolted and guarded, now void of any meaning. It impressed me, I remember, from the first; so perhaps it may be said that my mind was prepared to attach to it an importance which nothing justified.

The summer was a very happy period of repose for us all; and it was when the family had settled down for the winter, when the days were short and dark, and the rigorous reign of frost upon us, that the incidents occurred which alone could justify me in intruding upon the world my private affairs.

I was absent in London when these events began. In London an old Indian plunges back into the interests with which all his previous life has been associated, and meets old friends at every step. I had been circulating among some half-dozen of these and had missed some of my home letters. It is never safe to miss one's letters. In this transitory life, as the Prayer-book says, how can one ever be certain what is going to happen? All was well at home. I knew exactly (I thought) what they would have to say to me: 'The weather has been so fine, that Roland has not once gone by train, and he enjoys the ride beyond anything.' 'Dear papa, be sure that you don't forget anything, but bring us so-and-so, and so-and-so,' – a list as long as my arm. Dear girls and dearer mother! I would not for the world have forgotten their commissions, or lost their little letters!

When I got back to my club, however, three or four letters were lying for me, upon some of which I noticed the 'immediate', 'urgent', which old-fashioned people and anxious people still believe will influence the post-office and quicken the speed of the mails. I was about to open one of these, when the club porter brought me two telegrams, one of which, he said, had arrived the night before. I opened, as was to be expected, the last first, and this was what I read:

Why don't you come or answer? For God's sake, come. He is much worse.

This was a thunderbolt to fall upon a man's head who had one only son, and he the light of his eyes! The other telegram, which I opened with hands trembling so much that I lost time by my haste, was to much the same purpose:

No better; doctor afraid of brain-fever. Calls for you day and night. Let nothing detain you.

The first thing I did was to look up the time-tables to see if there was any way of getting off sooner than by the night-train, though I knew well enough there was not; and then I read the letters, which furnished – alas! – too clearly, all the details. They told me that the boy had been pale for some time, with a scared look. His mother had noticed it before I left home, but would not say anything to alarm me. This look had increased day by day; and soon it was observed that Roland came home at a wild gallop through the park, his pony panting and in foam, himself 'as white as a sheet', but with the perspiration streaming from his forehead. For a long time he had resisted all questioning, but at length had developed such strange changes of mood, showing a reluctance to go to school, a desire to be fetched in the carriage at night – which was a ridiculous piece of luxury – an unwillingness to go out into the grounds, and nervous start at every sound, that his mother had insisted upon an explanation. When the boy – our boy Roland, who had never known what fear was – began to talk to her of voices he had heard in the park, and shadows that had appeared to him among the ruins, my wife promptly put him to bed and sent for Dr. Simson, which, of course, was the only thing to do.

I hurried off that evening, as may be supposed, with an anxious heart. How I got through the hours before the starting of the train, I cannot tell. We must all be thankful for the quickness of the railway when in anxiety; but to have thrown myself into a post-chaise as soon as horses could be put to, would have been a relief. I got to Edinburgh very early in the blackness of the winter morning, and scarcely dared look the man in the face, at whom I gasped, "What news?" My wife had sent the brougham for me, which I concluded, before the man spoke, was a bad sign. His answer was that stereotyped answer which leaves the imagination so wildly free – "Just the same." Just the same! What might that mean? The horses seemed to me to creep along the long dark country road. As we dashed through the park, I thought I heard someone moaning among the trees, and clenched my fist at him (whoever he might be) with fury. Why had the fool of a woman at the gate allowed anyone to come in to disturb the quiet of the place? If I had not been in such hot haste to get home, I think I should have stopped the carriage and got out to see what tramp it was that had made an entrance, and chosen my grounds, of all places in the world – when my boy was ill! – to grumble and groan in. But I had no reason to complain of our slow pace here. The horses flew like lightning along the intervening path, and drew up at the door all panting, as if they had run a race.

My wife stood waiting to receive me, with a pale face, and a candle in her hand, which made her look paler still as the wind blew the flame about. "He is sleeping," she said in a whisper, as if her voice might wake him. And I replied, when I could find my voice, also in a whisper, as though the jingling of the horses' furniture and the sound of their hoofs must not have been more dangerous. I stood on the steps with her a moment, almost afraid to go in, now that I was here; and it seemed to me that I saw without observing, if I may so say, that the horses were unwilling to turn round, though their stables lay that way, or that the men were unwilling. These things occurred to me afterwards, though at the moment I was not capable of anything but to ask questions and to hear of the condition of the boy.

I looked at him from the door of his room, for we were afraid to go near, lest we should disturb that blessed sleep. It looked like actual sleep, not the lethargy into which my wife told me he would sometimes fall. She told me everything in the next room, which communicated with his, rising now and then and going to the door of the communication; and in this there was much that was very startling and confusing to the mind. It appeared that ever since the winter began – since it was early dark, and night had fallen before his return from school – he had been hearing voices among the ruins; at first only a groaning, he said, at which his pony was as much alarmed as he was, but by degrees a voice. The tears ran down my wife's cheeks as she described to me how he would start up in the night and cry out. "Oh, mother, let me in! Oh, mother, let me in!" with a pathos which rent her heart. And she sitting there all the time, only longing to do everything his heart could desire! But though she would try to soothe him, crying, "You are at home, my darling. I am here. Don't you know me? Your mother is here!" he would only stare at her, and after a while spring up again with the same cry. At other times he would be quite reasonable, she said, asking eagerly when I was coming, but declaring that he must go with me as soon as I did so, 'to let them in'.

"The doctor thinks his nervous system must have received a shock," my wife said. "Oh, Henry, can it be that we have pushed him on too much with his work – a delicate boy like Roland? And what is his work in comparison with his health? Even you would think little of honours or prizes if it hurt the boy's health." Even I! – as if I were an inhuman father sacrificing my child to my ambition. But I would not increase her trouble by taking any notice.

There was just daylight enough to see his face when I went to him; and what a change in a fortnight! He was paler and more worn, I thought, than even in those dreadful days in the plains before we left India. His hair seemed to me to have grown long and lank; his eyes were like blazing lights projecting out of his white face. He got hold of my hand in a cold and tremulous clutch, and waved to everybody to go away. "Go away – even mother," he said; "go away." This went to her heart; for she did not like that even I should have more of the boy's confidence than herself; but my wife has never been a woman to think of herself, and she left us alone. "Are they all gone?" he said eagerly. "They would not let me speak. The doctor treated me as if I were a fool. You know I am not a fool, papa."

"Yes, yes, my boy, I know. But you are ill, and quiet is so necessary. You are not only not a fool, Roland, but you are reasonable and understand. When you are ill you must deny yourself; you must not do everything that you might do being well."

He waved his thin hand with a sort of indignation. "Then, father, I am not ill," he cried. "Oh, I thought when you came you would not stop me – you would see the sense of it! What do you think is the matter with me, all of you? Simson is well enough; but he is only a doctor. What do you think is the matter with me? I am no more ill than you are. A doctor, of course, he thinks you are ill the moment he looks at you – that's what he's there for – and claps you into bed."

"Which is the best place for you at present, my dear boy."

"I made up my mind," cried the little fellow, "that I would stand it till you came home. I said to myself, I won't frighten mother and the girls. But now, father," he cried, half jumping out of bed, "it's not illness: it's a secret."

His eyes shone so wildly, his face was so swept with strong feeling, that my heart sank within me. It could be nothing but fever that did it, and fever had been so fatal. I got him into my arms to put him back into bed. "Roland," I said, humouring the poor child, which I knew was the only way, "if you are going to tell me this secret to do any good, you know you must be quite quiet, and not excite yourself. If you excite yourself, I must not let you speak."

"Yes, father," said the boy. He was quiet directly, like a man, as if he quite understood. When I had laid him back on his pillow, he looked up at me with that grateful, sweet look with which children, when they are ill, break one's heart, the water coming into his eyes in his weakness. "I was sure as soon as you were here you would know what to do," he said.

"To be sure, my boy. Now keep quiet, and tell it all out like a man." To think I was telling lies to my own child! For I did it only to humour him, thinking, poor little fellow, his brain was wrong.

"Yes, father. Father, there is someone in the park – someone that has been badly used."

"Hush, my dear; you remember there is to be no excitement. Well, who is this somebody, and who has been ill-using him? We will soon put a stop to that."

"Ah," cried Roland, "but it is not so easy as you think. I don't know who it is. It is just a cry. Oh, if you could hear it! It gets into my head in my sleep. I heard it as clear – as clear; and they think that I am dreaming, or raving perhaps," the boy said, with a sort of disdainful smile.

This look of his perplexed me; it was less like fever than I thought. "Are you quite sure you have not dreamed it, Roland?" I said.

"Dreamed? – That!" He was springing up again when he suddenly bethought himself, and lay down flat, with the same sort of smile on his face. "The pony heard it, too," he said. "She jumped as if she had been shot. If I had not grasped at the reins – for I was frightened, father –"

"No shame to you, my boy," said I, though I scarcely knew why.

"If I hadn't held to her like a leech, she'd have pitched me over her head, and never drew breath till we were at the door. Did the pony dream it?" he said, with a soft disdain, yet indulgence for my foolishness. Then he added slowly, "It was only a cry the first time, and all the time before you went away. I wouldn't tell you, for it was so wretched to be frightened. I thought it might be a hare or a rabbit snared, and I went in the morning and looked; but there was nothing. It was after you went I heard it really first; and this is what he says." He raised himself on his elbow close to me, and looked me in the face: "Oh, mother, let me in! Oh, mother, let me in!" As he said the words a mist came over his face, the mouth quivered, the soft features all melted and changed, and when he had ended these pitiful words, dissolved in a shower of heavy tears.

Was it a hallucination? Was it the fever of the brain? Was it the disordered fancy caused by great bodily weakness? How could I tell? I thought it wisest to accept it as if it were all true.

"This is very touching, Roland," I said.

"Oh, if you had just heard it, father! I said to myself, if father heard it he would do something; but mamma, you know, she's given over to Simson, and that fellow's a doctor, and never thinks of anything but clapping you into bed."

"We must not blame Simson for being a doctor, Roland."

"No, no," said my boy, with delightful toleration and indulgence; "oh, no: that's the good of him; that's what he's for; I know that. But you – you are different; you are just father; and you'll do something – directly, papa, directly; this very night."

"Surely," I said. "No doubt it is some little lost child."

He gave me a sudden, swift look, investigating my face as though to see whether, after all, this was everything my eminence as 'father' came to – no more than that. Then he got hold of my shoulder, clutching it with his thin hand: "Look here," he said, with a quiver in his voice: "suppose it wasn't – living at all!"

"My dear boy, how then could you have heard it?" I said.

He turned away from me with a pettish exclamation – "As if you didn't know better than that!"

"Do you want to tell me it is a ghost?" I said.

Roland withdrew his hand; his countenance assumed an aspect of great dignity and gravity; a slight quiver remained about his lips. "Whatever it was – you always said we were not to call names. It was something – in trouble. Oh, father, in terrible trouble!"

"But, my boy," I said (I was at my wits' end), "if it was a child that was lost, or any poor human creature – but, Roland, what do you want me to do?"

"I should know if I was you," said the child eagerly. "That is what I always said to myself – Father will know. Oh, papa, papa, to have to face it night after night, in such terrible, terrible trouble, and never to be able to do it any good! I don't want to cry; it's like a baby, I know; but what can I do else? Out there all by itself in the ruin, and nobody to help it! I can't bear it!" cried my generous boy. And in his weakness he burst out, after many attempts to restrain it, into a great childish fit of sobbing and tears.

I do not know that I was ever in a greater perplexity in my life; and afterwards, when I thought of it, there was something comic in it too. It is bad enough to find your child's mind possessed with the conviction that he had seen, or heard, a ghost; but that he should require you to go instantly and help that ghost was the most bewildering experience that had ever come my way. I did my best to console my boy without giving any promise of this astonishing kind; but he was too sharp for me; he would have none of my caresses. With sobs breaking in at intervals upon his voice, and the rain-drops hanging on his eyelids, he yet returned to the charge.

"It will be there now! – It will be there all the night! Oh, think, papa – think if it was me! I can't rest for thinking of it. Don't!" he cried, putting away my hand – "Don't! You go and help it, and mother can take care of me."

"But, Roland, what can I do?"

My boy opened his eyes, which were large with weakness and fever, and gave me a smile such, I think, as sick children only know the secret of. "I was sure you would know as soon as you came. I always said, 'Father will know.' And mother," he cried, with a softening of repose upon his face, his limbs relaxing, his form sinking with a luxurious ease in his bed – "mother can come and take care of me."

I called her, and saw him turn to her with the complete dependence of a child; and then I went away and left them, as perplexed a man as any in Scotland. I must say, however, I had this consolation, that my mind was greatly eased about Roland. He might be under a hallucination; but his head was clear enough, and I did not think him so ill as everybody else did. The girls were astonished even at the ease with which I took it. "How do you think he is?" they said in a breath, coming round me, laying hold of me. "Not half so ill as I expected," I said; "not very bad at all."

"Oh, papa, you are a darling!" cried Agatha, kissing me, and crying upon my shoulder; while little Jeanie, who was as pale as Roland, clasped both her arms round mine, and could not speak at all. I knew nothing about it, not half so much as Simson; but they believed in me: they had a feeling that all would go right now. God is very good to you when your children look to you like that. It makes one humble, not proud. I was not worthy of it; and then I recollected that I had to act the part of a father to Roland's ghost – which made me almost laugh, though I might just as well have cried. It was the strangest mission that ever was intrusted to mortal man.

It was then I remembered suddenly the looks of the men when they turned to take the brougham to the stables in the dark that morning. They had not liked it, and the horses had not liked it. I remembered that even in my anxiety about Roland I had heard them tearing along the avenue back to the stables, and had made a memorandum mentally that I must speak of it. It seemed to me that the best thing I could do was to go to the stables now and make a few inquiries. The coachman was the head of this little colony, and it was to his house I went to pursue my investigations. He was a native of the district, and had taken care of the place in the absence of the family for years; it was impossible but that he must know everything that was going on, and all the traditions of the place. The men, I could see, eyed me anxiously when I thus appeared at such an hour among them, and followed me with their eyes to Jarvis's house, where he lived alone with his old wife, their children being all married and out in the world. Mrs. Jarvis met me with anxious questions. How was the poor young gentleman? But the others knew, I could see by their faces, that not even this was the foremost thing in my mind.

After a while I elicited without much difficulty the whole story. In the opinion of the Jarvises, and of everybody about, the certainty that the place was haunted was beyond all doubt. As Sandy and his wife warmed to the tale, one tripping up another in their eagerness to tell everything, it gradually developed as distinct a superstition as I ever heard, and not without poetry and pathos. How long it was since the voice had been heard first, nobody could tell with certainty. Jarvis's opinion was that his father, who had been coachman at Brentwood before him, had never heard anything about it, and that the whole thing had arisen within the last ten years, since the complete dismantling of the old house; which was a wonderfully modern date for a tale so well authenticated. According to these witnesses, and to several whom I questioned afterwards, and who were all in perfect agreement, it was only in the months of November and December that 'the visitation' occurred.

During these months, the darkest of the year, scarcely a night passed without the recurrence of these inexplicable cries. Nothing, it was said, had ever been seen – at least, nothing that could be identified. Some people, bolder or more imaginative than the others, had seen the darkness moving, Mrs. Jarvis said, with unconscious poetry. It began when night fell, and continued at intervals till day broke. Very often it was only an inarticulate cry and moaning, but sometimes the words which had taken possession of my poor boy's fancy had been distinctly audible – "Oh, mother, let me in!" The Jarvises were not aware that there had ever been any investigation into it. The estate of Brentwood had lapsed into the hands of a distant branch of the family, who had lived but little there; and of the many people who had taken it, as I had done, few had remained through two Decembers. And nobody had taken the trouble to make a very close examination into the facts. "No, no," Jarvis said, shaking his head, "No, no, Cornel. Wha wad set themsels up for a laughin'-stock to a' the country-side, making a wark about a ghost? Naebody believes in ghosts. It bid to be the wind in the trees, the last gentleman said, or some effec' o' the water wrastlin' among the rocks. He said it was a' quite easy explained; but he gave up the hoose. And when you cam, Cornel, we were awfu' anxious you should never hear. What for should I have spoiled the bargain and hairmed the property for no-thing?"

"Do you call my child's life nothing?" I said in the trouble of the moment, unable to restrain myself. "And instead of telling this all to me, you have told it to him – to a delicate boy, a child unable to sift evidence or judge for himself, a tender-hearted young creature –"

I was walking about the room with an anger all the hotter that I felt it to be most likely quite unjust. My heart was full of bitterness against the stolid retainers of a family who were content to risk other people's children and comfort rather than let a house lie empty. If I had been warned I might have taken precautions, or left the place, or sent Roland away, a hundred things which now I could not do; and here I was with my boy in a brain-fever, and his life, the most precious life on earth, hanging in the balance, dependent on whether or not I could get to the reason of a commonplace ghost-story!

"Cornel," said Jarvis solemnly, "and *she'll* bear me witness – the young gentleman never heard a word from me – no, nor from either groom or gardner; I'll gie ye my word for that. In the first place, he's no a lad that invites ye to talk. There are some that are, and that arena. Some will draw ye on, till ye've tellt them a' the clatter of the toun, and a' ye ken, and whiles mair. But Maister Roland, his mind's fu' of his books. He's aye civil and kind, and a fine lad; but no that sort. And ye see it's for a' our interest, Cornel, that you should stay at Brentwood. I took it upon me mysel to pass the word – 'No a syllable to Maister Roland, nor to the young leddies – no a syllable.' The women-servants, that have little reason to be out at night, ken little or nothing about it. And some think it grand to have a ghost so long as they're no in the way of coming across it. If you had been tellt the story to begin with, maybe ye would have thought so yoursel'."

This was true enough. I should not have been above the idea of a ghost myself! Oh, yes, I claim no exemption. The girls would have been delighted. I could fancy their eagerness, their interest, and excitement. No; if we had been told, it would have done no good – we should have made the bargain all the more eagerly, the fools that we are.

"Come with me, Jarvis," I said hastily, "and we'll make an attempt at least to investigate. Say nothing to the men or to anybody. Be ready for me about ten o'clock."

"Me, Cornel!" Jarvis said, in a faint voice. I had not been looking at him in my own preoccupation, but when I did so, I found that the greatest change had come over the fat and ruddy coachman. "Me, Cornel!" he repeated, wiping the perspiration from his brow. "There's nothin' I wouldna do to pleasure ye, Cornel, but if ye'll reflect that I am no used to my feet. With a horse atween my legs, or the reins in my hand, I'm maybe nae worse than other men;

but on fit, Cornel – it's no the – bogles; – but I've been cavalry, ye see," with a little hoarse laugh, "a' my life. To face a thing ye dinna understan' – on your feet, Cornel."

"He believes in it, Cornel, and you dinna believe in it," the woman said.

"Will you come with me?" I said, turning to her.

She jumped back, upsetting her chair in her bewilderment. "Me!" with a scream, and then fell into a sort of hysterical laugh. "I wouldna say but what I would go; but what would the folk say to hear of Cornel Mortimer with an auld silly woman at his heels?"

The suggestion made me laugh too, though I had little inclination for it. "I'm sorry you have so little spirit, Jarvis," I said. "I must find someone else, I suppose."

Jarvis, touched by this, began to remonstrate, but I cut him short. My butler was a soldier who had been with me in India, and was not supposed to fear anything – man or devil – certainly not the former; and I felt that I was losing time. The Jarvises were too thankful to get rid of me. They attended me to the door with the most anxious courtesies. Outside, the two grooms stood close by, a little confused by my sudden exit. I don't know if perhaps they had been listening – at least standing as near as possible, to catch any scrap of the conversation. I waved my hand to them as I went past, in answer to their salutations, and it was very apparent to me that they also were glad to see me go.

And it will be thought very strange, but it would be weak not to add, that I myself, though bent on the investigation I have spoken of, pledged to Roland to carry it out, and feeling that my boy's health, perhaps his life, depended on the result of my inquiry – I felt the most unaccountable reluctance, now that it was dark, to pass the ruins on my way home. My curiosity was intense; and yet it was all my mind could do to pull my body along. I dare say the scientific people would describe it the other way, and attribute my cowardice to the state of my stomach. I went on; but if I had followed my impulse, I should have turned and bolted. Everything in me seemed to cry out against it; my heart thumped, my pulses all began, like sledge-hammers, beating against my ears and every sensitive part. It was very dark, as I have said; the old house, with its shapeless tower, loomed a heavy mass through the darkness, which was only not entirely so solid as itself. On the other hand, the great dark cedars of which we were so proud seemed to fill up the night.

My foot strayed out of the path in my confusion and the gloom together, and I brought myself up with a cry as I felt myself knocked against something solid. What was it? The contact with hard stone and lime and prickly bramble-bushes restored me a little to myself. "Oh, it's only the old gable," I said aloud, with a little laugh to reassure myself. The rough feeling of the stones reconciled me. As I groped about thus, I shook off my visionary folly. What so easily explained as that I should have strayed from the path in the darkness? This brought me back to common existence, as if I had been shaken by a wise hand out of all the silliness of superstition. How silly it was, after all! What did it matter which path I took? I laughed again, this time with better heart, when suddenly, in a moment, the blood was chilled in my veins, a shiver stole along my spine, my faculties seemed to forsake me. Close by me, at my side, at my feet, there was a sigh. No, not a groan, not a moaning, not anything so tangible – a perfectly soft, faint, inarticulate sigh. I sprang back, and my heart stopped beating. Mistaken! no, mistake was impossible. I heard it as clearly as I hear myself speak; a long, soft, weary sigh, as if drawn to the utmost, and emptying out a load of sadness that filled the breast. To hear this in the solitude, in the dark, in the night (though it was still early), had an effect which I cannot describe. I feel it now – something cold creeping over me up into my hair, and down to my feet, which refused to move. I cried out, with a trembling voice, "Who is there?" as I had done before; but there was no reply.

I got home I don't quite know how; but in my mind there was no longer any indifference as to the thing, whatever it was, that haunted these ruins. My scepticism disappeared like a mist. I was as firmly determined that there was something as Roland was. I did not for a moment pretend to myself that it was possible I could be deceived; there were movements and noises which I understood all about – cracklings of small branches in the frost, and little rolls of gravel on the path, such as have a very eerie sound sometimes, and perplex you with wonder as to who has done it, *when there is no real mystery*; but I assure you all these little movements of nature don't affect you one bit *when there is something*. I understood *them*. I did not understand the sigh. That was not simple nature; there was meaning in it, feeling, the soul of a creature invisible. This is the thing that human nature trembles at – a creature invisible, yet with sensations, feelings, a power somehow of expressing itself. Bagley was in the hall as usual when I went in. He was always there in the afternoon, always with the appearance of perfect occupation, yet, so far as I know, never doing anything. The door was open, so that I hurried in without any pause, breathless; but the sight of his calm regard, as he came to help me off with my overcoat, subdued me in a moment. Anything out of the way, anything incomprehensible, faded to nothing in the presence of Bagley. You saw and wondered how *he* was made: the parting of his hair, the tie of his white neckcloth, the fit of his trousers, all perfect as works of art: but you could see how they were done, which makes all the difference. I flung myself upon him, so to speak, without waiting to note the extreme unlikeness of the man to anything of the kind I meant. "Bagley," I said, "I want you to come out with me tonight to watch for –"

"Poachers, Colonel?" he said, a gleam of pleasure running all over him.

"No, Bagley; a great deal worse," I cried.

"Yes, Colonel; at what hour, sir?" the man said; but then I had not told him what it was.

It was ten o'clock when we set out. All was perfectly quiet indoors. My wife was with Roland, who had been quite calm, she said, and who (though, no doubt, the fever must run its course) had been better ever since I came. I told Bagley to put on a thick greatcoat over his evening coat, and did the same myself, with strong boots; for the soil was like a sponge, or worse. Talking to him, I almost forgot what we were going to do. It was darker even than it had been before, and Bagley kept very close to me as we went along. I had a small lantern in my hand, which gave us a partial guidance. We had come to the corner where the path turns. On one side was the bowling-green, which the girls had taken possession of for their croquet-ground – a wonderful enclosure surrounded by high hedges of holly, three hundred years old and more; on the other, the ruins. Both were black as night; but before we got so far, there was a little opening in which we could just discern the trees and the lighter line of the road. I thought it best to pause there and take breath. "Bagley," I said, "there is something about these ruins I don't understand. It is there I am going. Keep your eyes open and your wits about you. Be ready to pounce upon any stranger you see – anything, man or woman. Don't hurt, but seize – anything you see."

"Colonel," said Bagley, with a little tremor in his breath, "they do say there's things there – as is neither man nor woman." There was no time for words. "Are you game to follow me, my man? that's the question," I said. Bagley fell in without a word, and saluted. I knew then I had nothing to fear.

We went, so far as I could guess, exactly as I had come, when I heard that sigh. The darkness, however, was so complete that all marks, as of trees or paths, disappeared. One moment we felt our feet on the gravel, another sinking noiselessly into the slippery grass, that was all. I had shut up my lantern, not wishing to scare anyone, whoever it might be. Bagley followed, it seemed to me, exactly in my footsteps as I made my way, as I supposed, towards the mass of the ruined house. We seemed to take a long time groping along seeking this; the squash of the wet soil under our feet was the only thing that marked our progress. After a while I stood still to see, or rather feel, where we were. The darkness was very still, but no stiller than is usual in a winter's night. The sounds I have mentioned – the crackling of twigs, the roll of a pebble, the sound of some rustle in the dead leaves, or creeping creature on the grass – were audible when you listened, all mysterious enough when your mind is disengaged, but to me cheering now as signs of the livingness of nature, even in the death of the frost. As we stood still there came up from the trees in the glen the prolonged hoot of an owl. Bagley started with alarm, being in a state of general nervousness, and not knowing what he was afraid of. But to me the sound was encouraging and pleasant, being so comprehensible. "An owl," I said, under my breath. "Y–es, Colonel," said Bagley, his teeth chattering. We stood still about five minutes, while it broke into the still brooding of the air, the sound widening out in circles, dying upon the darkness. This sound, which is not a cheerful one, made me almost gay. It was natural, and relieved the tension of the mind. I moved on with new courage, my nervous excitement calming down.

When all at once, quite suddenly, close to us, at our feet, there broke out a cry. I made a spring backwards in the first moment of surprise and horror, and in doing so came sharply against the same rough masonry and brambles that had struck me before. This new sound came upwards from the ground – a low, moaning, wailing voice, full of suffering and pain. The contrast between it and the hoot of the owl was indescribable – the one with a wholesome wildness and naturalness that hurt nobody; the other, a sound that made one's blood curdle, full of human misery. With a great deal of fumbling – for in spite of everything I could do to keep up my courage my hands shook – I managed to remove the slide of my lantern. The light leaped out like something living, and made the place visible in a moment. We were what would have been inside the ruined building had anything remained but the gable-wall which I have described. It was close to us, the vacant door-way in it going out straight into the blackness outside. The light showed the bit of wall, the ivy glistening upon it in clouds of dark green, the bramble-branches waving, and below, the open door – a door that led to nothing. It was from this the voice came which died out just as the light flashed upon this strange scene. There was a moment's silence, and then it broke forth again. The sound was so near, so penetrating, so pitiful, that, in the nervous start I gave, the light fell out of my hand. As I groped for it in the dark my hand was clutched by Bagley, who, I think, must have dropped upon his knees; but I was too much perturbed myself to think much of this. He clutched at me in the confusion of his terror, forgetting all his usual decorum. "For God's sake, what is it, sir?" he gasped. If I yielded, there was evidently an end of both of us. "I can't tell," I said, "any more than you; that's what we've got to find out. Up, man, up!" I pulled him to his feet. "Will you go round and examine the other side, or will you stay here with the lantern?" Bagley gasped at me with a face of horror. "Can't we stay together, Colonel?" he said; his knees were trembling under him. I pushed him against the corner of the wall, and put the light into his hands. "Stand fast till I come back; shake yourself together, man; let nothing pass you," I said. The voice was within two or three feet of us; of that there could be no doubt.

I went myself to the other side of the wall, keeping close to it. The light shook in Bagley's hand, but, tremulous though it was, shone out through the vacant door, one oblong block of light marking all the crumbling corners and hanging masses of foliage. Was that something dark huddled in a heap by the side of it? I pushed forward across the light in the door-way, and fell upon it with my hands; but it was only a juniper-bush growing close against the wall. Meanwhile, the sight of my figure crossing the door-way had brought Bagley's nervous excitement to a height; he flew at me, gripping my shoulder. "I've got him, Colonel! I've got him!" he cried, with a voice of sudden exultation. He thought it was a man, and was at once relieved. But at the moment the voice burst forth again between us, at our feet – more close to us than any separate being could be. He dropped off from me, and fell against the wall, his jaw dropping as if he were dying. I suppose, at the same moment, he saw that it was me whom he had clutched. I for my part, had scarcely more command of myself. I snatched the light out of his hand, and flashed it all about me wildly. Nothing – the juniper-bush which I thought I had never seen before, the heavy growth of the glistening ivy, the brambles waving. It was close to my ears now, crying, crying, pleading as if for life. Either I heard the same words Roland had heard, or else, in my excitement, his imagination got possession of mine. The voice went on, growing into distinct articulation, but wavering about, now from one point, now from another, as if the owner of it were moving slowly back and forward. "Mother! Mother!" and then an outburst of wailing. As my mind steadied, getting accustomed (as one's mind gets accustomed to anything), it seemed to me as if some uneasy, miserable creature was pacing up and down before a closed door. Sometimes – but that must have been excitement – I thought I heard a sound like knocking, and then another burst, "Oh, mother! Mother!" All this close, close to the space where I was standing with my lantern, now before me, now behind me: a creature restless, unhappy, moaning, crying, before the vacant door-way, which no one could either shut or open more.

"Do you hear it, Bagley? Do you hear what it is saying?" I cried, stepping in through the door-way. He was lying against the wall, his eyes glazed, half dead with terror. He made a motion of his lips as if to answer me, but no sounds came; then lifted his hand with a curious imperative movement as if ordering me to be silent and listen. And how long I did so I cannot tell. It began to have an interest, an exciting hold upon me, which I could not describe. It seemed to call up visibly a scene anyone could understand – a something shut out, restlessly wandering to and fro; sometimes the voice dropped, as if throwing itself down, sometimes wandered off a few paces, growing sharp and clear. "Oh, mother, let me in! Oh, mother, mother, let me in! Oh, let me in." Every word was clear to me. No wonder the boy had gone wild with pity. I tried to steady my mind upon Roland, upon his conviction that I could do something, but my head swam with the excitement, even when I partially overcame the terror. At last the words died away, and there was a sound of sobs and moaning. I cried out, "In the name of God who are you?" with a kind of feeling in my mind that to use the name of God was profane, seeing that I did not believe in ghosts or anything supernatural; but I did it all the same, and waited, my heart giving a leap of terror lest there should be a reply. Why this should have been I cannot tell, but I had a feeling that if there was an answer it would be more than I could bear. But there was no answer, the moaning went on, and then, as if it had been real, the voice rose a little higher again, the words recommenced, "Oh, mother, let me in! Oh, mother, let me in!" with an expression that was heart-breaking to hear.

As if it had been real! What do I mean by that? I suppose I got less alarmed as the thing went on. I began to recover the use of my senses – I seemed to explain it all to myself by saying that this had once happened, that it was a recollection of a real scene. Why there should have seemed something quite satisfactory and composing in this explanation I cannot tell, but so it was. I began to listen almost as if it had been a play, forgetting Bagley, who, I almost think, had fainted, leaning against the wall. I was started out of this strange spectatorship that had fallen upon me by the sudden rush of something which made my heart jump once more, a large black figure in the door-way waving its arms. "Come in! Come in! Come in!" it shouted out hoarsely at the top of a deep bass voice, and then poor Bagley fell down senseless across the threshold. He was less sophisticated than I – he had not been able to bear it any longer. I took him for something supernatural, as he took me, and it was some time before I awoke to the necessities of the moment. I remembered only after, that from the time I began to give my attention to the man, I heard the other voice no more. It was some time before I brought him to. It must have been a strange scene: the lantern making a luminous spot in the darkness, the man's white face lying on the black earth, I over him, doing what I could for him. Probably I should have been thought to be murdering him had anyone seen us. When at last I succeeded in pouring a little brandy down his throat, he sat up and looked about him wildly. "What's up?" he said; then recognizing me, tried to struggle to his feet with a faint "Beg your pardon, Colonel." I got him home as best I could, making him lean upon my arm. The great fellow was as weak as a child. Fortunately he did not for some time remember what had happened. From the time Bagley fell the voice had stopped, and all was still.

* * *

"You've got an epidemic in your house, Colonel," Simson said to me next morning. "What's the meaning of it all? Here's your butler raving about a voice. This will never do, you know; and so far as I can make out, you are in it too."

"Yes, I am in it, Doctor. I thought I had better speak to you. Of course you are treating Roland all right, but the boy is not raving, he is as sane as you or me. It's all true."

"As sane as – I – or you. I never thought the boy insane. He's got cerebral excitement, fever. I don't know what you've got. There's something very queer about the look of your eyes."

"Come," said I, "you can't put us all to bed, you know. You had better listen and hear the symptoms in full."

The Doctor shrugged his shoulders, but he listened to me patiently. He did not believe a word of the story, that was clear; but he heard it all from beginning to end. "My dear fellow," he said, "the boy told me just the same. It's an epidemic. When one person falls a victim to this sort of thing, it's as safe as can be – there's always two or three."

"Then how do you account for it?" I said.

"Oh, account for it! – That's a different matter; there's no accounting for the freaks our brains are subject to. If it's delusion, if it's some trick of the echoes or the winds – some phonetic disturbance or other –"

"Come with me tonight and judge for yourself," I said.

Upon this he laughed aloud, then said, "That's not such a bad idea; but it would ruin me forever if it were known that John Simson was ghost-hunting."

"There it is," said I; "you dart down on us who are unlearned with your phonetic disturbances, but you daren't examine what the thing really is for fear of being laughed at. That's science!"

"It's not science – it's common-sense," said the Doctor. "The thing has delusion on the front of it. It is encouraging an unwholesome tendency even to examine. What good could come of it? Even if I am convinced, I shouldn't believe."

"I should have said so yesterday; and I don't want you to be convinced or to believe," said I. "If you prove it to be a delusion, I shall be very much obliged to you for one. Come; somebody must go with me."

"You are cool," said the Doctor. "You've disabled this poor fellow of yours, and made him – on that point – a lunatic for life; and now you want to disable me. But, for once, I'll do it. To save appearance, if you'll give me a bed, I'll come over after my last rounds."

It was agreed that I should meet him at the gate, and that we should visit the scene of last night's occurrences before we came to the house, so that nobody might be the wiser. It was scarcely possible to hope that the cause of Bagley's sudden illness should not somehow steal into the knowledge of the servants at least, and it was better that all should be done as quietly as possible. The day seemed to me a very long one. I had to spend a certain part of it with Roland, which was a terrible ordeal for me, for what could I say to the boy? The improvement continued, but he was still in a very precarious state, and the trembling vehemence with which he turned to me when his mother left the room filled me with alarm. "Father?" he said quietly. "Yes, my boy, I am giving my best attention to it; all is being done that I can do. I have not come to any conclusion – yet. I am neglecting nothing you said," I cried. What I could not do was to give his active mind any encouragement to dwell upon the mystery. It was a hard predicament, for some satisfaction had to be given him. He looked at me very wistfully, with the great blue eyes which shone so large and brilliant out of his white and worn face. "You must trust me," I said. "Yes, father. Father understands," he said to himself, as if to soothe some inward doubt. I left him as soon as I could. He was about the most precious thing I had on earth, and his health my first thought; but yet somehow, in the excitement of this other subject, I put that aside, and preferred not to dwell upon Roland, which was the most curious part of it all.

That night at eleven I met Simson at the gate. He had come by train, and I let him in gently myself. I had been so much absorbed in the coming experiment that I passed the ruins in going to meet him, almost without thought, if you can understand that. I had my lantern; and he showed me a coil of taper which he had ready for use. "There is nothing like light," he said in his scoffing tone. It was a very still night, scarcely a sound, but not so dark. We could keep the path without difficulty as we went along. As we approached the spot we could hear a low moaning, broken occasionally by a bitter cry. "Perhaps that is your voice," said the Doctor; "I thought it must be something of the kind. That's a poor brute caught in some of these infernal traps of yours; you'll find it among the bushes somewhere." I said nothing. I felt no particular fear, but a triumphant satisfaction in what was to follow. I led him to the spot where Bagley and I had stood on the previous night. All was silent as a winter night could be – so silent that we heard far off the sound of the horses in the stables, the shutting of a window at the house. Simson lighted his taper and went peering about, poking into all the corners. We looked like two conspirators lying in wait for some unfortunate traveller; but not a sound broke the quiet. The moaning had stopped before we came up; a star or two shone over us in the sky, looking down as if surprised at our strange proceedings. Dr. Simson did nothing but utter subdued laughs under his breath. "I thought as much," he said. "It is just the same with tables and all other kinds of ghostly apparatus; a sceptic's presence stops everything. When I am present nothing ever comes off. How long do you think it will be necessary to stay here? Oh, I don't complain; only when *you* are satisfied I am – quite."

I will not deny that I was disappointed beyond measure by this result. It made me look like a credulous fool. It gave the Doctor such a pull over me as nothing else could. I should point all his morals for years to come; and his materialism, his scepticism, would be increased beyond endurance. "It seems, indeed," I said, "that there is to be no –"

"Manifestation," he said, laughing; "that is what all the mediums say. No manifestations, in consequence of the presence of an unbeliever." His laugh sounded very uncomfortable to me in the silence; and it was now near midnight. But that laugh seemed the signal; before it died away the moaning we had heard before was resumed. It started from some distance off, and came towards us, nearer and nearer, like someone walking along and moaning to himself. There could be no idea now that it was a hare caught in a trap. The approach was slow, like that of a weak person, with little halts and pauses. We heard it coming along the grass straight towards the vacant door-way. Simson had been a little startled by the first sound. He said hastily, "That child has no business to be out so late." But he felt, as well as I, that this was no child's voice.

As it came nearer, he grew silent, and, going to the door-way with his taper, stood looking out towards the sound. The taper being unprotected blew about in the night air, though there was scarcely any wind. I threw the light of my lantern steady and white across the same space. It was in a blaze of light in the midst of the blackness. A little icy thrill had gone over me at the first sound, but as it came close, I confess that my only feeling was satisfaction. The scoffer could scoff no more. The light touched his own face, and showed a very perplexed countenance. If he was afraid, he concealed it with great success, but he was perplexed. And then all that had happened on the previous night was enacted once more. It fell strangely upon me with a sense of repetition. Every cry, every sob seemed the same as before. I listened almost without any emotion at all in my own person, thinking of its effect upon Simson. He maintained a very bold front, on the whole. All that coming and going of the voice was, if our ears could be trusted, exactly in front of the vacant, blank door-way, blazing full of light, which caught and shone in the glistening leaves of the great hollies at a little distance. Not a rabbit could have crossed the turf without being seen; but there was nothing.

After a time, Simson, with a certain caution and bodily reluctance, as it seemed to me, went out with his roll of taper into this space. His figure showed against the holly in full outline. Just at this moment the voice sank, as was its custom, and seemed to fling itself down at the door. Simson recoiled violently, as if someone had come up against him, then turned, and held his taper low, as if examining something. "Do you see anybody?" I cried in a whisper, feeling the chill of nervous panic steal over me at this action. "It's nothing but a – confounded juniper-bush," he said. This I knew very well to be nonsense, for the juniper-bush was on the other side. He went about after this, round and round, poking his taper everywhere, then returned to me on the inner side of the wall. He scoffed no longer; his face was contracted and pale. "How long does this go on?" he whispered to me, like a man who does not wish to interrupt someone who is speaking. I had become too much perturbed myself to remark whether the successions and changes of the voice were the same as last night. It suddenly went out in the air almost as he was speaking, with a soft reiterated sob dying away. If there had been anything to be seen, I should have said that the person was at that moment crouching on the ground close to that door.

We walked home very silent afterwards. It was only when we were in sight of the house that I said, "What do you think of it?"

"I can't tell what to think of it," he said quickly. He took – though he was a very temperate man – not the claret I was going to offer him, but some brandy from the tray, and swallowed it almost undiluted. "Mind you, I don't believe a word of it," he said, when he had lighted his candle; "but I can't tell what to think," he turned round to add, when he was half-way upstairs.

All of this, however, did me no good with the solution of my problem. I was to help this weeping, sobbing thing, which was already to me as distinct a personality as anything I knew; or what should I say to Roland? It was on my heart that my boy would die if I could not find some way of helping this creature. You may be surprised that I should speak of it in this way. I did not know if it was man or woman; but I no more doubted that it was a soul in pain than I doubted my own being; and it was my business to soothe this pain – to deliver it, if that was possible. Was ever such a task given to an anxious father trembling for his only boy? I felt in my heart, fantastic as it may appear, that I must fulfil this somehow, or part with my child; and you may conceive that rather than do that I was ready to die. But even my dying would not have advanced me, unless by bringing me into the same world with that seeker at the door.

* * *

Next morning Simson was out before breakfast, and came in with evident signs of the damp grass on his boots, and a look of worry and weariness, which did not say much for the night he had passed. He improved a little after breakfast, and visited his two patients – for Bagley was still an invalid. I went out with him on his way to the train, to hear what he had to say about the boy. "He is going on very well," he said; "there are no complications as yet. But mind you, that's not a boy to be trifled with, Mortimer. Not a word to him about last night." I had to tell him then of my last interview with Roland, and of the impossible demand he had made upon me, by which, though he tried to laugh, he was much discomposed, as I could see. "We must just perjure ourselves all round," he said, "and swear you exorcised it"; but the man was too kind-hearted to be satisfied with that. "It's frightfully serious for you, Mortimer. I can't laugh as I should like to. I wish I saw a way out of it, for your sake. By the way," he added shortly, "didn't you notice that juniper-bush on the left-hand side?"

"There was one on the right hand of the door. I noticed you made that mistake last night."

"Mistake!" he cried, with a curious low laugh, pulling up the collar of his coat as though he felt the cold – "There's no juniper there this morning, left or right. Just go and see." As he stepped into the train a few minutes after, he looked back upon me and beckoned me for a parting word. "I'm coming back tonight," he said.

I don't think I had any feeling about this as I turned away from that common bustle of the railway which made my private preoccupations feel so strangely out of date. There had been a distinct satisfaction in my mind before, that his scepticism had been so entirely defeated. But the more serious part of the matter pressed upon me now. I went straight from the railway to the manse, which stood on a little plateau on the side of the river opposite to the woods of Brentwood. The minister was one of a class which is not so common in Scotland as it used to be. He was a man of good family, well educated in the Scotch way, strong in philosophy, not so strong in Greek, strongest of all in experience – a man who had 'come across', in the course of his life, most people of note that had ever been in Scotland, and who was said to be very sound in doctrine, without infringing the toleration with which old men, who are good men, are generally endowed. He was old-fashioned; perhaps he did not think so much about the troublous problems of theology as many of the young men, nor ask himself any hard questions about the Confession of Faith; but he understood human nature, which is perhaps better. He received me with a cordial welcome. "Come away, Colonel Mortimer," he said; "I'm all the more glad to see you, that I feel it's a good sign for the boy. He's doing well? – God be praised – and the Lord bless him and keep him. He has many a poor body's prayers, and that can do nobody harm."

"He will need them all, Dr. Moncrieff," I said, "and your counsel, too." And I told him the story – more than I had told Simson. The old clergyman listened to me with many suppressed exclamations, and at the end the water stood in his eyes.

"That's just beautiful," he said. "I do not mind to have heard anything like it; it's as fine as Burns when he wished deliverance to one – that is prayed for in no kirk. Ay, ay! So he would have you console the poor lost spirit? God bless the boy! There's something more than common in that, Colonel Mortimer. And also the faith of him in his father! – I would like to put that into a sermon." Then the old gentleman gave me an alarmed look, and said, "No, no; I was not meaning a sermon; but I must write it down for the 'Children's Record'." I saw the thought that passed through his mind. Either he thought, or he feared I would think, of a funeral sermon. You may believe this did not make me more cheerful.

I can scarcely say that Dr. Moncrieff gave me any advice. How could anyone advise on such a subject? But he said, "I think I'll come too. I'm an old man; I'm less liable to be frightened than those that are further off the world unseen. It behooves me to think of my own journey there. I've no cut-and-dry beliefs on the subject. I'll come too; and maybe at the moment the Lord will put into our heads what to do."

This gave me a little comfort – more than Simson had given me. To be clear about the cause of it was not my grand desire. It was another thing that was in my mind – my boy. As for the poor soul at the open door, I had no more doubt, as I have said, of its existence than I had of my own. It was no ghost to me. I knew the creature, and it was in trouble. That was my feeling about it, as it was Roland's. To hear it first was a great shock to my nerves, but not now; a man will get accustomed to anything. But to do something for it was the great problem; how was I to be serviceable to a being that was invisible, that was mortal no longer? "Maybe at the moment the Lord will put it into our heads." This is very old-fashioned phraseology, and a week before, most likely, I should have smiled (though always with kindness) at Dr. Moncrieff's credulity; but there was a great comfort, whether rational or otherwise I cannot say, in the mere sound of the words.

The road to the station and the village lay through the glen, not by the ruins; but though the sunshine and the fresh air, and the beauty of the trees, and the sound of the water were all very soothing to the spirits, my mind was so full of my own subject that I could not refrain from turning to the right hand as I got to the top of the glen, and going straight to the place which I may call the scene of all my thoughts. It was lying full in the sunshine, like all the rest of the world. The ruined gable looked due east, and in the present aspect of the sun the light streamed down through the door-way as our lantern had done, throwing a flood of light upon the damp grass beyond. There was a strange suggestion in the open door – so futile, a kind of emblem of vanity: all free around, so that you could go where you pleased, and yet that semblance of an enclosure – that way of entrance, unnecessary, leading to nothing. And why any creature should pray and weep to get in – to nothing, or be kept out – by nothing! You could not dwell upon it, or it made your brain go round. I remembered, however, what Simson said about the juniper, with a little smile on my own mind as to the inaccuracy of recollection which even a scientific man will be guilty of. I could see now the light of my lantern gleaming upon the wet glistening surface of the spiky leaves at the right hand – and he ready to go to the stake for it that it was the left! I went round to make sure.

And then I saw what he had said. Right or left there was no juniper at all! I was confounded by this, though it was entirely a matter of detail: nothing at all – a bush of brambles waving, the grass growing up to the very walls. But after all, though it gave me a shock for a moment, what did that matter? There were marks as if a number of footsteps had been up and down in front of the door, but these might have been our steps; and all was bright and peaceful and still. I poked about the other ruin – the larger ruins of the old house – for some time, as I had done before. There were marks upon the grass here and there – I could not call them footsteps – all about; but that told for nothing one way or another. I had examined the ruined rooms closely the first day. They were half-filled up with soil and debris, withered brackens and bramble – no refuge for anyone there. It vexed me that Jarvis should see me coming from that spot when he came up to me for his orders. I don't know whether my nocturnal expeditions had got wind among the servants. But there was a significant look in his face. Something in it I felt was like my own sensation when Simson in the midst of his scepticism was struck dumb. Jarvis felt satisfied that his veracity had been put beyond question. I never spoke to a servant of mine in such a peremptory tone before. I sent him away 'with a flea in his lug', as the man described it afterwards. Interference of any kind was intolerable to me at such a moment.

But what was strangest of all was, that I could not face Roland. I did not go up to his room, as I would have naturally done, at once. This the girls could not understand. They saw there was some mystery in it. "Mother has gone to lie down," Agatha said; "he has had such a good night."

"But he wants you so, papa!" cried little Jeanie, always with her two arms embracing mine in a pretty way she had. I was obliged to go at last, but what could I say? I could only kiss him, and tell him to keep still – that I was doing all I could. There is something mystical about the patience of a child. "It will come all right, won't it, father?" he said. "God grant it may! I hope so, Roland."

"Oh, yes, it will come all right." Perhaps he understood that in the midst of my anxiety I could not stay with him as I should have done otherwise. But the girls were more surprised than it is possible to describe. They looked at me with wondering eyes. "If I were ill, papa, and you only stayed with me a moment, I should break my heart," said Agatha. But the boy had a sympathetic feeling. He knew that of my own will I would not have done it. I shut myself up in the library, where I could not rest, but kept pacing up and down like a caged beast. What could I do? And if I could do nothing, what would become of my boy? These were the questions that, without ceasing, pursued each other through my mind.

Simson came out to dinner, and when the house was all still, and most of the servants in bed, we went out and met Dr. Moncrieff, as we had appointed, at the head of the glen. Simson, for his part, was disposed to scoff at the Doctor. "If there are to be any spells, you know, I'll cut the whole concern," he said. I did not make him any reply. I had not invited him; he could go or come as he pleased. He was very talkative, far more so than suited my humour, as we went on. "One thing is certain, you know; there must be some human agency," he said. "It is all bosh about apparitions. I never have investigated the laws of sound to any great extent, and there's a great deal in ventriloquism that we don't know much about."

"If it's the same to you," I said, "I wish you'd keep all that to yourself, Simson. It doesn't suit my state of mind."

"Oh, I hope I know how to respect idiosyncrasy," he said. The very tone of his voice irritated me beyond measure. These scientific fellows, I wonder people put up with them as they do, when you have no mind for their cold-blooded confidence.

Dr. Moncrieff met us about eleven o'clock, the same time as on the previous night. He was a large man, with a venerable countenance and white hair – old, but in full vigour, and thinking less of a cold night walk than many a younger man. He had his lantern, as I had. We were fully provided with means of lighting the place, and we were all of us resolute men. We had a rapid consultation as we went up, and the result was that we divided to different posts. Dr. Moncrieff remained inside the wall – if you can call that inside where there was no wall but one. Simson placed himself on the side next the ruins, so as to intercept any communication with the old house, which was what his mind was fixed upon. I was posted on the other side. To say that nothing could come near without being seen was self-evident. It had been so also on the previous night. Now, with our three lights in the midst of the darkness, the whole place seemed illuminated. Dr. Moncrieff's lantern, which was a large one, without any means of shutting up – an old-fashioned lantern with a pierced and ornamental top – shone steadily, the rays shooting out of it upward into the gloom. He placed it on the grass, where the middle of the room, if this had been a room, would have been. The usual effect of the light streaming out of the door-way was prevented by the illumination which Simson and I on either side supplied. With these differences, everything seemed as on the previous night.

And what occurred was exactly the same, with the same air of repetition, point for point, as I had formerly remarked. I declare that it seemed to me as if I were pushed against, put aside, by the owner of the voice as he paced up and down in his trouble – though these are perfectly futile words, seeing that the stream of light from my lantern, and that from Simson's taper, lay broad and clear, without a shadow, without the smallest break, across the entire breadth of the grass. But just as it threw itself sobbing at the door (I cannot use other words), there suddenly came something which sent the blood coursing through my veins, and my heart into my mouth. It was a voice inside the wall – my minister's well-known voice. I would have been prepared for it in any kind of adjuration, but I was not prepared for what I heard. It came out with a sort of stammering, as if too much moved for utterance. "Willie, Willie! Oh, God preserve us! Is it you?"

I made a dash round to the other side of the wall. The old minister was standing where I had left him, his shadow thrown vague and large upon the grass by the lantern which stood at his feet. I lifted my own light to see his face. He was very pale, his eyes wet and glistening, his mouth quivering with parted lips. He neither saw nor heard me. His whole being seemed absorbed in anxiety and tenderness. He held out his hands, which trembled, but it seemed to me with eagerness, not fear. He went on speaking all the time. "Willie, if it is you – and it's you, if it is not a delusion of Satan – Willie, lad! Why come ye here frighting them that know you not? Why came ye not to me? Your mother's gone with your name on her lips. Do you think she would ever close her door on her own lad? Do ye think the Lord will close the door, ye faint-hearted creature? No! – I forbid ye! I forbid ye!" cried the old man. The sobbing voice had begun to resume its cries. He made a step forward, calling out the last words in a voice of command. "I forbid ye! Cry out no more to man. Go home, ye wandering spirit! Go home! Do you hear me? – Me that christened ye, that have struggled with ye, that have wrestled for ye with the Lord!" Here the loud tones of his voice sank into tenderness. "And her too, poor woman! Poor woman! Her you are calling upon. She's no here. You'll find her with the Lord. Go there and seek her, not here. Do you hear me, lad? Go after her there. He'll let you in, though it's late. Man, take heart! If you will lie and sob and greet, let it be at heaven's gate, and no your poor mother's ruined door."

He stopped to get his breath; and the voice had stopped, not as it had done before, when its time was exhausted and all its repetitions said, but with a sobbing catch in the breath as if overruled. Then the minister spoke again, "Are you hearing me, Will? Oh, laddie, you've liked the beggarly elements all your days. Be done with them now. Go home to the Father – the Father! Are you hearing me?" Here the old man sank down upon his knees, his face raised upwards, his hands held up with a tremble in them, all white in the light in the midst of the darkness. I resisted as long as I could, though I cannot tell why; then I, too, dropped upon my knees. Simson all the time stood in the door-way, with an expression in his face such as words could not tell, his under lip dropped, his eyes wild, staring. It seemed to be to him, that image of blank ignorance and wonder, that we were praying. All the time the voice, with a low arrested sobbing, lay just where he was standing, as I thought.

"Lord," the minister said – "Lord, take him into Thy everlasting habitations. The mother he cries to is with Thee. Who can open to him but Thee? Lord, when is it too late for Thee, or what is too hard for Thee? Lord, let that woman there draw him inower! Let her draw him inower!"

I sprang forward to catch something in my arms that flung itself wildly within the door. The illusion was so strong, that I never paused till I felt my forehead graze against the wall and my hands clutch the ground – for there was nobody there to save from falling, as in my foolishness I thought. Simson held out his hand to me to help me up. He was trembling and cold, his lower lip hanging, his speech almost inarticulate. "It's gone," he said, stammering – "it's gone!"

As long as I live I will never forget the shining of the strange lights, the blackness all round, the kneeling figure with all the whiteness of the light concentrated on its white venerable head and uplifted hands. I never knew how long we stood, like sentinels guarding him at his prayers. But at last the old minister rose from his knees, and standing up at his full height, raised his arms, as the Scotch manner is at the end of a religious service, and solemnly gave the apostolical benediction – to what? To the silent earth, the dark woods, the wide breathing atmosphere; for we were but spectators gasping an Amen!

It seemed to me that it must be the middle of the night, as we all walked back. It was in reality very late. Dr. Moncrieff himself was the first to speak. "I must be going," he said; "I will go down the glen, as I came."

"But not alone. I am going with you, Doctor."

"Well, I will not oppose it. I am an old man, and agitation wearies more than work. Yes; I'll be thankful of your arm. Tonight, Colonel, you've done me more good turns than one."

I pressed his hand on my arm, not feeling able to speak. But Simson, who turned with us, and who had gone along all this time with his taper flaring, in entire unconsciousness, became himself, sceptical and cynical. "I should like to ask you a question," he said. "Do you believe in Purgatory, Doctor? It's not in the tenets of the Church, so far as I know."

"Sir," said Dr. Moncrieff, "an old man like me is sometimes not very sure what he believes. There is just one thing I am certain of – and that is the loving-kindness of God."

"But I thought that was in this life. I am no theologian –"

"Sir," said the old man again, with a tremor in him which I could feel going over all his frame, "if I saw a friend of mine within the gates of hell, I would not despair but his Father would take him by the hand still, if he cried like *you*."

"I allow it is very strange, very strange. I cannot see through it. That there must be human agency, I feel sure. Doctor, what made you decide upon the person and the name?"

The minister put out his hand with the impatience which a man might show if he were asked how he recognized his brother. "Tuts!" he said, in familiar speech; then more solemnly, "How should I not recognize a person that I know better – far better – than I know you?"

"Then you saw the man?"

Dr. Moncrieff made no reply. He moved his hand again with a little impatient movement, and walked on, leaning heavily on my arm. We parted with him at his own door, where his old housekeeper appeared in great perturbation, waiting for him. "Eh, me, minister! The young gentleman will be worse?" she cried.

"Far from that – better. God bless him!" Dr. Moncrieff said.

I think if Simson had begun again to me with his questions, I should have pitched him over the rocks as we returned up the glen; but he was silent, by a good inspiration. And the sky was clearer than it had been for many nights, shining high over the trees, with here and there a star faintly gleaming through the wilderness of dark and bare branches. We went up to the boy's room when we went in. There we found the complete hush of rest. My wife looked up out of a doze, and gave me a smile; "I think he is a great deal better; but you are very late," she said in a whisper, shading the light with her hand that the Doctor might see his patient. The boy had got back something like his own colour. He woke as we stood all round his bed. His eyes had the happy, half-awakened look of childhood, glad to shut again, yet pleased with the interruption and glimmer of the light. I stooped over him and kissed his forehead, which was moist and cool. "All is well, Roland," I said. He looked up at me with a glance of pleasure, and took my hand and laid his cheek upon it, and so went to sleep.

* * *

For some nights after, I watched among the ruins, spending all the dark hours up to midnight patrolling about the bit of wall which was associated with so many emotions; but I heard nothing, and saw nothing beyond the quiet course of nature; nor, so far as I am aware, has anything been heard again. Dr. Moncrieff gave me the history of the youth, whom he never hesitated to name. I did not ask, as Simson did, how he recognized him. He had been a prodigal – weak, foolish, easily imposed upon, and 'led away', as people say. All that we had heard had passed actually in life, the Doctor said. The young man had come home thus a day or two after his mother died – who was no more than housekeeper in the old house – and distracted with the news, had thrown himself down at the door and called upon her to let him in. The old man could scarcely speak of it for tears. He was not terrified, as I had been myself, and all the rest of us. It was no 'ghost', as I fear we all vulgarly considered it, to him – but a poor creature whom he knew under these conditions, just as he had known him in the flesh, having no doubt of his identity. And to Roland it was the same. This spirit in pain – if it was a spirit – this voice out of the unseen – was a poor fellow-creature in misery, to be succoured and helped out of his trouble, to my boy. He spoke to me quite frankly about it when he got better. "I knew father would find out some way," he said. And this was when he was strong and well, and all idea that he would turn hysterical or become a seer of visions had happily passed away.

* * *

I must add one curious fact, which does not seem to me to have any relation to the above, but which Simson made great use of, as the human agency which he was determined to find somehow. One Sunday afternoon Simson found a little hole – for it was more a hole than a room – entirely hidden under the ivy and ruins, in which there was a quantity of straw laid in a corner, as if someone had made a bed there, and some remains of crusts about the floor. Someone had lodged there, and not very long before, he made out; and that this unknown being was the author of all the mysterious sounds we heard he is convinced. "I was puzzled myself – I could not make it out – but I always felt convinced human agency was at the bottom of it. And here it is – and a clever fellow he must have been," the Doctor says. There is no argument with men of this kind.

Bagley left my service as soon as he got well. He assured me it was no want of respect, but he could not stand 'them kind of things'; and the man was so shaken and ghastly that I was glad to give him a present and let him go. For my own part, I made a point of staying out the time – two years – for which I had taken Brentwood; but I did not renew my tenancy. By that time we had settled, and found for ourselves a pleasant home of our own.

I must add, that when the Doctor defies me, I can always bring back gravity to his countenance, and a pause in his railing, when I remind him of the juniper-bush. To me that was a matter of little importance. I could believe I was mistaken. I did not care about it one way or other; but on his mind the effect was different. The miserable voice, the spirit in pain, he could think of as the result of ventriloquism, or reverberation, or – anything you please: an elaborate prolonged hoax, executed somehow by the tramp that had found a lodging in the old tower; but the juniper-bush staggered him. Things have effects so different on the minds of different men.

Orpheus and Eurydice
A Retelling of the Myth from Ovid's Metamorphoses

THE MUSIC OF ORPHEUS was known across the lands. With his lyre, he played the sweetest strains which lulled even the fiercest beasts into a peaceful rapture. For his music Orpheus was loved, and he travelled far and wide, issuing forth melodies that were pure, sublime.

Orpheus was the son of Apollo and the muse Calliope. He lived in Thrace and spent his days singing, playing the music that spread his fame still further. One day, Orpheus came across a gentle and very beautiful young nymph, who danced to his music as if she was born to do so. She was called Eurydice, and wings seemed to lift her heels, as she played and frolicked to his music. And then, when their eyes caught, it was clear that it was love at first sight and that their destiny was to be shared.

It was only a few days later that they were joined in marriage, and never before had such an angelic couple existed. As they danced on the eve of their wedding, the very trees and flowers, the winds and rushing streams paused and then shouted their congratulations. The world stopped to watch, to approve, to celebrate.

And then that most sinister of animals, a stealthy viper, made its way into the babbling midst and struck at the ankle of Eurydice, sending her to an icy, instant death. Eurydice sank down in the circle, and all efforts to revive her failed. Time seemed to stop. Certainly there was no music, anywhere.

Orpheus was disconsolate with grief. He could not even bring himself to bury her, and he played on his lyre such tunes that even the rocks, the hardened fabric of the caves, shed tears. After several days he came to a decision which seemed at once as clear and as necessary as anything he had ever undertaken.

Orpheus made his way to the Underworld, determined to rescue his great love. His lyre in hand, his heart pounding with emotion, he reached the river Styx, the black waterway which snakes its way into the Underworld, which divides the other world from our own. There he played his lute so tunefully, so eloquently, that Charon, the ferryman, took him across the river at no charge, granted access to a place into which no mortal must go.

As Orpheus was drawn deeper into the Underworld, grisly, frightening sights greeted his eyes, but he continued to play his soulful tune, filling with tears the eyes of those cast in wretched purgatory, the ghosts of beings who had done ill deeds, the spirits of men who had been cursed. He played on and on, his music seeping into the blackness and creating an effortless light which guided the way.

At the end of his journey King Hades and Queen Persephone sat, entranced by his music. They knew of his mission. They would allow him to take Eurydice. His music had unwound the rigours of their rules, of their laws, and momentarily appeased, temporarily relaxed, they permitted Orpheus to take one of their own.

There was a condition, as there is in all such matters. Orpheus could have his bride returned to him; she would follow him as his shadow. But he must not look back on his trip from their world. The music from Orpheus' lyre picked up the timbre of his pleasure and took on a jaunty character which brought a look of surprise to the stony faces of Hades' guards. Orpheus turned and made his way back to the Styx, to his world, to home and Eurydice.

The gate of the Underworld was in sight when Orpheus felt an overwhelming need to confirm that Eurydice was there. Instinctively, he turned towards his great love, and there she stood, shrouded in a dark cape. As he reached for her, just as he felt the warmth of her skin, her breath on his cheek, she vanished, drawn back into death, into the darkened world of the afterlife.

Orpheus left the Underworld alone, and when he returned to his land, he lay broken and wasted on the shores of the Styx. For the rest of his short life he wandered among the hills, carrying a broken lyre which he would not mend and could not play. He cared for nothing. He was attacked, one day, without the powers to play, to appease his enemy. His attackers were a throng of Thracian women who killed him, and tore him to pieces. His lyre was taken to Lesbos, where it became a shrine, and some years later, his head was washed upon the shores of the island. There it was joined with his sacred lyre, its broken strings representing forever the broken heart of Orpheus.

The Phone Call

Michael Penncavage

I PLACE my empty tumbler onto the bar.

"You want another?" Peter asks as he takes a final swig from his bottle.

"Sure." I loosen my tie and lean up against the edge of the bar. "Tell me again why we are here?"

"To cheer you up."

I glance down at the running tab. "If you think ten dollar mix drinks are going to make me happy, you have another thing coming."

Peter leans over to me and mumbles, "Not the drinks. The company."

I glance around. We're at an Upper West Side bar and the pretty people are out in force. "Sorry, Doctor Love. I'm not in the mood."

Peter motions to the bartender for another bottle. "If not tonight, when? No disrespect, but it's going on two years since she died."

"So?" I look at my reflection in the mirror behind the bar. The hair seems a little grayer, the cheeks a little more sullen.

"Kate wouldn't have wanted for you to be alone."

"I'm sure she wouldn't. But if I don't feel like dating, then I don't feel like dating. Even if it's with someone you are trying to set me up with."

"It's only a blind date," he answers. "Maria's a nice girl. Dinner. Drink. No sparks, no problem. It's adios before midnight." Peter takes a moment to size up a brunette at the other end of the bar before turning to me. "Well, I suppose I wouldn't feel like dating either if I put in 80 hour work weeks."

"Hey, there's a lot of shit going on there. It's not like I can help it."

"Oh, no. Of course not. The fate of the 6 billion in annual revenues falls squarely on your shoulders."

"Touché. Bad excuse." I take a sip from my fresh glass. "I don't know, Peter. This dating thing; it just feels weird. I know this might sound strange, but sometimes when I am in the apartment, it feels like she is still there with me."

"Well of course it does, John. Let me ask you – have you gotten rid of any of her stuff since she died?"

"No."

"All of those personal effects that you surround yourself with, it's no wonder you feel like she is around."

"I haven't had the need to make extra room."

"I think you should. You really need to start putting her behind you. It's the only way."

* * *

My cell-phone tweets as I walk into the apartment. Work. Peterson from New Business. I glanced at my watch. 11:10 p.m. Another tweet.

"Damn-it!" It tweets again in defiance. I unhook the battery and toss the phone onto the counter. Peterson will have to wait until the morning.

I take two aspirin. My head hurts and a foul taste is in my mouth. Damn alcohol. I feel like shit.

I click on the television. *Charlie Rose* is on and he is interviewing some no-name politician who is explaining how he can eliminate the deficit. The apartment phone begins to ring.

"Son of a…" I reach for the cordless. If it's Peterson he's a dead-man.

"Hello?"

"Oh, I'm sorry." Not Peterson. A woman's voice instead. "I dialed the wrong number."

"No problem." I click off the phone and turn back to *Charlie Rose*. Before I can grab the remote the phone rings again.

"Hello?"

"Uh, sorry. It's me. I seem to have misdialed again."

"What number are you trying to reach?"

"555-6269."

"That's me. What about the area code?"

"212."

"Sorry. It looks like you wrote down the wrong number."

"No. I don't think that is possible. This is my phone number. I was calling in for my messages."

I mute *Charlie Rose*. "I guess the phone-company screwed up by giving you a number that already exists."

"I've had this number for quite some time."

"As have I." My headache continues to paramount. It's late and thoughts of having to get up early to deal with Peterson makes my patience run out. "Listen. This is probably just some sort of weird case of the telephone lines getting crossed. I'm sure in the morning it will all be fixed." Nut case.

Silence on the other end for a moment. "Perhaps I should get your name, if you don't mind."

"Why?"

"In case your charges end up on my bill. I can have the phone-company fix them so you can get charged."

"Well, gee, thanks." I chuckle. "Fine. My names John. John Bentonn. With two n's at the end."

"Is that supposed to be some sort of joke?"

"Excuse me?"

"Who is this?"

"I just told you. Listen, I don't mean to be rude, but it's late and I'm…"

"Where are you right now?"

"I'm sorry? I'm not following you."

"Oh my god. You're *there*. I'm calling the police."

"Police?" I begin rubbing my temple. "Well, considering you have no idea where I live I suppose you can call whoever you want."

"1514 East 45th Street. 24th Floor. Apartment 2423."

I sit up so quickly my glass flies off the coffee table, sending water across the floor. "How did you know that?"

"Because that is where I live! You're trespassing in my apartment and I'm calling 911!"

"You go do that! When they arrive I'll be sure to show them the lease with my name on it!"

Her voice began to shake. "How dare you break into my apartment, pretending to be my late husband!"

"Who is this?"

"Kate. Kate Bentonn."

"Really? So who's playing games now? You accuse me of being your dead husband, yet now you tell me you're my dead wife! Why don't you just hang up and wander back to whatever mental ward they let you out of!"

"That's not funny. You're a sick man! First you tell me you're my husband and then you claim *I'm* supposed to be dead!"

"My wife *is* dead! She was killed in a car accident when our truck went off the road and wrapped itself around a tree!" I'm so angry sweat begins to trickle down my shirt.

"Really? So I guess the doctors that pronounced you dead were all wrong?"

"Lady, I'm *really* getting tired of listening to your nonsense!" My head is throbbing. I begin to hang up, but decide to end this another way so that hopefully she won't call back. "If you're my wife, what nickname did she call me? Only Kate knew that."

"Nookums"

I lean against the wall for support. "How…did…you…know…that?" I hear her breathing heavily on the other end. A minute passes, maybe more. "Ask me a question."

"This is ridiculous," she says.

"Go on. Ask me something."

"All right, on our first date, something happened that made you very embarrassed."

"I knocked the table over in the restaurant." Words begin spewing from my mouth. "You ordered a Caesar Salad. I got a Rueben. Afterwards we went to see a wretched movie with Kurt Douglas."

"In a theater that the lights kept flashing on and off." The room is spinning. My legs buckle and I slump to the floor. *I must be dreaming. I fell asleep watching Charlie Rose. Talking about Kate with Peter has caused me to have some sort of delusional dream.*

The clock above the television reads 11:45 p.m. Charlie is interviewing Brad Pitt. I change the channel. Letterman is chatting with Val Kilmer. *Were dreams normally this vivid?*

"Are you still there?"

"Yes."

"If you're really my husband tell me something else. Something only he would know."

I do, telling her about the places we vacationed, restaurants we dined, places we made love.

"John, if it is you, how is this possible?"

"I…don't know."

"Where are you?"

"I told you. I'm in the apartment."

Another pause. "I've been in a taxi talking on my cell-phone this whole time."

I interpret what she is saying. "You're at the building?"

"Yes. In the lobby."

I go to the door and flip the tumbler. "Door's open."

"I'm in the elevator," I hear her say.

The reality of the situation hits me. My dead wife is stopping by to visit me. A golf ball forms in my throat. *Was I losing my mind? What sort of psychopath might be coming through the door?* As I'm walking over to the door I hear her through the telephone.

"Where are you?"

"What?" I flip the lock.

"I'm here. In the hallway. Why was the door locked? And why are the lights out?"

"What room are you in?" I instinctively whirl around towards the kitchen, as if she would have been able to pass me in the narrow hallway. "I don't see you."

"I'm in the living room," she answers.

From where I am standing I can look into that room. "Really? Where? Under the sofa?"

"By the windowsill. The one with the gouge from when you dropped the paperweight onto it."

I walk over to the window and place my hand on the frame. The wood is smooth and unblemished. "I had the scrape fixed a year ago when the windows were replaced."

"What are you talking about? The windows haven't been replaced. They're still the same old drafty ones we've always had."

The window looks out over the park. I stare at the trees for a moment, saying nothing. *Those comments. How would anyone else know?* I try to make some sense of it all.

"John?"

"Yes."

"How is this possible? How can I be talking to you?"

"I'm not sure, Kate. I think it might have something to do with the accident. Somehow you died and I lived. But at the same time I died and you lived."

Kate chuckles and I can almost visualize the smile on her face. "You sound ridiculous. For all I know this can all be some sort of wild prank. At any moment I'm expecting someone to jump out of hiding and tell me I'm on *Candid Camera*."

To the left of me the floor creaks softy. *Perhaps a building settling?* A shadow flashes across the wall. *A passing car?*

We talk and the conversation becomes a mix of updates and trivia as if we are trying to debunk each other. We both fail.

"How do you explain the telephone call, Kate?"

"I can't. Some sort of weird, passing interference, I guess."

"If you're right then when we hang up..."

"I think you know the answer to that." I sit down on the couch. "Well, I suppose I just won't hang up then. We can continue our marriage via telephone."

She giggles again.

A thought pops into my head. "Are you seeing anyone?"

"Yes."

"Is it serious?"

"We've only been dating for a few months."

"Oh."

"How about yourself?"

"No."

"John, I..."

"Kate, you don't need to explain yourself."

"I feel guilty."

"Don't be ridiculous. Listen to me. Once we hang up it will be as if none of this happened."

"But, John..."

"Does this guy treat you right?"

"Yes."

"Well, then, don't let this ruin that. All right?"

Silence for a moment. "What about you?"

"What about me?"

"We were married for eleven years. I have a pretty good idea of how you must be treating yourself."

"It's been difficult, Kate."

"I know it has. But I want you to find someone, John. You deserve happiness. I want you to do it. For me."

I don't answer.

"Promise me."

"I can't promise something like that."

"I want you to go out and meet people. I want you to try."

"All right. I promise."

"I love you, John."

"I love you, too. Goodbye, Kate."

"Goodbye."

Before I can second-guess myself, I press the power button. I wait a moment, thinking it is going to start ringing again. But it doesn't.

She's gone.

The phone slips from my hand.

My head is still throbbing so I take two more Tylenol and head off to bed.

The following day I call the Salvation Army and make an appointment to have them come by. A week later all of Kate's stuff, with the exception of two crates, are gone.

A month later I finally get around to having Peter set me up on the blind date with Maria.

The seasons change. I no longer hear any creaks in the floor nor spot any fleeting shadows.

And I never get the phone call again.

Morella

Edgar Allan Poe

'Itself, by itself, solely, one everlasting, and single.'
Plato, Sympos

WITH A FEELING of deep yet most singular affection I regarded my friend Morella. Thrown by accident into her society many years ago, my soul from our first meeting burned with fires it had never before known; but the fires were not of Eros, and bitter and tormenting to my spirit was the gradual conviction that I could in no manner define their unusual meaning or regulate their vague intensity. Yet we met; and fate bound us together at the altar, and I never spoke of passion nor thought of love. She, however, shunned society, and, attaching herself to me alone rendered me happy. It is a happiness to wonder; it is a happiness to dream.

Morella's erudition was profound. As I hope to live, her talents were of no common order – her powers of mind were gigantic. I felt this, and, in many matters, became her pupil. I soon, however, found that, perhaps on account of her Presburg education, she placed before me a number of those mystical writings which are usually considered the mere dross of the early German literature. These, for what reason I could not imagine, were her favourite and constant study – and that in process of time they became my own, should be attributed to the simple but effectual influence of habit and example.

In all this, if I err not, my reason had little to do. My convictions, or I forget myself, were in no manner acted upon by the ideal, nor was any tincture of the mysticism which I read to be discovered, unless I am greatly mistaken, either in my deeds or in my thoughts. Persuaded of this, I abandoned myself implicitly to the guidance of my wife, and entered with an unflinching heart into the intricacies of her studies. And then – then, when poring over forbidden pages, I felt a forbidden spirit enkindling within me – would Morella place her cold hand upon my own, and rake up from the ashes of a dead philosophy some low, singular words, whose strange meaning burned themselves in upon my memory. And then, hour after hour, would I linger by her side, and dwell upon the music of her voice, until at length its melody was tainted with terror, and there fell a shadow upon my soul, and I grew pale, and shuddered inwardly at those too unearthly tones. And thus, joy suddenly faded into horror, and the most beautiful became the most hideous, as Hinnon became Ge-Henna.

It is unnecessary to state the exact character of those disquisitions which, growing out of the volumes I have mentioned, formed, for so long a time, almost the sole conversation of Morella and myself. By the learned in what might be termed theological morality they will be readily conceived, and by the unlearned they would, at all events, be little understood. The wild Pantheism of Fichte; the modified Paliggenedia of the Pythagoreans; and, above all, the doctrines of Identity as urged by Schelling, were generally the points of discussion presenting the most of beauty to the imaginative Morella. That identity which is termed personal, Mr. Locke, I think, truly defines to consist in the saneness of rational being. And since by person we understand an intelligent essence having reason, and since there is a consciousness which always accompanies thinking, it is this which makes us all to be that which we call ourselves, thereby distinguishing us from other beings that think, and giving us our personal identity. But the *principium indivduationis,* the notion of that identity which at death is or is not lost for ever, was to me, at all times, a consideration of intense interest; not more from the perplexing and exciting nature of its consequences, than from the marked and agitated manner in which Morella mentioned them.

But, indeed, the time had now arrived when the mystery of my wife's manner oppressed me as a spell. I could no longer bear the touch of her wan fingers, nor the low tone of her musical language, nor the lustre of her melancholy eyes. And she knew all this, but did not upbraid; she seemed conscious of my weakness or my folly, and, smiling, called it fate. She seemed also conscious of a cause, to me unknown, for the gradual alienation of my regard; but she gave me no hint or token of its nature. Yet was she woman, and pined away daily. In time the crimson spot settled steadily upon the cheek, and the blue veins upon the pale forehead became prominent; and one instant my nature melted into pity, but in the next I met the glance of her meaning eyes, and then my soul sickened and became giddy with the giddiness of one who gazes downward into some dreary and unfathomable abyss.

Shall I then say that I longed with an earnest and consuming desire for the moment of Morella's decease? I did; but the fragile spirit clung to its tenement of clay for many days, for many weeks and irksome months, until my tortured nerves obtained the mastery over my mind, and I grew furious through delay, and, with the heart of a fiend, cursed the days and the hours and the bitter moments, which seemed to lengthen and lengthen as her gentle life declined, like shadows in the dying of the day.

But one autumnal evening, when the winds lay still in heaven, Morella called me to her bedside. There was a dim mist over all the earth, and a warm glow upon the waters, and amid the rich October leaves of the forest, a rainbow from the firmament had surely fallen.

"It is a day of days," she said, as I approached; "a day of all days either to live or die. It is a fair day for the sons of earth and life – ah, more fair for the daughters of heaven and death!"

I kissed her forehead, and she continued:

"I am dying, yet shall I live."

"Morella!"

"The days have never been when thou couldst love me – but her whom in life thou didst abhor, in death thou shalt adore."

"Morella!"

"I repeat I am dying. But within me is a pledge of that affection – ah, how little! – which thou didst feel for me, Morella. And when my spirit departs shall the child live – thy child and mine, Morella's. But thy days shall be days of sorrow – that sorrow which is the most lasting of impressions, as the cypress is the most enduring of trees. For the hours of thy happiness are over and joy is not gathered twice in a life, as the roses of Paestum twice in a year. Thou shalt no longer, then, play the Teian with time, but, being ignorant of the myrtle and the vine, thou shalt bear about with thee thy shroud on the earth, as do the Moslemin at Mecca."

"Morella!" I cried, "Morella! How knowest thou this?" but she turned away her face upon the pillow and a slight tremor coming over her limbs, she thus died, and I heard her voice no more.

Yet, as she had foretold, her child, to which in dying she had given birth, which breathed not until the mother breathed no more, her child, a daughter, lived. And she grew strangely in stature and intellect, and was the perfect resemblance of her who had departed, and I loved her with a love more fervent than I had believed it possible to feel for any denizen of earth.

But, ere long the heaven of this pure affection became darkened, and gloom, and horror, and grief swept over it in clouds. I said the child grew strangely in stature and intelligence. Strange, indeed, was her rapid increase in bodily size, but terrible, oh! terrible were the tumultuous thoughts which crowded upon me while watching the development of her mental being. Could it be otherwise, when I daily discovered in the conceptions of the child the adult powers and faculties of the woman? When the lessons of experience fell from the lips of infancy? And when the wisdom or the passions of maturity I found hourly gleaming from its full and speculative eye? When, I say, all this became evident to my appalled senses, when I could no longer hide it from my soul, nor throw it off from those perceptions which trembled to receive it, is it to be wondered at that suspicions, of a nature fearful and exciting, crept in upon my spirit, or that my thoughts fell back aghast upon the wild tales and thrilling theories of the entombed Morella? I snatched from the scrutiny of the world a being whom destiny compelled me to adore, and in the rigorous seclusion of my home, watched with an agonizing anxiety over all which concerned the beloved.

And as years rolled away, and I gazed day after day upon her holy, and mild, and eloquent face, and poured over her maturing form, day after day did I discover new points of resemblance in the child to her mother, the melancholy and the dead. And hourly grew darker these shadows of similitude, and more full, and more definite, and more perplexing, and more hideously terrible in their aspect. For that her smile was like her mother's I could bear; but then I shuddered at its too perfect identity, that her eyes were like Morella's I could endure; but then they, too, often looked down into the depths of my soul with Morella's own intense and bewildering meaning. And in the contour of the high forehead, and in the ringlets of the silken hair, and in the wan fingers which buried themselves therein, and in the sad musical tones of her speech, and above all – oh, above all, in the phrases and expressions of the dead on the lips of the loved and the living, I found food for consuming thought and horror, for a worm that would not die.

Thus passed away two lustra of her life, and as yet my daughter remained nameless upon the earth. 'My child', and 'my love', were the designations usually prompted by a father's affection, and the rigid seclusion of her days precluded all other intercourse. Morella's name died with her at her death. Of the mother I had never spoken to the daughter, it was impossible to speak. Indeed, during the brief period of her existence, the latter had received no impressions from the outward world, save such as might have been afforded by the narrow limits of her privacy. But at length the ceremony of baptism presented to my mind, in its unnerved and agitated condition, a present deliverance from the terrors of my destiny. And at the baptismal font I hesitated for a name. And many titles of the wise and beautiful, of old and modern times, of my own and foreign lands, came thronging to my lips, with many, many fair titles of the gentle, and the happy, and the good. What prompted me then to disturb the memory of the buried dead? What demon urged me to breathe that sound, which in its very recollection was wont to make ebb the purple blood in torrents from the temples to the heart? What fiend spoke from the recesses of my soul, when amid those dim aisles, and in the silence of the night, I whispered within the ears of the holy man the syllables – Morella? What more than fiend convulsed the features of my child, and overspread them with hues of death, as starting at that scarcely audible sound, she turned her glassy eyes from the earth to heaven, and falling prostrate on the black slabs of our ancestral vault, responded – "I am here!"

Distinct, coldly, calmly distinct, fell those few simple sounds within my ear, and thence like molten lead rolled hissingly into my brain. Years – years may pass away, but the memory of that epoch never. Nor was I indeed ignorant of the flowers and the vine – but the hemlock and the cypress overshadowed me night and day. And I kept no reckoning of time or place, and the stars of my fate faded from heaven, and therefore the earth grew dark, and its figures passed by me like flitting shadows, and among them all I beheld only – Morella. The winds of the firmament breathed but one sound within my ears, and the ripples upon the sea murmured evermore – Morella. But she died; and with my own hands I bore her to the tomb; and I laughed with a long and bitter laugh as I found no traces of the first in the channel where I laid the second – Morella.

Last Long Night
Lina Rather

TWO MONTHS after the last broken transmission from Earth, somewhere in the unexplored dark, we found a voice.

At first we thought it was a mass hallucination. We'd been alone in space too long. Back home, we'd be treated for space sickness and starlust, our brains scanned and studied for signs that our grey matter had deteriorated in the vacuum. We'd be swaddled in hospitals, kept barefoot and away from the night sky until we stopped dreaming of plumed nebulas and stopped thinking we could hear the music of the spheres in C minor.

But there was no more Earth, and we were lost, limping along to a semi-terraformed planet we were supposed to be studying and would now be colonizing. We'd taken to talking each other away from the airlock when the stars started looking like houses in the distance and confirming reality as a matter of course. We might all lose our minds, but probably not at the same time.

"Does this taste like banana?" Lucinda asked, chewing on a freeze-dried ration. And we'd all nod.

"I hear someone breathing out there," Antin murmured, standing at one of the portholes. And we'd all say *no, it's only rock and plasma, come away from there, look at us instead.*

So when Carl found the signal and the voice crackled through the speakers, he asked, "Do you hear a voice?"

"Yes," said Jane, and Lucinda, and then one by one we all confirmed that we did hear a voice. Muttering, male, half-covered in static. We all bent close to the speakers.

The voice coughed, and paused, and Lucinda covered her mouth.

Breath rattled. More words.

"It's Russian," Antin whispered. None of the rest of us spoke it. Hardly anyone in the space programs did anymore. Russia died at the beginning of the slow end. He swayed in time with the enunciation. "He says he's lost. Over and over. He's lost."

He grabbed the mic before the rest of us could stop him and broadcast out into the black. "*Zdravstvujtye? Zdravstvujtye?*"

A pause. We held our breath, our hearts waiting for the next word to start beating again. It had been so long since we'd savored the sound of a stranger's voice.

He began again. The same pattern.

"It's a recording," Carl said. He had tears in his eyes. One ended up in his mustache, a shimmer in the energy-efficient lighting.

We let the voice play all night, damn the fuel reserves, damn the razor-thin margins between death and life on a barely-habitable planet.

* * *

The next day, we found the ship. Late twentieth century as near as anyone could guess. Our scanners were calibrated for geological identifications only. We didn't know what trick of folding space brought it here. The hull was pitted with burn marks and long scratches from debris. It was just big enough for one person who wasn't claustrophobic.

Matt and Amal volunteered to go aboard. Amal was forty, probably too old to have children when we made landfall. Matt insisted. We could have debated the impact their possible deaths would have on our as-yet-hypothetical colony, but none of the rest of us wanted to stop them. We helped them put on the suits and tethers.

"It's cold," Amal said when she made it aboard. Her chattering teeth made the radio pop. "There he is. Look."

They had a camera and we tumbled over each other in a mess of arms and legs and sweating palms to get close to the screen. Lucinda and Regan – who loved each other so secretly that even they didn't know it yet – held onto each other's forearms so tight that Lucinda had waning moon scars from Regan's nails for the rest of her life. Antin's mouth twitched, and we all knew he was aching for the cigarettes he'd given up to see the stars.

Amal held the camera up to where the cosmonaut's eyes used to be. He'd been handsome. He had a vintage face out of the days of Hugo Boss and ships caught in the orbit of a single planet.

"Do you know who he is?" Carl asked.

Antin shook his head. His hands still didn't know what to do. "There were so many lost in the early days. When my mother was a child, her class listened to the audio of Vladimir Komarov sobbing."

Matt's breath was the rush of the ocean half-remembered. In and out and in and out. "I don't want to die up here like that."

Amal touched the dead man's cheek with one gloved finger. With all the air gone, he was a facsimile of human still, even after these hundreds of years. "Hush. We won't die. Think of everything that aligned for you to be here, at the right moment and the right velocity, at the same time as he is. We are in the presence of a miracle. Of a universal astronomical improbability. No one is going to die."

"I don't believe in signs," Lucinda said from the deck of our ship, with her arms still bleeding in Regan's hands. She didn't mean it.

Matt went to his knees. Amal smoothed her other hand over his helmet and it would have been comforting had they not been separated by six layers of Mylar and mysterious alloys. She kept her other hand on the cosmonaut, and for a moment the dead Earth and the new were separated by only a touch.

* * *

We stripped the old ship for precious metals and spare parts, liquefied the body for the carbon. Our fuel reserves rose above the margin of error. We collected the ice crystals from the interior and thrilled at the taste of unfiltered water. It tasted like dust and dirt and everything else we wouldn't see again for months.

We kept the recording. Matt played it when we dimmed the lights for nighttime. A voice in the dark, the last stranger, who found us all this way from home.

A Good Thing and a Right Thing

Alexandra Renwick

MY KNEES are beginning to ache from cold soaking up out of the lichen-covered rocks. The rest of the archaeological team is gathering near the tallest remaining ruins, perching their asses on walls a meter thick and a thousand years old to eat peanut butter sandwiches and slurp instant coffee from styrofoam cups. Between there and here, abandoned digging and sifting tools lie scattered on the moss-green ground, glinting in the hard near-arctic sunlight that passes for summer in Greenland.

I turn my attention back to the private little square where I kneel, its parameters neatly marked with twine and pegs, tiny flags planted to show the exact location of artifacts already excavated. I know those pieces so well I can close my eyes and see them, practically smell the millennium-old damp earth hint of rot clinging to their surfaces: three bits of a badly deteriorated iron staff and a silver amulet the shape of a chair carved from a tree-stump, a typical Freyja's necklace pendant....

This is a woman's grave.

My back goes cool where light suddenly ceases to fall. It's Anders, come to stand behind me, blocking warmth from above. With the bright afternoon sun behind him he's only a looming shape of blackness, no human features at all. He extends a hand to help me to my feet, the hand of a fisherman rather than an academic. His fingers are square and blunt, thick as callused sausages, like my father's.

Ignoring his hand I stand by myself and dust lichen from my aching knees.

"Anything new, Christina?" he says, letting his hand drop to his side. "Anything to report to your Institute? Any insights into what might've happened here a thousand years ago?"

Between his words I hear all the things he isn't saying. He isn't saying, *go home*. He isn't saying, *your Institute and its psychic stuff is a load of crap, no matter what the University thinks*. He isn't saying, *why don't you close your eyes, let me do whatever I want to you, and get it over with*.

Glancing back at the dig team lunching far across the rocky field, I can't help thinking the others look farther away than before. The outlines of the heathen hof ruins divide the field into a pattern of rough squares the approximate dimensions of a longhouse, of outbuildings, sheds, long-gone sod huts. Slight variations in the sheath of ground vegetation show where the soil is less deep or its composite elements slightly altered. Here and there are darker patches of naked earth with its thin green skin peeled back, shallow troughs outlined in twine to show where human remains have been unearthed, or ceremonially staved-in animal skulls, or small bowls and knives and awls and other tools. The ancient hearth in the center of the hof is obvious, its soil rich with nutrients from hundreds of sacrifices to Thor, to Odin, to Freyja, fertilized by the ancient liters of blood which once soaked the ground or by the ash of countless bodies burned, human and animal mingling together in an orgy of tooth and bone fragments. To most it would look like nothing, now. To me it's everything.

Meeting Anders's eyes, I say, "No. Nothing new. It's all just the same as it ever was." I turn to trudge away from the hof ruins and the picnicking archaeologists, angling over the rise toward the tents scattered across the rocky ground, bright domes like big nylon gumdrops tossed onto the rough hillside. I unzip the flap of my tent and crawl inside, pretending to myself I don't feel the weight of Anders's gaze on the backs of my legs as I pull them in behind me.

* * *

Gudrun knew she shouldn't, but she pressed her daughters' faces into the folds of her skirts as blood spurted from the old woman's neck into the hlautbolli. The sacrificial bowl was already filled to the rim with red, thick and shiny and viscous. Erik's bare arms were smeared up to his chest, splatters marking his face like fever spots. His eyes shone particularly green in the light of the hof hearth, his braided beard particularly golden.

The old woman, nurse to Gudrun's own daughters, slumped to the ground at last and her body was carried away by thralls, the third blót sacrifice in as many days. Gudrun thought soon Erik would run out of old women and sheep, and wondered whose blood would fill his hlautbolli then.

Inga whimpered slightly into Gudrun's skirts and Hilda put her arm around her sister. They were good girls, her daughters. Kind and obedient. It spoke to some failing in their mother that she turned their faces away when their father made sacrifices to Thor, rather than letting them watch. It was for the girls he held the blót. For them, and for Gudrun, and for all the people of Grønland.

The girls were too young to remember when the settlement had been lush, with sheep like puffy clouds dotting every hillside, grain overflowing every granary, thick tapestries warming every wall of every sod house, and milk enough to pour onto the ground if it took even a hint of sour. Gudrun looked around – at the barren hof walls, at the angular ribs nearly poking through the skin on Erik's bloody chest, at the starvation-hollow eyes sunk deep in the faces upturned to catch some of the old woman's blood as their gothi sprinkled the crowd with his hlaut-stave – and imagined all as it had been.

A few drops of hlaut rained across Gudrun's face, warm and slightly sticky. The backs of her daughters' gowns would need to be washed again, and of course the gown Gudrun wore, though the wool was beginning to show threadbare patches with the precise outlines of the rocks where she always pounded her clothes by the water. Her thralls used to do all that work, twin Icelander girls with quick hands and silenced tongues who'd been chosen for the first blót of the year. Erik had thought the sacrifice of twins would be especially pleasing to Thor, that their hlaut-blood would move the gods to bring back the days of barley and wool, restore the hof to the glory it had seen in his father's time, and in that of his father's father, who Erik son of Erik liked to claim was descended from Erik the Red himself though every boy baby born in the fjords for a hundred years had been named after the great man who'd discovered Grønland and brought wealth and the gods' favor for the Norse.

But now the little thrall twins with their sweet shy smiles and nimble hands were gone, and Gudrun pounded her gowns to threads in the icy waters herself, and her daughters cried themselves to sleep each night while their stomachs ate at them from the inside, having nothing else to churn.

Avoiding her husband's gaze as he spoke his gothi ritual to each of the three gods rendered on enormous driftwood pillars around the central hearth, Gudrun turned and left the hof, sweeping her girls with her as they clutched her skirts, bilious smoke smelling of burnt flesh making her throat close up and her eyes sting.

* * *

It's far later than I intended when I emerge from my tent. A bad habit, sleeping through the middle of the day, but so easy to do this far north, where light in summer never goes away. It's not uncommon to see people squatting at the dig site, sifting soil and scraping rock in the middle of the night, the sky nearly as bright as it is in the morning or the evening.

The group is eating by the fire pit. I blink back the dream memory of tears tinted with smoking wool and burnt human hair. This fire smells like paper and coffee and the mild chemical used in the slow-burning manufactured logs we cart up to the camp from the port at Qaqortoq, where they arrive from Canada by the boatload, since trees on these rocky hillsides are stunted and scarce.

The others smile and nod, but I'm not really one of them and they know it. Even when in English, their arcane archaeological discussions have an academic quality which leaves me feeling isolated and ignorant. I pour myself a cup of coffee and leave, the fire's warmth fading behind me.

The taller standing ruins loom dusky against the pale night sky. These date later than the heathen hof and other buildings, a Christian church probably built close to the end of the earliest Norse inhabitation, at the onset of the Little Ice Age. The church footprint is smaller than the hof's, but its walls are of rock rather than sod. In my dream the hof's four support pillars were made of stones fitted together one on top of the other, plastered with ground mussel shells, rising to the humped turf roof. Coffee in one hand, I reach out with the other to touch the crumbling church wall, wondering which of these lichen-covered stones were scavenged from the older building, picked from among the rubble mingled with skeletons then not even a century old.

Closing my eyes I brush my hand over the rocks, across the pitted surfaces and rough lichen. The scene of my dream returns with startling clarity, bodies dangling from the hof walls in various states of decay, sheep next to woman next to cow. Another woman. Two smaller bodies, children maybe, or at least people of an age we'd consider children now: the thrall twins.

The flare of a match jolts me, my eyes snapping open. Sharp sweet tobacco scent curls through the air. A boot crunches on the pebbled ground. Anders steps into view on the other side of the church wall, looks at me through the rounded arch of the empty window. The ancient wall between us is a meter thick, but he could lunge across and grab me if he wanted.

Watching me watch him, he draws a long slow pull on his handrolled cigarette, then steps past the window out of sight.

* * *

Even nine years earlier at the last great blót, Gudrun's neighbors and everyone in the fjords had still come together with a sense of hope. She'd been their völva then: their seer, their healer, their conduit to Freyja's favor. But she'd never regretted her decision to set aside her iron staff and blue cloak and necklace to commit to family life. Not until recently.

On the other side of the hearth her daughters lay sleeping, curled together like two kittens in a basket. It was a shame nobody kept cats anymore. Gudrun missed kittens; they were so uncomplicated.

Marrying Erik had complicated everything. People had been happy at first, saying the völva's strength wedded to the gothi's would return the favor of the gods to the land, end the famine and ease the cold. But the cattle continued to die, and the barley to rot in the fields before ripening. Each winter was more bitter than the last, its months of darkness harder to bear, the stacks of corpses on the ice outside the longhouse higher as more and more died before the sky grew bright again and the ground softened enough for burial. And lately Gudrun had heard whispers, down by the water where she pounded her daughters' hlaut-spattered dresses on the rocks, or behind the shearing pens where the few remaining flocks straggled in one by one and were robbed of their thin wool for the season.

It's the woman, said the whispers. *Freyja is displeased, and Thor, and Odin. It's the woman, sapping the strength of our gothi. The woman, and her children....*

* * *

One of the young archaeologists, Anneliese, calls out in English, excitement making her voice shrill. "Another grave!" she says. "Anders, quick! Bring your camera!"

Everybody drops what they're doing and clambers over rocks and mounds of dirt, carefully traversing the twine grids crisscrossing the site. We all like a new discovery at the dig. Soon we're crowded around Anneliese where she squats, pointing with the tip of her brush *here* and *there* in the dark loam. The other archaeologists speculate in at least three languages, milling, happy to have something new to get excited about after a week of nothing.

The find turns out to be a double grave, though the bones are fragile and will take lots of painstaking work to excavate. Certainly human, though age, gender, and other definitive details will have to come later, after samples and photos and diagrams are sent to the Institute and to universities in Copenhagen and Halifax.

During the communal dinner hour, Anneliese seeks me out. "Christina," she says, her round face still flushed with pleasure at the find, "what do you think? Any – what does your Institute call it? Intuitive flashes? – about who they were, or how they died? Could the remains date back as old as the church?"

Lots of questions. I laugh with her at her enthusiasm. "Older than the church," I say. "And it's girls. Two of them. Ages..." I breathe deep, try to remember the red-spattered faces of the little girls clinging to their mother's skirts. "...Ages about three and five, I think. Maybe a little older, but not much. They slept curled together, like kittens in a basket."

She stares at me a moment, her mouth open. Then she laughs, shaking her head. "I love your approach, blending cultural and mythic and forensic stuff all together to theorize. I know some people don't appreciate the University hiring you through the Institute..." I pretend not to notice she's looking at Anders. He's standing over the new discovery, smoking a loose-rolled cigarette, camera balanced on one hip. "...But, well, I think it's cool, is all. A much more modern approach to anthropological re-imagining of lost societies. Very holistic. Forward thinking, for sure."

Late into the bright night the team works on the gravesite, carefully dusting the little bones and the little rings and other decorations embedded in the soil where the little feet and hands would've lain.

That night I go to sleep early. I close my eyes, breathing shallowly to avoid inhaling the acrid tang of handrolled cigarettes being smoked somewhere near my tent, and I dream.

* * *

Gudrun knew Erik the gothi had heard the whispers too, and that in his own way he sought to placate them.

At first it was only old women he chose for his endless blót. Never had the fjords seen such a bloody year outside the usual small skirmishes for land and cattle and wood. But in times of privation, the helpless and the hapless went first. Gudrun had heard Norse settlements farther up the coast routinely killed the very old and the very young in harsh winters, and threw their bodies over the cliffs into the sea.

At least their gothi brought meaning to the killing. At least he dedicated those deaths to the gods, and dutifully said the rituals, and spattered his hof and his people with the sacrificial blood to bring blessings. This was a good thing, and a right thing. And when he ran out of all the women too old for childbearing, all the girl thralls too small to be useful in the field or on the sea, he moved to the children. The female children, who were weak compared to the boys, who'd never be as big or as strong, who'd never be able to take on the duties of men and return the land to what it had been when at last Thor and Odin decided to smile on the Norse again.

Gudrun crouched in a dark corner of the abandoned sod hut, an arm around the shoulders of each daughter. Inga curled in her mother's embrace, bored, sucking a well-worn thumb. Hilda had told her sister they played a hiding game and that's why they stayed quiet in the crumbling dirt of an abandoned house while men with torches outside shouted their names into the darkness.

Hilda started shaking despite the heavy blanket Gudrun had wrapped around her before rushing her daughters from the house. "Hilda," she said calmly, very softly, almost whispering in the girl's ear. "Hilda, can you name the gods for me? Quiet as you can, so we can keep playing our game."

The old sod hut was very dark. The only light came from the hole in the ceiling, where smoke would've spiraled out had the hearth been lit. But the crisp air was clear and the moon was bright, enough silver light filtering through the gloom to limn the pale roundness of the child's face as she nodded.

Tightening her embrace, Gudrun pulled her daughter closer. Hilda leaned in, wrapped her arms around her mother's neck and whispered into her ear: "First is Freyja, who gave you your necklace and your pretty iron staff."

Gudrun smiled into the dark. "Very good," she whispered back. "Who else?"

"Frigg, wife of Odin."

Shifting her hold on Inga as the smaller girl went slack with sleep at last, Gudrun nodded. "Who else? Quietly now."

"Syn, who defends. And then there's Sól and Máni, the Sun and the Moon."

Gudrun laughed softly. "Interesting choices. Let's see how many we can think of together. Keep whispering, so we don't wake your sister."

* * *

I wake with my heart pounding against my ribs, sweat prickling my neck and chest. My feet are hard lumps of ice despite the tight binding of the sleeping bag.

Gulping, gulping, gulping for air, I kick free of the sleeping bag and crawl to the tent flap. Outside the sun is high, the sky clean and crisp with early morning and with arctic breezes.

Shivering, I draw on thick socks and jeans. Quilted jacket. Boots. Thrusting aside the front flap I emerge into morning. All the other tents are still quiet, everybody having grown accustomed to sleeping through nights without darkness.

It's cooler this morning than it has been these last two weeks. My breath forms little puffs in the air. My hair feels dry and brittle from too many days without proper washing. My fingernails are tipped with the same dirt crescent moons as all the archaeologists. I might not be university-trained like the rest of them, but I'm down there in the soil with them every day, poking and prodding and brushing at the earth.

My steps take me to the church ruins. Four meters of wall left standing at its tallest point, the sod and timber roof long since disintegrated, folding itself back into the landscape. Inside, the open rectangular structure feels even colder than outside, as though the scavenged hof pillar rocks infect the other stones in the thick walls with the coldness of famine and sacrifice, of gods long forgotten. Of death.

The crunch of a bootfall makes me spin to face Anders. Nobody else will be up this time of day, roaming the windy ruins. The camp is over the rise on the other side of the excavation site. People would probably hear me scream, unless my mouth were covered with a hand. A large square-fingered hand, with nails dirty at the tips, and cuticles rough and chapped from wind and sun and dry, dry air.

Anders lifts his hand toward my face and I go utterly still. The gothi flashes though my mind, an image of his hand as he slit the old woman's throat. His hand had been as work-roughened, though his fingers bony and narrow with years of starvation. His nails too had been dark at their ragged ends, blood and dirt caught beneath.

"Touch me," I say softly, "and the gods will curse you, and ravens tear your heart asunder."

His hand freezes midair. Surprise flits across his face, then a genuinely puzzled look, before he flushes deeply red and steps back. "Just thought you might like a cigarette," he says, reaching into his jacket pocket, the same hand he'd reached out to me. He steps away to strike the match, gazes out the empty window of the church ruin toward the water. Even this time of year, big melting chunks of ice float offshore, shaped like enormous anvils, or small steamships, or hunched fantastical creatures out of Scandinavian fairy tales.

Anders turns to me, holds the lit cigarette my direction. "You know your namesake, Christina? A Scandinavian saint, Saint Christina, tortured by her pagan father."

After a long moment of me not answering, not moving, not even twitching, he shrugs, his flush fading. Lifting the cigarette to his mouth he turns and walks out the gaping doorway leading back to the hof ruins, leaving me standing as still as a pillar of fitted stones plastered with mussel shells. As still as a dead woman with her throat slit over the sacrificial bowl. As still as the bones of two little girls laid to rest together, a thousand years ago.

* * *

Gudrun/I sag with my/her back to the small bodies by the hearth. Two fjordsmen stand, one to each side, gripping her/my arms and holding me/her upright. The warm hlaut of the sacrifice rains down from above as Erik the gothi dutifully splatters the gaunt gathered remnants of his men with his hlaut-stave. The hof air is thick and sweet and sickening. The walls run with blood. The three columns carved to the likenesses of gods shimmer in the smoke and heat and the tears in my/Gudrun's eyes.

Erik recites the rituals, asking for the blessings of all the gods, asking for times of warmth and wool and barley to return to Grønland, and for Norsemen to flourish in the fjords.

A strange eerie gurgling erupts from the crowd. The sound swells, strengthens until Erik can't ignore its effect on his men, on the sanctity of his ritual as he smears his hearth with the last of the cooling hlaut-blood from his latest, greatest sacrifice. The raw gurgling gets louder, rises in tone and pitch until it assumes the unmistakable edge of keening. Like iced winter wind rushing through gaping stones in the longhouse wall. Like wounded whales caught in shallow shoals, separated from their young.

It's his wife, the völva, laughing.

The gothi lets the slick hlautbolli slide from his fingers as his wife's gaze scorches him. "You," she says. "What exactly do you think you're blessing? Everything worth blessing is gone now." The völva laughs again, no other sound in the room but the crackle of smoky hearth fire, the whipping of cold wind beyond the hof door. "I hope your grain grows tall as longships next year, and your cattle fat as houses, so you and your men feast well, alone at your cold hearths. Look at you."

Erik son of Erik looks around the hof at the men he's known all his life, the men still remaining, the ones strong enough to plow, to run cattle and sheep, to carry the oar and the axe. All the old ones are gone, and the women. The children, all gone. Gone to appease the gods and their terrible appetites.

The völva draws herself upright, shakes off the hands of the men gripping her/my arms. "May ravens tear your hearts asunder. You. All of you, whose daughters meant so little to you…." My/her gaze sweeps the room, and the men look away from their völva's scorn, grow smaller under her stare. Even the gothi. "Who do you think will give you your next generation of sons? Who? *Who?*"

But none of the men answer, as there is no answer to give.

Scare Tactics

Aeryn Rudel

LINDSEY PULLED UP to the curb beside a small well-kept house in an agreeably upper middleclass neighborhood. The newish Lexus ES 350 in the driveway said her prospective clients had money – not millions or anything, but more than enough to afford her services.

She got out of the car, popped open the trunk, and made a face at the awful stink within. A pungent mix of the worst fart overlaid with rotting meat and old garbage wafted up from the dark enclosure.

"Jesus," Lindsey said, covering her mouth. "Can't you control that?"

A jumbo-sized Raggedy Ann doll that had seen better days lay face-up in the trunk. Moth holes pocked its pinkish cotton, and its once-bright dress was dirty and stained. Only the red yarn that served as its hair retained its original color.

Adramelech's voice drifted up from the doll, faint and irritated. "You know I can't help it," the demon said. "You keep a demon in physical form, you get the stink. That's the way it is. Maybe you shouldn't stick me in a small, enclosed space."

"And have that stench up front with me? No thanks. Hey, switch to silent mode. It's almost show time."

Are we doing this again? Adramelech's voice spoke in Lindsey's head now, as she'd requested. It wasn't quite telepathy. He couldn't read her thoughts, like she couldn't read his, but they could 'hear' each other when they wanted. *It's demeaning, you know. I'm a demon of the first order, a goddamn chancellor of Hell. I'm not some bullshit scare artist.*

Lindsey stifled a chuckle. *Chancellor, my ass. I've read de Plancy. He says you were nothing more than Satan's fashion consultant.*

Adramelech's anger surged against the back of her brain, a red haze of power that would be terrifying if she didn't have complete control over its source.

De Plancy was an asshole and a liar. Adramelech's voice was a droning buzz, like a thousand angry flies. *Most of what's in the* Dictionnaire Infernal *he got from Titivillus, the biggest fucking liar in Hell, and I don't need to tell you that's saying something. I commanded fifteen infernal legions, and I –*

Yeah, yeah, I've heard this before. Lindsey rolled her eyes. *You were a big deal in Hell. Well, if that's the case, you should have stayed there rather than acting like the boogeyman in a cheap horror flick.* She'd had Adramelech for five years, acquiring him in the one and only truly supernatural case in her entire parapsychology career.

Don't be a bitch, Adramelech said, a noticeable sulk softening his insectile rasp. *Eternity is boring. Possession breaks the monotony. How was I to know you would know the one spell that (a) actually works and (b) would bind me to this stupid doll?*

When she'd encountered Adramelech and the college girls he'd been tormenting, she had immediately realized the opportunity. She'd performed an exorcism that contained a bit of Haitian voodoo mixed into the Latin. The exorcism was for show, but the Haitian spell had trapped Adramelech in the doll he'd been using to terrorize sorority row for the term of sixty-six years. The spell also bound him to her will for that same period of time.

Self-pity is an unbecoming trait in a demon, Lindsey said. *Face it. You're stuck, and this is how I – check that, we – make a living.* She scooped the doll out of the trunk and held it up, staring into the vacant depths of its glassy eyes. *Don't make me give you a command. We're past that now, aren't we?*

Adramelech went silent for a moment, his anger festering in the back of her mind like an old wound. *Fine,* the demon said at last, and his anger faded. *What's the play?*

Good boy. Lindsey walked up the driveway toward the front door, cradling the doll in her arms. She told people the doll housed her 'spirit medium', a friendly Native American soul who helped her identify and remove supernatural activity. Most clients ate that shit up. Those that didn't just accepted the doll as part of the whole kooky parapsychologist thing.

It's pretty typical, she said. *A couple of yuppies are hearing noises – rattling, babies crying, that kind of stuff – and smelling smoke when there's no fire. They've got overactive imaginations, and they're convinced their home is haunted. We are going to make sure they believe it one-hundred percent before we leave. Then we come back, do the clearing, collect the fee, and we're down the road.*

Babies crying? Smoke? Adramelech said.

Lindsey detected a hint of interest from the demon and stopped a few yards from the front door. *Does that mean something to you?*

Nope. It's just out of the ordinary.

Lindsey hesitated, trying to tell if the demon was lying. He could still do that, despite the spell that bound him to her service. Adramelech hadn't held anything back from her as far as she knew, but fair dealing wasn't exactly in the demon's nature. She elected to hedge her bets with a bribe.

Look, if this thing goes smoothly, we'll pick up another season of Buffy the Vampire Slayer *on the way home.* To keep the demon occupied, she often set his doll in front of the TV and let him watch what he wanted. Adramelech's tastes ran to reality shows and anything that dealt with the supernatural, which the demon found hilarious. *Buffy the Vampire Slayer* was one of his favorites.

Really? Lindsey smiled at Adramelech's naked eagerness. *Season four?*

Yep. Do your part, help me without any bitching, and you've got twenty-plus hours of Sarah Michelle Gellar and company headed your way. Lindsey suppressed a smile. She knew the demon would take the bait.

Deal.

* * *

Sandy Miller was hands-down the most ordinary human Adramelech had ever seen. Her soul looked like a bunch of vanilla custard dumped inside a boring sad-sack body. Lindsey had set his doll in the loveseat next to her so he could see and hear everything happening in the Miller's living room.

"And when did the disturbances begin, Sandy?" Lindsey said, directing her question to Mrs. Miller seated on the couch across from her.

"About a month ago," Robert Miller said before his wife could speak. He sat next to her, one hand resting on her leg. Whereas Sandy Miller might be white-bread dull, her husband was a malignant diamond. His soul was a lump of black slime pulsating in the middle of his chest: wretched, warped, and wonderful. To put it in no uncertain terms, Robert Miller was a monster to make a demon proud.

"Uh huh." Lindsey nodded. "Can you describe the events?" She glanced at Adramelech's doll seated on the loveseat next to her. *You getting anything?* she thought at him.

Adramelech considered telling Lindsey about Robert Miller, but then decided against it. A small rebellion, but small rebellions were all he had. *Nope. This place is clean as a nun's twat,* he said.

Gross. Let me know if that changes.

"Well, we started hearing noises a week ago," Sandy Miller said. "Bumps in the wall, and what sounded like babies crying in the middle of the night."

"That's pretty common with a haunting," Lindsey said, nodding sagely. "Anything else?"

"The smoke," Robert Miller said. "Like I told you on the phone, we've been smelling smoke in the house for the past week. Like burnt pork or something."

"Do you think we're haunted?" Mrs. Miller asked, her eyes wide and fearful.

"I'll do a thorough investigation of your home, Mrs. Miller," Lindsey said. "I'll determine if a supernatural presence is the source of your problems. If there is a paranormal factor, I *will* remove it."

Adramelech had heard Lindsey lay down her shtick a dozen times, scaring gullible idiots into paying thousands of dollars to be rid of ghosts. It was all nonsense, of course. There were no ghosts. Human souls didn't linger; they went to Heaven or Hell as intended. The few real hauntings were demons creating havoc for kicks.

Still, Adramelech's interest piqued at some of the details of this case. It wasn't your typical bump-in-the-night bullshit. In fact, it felt pretty damn specific…and familiar. He moved his focus away from the Lindsey and the Millers, scanning the house. He was supposed to be waiting for cues from Lindsey to shake some picture frames, rattle the floorboards, or even throw his voice down the hall. It was all the demon mojo he could muster in his current form – well, and the stink, which he *could* control, but told Lindsey otherwise to fuck with her.

He wanted to turn his head, but moving the doll so overtly would piss off Lindsey. Still, he had other senses beyond sight and hearing. It only took a few seconds to locate the *other*, a familiar sensation, comforting almost. It'd been a long time since he'd encountered another demon.

You look ridiculous, Adramelech, Baal said from across the room, revealing himself as a shadowy bat-winged shape hunched on the floor next to Mr. Miller, visible only to Adramelech. Baal clutched the man's leg with one smoky, spade-claw hand. Adramelech could feel his fellow demon's corruption worming its way through the human's body and soul. He became instantly jealous.

Have pity, Adramelech said. *I'm trapped like this for another sixty years.*

We're demons. We don't have pity. Who's the woman? Baal nodded his shadowy head toward Lindsey.

Parapsychologist and charlatan, Adramelech said. *She's studied some real demonology, though, so be careful.*

Bullshit, Baal said. *She's no priest.*

Suit yourself. If you wind up bound to a My Pretty Pony, don't complain to me.

Baal's bravado wasn't entirely unwarranted; as a demon of the first order, he'd been a Great Duke who commanded sixty legions in the infernal army. Of course that army hadn't done jack shit since the beginning of time, leaving one of its most important generals free to slum it on Earth.

You working for her or something? Baal said. His eyes flashed crimson in the wispy darkness of his face. *That's kind of pathetic.*

I'm making the best of a bad situation, Adramelech replied. *I'd appreciate it if you wouldn't piss on my parade.*

Are you going to tell her about me? Mr. Miller has given me quite a bit of enjoyment.

I won't say anything if I don't have to, Adramelech said. *What's this guy's deal anyway? His soul looks like liquefied dog shit. You do that?*

Baal laughed. *Found him that way. All I've been doing is nudging him a bit, adding some spice to that rotten little soul of his.*

Hey! You paying attention? Lindsey's voice broke into Adramelech's mind.

Adramelech pushed Baal's thoughts away and focused on Lindsey. *I'm here. I don't think you've convinced hubby yet.*

Robert Miller stared fixedly at Lindsey, and his right hand clenched and unclenched around the arm of his chair.

Understood, Lindsey said. *I'll look for a way to nudge him along. Be ready.*

"It might help if I showed you where the disturbances are most common, Ms. Wallace," Robert Miller said. Adramelech heard the unmistakable eagerness in his voice, and malice surged through the room. Like sweet perfume, the rotten scent of human evil was ambrosia to a demon.

My boy's about to make his pitch, Baal said.

"Yes, please," Mrs. Miller said, also quite eager. "Something might happen while you're here."

"Okay, um, where have the disturbances been concentrated?" Lindsey said.

"The basement," Robert Miller answered. "I have a workshop down there – I like to tinker a bit – and I've smelled smoke and heard strange noises more times than I can count."

These two are starting to creep me out, Lindsey said to Adramelech. *You getting any weird vibes?*

She's talking to you, isn't she? Baal said. *She's getting nervous, right?*

Adramelech weighed his options, then replied to Lindsey, stalling for time. *Nah, they're fine. I'll see about making some noise in the basement when you get down there.*

Nice, Lindsey said. *That should seal the deal.*

Why don't we work together on this one? Baal said, his eyes glinting. His excitement caused him to become more visible, revealing the scaly ruin of his face. Baal was ugly even by demonic standards.

A tempting offer, Adramelech admitted. *But after, could you free me?* He tried not to sound too desperate.

He saw something that looked like a frown in the shifting mass of shadows that made up Baal's face. *No,* the demon said after a long pause. *But we could make your handler pay.* The malevolence in Baal's voice was immensely pleasing.

"I'm not surprised," Lindsey said. "Spirits often seek the lowest points of a house – psychic energy tends to gather there."

If Adramelech had eyes, he would have rolled them. Lindsey was ad-libbing, but she delivered her bullshit with such conviction no one ever called her on it. She was in full snake-oil-salesman mode again, confident as hell with her pet demon by her side. It made him sick and angry.

Robert Miller stood. "Let me show you the basement, Ms. Wallace."

Lindsey stood as well and picked up her purse. "Sure. Let's go have a look."

Time to shit or get off the pot, Baal said. *You joining me for playtime?*

Adramelech did not reply, and he moved the doll's head an imperceptible few inches to watch Lindsey and Robert disappear down the hall to the basement door.

* * *

Robert Miller opened the door to the basement, trying to control the shaking in his hands. She was so pretty, so vulnerable, so full of life and energy. If it wasn't for the whisperer urging him to wait, to hold off because it would be so much better when they got down to the workshop, he might have given in right there.

"Let me get the light, Ms. Wallace," he said, reaching past her to flick the switch. The motion brought him close to her, and he could smell her perfume, the shampoo in her hair, and, yes, the subtle hint of her sweat. That personal stink excited him; he loved the smells both inside and out. It was the best part. He began reaching for the short, hooked Spyderco folding knife in his back pocket.

No. Not yet, the whisperer said, and Robert's excitement dwindled, became more manageable. He moved his hand away from the knife.

"Thank you," Ms. Wallace said. "You can call me Lindsey."

"After you, Lindsey," Robert said, smiling. It was the fake smile, the one the whisperer had taught him, the one that made the women trust him. He looked over his shoulder at his wife; she stood at the end of the hall, her hands clasped before her. He smiled at her. A different smile, the one he only showed her. It said, "Let me do what I need to do, and things will be normal again."

He had told Sandy the noises and smells came from the whisperer. She believed him, even though she couldn't hear it. They scared her, but when Robert did his work, she knew they stopped for a while, and her husband was hers again. He didn't let her go down to the basement, and she didn't ask questions. Sandy knew her place, and she wanted to keep it.

Lindsey started down the steps, and Robert followed, pulling the door closed behind him. The steps led down into an expansive basement, mostly unfinished. Robert had installed fluorescent lights overhead, and they cast a bright white glow over a new washer and dryer, racks containing bleach, detergent, and other household cleaners, and two wooden work tables. The tables were for show; he did his real work elsewhere.

"What do you do down here?" Lindsey asked, moving into the center of the room.

"Tinker, mostly," Robert replied.

"Do you build things?"

He smiled. "No, I'm much better at taking things apart."

Soon. Wait. Let her put it together; let her be afraid before you begin. The whisperer always knew how to make it right, how to make it better.

"What's behind that?" Lindsey asked, pointing to a door in the wall he'd put up to separate the basement into two large rooms.

"That's where I keep my tools," he said. "Most of the noises and smells have been coming from there."

"We should take a look," Lindsey said. She sounded confident, no hint of fear or even unease in her voice. It bothered him. It felt like she was in control. That could not stand; not in *his* space.

Patience, the whisperer said.

"Absolutely," Robert said to Lindsey, and reached into his pocket for the key. He opened the door, and put his hand on the light switch inside, but he didn't turn it on. Not yet.

Lindsey took a step into the room and then another. "Dark in here. Can you turn on the light?"

"Sure," Robert said. He trembled with excitement. She was so close. He flicked on the light, revealing his tools in racks on the walls and his work table, its granite top stained with the leavings of his last project. He had left them because he liked the smell: an old coppery tang and the ripe odor of opened bowels. It was enough to remind of him of the work until the whisperer said he could begin another project. He had assembled his tools from a variety of cutlery and butcher shops: hooks for hanging, small knives for delicate work, big knives for opening and digging, saws for removing unneeded parts.

Robert shut the door behind him and locked it with the key. Lindsey had her back to him. What terror she must feel. She had to realize what would happen, that she was his. He reached into his back pocket and pulled out the Spyderco. He'd start with that. He opened the knife with an audible click, its hooked blade gleaming, hungry.

"This is where I do my real work," Robert said. "What do you think?"

Lindsey didn't turn around, but he could hear her saying something under her breath. Words he didn't recognize.

KILL HER! The whisperer's voice filled his head. *NOW.* It sounded desperate, afraid, and that made *him* afraid. He took a step forward, and Lindsey turned to face him.

Robert stopped midstride. Lindsey held a very large automatic pistol in her right hand, and she pointed it at his head. She must have had it in her purse. In her other hand she held a doll – a Barbie doll in a pink dress.

She smiled, a crooked mocking smile that enraged and terrified Robert. And still she spoke, louder now. The words were in a language he didn't understand. Some of them sounded like Latin, others more like grunts than actual words.

KILL HER. KILL HER. KILL HER, the whisperer howled in Robert's head. Its power was undeniable, unstoppable. He brought the knife up and lunged.

The world ended in thunder and darkness.

* * *

The cop was a good-looking guy, youngish and well built, and he ate up her damsel in distress act. They stood in front of the Millers' house in the strobing lights of six police cars, a fire truck, and two ambulances. There were cops and paramedics all over the place.

"You're very lucky, Ms. Wallace," Sergeant Victors said. "Robert Miller was a very bad man."

"I was so scared," Lindsey said, tears streaming down her face. She clutched Adramelech's doll to her chest. "He came at me with the knife, and I…and I…."

Oh, Jesus fucking Christ, Lindsey, Adramelech said. *Laying it on a bit thick, aren't you?*

Sergeant Victors reached out and put a hand on Lindsey's shoulder. "You did the right thing. He would have hurt you."

Just thick enough, I think, Lindsey thought back.

"I didn't want to kill him," Lindsey said, continuing the show. "I tried to shoot him in the leg, to stop him, but the gun kicked so much. I've only fired it once or twice." Bullshit, of course. She'd put three thousand rounds through her Sig 220 and could shoot one-inch groups at 20 yards. She'd been carrying the gun in her purse for years. Parapsychology attracted all kinds of freaks.

Sergeant Victors stepped close. "I'm *glad* you killed that son-of-a-bitch. Who knows how many women you saved tonight, starting with his wife."

Lindsey glanced over to where Sandy Miller sat in the back of one of the ambulances, a blanket wrapped around her, expression vacant. *She was long past saving*, Lindsey thought.

"Do you think he's killed a lot of people?" Lindsey asked, genuinely curious.

Sergeant Victors licked his lips and glanced around. "I shouldn't tell you this, but I will because I want you to understand that you did the right thing and that you had no other choice. We found evidence of at least two victims. He kept...trophies." As soon as the words were out of his mouth, he looked guilty for saying them.

Lindsey repressed a real shudder. "Can I go home now?" she asked, squeezing a few more tears out to seal the deal.

Sergeant Victors nodded, eager to change the subject. "We need to get a complete statement from you, but I don't see why we can't do that tomorrow after you've had some time to get yourself together. Officer Johnson will follow you home." He indicated another cop standing a few feet away.

"Thank you, sergeant," Lindsey said. "Should I ask for you at the station tomorrow?"

"Yes, ma'am," He said and smiled at her. "I'll take your statement personally. Now get some rest."

Lindsey reached out and took one of Sergeant Victors' hands and squeezed it. "You've been so kind. Thank you."

"I'm...I'm just doing my job." He blushed, but held Lindsey's hand for few seconds before letting go.

No wedding ring, Lindsey thought at Adramelech as they walked toward the Honda.

Couldn't hurt to have a friend in the police department, the demon admitted.

They reached the car and Lindsey popped the trunk. She put Adramelech inside. *You did a hell of a job tonight,* she said and meant it. She had no doubt things could have gone very badly, that Baal and Robert Miller could have ended her life in a way she could hardly imagine. She also knew that Adramelech had had a choice, and he'd chosen her. She didn't know why, but it didn't matter. She was never one to focus on what could have been. Maybe the demon had some infernal version of the Stockholm syndrome. Still, he had been loyal. He had warned her, and for that he deserved a reward.

You know, she said. *I see two full seasons of* Buffy *in your future.*

Really? Adramelech replied, so eager. *Four and five?*

You got it. She reached into her purse and pulled out the Birthday Wishes Barbie doll, smoothing down its pink, frilly dress. *How you doing in there?* she thought at Baal. There were no words in the reply, just a hurricane of rage and power that buckled her knees. She pulled away, shaking her head. It might take a little longer to tame this one. Adramelech might help with that.

Lindsey put the Barbie doll next to the Raggedy Ann. "Play nice," she said out loud, and before she closed the trunk, she heard Adramelech's muffled voice.

"Hey, Baal, do you like *Buffy the Vampire Slayer?*"

The Tapestried Chamber
or, The Lady in the Sacque
Walter Scott

THE FOLLOWING NARRATIVE is given from the pen, so far as memory permits, in the same character in which it was presented to the author's ear; nor has he claim to further praise, or to be more deeply censured, than in proportion to the good or bad judgment which he has employed in selecting his materials, as he has studiously avoided any attempt at ornament which might interfere with the simplicity of the tale.

At the same time, it must be admitted that the particular class of stories which turns on the marvellous possesses a stronger influence when told than when committed to print. The volume taken up at noonday, though rehearsing the same incidents, conveys a much more feeble impression than is achieved by the voice of the speaker on a circle of fireside auditors, who hang upon the narrative as the narrator details the minute incidents which serve to give it authenticity, and lowers his voice with an affectation of mystery while he approaches the fearful and wonderful part. It was with such advantages that the present writer heard the following events related, more than twenty years since, by the celebrated Miss Seward of Litchfield, who, to her numerous accomplishments, added, in a remarkable degree, the power of narrative in private conversation. In its present form the tale must necessarily lose all the interest which was attached to it by the flexible voice and intelligent features of the gifted narrator. Yet still, read aloud to an undoubting audience by the doubtful light of the closing evening, or in silence by a decaying taper, and amidst the solitude of a half-lighted apartment, it may redeem its character as a good ghost story. Miss Seward always affirmed that she had derived her information from an authentic source, although she suppressed the names of the two persons chiefly concerned. I will not avail myself of any particulars I may have since received concerning the localities of the detail, but suffer them to rest under the same general description in which they were first related to me; and for the same reason I will not add to or diminish the narrative by any circumstance, whether more or less material, but simply rehearse, as I heard it, a story of supernatural terror.

About the end of the American war, when the officers of Lord Cornwallis's army, which surrendered at Yorktown, and others, who had been made prisoners during the impolitic and ill-fated controversy, were returning to their own country, to relate their adventures, and repose themselves after their fatigues, there was amongst them a general officer, to whom Miss S. gave the name of Browne, but merely, as I understood, to save the inconvenience of introducing a nameless agent in the narrative. He was an officer of merit, as well as a gentleman of high consideration for family and attainments.

Some business had carried General Browne upon a tour through the western counties, when, in the conclusion of a morning stage, he found himself in the vicinity of a small country town, which presented a scene of uncommon beauty, and of a character peculiarly English.

The little town, with its stately old church, whose tower bore testimony to the devotion of ages long past, lay amidst pastures and cornfields of small extent, but bounded and divided with hedgerow timber of great age and size. There were few marks of modern improvement. The environs of the place intimated neither the solitude of decay nor the bustle of novelty; the houses were old, but in good repair; and the beautiful little river murmured freely on its way to the left of the town, neither restrained by a dam nor bordered by a towing-path.

Upon a gentle eminence, nearly a mile to the southward of the town, were seen, amongst many venerable oaks and tangled thickets, the turrets of a castle as old as the walls of York and Lancaster, but which seemed to have received important alterations during the age of Elizabeth and her successor. It had not been a place of great size; but whatever accommodation it formerly afforded was, it must be supposed, still to be obtained within its walls. At least, such was the inference which General Browne drew from observing the smoke arise merrily from several of the ancient wreathed and carved chimney-stalks. The wall of the park ran alongside of the highway for two or three hundred yards; and through the different points by which the eye found glimpses into the woodland scenery, it seemed to be well stocked. Other points of view opened in succession – now a full one of the front of the old castle, and now a side glimpse at its particular towers, the former rich in all the bizarrerie of the Elizabethan school, while the simple and solid strength of other parts of the building seemed to show that they had been raised more for defence than ostentation.

Delighted with the partial glimpses which he obtained of the castle through the woods and glades by which this ancient feudal fortress was surrounded, our military traveller was determined to inquire whether it might not deserve a nearer view, and whether it contained family pictures or other objects of curiosity worthy of a stranger's visit, when, leaving the vicinity of the park, he rolled through a clean and well-paved street, and stopped at the door of a well-frequented inn.

Before ordering horses, to proceed on his journey, General Browne made inquiries concerning the proprietor of the chateau which had so attracted his admiration, and was equally surprised and pleased at hearing in reply a nobleman named, whom we shall call Lord Woodville. How fortunate! Much of Browne's early recollections, both at school and at college, had been connected with young Woodville, whom, by a few questions, he now ascertained to be the same with the owner of this fair domain. He had been raised to the peerage by the decease of his father a few months before, and, as the General learned from the landlord, the term of mourning being ended, was now taking possession of his paternal estate in the jovial season of merry, autumn, accompanied by a select party of friends, to enjoy the sports of a country famous for game.

This was delightful news to our traveller. Frank Woodville had been Richard Browne's fag at Eton, and his chosen intimate at Christ Church; their pleasures and their tasks had been the same; and the honest soldier's heart warmed to find his early friend in possession of so delightful a residence, and of an estate, as the landlord assured him with a nod and a wink, fully adequate to maintain and add to his dignity. Nothing was more natural than that the traveller should suspend a journey, which there was nothing to render hurried, to pay a visit to an old friend under such agreeable circumstances.

The fresh horses, therefore, had only the brief task of conveying the General's travelling carriage to Woodville Castle. A porter admitted them at a modern Gothic lodge, built in that style to correspond with the castle itself, and at the same time rang a bell to give warning of the approach of visitors. Apparently the sound of the bell had suspended the separation of the company, bent on the various amusements of the morning; for, on entering the court of the chateau, several young men were lounging about in their sporting dresses, looking at and criticizing the dogs which the keepers held in readiness to attend their pastime. As General Browne alighted, the young lord came to the gate of the hall, and for an instant gazed, as at a stranger, upon the countenance of his friend, on which war, with its fatigues and its wounds, had made a great alteration. But the uncertainty lasted no longer than till the visitor had spoken, and the hearty greeting which followed was such as can only be exchanged betwixt those who have passed together the merry days of careless boyhood or early youth.

"If I could have formed a wish, my dear Browne," said Lord Woodville, "it would have been to have you here, of all men, upon this occasion, which my friends are good enough to hold as a sort of holiday. Do not think you have been unwatched during the years you have been absent from us. I have traced you through your dangers, your triumphs, your misfortunes, and was delighted to see that, whether in victory or defeat, the name of my old friend was always distinguished with applause."

The General made a suitable reply, and congratulated his friend on his new dignities, and the possession of a place and domain so beautiful.

"Nay, you have seen nothing of it as yet," said Lord Woodville, "and I trust you do not mean to leave us till you are better acquainted with it. It is true, I confess, that my present party is pretty large, and the old house, like other places of the kind, does not possess so much accommodation as the extent of the outward walls appears to promise. But we can give you a comfortable old-fashioned room, and I venture to suppose that your campaigns have taught you to be glad of worse quarters."

The General shrugged his shoulders, and laughed. "I presume," he said, "the worst apartment in your chateau is considerably superior to the old tobacco-cask in which I was fain to take up my night's lodging when I was in the Bush, as the Virginians call it, with the light corps. There I lay, like Diogenes himself, so delighted with my covering from the elements, that I made a vain attempt to have it rolled on to my next quarters; but my commander for the time would give way to no such luxurious provision, and I took farewell of my beloved cask with tears in my eyes."

"Well, then, since you do not fear your quarters," said Lord Woodville, "you will stay with me a week at least. Of guns, dogs, fishing-rods, flies, and means of sport by sea and land, we have enough and to spare – you cannot pitch on an amusement but we will find the means of pursuing it. But if you prefer the gun and pointers, I will go with you myself, and see whether you have mended your shooting since you have been amongst the Indians of the back settlements."

The General gladly accepted his friendly host's proposal in all its points. After a morning of manly exercise, the company met at dinner, where it was the delight of Lord Woodville to conduce to the display of the high properties of his recovered friend, so as to recommend him to his guests, most of whom were persons of distinction. He led General Browne to speak of the scenes he had witnessed; and as every word marked alike the brave officer and the sensible man, who retained possession of his cool judgment under the most imminent dangers, the company looked upon the soldier with general respect, as on one who had proved himself possessed of an uncommon portion of personal courage – that attribute of all others of which everybody desires to be thought possessed.

The day at Woodville Castle ended as usual in such mansions. The hospitality stopped within the limits of good order. Music, in which the young lord was a proficient, succeeded to the circulation of the bottle; cards and billiards, for those who preferred such amusements, were in readiness; but the exercise of the morning required early hours, and not long after eleven o'clock the guests began to retire to their several apartments.

The young lord himself conducted his friend, General Browne, to the chamber destined for him, which answered the description he had given of it, being comfortable, but old-fashioned, The bed was of the massive form used in the end of the seventeenth century, and the curtains of faded silk, heavily trimmed with tarnished gold. But then the sheets, pillows, and blankets looked delightful to the campaigner, when he thought of his 'mansion, the cask'. There was an air of gloom in the tapestry hangings, which, with their worn-out graces, curtained the walls of the little chamber, and gently undulated as the autumnal breeze found its way through the ancient lattice window, which pattered and whistled as the air gained entrance. The toilet, too, with its mirror, turbaned after the manner of the beginning of the century, with a coiffure of murrey-coloured silk, and its hundred strange-shaped boxes, providing for arrangements which had been obsolete for more than fifty years, had an antique, and in so far a melancholy, aspect. But nothing could blaze more brightly and cheerfully than the two large wax candles; or if aught could rival them, it was the flaming, bickering fagots in the chimney, that sent at once their gleam and their warmth through the snug apartment, which, notwithstanding the general antiquity of its appearance, was not wanting in the least convenience that modern habits rendered either necessary or desirable.

"This is an old-fashioned sleeping apartment, General," said the young lord; "but I hope you find nothing that makes you envy your old tobacco-cask."

"I am not particular respecting my lodgings," replied the General; "yet were I to make any choice, I would prefer this chamber by many degrees to the gayer and more modern rooms of your family mansion. Believe me that, when I unite its modern air of comfort with its venerable antiquity, and recollect that it is your lordship's property, I shall feel in better quarters here than if I were in the best hotel London could afford."

"I trust – I have no doubt – that you will find yourself as comfortable as I wish you, my dear General," said the young nobleman; and once more bidding his guest goodnight, he shook him by the hand, and withdrew.

The General once more looked round him, and internally congratulating himself on his return to peaceful life, the comforts of which were endeared by the recollection of the hardships and dangers he had lately sustained, undressed himself, and prepared for a luxurious night's rest.

Here, contrary to the custom of this species of tale, we leave the General in possession of his apartment until the next morning.

The company assembled for breakfast at an early hour, but without the appearance of General Browne, who seemed the guest that Lord Woodville was desirous of honouring above all whom his hospitality had assembled around him. He more than once expressed surprise at the General's absence, and at length sent a servant to make inquiry after him. The man brought back information that General Browne had been walking abroad since an early hour of the morning, in defiance of the weather, which was misty and ungenial.

"The custom of a soldier," said the young nobleman to his friends. "Many of them acquire habitual vigilance, and cannot sleep after the early hour at which their duty usually commands them to be alert."

Yet the explanation which Lord Woodville thus offered to the company seemed hardly satisfactory to his own mind, and it was in a fit of silence and abstraction that he waited the return of the General. It took place near an hour after the breakfast bell had rung. He looked fatigued and feverish. His hair, the powdering and arrangement of which was at this time one of the most important occupations of a man's whole day, and marked his fashion as much as in the present time the tying of a cravat, or the want of one, was dishevelled, uncurled, void of powder, and dank with dew. His clothes were huddled on with a careless negligence, remarkable in a military man, whose real or supposed duties are usually held to include some attention to the toilet; and his looks were haggard and ghastly in a peculiar degree.

"So you have stolen a march upon us this morning, my dear General," said Lord Woodville; "or you have not found your bed so much to your mind as I had hoped and you seemed to expect. How did you rest last night?"

"Oh, excellently well! Remarkably well! Never better in my life," said General Browne rapidly, and yet with an air of embarrassment which was obvious to his friend. He then hastily swallowed a cup of tea, and neglecting or refusing whatever else was offered, seemed to fall into a fit of abstraction.

"You will take the gun today, General?" said his friend and host, but had to repeat the question twice ere he received the abrupt answer, "No, my lord; I am sorry I cannot have the opportunity of spending another day with your lordship; my post horses are ordered, and will be here directly."

All who were present showed surprise, and Lord Woodville immediately replied "Post horses, my good friend! What can you possibly want with them when you promised to stay with me quietly for at least a week?"

"I believe," said the General, obviously much embarrassed, "that I might, in the pleasure of my first meeting with your lordship, have said something about stopping here a few days; but I have since found it altogether impossible."

"That is very extraordinary," answered the young nobleman. "You seemed quite disengaged yesterday, and you cannot have had a summons today, for our post has not come up from the town, and therefore you cannot have received any letters."

General Browne, without giving any further explanation, muttered something about indispensable business, and insisted on the absolute necessity of his departure in a manner which silenced all opposition on the part of his host, who saw that his resolution was taken, and forbore all further importunity.

"At least, however," he said, "permit me, my dear Browne, since go you will or must, to show you the view from the terrace, which the mist, that is now rising, will soon display."

He threw open a sash-window, and stepped down upon the terrace as he spoke. The General followed him mechanically, but seemed little to attend to what his host was saying, as, looking across an extended and rich prospect, he pointed out the different objects worthy of observation. Thus they moved on till Lord Woodville had attained his purpose of drawing his guest entirely apart from the rest of the company, when, turning round upon him with an air of great solemnity, he addressed him thus:

"Richard Browne, my old and very dear friend, we are now alone. Let me conjure you to answer me upon the word of a friend, and the honour of a soldier. How did you in reality rest during last night?"

"Most wretchedly indeed, my lord," answered the General, in the same tone of solemnity – "so miserably, that I would not run the risk of such a second night, not only for all the lands belonging to this castle, but for all the country which I see from this elevated point of view."

"This is most extraordinary," said the young lord, as if speaking to himself; "then there must be something in the reports concerning that apartment." Again turning to the General, he said, "For God's sake, my dear friend, be candid with me, and let me know the disagreeable particulars which have befallen you under a roof, where, with consent of the owner, you should have met nothing save comfort."

The General seemed distressed by this appeal, and paused a moment before he replied. "My dear lord," he at length said, "what happened to me last night is of a nature so peculiar and so unpleasant, that I could hardly bring myself to detail it even to your lordship, were it not that, independent of my wish to gratify any request of yours, I think that sincerity on my part may lead to some explanation about a circumstance equally painful and mysterious. To others, the communication I am about to make, might place me in the light of a weak-minded, superstitious fool, who suffered his own imagination to delude and bewilder him; but you have known me in childhood and youth, and will not suspect me of having adopted in manhood the feelings and frailties from which my early years were free." Here he paused, and his friend replied:

"Do not doubt my perfect confidence in the truth of your communication, however strange it may be," replied Lord Woodville. "I know your firmness of disposition too well, to suspect you could be made the object of imposition, and am aware that your honour and your friendship will equally deter you from exaggerating whatever you may have witnessed."

"Well, then," said the General, "I will proceed with my story as well as I can, relying upon your candour, and yet distinctly feeling that I would rather face a battery than recall to my mind the odious recollections of last night."

He paused a second time, and then perceiving that Lord Woodville remained silent and in an attitude of attention, he commenced, though not without obvious reluctance, the history of his night's adventures in the Tapestried Chamber.

"I undressed and went to bed so soon as your lordship left me yesterday evening; but the wood in the chimney, which nearly fronted my bed, blazed brightly and cheerfully, and, aided by a hundred exciting recollections of my childhood and youth, which had been recalled by the unexpected pleasure of meeting your lordship, prevented me from falling immediately asleep. I ought, however, to say that these reflections were all of a pleasant and agreeable kind, grounded on a sense of having for a time exchanged the labour, fatigues, and dangers of my profession for the enjoyments of a peaceful life, and the reunion of those friendly and affectionate ties which I had torn asunder at the rude summons of war.

"While such pleasing reflections were stealing over my mind, and gradually lulling me to slumber, I was suddenly aroused by a sound like that of the rustling of a silken gown, and the tapping of a pair of high-heeled shoes, as if a woman were walking in the apartment. Ere I could draw the curtain to see what the matter was, the figure of a little woman passed between the bed and the fire. The back of this form was turned to me, and I could observe, from the shoulders and neck, it was that of an old woman, whose dress was an old-fashioned gown, which I think ladies call a sacque – that is, a sort of robe completely loose in the body, but gathered into broad plaits upon the neck and shoulders, which fall down to the ground, and terminate in a species of train.

"I thought the intrusion singular enough, but never harboured for a moment the idea that what I saw was anything more than the mortal form of some old woman about the establishment, who had a fancy to dress like her grandmother, and who, having perhaps (as your lordship mentioned that you were rather straitened for room) been dislodged from her chamber for my accommodation, had forgotten the circumstance, and returned by twelve to her old haunt. Under this persuasion I moved myself in bed and coughed a little, to make the intruder sensible of my being in possession of the premises. She turned slowly round, but, gracious Heaven! My lord, what a countenance did she display to me! There was no longer any question what she was, or any thought of her being a living being. Upon a face which wore the fixed features of a corpse were imprinted the traces of the vilest and most hideous passions which had animated her while she lived. The body of some atrocious criminal seemed to have been given up from the grave, and the soul restored from the penal fire, in order to form for a space a union with the ancient accomplice of its guilt. I started up in bed, and sat upright, supporting myself on my palms, as I gazed on this horrible spectre. The hag made, as it seemed, a single and swift stride to the bed where I lay, and squatted herself down upon it, in precisely the same attitude which I had assumed in the extremity of horror, advancing her diabolical countenance within half a yard of mine, with a grin which seemed to intimate the malice and the derision of an incarnate fiend."

Here General Browne stopped, and wiped from his brow the cold perspiration with which the recollection of his horrible vision had covered it.

"My lord," he said, "I am no coward, I have been in all the mortal dangers incidental to my profession, and I may truly boast that no man ever knew Richard Browne dishonour the sword he wears; but in these horrible circumstances, under the eyes, and, as it seemed, almost in the grasp of an incarnation of an evil spirit, all firmness forsook me, all manhood melted from me like wax in the furnace, and I felt my hair individually bristle. The current of my life-blood ceased to flow, and I sank back in a swoon, as very a victim to panic terror as ever was a village girl, or a child of ten years old. How long I lay in this condition I cannot pretend to guess.

"But I was roused by the castle clock striking one, so loud that it seemed as if it were in the very room. It was some time before I dared open my eyes, lest they should again encounter the horrible spectacle. When, however, I summoned courage to look up, she was no longer visible. My first idea was to pull my bell, wake the servants, and remove to a garret or a hay-loft, to be ensured against a second visitation. Nay, I will confess the truth that my resolution was altered, not by the shame of exposing myself, but by the fear that, as the bell-cord hung by the chimney, I might, in making my way to it, be again crossed by the fiendish hag, who, I figured to myself, might be still lurking about some corner of the apartment.

"I will not pretend to describe what hot and cold fever-fits tormented me for the rest of the night, through broken sleep, weary vigils, and that dubious state which forms the neutral ground between them. A hundred terrible objects appeared to haunt me; but there was the great difference betwixt the vision which I have described, and those which followed, that I knew the last to be deceptions of my own fancy and over-excited nerves.

"Day at last appeared, and I rose from my bed ill in health and humiliated in mind. I was ashamed of myself as a man and a soldier, and still more so at feeling my own extreme desire to escape from the haunted apartment, which, however, conquered all other considerations; so that, huddling on my clothes with the most careless haste, I made my escape from your lordship's mansion, to seek in the open air some relief to my nervous system, shaken as it was by this horrible rencounter with a visitant, for such I must believe her, from the other world. Your lordship has now heard the cause of my discomposure, and of my sudden desire to leave your hospitable castle. In other places I trust we may often meet, but God protect me from ever spending a second night under that roof!"

Strange as the General's tale was, he spoke with such a deep air of conviction that it cut short all the usual commentaries which are made on such stories. Lord Woodville never once asked him if he was sure he did not dream of the apparition, or suggested any of the possibilities by which it is fashionable to explain supernatural appearances as wild vagaries of the fancy, or deceptions of the optic nerves. On the contrary, he seemed deeply impressed with the truth and reality of what he had heard; and, after a considerable pause regretted, with much appearance of sincerity, that his early friend should in his house have suffered so severely.

"I am the more sorry for your pain, my dear Browne," he continued, "that it is the unhappy, though most unexpected, result of an experiment of my own. You must know that, for my father and grandfather's time, at least, the apartment which was assigned to you last night had been shut on account of reports that it was disturbed by supernatural sights and noises. When I came, a few weeks since, into possession of the estate, I thought the accommodation which the castle afforded for my friends was not extensive enough to permit the inhabitants of the invisible world to retain possession of a comfortable sleeping apartment. I therefore caused the Tapestried Chamber, as we call it, to be opened, and, without destroying its air of antiquity, I had such new articles of furniture placed in it as became the modern times. Yet, as the opinion that the room was haunted very strongly prevailed among the domestics, and was also known in the neighbourhood and to many of my friends, I feared some prejudice might be entertained by the first occupant of the Tapestried Chamber, which might tend to revive the evil report which it had laboured under, and so disappoint my purpose of rendering it a useful part of the house. I must confess, my dear Browne, that your arrival yesterday, agreeable to me for a thousand reasons besides, seemed the most favourable opportunity of removing the unpleasant rumours which attached to the room, since your courage was indubitable, and your mind free of any preoccupation on the subject. I could not, therefore, have chosen a more fitting subject for my experiment."

"Upon my life," said General Browne, somewhat hastily, "I am infinitely obliged to your lordship – very particularly indebted indeed. I am likely to remember for some time the consequences of the experiment, as your lordship is pleased to call it."

"Nay, now you are unjust, my dear friend," said Lord Woodville. "You have only to reflect for a single moment, in order to be convinced that I could not augur the possibility of the pain to which you have been so unhappily exposed. I was yesterday morning a complete sceptic on the subject of supernatural appearances. Nay, I am sure that, had I told you what was said about that room, those very reports would have induced you, by your own choice, to select it for your accommodation. It was my misfortune, perhaps my error, but really cannot be termed my fault, that you have been afflicted so strangely."

"Strangely indeed!" said the General, resuming his good temper; "and I acknowledge that I have no right to be offended with your lordship for treating me like what I used to think myself – a man of some firmness and courage. But I see my post horses are arrived, and I must not detain your lordship from your amusement."

"Nay, my old friend," said Lord Woodville, "since you cannot stay with us another day – which, indeed, I can no longer urge – give me at least half an hour more. You used to love pictures, and I have a gallery of portraits, some of them by Vandyke, representing ancestry to whom this property and castle formerly belonged. I think that several of them will strike you as possessing merit."

General Browne accepted the invitation, though somewhat unwillingly. It was evident he was not to breathe freely or at ease till he left Woodville Castle far behind him. He could not refuse his friend's invitation, however; and the less so, that he was a little ashamed of the peevishness which he had displayed towards his well-meaning entertainer.

The General, therefore, followed Lord Woodville through several rooms into a long gallery hung with pictures, which the latter pointed out to his guest, telling the names, and giving some account of the personages whose portraits presented themselves in progression. General Browne was but little interested in the details which these accounts conveyed to him. They were, indeed, of the kind which are usually found in an old family gallery. Here was a Cavalier who had ruined the estate in the royal cause; there a fine lady who had reinstated it by contracting a match with a wealthy Roundhead. There hung a gallant who had been in danger for corresponding with the exiled Court at Saint Germain's; here one who had taken arms for William at the Revolution; and there a third that had thrown his weight alternately into the scale of Whig and Tory.

While lord Woodville was cramming these words into his guest's ear, 'against the stomach of his sense', they gained the middle of the gallery, when he beheld General Browne suddenly start, and assume an attitude of the utmost surprise, not unmixed with fear, as his eyes were suddenly caught and riveted by a portrait of an old lady in a sacque, the fashionable dress of the end of the seventeenth century.

"There she is!" he exclaimed – "there she is, in form and features, though Inferior in demoniac expression to the accursed hag who visited me last night!"

"If that be the case," said the young nobleman, "there can remain no longer any doubt of the horrible reality of your apparition. That is the picture of a wretched ancestress of mine, of whose crimes a black and fearful catalogue is recorded in a family history in my charter-chest. The recital of them would be too horrible; it is enough to say, that in yon fatal apartment incest and unnatural murder were committed. I will restore it to the solitude to which the better judgment of those who preceded me had consigned it; and never shall anyone, so long as I can prevent it, be exposed to a repetition of the supernatural horrors which could shake such courage as yours."

Thus the friends, who had met with such glee, parted in a very different mood – Lord Woodville to command the Tapestried Chamber to be unmantled, and the door built up; and General Browne to seek in some less beautiful country, and with some less dignified friend, forgetfulness of the painful night which he had passed in Woodville Castle.

This House Is My Cage

Lizz-Ayn Shaarawi

THE DOOR HINGES scream in protest, forced open for the first time this year. He's back. Like clockwork, for the past five years, he's returned to gawk and stare at me. Like I'm an animal in a zoo. Like I exist just for his amusement. From an upper landing's corner, I stare down to find him pacing with excitement. Without thinking, I groan. The sound reverberates down the staircase, causing the TV crew in the foyer to glance around nervously.

He brought a TV crew this time. Ugh.

Ben, in a tight black tee shirt with ridiculously coiffed hair beams at the sound. "I told you this was an active house," he says. A few murmurs travel through the group. "Let's set up multiple points here and here," he directs. "And don't forget to light the staircase. I want this to be perfect."

I am an animal in a zoo; this house, my cage.

The crew wears matching tee shirts with the show's name printed across the back. They scurry around the room, taping down cables and setting up lighting rigs. I watch for a while, impressed by the neat economy and precision of the entire operation, though I remain wary of what sort of stunt Ben will pull this time. He reminds me of a little general, commanding the troops in his tight black clothes, the goth eyeliner lending an air of theater. All for the camera, I suppose.

Before long, boredom sets in. I shake my head at the carnival below and drift away, back to my happy place. Which is, ironically, a dark place. The upstairs linen closet with its ornate double doors and crown molded frame serves as my refuge. I like to imagine I can still smell sunshine on the sheets, which were at one time dried on a clothesline in the back garden. In truth, they're mildewed, moth-eaten, and stained. But pretending brings me joy. You can't fault me that, especially under the current circumstances. Yes, the linen closet is my sanctuary. It's where I go whenever visitors invade my home to check out the freakshow. Not that the happy place protects me. Every year at the same date and time, I'm forced to act out my death. It's a horrible existence. I can roam the house if I want; I can even step out on the front porch or the back patio. But I can't stand in the sunshine or feel grass between my toes. I can touch people, if by touch you meant violently shove. I can feel people, if by feel you meant a horrible, revolting tremor when they walk through me. This house is my cage.

This is the fifth time Ben has visited me. I hate when they get like this, romantic men who want to save me, be my white knight and release me from my imprisonment in this limbo of existence. It would be great if anything they tried actually worked, but it never did. They only end up obsessed with me which causes them to become increasingly strange and erratic. They never really help and, though it does relieve some of the boredom at first, in the end they became annoyances and I'm always glad to see them gone.

Ben directed the members of his team on where to set up the cameras (HD and infrared), how to set up the temperature monitors, and what to adjust on the EVP recorder. Once the work is completed, he gathers them around. The crew consists of three men and one woman. They all regard Ben with the utmost respect and awe.

"Are we rolling?" Ben glances around at the cameras stationed around the room, all pointing at him. "Good." He climbs the stairs and stops at the top, illuminated by a multitude of lights, a man in his element. Two cameras follow his movements.

"Sound," a voice says off to the side.

A man in a baseball cap holds up his index finger as he stares into a monitor, waits for a moment, then points at Ben.

"Not to be a broken record, but I want to make sure all of you know what to expect tonight," Ben says. "Cassandra Middleton died a violent death on March 18, 1963, at 10:17 p.m. There are three theories on what actually occurred that night. The first is that her brother, Reginald, was jealous of the inheritance she had recently received from their late grandmother."

I snort. As if Reggie would have the guts to do anything that brave.

Ben strides down a couple of stairs. "The second is that a burglar broke in this beautiful, palatial home. When Cassandra ran to the staircase to check on the noise, he panicked and attacked her, killing her in the ensuing fight." He casually hops down a few more steps.

Wrong again, I think.

"The third theory is that it was a crime of passion." He steps off onto the foyer floor and turns to a nearby camera.

I shake my head. Nope, I can't think about it. Ben's words drone on but I'm already retreating into the dark space, my happy place. Instead of the drone of white noise that accompanies me, my mind drifts back five years.

The first time Ben visited me, it was as a fraternity pledge. He stood at the bottom of the stairs with two other dopes, all three in their blue kappa-gamma-whoever shirts, quivering in anticipation. They whispered between each other, the mock bravado betrayed by trembling hands holding warming beers. Electricity filled the air and the moment approached. When I made my grand entrance the other two pledges bolted from the house screaming but Ben stayed. For a minute I thought he must have gone into shock, the way he just stood there, mouth agape. But no, he reached down and touched my cheek.

It was revolting.

The next year he was back, this time with a group of friends. They drank and told stupid ghost stories to each other to pass the time. Ben kept glancing at the stairs, becoming more and more anxious as the minutes passed. The girls screamed shrilly and giggled as the boys tickled and poked them at the scariest parts of the stories. The girl sitting beside Ben began to look bored, then irritated at his inattention. At 10:16, Ben was practically a bundle of nerves while his friends laughed and joked around him. At 10:18, he was the only one left in the house.

One year later, he was back, this time on his own. He brought flowers, lit candles, and laid out a picnic blanket at the bottom of the stairs. When the big show kicked off, he actually tried to jump in and save me, not realizing it was only a skip in a record that would go round and round until a force, much more powerful that he could ever be, would knock the cosmic turntable. When I hit the bottom of the stairs, I forced the candles to go out, not only to scare him away but also to keep the idiot from burning the house down. My home was the only thing I had left. He sat in the dark, on the bottom step where I'd just disappeared from. Then he started to talk. On and on for hours, he told me his whole life story. In the beginning, I hung around. It was something different, after all. But soon enough, he began to bore me and I wandered off to the linen closet.

After that, he came by the house more often, sometimes camping out in the moldy old living room, but mainly staying in the foyer where he could keep sight of the stairs, though I never made an appearance. He brought Ouija boards and psychics, mystics and crackpots. They trailed through my house but I kept myself hidden. Then he crossed the line.

The fourth year.

The year of the exorcism.

The prince charming that he was decided he would release me from the shackles of this earthly plane. I have no idea what parish he dug the priest up from but judging by the state of his vestments and the smell wafting up from him, it was somewhere around Our Lady of Mad Dog 20/20.

It was horrible. The priest mumbled through the exorcism, throwing holy water all over everything, leaving water spots on the wallpaper and furniture. It infuriated me. I might be dead but I'm still rather house-proud. The censure belched incense, making the room so sickly sweet, I was relieved that I no longer need to breathe. Then came my reluctant performance. As I went through the same motions, the priest looked genuinely surprised to see me. The chanting and incantations, which to this point had been very half-hearted, suddenly flared from him with religious conviction I doubt he'd felt in twenty years.

"Out, poor spirit!" the priest yelled. "Release yourself!" It was almost sad how disappointed he was when the show just kept right on going as if he wasn't even there. He tried Latin and Greek, holy water and Hail Marys. I still ended up at the bottom of the stairs.

Ben was furious. He cursed God and his poor hung-over representative before him. The sad little priest was practically chased out of the house by Ben, railing against the heavens and all within. I had hoped that would be the end of it. A botched exorcism should put anyone off. Genuinely, sincerely, I had hoped to find the house empty so I could repeat my death with a bit of privacy, just get the whole thing over with, if only so I could have 364 days of peace. But ghosts don't get much say in what *they* want.

It's a year later and he's back. This time he brought some reality show hacks with him. Surely, this will be a real rating coup for them. I hate him more than ever.

Soon, too soon, the show will begin against my will. A trickle of nervous anticipation fills me, like an old engine slowly gearing up after a long rest. Unpleasant prickles of cold energy flick against my scalp, arms, legs, becoming more rapid, more insistent as they move inward towards my core. Out from the black, a force yanks me into the upstairs corridor with sickening speed. Bright lights flood my face.

With a gasp, I find myself racing down the hallway, the well-worn story starting over again. At the top of the stairs stands Ben and a camera man. The poor fellow quakes in his boots at the sight of me. Ben smiles, triumphant. "There you have it! Proof of life after death! Proof of the world beyond!" Ben announces for the camera's benefit.

I glance over my shoulder and, though I can never see the actual face of who attacks me, I cry out. The words "Please, no!" fall from my lips before I tear my gaze back to the upcoming staircase.

Ben hasn't moved. He watches me, his chest heaving with excitement. Below Ben, the rest of the crew shine lights up the staircase. The multiple cameras capture my death in as many angles as they can.

The staircase looms close, so close. I stretch out my fingers in front of me. Maybe this time I'll make it. Maybe this time –

An unseen force grabs me by the hair and yanks me from my feet. I fall on my back. The force pins my arms to the ground and viciously pummels my face. I manage to pull one arm free and scratch at my attacker's cheek. A brief look of triumph crosses my face, only to be quickly crushed by hands squeezing my throat. My body bucks and writhes in protest as the last bit of life is extinguished. As one last insult, my attacker gives my dead body a hearty kick, sending it rolling down the long, ornate staircase.

A scream rings out. No doubt one of the crew members, shocked to finally see a real ghost. But, no. I'm not the cause of the scream. At the top of the stairs, on camera, Ben stretches his arms out to the side, rocks on his feet, just before leaping into the air. He hovers, for one brief moment, then comes crashing down the marble steps. The air fills with the bone-crunching thuds and cracks of 175 pounds of flesh falling head over heels. His head lands on the step beside mine and with his last ounce of strength, his trembling hand strokes my cheek.

It's still revolting. But that isn't the worst part.

He's here now. Never leaving, always with me. I still find ways to escape him, to go to my happy place, but whenever I come back he's waiting with his big plan on how he's figured it all out. He'll really save me this time. In death, he'll fight my killer. This time, he'll get it right.

Ben doesn't realize that my killer has gone on to live a full life and now runs one of the highest grossing mid-level sedan dealerships in three counties. My killer walks the earth, alive, beside his wife, children, and grandchildren, with only a small scar on his cheek to remember me by.

The only thing left to do is hide in the linen closet, and wait for the next year, the next big performance, the coil I'm forever shuffling on. Unfortunately, now I have company, Ben and his big ideas, to haunt me for eternity. This house is my cage but now I must share it.

Lullaby for the Dead

Erin Skolney

IT ALMOST CAME as no surprise when the dead child first arrived.

That morning, Natalie Morris sat on the porch, sipping coffee that had long gone cold. The clouds and rain had made the sky nearly the same gray as the lake water. Gravestone gray. When her husband, Scott, had built the lakeside home by hand, it had been the place where she'd envisioned her entire life unfolding. Natalie no longer saw anything but death in the depths. She could spend hours staring over the water, imagining it swallowing her.

A pair of yellow rubber boots were first to catch Natalie's eye; the color where none had been before. The boy stood still on the rocky beach, watching Natalie. His clothes were heavy with water, clinging to his small frame. Pieces of seaweed were caught in his pockets and tangled in his hair; a long, green rope of it wrapped around his neck.

Natalie's throat closed and her chest tightened. She put down her coffee and approached him. Kneeling, she looked over the small dead child. She knew he was dead because his flesh was pallid and puffy from all the water – so much water that it leaked from him; from his eyes, his nose, his mouth, his flesh.

She also knew he was dead because she had buried him five years ago.

"Noah," she whispered.

The boy's eyes used to be blue, but now his irises were milky and clouded. His dead gaze made Natalie's stomach crawl with guilt.

Natalie reached to stroke Noah's cheek. He didn't move, didn't respond to her touch, just blinked at her. Natalie's eyes trailed over the little, bloated body standing there.

She had watched as the rescue divers had pulled him from the water. He had been dried off and placed in a cushioned casket with his stuffed elephant tucked under his little arm, still chubby with baby fat. She had watched as they had lowered him into the ground and shoveled the earth on top of him. He couldn't be here, dripping wet, cold, and alone. And yet Natalie could feel his icy flesh beneath her fingers.

She pulled seaweed from the boy's hair, smoothing the wet blond tangle.

"Natalie?" Scott's voice cut through the wet silence.

Noah raised a hand and curled his fingers into a wave.

"Come inside. You've been out in the cold for hours."

Natalie turned toward her husband who stood barefoot on the porch, still wearing his flannel boxers and white sleep shirt even though it was late into the morning.

"Scott," she began, and turned back toward Noah, but he was gone.

"What is it?" Scott moved off the porch toward her in concern, scanning the rocky beach.

"He's gone." Natalie's voice sounded distant, even to her own ears.

Scott looked around, confusion evident on his face. "Who's gone?"

"Noah. He was here. Standing right in front of me."

Scott's expression broke into grief. "Natalie, come inside." His voice was laced with pity.

"I know how it sounds, but I saw him. I touched his hair. He was here."

Scott put a hand on Natalie's forehead, as though checking for a fever. "You need rest. You've hardly slept this week. I know it's hard with a baby, but he's asleep now and you should be too. Sitting out in the cold like this, it's not good for you."

"He was here," Natalie urged, needing him to understand. "His eyes...they were all clouded; but do you remember how they used to be? Oliver has the exact same eyes. That exact same sunshiny blue. I didn't notice until today, but when he stood there in front of me, I remembered. Noah was here. He was *real*."

Scott shook his head. "Please stop. Noah died. I know having Oliver here now reminds you of him, but Noah is still gone."

"He was –"

"Come inside," Scott said, turning to leave Natalie by the edge of the lake.

Natalie looked at where Noah had been standing only moments earlier. The beach was empty, achingly so. She could nearly see Noah's name etched into the gray lake; her son's watery headstone. His date of birth. Date of death. He was there, under the water, waiting for her to comfort him.

* * *

He came again the next day, and the day after, and the day after that. Each time, he would stand by the water and Natalie would go to him. She would pluck the seaweed from him and straighten his hair and clothes, but her dead son never responded. Noah would remain still and unforgiving, while Natalie would ache to hold him. Death, she imagined, was a dark and lonely place.

"Forgive me," she would whisper, reaching her arms to him. But he would never move toward her.

On the day Noah had drowned, Natalie had been busy finishing laundry, taking phone calls, and preparing dinner. Noah had followed her through the house, tugging on her shirt and inundating her with need – *"Mama, come look at my tower." "Mama, I'm hungry." "Mama, come play with me."* She had shooed him to play by himself, and he had gone to play at the lake.

Now that Noah had returned, Natalie made a point of taking her coffee outside at six every morning, and she would wait as long as it took until he appeared. And so it went until the ninth day, when no sooner than she sat down, Noah appeared right beside her, rather than on the rocky beach.

"Good morning," Natalie said, meeting his wide, wet eyes.

In response, Noah climbed into Natalie's lap. The move surprised Natalie but she quickly accommodated him, setting down her coffee and wrapping her little boy in her arms. Noah was cold and wet, but she still pulled him close, slowly rocking him back and forth.

Noah snuggled into Natalie's lap with the most pained little whimper she could have imagined. Her heart shattered. She kissed his cold, wet hair.

"I'm here now," Natalie said as she rocked the corpse. "It's okay. I've got you."

Noah's pained whimper turned into a wail, and Natalie held him as he cried against her. His tiny chest heaved from the force of his violent sobs, until suddenly he stopped, wiped his eyes, and climbed off Natalie's lap. Noah vanished, leaving Natalie cold and alone.

"Natalie? Are you okay?" Scott asked, appearing in the doorway. "I heard you crying from the nursery."

Natalie continued staring toward the lake, hoping to catch sight of her child. "I'm fine. It wasn't me you heard, it was Noah."

"Enough. Noah died. He's been gone now for five years."

Natalie shook her head, and Scott moved toward her.

Concern creased his face. "Why are you all wet? Were you in the lake?"

"I'm not –" Natalie began, but then noticed she was, in fact, soaked. Not just her lap and arms, which had held her drowned boy, but all her clothes; her cardigan, her sweatpants, and even her socks. "He was so wet from the lake. I held him and I rocked him, and he was wet all the way down inside from all the water. I must be wet from holding Noah."

"You could have drowned," Scott said, as though Natalie had not spoken at all. "And you're shivering."

Natalie hardened against the implicit accusation of Scott's words. He thought she was lying, that she was making it all up. Or worse, that she was crazy and only imagining Noah standing in front of her. Natalie didn't know how Noah had come back to her, but when she had held him, she had felt his weight against her, and she knew he was as real as either Scott or Oliver.

From inside the house came the muted sound of a baby crying.

"Oliver's awake," Scott said, and went inside without giving Natalie another glance.

Natalie followed him and peeled off her soggy clothes in the bathroom. She toweled dry and slipped into a bathrobe. When she entered the nursery, she saw Scott sitting in the recliner, holding a bottle for Oliver.

"I need you," Scott said to Natalie without looking up from their son. "*Oliver* needs you."

But Natalie could see they didn't need her.

"I know it's been hard," Scott said. "It's been hard for me too. Of course, having Oliver reminds me of what we lost. He doesn't replace Noah, and he can't bring Noah back."

"You don't understand."

"But I *do*. We have Oliver. He's alive and he needs us. We'll never stop loving Noah, but we need to love our living boy now."

Natalie *did* love Oliver. She loved him more than anything in the entire world. But Oliver didn't need her. He didn't cry for her from the bottom of the lake, not like Noah did.

* * *

Natalie awoke shivering shortly after midnight. There was a wet chill in the air and a faint foul odor. She felt death's oppressive presence in the room.

"Noah?" she whispered, pulling back the covers.

Her dead boy was not there. Still, she knew she and Scott were not alone in the room. Natalie's spine prickled with fear. Her breath was shallow and her chest was tight. She felt the whisper, more than she heard it. The single phrase echoed through all the lonely spaces in her heart.

"*Mama, come play.*"

Natalie knew what was needed of her.

Scott snored lightly beside her. Natalie watched him sleep, her gaze tracing the lines on his face that had not been there when they had first met. She recalled their first date, like it had been only yesterday, and yet a lifetime had happened in the time they had been together.

Natalie leaned over and kissed his cheek, then slipped out of bed, careful not to make a sound as she pulled the bedroom door closed behind her.

She needed to see Oliver first. She went to his room and studied her sleeping baby. She brushed her fingers over his feather-light blond wisps of hair. His cheeks were chubby and pink, and he sucked his bottom lip in and out as he slept. He was so new that his tiny round nose still had a white dusting of milia.

Natalie began to sing.

"*Rock-a-bye baby, in the treetop...*"

Oliver squirmed and Natalie picked him up, clutching him close to her.

"*When the wind blows, the cradle will rock...*"

He opened his eyes and looked at her. Noah used to look at her like that, his gaze sleepy and content.

"*When the bough breaks, the cradle will fall...*"

Natalie brushed her lips over his forehead. She breathed his sweet scent of milk and baby lotion.

"*And down will come baby, cradle and all.*"

The door creaked and she turned toward the sound, expecting to see Scott. Instead, Noah stood in the entrance to the room that had once been his. Natalie watched as Noah surveyed the nursery. The race car bed had been replaced with a crib. The lettering on the wall now said *Oliver*, not *Noah*. The spaceship wall decals had been stripped and replaced with clouds and trees.

Natalie's heart twisted with guilt. She returned Oliver to his crib and then turned to Noah, but he was already gone.

Scott had said she had to love her living boy, but everybody loved the living boys. The dead were the ones who had nobody. Noah had nobody.

Natalie glanced at Oliver one last time and then left the nursery. There was a boy at the lake who needed her more.

* * *

Scott woke to the sound of Oliver crying over the baby monitor. He groaned and turned to look at the clock. 2:12 a.m. As he rubbed the sleep from his eyes, he became aware of the empty bed. Perhaps Natalie had already woken to tend to Oliver. He waited, but when his wife's voice did not come through the baby monitor, he was forced to accept that she was not with their son. Anger and concern warred within him.

Although he didn't know where his wife was, he was hardly surprised to find Natalie gone in the middle of the night. She was absent more often than she was present these days. He supposed he would find her somewhere dreaming of Noah. At first, Scott had thought Natalie was just going through a rough patch. He had expected the new baby would be an adjustment for them, but this was more than that. She needed help. Scott decided he would try to convince Natalie to talk to a doctor.

Oliver continued to fuss. Scott swung his feet over the edge of the bed. The floor was wet and cold. He looked at the ceiling. There didn't appear to be a leak. He frowned and switched on a light. Little circles of water pooled in a line across the floor, leading a trail out the door.

Perhaps they had come from Natalie.

Scott would worry about the water later. Oliver's cries were intensifying. When Scott entered the nursery, he found Oliver squirming and red-faced from crying. He scooped up his son and pulled him close.

"Hey, buddy."

Oliver continued to cry, but with less intensity.

"Let's go get you some milk, eh?" Scott said, carrying Oliver to the kitchen to warm a bottle.

All the lights were off. There was no sign that Natalie had come into the kitchen. He had expected lights and coffee, and his distant wife sitting outside in the cold. That was where he usually found her. Instead, he hit the light switch and saw the door swinging open.

"Natalie?" Scott called, forgetting about the baby in his arms demanding milk. His stomach tightened as he approached the door. He hoped to find her sitting in her chair.

The chair was empty. Well, almost empty. Scott's eyes went straight to the worn little gray elephant tossed on its side on the chair.

Scott hadn't seen the elephant in years. Five years. It had been buried with his son.

"Natalie?" Scott called, louder this time.

The volume and intensity frightened Oliver and he began to scream, beating his tiny fists and feet against Scott.

Without thought, Scott went inside and grabbed the phone from the counter. He dialed 9-1-1.

As the phone rang, Scott noticed little pieces of seaweed on the kitchen floor, along with little puddles, trailing out of the house.

Scott followed the puddles outside, calling his wife's name.

The phone rang.

The baby cried.

And over it all, Scott heard singing. The familiar voice and the familiar lullaby. But the notes were wet and muffled, coming from the lake.

Abandonment Option

by Lucy A. Snyder

MARTIN BENNINGTON graduated at the top of his Harvard MBA class, sat on the boards of the noblest charities, dined at the most lavish restaurants, bedded the most beautiful models, and ran the best-respected investment firm on Wall Street.

Now, he was standing naked before a bored Bureau of Prisons officer at the Lynchwood Federal Correctional Institution. The gray, vinyl-tiled floor was simultaneously gritty and sticky underneath his bare feet.

"Lift up your scrotum," ordered the officer.

Martin did as he was told, chagrined to see how far his penis had retreated from the chilly room. He also wondered what any man could possibly hide behind his testicles. A file? A knife? Plastic explosives? That would take quite a pair.

"Turn around, bend over, and spread your cheeks."

His lawyer had advised him to go to his 'happy place' once those words were uttered. Martin was a man who usually liked to live in the moment. And so, as unfriendly gloved fingers probed his most tender places, it was difficult to imagine he'd ever spent pleasant days entertaining starlets at the Isle of Capri and Bora Bora, but he closed his eyes and did his best.

Finally, the strip-search was over, and the officer told him to gather up his clothes. He led Martin into another room where he received a pair of tan polyester prison pants and matching shirt along with scratchy white underwear, undershirt and socks. Tacky slip-on sneakers completed the ensemble. Martin gave his street clothes to the receiving clerk, who dropped them into a cardboard box that would be shipped back to Martin's wife. She probably wouldn't even notice the delivery; she was too busy fending off the Feds in an effort to keep the Florida mansion he'd put in her name. The media probably weren't helping, either.

After getting dressed and signing off on the inventory form, the guards took Martin to yet another room where he was photographed for his prison ID card and then fingerprinted. A male nurse came in with more paperwork but no blood pressure cuff or stethoscope.

"How's your health?" asked the nurse, not looking up from the clipboard.

"Fit as a fiddle," Martin lied.

* * *

Not quite twelve months before, Martin was sitting in his doctor's office.

"You know the fatigue you've been feeling, and the shortness of breath you've been experiencing at the gym?"

Martin nodded, already suspecting and fearing the answer.

"The tests confirmed it's congestive heart failure: your heart muscle has gotten stiff and so the chambers aren't filling like they should. It's causing fluid to back up in your lungs. But I don't want you to panic…this is treatable. We're going to keep you on the Lotensin but also put you on Lasix, which is a diuretic that should help reduce a lot of your symptoms.

"Your diet's really important here," his doctor continued. "Stick to chicken and fish and eat lots of veggies. And I really want you to watch your salt intake. If I see you eating any more caviar canapés down at the country club, I'm going to kick your well-insured ass from here to Honolulu. If your ticker gets worse, we'll have to find you a replacement – and even with *your* resources, that won't be easy."

"I'll watch my diet," Martin said, lifting his hand with three fingers raised. "Scout's honor."

* * *

Before reporting for his 10-year prison sentence, Martin had his driver take him to a nearby steakhouse, where he dropped what was left of his pocket money on a lunch of fried shrimp and a thick New York strip. He limited himself to a single glass of mediocre Bordeaux; his lawyer had warned of dire consequences if he showed up at the FCI even slightly inebriated.

The briny red meat had worked its way into his blood, and his vision twitched with every beat of his straining heart.

"For some reason, we haven't received your PSI paperwork yet." The unit manager handed Martin a package of flimsy white towels and sheets topped with a package of basic toiletries. The manager's hands shook ever so slightly, and Martin saw a few drops of sweat on the man's tanned brow. "So you'll have to go to the Secure Housing Unit until we get those documents and can finish processing you. Then you'll be transferred to the Camp dorm."

Martin slipped his fingers inside the towel stack to ensure that the object he'd requested was there, then indulged in a grim smile. If his lawyers had done their jobs, he'd never have to see the inside of the inmate dormitory, and he'd have to endure the cell for a few hours at the most. He took a deep breath, trying to steady himself for what was going to happen next....

* * *

"Money isn't everything," his father had told him once they were ensconced in the back of the limo after Martin's MBA graduation ceremony. "Luck matters a whole lot more in this world. If you have enough luck, the money comes practically on its own. The thing that they probably didn't tell you in those fancy economics classes of yours is that the phenomenon we call luck is actually a commodity just like everything else. It can be bought and sold, although only a fool sells off his own luck."

The elder Bennington drained his martini glass down to the olive; Martin was quick to pour the old man another from the limousine's wet bar. The old man grinned. "Do you think you're ready to find out why our family has been so damn lucky?"

Something in his father's tone sent a chill up young Martin's spine. "Of course I am, Dad."

His father laughed and steadied his drink with a practiced hand as the driver slammed the accelerator and the limo lurched up the I-84 onramp. "Of course you think you're ready. When I was your age, I was ready to drink the whisky barrels dry, ready to fuck a thousand girls, ready to take Wall Street by the balls and make 'em all beg for mercy. But I was most definitely not ready to see what my father showed me. What I'm going to show you tonight. We'll see what you're made of after that."

Once they were back at the family mansion in Westport, Martin's father took him into his study.

"Someone once said that sufficiently advanced technology is indistinguishable from magic," his father said as he pulled some old leather-bound law texts off one of his polished bookshelves to reveal a keypad behind them. "I would disagree with that; once you've seen magic – the real kind, not that David Copperfield bullshit – you're not going to confuse it with a Cray or a jumbo jet."

The old man finished punching in a long string of numbers, and one of the bookshelves at the back of the room emitted a click and swung a few inches away from the wall.

"But I will make a truer version of that statement: possessing sufficient amounts of accurate information becomes indistinguishable from possessing an unusual amount of luck." Martin's father crossed the room to the bookshelf door and swung it wide, revealing an old iron door that looked like it might go down to a cellar. "Go to Atlantic City and sit down at the poker tables – if you know exactly how the cards will fall, you'll break every bastard in the room. Go to Wall Street – if you know how the markets will swing five months, ten months, ten years down the road – well. You'll do pretty well for yourself, won't you?"

"But that's...not possible, is it?" Martin said.

His father laughed and dug in the inside breast pocket of his tuxedo, producing a wrought-iron key. "It is very much possible, son. But I'm not talking about the kind of information that ordinary people – even your fancy Harvard mathematics whiz kids – could ever get their hands on."

He put the key in the heavy lock and opened the forbidding door with some effort. "I know of exactly one source in the whole world for that kind of information, and you're about to meet him."

Martin followed his father down marble steps into a subterranean room lit with old-fashioned gaslight sconces. Near the door, there was an old oak table littered with various arcane-looking implements, but the room was completely dominated by what sat at the far end: a golden skeleton on some kind of throne. Even though the metal bones glittered, they also seemed to draw the light from the room.

"Meet the man John D. Rockefeller once said was the most skilled businessman he'd ever known," Martin's father said. "Or what his dusty corpse became, anyhow."

"That's Gould?" Martin asked, incredulous. "Jay Gould, the robber baron?"

Martin stepped closer to the precious revenant. Its skull had polished rubies in the eyesockets. The top of the cranium bore a threaded screw hole. There was a buildup of some kind of dried, tarry substance that, when liquid, had apparently spilled down from the foramen magnum over the spinal column and the ribs, staining a dark pool on the red velvet seat of the throne.

"Now, don't call the old boy names," his father said, a perverse smile playing on his face. "He still has feelings, you know. *Pride*, anyhow. Best to stay on his good side if you want his help. And believe me, son, you *do* want his help."

"But...how...." A million questions were crowding in Martin's head, and he found himself unable to articulate a single one of them.

"How, indeed," his father said, looking tremendously amused at Martin's confusion. "About fifteen years after Jay Gould died, your grandfather met a prospective business partner, a nephew of King Carol of Romania, who claimed to have a plan for generating great riches for them both. The pair of them broke into Gould's mausoleum, replaced his remains with the corpse of a transient, and smuggled Jay's body out to a monastery in the Carpathians where the monks were known to be skilled in, well, *certain mysteries*. Once your grandfather acquired all the gold and jewels necessary for the ritual, the monks gilded and enchanted the skeleton as if it were a holy relic, summoning and binding Jay's soul to the bones and giving it clairvoyance into all possible futures.

"When Jay's skeleton was completed, the king's nephew of course tried to double-cross your grandfather and have him murdered, but he was too tough and far too sly to fall for that kind of a trick. Your grandfather took the skeleton for himself, and hightailed back to the States. Old Jay's been down here ever since.

"The throne was my idea," his father continued. "Jay wasn't too happy with your grandfather after a while, and so I got him the chair as sort of a peace offering when I took over. It belonged to King Louis XIV of France…it's not magic, but it is a very fine place to sit."

"What's that black stuff on the bones and seat?" Martin asked.

"Blood," his father replied. "Even spirits need to eat. I can get an answer with, say, fresh chicken blood, but old Jay always did have a taste for human juice."

Martin's father leaned over the cluttered table and picked up a bronze funnel with a threaded tip, a bronze dish, and a very sharp-looking silver dagger. "I haven't fed him in a while, so he's sleeping now, but I might as well get you two introduced. Give me your hand, son…."

* * *

Two guards flanked Martin as he carried his pack of linens and towels down the gray hall to the Secure Housing Unit. Most of the men crammed by twos and threes in the 8'x10' cells were dressed in bright orange jumpsuits. At the far end was a cell occupied by one young, worried-looking man in the same tan clothing Martin had been issued. The young fellow's skin was fair, but his broad nose and close-cropped curly hair spoke of a mixed ethnic ancestry. His solemn green eyes blinked behind thick glasses.

"Hey, any word on my paperwork?" the young man called out to the guards.

"No paperwork, but we brought you a new bunky," one of the guards replied. They marched Martin up to the cell, unlocked it, and put him inside. "You boys play nice, y'hear?"

"Whoa." The gangly young man's eyes widened. "Are you Bennington?"

Martin set his stack of towels and linens on the small desk. "That I am."

"Oh, wow, it's an honor, sir…I mean, the circumstances aren't – look, you can take the bottom bunk, a man like you shouldn't have to climb up on this rickety thing."

"Thank you," Martin said, unfolding one of the steel chairs and taking a seat. "But don't worry about all that now. Tell me about yourself."

"Uh, my name's Raymond Greene, and I used to work for Groshawk Investments. I was only there eleven months. I got a job there right out of college. I thought I had it made, but…." His voice faltered.

"Did you get caught in the embezzlement scam Hobson was running?" Martin asked gently.

"Yes," Raymond replied, looking profoundly depressed. His glasses were slipping down his nose, and he pushed them up with a long forefinger. "And I know this makes me sound like a liar or an idiot, but I had *no* idea what was going on. Those papers they found…they had my signature on them, but I know I never saw those docs before the trial. And that money that showed up in my bank account…I had no idea. It's like I got set up, but there's no reason to set up a guy like me, so my own lawyer didn't even believe me."

"Well, my lawyer's pretty good, not to mention open-minded; maybe I can get him to look at your case," Martin said.

"You'd do that? Wow, thanks, bro. Sir, I mean."

Martin smiled. "Always glad to help out a fellow in need."

"What, um…what about you, sir? I mean, I know they convicted you and all, but was the prosecution telling the truth?"

"Parts of it," Martin replied.

"What about the hedge fund? Was it *ever* legit, or was it a Ponzi from the start like they said?"

"It started as a legitimate thing," Martin lied. "Things just…got out of hand. It's hard to give up on that kind of money; you just keep hoping the tide will turn before it's too late."

Martin hadn't needed anything as flimsy as hope. He knew going in exactly what would happen; he'd started the scam to feather his nest against the impending economic collapse Jay Gould's ghost had foreseen. His reputation had been ruined and he'd been sent to prison, but he'd achieved his ultimate goal. For every dollar the feds had confiscated, there was another ten hidden as well-protected caches of precious metals and weapons around the country.

"Sixty billion is a lot to walk away from," Raymond agreed. "And you had, what, four hundred million in liquid assets?"

"About that, yes."

"So why didn't you…you know, disappear?"

The young man's shyness finally seemed to be falling away. It was about damn time, Martin figured. The timid didn't belong on Wall Street, and Martin hated to think the kid had taken a good job away from someone more competent, even if the ship *was* going down.

"I mean, people have killed themselves over the money they lost. There are angry mothers and fathers and husbands and wives out there. Angry mobsters, too, I heard." Raymond leaned in close, lowering his voice to a whisper. "When I was on the prison bus, I heard some talk about how there's a hit out on you. And you have to have heard that, too. So why didn't you run?"

"That's a little complicated," Martin said.

* * *

A few hours after Martin got his congestive heart failure diagnosis, he went down into the secret cellar to talk to Jay. It had been a while since he'd consulted his silent partner. Once he'd poured a half-pint of fresh blood (courtesy of a local med tech on his payroll) into the golden skull, the skeleton's ruby eyes lit up with the faint smoky fire that let him know Mr. Gould was awake and ready to talk.

"You told me that there was only a 10% chance my heart would start to fail," Martin said, his arms crossed.

"I'm sorry that mortality is touching you so soon, but a 10% chance is not the same as a zero chance," the skeleton replied. Its thin voice seemed to be nowhere and everywhere.

"What am I supposed to do now?"

"Stick with the plan you've set in motion. Only now, your goal will be securing your daughters' futures. You'll need to step aside as your father did and pick one of them to introduce to me."

Martin shook his head. "I'm not ready. I don't want to step aside, I don't want to go to prison, not even for a day. Surely – surely Japan or Switzerland have better treatments, better access to fresh hearts."

"You'll be apprehended in any country with a decent medical system. And you'll die in any that don't. Medicine will have a cure for what ails you, but not for another ten years. And there's a 40% chance they'll *never* have a cure if the collapse comes. I feel your pain, Martin, really I do…a shot of cheese mold extract would have kept me from dying of consumption, but the doctors in my day couldn't figure out something as simple as that."

"What can I do, sir? Is there *anything* I can do?"

"You can reverse course and come clean to the authorities, if you want. It'll cost your family their fortune, but the fraud we've engineered has added 15% to the probability that the nation will collapse. If you reverse the economic damage, things may stabilize. And then, you have a 60% chance of pleading down to probation if you pay back all the money, and if that happens you'll be very likely to die in your eighties, as your father did. Comfortable, once again a respected pillar of the community, forgiven of your sins in society's eyes, provided you can resist the temptation to sell me off."

Martin almost said "I wouldn't sell you", but clearly Jay knew what lay in the basement of his heart. It did no good to lie to his deathly confidante.

"So I come clean and maybe get thirty more years of living," Martin mused. "What's thirty years?"

"To many, it is a lifetime," the skeleton observed.

"But in the grand scheme, it's nothing," Martin replied, pacing. "All my money, all my power, gone, like *that*. And then what? To be mostly forgotten in fifty years, entirely forgotten in two hundred?"

"I don't know what lies beyond," Jay replied. "I surely tasted it before I was bound to these bones, but I cannot remember whether I took my leisure in Heaven, suffered in Hell, or simply waited in darkness."

"I can't count on a happy afterlife, not after everything I've done. Is there any other option for me here? Is there a way…to continue?"

The skeleton was silent for a moment. "I do know of a way you could become immortal, but be warned that it involves great sacrifice and the blackest of magic. Among other debasements, you will have to spill the heart's blood of your close kin, and then do worse. One of your daughters would do."

Martin flinched. "I couldn't murder one of my babies. They're spoiled little brats like their mother most of the time and I'll be damned if I want to hand my companies over to them…but I could never hurt either one of them." He took a deep breath. "Would anyone else fit the bill?"

"As a matter of fact, yes; there are others, and one in particular who can best be put to use…."

* * *

"On second thought, maybe the question of why I didn't run away isn't so complicated after all," Martin said to Raymond. "Ultimately, I knew that trying to escape to another country wouldn't work out so well for me, whether there's a bounty on my life or not."

"What are you going to do to protect yourself?" Raymond asked.

"Nothing," Martin replied.

In response to Raymond's shocked expression, he replied: "Now, don't get me wrong, I'm not suicidal – I love life and being alive. *Love* it. Maybe I'm not quite as indulgent as my father. He loved his drink, and he loved his women, right to the end. He was still tomcatting around in his seventies, and he even fathered a son the rest of us never knew about. You, in fact."

It took a moment for Martin's words to sink in. "W-what? You mean I'm –"

"My half-brother. Exactly! Nice to finally meet you, half-brother!" Martin clapped him on the arm.

Raymond seemed dumbfounded, so Martin continued, speaking fast as a salesman. "It might seem like an amazing coincidence we'd encounter each other in prison, but let me tell you, I took great pains to make sure we'd meet right in this very cell. All told, I must have paid out two million dollars in bribes to prison officials, FBI agents, forgers, and the recruiting director and your bosses at Groshawk, all so we'd be able to spend a little quality time together."

Raymond's mouth hung open, and for the first time, Martin saw a definite family resemblance: two of his lower front teeth overlapped crookedly, just as his father's had.

Martin reached into his towel stack and quickly pulled out the silver dagger planted by the bribed unit manager and – in a motion he'd practiced a thousand times over the past year – he slashed the scalpel-sharp blade across his brother's throat. Raymond's hands went to his neck as his carotid artery began to jet out, but Martin didn't flinch, didn't pause, simply shoved the kid down onto the concrete floor and quickly began smearing the magic symbols with bloodied fingers, chanting the words Jay had taught him, and when the symbols were complete and Raymond was twitching and gurgling horribly, there wasn't a moment to lose. Martin ripped open Raymond's scarlet-soaked shirt and carved into the taut flesh of the kid's upper abdomen to get at his heart from beneath. He grabbed the slippery pulsing muscle with his fingers, and his own heart was straining, aching sympathetically in his own chest when he finally managed to cut and tear the organ free. He shouted the last of the incantation, and took a bite of his half-brother's still-shuddering flesh and swallowed it like a chunk of unusually tough carpaccio.

The ritual was done, and the guard outside was shouting for help, fumbling with the keys, and when they finally got inside Martin screeched at them like a madman and flung himself at their knees. They hit him with their batons, and another primed his Taser and shot the electrified darts into Martin's back. The sudden current overwhelmed his weakened heart, and he felt himself sinking down, down into blackness.

* * *

When Martin came to, his bones hurt so much it seemed like they were on fire. He was able to hear before he was able to see, and when he tried to blink to clear his blurred vision, he discovered he couldn't move.

"Ask it a question," a young voice said.

"Shush! It needs tribute first," said another.

Something warm and delicious was pouring into him from the top of his head, and for a moment he could imagine it was a fine cocktail going down his throat, and not a cup of hot salty gore trickling through what was left of him, tarring the shining cage of bone that enclosed the dusty nothingness where his heart and guts used to live.

His ruby eyes focused, and he saw a muscular, battle-scarred young man standing before him in a motley of salvaged leathers and rough homespuns. A few other feral-looking youngsters lurked behind. Martin instantly knew everything about this hard youth: barely out of his teens, he'd already slaughtered a hundred men, but along with his sociopathic blood-lust he had a cunning intelligence. More important, his belly was fired with a thirst for power beyond the ruined section of Pittsburgh he'd staked out as his own kingdom. The boy knew he was still just a gangster, but his aspirations weren't yet sharpened to their deadliest points.

"Skeleton," the youth ordered. "Tell me about the future."

The doors of perception opened inside Martin's enslaved mind, and he saw the cities on fire and the streets running red with the blood of the boy's foes. The speck of humanity that remained inside Martin cursed Jay Gould and wept at these visions, but the rest of him, the part that had wanted more and more and more, was grimly pleased. He'd see the race through until the bitter end, even if he was just a consultant.

"As you wish, Lord John," Martin replied. "What part of the future unwritten did you want to see?"

"All, skeleton," the boy replied. "Give me everything."

Casualty of Peace

David Tallerman

IT'S SUNDAY, and we're drawing lots in the church hall.

The vicar calls them straws, but really they're only strips of paper. He shows them, each time, before we start: most are longer than his middle finger, a few – two, three, never more than six – are shorter than his thumb. Today, three are short. He fans the entire handful, with a smile, so that we all can see. Then he goes among the rows of weary women, and we each take a strip.

By the time he comes to me, my hand is shaking. I curl my fist and dig in my nails to make it be still. The vicar continues to smile. As I reach to draw my straw, his fingertips brush my own. His are warm, much warmer than mine. Then he moves on. Rather than look at the paper, I ball it in my hand. I wonder if I can tell from feel alone whether it's long or short. I roll it within my fingers, back and forth, over and over.

Kathy, beside me, is looking at her slip. I know, perhaps only from how her body tenses, that her straw isn't short. Then her eyes are on me, on my hands where they press against my stomach, turning the scrap there. So I stop and unroll it, careful not to tear the sweat-moistened paper. I hold it up so that she can see, and she holds hers up, and we can both see than neither one is short.

Behind us, a woman cries out. She is saying, "Oh, oh, oh," again and again, a sound neither happy nor sad, like a pause between thoughts. I don't recognize her voice. The women here are from five villages and farther, and I know only a few by name; less than that I'd call friends. But the woman making the *oh, oh* noise – which is more rapid now, as though she's having trouble breathing – has her own friends, and they're talking to her, telling her how lucky she is, telling her how glad she must be, ignoring her strange almost-sobs.

Eventually, the woman quiets. I wish I could leave. I wish we didn't have to stay until everyone has drawn their straw. Is that uncharitable of me? To find this cruel? Anyway, there's no use in wishing. We all must wait until the end.

At least there are only two short straws left. The woman who receives the second says a man's name, which I don't quite catch – Gerard? Gerald? – and then nothing more. The woman who finds the third won't stop laughing, a sound not very different from the first woman's sobs. Couldn't we stop now, when there's no more hope for anyone? But no, we carry on until the end. Anything else would be cowardice, I suppose.

Finally it's over. Once we get outside, it takes Kathy and me three streets to separate ourselves from the diminishing throng. When we're out of anyone's earshot, Kathy says, "I wish it had been me."

"Yes," I agree.

"Who were those women, anyway? They weren't from our village."

"No."

"Don't you wish it had been you, Aggy?"

"Yes, I do."

How can I tell her the truth? How can I tell if she's afraid, just as afraid as me? I can't, so I hide what I feel. Then, not knowing how to feel, I feel nothing.

On the main street, we lapse into silence. Even Kathy's limitless good spirits seem to have exhausted her. I find my eyes drawn to part-curtained windows, against my will. From the far side of the street, a shadow gazes back at me, unmoving, a featureless face halved by flower-patterned fabric. Seeing no eyes to meet, I look away, and fail to suppress a shudder.

Kathy doesn't notice – or if she notices, doesn't comment.

When we reach the store, we enter and join the line before the counter. Arriving at its end, we hand over our cards. A chalked sign lists the week's privations: today there is no salt; there are potatoes but no eggs; there's sugar, in small quantities, not enough for baking.

"I was hoping to make scones," Kathy says sorrowfully. She's always had a sweet tooth; this must be hard on her. I suppose I'm lucky, having long since stopped caring what I eat or in what quantities. Apathy makes making do much easier.

We part on Soot Lane. I travel the last distance alone, more careful not to look at windows. I'm glad to be home, until I step through the door. Then the emptiness strikes me like an open-handed slap. I can feel it, smell it, taste it in my mouth.

A year ago I never knew that emptiness had a taste. Strange how much you can learn in a mere twelve months.

* * *

During the week, we build bombs.

The bombs look like mushrooms – like a field of fungi stretching to every horizon. In the low light, the factory floor is without walls, without ceiling. There are only us and the bombs – and there are so many more of them than us.

Is that how it feels for you? Out there, where you are, have the munitions already outnumbered those they're supposed to kill? While I work, I think of you. We build bombs to kill young men. We build bombs to make widows of girls like us. We build bombs to make money, to buy food, to stay alive, to build more bombs.

Some of the women talk and joke. Some of them even sing. I wonder how they can.

* * *

In the evenings, I don't know what to do with myself. Sometimes I clean, though there's little to be done. A house doesn't get so dirty with one person, it seems. There are never enough jobs to keep me occupied, however much I hunt. Cooking, cleaning, washing – done for one, they still leave too much time.

Sometimes Kathy comes over, but not this week. I remember that her mother has been sick, and probably she's busy nursing. Didn't I used to have more friends? If I did then I don't miss them. It's hard even to remember their names. They are people in a book that's closed and can't be read, and it's so rare now that I want company.

When I do, there's always the radio. I like the dramas, and a few of the songs: the ones that are slow and sad and say nothing about anything. But I can't tolerate the news. Whenever I hear the announcer's voice, I long, irrationally, for him to say your name, as though the war is a dark water and your one small life could bob alone to the surface. But all they talk about is places and important men, numbers, statistics, battles lost and battles won. When the announcer's voice comes on, I turn the radio off, and the silence lies thicker than old dust.

At night I lie awake in the darkness. Sleep doesn't come easily these days. Not even exhaustion brings peace readily. Often I'll lie until I hear the train: its approaching rumble, its whistle like a gull's shriek, long and desperate. Once a week it will stop. Once a week it will discharge its burdens. In that caesura of deadened noise, I imagine its snaking body waiting patiently, smoke curling like steam from an old carthorse's flank, as silent feet tread the silent platform. I wait for the train to stumble back into life, to recede – and in my mind's eye, shadows drift along nighttime streets.

* * *

It's Sunday, and we're drawing lots in the church hall.

The vicar holds up ribbons of paper for us all to see. There are five short, and more long than I can count. I can't remember the last time there were so many short straws. I feel a fluttering in my chest, like a frantic moth beating broken wings against my ribs – and I realize, to my horror, that what I'm feeling is hope.

I hold my breath until my heart grows still. I can bear many things, but not that.

My slip is long. I know it even as my fingers touch coarse paper, know without having to look. Kathy's will be too.

Hope is always a liar. Hope always betrays.

* * *

Kathy and I walk back together as far as the store. Today, even Kathy is quiet. Perhaps hope infected her too.

Today there is no salt. There's no butter or bacon. Sugar is rationed, and so is flour. There's bread, but the loaves are small and hard and dark, little like the bread we had before. I can remember the texture of proper bread, but not its taste. I've always found tastes hard to remember, and smells too. Now I wonder if that isn't a small kindness of memory; scarcity is easiest to tolerate with nothing to compare it to.

But oh, I can remember your smell: coal dust and musk and pipe smoke. It hangs around the house, loiters in nooks and crannies and surprises me. When I think I have no more tears, your scent finds ways to make me cry.

So maybe memory is no kinder than hope.

* * *

This week I'm on night shifts.

The factory is dark in the day; by night it's Stygian. I work in an oasis of acid yellow light, an island where there's only me and the bombs. Sometimes I hear voices from beyond the edge of my island. Sometimes I imagine that it's the bombs, whispering together, sharing their jokes, singing their tuneless songs. They are inheriting the earth. They have so much more to celebrate than we do.

The shifts are from seven at night until seven in the morning. It's night when I begin and night when I leave. By Saturday I don't remember what day looks like; my recollections of sunlight feel frail and doubtful. I would like to sleep and sleep. I'd like to grow drunk on sleep, to become sick with it, to drown in its depths.

What would happen if I didn't get up tomorrow? What would happen if my place in line was left empty? If my straw was short and I wasn't there to receive it?

Useless questions. Of course I'll go. Hope may be a liar, but it can't be hidden from for long.

* * *

It's Sunday, and we're drawing lots in the church hall.

Today there are four short slips. The vicar displays them delicately, before folding them into the greater mass. He shuffles them clumsily in slender white fingers, and we all watch, as if we were the audience of a magic trick.

Today my hand is still. I'm too tired for emotion, too disorientated by being awake during the day. The significance of all this washes over me, leaving me unmoved. I take my slip, and Kathy takes hers. I look at my slip. It's as long as the distance from the base of my thumb to the tip of my middle finger. I look at Kathy's slip. It's exactly as long as her littlest finger. My slip is long. And hers is short.

Kathy stares, just as I do. As we watch, the paper slides from her fingers. She looks at me, and there are fat tears in the corners of her eyes, refusing to fall. Then she collapses into my arms, as though there's no strength left in her. I hold her, not knowing what else to do, and her body shudders and heaves. I don't know how to identify the emotion surging through her, nor do I want to. All the while the vicar smiles at us, beneficent. I make no effort to smile back.

Outside in the street, Kathy's stupor slips away, and suddenly she becomes bright. "I'll have to bake a cake," she says. She considers, frowning with the intensity of her thoughts. "But, oh – there's no sugar."

"I might have some," I say.

Her pleasure is radiant and brittle. "Oh! Then that's what I'll do. With currants, just how he likes it."

I don't tell her that no amount of effort will do any good. She knows – or else, somehow, she doesn't.

"I'll have to clean. Wash the floors. Scrub the doorstep."

Neither will cleaning help. She must know this; she can't not. "I'm sure he'd like that."

"Do you think so?" She looks at me then, the question repeated in her eyes. Could I be telling the truth? Knowing how badly she'd like to believe, my heart breaks for her.

"I'm sure," I repeat, and wish I convinced myself, so that perhaps I could convince Kathy.

* * *

That night I lie awake, waiting for the whistle of the train – listening, as I know Kathy will be, with bated breath. The wind has died to nothing, and when finally the sound comes it carries clearly, like the shriek of a hunting bird. In its wake comes the slowing *clack-clack*, as metal wheels grind to a halt upon metal rails.

Perhaps if I were to look out my window I'd just be able to make out a pall of steam rising, to hover spectral on the still air. Perhaps if I strained my eyes I'd see shadows drifting through distant, silent streets. But I don't need to look. Behind my eyelids I can see clearly. There one figure detaches from the others, and there in a doorway Kathy waits, oblivious of the cold.

I sleep little that night.

All through the next days I think about Kathy. We've been friends since we were little girls; we went to school together, started work at the same time, married within a few months of each other. Maybe we've never been truly close – but nor have we ever been so far apart. There's a breach between us now that I know can't be bridged.

So it surprises me when on the Wednesday, as I'm leaving work through the wrought iron gates, caught amid the crowd of other dark-eyed women with skin stained the yellow of old lemons, I spy her across the street. She doesn't wave or cry out, but I know immediately that she's waiting for me.

Kathy looks gaunt. But when she sees that I've seen her, her face lights. I force my way nearer, fearful of sharp elbows and sharp tongues, glad when I'm free and the crowd swells on without me.

"Hello, Kathy," I say. And then, because I must, "How are you?"

"Oh, wonderful," she replies – even as her eyes eagerly reveal the lie. "It's funny…didn't realize, but while he was away, the house stopped feeling like a home. Now everything's back the way it should be."

"I'm glad." If what she said were true then, oh, I would be. I'd give anything to see Kathy happy, because if she was then, perhaps, one day I could be too.

"Why don't you come over? After your shift tomorrow?"

The question takes me by surprise – though now that it's out, I understand I'd been expecting it. I make the first sound of an excuse, without knowing what I can possibly say.

"Oh please! George would be so glad to see you. Just for an hour. Won't you?"

I can't say no. Her desperation is like a net, holding me tight, reeling me near.

"Of course," I tell her.

* * *

I feel his presence the moment I walk through the door. But I don't see him at first.

He's sitting in his armchair – the chair that was always his, with the frayed arms, the bald patches where elbows and palms have rested. But now that chair is in the corner, where the shadows fall deepest. I wouldn't have noticed him but for the cold, the silence: there's a chill from that direction, like the blast through a part-opened door in winter, and he makes no noise at all.

Not knowing what to say, I say nothing. Neither does he – and I'm glad, for who can tell what those invisible lips would utter? I shudder at the thought, and it's left to Kathy to make conversation for three.

She bustles about, calling from the kitchen as the kettle whistles upon the stove. I take the chair farthest from his, looking anywhere but at him. But I can't ignore the smell in the air, both familiar and strange: peat soaked by long rains. Nor can I help but notice the cake on the sideboard. It sits untouched, already growing stale. She'll offer me a slice, I know, and I'll have to say yes. Perhaps she'll set another piece on the small table within reach of that grey-fingered hand – which will not ever reach to take it.

Kathy is still talking from the kitchen. Her words are drowned by the kettle's shriek. I can't bear to be here. I can't stand to see what my friend's life has become, what it will be forever more.

I get up and walk on tiptoes to the front door. Do hollow eyes follow me from the gloom? Do unspoken words tremble on the cold air? I open the door and let myself out and close it softly behind me. In the street, the air tastes clean. In the street, the shadows are only shadows. And as I hurry through the dying evening, I hope Kathy will find a way to forgive one more betrayal.

* * *

It's Sunday, and we're drawing lots in the church hall.

I miss Kathy. It's strange to be here without her. I don't know the woman standing beside me. She's small and her face has no kindness in it, no hope either. I wonder how I must look to her. Have I grown hard? Do I seem bitter? Probably I do, for certainly I'm both of those things.

The vicar shows us the fanned ribbons of paper in his hands. At first I'm sure that they're all long; finally my eyes pick out the one that isn't. Just one for all of us, for this entire shuffling, throat-clearing, sad-eyed crowd. Then he jumbles them together, and that lone short strip is so easily lost, as though it never was.

Just one short straw. At least this week we have a small mercy: there'll be no hope.

The vicar moves along the lines. Sometimes he mumbles platitudes; sometimes he makes small jokes that only he laughs at. He has a particular scent, of starch and cough drops, that I can trace his slow progress by, though his footsteps are silent on the lacquered boards. Then, almost without my realizing, he's before me, hands outstretched, a fringe of white teasing from between his fingers. His smile is kindly and just slightly impatient. I reach and draw free a slip and fold my palm around it, and he moves on, like a well-oiled machine.

I look at the rectangle of paper in my hand, ready to crumple it, ready to dismiss this grotesque ritual from my mind for one more week.

My slip is short.

Not believing, I wish desperately that Kathy were beside me, so that I could compare my slip to hers. I don't dare look at the women on either side of me. Have they seen? Maybe they'll try and take my short straw from me. I close my fist hurriedly and then, no longer able to believe, have to open it again. A part of me is sure the slip will be long this time. A part of me breaks when it isn't.

The church hall is too warm. There are eyes on me, eyes everywhere. They must know what I'm thinking – even though I don't. I want to run. So I do. Outside the wind teases the slip from my fingers, and I watch as it dances along the street, as it flutters beyond the last of the buildings and is lost.

I expect someone to follow after me: the vicar, or else kindly busybody women. No one comes. After a while I have no choice but to start home. I imagine a white slip of paper cavorting among the dark-limbed trees. Will its loss change what's coming? What if someone else were to find it? For a moment I think of chasing after, past the edge of the village and off the road, into the forest, to hunt for hours amid the black trunks.

Instead I start to walk home. My feet guide themselves, my thoughts are a numbness inside my mind, and it surprises me when I see the store before me. I hadn't meant to come this way. I reach out a hand, open the door, wince at the jangle of the bell. I step inside, and still I'm thinking nothing at all.

Today there is no red meat. There are tinned goods, but no flour. There's no sugar, but there's salt. I can see the bags piled on the shelf behind the storekeeper, in regimental rows. They are blue and white, and make me think of sailors' uniforms.

I point. "How much can I buy?"

The shopkeeper looks at me queerly. "How much do you want?"

I'd buy it all if he'd let me. "As much as I'm allowed."

In the end, he sells me four small bags. He lays them out slowly upon the counter, hoisting each in his one good hand as I watch without impatience. He places them one after the other, as though at any moment I'll change my mind. But I won't. I don't know what I'm doing or why, but I'll do it anyway.

I hurry the last distance home, paper sack gripped in my arms, fearful of dropping it – watching in my mind's eye as it bursts and spills its precious contents upon the rain-damp cobbles. By the time I reach my doorstep, my breath is coming in harsh tugs. I lay the sack down though I leave the door unopened. I know now what I have to do, what I've been planning all along.

I remove my bags of salt, to set them out carefully. I empty one across the window ledge, a second along the rim where doorstep meets frame – the step I only cleaned the day before. That's two bags gone, but I daren't risk that these lines should break. The third I tease into a thread that just barely covers the entire boundary where house meets street. Then finally I let myself inside. The fourth bag I carry upstairs, for the bedroom window.

For *our* bedroom window.

Then the tears come. I can't help them. It's as though I've somehow hidden what I'm doing from myself until this moment, and now the reality is too much to bear.

Only, it must be borne, because the alternative is worse. I wipe my eyes, afraid that grief will blind me – that it will stop me from doing what must be done.

When I'm finished, silvery lines just visible in the dying autumn light trace every border, every entry. I consider cooking and know that I couldn't eat, that perhaps I'll never want to eat again. In any case, I've spent everything I have: I have no money and no food. A part of me thinks, with an intensity akin to pain, of what a terrible wife I am. You're coming home to me and the larder is bare.

A foolish thought. A silly worry, when what I've done is so much worse.

I go downstairs. Realizing I've left the front door open, I close it. My body feels heavy and useless, so I sit. Through the open curtains I can feel the dying of the light, as the sun dips toward the rooftops. I get up and close them. I want to cry and can't. I want to scream but know I wouldn't stop.

The silence is vast. I know it will drown me if I let it. I turn on the radio. Even the news might be bearable; perhaps, this day of all days, they really will say your name. But it's a song that greets me, aching in its cheerfulness:

> *When life's a beach,*
> *Just out of reach,*
> *Look on the sunny side of love.*

The song is worse than the silence, and I'd like to turn it off. Only, I haven't the strength; suddenly I have no strength at all. I sit down again. I could reach for the dial, but my hands are a leaden weight in my lap. The song has no meaning, and won't be stopped.

> *When life's a boat,*
> *Pushed out to float,*
> *Look on the sunny side of love.*

The song trickles to an end. Another takes its place. This time I find that I can ignore the words. The radio becomes just noise, then nothing at all.

Have I slept? I don't think so. But now the radio is only playing static, a shivering hum like a voice just beyond hearing. I get up to turn it off, and afterwards the silence is thick as falling snow. Then, far away, I hear the whistle of the train: long, low, and impossibly mournful. Beneath I can make out the declining rattle of wheels on tracks, like clockwork winding down.

I know what will happen now. The train has come to rest; steam writhes upon its flanks. Someone will open a door for you, but you'll depart alone, and no one will be waiting to meet you. As you step to the platform, your feet will make no sound. As you walk into the empty streets, your feet will make no sound. As you drift through familiar passages, past familiar landmarks, over familiar cobbles, you will make no sound.

And just like that, I realize you're outside.

You're standing on the doorstep, and you're looking up, at a home made strange by all that's passed since last you stood here. You're reaching out a hand. You're back, finally back.

And you can't come in.

You won't understand why. No moonlight falls to light the line at your feet silver. Even if it did, the sight would make no sense to you. Are you hurt by this obstruction, this rejection? No, I think that it makes you angry. I can feel your fury through wood and brick.

Your shout is a whisper in grass. Your hammering is far-off footsteps, as of a figure pacing distant, vacant streets.

But you aren't you. I know this, love. I know.

You went away, went to war, and what's come back is only a silhouette. I know this to be true, because I've seen it happen to so many: to sons and fathers, husbands and brothers. So many men gone, and not one returned close to whole.

Hope is a lie. You are a lie. I miss you so, so much. But what I miss isn't what's outside our door, not what rattles my window with pale hands, hands that would be colder than ice if I should dare open the pane and reach for them. You're nothing I could hold, nothing I could ever warm.

I'm sorry. I'm sorry, I'm sorry, I'm sorry.

But I can't let you in, my love.

* * *

I must have slept. I don't remember doing so, but I must have – for I'm curled in the armchair, and there's light pricking at the gap between the curtains. For an instant I worry that I'm late for work. Then I remember that this week I'm on nightshifts once more, and no amount of oversleeping could make me late.

I remember, too, that in any case it doesn't matter anymore – that nothing matters now.

I get up and open the front door. I don't know what to expect, or if I expect anything at all. But there's nothing to see: only a faint perimeter, like a snail's trail, that navigates house front and windowsill and doorstep. The line of salt is undisturbed, not marred by footsteps or by the wind that rattles the chimneypots above.

You've gone. I don't know where, but you've gone – and this time you won't return.

I go back inside. The day is mine to waste. Then tonight, I'll go to work and I'll build bombs. I will build bombs to kill young men. I'll build bombs to make widows of young girls. I'll take from others what has been taken from me.

And from now on, I'll sing as I work.

The Storm

Sarah Elizabeth Utterson

> – *Of shapes that walk*
> *At dead of night, and clank their chains, and wave*
> *The torch of hell around the murderer's bed.*
> **Pleasures of Imagination**

ON THE EVENING of the 12th of June 17—, a joyous party was assembled at Monsieur de Montbrun's château to celebrate the marriage of his nephew, who had, in the morn of that day, led to the altar the long-sought object of his fond attachment. The mansion, which was on this occasion the scene of merriment, was situated in the province of Gascony, at no very great distance from the town of —.

It was a venerable building, erected during the war of the League, and consequently discovered in its exterior some traces of that species of architecture which endeavoured to unite strength and massiveness with domestic comfort. Situated in a romantic, but thinly peopled district, the family of Monsieur de Montbrun was compelled principally to rely on itself for amusement and society. This family consisted of the chevalier, an old soldier of blunt but hospitable manners; his nephew the bridegroom, whom (having no male children) he had adopted as his son, and Mademoiselle Emily, his only daughter: the latter was amiable, frank, and generous; warm in her attachments, but rather romantic in forming them. Employed in rural sports and occupations, and particularly attached to botany, for which the country around afforded an inexhaustible field, the chevalier and his inmates had not much cultivated the intimacy of the few families which disgust to the world or other motives had planted in this retired spot. Occasional visits exchanged with the nearest of their neighbours sometimes enlivened their small circle; with the greater part of those who lived at a distance, they were scarcely acquainted even by name.

The approaching nuptials, however, of Theodore (which was the name of Monsieur de Montbrun's adopted son) excited considerable conversation in the adjacent district: and the wedding of her cousin, it was determined by Emily, should not pass off unaccompanied by every festivity which the nature of their situation and the joyfulness of the event would allow. On this occasion, therefore, inquiries were made as to all the neighbouring gentry within a considerable distance around; and there were none of the least note neglected in the invitations, which were scattered in all directions. Many persons were consequently present, with whose persons and character the host and his family were unacquainted: some also accepted the summons, who were strangers to them even in name.

Emily was attentive and courteous to all; but to one lady in particular she attached herself during the entertainment with most sedulous regard. Madame de Nunez, the immediate object of Emily's care, had lately settled in the neighbourhood, and had hitherto studied to shun society. It was supposed that she was the widow of a Spanish officer of the Walloon guards, to whom she had been fondly attached; indeed so much so, that, notwithstanding he had been dead several years, the lady never appeared but in the garb of mourning. She had only lately settled in Gascony; but her motives for retiring from Spain and fixing on the French side of the Pyrenees were not known, and but slightly conjectured. Isabella de Nunez was about twenty-eight years of age, tall and well-formed: her countenance was striking, nay even handsome; but a nice physiognomist would have traced in her features evidence of the stronger passions of human nature. He would have seen pride softened by distress; and would have fancied, at times, that the effects of some concealed crime were still evident in her knit brow and retiring eye, when she became the object of marked scrutiny.

She had never before entered the château de Montbrun, and her person had hitherto been unnoticed by Emily; but who, having now seen her, devoted herself with ardour to her new friend. The lady received the attentions of her amiable hostess with grateful but dignified reserve.

The morning had been extremely sultry, and an oppressive sensation in the air, which disordered respiration, threw, as the day closed, an air of gloom over the company, ill suited to the occasion of their meeting. Madame de Nunez appeared more than anyone else to feel the effects of the lurid atmosphere; the occasional sparks of gaiety which she had discovered, gradually disappeared; and before the day had entirely shut in, she seemed at times perfectly abstracted, at other times to start with causeless apprehension. In order to divert or dispel this increasing uneasiness, which threatened to destroy all the pleasure of the festival, dancing was proposed; and the enlivening sounds of the music in a short time dissipated the temporary gloom. The dancing had not however long continued, ere the expected storm burst in all its fury on the château: the thunder, with its continued roar, reverberated by the adjoining mountains, caused the utmost alarm in the bosom of the fair visitors; the torrents of rain which fell, might almost be said to swell the waters of the neighbouring Garonne, whilst sheets of lightning, reflected on its broad waves, gave a deeper horror to the pitchy darkness which succeeded. The continuance of the storm gradually wound up the apprehensions of the greater part of the females to horror; and they took refuge in the arched vaults, and long subterranean passages which branched beneath the *château*, from the vivid glare of the lightning; although unable to shut their ears to the reiterated claps of thunder which threatened to shake the building to its foundations. In this general scene of horror, Isabella alone appeared unappalled. The alternate abstraction and alarm, which before seemed to harass her mind, had now vanished, and had given place to a character of resignation which might almost be considered as bordering on apathy. While the younger females yielded without resistance to the increasing horrors of the tempest, and by frequent shrieks and exclamations of dread bore testimony to the terror excited in their bosoms by the aggravated circumstances of the scene, she suffered no symptom of apprehension to be visible in her now unvarying features. Agitation had yielded to quiet: she sat ostensibly placid; but her apparent inattention was evidently not the effect of tranquillity, but the result of persevering exertion.

The hour was approaching towards midnight; and the storm, instead of blowing over, having increased in violence, the hospitable owner of the mansion proposed to his guests, that they should abandon the idea of returning home through the torrents of rain, which had already deluged the country, and rendered the roads in the vicinity impassable; but should accommodate themselves, with as little difficulty as possible, to the only plan now to be devised – of making themselves easy during the remainder of this dismal night. Although his mansion was not extensive, yet he proposed (with the aid of temporary couches, and putting the ladies to the inconvenience of sleeping two in each room) to render the party as comfortable as his means would allow; and which would, at all events, be more agreeable than braving abroad the horrors of the tempest.

Reasonable as such a plan was in itself, it was still more strongly recommended by the circumstance, that the carriages which were expected to convey the parties to their respective abodes had not arrived; and from the state of the roads, and the continuance of the still pitiless storm, it seemed visionary to expect them.

The party, therefore, yielded without regret to the offered arrangement, save with one dissenting voice. The fair Spaniard alone positively declined the offered accommodation. Argument in vain was used for a considerable space of time to detain her; she positively insisted on returning home: and would alone in the dark have faced the storm, had not an obstacle which appeared invincible, militated against her resolve; this was too imperious to be resisted – her carriage and servants were not arrived; and from the representation of Monsieur de Montbrun's domestics (some of whom had been detached to examine the condition of the neighbouring roads), it was perfectly clear that with that part of the district in which she resided no communication could for several hours take place. Madame de Nunez, therefore, at length yielded to necessity; although the pertinacity of her resistance had already excited much surprise, and called forth innumerable conjectures.

The arrangements between the respective parties were soon made, and the greater part of the ladies gladly retired to seek repose from the harassing events of the day. Emily, who had not relaxed in her marked attention to her interesting friend, warmly pressed her to share her own room, in which a sofa had been prepared as a couch, and to which she herself insisted on retiring, while Madame de Nunez should take possession of the bed. The latter, however, again strenuously objected to this plan, asserting, that she should prefer remaining all night in one of the sitting-rooms, with no other companion than a book. She appeared obstinately to adhere to this resolution, until Emily politely, yet positively, declared, that were such the intention of her new friend, she would also join her in the saloon, and pass the time in conversation until the day should break, or until Madame's servants should arrive. This proposition, or rather determination, was received by the frowning Isabella with an air of visible chagrin and disappointment, not altogether polite. She expressed her unwillingness that Mademoiselle should be inconvenienced, with some peevishness; but which, however, soon gave place to her former air of good-breeding.

She now appeared anxious to hurry to her room; and the rest of the party having some time retired, she was escorted thither by the ever-attentive Emily. No sooner had they reached the chamber, than Isabella sunk into a chair; and after struggling for some time in evident emotion for utterance, at length exclaimed:

"Why, dearest Emily, would you insist on sharing with me the horrors of this night? To me the punishment is a merited one: but to you –"

"What, my dearest madam, do you say?" replied Emily affectionately – "The terrors of the night are over, the thunder appears retiring, and the lightning is less vivid; and see in the west (added she, as she went to the window) there are still some remains of the summer twilight. Do not any longer, then, suffer the apprehension of the storm which has passed over us, to disturb the repose which you will, I hope, so shortly enjoy."

"Talk you of repose!" said Madame de Nunez, in a voice almost choked with agitation – "Know you not, then, that on the anniversary of this horrid night? – But what am I saying! To you, at present, all this is mystery; too soon your own feelings will add conviction to the terrible experience which six revolving years have afforded me, and which, even now but to think on, harrows up my soul. But no more."

Then darting suddenly towards the door, which had hitherto remained a-jar, she closed it with violence; and locking it, withdrew the key, which she placed in her own pocket. Emily had scarcely time to express her surprise at this action and the apparent distraction which accompanied it, ere Madame de Nunez seized both her hands with more than female strength, and with a maddened voice and eye straining on vacancy, exclaimed:

"Bear witness, ye powers of terror! That I imposed not this dreadful scene on the female whose oath must now secure her silence."

Then staring wildly on Mademoiselle de Montbrun, she continued:

"Why, foolish girl, wouldst thou insist on my partaking thy bed? The viper might have coiled in thy bosom; the midnight assassin might have aimed his dagger at thy breast – but the poison of the one would have been less fatal, and the apprehension of instant annihilation from the other would have been less oppressive, than the harrowing scene which thou art doomed this night to witness – doomed, I say; for all the powers of hell, whose orgies you must behold, cannot release you from the spectacle which you have voluntarily sought."

"To *what* am I doomed!" cried Emily, whose fears for herself were lessened in the dread she felt for her friend's intellects, which she supposed were suddenly become affected by illness, or from the incidents of the past day.

Isabella, after a silence of several minutes, during which she endeavoured to recover some degree of composure, in a softened but determined voice, said:

"Think not, my friend, (if I may use that endearing expression to one whose early prospects and happier days I am unwillingly condemned to blast,) that disorder has produced the agitation which, spite of myself, you have witnessed. Alas! Great as have been my sorrows, and heavy as my crime weighs on me, my reason has still preserved its throne: to seek oblivion in idiocy; to bury the remembrance of my fatal error in temporary derangement; would, I might almost say, be happiness to me. But fate has forbidden such an alleviation, and my impending destiny is not to be guarded against by precaution, cannot be avoided by repentance."

"Nay," said Emily, "exaggerated as your self-condemnation makes the fault to which you allude appear, in religion you may find a solace which could efface crimes of much deeper dye than any with which you can possibly charge yourself."

"Ah! No," replied the fair Spaniard. "Religion, it is true, holds out her benignant hand to receive the wandering sinner; she offers to the stranger a home; she welcomes to her bosom the repentant though blood-stained criminal; but for crimes like mine, what penitence can atone? But we waste time," added she; "the midnight hour approaches; and ere the clock in the turret first announces that dreaded period, much must be done."

Thus saying, she went into the adjoining oratory, and finding on the little altar at which Emily offered her daily oraisons, an ivory crucifix, she returned with it in her hand; and again seizing and forcibly grasping the hand of her now really alarmed hostess, she exclaimed in a hollow, yet determined voice:

"Swear, that whatsoever you may this night, this eventful night, be a witness to, not all the apprehensions of hell, not all your hopes of heaven, shall tempt you to reveal, until I am committed to the silent tomb – swear!"

Emily for a moment hesitated to adopt an oath imposed under circumstances of such an extraordinary nature: but whilst she was debating, Madame de Nunez, more violently grasping her hand, exclaimed, in a voice harsh from agitation:

"Swear; or dread the event!"

"Swear!" Emily fancied she heard echoed from the oratory. Almost sinking with horror, she faintly repeated the solemn oath, which the frantic female, whose character appeared so perfectly changed, thus dictated to her.

She had no sooner thus solemnly bound herself to silence, than Madame de Nunez's agitation appeared to subside; she replaced the crucifix on the altar, and sinking on her knees before the chair in which Emily, almost void of animation, was seated, she feebly exclaimed:

"Pardon, dearest Emily, the madness of my conduct; necessity has dictated it towards you; and your wayward fate, and not your suffering friend, is answerable for it. For six long years have I confined to my own bosom the horrors which we this night must jointly witness. On the anniversary of this day – but I dare not yet communicate the dreadful event; some hours hence I *may* recover composure to relate it: but remember your oath. While I live, the secret is buried in your bosom. You must have remarked my unwillingness to remain in your dwelling; you could not have been inattentive to my repugnance to share your room – too soon you will have a dreadful explanation of the cause. Be not angry with me – I must endeavour to conceal the circumstances which appal my soul: I must still preserve the respect of society, although I have for ever forfeited my own – hence the oath I have imposed on you. But –"

Here further conversation was interrupted by the sound of the turret clock, which began to strike the hour of midnight. It had scarcely finished, ere the slow rolling of a carriage was heard in the paved court-yard; at the noise of which, Madame de Nunez started from the posture in which she had continued at the feet of Emily, and rushed towards the door, which she had previously locked. Emily now heard heavy footsteps ascending the oaken stair-case; and before she could recall her recollection, which so singular a circumstance had bewildered, the door of the room in which they were sitting, spite of its fastening, slowly moved on its hinges; and in the next minute – Emily sunk on the earth in a state of stupefaction.

It is well for the human frame, that when assailed by circumstances too powerful to support, it seeks shelter in oblivion. The mind recoils from the horrors which it cannot meet, and is driven into insensibility.

At an early hour of the ensuing morning Madame de Nunez quitted Monsieur de Montbrun's château, accompanied by her servants, whom the retiring torrents had permitted to await their mistress's commands. She took a hasty farewell of the master of the mansion, and without making any inquiries as to the rest of the party, departed.

At the usual hour of breakfast, Emily did not appear; and her father at length went to her room door, and receiving no answer to his inquiries, went in. Judge his horror, when he discovered his daughter lying on the bed in the clothes she had worn the preceding day, but in a state of apparent insensibility. Immediate medical assistance was procured, and she at length discovered symptoms of returning life; but no sooner had she recovered her recollection, than, looking with horror and affright around her, she again relapsed into a state of inanimation. Repeated cordials being administered, she was again restored to life; but only to become the victim of a brain-fever, which in a few days put a period to her existence. In a short interval of recollection, in the early part of her illness, she confided what we have here related to her father; but conscientiously kept from his knowledge what she was bound by her oath to conceal. The very remembrance of what she had witnessed on that fatal night, hurried her into delirium, and she fell a victim to the force of recollection.

Madame de Nunez did not long survive her; but expired under circumstances of unexampled horror.

Sing Me Your Scars

Damien Angelica Walters

THIS IS NOT my body.

Yes, there are the expected parts – arms, legs, hips, breasts – each in its proper place and of the proper shape.

Is he a monster, a madman, a misguided fool? I don't know. I don't want to know. But this is not my body.

* * *

The rot begins, as always, around the stitches. This time, the spots of greyish-green appear on the left wrist, and there is an accompanying ache, but not in the expected way. It feels as though there is a great disconnect between mind and flesh, a gap that yearns to close but cannot. I say nothing, but there is no need; Lillian's weeping says it with more truth than words.

The hands are hers.

"Please don't show him yet. Please," she whispers. "I'm not ready."

"I must," I say. "You will be fine."

"Please, please, wait until after the party."

I ignore her. I have learned the hard way that hiding the rot is not acceptable, and while the flesh may be hers, the pain is mine and mine alone. I remember hearing him offer an explanation, but the words, the theories, were too complex for me to understand. I suspect that was his intention.

Lillian will still be with us; she is simply grasping for an excuse, any excuse at all. I understand her fear, but the rot could destroy us all.

My stride is long. Graceful. Therese was a dancer, and she taught me the carriage of a lady. I pass old Ilsa in the hallway, and she offers a distracted nod over the mound of bed linens she carries. All the servants are busy with preparations for the upcoming annual party, which I'm not allowed to attend, of course.

I wonder what sort of fiction he has spun to the servants. Am I an ill cousin, perhaps, or someone's cast-off bastard that he has taken in? Either way, I'm certain they call him the good doctor, but they're not here at night. They don't know everything.

They never speak to me, nor do they offer anything more than nods or waves of the hand, and none of them can see my face through the veil I must wear when I venture beyond my rooms. All my gowns have high necklines and long, flowing sleeves; not a trace of flesh is exposed.

For my safety, he says. They will not understand. They will be afraid and people in fear often act in a violent manner. His mouth never says what sort of violence he expects, but his eyes do.

When I knock on the half-open door to his study, he glances up from his notebooks. I shut the door behind me, approach his desk slowly, and hold out Lillian's hand.

"Oh, Victoria," he says, shaking his head. "I had hoped we were past this. This configuration is as close to perfect as I could hope."

I bite my tongue. Victoria is not my name, simply a construct.

I asked him once why he had done such a thing; he called me an ungrateful wretch and left his handprint on my cheek. I wonder if he even knows why. Perhaps the answer is so ugly he has buried it deep inside.

Without another word, he leads me to the small operating theater, unlocks the door, and steps aside to let me enter first. The room smells of antiseptic and gauze, but it's far better than the wet flesh reek of the large theater. My visual memories are vague, but the smell will not leave, no matter how hard I try to forget.

I sit on the edge of the examination table without prompting. His face is grim, studied, as he inspects the wrist, and even though his touch is gentle, I watch his eyes for signs of anger. I know the rot is not my fault, but innocence is no guard against rage.

He makes a sound deep in his throat. Of sorrow? Condemnation?

Lillian weeps, then begs, then prays. None of which will make any difference.

The rot binds us to him as the stitches bind them to me. A prison, not of bars, but circumstance. I have entertained thoughts of the scissors and the thread, the undoing to set us free, but I have no wish to die again, and neither do the others. While not perfect, this existence is preferable. And what if we did not die? What if our pieces remained alive and sentient? A crueler fate I cannot imagine.

He scrapes a bit of the rot away, revealing a darker patch beneath. When he lets out a heavy sigh, I note the absence of liquor on his breath.

He busies himself with the necessary preparations, and Lillian begins to cry again. The others remain silent. He paints the wrist with an anesthetic, which surprises me. My tears have never stopped him from his work. I close my eyes and feel pressure. Hear the blades snipping through the stitches. Smell the foul scent of decay as it reaches out from beneath.

He places the hand in a small metal tray, then coats the remaining flesh in an ointment that smells strongly of pine and wraps it in gauze.

"We shall know in a few days."

Diana's worry is as strong as mine. Lillian tries to speak but cannot force the words through her sorrow and fear.

* * *

When the anesthetic wears off, the skin gives a steady thump of pain from beneath the gauze and I do my best to ignore it.

"At least it was only the one," Grace says.

"You wouldn't understand," Lillian snaps.

"What if it spreads?" Diana asks.

Molly mutters something I cannot decipher, but it makes Lillian weep again.

"Hush," says Therese. "Remember Emily? She had reason to weep. You do not."

Sophie laughs. The sound is cruel. Hard.

"Stop, please, all of you," I finally say. "I need to sleep. To heal."

Heal is not the right term, perhaps *remain* would be better.

"I'm sorry, Kimberly," Lillian says softly.

The sound of my real name hurts, but not as much as the false one. At least Kimberly is, was, real.

The rest apologize as well, even Sophie, and fall silent. I toss and turn beneath the blankets and eventually slip from my bed. The others say nothing when I open the small door hidden behind a tapestry on the wall. The passageway is narrow and dusty and spiders scurry out of my way; it travels around the east wing of the house – the only part of the house where I'm allowed – then leads to the central part, the main house. There are small covered holes here and there that open to various rooms, to carpets my feet will never touch and sofas I will never recline upon. The passageway also goes to the west wing of the house, but the rooms are unused and the furniture nothing more than cloth-covered shapes in the darkness. The only doors I have found lead to bedrooms – mine, his, and one other designed for guests, although we never have guests stay – and one near the music room.

There is, as always, a race in the heartbeat, a dryness to the mouth, when I creep from the passage and make my way to the servants' entrance. The air outside is cold enough to take my breath away as I follow the narrow path that leads to the gate in the outer wall. There is another path that leads down the hill and into the town, but the gate is locked.

I pretend that one day I will walk through the gate and down that path. Leave this house behind; leave him behind for good. But if I ran away and the rot returned, who would fix me? The rot would not stop until it consumed me whole.

I know this for truth because he left it alone the first time to see what would happen, and the rot crept its way up until he had no choice but to remove the entire arm. Her name was Rachael, and he removed both arms so he could then attach a matching set.

Most of the windows in town are dark. The church's steeple rises high, a glint of moonlight on the spire. I have heard the servants talk about the market, the church. Beyond the town, a road winds around a bend and disappears from sight.

My parents' farm is half a day's travel from the town by horse and carriage. It would be a long, difficult walk but not impossible.

I wonder if Peter, my eldest brother, has asked for Ginny's hand in marriage yet. I wonder if Tom, younger than I by ten months, has stopped growing (when I fell ill, he already towered over all of us). I wonder if my mother still sings as she churns butter. And my father…the last thing I remember are the tears in his eyes. I hope he has found a way to smile again; I wish I could see them all once more, even if only from a distance.

I wait for someone to speak, to mention escape and freedom, but they remain silent. After a time, I return to my bed and press my hand to Molly's chest. The heart belongs to someone else, someone not us. Sometimes I think I feel her presence, like a ghostly spirit in an old house, but she never speaks. Perhaps there is not enough of her here to have a voice. Perhaps she simply refuses to speak.

I wish I knew her name.

* * *

Although the stump shows no more signs of rot, he doesn't replace Lillian's hand. It makes dressing difficult at best, but I manage.

After supper, when all the servants have gone, I join him in the music room. I sing the songs he has taught me. Melodies which were strange and awkward at first now flow with ease; foreign words that fumbled on my tongue now taste of familiarity.

He accompanies me on the piano he says belonged to his mother. Only two songs tonight, and after the second, he waves his hand in dismissal, and I notice the red in his eyes and the tremble in his fingers. Perhaps he is worried about the party.

When he comes to my room in the middle of the night, I hide my surprise. He usually doesn't touch me unless I'm whole, but by now I know what is expected, so I raise my chemise and part Therese's legs. When he kisses my neck, I pretend it belongs to someone else. Anyone else. The others whisper to me of nonsense as a distraction. Thankfully, he doesn't take long.

After he leaves, I use Lillian's finger to trace the stitches. They divide us into sections like countries on a map. The head, neck, and shoulders are mine; the upper torso, Molly's; the lower torso, Grace's; Diana, the arms; Lillian, the hand; Therese, the legs and feet; Sophie, the scalp and hair.

I make all the pieces of this puzzle move, I feel touches or insult upon them, but they never feel as if they belong completely to me. He may know how everything works on the outside, but he doesn't know that they are here with me on the inside, too. We plan to keep it this way.

* * *

Once a week, in the small operating theater, he has me strip and he inspects all the stitches, all the parts. He checks my heart and listens to me breathe. I hate the feel of his eyes upon me; it's far worse than enduring his weight in my bed.

Not long after he brought me back, I tried to stab myself with a knife. At the last moment, I held back and only opened a small wound above the left breast. Stitches hold it closed now.

He says the mind of all things, from the smallest insect to the largest animal, desires life, no matter the flesh. He says I am proof of this.

But it was Emily's doing. She was with me from the beginning, and she was always kind, always patient. She helped me stay sane. Like a mother, she whispered soft reassurances to me when I cried; told me I was not a monster when I insisted otherwise; promised me everything would be all right. She taught me how to strip the farm from my speech.

He tried hard to save her, carving away at the rot a bit at a time, but in the end he could not halt its progress. She screamed when he split apart the stitches. I did, too. Sometimes I feel as if her echo is still inside me and it offers a small comfort. Therese is kind, but I preferred my walk when it carried Emily's strength.

* * *

"I will unlock your door when the party is over," he says.

I nod.

"You will stay silent?"

"Yes."

"I would not even hold this party if not for my father's insufferable tradition. I curse him for beginning it in the first place, and I should have ended it when he died."

I know nothing of his father other than a portrait in the music room. He, too, was a doctor. I wonder if he taught his son how to make me.

The key turns in the door. I sit, a secret locked in with the shadows.

* * *

Even from my room, I can hear the music. The laughter. I creep in the passageway with small, quiet steps, extinguish my lamp, and swing open the spyhole. The year before, I was recovering and did not know about the passageway; the year before that, I was not here.

I twine a lock of Sophie's hair around my finger and watch the men and women spinning around on the dance floor, laughing with goblets of wine in hand, talking in animated voices. He is there, resplendent in a dark suit, but I don't allow my eyes to linger on him for too long. This smiling man is as much a construct as I am.

"I had a gown like that blue one," Grace says. "Oh, how I miss satin and lace."

"Please," Lillian says. "Let us go back. I can't bear to see this. The reminder hurts too much."

"Hush," Molly says.

"I wish we could join them," Diana says.

Sophie says, "Perhaps he will bring us some wine later. And look, look at the food."

Therese makes a small sound. "Look at the way they dance. Clumsy, so clumsy."

I sway back and forth, my feet tracing a pattern not from Therese, but a dance from my childhood. I remember the harvest festival, the bonfire, the musicians. My father placed my feet atop his to teach me the steps, and then he spun me around and around until we were both too dizzy to stand.

Therese laughs, but there is no mockery in the sound. I close my eyes, lost in the memory of my father's arms around me, how safe and secure I always felt. I would give anything to feel that way again.

The music stops, and my eyes snap open. A young woman in a dark blue gown approaches the piano, sits, and begins to play. The music is filled with tiny notes that reach high in the air then swoop back down, touching on melancholia. It's the most beautiful thing I have ever heard. Everyone falls silent, even Lillian.

Then I see him watching the girl at the piano. His brow is creased; his mouth soft. I hear a strange sound from Sophie. She recognizes the intensity of his gaze. As a kindness, I let go of her hair. Does he covet this girl's arms? Her hair? Her face?

Lillian begins to weep again, and it doesn't take long for the rest to join her. All except Sophie. She never cries.

* * *

"He will not," I say.

"He will do whatever he wants. You know that," Sophie says.

"She is not sick," Grace says.

"Neither was I," Sophie hisses. "He saw me in the Hargrove market. He gave me *that* look, then I woke up here."

"But you do not know for certain," Therese says. "The influenza took so many."

"I was not sick." Sophie's voice is flat. Then, she says nothing more.

Hargrove is even further away than my parents' farm. I bend my head forward, and Sophie's hair spills down, all chestnut brown and thick curls. My hair was straight and thin, best suited for tucking beneath roughspun scarves, not hanging free, but still I cried when he replaced it.

* * *

He is drunk again. His voice is loud. Angry. I pull the sheets up to my shoulders and hope he doesn't come to visit. When he is drunk, it takes longer.

Sometimes I want to sneak into his study and take one of the bottles and hide it in my room. On nights when I can still hear my mother saying my name; when I can remember the illness that confined me to my bed and eventually took my life; when I recall the confusion when I woke here and knew something was wrong.

But those nights happen less and less, and I'm afraid I will forget my mother's voice completely. Would she even recognize me with Sophie's hair in place of my own? Would she run screaming?

* * *

On Sunday morning, I creep through the passageway. Step outside. The servants have the day off, and he has gone to mass. Even here, I can hear voices in song. I remember these songs from my own church where I sang with the choir. I have never known if he heard me somehow and chose me because of my voice, but I remember seeing him on the farm in my fifteenth year when Peter broke his arm, two years before the influenza epidemic.

"We should leave," Sophie says.

"Yes, we should run far away," Lillian says.

"And where would we go?" Molly asks.

"Anywhere."

Therese laughs. "And who will fix us if we rot?"

"Better that we rot away to nothing than remain here," Sophie says.

The others start speaking over each other, denying her words. In truth, I do not know what I want. When I head back inside, the voices outside are still singing and those inside still arguing.

* * *

Days pass, then weeks. The stump remains rot free, but he says nothing of it, only nods when he does his inspection.

He spends his days in the town, ministering to the sick. I spend mine in the library, reading of wars and dead men and politics. Rachael taught me how to read; now Sophie helps when I find myself stuck on a word.

* * *

"Wake up."

His voice is rough, scented with whiskey.

"Now?"

"Yes, hurry."

"No, oh, no," someone says as we approach the small operating theater, but I cannot tell who it is.

He tears away my chemise. Pushes me down on the table.

"But there is nothing wrong," I say.

"Don't let him do this," Lillian screams. "Please, don't let him do this to me."

He lifts a blade. I grab his forearm, dig Lillian's nails in hard enough to make him wince.

"Please, no."

He slaps me across the face with his free hand. The others are shrieking, shouting. Lillian is begging, pleading, screaming for me to make him stop. I grab his arm again and try to swing

Therese's legs off the table. He slaps me twice more and presses a sharp-smelling cloth over my mouth and nose. I hold my breath until my chest tightens; he pushes the cloth harder.

I breathe in, and everything goes grey – *I'm sorry, Lillian. So sorry.* – then black.

* * *

I wake in my bed, the sheets tucked neatly around me. The others are weeping, and Lillian is gone. I choke back my tears because I don't wish to frighten the newcomer.

"What has happened to me?" she asks. Her voice is small and trembling.

"What is your name?" I ask.

"Anna," she says.

"Welcome to madness," Sophie says, her voice strangely flat.

"Hush," Molly says.

"Who is that? What is this? Please, I want to go home."

"I told you," Sophie says, still in that strange, lifeless tone. "We should have run away."

"Where am I?" Anna says. "How did I get here?"

I try to explain, but nothing I say helps. Nothing can make it right, and in the end, we are all weeping, even Sophie, and that frightens me more than I could have imagined.

* * *

I don't see him for several days. The music room remains dark, the door to the operating theater locked. I retreat to the library, lose myself in books, and pretend not to hear Anna cry. We have all tried to offer support, but she rebuffs every attempt so there is nothing to do but wait. Eventually, she will accept the way things are now, the way we've all been forced into acceptance.

There are no signs of rot along the new stitches. They're uneven both in length and spacing – not nearly as neat as the others – but they hold firm. Anna's hands are delicate with long slender fingers, the skin far paler than Diana's. The weight is wrong; they're far too light, as if I'm wearing gloves instead of hands.

I miss Lillian so very much. I didn't even have a chance to say goodbye.

* * *

When he enters the library, I notice first his disheveled clothes, then the red of his eyes. He tosses my book aside, drags me to the music room, and shoves me toward the piano.

"Tell her to play."

Everyone falls silent. Surely we have heard him wrong.

"I don't understand."

He steps close enough for me to smell the liquor. "Tell Anna to play," he says, squeezing each word out between clenched teeth.

I sit down and thump on the keys, the notes painful enough to make me grit my teeth. I poke and prod, but Anna is hiding the knowledge deep inside, and I cannot pull it free. I offer a tentative smile even though I want to scream.

"Shall I sing instead?"

He groans and pulls me from the bench. The skirts tangle and twist, and I stumble. He digs his fingers into my shoulders, brings my face close to his. "Did you truly believe I didn't know? I have heard you speak to them. I know they are in there with you. You tell her to play. Or else."

"Never," Anna says.

Therese's legs are no longer strong enough to hold us up, and I sink to the floor. He smiles, the gesture like a whip. Eventually, he stalks from the room, and I sit with Diana's arms around me.

Sophie hisses, "Bastard."

"You must teach me how to play," I tell Anna.

"I will not."

"Please, you must. If you don't, he will kill you."

"It doesn't matter. I am already dead."

"But he may kill us all, and we don't want to die."

The others chime in in agreement.

"I do not care," Anna says. "I will give him nothing. He killed me. Don't you understand? He killed me!"

"Yes, I do," says Sophie, "We do. But this is what we have now."

"I do not want this. It is monstrous, and you, all of you, you're as dead as I am."

"Please," I say. "Teach me something, anything that will make him happy. I'm begging you, please."

She doesn't respond.

* * *

Three more trips to the music room. Three more refusals that leave me with a circlet of bruises around the arms; red marks on my cheeks in the shape of his hand; more bruises on the soft skin between breasts and belly. The others scream at Anna when he strikes me, but she doesn't give in.

She is strong. Stronger than any of us.

* * *

The fourth trip. The fourth refusal. He pulls me from the bench with his hands around my neck. His fingers squeeze tighter and tighter until spots dance in my eyes and when he lets go, I fall to the floor gasping for air as he walks away without even a backward glance.

* * *

I wake to find his face leering over mine. I bite back the tears, begin to lift my chemise, and he slaps my hand.

"If you cannot make her play, I will find someone else who will." He traces the stitches just above the collarbone, spins on his heel, and lurches from the room.

I sit in the darkness and let the tears flow. I don't want to die again. I will not.

* * *

I creep into the passageway and make my way into the kitchen. Cheese, bread, a few apples. An old cloak hangs from a hook near the servants' entrance. I slip it on and pull up the hood before I step outside. The air is cold enough to sting my cheeks, too cold for the thin cloak, but I head toward the gate, searching the ground for a rock large enough to break the lock.

Perhaps my mother will scream, perhaps my father and brothers will threaten me with violence, but they cannot hurt me more than he has.

I'm five steps away from the gate when he grabs me from behind. All the air rushes from my lungs. I draw another breath to scream, and his hand covers my mouth. He leans close to my ear.

"I had such high hopes for you. Perhaps I will have better luck with the next one."

I fight to break free. The gate is so close. So close.

He laughs. "Do you have any idea what they would do to you? Even your own parents would tear you limb from limb and toss you into the fire. If I didn't need the rest of them, I'd let you go so you could find out."

He presses a cloth to my mouth, and I try not to breathe in.

I fail.

* * *

I wake in the large operating theater. The smell is blood and decay, pain and suffering. I scream and pound on the door, but it's barred from the outside. I sink down and cover my eyes; I don't want to see the equipment, the tools, the knives, and the reddish-brown stains. There are no windows, no hidden doors, no secret passageways. There is no hope.

I have no idea how much time passes before he comes. "This is your last chance," he says. "Will you play?"

"No," Anna says.

"Please, please," the others beg.

"I will not."

"She will not play," I say, my voice little more than a whisper.

He smiles. "I thought not." He closes the door again.

Does he mean to leave us locked here until we die? I bang on the door until tiny smears of blood mark the wood, then I curl up into a small ball in the corner.

I wake when he opens the door again and drags something in wrapped in a sheet. No, not a something. A body. I lurch to my feet.

"No, no, you cannot do this. Please."

"I can do whatever I want. I made you, and I can unmake you."

He approaches me with another cloth in his hand. I know if I breathe this time, I will never wake again. Sophie is shrieking. They all are.

I stumble against a table and instruments clatter to the floor with a metallic tangle. I reach blindly with Anna's hand, find a handle, and swing. He steps into the blade's path, and it sinks deep into his chest. He drops the cloth; his mouth opens and closes, opens and closes again, then he collapses to the floor as if boneless. Anna lets out a sound of triumph, but I cannot speak, cannot breathe, cannot move.

"No, no," Sophie shouts. "What have you done?"

Therese and Grace scream, Diana lets out a keening wail, Molly babbles incoherencies that sound of madness, and all the while, Anna laughs.

His eyes flutter shut, and his chest rises, falls, rises. I drop to his side and pull the blade free, grimacing at the blood that fountains forth. His eyes seek mine. His mouth moves, and it sounds as if he is trying to say, "I'm sorry," but perhaps that is only what I wish he would say.

Nonetheless, I say, "I'm sorry, too."

Then, I begin to cut.

* * *

"Thank you," Anna whispers, right before the blade touches the last stitch and she is set free. I close my eyes for a brief moment to wish her well on her journey, but there is not enough time to mourn her properly.

My stitches are clumsy, ugly, but they seem sturdy enough for now. His hands are too large, the movements awkward, but gloves will hide them, and soon I will know how to make everything work the way it's supposed to.

He whispers he will never tell us how. We laugh because we know he will eventually; he will not want his creation, his knowledge, to fall apart or to rot away and die. He mutters obscenities, names, and threats, but we ignore him.

We are not afraid of him anymore.

In the ballroom, I set fire to the drapes and wait long enough to see the flames spread to the ceiling and across the floor in a roiling carpet of destruction.

"Where shall we go?" Therese asks.

"I don't know," I say.

Sophie gives a small laugh. "We can go anywhere we wish."

The heat of the blaze follows us out. The air is thick with the stench of burning wood and the death of secrets. The promise of freedom. We pause at the gate and glance back. A section of the roof caves in with a rush of orange sparks, flames curl from the windows, and the fire's rage growls and shrieks.

When we hear shouts emerge from the town below, we slip into the shadows. This is our, *my*, body, and I will be careful. I will keep us safe.

The Triumph of Night
Edith Wharton

I

IT WAS CLEAR that the sleigh from Weymore had not come; and the shivering young traveller from Boston, who had counted on jumping into it when he left the train at Northridge Junction, found himself standing alone on the open platform, exposed to the full assault of night-fall and winter.

The blast that swept him came off New Hampshire snow-fields and ice-hung forests. It seemed to have traversed interminable leagues of frozen silence, filling them with the same cold roar and sharpening its edge against the same bitter black-and-white landscape. Dark, searching and sword-like, it alternately muffled and harried its victim, like a bull-fighter now whirling his cloak and now planting his darts. This analogy brought home to the young man the fact that he himself had no cloak, and that the overcoat in which he had faced the relatively temperate air of Boston seemed no thicker than a sheet of paper on the bleak heights of Northridge. George Faxon said to himself that the place was uncommonly well-named. It clung to an exposed ledge over the valley from which the train had lifted him, and the wind combed it with teeth of steel that he seemed actually to hear scraping against the wooden sides of the station. Other building there was none: the village lay far down the road, and thither – since the Weymore sleigh had not come – Faxon saw himself under the necessity of plodding through several feet of snow.

He understood well enough what had happened: his hostess had forgotten that he was coming. Young as Faxon was, this sad lucidity of soul had been acquired as the result of long experience, and he knew that the visitors who can least afford to hire a carriage are almost always those whom their hosts forget to send for. Yet to say that Mrs. Culme had forgotten him was too crude a way of putting it. Similar incidents led him to think that she had probably told her maid to tell the butler to telephone the coachman to tell one of the grooms (if no one else needed him) to drive over to Northridge to fetch the new secretary; but on a night like this, what groom who respected his rights would fail to forget the order?

Faxon's obvious course was to struggle through the drifts to the village, and there rout out a sleigh to convey him to Weymore; but what if, on his arrival at Mrs. Culme's, no one remembered to ask him what this devotion to duty had cost? That, again, was one of the contingencies he had expensively learned to look out for, and the perspicacity so acquired told him it would be cheaper to spend the night at the Northridge inn, and advise Mrs. Culme of his presence there by telephone. He had reached this decision, and was about to entrust his luggage to a vague man with a lantern, when his hopes were raised by the sound of bells.

Two sleighs were just dashing up to the station, and from the foremost there sprang a young man muffled in furs.

"Weymore? – No, these are not the Weymore sleighs."

The voice was that of the youth who had jumped to the platform – a voice so agreeable that, in spite of the words, it fell consolingly on Faxon's ears. At the same moment the wandering station-lantern, casting a transient light on the speaker, showed his features to be in the pleasantest harmony with his voice. He was very fair and very young – hardly in the twenties, Faxon thought – but his face, though full of a morning freshness, was a trifle too thin and fine-drawn, as though a vivid spirit contended in him with a strain of physical weakness. Faxon was perhaps the quicker to notice such delicacies of balance because his own temperament hung on lightly quivering nerves, which yet, as he believed, would never quite swing him beyond a normal sensibility.

"You expected a sleigh from Weymore?" the newcomer continued, standing beside Faxon like a slender column of fur.

Mrs. Culme's secretary explained his difficulty, and the other brushed it aside with a contemptuous "Oh, *Mrs. Culme!*" that carried both speakers a long way toward reciprocal understanding.

"But then you must be –" The youth broke off with a smile of interrogation.

"The new secretary? Yes. But apparently there are no notes to be answered this evening." Faxon's laugh deepened the sense of solidarity which had so promptly established itself between the two.

His friend laughed also. "Mrs. Culme," he explained, "was lunching at my uncle's today, and she said you were due this evening. But seven hours is a long time for Mrs. Culme to remember anything."

"Well," said Faxon philosophically, "I suppose that's one of the reasons why she needs a secretary. And I've always the inn at Northridge," he concluded.

"Oh, but you haven't, though! It burned down last week."

"The deuce it did!" said Faxon; but the humour of the situation struck him before its inconvenience. His life, for years past, had been mainly a succession of resigned adaptations, and he had learned, before dealing practically with his embarrassments, to extract from most of them a small tribute of amusement.

"Oh, well, there's sure to be somebody in the place who can put me up."

"No one *you* could put up with. Besides, Northridge is three miles off, and our place – in the opposite direction – is a little nearer." Through the darkness, Faxon saw his friend sketch a gesture of self-introduction. "My name's Frank Rainer, and I'm staying with my uncle at Overdale. I've driven over to meet two friends of his, who are due in a few minutes from New York. If you don't mind waiting till they arrive I'm sure Overdale can do you better than Northridge. We're only down from town for a few days, but the house is always ready for a lot of people."

"But your uncle –?" Faxon could only object, with the odd sense, through his embarrassment, that it would be magically dispelled by his invisible friend's next words.

"Oh, my uncle – you'll see! I answer for *him!* I daresay you've heard of him – John Lavington?"

John Lavington! There was a certain irony in asking if one had heard of John Lavington! Even from a post of observation as obscure as that of Mrs. Culme's secretary the rumour of John Lavington's money, of his pictures, his politics, his charities and his hospitality, was as difficult to escape as the roar of a cataract in a mountain solitude. It might almost have been said that the one place in which one would not have expected to come upon him was in just such a solitude as now surrounded the speakers – at least in this deepest hour of its desertedness. But it was just like Lavington's brilliant ubiquity to put one in the wrong even there.

"Oh, yes, I've heard of your uncle."

"Then you *will* come, won't you? We've only five minutes to wait." young Rainer urged, in the tone that dispels scruples by ignoring them; and Faxon found himself accepting the invitation as simply as it was offered.

A delay in the arrival of the New York train lengthened their five minutes to fifteen; and as they paced the icy platform Faxon began to see why it had seemed the most natural thing in the world to accede to his new acquaintance's suggestion. It was because Frank Rainer was one of the privileged beings who simplify human intercourse by the atmosphere of confidence and good humour they diffuse. He produced this effect, Faxon noted, by the exercise of no gift but his youth, and of no art but his sincerity; and these qualities were revealed in a smile of such sweetness that Faxon felt, as never before, what Nature can achieve when she deigns to match the face with the mind.

He learned that the young man was the ward, and the only nephew, of John Lavington, with whom he had made his home since the death of his mother, the great man's sister. Mr. Lavington, Rainer said, had been 'a regular brick' to him – "But then he is to everyone, you know" – and the young fellow's situation seemed in fact to be perfectly in keeping with his person. Apparently the only shade that had ever rested on him was cast by the physical weakness which Faxon had already detected. Young Rainer had been threatened with tuberculosis, and the disease was so far advanced that, according to the highest authorities, banishment to Arizona or New Mexico was inevitable. "But luckily my uncle didn't pack me off, as most people would have done, without getting another opinion. Whose? Oh, an awfully clever chap, a young doctor with a lot of new ideas, who simply laughed at my being sent away, and said I'd do perfectly well in New York if I didn't dine out too much, and if I dashed off occasionally to Northridge for a little fresh air. So it's really my uncle's doing that I'm not in exile – and I feel no end better since the new chap told me I needn't bother." Young Rainer went on to confess that he was extremely fond of dining out, dancing and similar distractions; and Faxon, listening to him, was inclined to think that the physician who had refused to cut him off altogether from these pleasures was probably a better psychologist than his seniors.

"All the same you ought to be careful, you know." The sense of elder-brotherly concern that forced the words from Faxon made him, as he spoke, slip his arm through Frank Rainer's.

The latter met the movement with a responsive pressure. "Oh, I *am*: awfully, awfully. And then my uncle has such an eye on me!"

"But if your uncle has such an eye on you, what does he say to your swallowing knives out here in this Siberian wild?"

Rainer raised his fur collar with a careless gesture. "It's not that that does it – the cold's good for me."

"And it's not the dinners and dances? What is it, then?" Faxon good-humouredly insisted; to which his companion answered with a laugh: "Well, my uncle says it's being bored; and I rather think he's right!"

His laugh ended in a spasm of coughing and a struggle for breath that made Faxon, still holding his arm, guide him hastily into the shelter of the fireless waiting-room.

Young Rainer had dropped down on the bench against the wall and pulled off one of his fur gloves to grope for a handkerchief. He tossed aside his cap and drew the handkerchief across his forehead, which was intensely white, and beaded with moisture, though his face retained a healthy glow. But Faxon's gaze remained fastened to the hand he had uncovered: it was so long, so colourless, so wasted, so much older than the brow he passed it over.

"It's queer – a healthy face but dying hands," the secretary mused: he somehow wished young Rainer had kept on his glove.

The whistle of the express drew the young men to their feet, and the next moment two heavily-furred gentlemen had descended to the platform and were breasting the rigour of the night. Frank Rainer introduced them as Mr. Grisben and Mr. Balch, and Faxon, while their luggage was being lifted into the second sleigh, discerned them, by the roving lantern-gleam, to be an elderly greyheaded pair, of the average prosperous business cut.

They saluted their host's nephew with friendly familiarity, and Mr. Grisben, who seemed the spokesman of the two, ended his greeting with a genial – "and many many more of them, dear boy!" which suggested to Faxon that their arrival coincided with an anniversary. But he could not press the enquiry, for the seat allotted him was at the coachman's side, while Frank Rainer joined his uncle's guests inside the sleigh.

A swift flight (behind such horses as one could be sure of John Lavington's having) brought them to tall gateposts, an illuminated lodge, and an avenue on which the snow had been levelled to the smoothness of marble. At the end of the avenue the long house loomed up, its principal bulk dark, but one wing sending out a ray of welcome; and the next moment Faxon was receiving a violent impression of warmth and light, of hot-house plants, hurrying servants, a vast spectacular oak hall like a stage-setting, and, in its unreal middle distance, a small figure, correctly dressed, conventionally featured, and utterly unlike his rather florid conception of the great John Lavington.

The surprise of the contrast remained with him through his hurried dressing in the large luxurious bedroom to which he had been shown. "I don't see where he comes in," was the only way he could put it, so difficult was it to fit the exuberance of Lavington's public personality into his host's contracted frame and manner. Mr. Lavington, to whom Faxon's case had been rapidly explained by young Rainer, had welcomed him with a sort of dry and stilted cordiality that exactly matched his narrow face, his stiff hand, and the whiff of scent on his evening handkerchief. "Make yourself at home – at home!" he had repeated, in a tone that suggested, on his own part, a complete inability to perform the feat he urged on his visitor. "Any friend of Frank's... delighted... make yourself thoroughly at home!"

II

IN SPITE OF the balmy temperature and complicated conveniences of Faxon's bedroom, the injunction was not easy to obey. It was wonderful luck to have found a night's shelter under the opulent roof of Overdale, and he tasted the physical satisfaction to the full. But the place, for all its ingenuities of comfort, was oddly cold and unwelcoming. He couldn't have said why, and could only suppose that Mr. Lavington's intense personality – intensely negative, but intense all the same – must, in some occult way, have penetrated every corner of his dwelling. Perhaps, though, it was merely that Faxon himself was tired and hungry, more deeply chilled than he had known till he came in from the cold, and unutterably sick of all strange houses, and of the prospect of perpetually treading other people's stairs.

"I hope you're not famished?" Rainer's slim figure was in the doorway. "My uncle has a little business to attend to with Mr. Grisben, and we don't dine for half an hour. Shall I fetch you, or can you find your way down? Come straight to the dining-room – the second door on the left of the long gallery."

He disappeared, leaving a ray of warmth behind him, and Faxon, relieved, lit a cigarette and sat down by the fire.

Looking about with less haste, he was struck by a detail that had escaped him. The room was full of flowers – a mere 'bachelor's room', in the wing of a house opened only for a few days, in the dead middle of a New Hampshire winter! Flowers were everywhere, not in senseless profusion, but placed with the same conscious art that he had remarked in the grouping of the blossoming shrubs in the hall. A vase of arums stood on the writing-table, a cluster of strange-hued carnations on the stand at his elbow, and from bowls of glass and porcelain clumps of freesia-bulbs diffused their melting fragrance. The fact implied acres of glass – but that was the least interesting part of it. The flowers themselves, their quality, selection and arrangement, attested on someone's part – and on whose but John Lavington's? – a solicitous and sensitive passion for that particular form of beauty. Well, it simply made the man, as he had appeared to Faxon, all the harder to understand!

The half-hour elapsed, and Faxon, rejoicing at the prospect of food, set out to make his way to the dining-room. He had not noticed the direction he had followed in going to his room, and was puzzled, when he left it, to find that two staircases, of apparently equal importance, invited him. He chose the one to his right, and reached, at its foot, a long gallery such as Rainer had described. The gallery was empty, the doors down its length were closed; but Rainer had said: "The second to the left," and Faxon, after pausing for some chance enlightenment which did not come, laid his hand on the second knob to the left.

The room he entered was square, with dusky picture-hung walls. In its centre, about a table lit by veiled lamps, he fancied Mr. Lavington and his guests to be already seated at dinner; then he perceived that the table was covered not with viands but with papers, and that he had blundered into what seemed to be his host's study. As he paused Frank Rainer looked up.

"Oh, here's Mr. Faxon. Why not ask him –?"

Mr. Lavington, from the end of the table, reflected his nephew's smile in a glance of impartial benevolence.

"Certainly. Come in, Mr. Faxon. If you won't think it a liberty –"

Mr. Grisben, who sat opposite his host, turned his head toward the door. "Of course Mr. Faxon's an American citizen?"

Frank Rainer laughed. "That's all right!... Oh, no, not one of your pin-pointed pens, Uncle Jack! Haven't you got a quill somewhere?"

Mr. Balch, who spoke slowly and as if reluctantly, in a muffled voice of which there seemed to be very little left, raised his hand to say: "One moment: you acknowledge this to be –?"

"My last will and testament?" Rainer's laugh redoubled. "Well, I won't answer for the 'last'. It's the first, anyway."

"It's a mere formula," Mr. Balch explained.

"Well, here goes." Rainer dipped his quill in the inkstand his uncle had pushed in his direction, and dashed a gallant signature across the document.

Faxon, understanding what was expected of him, and conjecturing that the young man was signing his will on the attainment of his majority, had placed himself behind Mr. Grisben, and stood awaiting his turn to affix his name to the instrument. Rainer, having signed, was about to push the paper across the table to Mr. Balch; but the latter, again raising his hand, said in his sad imprisoned voice: "The seal –?"

"Oh, does there have to be a seal?"

Faxon, looking over Mr. Grisben at John Lavington, saw a faint frown between his impassive eyes. "Really, Frank!" He seemed, Faxon thought, slightly irritated by his nephew's frivolity.

"Who's got a seal?" Frank Rainer continued, glancing about the table. "There doesn't seem to be one here."

Mr. Grisben interposed. "A wafer will do. Lavington, you have a wafer?"

Mr. Lavington had recovered his serenity. "There must be some in one of the drawers. But I'm ashamed to say I don't know where my secretary keeps these things. He ought to have seen to it that a wafer was sent with the document."

"Oh, hang it –" Frank Rainer pushed the paper aside: "It's the hand of God – and I'm as hungry as a wolf. Let's dine first, Uncle Jack."

"I think I've a seal upstairs," said Faxon.

Mr. Lavington sent him a barely perceptible smile. "So sorry to give you the trouble –"

"Oh, I say, don't send him after it now. Let's wait till after dinner!"

Mr. Lavington continued to smile on *his* guest, and the latter, as if under the faint coercion of the smile, turned from the room and ran upstairs. Having taken the seal from his writing-case he came down again, and once more opened the door of the study. No one was speaking when he entered – they were evidently awaiting his return with the mute impatience of hunger, and he put the seal in Rainer's reach, and stood watching while Mr. Grisben struck a match and held it to one of the candles flanking the inkstand. As the wax descended on the paper Faxon remarked again the strange emaciation, the premature physical weariness, of the hand that held it: he wondered if Mr. Lavington had ever noticed his nephew's hand, and if it were not poignantly visible to him now.

With this thought in his mind, Faxon raised his eyes to look at Mr. Lavington. The great man's gaze rested on Frank Rainer with an expression of untroubled benevolence; and at the same instant Faxon's attention was attracted by the presence in the room of another person, who must have joined the group while he was upstairs searching for the seal. The new-comer was a man of about Mr. Lavington's age and figure, who stood just behind his chair, and who, at the moment when Faxon first saw him, was gazing at young Rainer with an equal intensity of attention. The likeness between the two men – perhaps increased by the fact that the hooded lamps on the table left the figure behind the chair in shadow – struck Faxon the more because of the contrast in their expression. John Lavington, during his nephew's clumsy attempt to drop the wax and apply the seal, continued to fasten on him a look of half-amused affection; while the man behind the chair, so oddly reduplicating the lines of his features and figure, turned on the boy a face of pale hostility.

The impression was so startling that Faxon forgot what was going on about him. He was just dimly aware of young Rainer's exclaiming; "Your turn, Mr. Grisben!" of Mr. Grisben's protesting: "No – no; Mr. Faxon first," and of the pen's being thereupon transferred to his own hand. He received it with a deadly sense of being unable to move, or even to understand what was expected of him, till he became conscious of Mr. Grisben's paternally pointing out the precise spot on which he was to leave his autograph. The effort to fix his attention and steady his hand prolonged the process of signing, and when he stood up – a strange weight of fatigue on all his limbs – the figure behind Mr. Lavington's chair was gone.

Faxon felt an immediate sense of relief. It was puzzling that the man's exit should have been so rapid and noiseless, but the door behind Mr. Lavington was screened by a tapestry hanging, and Faxon concluded that the unknown looker-on had merely had to raise it to pass out. At any rate he was gone, and with his withdrawal the strange weight was lifted. Young Rainer was lighting a cigarette, Mr. Balch inscribing his name at the foot of the document, Mr. Lavington – his eyes no longer on his nephew – examining a strange white-winged orchid in the vase at his elbow. Everything suddenly seemed to have grown natural and simple again, and Faxon found himself responding with a smile to the affable gesture with which his host declared: "And now, Mr. Faxon, we'll dine."

III

"I WONDER how I blundered into the wrong room just now; I thought you told me to take the second door to the left," Faxon said to Frank Rainer as they followed the older men down the gallery.

"So I did; but I probably forgot to tell you which staircase to take. Coming from your bedroom, I ought to have said the fourth door to the right. It's a puzzling house, because my uncle keeps adding to it from year to year. He built this room last summer for his modern pictures."

Young Rainer, pausing to open another door, touched an electric button which sent a circle of light about the walls of a long room hung with canvases of the French impressionist school.

Faxon advanced, attracted by a shimmering Monet, but Rainer laid a hand on his arm.

"He bought that last week. But come along – I'll show you all this after dinner. Or *he* will, rather – he loves it."

"Does he really love things?"

Rainer stared, clearly perplexed at the question. "Rather! Flowers and pictures especially! Haven't you noticed the flowers? I suppose you think his manner's cold; it seems so at first; but he's really awfully keen about things."

Faxon looked quickly at the speaker. "Has your uncle a brother?"

"Brother? No – never had. He and my mother were the only ones."

"Or any relation who – who looks like him? Who might be mistaken for him?"

"Not that I ever heard of. Does he remind you of someone?"

"Yes."

"That's queer. We'll ask him if he's got a double. Come on!"

But another picture had arrested Faxon, and some minutes elapsed before he and his young host reached the dining-room. It was a large room, with the same conventionally handsome furniture and delicately grouped flowers; and Faxon's first glance showed him that only three men were seated about the dining-table. The man who had stood behind Mr. Lavington's chair was not present, and no seat awaited him.

When the young men entered, Mr. Grisben was speaking, and his host, who faced the door, sat looking down at his untouched soup-plate and turning the spoon about in his small dry hand.

"It's pretty late to call them rumours – they were devilish close to facts when we left town this morning," Mr. Grisben was saying, with an unexpected incisiveness of tone.

Mr. Lavington laid down his spoon and smiled interrogatively. "Oh, facts – what *are* facts? Just the way a thing happens to look at a given minute…."

"You haven't heard anything from town?" Mr. Grisben persisted.

"Not a syllable. So you see…. Balch, a little more of that *petite marmite*. Mr. Faxon… between Frank and Mr. Grisben, please."

The dinner progressed through a series of complicated courses, ceremoniously dispensed by a prelatical butler attended by three tall footmen, and it was evident that Mr. Lavington took a certain satisfaction in the pageant. That, Faxon reflected, was probably the joint in his armour – that and the flowers. He had changed the subject – not abruptly but firmly – when the young men entered, but Faxon perceived that it still possessed the thoughts of the two elderly visitors, and Mr. Balch presently observed, in a voice that seemed to come from the last survivor down a mine-shaft: "If it *does* come, it will be the biggest crash since '93."

Mr. Lavington looked bored but polite. "Wall Street can stand crashes better than it could then. It's got a robuster constitution."

"Yes; but –"

"Speaking of constitutions," Mr. Grisben intervened: "Frank, are you taking care of yourself?"

A flush rose to young Rainer's cheeks.

"Why, of course! Isn't that what I'm here for?"

"You're here about three days in the month, aren't you? And the rest of the time it's crowded restaurants and hot ballrooms in town. I thought you were to be shipped off to New Mexico?"

"Oh, I've got a new man who says that's rot."

"Well, you don't look as if your new man were right," said Mr. Grisben bluntly.

Faxon saw the lad's colour fade, and the rings of shadow deepen under his gay eyes. At the same moment his uncle turned to him with a renewed intensity of attention. There was such solicitude in Mr. Lavington's gaze that it seemed almost to fling a shield between his nephew and Mr. Grisben's tactless scrutiny.

"We think Frank's a good deal better," he began; "this new doctor –"

The butler, coming up, bent to whisper a word in his ear, and the communication caused a sudden change in Mr. Lavington's expression. His face was naturally so colourless that it seemed not so much to pale as to fade, to dwindle and recede into something blurred and blotted-out. He half rose, sat down again and sent a rigid smile about the table.

"Will you excuse me? The telephone. Peters, go on with the dinner." With small precise steps he walked out of the door which one of the footmen had thrown open.

A momentary silence fell on the group; then Mr. Grisben once more addressed himself to Rainer. "You ought to have gone, my boy; you ought to have gone."

The anxious look returned to the youth's eyes. "My uncle doesn't think so, really."

"You're not a baby, to be always governed by your uncle's opinion. You came of age today, didn't you? Your uncle spoils you.... that's what's the matter...."

The thrust evidently went home, for Rainer laughed and looked down with a slight accession of colour.

"But the doctor –"

"Use your common sense, Frank! You had to try twenty doctors to find one to tell you what you wanted to be told."

A look of apprehension overshadowed Rainer's gaiety. "Oh, come – I say!... What would *you* do?" he stammered.

"Pack up and jump on the first train." Mr. Grisben leaned forward and laid his hand kindly on the young man's arm. "Look here: my nephew Jim Grisben is out there ranching on a big scale. He'll take you in and be glad to have you. You say your new doctor thinks it won't do you any good; but he doesn't pretend to say it will do you harm, does he? Well, then – give it a trial. It'll take you out of hot theatres and night restaurants, anyhow.... And all the rest of it.... Eh, Balch?"

"Go!" said Mr. Balch hollowly. "Go *at once*," he added, as if a closer look at the youth's face had impressed on him the need of backing up his friend.

Young Rainer had turned ashy-pale. He tried to stiffen his mouth into a smile. "Do I look as bad as all that?"

Mr. Grisben was helping himself to terrapin. "You look like the day after an earthquake," he said.

The terrapin had encircled the table, and been deliberately enjoyed by Mr. Lavington's three visitors (Rainer, Faxon noticed, left his plate untouched) before the door was thrown open to re-admit their host. Mr. Lavington advanced with an air of recovered composure. He seated himself, picked up his napkin and consulted the gold-monogrammed menu. "No, don't bring back the filet.... Some terrapin; yes...." He looked affably about the table. "Sorry to have deserted you, but the storm has played the deuce with the wires, and I had to wait a long time before I could get a good connection. It must be blowing up for a blizzard."

"Uncle Jack," young Rainer broke out, "Mr. Grisben's been lecturing me."

Mr. Lavington was helping himself to terrapin. "Ah – what about?"

"He thinks I ought to have given New Mexico a show."

"I want him to go straight out to my nephew at Santa Paz and stay there till his next birthday." Mr. Lavington signed to the butler to hand the terrapin to Mr. Grisben, who, as he took a second helping, addressed himself again to Rainer. "Jim's in New York now, and going back the day after tomorrow in Olyphant's private car. I'll ask Olyphant to squeeze you in if you'll go. And when you've been out there a week or two, in the saddle all day and sleeping nine hours a night, I suspect you won't think much of the doctor who prescribed New York."

Faxon spoke up, he knew not why. "I was out there once: it's a splendid life. I saw a fellow – oh, a really *bad* case – who'd been simply made over by it."

"It *does* sound jolly," Rainer laughed, a sudden eagerness in his tone.

His uncle looked at him gently. "Perhaps Grisben's right. It's an opportunity –"

Faxon glanced up with a start: the figure dimly perceived in the study was now more visibly and tangibly planted behind Mr. Lavington's chair.

"That's right, Frank: you see your uncle approves. And the trip out there with Olyphant isn't a thing to be missed. So drop a few dozen dinners and be at the Grand Central the day after tomorrow at five."

Mr. Grisben's pleasant grey eye sought corroboration of his host, and Faxon, in a cold anguish of suspense, continued to watch him as he turned his glance on Mr. Lavington. One could not look at Lavington without seeing the presence at his back, and it was clear that, the next minute, some change in Mr. Grisben's expression must give his watcher a clue.

But Mr. Grisben's expression did not change: the gaze he fixed on his host remained unperturbed, and the clue he gave was the startling one of not seeming to see the other figure.

Faxon's first impulse was to look away, to look anywhere else, to resort again to the champagne glass the watchful butler had already brimmed; but some fatal attraction, at war in him with an overwhelming physical resistance, held his eyes upon the spot they feared.

The figure was still standing, more distinctly, and therefore more resemblingly, at Mr. Lavington's back; and while the latter continued to gaze affectionately at his nephew, his counterpart, as before, fixed young Rainer with eyes of deadly menace.

Faxon, with what felt like an actual wrench of the muscles, dragged his own eyes from the sight to scan the other countenances about the table; but not one revealed the least consciousness of what he saw, and a sense of mortal isolation sank upon him.

"It's worth considering, certainly –" he heard Mr. Lavington continue; and as Rainer's face lit up, the face behind his uncle's chair seemed to gather into its look all the fierce weariness of old unsatisfied hates. That was the thing that, as the minutes laboured by, Faxon was becoming most conscious of. The watcher behind the chair was no longer merely malevolent: he had grown suddenly, unutterably tired. His hatred seemed to well up out of the very depths of balked effort and thwarted hopes, and the fact made him more pitiable, and yet more dire.

Faxon's look reverted to Mr. Lavington, as if to surprise in him a corresponding change. At first none was visible: his pinched smile was screwed to his blank face like a gas-light to a white-washed wall. Then the fixity of the smile became ominous: Faxon saw that its wearer was afraid to let it go. It was evident that Mr. Lavington was unutterably tired too, and the discovery sent a colder current through Faxon's veins. Looking down at his untouched plate, he caught the soliciting twinkle of the champagne glass; but the sight of the wine turned him sick.

"Well, we'll go into the details presently," he heard Mr. Lavington say, still on the question of his nephew's future. "Let's have a cigar first. No – not here, Peters." He turned his smile on Faxon. "When we've had coffee I want to show you my pictures."

"Oh, by the way, Uncle Jack – Mr. Faxon wants to know if you've got a double?"

"A double?" Mr. Lavington, still smiling, continued to address himself to his guest. "Not that I know of. Have you seen one, Mr. Faxon?"

Faxon thought: "My God, if I look up now they'll *both* be looking at me!" To avoid raising his eyes he made as though to lift the glass to his lips; but his hand sank inert, and he looked up. Mr. Lavington's glance was politely bent on him, but with a loosening of the strain about his heart he saw that the figure behind the chair still kept its gaze on Rainer.

"Do you think you've seen my double, Mr. Faxon?"

Would the other face turn if he said yes? Faxon felt a dryness in his throat. "No," he answered.

"Ah? It's possible I've a dozen. I believe I'm extremely usual-looking," Mr. Lavington went on conversationally; and still the other face watched Rainer.

"It was…a mistake…a confusion of memory…." Faxon heard himself stammer. Mr. Lavington pushed back his chair, and as he did so Mr. Grisben suddenly leaned forward.

"Lavington! What have we been thinking of? We haven't drunk Frank's health!"

Mr. Lavington reseated himself. "My dear boy!… Peters, another bottle…." He turned to his nephew. "After such a sin of omission I don't presume to propose the toast myself…but Frank knows…. Go ahead, Grisben!"

The boy shone on his uncle. "No, no, Uncle Jack! Mr. Grisben won't mind. Nobody but *you* – today!"

The butler was replenishing the glasses. He filled Mr. Lavington's last, and Mr. Lavington put out his small hand to raise it…. As he did so, Faxon looked away.

"Well, then – all the good I've wished you in all the past years…. I put it into the prayer that the coming ones may be healthy and happy and many…and *many*, dear boy!"

Faxon saw the hands about him reach out for their glasses. Automatically, he reached for his. His eyes were still on the table, and he repeated to himself with a trembling vehemence: "I won't look up! I won't…. I won't…."

His fingers clasped the glass and raised it to the level of his lips. He saw the other hands making the same motion. He heard Mr. Grisben's genial "Hear! Hear!" and Mr. Batch's hollow echo. He said to himself, as the rim of the glass touched his lips: "I won't look up! I swear I won't! –" and he looked.

The glass was so full that it required an extraordinary effort to hold it there, brimming and suspended, during the awful interval before he could trust his hand to lower it again, untouched, to the table. It was this merciful preoccupation which saved him, kept him from crying out, from losing his hold, from slipping down into the bottomless blackness that gaped for him. As long as the problem of the glass engaged him he felt able to keep his seat, manage his muscles, fit unnoticeably into the group; but as the glass touched the table his last link with safety snapped. He stood up and dashed out of the room.

IV

IN THE GALLERY, the instinct of self-preservation helped him to turn back and sign to young Rainer not to follow. He stammered out something about a touch of dizziness, and joining them presently; and the boy nodded sympathetically and drew back.

At the foot of the stairs Faxon ran against a servant. "I should like to telephone to Weymore," he said with dry lips.

"Sorry, sir; wires all down. We've been trying the last hour to get New York again for Mr. Lavington."

Faxon shot on to his room, burst into it, and bolted the door. The lamplight lay on furniture, flowers, books; in the ashes a log still glimmered. He dropped down on the sofa and hid his face. The room was profoundly silent, the whole house was still: nothing about him gave a hint of what was going on, darkly and dumbly, in the room he had flown from, and with the covering of his eyes oblivion and reassurance seemed to fall on him. But they fell for a moment only; then his lids opened again to the monstrous vision. There it was, stamped on his pupils, a part of him forever, an indelible horror burnt into his body and brain. But why into his – just his? Why had he alone been chosen to see what he had seen? What business was it of *his*, in God's name? Any one of the others, thus enlightened, might have exposed the horror and defeated it; but *he*, the one weaponless and defenceless spectator, the one whom none of the others would believe or understand if he attempted to reveal what he knew – *he* alone had been singled out as the victim of this dreadful initiation!

Suddenly he sat up, listening: he had heard a step on the stairs. Someone, no doubt, was coming to see how he was – to urge him, if he felt better, to go down and join the smokers. Cautiously he opened his door; yes, it was young Rainer's step. Faxon looked down the passage, remembered the other stairway and darted to it. All he wanted was to get out of the house. Not another instant would he breathe its abominable air! What business was it of *his*, in God's name?

He reached the opposite end of the lower gallery, and beyond it saw the hall by which he had entered. It was empty, and on a long table he recognized his coat and cap. He got into his coat, unbolted the door, and plunged into the purifying night.

The darkness was deep, and the cold so intense that for an instant it stopped his breathing. Then he perceived that only a thin snow was falling, and resolutely he set his face for flight. The trees along the avenue marked his way as he hastened with long strides over the beaten snow. Gradually, while he walked, the tumult in his brain subsided. The impulse to fly still drove him forward, but he began feel that he was flying from a terror of his own creating, and that the most urgent reason for escape was the need of hiding his state, of shunning other eyes till he should regain his balance.

He had spent the long hours in the train in fruitless broodings on a discouraging situation, and he remembered how his bitterness had turned to exasperation when he found that the Weymore sleigh was not awaiting him. It was absurd, of course; but, though he had joked with Rainer over Mrs. Culme's forgetfulness, to confess it had cost a pang. That was what his rootless life had brought him to: for lack of a personal stake in things his sensibility was at the mercy of such trifles.... Yes; that, and the cold and fatigue, the absence of hope and the haunting sense of starved aptitudes, all these had brought him to the perilous verge over which, once or twice before, his terrified brain had hung.

Why else, in the name of any imaginable logic, human or devilish, should he, a stranger, be singled out for this experience? What could it mean to him, how was he related to it, what bearing had it on his case?... Unless, indeed, it was just because he was a stranger – a stranger everywhere – because he had no personal life, no warm screen of private egotisms to shield him from exposure, that he had developed this abnormal sensitiveness to the vicissitudes of others. The thought pulled him up with a shudder. No! Such a fate was too abominable; all that was strong and sound in him rejected it. A thousand times better regard himself as ill, disorganized, deluded, than as the predestined victim of such warnings!

He reached the gates and paused before the darkened lodge. The wind had risen and was sweeping the snow into his race. The cold had him in its grasp again, and he stood uncertain. Should he put his sanity to the test and go back? He turned and looked down the dark drive to the house. A single ray shone through the trees, evoking a picture of the lights, the flowers, the faces grouped about that fatal room. He turned and plunged out into the road....

He remembered that, about a mile from Overdale, the coachman had pointed out the road to Northridge; and he began to walk in that direction. Once in the road he had the gale in his face, and the wet snow on his moustache and eye-lashes instantly hardened to ice. The same ice seemed to be driving a million blades into his throat and lungs, but he pushed on, the vision of the warm room pursuing him.

The snow in the road was deep and uneven. He stumbled across ruts and sank into drifts, and the wind drove against him like a granite cliff. Now and then he stopped, gasping, as if an invisible hand had tightened an iron band about his body; then he started again, stiffening himself against the stealthy penetration of the cold. The snow continued to descend out of a pall of inscrutable darkness, and once or twice he paused, fearing he had missed the road to Northridge; but, seeing no sign of a turn, he ploughed on.

At last, feeling sure that he had walked for more than a mile, he halted and looked back. The act of turning brought immediate relief, first because it put his back to the wind, and then because, far down the road, it showed him the gleam of a lantern. A sleigh was coming – a sleigh that might perhaps give him a lift to the village! Fortified by the hope, he began to walk back toward the light. It came forward very slowly, with unaccountable zigzags and waverings; and even when he was within a few yards of it he could catch no sound of sleigh-bells. Then it paused and became stationary by the roadside, as though carried by a pedestrian who had stopped, exhausted by the cold. The thought made Faxon hasten on, and a moment later he was stooping over a motionless figure huddled against the snow-bank. The lantern had dropped from its bearer's hand, and Faxon, fearfully raising it, threw its light into the face of Frank Rainer.

"Rainer! What on earth are you doing here?"

The boy smiled back through his pallour. "What are *you*, I'd like to know?" he retorted; and, scrambling to his feet with a clutch oh Faxon's arm, he added gaily: "Well, I've run you down!"

Faxon stood confounded, his heart sinking. The lad's face was grey.

"What madness –" he began.

"Yes, it *is*. What on earth did you do it for?"

"I? Do what?... Why I.... I was just taking a walk.... I often walk at night...."

Frank Rainer burst into a laugh. "On such nights? Then you hadn't bolted?"

"Bolted?"

"Because I'd done something to offend you? My uncle thought you had."

Faxon grasped his arm. "Did your uncle send you after me?"

"Well, he gave me an awful rowing for not going up to your room with you when you said you were ill. And when we found you'd gone we were frightened – and he was awfully upset – so I said I'd catch you.... You're *not* ill, are you?"

"Ill? No. Never better." Faxon picked up the lantern. "Come; let's go back. It was awfully hot in that dining-room."

"Yes; I hoped it was only that."

They trudged on in silence for a few minutes; then Faxon questioned: "You're not too done up?"

"Oh, no. It's a lot easier with the wind behind us."

"All right. Don't talk anymore."

They pushed ahead, walking, in spite of the light that guided them, more slowly than Faxon had walked alone into the gale. The fact of his companion's stumbling against a drift gave Faxon a pretext for saying: "Take hold of my arm," and Rainer obeying, gasped out: "I'm blown!"

"So am I. Who wouldn't be?"

"What a dance you led me! If it hadn't been for one of the servants happening to see you –"

"Yes; all right. And now, won't you kindly shut up?"

Rainer laughed and hung on him. "Oh, the cold doesn't hurt me...."

For the first few minutes after Rainer had overtaken him, anxiety for the lad had been Faxon's only thought. But as each labouring step carried them nearer to the spot he had been fleeing, the reasons for his flight grew more ominous and more insistent. No, he was not ill, he was not distraught and deluded – he was the instrument singled out to warn and save; and here he was, irresistibly driven, dragging the victim back to his doom!

The intensity of the conviction had almost checked his steps. But what could he do or say? At all costs he must get Rainer out of the cold, into the house and into his bed. After that he would act.

The snow-fall was thickening, and as they reached a stretch of the road between open fields the wind took them at an angle, lashing their faces with barbed thongs. Rainer stopped to take breath, and Faxon felt the heavier pressure of his arm.

"When we get to the lodge, can't we telephone to the stable for a sleigh?"

"If they're not all asleep at the lodge."

"Oh, I'll manage. Don't talk!" Faxon ordered; and they plodded on....

At length the lantern ray showed ruts that curved away from the road under tree-darkness. Faxon's spirits rose. "There's the gate! We'll be there in five minutes."

As he spoke he caught, above the boundary hedge, the gleam of a light at the farther end of the dark avenue. It was the same light that had shone on the scene of which every detail was burnt into his brain; and he felt again its overpowering reality. No – he couldn't let the boy go back!

They were at the lodge at last, and Faxon was hammering on the door. He said to himself: "I'll get him inside first, and make them give him a hot drink. Then I'll see – I'll find an argument...."

There was no answer to his knocking, and after an interval Rainer said: "Look here – we'd better go on."

"No!"

"I can, perfectly –"

"You shan't go to the house, I say!" Faxon redoubled his blows, and at length steps sounded on the stairs. Rainer was leaning against the lintel, and as the door opened the light from the hall flashed on his pale face and fixed eyes. Faxon caught him by the arm and drew him in.

"It *was* cold out there." he sighed; and then, abruptly, as if invisible shears at a single stroke had cut every muscle in his body, he swerved, drooped on Faxon's arm, and seemed to sink into nothing at his feet.

The lodge-keeper and Faxon bent over him, and somehow, between them, lifted him into the kitchen and laid him on a sofa by the stove.

The lodge-keeper, stammering: "I'll ring up the house," dashed out of the room. But Faxon heard the words without heeding them: omens mattered nothing now, beside this woe fulfilled. He knelt down to undo the fur collar about Rainer's throat, and as he did so he felt a warm moisture on his hands. He held them up, and they were red....

V

THE PALMS THREADED their endless line along the yellow river. The little steamer lay at the wharf, and George Faxon, sitting in the verandah of the wooden hotel, idly watched the coolies carrying the freight across the gang-plank.

He had been looking at such scenes for two months. Nearly five had elapsed since he had descended from the train at Northridge and strained his eyes for the sleigh that was to take him to Weymore: Weymore, which he was never to behold!... Part of the interval – the first part – was still a great grey blur. Even now he could not be quite sure how he had got back to Boston, reached the house of a cousin, and been thence transferred to a quiet room looking out on snow under bare trees. He looked out a long time at the same scene, and finally one day a man he had known at Harvard came to see him and invited him to go out on a business trip to the Malay Peninsula.

"You've had a bad shake-up, and it'll do you no end of good to get away from things."

When the doctor came the next day it turned out that he knew of the plan and approved it. "You ought to be quiet for a year. Just loaf and look at the landscape," he advised.

Faxon felt the first faint stirrings of curiosity.

"What's been the matter with me, anyway?"

"Well, over-work, I suppose. You must have been bottling up for a bad breakdown before you started for New Hampshire last December. And the shock of that poor boy's death did the rest."

Ah, yes – Rainer had died. He remembered....

He started for the East, and gradually, by imperceptible degrees, life crept back into his weary bones and leaden brain. His friend was patient and considerate, and they travelled slowly and talked little. At first Faxon had felt a great shrinking from whatever touched on familiar things. He seldom looked at a newspaper and he never opened a letter without a contraction of the heart. It was not that he had any special cause for apprehension, but merely that a great trail of darkness lay on everything. He had looked too deep down into the abyss.... But little by little health and energy returned to him, and with them the common promptings of curiosity. He was beginning to wonder how the world was going, and when, presently, the hotel-keeper told him there were no letters for him in the steamer's mail-bag, he felt a distinct sense of disappointment. His friend had gone into the jungle on a long excursion, and he was lonely, unoccupied and wholesomely bored. He got up and strolled into the stuffy reading-room.

There he found a game of dominoes, a mutilated picture-puzzle, some copies of *Zion's Herald* and a pile of New York and London newspapers.

He began to glance through the papers, and was disappointed to find that they were less recent than he had hoped. Evidently the last numbers had been carried off by luckier travellers. He continued to turn them over, picking out the American ones first. These, as it happened, were the oldest: they dated back to December and January. To Faxon, however, they had all the flavour of novelty, since they covered the precise period during which he had virtually ceased to exist. It had never before occurred to him to wonder what had happened in the world during that interval of obliteration; but now he felt a sudden desire to know.

To prolong the pleasure, he began by sorting the papers chronologically, and as he found and spread out the earliest number, the date at the top of the page entered into his consciousness like a key slipping into a lock. It was the seventeenth of December: the date of the day after his arrival at Northridge. He glanced at the first page and read in blazing characters: 'Reported Failure of Opal Cement Company. Lavington's name involved. Gigantic Exposure of Corruption Shakes Wall Street to Its Foundations.'

He read on, and when he had finished the first paper he turned to the next. There was a gap of three days, but the Opal Cement 'Investigation' still held the centre of the stage. From its complex revelations of greed and ruin his eye wandered to the death notices, and he read: "Rainer. Suddenly, at Northridge, New Hampshire, Francis John, only son of the late...."

His eyes clouded, and he dropped the newspaper and sat for a long time with his face in his hands. When he looked up again he noticed that his gesture had pushed the other papers from the table and scattered them at his feet. The uppermost lay spread out before him, and heavily his eyes began their search again. 'John Lavington comes forward with plan for reconstructing Company. Offers to put in ten millions of his own – The proposal under consideration by the District Attorney.'

Ten millions... ten millions of his own. But if John Lavington was ruined?... Faxon stood up with a cry. That was it, then – that was what the warning meant! And if he had not fled from it, dashed wildly away from it into the night, he might have broken the spell of iniquity, the powers of darkness might not have prevailed! He caught up the pile of newspapers and began to glance through each in turn for the headline: 'Wills Admitted to Probate.' In the last of all he found the paragraph he sought, and it stared up at him as if with Rainer's dying eyes.

That – *that* was what he had done! The powers of pity had singled him out to warn and save, and he had closed his ears to their call, and washed his hands of it, and fled. Washed his hands of it! That was the word. It caught him back to the dreadful moment in the lodge when, raising himself up from Rainer's side, he had looked at his hands and seen that they were red....

THE END

Biographies & Sources

Sara Dobie Bauer
They Lived in the House on Cherry Street
(First Publication)
Sara Dobie Bauer is a bestselling, award-winning author, model, and mental health advocate with a creative writing degree from Ohio University. Her short story 'Don't Ball the Boss', inspired by her shameless crush on Benedict Cumberbatch, was nominated for the Pushcart Prize. She lives in Northeast Ohio, although she'd really like to live in a Tim Burton film. She is author of the paranormal rom-com *Bite Somebody* from World Weaver Press, among other ridiculously entertaining things. Learn more at SaraDobieBauer.com.

E.F. Benson
The Outcast
(Originally Published in *Hutchinson's Magazine,* April 1922)
Edward Frederic ('E.F.') Benson (1867–1940) was born at Wellington College in Berkshire, England, where his father, the future Archbishop of Canterbury Edward White Benson, was headmaster. Benson is widely known for being a writer of reminiscences, fiction, satirical novels, biographies and autobiographical studies. His first published novel, *Dodo*, initiated his success, followed by a series of comic novels such as *Queen Lucia* and *Trouble for Lucia*. Later in life, Benson moved to Rye where he was elected mayor. It was here that he was inspired to write several macabre ghost story and supernatural collections and novels, including *Paying Guests* and *Mrs Ames*.

Ambrose Bierce
An Inhabitant of Carcosa
(Originally Published in *San Fransisco News Letter and California Advertiser,* December 1886)
The Moonlit Road
(Originally published in *Cosmopolitan*, January 1907)
Ambrose Bierce (1824–c. 1914) was born in Meigs County, Ohio. He was a famous journalist and author known for writing *The Devil's Dictionary*. After fighting in the American Civil War, Bierce used his combat experience to write stories based on the war, such as in 'An Occurrence at Owl Creek Bridge'. Following the separate deaths of his ex-wife and two of his three children he gained a sardonic view of human nature and earned the name 'Bitter Bierce'. His disappearance at the age of 71 on a trip to Mexico remains a great mystery and continues to spark speculation.

Mary Elizabeth Braddon
The Cold Embrace
(Originally Published in *The Welcome Guest*, September 1860)
Mary Elizabeth Braddon (1835–1915) was born in London, England. During her lifetime, Braddon was a productive writer, producing over 80 novels. Her most notable novel, *Lady Audley's Secret* (1892), brought Braddon much recognition and fortune. In addition to her tales of intrigue, Braddon wrote a number of works on the supernatural, including 'Gerald

or the World, the Flesh and the Devil', 'The Cold Embrace' and 'At Chrighton Abbey'. Beyond her literary endeavours, Braddon founded *Belgravia Magazine* (1866), showcasing the latest serialized sensation novels, poems and travel narratives alongside essays on fashion, history and science.

Sarah L. Byrne
Joined
(Originally Published in *Aliterate: Volume 1*, 2016)
Sarah L. Byrne is a writer and editor in London, UK. Her short speculative fiction has appeared in various publications, including *Nature* magazine and *Best of British Science Fiction 2016 and 2017*, and has been performed live at a Liars' League event in London. Her scientific non-fiction has been published in *Chemistry World* and *The Scientist*. She has also worked as an editor on various scientific and medical journals, on subjects ranging from molecular biology to psychiatry – material which provides unending inspiration for her fiction.

F. Marion Crawford
The Doll's Ghost
(Originally Published in *Uncanny Tales*, T. Fisher Unwin, 1911)
Francis Marion Crawford (1854–1909) was born in Bagni di Lucca, Italy. He is well known for his classically weird and fantastical stories. Travelling to and from Italy, England, Germany and the United States, Crawford became an extraordinary linguist and his first novel *Mr. Isaacs: A Tale of Modern India* was an instant success. His body of work in the horror genre is immense, with H.P. Lovecraft praising 'The Upper Berth' as Crawford's 'weird masterpiece' and 'one of the most tremendous horror-stories in all literature'.

Rachael Cudlitz
Some Souls Stay
(First Publication)
Rachael Cudlitz is the rare, native-born Angeleno who still resides in Los Angeles. She attended CalArts, where she received a BA in Theatre: a degree she no longer uses as she has spent most of the last 21 years parenting identical twins and traveling the world with her family. She started writing seriously four years ago and loves the challenge of both short and long form. She has just completed her first novel *Mother's Girl, a Magical Realism Mystery*, and is currently working on the sequel *The Girl in the Cage*. 'Some Souls Stay' is her first published work.

Dante
Purgatorio (First Terrace – Pride)
(Originally Published in *The Divine Comedy*, completed in 1320; printed in
1472. This text was translated by Rev. Henry Francis Cary, c. 1890.)
Dante Alighieri (c. 1265–1321) was a prolific poet born in Florence, Italy. Renowned for his epic poem *The Divine Comedy*, he is regarded as one of the central figures of Medieval European literature. A deeply reflective body of work, the allegory explores Dante's spiritual journey through Inferno, Purgatory and Paradise, which draws from Christian theology and philosophy. His vivid descriptions established him as the 'Father' of the modern Italian language, as he eschewed Latin in favour of the vernacular Tuscan dialect, bringing forth a new era of literature.

Charles Dickens
The Trial for Murder
(Originally Published in *All the Year Round Christmas Number,* 1865)
The iconic and much-loved Charles Dickens (1812–70) was born in Portsmouth, England, though he spent much of his life in Kent and London. At the age of 12 Charles was forced into working in a factory for a couple of months to support his family. He never forgot his harrowing experience there, and his novels always reflected the plight of the working class. A prolific writer, Dickens kept up a career in journalism as well as writing short stories and novels, with much of his work being serialized before being published as books. He gave a view of contemporary England with a strong sense of realism, yet incorporated the occasional ghost and horror elements. He continued to work hard until his death in 1870, leaving *The Mystery of Edwin Drood* unfinished.

Amelia B. Edwards
Was It an Illusion?
(Originally Published in 1881)
Amelia B. Edwards (1831–92) was born in London, England. Enjoying a rich and varied career as a writer, journalist and Egyptologist, Edwards was a precocious talent, as her first poem was published when she was only seven years old. Her most successful works included the short story 'The Phantom Coach' – one of her many ghost stories, and the novels *Barbara's History* and *Lord Brackenbury*, alongside her Egyptian travelogue *A Thousand Miles up the Nile*, which detailed her extensive 1873–74 voyage through the country.

C.R. Evans
Shut-In (First Publication)
C.R. Evans resides in Sydney with her boyfriend and their entirely unreasonable cat. This is C.R. Evans' first published work, however she has been writing and sharing her ghost stories since childhood, much to the regret of her peers. She has dabbled in painting, sculpting and composing music, most of which (usually unintentionally) incorporate elements of horror. Worryingly, so does her baking. C.R. Evans has a longstanding interest in sci-fi, fantasy and horror and believes that in stories, the unknown elements are the most disturbing.

Sheridan le Fanu
The Child That Went with the Fairies
(Originally Published in *All the Year Round*, February 1870)
The remarkable father of Victorian ghost stories Joseph Thomas Sheridan Le Fanu (1814–73) was born in Dublin, Ireland. His gothic tales and mystery novels led to him become a leading ghost story writer of the nineteenth century. Three oft-cited works of his are *Uncle Silas, Carmilla* and *The House by the Churchyard,* which all are assumed to have influenced Bram Stoker's *Dracula*. Le Fanu wrote his most successful and productive works after his wife's tragic death and he remained a relatively strong writer up until his own death.

Geneve Flynn
The Pontianak's Doll
(Originally Published in *Play Things and Past Times*, 2015)
Geneve Flynn is a freelance editor from Australia who specializes in speculative fiction. She has two psychology degrees and has only ever used them for nefarious purposes. She

has had her short horror fiction published by KnightWatch Press, the Australasian Horror Writers' Association, Oz Horror Con, and TANSTAAFL Press. She loves tales that unsettle, all things writerly, and B-grade action movies. If that sounds like you, check out her website at geneveflynn.com.au or you can find her at facebook.com/geneveflynn.

Mary E. Wilkins Freeman
The Lost Ghost
(Originally Published in *The Wind in the Rose-Bush and Other Stories of the Supernatural*, Doubleday, Page& Company, 1903)
The American author Mary Eleanor Wilkins Freeman (1852–1930) was born in Randolph, Massachusetts. Most of Freeman's works were influenced by her strict childhood, as her parents were orthodox Congregationalists and harboured strong religious views. While working as a secretary for the author Oliver Wendell Holmes, Sr., she was inspired to write herself. Supernatural topics kept catching her attention, and she began to write many short stories with a combination of supernatural and domestic realism, her most famous being 'A New England Nun'. She wrote a number of ghost tales, which were turned into famous ghost story collections after her death.

Adele Gardner
Soul Cakes
(First Publication)
Cat-loving cataloguing librarian Adele Gardner (gardnercastle.com) hails from Tidewater Virginia, USA. With a poetry book (*Dreaming of Days in Astophel*), 238 poems, and 43 stories published in venues like *Strange Horizons, Legends of the Pendragon*, and *The Doom of Camelot*, she's an active member of SFWA with a master's degree in English literature (thesis on William Morris). Adele loves the legends of the Round Table and recently guest-edited the Arthuriana issue of *Eye to the Telescope* (#27, Jan. 2018, eyetothetelescope.com/archives/027issue.html). She serves as literary executor for her father, mentor, and namesake, WWII veteran Delbert R. Gardner (8th Air Force, Rackheath).

Anne Gresham
Perfect Mother
(First Publication)
Anne Gresham is a writer and librarian living in Northwest Arkansas in the United States with her husband, daughter, and various small carnivores. Her work has appeared in *I Don't Want to Play This Game Anymore* (Unnerving, 2018), and Grindstone Literary Services' 2017 *Anthology*. Her horror influences and heroes include Mary Shelley, Stephen Graham Jones, Gemma Files, Paul Tremblay, Victor LaValle, Carmen Maria Machado, and Shirley Jackson. She is happiest spending time with her family, running on dark trails under a full moon, and paging through the gossip sections of turn-of-the-century newspapers on microfilm. For more, visit annegresham.com.

Sara M. Harvey
Thalassa's Pool
(First Publication)
Sara M. Harvey lives and writes fantasy and horror in (and sometimes about) Nashville, TN. She is also a clothing historian, costume designer, and art history and fashion teacher. She has three spoiled dogs, one awesome daughter, and one feisty son; her husband falls somewhere in between. Sara's fiction has appeared in anthologies such as *Upside Down:*

Inverted Tropes in Storytelling, *Submerged*, and Flame Tree's *Lost Worlds*. Her novels include *A Year and a Day*, *Seven Times a Woman*, *Music City*, and *The Blood of Angels* trilogy. She tweets @saraphina_marie, wastes time on facebook.com/saramharvey, and her website is saramharvey.com.

W.F. Harvey
The Beast with Five Fingers
(Originally Published in 1919)
William Fryer Harvey (1885–1937) was born in Yorkshire, England. As a young man, Harvey pursued a degree in Medicine at Leeds, however ill health was to be a frequent presence in his life. Despite the hardships of illness, Harvey dedicated himself to personal projects which resulted in his first collection of short stories, *Midnight House*. Alongside his literary accomplishments, Harvey served as a surgeon-lieutenant in the Royal Navy during the First World War, and was recognized for his bravery, as he received the Albert Medal for Lifesaving. Building upon his initial success as a writer, he went on to write collections of short stories, including *The Beast with Five Fingers* and *Moods and Tenses*.

William Hope Hodgson
The Searcher of the End House
(Originally Published in *The Idler*, June 1910)
William Hope Hodgson (1877–1918) was born in Essex, England but moved several times with his family, including living for some time in County Galway, Ireland – a setting that would later inspire *The House on the Borderland*. Hodgson made several unsuccessful attempts to run away to sea, until his uncle secured him some work in the Merchant Marine. This association with the ocean would unfold later in his many sea stories. After some initial rejections of his writing, Hodgson managed to become a full-time writer of both novels and short stories, which form a fantastic legacy of adventure, mystery and horror fiction.

E.T.A. Hoffmann
The Elementary Spirit
(Originally Published in German in 1841. This English translation was originally published in *Tales from the German*, Chapman and Hall, London, 1844. Translated by John Oxenford And C.A. Feiling.)
Ernst Theodor Amadeus Hoffmann (1776–1822) was a musician and a painter as well as a successful writer. Born in Germany and raised by his uncle, Hoffmann followed a legal career until his interests drew him to composing operas and ballets. He began to write richly imaginative stories that helped secure his reputation as an influential figure during the German Romantic movement, with many of his tales inspiring stage adaptations, such as *The Nutcracker* and *Coppélia*. Hoffmann's chilling tale 'The Sandman' has influenced many, including Neil Gaiman, whose popular graphic novel series *The Sandman* also features a character who steals peoples' eyes.

James Hogg
Mary Burnet
(Originally Published in *The Shepherd's Calendar*, 1828)
James Hogg (1779–1835) was a prolific poet, novelist, journalist and essayist. Born in Ettrick, Scotland, Hogg spent his early youth on a farm, working as a shepherd and farmhand. Despite

the unconventional beginnings of the writer, he successfully educated himself by reading widely. Nicknamed 'Ettrick the Shephard', Hogg cemented his writing career through works such as *Noctes Ambrosianae*, published in *Blackwood's Magazine*. He is best known for his novel *The Private Memoirs and Confessions of a Justified Sinner*, an early example of modern crime fiction written from the perspective of the anti-hero.

Kurt Hunt
Only Bella
(First Publication)
Kurt Hunt was formed in the swamps and abandoned gravel pits of post-industrial Michigan. Tolkien and Alexander seeded his life-long love of genre, Le Guin and Zelazny expanded it, but he's convinced that we're currently living in the best and most transformative era of science fiction and fantasy. His short fiction has been published at *Strange Horizons, Beneath Ceaseless Skies, PodCastle, Orson Scott Card's InterGalactic Medicine Show, Kaleidotrope*, and more. He is also a co-author of *Archipelago*, a collaborative serial fantasy adventure.

Washington Irving
The Adventure of the German Student
(Originally Published in *Tales of a Traveller, John Murray* 1824)
Washington Irving (1783–1859) was a famous American author, essayist, biographer and historian born in New York City. He was influenced by his private education and law school studies to begin writing essays for periodicals. Travelling and working all over the globe, Irving established a name for himself with his successful short stories 'Rip Van Winkle' and 'The Legend of Sleepy Hollow'. These works in particular reflected the mischievous and adventurous behaviour of his childhood. Years later, Irving lived in Spain as a US Ambassador. He returned to America towards the end of life, where he wrote several successful historical and biographical works including a five-volume biography of George Washington.

Henry James
The Jolly Corner
(Originally Published in *The English Review*, December 1908)
Henry James (1843–1916) was born in New York City, though spent a lot of time in England, with the dynamic between Europe and America playing a key role in his novels. Writing a massive amount of literary works throughout his lifetime, he published over 112 tales, 20 novels, 16 plays and various other autobiographies and literary criticisms. Each work is filled with characters of great social complexity as most of his works reflect his own complicated perspectives and satirical personality. James's works include *Daisy Miller, The Turn of the Screw, The Ambassadors, The Golden Bowl* and *The Portrait of a Lady*. James strongly believed novels had to be a recognizable representation of the realistic truth as well as filled with imaginative action.

M.R. James
The Haunted Dolls' House
(Originally Published in *The Empire Review*, February 1923)
Montague Rhodes James (1862–1936), whose works are regarded as being at the forefront of the ghost story genre, was born in Kent, England. James dispensed with the traditional, predictable techniques of ghost story construction, instead using realistic contemporary

settings for his works. He was also a British medieval scholar, so his stories often incorporated antiquarian elements. His stories often reflect his childhood in Suffolk and talented acting career, which both seem to have assisted in the build-up of tension and horror in his works.

Jerome K. Jerome
The Man of Science
(Originally Published in 1892)
Jerome Klapka Jerome (1859–1927) was born in Staffordshire, England. A novelist, playwright and editor, his humour secured his popularity. Inspired by his sister Blandina's love for the theatre, a young Jerome tried his hand at acting under the name of 'Harold Crichton'. After three difficult years, Jerome departed from the stage and pursued a number of odd jobs as a teacher, journalist and essayist – to no avail. However, success eventually arrived through his memoir, *On the Stage – and Off*. Building upon the strength of his writing, Jerome's best-known novel, *Three Men in a Boat* (1889), exemplified his comic talent. However he also delved into more genre tales, like the chilling ghost story 'The Man of Science' or the early robotic story 'The Dancing Partner'.

Perceval Landon
Thurnley Abbey
(Originally Published in 1908)
Perceval Landon (1868–1927) was born in Hastings, England. In his early adulthood, Landon attended Oxford University, obtaining a degree in Law. Landon was the war correspondent for *The Times* during the Second Boer War in South Africa, and it was during this period, an enduring friendship with the iconic writer Rudyard Kipling developed. Moreover, this fundamental experience in South Africa launched a successful career of international travel and journalism. In 1908, *Raw Edges,* a collection of 13 short stories, was published. The most memorable of these tales is 'Thurnley Abbey', a ghost story that proved the endless possibilities of the popular horror genre.

Friedrich Laun
The Death-Bride
(Originally Published in *Das Gespensterbuch* vol. 2, by Johann August Apel and Friedrich Laun, *c.* 1811/12. This English translation is from *Tales of the Dead*, by Sarah Elizabeth Utterson, 1813)
Friedrich August Schulze (1770–1849) was a German novelist who wrote under the pen name Friedrich Laun. Born in Dresden, Germany, his first novel, *Der Mann, auf Freiersfüssen*, was well received. He collaborated with Johann August Apel on a book of ghost stories called *Gespensterbuch*, some of which were included in the French collection *Fantasmagoria*, which inspired both Shelley's *Frankenstein* and Polidori's *The Vampyre*.

H.P. Lovecraft
The Strange High House in the Mist
(Originally Published in *Weird Tales,* October 1931)
Master of weird fiction Howard Phillips Lovecraft (1890–1937) was born in Providence, Rhode Island. Featuring unknown and otherworldly creatures, his stories were one of the first to mix science fiction with horror. Plagued by nightmares from an early age, he was inspired to write his dark and strange fantasy tales; and the isolation he must have experienced from

suffering frequent illnesses can be felt as a prominent theme in his work. Lovecraft inspired many other authors, and his most famous story 'The Call of Cthulhu' has gone on to influence many aspects of popular culture.

Roger Luckhurst
Foreword: Lost Souls Short Stories
Roger Luckhurst is a professor in the School of Arts, at Birkbeck College, University of London. He is author of eight books, including *The Mummy's Curse* (2012) and *Zombies: A Cultural History* (2015). He has also edited Robert Louis Stevenson's *Jekyll and Hyde,* Bram Stoker's *Dracula,* and the collection *Late Victorian Gothic Tales* for the Oxford World's Classics series. He also writes on film for *Sight and Sound,* and has written books on the films *Alien* and *The Shining* for the British Film Institute 'Classics' series.

Arthur Machen
The Inmost Light
(Originally Published in *The Great God Pan and The Inmost Light,* John Lane, London, 1894)
The Bowmen
(Originally Published in *London Evening News,* September 1914)
Arthur Machen (1863–1947) was born in Monmouthshire, Wales. Machen was an author of horror, supernatural and fantasy fiction. A key figure of the horror genre, his early novella *The Great God Pan* cultivated a reputation as an iconic classic. Casting his net wide, Machen was also an accomplished journalist and actor. His literary forays into fantasy and supernatural realms led to interesting works such as *The Three Impostors* (1895) and *The Hill of Dreams* (1907). In his essay 'Supernatural Horror in Literature' Lovecraft praised Machen highly, describing his stories as those 'in which the elements of hidden horror and brooding fright attain an almost incomparable substance and realistic acuteness.'

Michael Matheson
Until There Is Only Hunger
(Originally Published in *Upside Down: Inverted Tropes in Storytelling*, 2016)
Based in Toronto, Canada, Michael Matheson is a genderfluid graduate of Clarion West ('14). Their work is published or forthcoming in *Nightmare, Shimmer,* and the anthology *Upside Down: Inverted Tropes in Storytelling,* among others. Their first anthology as editor, *The Humanity of Monsters,* was released by CZP in Autumn 2015. Michael is also co-founder and co-EIC of *Anathema: Spec from the Margins,* a tri-annual spec fic mag of work by queer POC/Indigenous/Aboriginal creators. Find more at michaelmatheson.wordpress.com, or on Twitter @sekisetsu.

Charles Maturin
Melmoth the Wanderer (abridged version)
(Originally Published by The Lock and Key Library, 1820)
Charles Maturin (1782–1824) was born in Dublin, Ireland. Alongside working as a Protestant clergyman, Maturin wrote Gothic plays and novels. His first three Gothic novels were critical and commercial failures. However, they caught the eye of Sir Walter Scott, who recommended Maturin's work to Lord Byron. With their encouragement, Maturin's play *Bertram* was staged in 1816, although financial success still escaped him. Shortly after, the Church of Ireland halted his progress as a clergyman, as it was discovered that he collected profits for his plays. Despite the difficulties, Maturin became a novelist and is best-known for his story about a Faustian pact, *Melmoth the Wanderer.*

J.A.W. McCarthy
Every Time She Kills Him
(First Publication)
J.A.W. McCarthy goes by Jen when she is not writing. She lives with her husband and assistant cat in Seattle, WA, where she prefers to enjoy the beauty of the Pacific Northwest with a drink in hand. When she's not coming up with disturbing story ideas in the shower or while trying to fall asleep at night, she enjoys reading and viewing other people's dark fiction. Her work has most recently appeared or is forthcoming in *Unfading Daydream*, A Murder of Storytellers' anthology *The Misbehaving Dead*, and *Ink Stains*. Visit her on Instagram: @jawmccarthy.

John M. McIlveen
The Price of Forever
(Originally Published in *Canopic Jars*, 2013)
John M. McIlveen is the author of the paranormal suspense novel *Hannahwhere*, which was nominated for the 2015 Bram Stoker Award (HWA), and winner of the 2015 Drunken Druid Award (Ireland). He has also authored two story collections, *Inflictions* and *Jerks, and Other Tales from a Perfect Man*. He is a father to five daughters, owner and editor-in-chief of Haverhill House Publishing, and works at MIT's Lincoln Laboratory. He lives in Rock's Village, Massachusetts, with his wife Roberta Colasanti. Watch for his forthcoming novels *Gone North* and *Corruption*. Please visit him at johnmcilveen.com and haverhillhouse.com.

E. Nesbit
Man-Size in Marble
(Originally Published in *Home Chimes,* December 1887)
Edith Nesbit (1858–1924) was born in Kennington, England. Nesbit established herself as a successful author and poet, writing a variety of literature ranging from children's books to adult horror stories. She co-founded the Fabian Society and was also a strong political activist. Marrying young and frequently moving home, Nesbit made many friendships with other writers including H.G. Wells and George Bernard Shaw. Although she gained most of her success from her children's books, like the ever-popular *The Railway Children*, she was also a well-known horror writer, with such collections as *Something Wrong* and *Grim Tales*.

Jessica Nickelsen
The Obstinate One (First Publication)
Jessica Nickelsen is originally from Vancouver, Washington, but moved to New Zealand in her teens. She now lives in Wellington with her husband, daughter, and a tribe of cats. Apart from New Zealand and the US, she has also lived in Italy and Ireland and now has an accent that confuses many people. When not making up stories she's a gamer, software tester and knitter of socks. She is terrified of ghosts. Find out more about Jessica at discombobulated.co.nz.

Margaret Oliphant
The Open Door
(Originally Published in *Blackwood's Magazine,* January 1882)
Margaret Oliphant (1828–97) was born in Wallyford, Scotland. As a young girl, Oliphant showed promise, dedicating her time to experimenting with story-telling. Success arrived in 1849 with her first novel *Passages in the Life of Margaret Maitland*,

marking the start of a rich and varied literary career. She was later invited by the esteemed publisher William Blackwood to contribute to *Blackwood's Magazine,* a crucial partnership that was to last throughout her life. Calling upon the themes of history, domesticity and the supernatural, Oliphant's unique blend of ideas led to the creation of over 120 works including novels, books on travel, histories and literary criticism.

Ovid
Orpheus and Eurydice
(Modern retelling of a poem from Ovid's *Metamorphoses*, 8 AD)
Publius Ovidius Naso (43 BC–17/18 AD) was a Roman poet, alive during the reign of the Emperor Augustus. He is known for such works as the *Ars Amatoria* ('The Art of Love') – a slightly tongue-in-cheek set of books giving amatory advice to both men and women, and *The Metamorphoses* ('Books of Transformations'), which was an epic work comprising over 250 myths. *The Metamorphoses* in particular has had a huge impact on Western literature, inspiring later authors like Dante, Chaucer and Shakespeare. Ovid died in exile, which the poet himself attributes to 'a poem and a mistake', but the exact cause remains a mystery. This modern retelling of 'Orpheus and Eurydice' is taken from Flame Tree's *Greek Myths and Tales* book; written, compiled and edited by a team of experts and enthusiasts on mythological traditions.

Michael Penncavage
The Phone Call
(Originally Published in *Escape Velocity Magazine*, 2009)
Michael Penncavage's fiction can be found in over 100 magazines and anthologies from 7 different countries, such as *Alfred Hitchcock Mystery Magazine* (USA), *Here and Now* (England), *Tenebres* (France) *Crime Factory* (Australia), *Reaktor* (Estonia), *Speculative Mystery* (South Africa), and *Visionarium* (Austria). His other stories include 'The Cost of Doing Business', which won the Derringer Award for best mystery; 'The Converts', which was filmed as a short movie; and 'The Landlord', which was adapted into a play. Michael has been an Associate Editor for *Space and Time Magazine* as well as the Editor of the horror/suspense anthology *Tales from a Darker State*.

Edgar Allan Poe
Morella
(Originally Published in *Southern Literary Messenger,* April 1835)
The versatile writer Edgar Allan Poe (1809–49) was born in Boston, Massachusetts. Poe is extremely well known as an influential author, poet, editor and literary critic that wrote during the American Romantic Movement. Poe is generally considered the inventor of the detective fiction genre, and his works are famously filled with terror, mystery, death and hauntings. Some of his better-known works include his poems 'The Raven' and 'Annabel Lee', and the short stories 'The Tell Tale Heart' and 'The Fall of the House of Usher'. The dark, mystifying characters of his tales have captured the public's imagination and reflect the struggling, poverty-stricken lifestyle he lived his whole life.

Lina Rather
Last Long Night
(Originally Published in *Daily Science Fiction*, 2017)
Lina Rather is a speculative fiction author from Michigan, now living in Washington, D.C. She wishes she could say she has a dog, but alas, she lives under the tyranny of landlords. When she isn't writing, she likes to cook, go hiking, and collect terrible 90's comic books. Her work has appeared in a variety of publications, including *Shimmer*, *Flash Fiction Online*, and *Lightspeed*. You can find more about her and her other stories on her website, linarather.wordpress.com. She also spends altogether too much time on Twitter as @LinaRather.

Alexandra Renwick
A Good Thing and a Right Thing
(Originally Published in *Ellery Queen Mystery Magazine*, 2013)
Alexandra Renwick is a US & Canadian writer whose genre-elastic stories have been translated into nine languages and adapted to stage and audio. Born in Los Angeles but raised in Yorkshire, Philadelphia, Toronto, Austin, and Denmark, she currently lives in a historic heritage manor in Canada's capital city of Ottawa. Find her most recent stories in *Asimov's*, *Interzone*, the *Alfred Hitchcock Mystery Magazine*, and in audio at *Cast of Wonders*. More information at alexcrenwick.com.

Aeryn Rudel
Scare Tactics
(Originally Published in *The Devilfish Review*, 2016)
Aeryn Rudel is a freelance writer and game designer from Seattle, Washington. He is the author of the Acts of War series published by Privateer Press, and his short fiction has appeared in *The Arcanist*, *Havok Magazine*, and *Pseudopod*, among others. Aeryn is a notorious dinosaur nerd, a baseball connoisseur, and has mastered the art of fighting with sword-shaped objects (but not actual swords). He occasionally offers dubious advice on the subjects of writing and rejection (mostly rejection) on his blog at rejectomancy.com or Twitter @Aeryn_Rudel.

Walter Scott
The Tapestried Chamber
(Originally Published in *The Keepsake* for 1829)
Walter Scott (1771–1832) was born in Edinburgh, Scotland, and was a historical novelist, poet and biographer. He was fascinated by the oral traditions of the Scottish Borders and later developed an interest in German Romanticism and Gothic novels. Scott is often credited with inventing the modern historical novel, and is known for such works as Ivanhoe and Rob Roy. His first novel, *Waverley*, was published anonymously along with the rest of his fictional works. Those familiar with the internationally celebrated poet though would come to recognize these stories as Scott's due to his unique narrative style.

Lizz-Ayn Shaarawi
This House Is My Cage
(First Publication)
Lizz-Ayn Shaarawi is a Texan lost in the Oregon wilderness. She's a screenwriter and author whose short stories have been featured in numerous anthologies. Her screenplays have

been recognized by The Austin Film Festival, The Nicholl Fellowship in Screenwriting, and The Page Awards. She enjoys cheap thrills, expensive shoes, and things that go bump in the night.

Erin Skolney
Lullaby for the Dead
(First Publication)
Erin Skolney is an emerging horror writer from Edmonton, Canada. In 2017, she graduated with an M.Sc. in Counselling from the University of North Texas, and her background in psychology influences much of her work. She grew up reading scary stories late into the night, and she hopes to write stories for readers to enjoy while hiding beneath the covers. When she is not writing, she enjoys playing the drums, riding her motorcycle, and exploring new places.

Lucy A. Snyder
Abandonment Option
(Originally Published in *What Fates Impose*, 2013)
Lucy A. Snyder is a five-time Bram Stoker Award-winning writer and is the author of a dozen books. Her work has been translated into French, Russian, Italian, Spanish, Czech, and Japanese editions and has appeared in publications such as *Asimov's Science Fiction*, *Apex Magazine*, *Nightmare Magazine*, *Pseudopod*, *Strange Horizons*, and *Best Horror of the Year*. She lives in Columbus, Ohio, and is faculty in Seton Hill University's MFA program in Writing Popular Fiction. You can learn more about her at lucysnyder.com.

David Tallerman
Casualty of Peace
(Originally Published in *Horror Library Volume 6*, 2017)
David Tallerman is the author of upcoming crime thriller *The Bad Neighbour*, YA fantasy series *The Black River Chronicles*, the *Tales of Easie Damasco* novels and the novella *Patchwerk*. His comics work includes the absurdist steampunk graphic novel *Endangered Weapon B: Mechanimal Science*, with artist Bob Molesworth. David's short fiction has appeared in around eighty markets, including *Clarkesworld*, *Nightmare*, *Alfred Hitchcock Mystery Magazine* and *Beneath Ceaseless Skies*. A number of his best dark fantasy and horror stories were gathered together in his debut collection *The Sign in the Moonlight and Other Stories*. David can be found online at davidtallerman.co.uk.

Sarah Elizabeth Utterson
The Storm
(Originally Published in *Tales of the Dead,* White, Cochrane & Co., London, 1813)
Most famously known for her anthology *Tales of the Dead*, Sarah Elizabeth Utterson (1781–1851) was also a contributor to the influential collection. Translated from a French collection of ghost stories titled *Fantasmagoriana*, Utterson selected the stories she felt to be most chilling, as well as adding her own story, 'The Storm'. *Fantasmagoriana* was famously read out at a gathering between Mary Shelley, Percy Shelley, Lord Byron, John Polidori and Claire Claremont at the Villa Diodati, inspiring their ghost-writing contest which eventually lead to Mary Shelley's *Frankenstein* and Polidori's 'The Vampyre'.

Damien Angelica Walters
Sing Me Your Scars
(Originally Published in *Sing Me Your Scars*, 2015)
Damien Angelica Walters is the author of *Cry Your Way Home*, *Paper Tigers*, and *Sing Me Your Scars*. Her short fiction has been nominated twice for a Bram Stoker Award, reprinted in *The Year's Best Dark Fantasy & Horror* and *The Year's Best Weird Fiction*, and published in various anthologies and magazines, including the Shirley Jackson Award Finalists *Autumn Cthulhu* and *The Madness of Dr. Caligari*, World Fantasy Award Finalist *Cassilda's Song, Nightmare Magazine*, and *Black Static*. She lives in Maryland with her husband and two rescued pit bulls. Find her on Twitter @DamienAWalters or on the web at damienangelicawalters.com.

Edith Wharton
The Triumph of Night
(Originally Published *in Scribner's,* August 1914)
Edith Wharton (1862–1937), the Pulitzer Prize-winning writer of *The Age of Innocence,* was born in New York. As well as her talent as an American novelist, Wharton was also known for her short stories and career as a designer. Wharton was born into a controlled New York society where women were discouraged from achieving anything beyond a proper marriage. Defeating the norms, Wharton not only grew to become one of America's greatest writers, she grew to become a very self-rewarding woman. Writing numerous ghost stories and murderous tales such as 'The Lady's Maid's Bell', 'The Eyes' and 'Afterward', Wharton is widely known for the ghost tours that now take place at her old home, The Mount.

FLAME TREE PUBLISHING
Short Story Series
New & Classic Writing

Flame Tree's Gothic Fantasy books offer a carefully curated series of new titles, each with combinations of original and classic writing:

Chilling Horror Short Stories
Chilling Ghost Short Stories
Science Fiction Short Stories
Murder Mayhem Short Stories
Crime & Mystery Short Stories
Swords & Steam Short Stories
Dystopia Utopia Short Stories
Supernatural Horror Short Stories
Lost Worlds Short Stories
Time Travel Short Stories
Heroic Fantasy Short Stories
Pirates & Ghosts Short Stories
Agents & Spies Short Stories
Endless Apocalypse Short Stories
Alien Invasion Short Stories
Robots & Artificial Intelligence Short Stories

as well as new companion titles which offer rich collections of classic fiction from masters of the gothic fantasy genres:

H.G. Wells Short Stories
Lovecraft Short Stories
Sherlock Holmes Collection
Edgar Allan Poe Collection
Mary Shelley Horror Stories

Available from all good bookstores, worldwide, and online at
flametreepublishing.com

...and coming soon:
FLAME TREE PRESS | FICTION WITHOUT FRONTIERS
New and original writing in Horror, Crime, SF and Fantasy
flametreepress.com

GOTHIC FANTASY

For our books, calendars, blog
and latest special offers please see:
flametreepublishing.com